**STEPHEN JONE** ... ... ...he winner of three World Fantasy Awards, four Horror Writers Association Bram Stoker Awards and three International Horror Guild Awards as well as being a twenty-one time recipient of the British Fantasy Award and a Hugo Award nominee. A former television producer/director and genre movie publicist and consultant (the first three *Hellraiser* movies, *Night Life*, *Nightbreed*, *Split Second*, *Mind Ripper*, *Last Gasp* etc.), he is the co-editor of *Horror: 100 Best Books*, *Horror: Another 100 Best Books*, *The Best Horror from Fantasy Tales*, *Gaslight & Ghosts*, *Now We Are Sick*, *H.P. Lovecraft's Book of Horror*, *The Anthology of Fantasy & the Supernatural*, *Secret City: Strange Tales of London*, *Great Ghost Stories*, *Tales to Freeze the Blood: More Great Ghost Stories* and the *Dark Terrors*, *Dark Voices* and *Fantasy Tales* series. He has written *Coraline: A Visual Companion*, *Stardust: The Visual Companion*, *Creepshows: The Illustrated Stephen King Movie Guide*, *The Essential Monster Movie Guide*, *The Illustrated Vampire Movie Guide*, *The Illustrated Dinosaur Movie Guide*, *The Illustrated Frankenstein Movie Guide* and *The Illustrated Werewolf Movie Guide*, and compiled *The Mammoth Book of Best New Horror* series, *The Mammoth Book of Terror*, *The Mammoth Book of Vampires*, *The Mammoth Book of Zombies*, *The Mammoth Book of Werewolves*, *The Mammoth Book of Frankenstein*, *The Mammoth Book of Dracula*, *The Mammoth Book of Vampire Stories by Women*, *The Mammoth Book of New Terror*, *The Mammoth Book of Monsters*, *The Mammoth Book of the Best of Best New Horror*, *Shadows Over Innsmouth*, *Weird Shadows Over Innsmouth*, *Dark Detectives*, *Dancing with the Dark*, *Dark of the Night*, *White of the Moon*, *Keep Out the Night*, *By Moonlight Only*, *Don't Turn Out the Light*, *H.P. Lovecraft's Book of the Supernatural*, *Travellers in Darkness*, *Summer Chills*, *Brighton Shock!*, *Zombie Apocalypse!*, *Visitants: Stories of Fallen Angels & Heavenly Hosts*, *A Book of Horrors*, *Exorcisms and Ecstasies* by Karl Edward Wagner, *The Vampire Stories of R. Chetwynd-Hayes*, *Phantoms and Fiends* and *Frights and Fancies* by R. Chetwynd-Hayes, *James Herbert: By Horror Haunted*, *Basil Copper: A Life in Books*, *Necronomicon: The Best Weird Tales of H.P. Lovecraft*, *Eldritch Tales* by H.P. Lovecraft, *The Complete Chronicles of Conan* and *Conan's Brethren* by Robert E. Howard, *The Emperor of Dreams: The Lost Worlds of Clark Ashton Smith*, *Sea-Kings of Mars and Otherworldly Stories* by Leigh Brackett, *The Mark of the Beast and Other Fantastical Tales* by Rudyard Kipling, *Darkness Mist & Shadow: The Collected Macabre Tales of Basil Copper*, *Pelican Cay & Other Disquieting Tales* by David Case, *Clive Barker's A–Z of Horror*, *Clive Barker's Shadows in Eden*, *Clive Barker's The Nightbreed Chronicles*, *The Hellraiser Chronicles* and volumes of poetry by H.P. Lovecraft, Robert E. Howard ar ̶ ̶Cl̶ ̶ ̶k̶ Ashton Smith. A Guest of Honour at the 2002 World Fantasy Co ... ... the 2004 World Horror Conventio ... ... at UCLA in California ... ...'s University College. Y ... ... .com

*Also available in the Mammoth series*

# THE MAMMOTH BOOK OF
# BEST NEW HORROR

## VOLUME 22

Edited and with an Introduction by

## STEPHEN JONES

RUNNING PRESS
PHILADELPHIA · LONDON

Constable & Robinson Ltd
55–56 Russell Square
London WC1B 4HP
www.constablerobinson.com

First published in the UK by Robinson,
an imprint of Constable & Robinson, 2011

A copy of the British Library Cataloguing in Publication
Data is available from the British Library

UK ISBN 978-1-84901-618-6

1 3 5 7 9 10 8 6 4 2

First published in the United States in 2011 by Running Press Book Publishers,
A Member of the Perseus Books Group

US ISBN: 978-0-7624-4270-6
US Library of Congress Control Number: 2010941550

9  8  7  6  5  4  3  2  1
Digit on the right indicates the number of this printing

Running Press Book Publishers
2300 Chestnut Street
Philadelphia, PA 19103-4371

Visit us on the web!
www.runningpress.com

Printed and bound by CPI Group (UK) Ltd, Croydon, CR0 4YY

# CONTENTS

# ACKNOWLEDGMENTS

I would like to thank David Barraclough, Mandy Slater, Amanda Foubister, Andrew I. Porter, Brian Mooney, Johnny Mains, Philip Harbottle, Sara and Randy Broecker, Vincent Chong, Rodger Turner and Wayne MacLaurin (*www.sfsite.com*), Peter Crowther and Nicky Crowther, Gordon Van Gelder, Ray Russell and Rosalie Parker, Andy Cox, Ellen Datlow, Charles Black and, especially, Duncan Proudfoot and Dorothy Lumley for all their help and support. Special thanks are also due to *Locus*, *Variety*, *Ansible* and all the other sources that were used for reference in the Introduction and the Necrology.

*Fiction*, No.44, September 2010. Reprinted by permission of the author.

OH I DO LIKE TO BE BESIDE THE SEASIDE copyright © Christopher Fowler 2010. Originally published in *Brighton Shock! The Souvenir Book of The World Horror Convention 2010*. Reprinted by permission of the author.

LOSENEF EXPRESS copyright © Mark Samuels 2010. Originally published in *The Man Who Collected Machen & Other Stories*. Reprinted by permission of the author.

LESSER DEMONS copyright © Norman Partridge 2010. Originally published in *Lesser Demons* and *Black Wings: New Tales of Lovecraftian Horror*. Reprinted by permission of the author.

TELLING copyright © Steve Rasnic Tem 2010. Originally published in *The Seventh Black Book of Horror*. Reprinted by permission of the author.

AS RED AS RED copyright © Caitlín R. Kiernan 2010. Originally published in *Haunted Legends*. Reprinted by permission of the author.

WITH THE ANGELS copyright © Ramsey Campbell 2010. Originally published in *Visitants: Stories of Fallen Angels & Heavenly Hosts*. Reprinted by permission of the author.

AUTUMN CHILL copyright © Richard L. Tierney 2010. Originally published in *Savage Menace and Other Poems of Horror*. Reprinted by permission of the author.

CITY OF THE DOG copyright © John Langan 2009. Originally published in *The Magazine of Fantasy & Science Fiction*, No.687, January/February 2010. Reprinted by permission of the author.

*In memory of my dear friend,*
*and one of the Chapel Hill Gang*
C. BRUCE HUNTER
*(1944–2009)*

# INTRODUCTION

## Horror in 2010

AFTER ONLY A YEAR, Angry Robot left HarperCollins UK and became an independent imprint, backed by Osprey Publishing, best known for its military history titles.

In March, the American Borders book-selling chain held off possible bankruptcy after securing two loans, totalling $790 million. This allowed the company to see if its recent restructuring, which included closing Waldenbooks stores, could halt a continuing decline in sales.

With so many pundits proclaiming the demise of the traditional bookstore in favour of the Internet and e-books, London's Foyles bookshop defied the trend and enjoyed its most successful year for more than a decade, with a 9.7 per cent increase in sales on the previous year. It was, however, the first time that the store had made a pre-tax profit since 1999.

Industry figures revealed that the UK book industry suffered a 5.6 per cent decline in sales overall.

For the second year in a row, national SAT results in England revealed that reading standards had fallen amongst 11-year-olds in primary schools. This was borne out by a survey of 2,000 UK schoolchildren which revealed that 11 per cent of them thought that Albert Einstein was Frankenstein's brother and one in five believed that Disney's Buzz Lightyear was the first person to step on the Moon, not Neil Armstrong. Even more dispiriting, one in six thought Darth Vader's Death Star was the furthest place from Earth, one in six believed that the Daleks occupied Britain, and 12 per cent of kids thought that the Battle of Britain took place in outer space.

In the annual rundown of the most popular names for newborn babies in 2009, issued by America's Social Security Administration at the beginning of May, "Cullen" was placed at #485 – a leap of almost 300 slots from the previous year, and the biggest increase for any boy's name. This was put down to the fact that it is the surname of moody vampire "Edward" in Stephenie Meyer's "Twilight Saga". Perhaps more worrying, "Jacob" (the name of Meyer's buff werewolf) was the most popular boy's name for the eleventh year running, while "Isabella" – the progenitor of Meyer's heroine "Bella" (which itself rated #58) – topped the list of girls' names.

Meanwhile, the Pacific Inn Motel in Forks, Washington – home to Meyer's fictional Cullen family of vampires – opened six *Twilight*-themed rooms decorated in black and red Gothic trappings.

Stephenie Meyer's *The Short Second Life of Bree Tanner: An Eclipse Novella* was about the "newborn" teenage vampire whom Bella met in *Eclipse*. It was originally written by the author as an exercise. Published with a first print run of 1.5 million copies, with a dollar from each sale donated to the American Red Cross International Response Fund, the slim hardcover was also available online as a free download in June, as a special thank-you to "Twi-hard" fans.

British horror writer James Herbert received an OBE in the 2010 Queen's Birthday Honours list. So, too, did scriptwriter/producer Brian Clemens, whose credits include TV's *The Avengers* and *Thriller*.

In October, J.K. Rowling was named the most influential woman in Britain. Victoria Beckham was the runner-up, followed by the Queen in third place. Earlier in the year, Rowling donated £10 million to set up a multiple sclerosis research clinic in Edinburgh.

English professor Justin Cronin's much-hyped *The Passage*, a large novel about an enigmatic young girl turned into an immortal vampire (called "virals") through a covert military experiment, was the subject of a bidding war amongst publishers, with Ballantine finally securing the rights. Ridley Scott's Scott Free Productions snapped up the movie rights and, inevitably, the author was planning two sequels.

A group of four college friends, whose lives had been ruined one night in 1966 during a secret occult ritual, revisited the past in an attempt finally to face their very different visions in Peter Straub's *A Dark Matter*. An earlier and longer version of the novel, entitled *The Skylark*, was published by Subterranean Press in a 500-copy signed edition and as a traycased and lettered edition of twenty-six copies ($250.00).

*Frankenstein: Lost Souls* was the fourth in the series by Dean Koontz, in which mad scientist Victor created a race of evil replicants who recycled their human counterparts into biological components. From the same author, *What the Night Knows* was a supernatural serial-killer novel.

In Joe Hill's eagerly anticipated second novel, *Horns*, a man let his inner devil loose when he found that he had grown horns and acquired the power to know the worst secrets and darkest desires of everyone he met. A 500-copy signed and slipcased edition was also available from PS Publishing, along with a 200-copy traycased edition signed by Hill and artist Vincent Chong (£200.00).

When a preserved giant squid mysteriously disappeared from London's Natural History Museum, a clueless tour guide found himself caught up in the city's criminal and magical underworld in China Miéville's sometimes Lovecraftian novel *Kraken*. Subterranean Press did a 500-copy signed and limited edition, along with twenty-six lettered and traycased copies ($250.00).

The body of an old Native American shaman held the ghost of General Custer after the Battle of Little Big Horn in Dan Simmons' sprawling historical fantasy *Black Hills*. Subterranean produced a signed, limited edition of 500 copies, plus a twenty-six copy lettered and traycased edition ($500.00).

Simmons' classic Nazi vampire novel *Carrion Comfort* was also reissued for the twentieth anniversary of its publication, in a revised edition with a new Introduction by the author.

An alcoholic father returned to the mysterious island where

his six-year-old daughter disappeared two years previously in John Ajvide Lindqvist's spooky third novel, *Harbour*.

New father and serial killer Dexter Morgan found himself dealing with a group of cannibal killers in the Everglades in *Dexter is Delicious*, the fifth volume in Jeff Lindsay's increasingly silly series.

*The Heavenstone Secrets* and *Secret Whispers* were the first two volumes in a new Gothic series credited to "V.C. Andrews®", while *Daughter of Darkness* was a vampire novel from the same long-dead, yet still prolific, author.

*Frankenstein's Monster* by Susan Heyboer O'Keefe was a sequel to Mary Shelley's classic novel that followed the creature down through the years following the death of its creator. Meanwhile, Michelle Lovric's equally literary *The Book of Human Skin* was a sweeping historical horror novel in which sibling rivalry took a decidedly evil turn during the late 18th century.

In *A Matter of Blood*, the first in Sarah Pinborough's crossover "The Dog-Faced Gods" crime/horror trilogy, Detective Inspector Cass Jones discovered that the three murder cases he was working on were somehow connected, including that of a serial killer who could turn himself into a swarm of flies.

Having moved to Pan Books, British author Adam Nevill's first title from his new publisher was *Apartment 16*, about a haunted building in Knightsbridge.

*The Chamber of Ten* by Christopher Golden and Tim Lebbon was the third book in the "Hidden Cities" series, this time set beneath the city of Venice, while the end of the world was only the beginning in *Coldbrook*, a solo novel by Lebbon.

*Fatal Error* was the latest novel about Repairman Jack by F. Paul Wilson, and a female arson investigator tried to avert the apocalypse in *Fire Spirit* by Graham Masterton.

*Ghost of a Chance* was the first book in the new "Ghostfinders" series by Simon R. Green, about agents from the Carnacki Institute.

Gary McMahon's *Pretty Little Dead Things* featured psychic investigator Thomas Usher, who looked into the violent death of the daughter of a local gangster. The novel came with glowing quotes from Ramsey Campbell, Stephen Volk, Christopher Fowler and Tim Lebbon.

In Yvonne Navarro's *Highborn*, a fallen angel seeking redemption teamed up with a Chicago detective tracking a serial killer in the first in a new series.

Those who desecrated an Etruscan tomb were apparently torn apart by a large beast in *The Ancient Curse* by Valerio Massimo Manfredi, while a recently widowed celebrity found himself at the mercy of his malicious mansion in *The Haunting of James Hastings* by Christopher Ramsom.

A future Hollywood director filmed his extras really being killed onscreen while battling mechanical monsters in *The Extra* by Michael Shea.

Former accountant Owen Pitt was stalked by the "Shadow Man" in *Monster Hunter: Vendetta* by Larry Correia, and the inhabitants of a small Californian town were infested by a worm-like parasite in Jeff Jacobson's *Wormfood*.

*Skinners: Teeth of Beasts* and *Skinners: Vampire Uprising* were the third and fourth books, respectively, in the monster-hunting series by Marcus Pelegrimas.

*Shift* by Tim Kring and Dale Peck was the first book in the "Gate of Orpheus" trilogy, about an LSD mind-control experiment in the 1960s, while supernatural creatures attached themselves to people in *Drift* by the pseudonymous "Sharon Carter Rogers".

*Ghost Shadow*, *Ghost Night* and *Ghost Moon* made up Heather Graham's "Bone Island" trilogy set in the Florida Keys.

A newly renovated spa hotel harboured ghosts in *So Cold the River* by Michael Koryta, and in Trish J. MacGregor's *Esperanza*, a female FBI agent ended up in the eponymous Ecuadorian city haunted by hungry ghosts.

When a woman opened a new guesthouse, she discovered that the property came with a pair of resident ghosts who wanted her to solve their murder, in *Night of the Living Deed* by E.J. Copperman (Jeffrey Cohen), the first book in the "Haunted Guesthouse" series.

*The Fuller Memorandum* was the third Lovecraftian spy novel in Charles Stross' "Laundry Files" series featuring computational demonologist Bob Howard.

*Dog Blood* was the sequel to David Moody's *Hater*, about a plague that sparked sudden rage and killing. Moody's horror novel *Autumn*, originally published free online, also finally received a mass-market edition.

After all of humanity blacked out, one girl partially remembered what happened in Dalia Roddy's *A Catch in Time*.

*Cat's Claw* was the second novel about Death's daughter, Calliope Reaper-Jones, by *Buffy* actress Amber Benson.

In *The Devil*, Ken Bruen's sixth novel about an Irish alcoholic "finder", Jack Taylor found himself up against the Prince of Lies himself, while *The Devil's Playground* was the fourth book in the series by Jenna Black featuring exorcist Morgan Kingsley.

Stephen Leather's *Nightfall* was the first in a series featuring former cop Jack Nightingale, and a drug-addicted investigator for the only surviving Church in a world filled with ghosts was the main protagonist of Stacia Kane's *Unholy Ghosts*.

Police detective Kara Gillian could also summon demons in Diana Rowland's mystery *Blood of the Demon*, and a sceptical homicide detective teamed up with a psychic to solve a ritualistic murder in *Book of Shadows* by Alexandra Sokoloff.

*Johannes Cabal the Detective* was the second volume in the series by Jonathan L. Howard, in which the titular necromancer found himself fleeing execution by escaping on a state-of-the-art flying ship beset with mysterious murders.

Sir Richard Burton investigated a series of sexual attacks in an alternate 1861 London in Mark Hodder's steampunk horror novel *The Strange Affair of Spring-Heeled Jack*, the first book in the "Burton & Swinburne" series.

Over at the struggling Leisure imprint, a group of travellers found themselves trapped in a snow-bound deserted town in *Snow* by Ronald Malfi, while a boy befriended a monster in the woods in *Dweller* by Jeff Strand.

The government agents of Department 18 had to deal with vampire-like "Breathers" in *Night Souls*, the latest in the series by L.H. Maynard and M.P.N. Sims.

Magus Levi Stoltzfus tried to protect a small town from five demonic creatures in Brian Keene's *A Gathering of Crows*, a grieving father was entranced by a legendary sea creature in John

Everson's *Siren*, and a group of rich teens on spring break were stalked by serial killers in Bryan Smith's *The Killing Kind*.

The teenagers in Nate Kenyon's *Sparrow Rock* were stalked by mutant monsters in a post-apocalyptic future. The novel was also available as a 100-copy signed edition and twenty-six lettered copies from Bad Moon Books.

Reprints from Leisure included John Skipp and Craig Spector's *The Bridge*, Gord Rollo's *Strange Magic*, Ray Garton's *Scissors*, Ramsey Campbell's *Creatures of the Pool*, Brian Keene's *Darkness on the Edge of Town* (in an expanded edition) and Jack Ketchum's *Joyride* (with an added novella). The late Richard Laymon's *Friday Night in Beast House* was an omnibus edition of two reprint novellas.

Edited by Chris Keeslar, *My Zombie Valentine* contained four paranormal romance stories (one reprint) about the walking dead by Katie MacAlister, Angie Fox, Marianne Mancusi and Lisa Cach.

In August, Dorchester Publishing, whose imprints include Leisure, Love Spell and Cosmos, announced that it was dropping its mass-market paperback lines for a revised business model that would move titles to e-books and print-on-demand formats immediately. Declining mass-market paperback sales were blamed.

Just two weeks later, Dorchester CEO John Prebich confirmed that the company had let go of two of its top editors: editorial director Leah Hultenschmidt and senior editor Don D'Auria (who was responsible for Leisure and other genre lines), along with all the sales reps. Prebich claimed that the departures were part of the company's new operating plan, and that Dorchester would still be publishing scheduled product through 2011. However, the changes came amid mounting complaints from Dorchester authors of late royalty payments and defaulted contracts, with several writers reclaiming the rights to their works.

Prebich himself left the company in November, as agents and authors revealed that Dorchester was continuing to sell e-book editions even after the rights had been reverted. Robert Anthony stepped into the top role and immediately reversed the earlier decision to stop publishing print editions.

\*      \*      \*

*Dead in the Family* was the tenth book in Charlaine Harris' phenomenally successful Southern vampire series featuring Sookie Stackhouse. The complicated plot involved the aftermath of the brief but deadly Faery War and a number of more personal problems that the telepathic waitress had to deal with.

*Flirt*, the eighteenth volume in Laurell K. Hamilton's "Anita Blake, Vampire Hunter" series, featured an Afterword by the author, in which she discussed where she got her ideas, and a graphic story illustrated by Jennie Breeden. It was followed by *Bullet*, in which the Mother of All Darkness attempted to possess Anita's body.

*The Fall* was the second volume in the "Strain" trilogy about a vampire plague, written by film director Guillermo del Toro and Chuck Hogan.

Syrie James' *Dracula, My Love: The Secret Journals of Mina Harker* retold Bram Stoker's novel from the viewpoint of Mina Harker, while a soap opera writer named "Meena Harker" fell for a talk, dark and fanged stranger in *Insatiable*, Meg Cabot's paranormal riff on *Dracula*.

Credited solely to actress Adrienne Barbeau, *Love Bites* was a sequel to *Vampires Over Hollywood* (co-written with Michael Scott).

Humans and vampires teamed up in an unlikely alliance to fight back against alien invaders in *Out of the Dark* by David Weber, and a vampire saved a waitress from a serial killer in *Murder in Vein* by Sue Ann Jaffarian.

An ordinary-seeming suburban family denied their unusual appetites in Matt Haig's English vampire novel *The Radleys*, which strangely attempted to hide its genre roots.

Set during Napoleonic times, a 150-year-old vampire tried to cure his affliction in *Blood Prophecy* by Stefan Petrucha, and a young 19th-century widow discovered she was a vampire hunter in Jacqueline Lepore's Gothic novel *Descent Into Dust*.

Alaya Johnson's *Moonshine* was about a vampire in 1920s New York, while an opera singer carried the composer's musical talent down through the centuries in *Mozart's Blood* by Louise Marley.

Nathaniel Cade was an undead secret agent who had protected successive American presidents down through the decades in

*Blood Oath*, the first in the "President's Vampire" series by Christopher Farnsworth.

A vampire agent and a human police detective teamed up to find a killer bloodsucker in *Uprising*, the first volume in Scott G. Mariani's "Vampire Federation" series.

Prisoners were transformed into the undead by a covert government experiment in *The Passage*, the first volume in a new vampire trilogy by Justin Cronin, and *Vampire Empire: The Gateway* was the first volume in Clay Griffith and Susan Griffith's steampunk trilogy.

*Blood & Sex: Michael* and *Blood & Sex: Jonas* were the first two volumes in Angela Cameron's erotic vampire series, originally published as e-books.

*Thirteen Years Later* was the second volume in Jasper Kent's historical vampire series that began with *Twelve*, while *The Girls with Games of Blood* was Alex Bledsoe's follow-up to *Blood Groove* and involved a century-old feud between a nest of vampires and two beautiful undead sisters in 1975 Memphis.

Terence Taylor's *Blood Pressure* was the second book in the "Vampire Testament" series, and *Blood Maidens* was the third volume in Barbara Hambly's "James Asher" series.

*Bite Me* was the third in the humorous vampire series by Christopher Moore that began with *Bloodsucking Fiends* and *You Suck*. This time San Francisco vampires Jody and Tommy found themselves pitted against an enormous vampire cat named "Chet".

*Memories of Envy* by Barb Hendee was the third in the "Vampire Memories" series, about a deadly bloodsucker who was turned into one of the undead during the Roaring Twenties.

*Demon Dance*, the third volume in Sam Stone's "Vampire Gene" series, was about a time-travelling female vampire, and *The Season of Risks* was the third in the "Ethical Vampire" series by Susan Hubbard.

Latino vampire PI Felix Gomez became involved in a turf war amongst rival werewolf gangs in *Werewolf Smackdown*, the fifth volume in the mystery series by Mario Acevedo, and *Chosen* was the sixth volume in Jeanne C. Stein's series about vampire Anna Strong.

*Vampire Mistress* was an erotic paranormal romance by Joey

W. Hill, while *The Vampire Maker* was the fourth book in Michael Schiefelbein's gay vampire series about Victor Decimus, who moved to New Orleans.

*Blood Sacraments* was an anthology of twenty gay erotica vampire stories edited by Todd Gregory, published by the aptly named Bold Strokes Books.

A descendant of the Homo Lupens who once ruled the world was forced to protect the woman he loved from those of his own blood in *A Taint in the Blood*, the first volume in S.M. Sterling's "Shadowspawn" series.

A TV bounty hunter set his sights on shape-shifter Mercy Thompson's werewolf boyfriend Adam in Patricia Briggs' *Silver Borne*, while *Wolfsbane* was the author's second book about female shape-shifting mercenary, Aralorn.

*Wolfsangel* was the first in a new series by M.D. Lachlan involving werewolves and Norse mythology, and a New York homicide detective hunted a rogue werewolf serial killer in *The Frenzy Way* by Gregory Lambertson.

In Gail Carriger's *Changeless*, the second Victorian steampunk adventure in the "Parasol Protectorate" series featuring the soulless Alexia Tarabotti, something had caused all the vampires, werewolves and ghosts in London suddenly to lose their supernatural powers, and it was up to Alexia and her alpha werewolf husband Conall to investigate.

S.A. Swann's *Wolf's Cross* was the second volume in the historical werewolf series that began with *Wolfbreed*, *Overwinter* was the follow-up to David Wellington's *Frostbite*, and *Wolf's Bluff* was the third book in W.D. Gagliani's series about werewolf homicide detective Nick Lupo.

*Never Cry Werewolf* and *Left for Undead* were the fifth and sixth volumes, respectively, in the "Crimson Moon" series by L.A. Banks, about a lycanthropic Special Ops team, while the leader of a werewolf special forces team went crazy in *Kitty Goes to War*, the eighth in the series by Carrie Vaughn.

*The Reapers Are the Angels* by Alden Bell (Joshua Gaylord) was a literary novel set in a post-holocaust world decimated by a zombie plague.

*Rise Again: A Zombie Thriller* was a post-apocalyptic novel by Ben Tripp, a nasty epidemic in Northern Island resulted in victims returning as the walking dead in Wayne Simmons' *Flu*, and *Zombie Britannica* by Thomas Emson was set in a London overrun by the reanimated dead.

A mysterious girl had the power to repel the zombie hordes in Bob Fingerman's *Pariah*, while the ordinary folk of a small Minnesota town found themselves battling the waking dead in the parody *The Zombies of Lake Woebegotten* by "Harrison Geillor".

"Created by" Stephen Jones, *Zombie Apocalypse!* was an ambitious "mosaic novel" set in the near future, when a possibly supernatural plague swept across the world. Told through a series of interconnected eyewitness narratives, including text messages, e-mails, blogs, letters, diaries and transcripts, contributors included Michael Marshall Smith, Christopher Fowler, Sarah Pinborough, Jo Fletcher, Kim Newman, Lisa Morton, Tanith Lee, Tim Lebbon, Peter Crowther, Robert Hood, Mark Samuels, Peter Atkins, Scott Edelman, Mandy Slater and others.

In *Desperate Souls* by Gregory Lamberson, a New York detective uncovered a mystery involving zombies, and Nancy Holzner's *Deadtown* introduced demon-slayer Victory Vaughn and her zombie apprentice.

A zombie cheerleader investigated the theft of students' brains in *My So-Called Death* by Stacey Jay, and a pair of sibling bloggers were the main protagonists of *Feed*, the first book in the futuristic "Newsflesh" zombie trilogy by "Mira Grant" (Seanan McGuire).

*Dead Love* by Linda Watanabe McFerrin was a zombie novel set in Japan. One chapter appeared both in a text version and as a sixteen-page *manga* comic illustrated by Botan Yamada.

An ex-forces hotel manager had to deal with an outbreak of a zombie virus during a Star Trek convention in *Night of the Living Trekkies* by Kevin David Anderson and Sam Stall.

David Moody's zombie novel *Autumn* was originally published free online and was the first in a series.

Walter Greatshell's *Xombies: Apocalypticon* was the second novel in the series that began with *Xombies* in 2004, and *Day by Day Armageddon: Beyond Exile* was the second volume in the seven-book zombie series by J.L. Bourne.

While working as a bodyguard to Lucifer, paranormal enforcer James Stark had also to deal with a zombie outbreak in Los Angeles in Richard Kadrey's *Kill the Dead*, the author's follow-up to *Sandman Slim*, and a mad scientist hired a pair of zombie exterminators in *Flip This Zombie*, the second book in the humorous series by Jesse Petersen.

*Battle of the Network Zombies* was the third volume in Mark Henry's comedic "Amanda Feral" series, set around the murder of a reality TV show host, while *Silver Zombie* was the fourth book in the series by Carole Nelson Douglas featuring paranormal investigator Delilah Street.

Abaddon Books' "Tomes of the Dead" series continued with *Tide of Souls* by Simon Bestwick, *Stronghold* by Paul Finch, *Empire of Salt* by Weston Ochse and *Way of the Barefoot Zombie* by Jasper Bark. *The Best of Tomes of the Dead Volume 1* reprinted three novels by Matthew Smith, Al Ewing and Rebecca Levene with new Introductions to their work by the authors.

*Brains* was a first novel by Robin Becker, set in a post-apocalyptic future where a reanimated professor attempted to bring zombies and humans peacefully together.

Nine years after she died in a car crash, a girl came back as a zombie in Joan Francis Turner's first book, *Dust*, and an entire Texas high-school football team was brought back from the dead in Ryan Brown's humorous debut *Play Dead*.

*State of Decay*, the debut novel by James Knapp, was the first in a new zombie series set in the near future, where reanimated "revivors" were used for cheap labour. It was followed by *The Silent Army*.

Written by former funeral director "Carnell" (he apparently doesn't need a first name), *No Flesh Shall Be Spared* was another debut novel set in the near future, where zombies were used as pit fighters.

When a couple moved to a remote old farmhouse in northwest England, they discovered an ancient evil waiting for them in Tom Fletcher's first novel, *The Leaping*.

A woman inherited a haunted house on a remote island in *The Tale of Halcyon Crane*, the debut novel from short-story writer Wendy Webb, while Robert Jackson Bennett's first novel, *Mr Shivers*, was a revenge thriller set during America's Great Depression.

F.J. Lennon's debut, *Soul Trapper*, featured a musician-turned-ghost-hunter and was based on the author's iPhone app game.

*Claire de Lune* was a young adult debut novel about a sixteen-year-old female werewolf by Christine Johnson, while Andrea Cremer's first novel, *Nighshade*, was set in a world where humans were subservient to werewolves.

*Entangled* was the first novel by best-selling non-fiction author and lecturer Graham Hancock. A troubled teenager's near-death experience hurled her soul 24,000 years into a parallel past, where she teamed up with a Stone Age woman to prevent a demon horde destroying humanity.

In Rachel Hawkins' YA debut *Hex Hall*, a teenage witch was sent to a special reform school for supernaturals, where somebody was killing the students, and a high-school student discovered that vampires were real in A.M. Robinson's first book, *Vampire Crush*.

An Edgar Allan Poe fan pulled a cheerleader into his Gothic dream world in Kelly Creagh's debut novel *Nevermore*.

Karen Kincy's debut YA novel, *Other*, was set in a small Washington town where supernatural creatures were turning up dead. A girl discovered on her sixteenth birthday that her parents had been murdered in *Dead Beautiful*, a first novel by Yvonne Woon, and a boy had the ability to enter the land of the dead in Anna Kendall's debut *Crossing Over*.

Throughout the year the publishing industry continued to flog the "literary mash-up" concept to death with such titles as *Pride and Prejudice and Zombies: Dawn of the Dreadfuls* by Steve Hockensmith, which was a prequel to the best-seller by Jane Austen and Seth Graham-Smith, describing how Elizabeth Bennet became a zombie-slayer.

A young Abe set out to revenge his mother's death armed with his trusty axe in *Abraham Lincoln: Vampire Hunter*, television writer Grahame-Smith's follow-up to the best-selling *Pride and Prejudice and Zombies* and supposedly based on the future President's secret journals.

*Emma and the Vampires* by Jane Austen and Wayne Josephson poked fun at another of Austen's books, while Jane was still alive as a vampire in Michael Thomas Ford's *Jane Bites Back*. Jane Austen joined the vampire resistance in an England invaded by France in *Jane and the Damned* by Janet Mullany.

*Jane Slayre* by Charlotte Brontë and Sherri Browning Erwin re-imagined Brontë's heroine Jane Eyre as a vampire-slayer. Meanwhile, *Little Vampire Women* was a teen mash-up of Louisa May Alcott's novel and the undead by Lynn Messina, and *Little Women and Werewolves* was meant to be an unexpurgated version of Alcott's classic, co-credited to Porter Grand.

Mark Twain's adventurous youngster confronted a zombie plague in Don Borchert's *The Adventures of Tom Sawyer and the Undead*. Predictably, neither the author nor his publisher (Tor) were aware – or probably cared – that "undead" refers to vampires, not zombies.

The monarchy protected the British Empire from zombies and other supernatural creatures in *Queen Victoria Demon Hunter* by A.E. Moorat (Andrew Holmes), and *Henry VIII: Wolfman* was another title from the same author.

*The Secret History of Elizabeth Tudor: Vampire Slayer* by Lucy Weston spoke for itself, while William Shakespeare was a vampire necromancer in Loris Handeland's humorous *Shakespeare Undead*.

*Paul is Undead: The British Zombie Invasion* by Alan Goldsher was a humorous retelling of the birth of the Beatles, with three members of the pop group as the living dead.

*The War of the Worlds, Plus Blood, Guts, and Zombies* by H.G. Wells and Eric S. Brown was enough to make anyone's heart sink.

Edited by Joyce Carol Oates for the prestigious Library of America imprint, *Shirley Jackson: Novels and Stories* reprinted the novels *The Haunting of Hill House* and *We Have Always Lived in the Castle*, along with the complete contents of the collection *The Lottery*, plus a further twenty-one stories and vignettes, the text of a talk given by Jackson, and a chronology of the author's work.

Dover reprinted Charles Brockden Brown's 1798 novel

*Wieland: or, The Transformation; An American Tale* with a new Introduction by John Matteson, while *The String of Pearls* (aka *Sweeney Todd*), Thomas Preskett Prest's 1850 expansion of his serial, was reissued by Pocket Penguin Classics in trade paperback.

Edited with an Introduction and notes by Michael Newton, *The Penguin Book of Ghost Stories: From Elizabeth Gaskell to Ambrose Bierce* contained nineteen classic reprints and quickly went into a second printing.

*Dracula's Guest: A Connoisseur's Collection of Victorian Vampire Stories* collected twenty-two classic tales from Bram Stoker, John Polidori and Mary E. Wilkins-Freeman, amongst others, edited by Michael Sims.

From Barnes & Noble's bargain books imprint Fall River, *Dracula's Guest & Other Tales of Terror* brought together Bram Stoker's 1914 title collection and the author's 1881 volume *Under the Sunset. The Horror of the Heights & Other Strange Tales* collected fourteen stories by Arthur Conan Doyle, *The Legend of Sleepy Hollow & Other Macabre Tales* featured nineteen stories by Washington Irving, and *The Picture of Dorian Gray & Other Fantastic Tales* was reprinted from *The Complete Works of Oscar Wilde*, and contained three extra stories and six prose poems. All four books included Introductions by Michael Kelahan.

For the same imprint, Kelahan edited the reprint anthologies *The Screaming Skull and Other Classic Horror Stories* featuring thirty tales by H.P. Lovecraft, A. Merritt, Robert W. Chambers, E. Nesbit and others, and *The End of the World*, which included twenty stories and one poem from such authors as Lovecraft, H.G. Wells and Nathaniel Hawthorne.

*Horrors: Great Stories of Fear and Their Creators* by Rocky Wood included versions of *Frankenstein, Dracula* and *Beowulf* illustrated by Glenn Chadbourne.

*El Borak and Other Desert Adventures* was a collection of thirteen adventure stories by Robert E. Howard, with an Introduction by Steve Tompkins and an Afterword by David A. Hardy, illustrated by Tim Bradstreet and Jim and Ruth Keegan.

Pan Books reissued the initial volume of *The Pan Book of Horror Stories* selected by Herbert van Thal as a trade paperback. First published in 1959 and boasting the original cover design, the classic anthology contained twenty-two stories by Joan Aiken, Jack Finney, L.P. Hartley, Hazel Heald, Nigel Kneale, Seabury Quinn, Muriel Spark, Bram Stoker and others, along with a new Foreword by *Pan Book of Horror* expert Johnny Mains.

*Who Fears the Devil? The Complete Tales of Silver John* from Paizo/Planet Storis contained thirty stories by Manly Wade Wellman about John the Balladeer (including two previously uncollected in the series), along with Introductions by Mike Resnick and the late Karl Edward Wagner.

Ira Levin's 1967 novel *Rosemary's Baby* was reissued by Pegasus Books with a new Introduction by Otto Penzler, along with the disappointing 1997 sequel, *Son of Rosemary*.

Adding to the John Newbery Medal he received in 2009 from the American Library Association for *The Graveyard Book*, in June Neil Gaiman also won the UK's most prestigious children's fiction prize, the Cilip Carnegie Medal, for the same title. It was the first book to have ever won both prizes.

In August, Ricky Gervais was sued in the British High Court by obscure author John Savage, who claimed that the comedian's illustrated children's book *Flanimals* was based on his own 1998 publication, *Captain Pottie's Wildlife Encyclopedia*.

*My Name is Mina* was a prequel to David Almond's acclaimed children's book *Skellig* and was written in diary format.

*The Saga of Larten Crepsley: Birth of a Killer* was the first book in a prequel series to "The Demonata" series by Darren Shan (Darren O'Shaughnessy), which itself apparently concluded with the tenth volume, *Hell's Heroes*.

Two boys investigated a locked park and uncovered a mystery involving the legendary Greek gorgon Medusa in Christopher Fowler's first young adult novel, *The Curse of Snakes: Hellion*.

A pair of siblings had to rescue their Egyptologist father from Ancient Egyptian gods and demons in Rick Riordan's *The Red Pyramid*, the first book in the "Kane Chronicles".

A young girl could see a mark on people who were destined to die within twenty-four hours in Jen Nadol's *The Mark*, while a girl discovered that she could heal the dying in *Banished* by Sophie Littlefield.

A young girl could see into people's minds just by touching them in *Angel* by L.A. Weatherly, and a pair of special glasses allowed a boy to see into another world in Andrew Smith's *The Marbury Lens*.

Jill Jekel teamed up with Tristen Hyde to create an old family formula in Beth Fantaskey's YA romance *Jekel Loves Hyde*, while a boy's disturbing drawings helped solve a murder from the past in *Draw the Dark* by Ilsa J. Bick.

A girl was stalked by strange creatures accidentally raised by her parents in Mara Purnhagen's *Past Midnight*, the first in a new series, and *Witchfinder: Dawn of the Demontide* was the first book in a new trilogy by William Hussey.

*Jack: Secret Circles* was the second volume in F. Paul Wilson's trilogy about a teenage Repairman Jack.

Rick Yancey's *The Curse of the Wendigo* was the second volume in the "Monstrumologist" series featuring apprentice monster hunter Will Henry.

Kate Brain's *The Book of Spells* involved a coven of school-girls and was a prequel to the author's "Private" series, while *The Haunted* was Jessica Verday's sequel to *The Hollow*, once again set in Sleepy Hollow.

*Darke Academy: Blood Ties* was the second book in the series by Gabriella Poole, and *Mr Monster* was a sequel to Dan Wells' *I Am Not a Serial Killer*.

A group of children found themselves trapped in an evil comic-book world in *Havoc*, Chris Wooding's follow-up to *Malice*. Dan Chernett supplied the illustrations.

*Factotum* was the third and final volume in D.M. Cornish's "Monster Book Tattoo" or "The Foundling's Tale" series, depending on whether you live in Australia or the US.

Lisa Fade's *Gone* was the third book in the series that began with *Wake* and *Fade*, *Fearscape* by Simon Holt was the third book in the "Devouring" series, and *My Soul to Keep* was the third book in Rachel Vincent's "Soul Screamers" series about a teenage banshee.

*Skulduggery Pleasant: Mortal Coil* was the fifth volume in the mystery series by Derek Landy.

A teenager found himself haunted following a car crash in Amelia Atwater-Rhodes' *Token of Darkness*, and in a world where teenagers could see ghosts, a girl's dead boyfriend decided to stay around in *Shade* by Jeni Smith-Ready.

A girl and her dead boyfriend's brother were haunted by ghosts in the YA novel *Chasing Brooklyn*, written by Lisa Schroeder in blank verse.

A teen could see dead people in Sarah Smith's *The Other Side of Dark*, while *Among the Ghosts* by actress Amber Benson was about a teenager who could also see spirits. Sina Grace supplied the illustrations.

After her parents went missing, a girl ended up at a New England prep school where she could communicate with ghosts in *Deception*, the first volume in Lee Nichols' "Haunting Emma" series.

A girl received a text from her apparently dead schoolfriends in *Three Quarters Dead* by Richard Peck, and the ghost of a dead homecoming queen needed the help of a loser at her high school in *The Ghost and the Goth* by Stacey Kade.

A young maidservant had to contend with ghosts and a scheming housekeeper in *The Poisoned House* by Michael Ford, while Clare B. Dunkle's *The House of Dead Maids* was a ghostly novella prequel to *Wuthering Heights* by Emily Brontë.

In *7 Souls* by Barnabas Miller and Jordan Orlando, a murdered teen had to re-experience her death through the eyes of the people who most hated her.

*The Evil Within* was the second volume in Nancy Holder's "Possession" series, set in a haunted boarding school.

The mayor's mansion was haunted by an evil spirit in Marley Gibson's *Ghost Huntress Book 3: The Reason*, the third in the trilogy about a girl with psychic powers.

*The Back Door of Midnight* was the fifth book in the "Dark Secrets" series by Elizabeth Chandler (Mary Claire Helldorfer).

*The Spook's Nightmare* (aka *The Last Apprentice: Rise of the Huntress*) was the seventh volume in Joseph Delaney's "Wardstone Chronicles" series about an apprentice ghost hunter, illustrated by Patrick Arrasmith. A companion work to the series, *The Spook's Bestiary*, also by Delaney, was illustrated by Julek Heller.

A fourteen-year-old discovered that he was destined to become a vampire hunter in *Alex Van Helsing: Vampire Rising* by Jason

Henderson, while Daphne Van Helsing fell for a rival vampire slayer in Amanda Marrone's *Slayed*.

*Jealousy* was the latest volume in Lili St. Crow's "Strange Angels" series, in which tough teen Dru Anderson was hunted by a 400-year-old nosferat and his bloodthirsty army of suckers.

A terminally ill girl discovered that she could be cured by a vampire's blood in *Crave* by J. Laura Burns and Melinda Metz.

An overweight fifteen-year-old was accidently turned into one of the undead in Adam Rex's humorous *Fat Vampire: A Never Coming of Age Story*, while a not very interesting 100-year-old vampire who looked like a teenager wanted to impress the new girl at school in Tim Collins' *Diary of a Wimpy Vampire* (aka *Notes from a Totally Lame Vampire*), illustrated by Andrew Pinder.

*Crusade* by Nancy Holder and Debbie Viguié was the first in a new vampire spin-off series from the best-selling *Wicked* books, and Mia James' *By Midnight* was the first book in the "Ravenwood" series.

Following on from *Nightfall*, *Shadow Souls* was the second volume in L.J. Smith's spin-off series *Vampire Diaries: The Return*, while Douglas Rees' *Vampire High: Sophomore Year* was a belated sequel to the author's 2003 novel.

*Still Sucks to Be Me* was the humorous sequel to Kimberly Pauley's *Sucks to Be Me*, about new vampire Mina, and Melissa Francis' *Love Sucks!* was a sequel to *Bite Me!*, about another teenage vampire.

*V is for . . . Vampire* was the third in the humorous "Vampire Island" series by Adele Griffin, about three vampire children living in New York who were fruit/vampire bat hybrids.

Two teenagers were recruited by the FBI to battle evil in *ReVamped* by Lucienne Diver (aka Kit Daniels), the follow-up to *Vamped*. *End of Days* was the second title in Max Turner's "Night Runner" series, and *Hourglass* was the third in the vampire school series by "Claudia Gray" (Amy Vincent).

Somewhat confusingly, *Thirst No. 3: The Eternal Dawn* by Christopher Pike followed two omnibus volumes containing six novels in the "Last Vampire" series.

*Bad Blood* was the fourth book in Mari Mancusi's "Blood

Coven" series, in which a pair of twins secretly attended a vampire convention in Las Vegas.

*Eleventh Grade Burns* and *Twelfth Grade Kills* were the fourth and fifth entries, respectively, in Heather Brewer's series *The Chronicles of Vladimir Tod*, about a half-vampire boy.

*Vampirates: Empire of Night* was the fifth book in the series by Justin Somper, and *Misguided Angel* was the fifth in the vampire "Blue Bloods" series from Melissa de la Cruz.

*Spirit Bound* was the fifth of Richelle Mead's "Vampire Academy" books, and the author concluded the series with the sixth volume, *Last Sacrifice*.

From P.C. Cast and Kristin Cast, *Burned* and *Awakened* were the seventh and eighth volumes, respectively, in the "House of Night" series.

*Kiss of Death* and *Ghost Town* were the eighth and ninth volumes in the best-selling "The Morganville Vampires" series by "Rachel Caine" (Roxanne Longstreet Conrad).

Sisters Scarlett Red and Rosie March hunted werewolves in Atlanta in Jackson Pearce's *Sisters Red*, a young adult variation on the "Little Red Riding Hood" story.

After meeting a new student at school, a girl finally remembered how her parents died in *Low Red Moon* by Ivy Devlin, while Jennifer Lynn Barnes' *Raised by Wolves* was the first in a new series about a human teenager who witnessed her parents being murdered by werewolves before being taken in by the pack's alpha male.

*Once in a Full Moon* was the first in a new werewolf romance series by Ellen Schreiber, *Linger* by Maggie Stiefvater was another YA werewolf romance, and Francesca Block's *The Frenzy* also featured a teenage werewolf.

*Blood Wolf* and *Demon Games* were the third and fourth books, respectively, in the *Changeling* werewolf series by Steve Feasey.

Michael Thomas Ford's *Z* was a YA zombie novel set in the gaming world.

*The Dead-Tossed Waves* was Carrie Ryan's companion volume to *The Forest of Hands and Teeth*, set in a post-apocalyptic zombie world, while Charlie Higson's *The Dead* was a follow-up to *The Enemy*, in which a worldwide sickness had turned the adult population into zombies.

Jonathan Mayberry's *Rot & Ruin* was also set in a world overrun by the walking dead, and a school newspaper critic fell for a zombie singer in Adam Selzer's *I Kissed a Zombie, and I Liked It*.

*Undead Much* was the second volume in Stacey Jay's series about Megan Berry, "Zombie Settler".

*The Poison Eaters* from Big Mouth House collected twelve predominantly YA stories (two original) by Holly Black, and *More Bloody Horowitz* (aka *Bloody Horowitz*) collected fourteen stories by Anthony Horowitz.

*Haunted Houses* was the first volume in the "Are You Scared Yet?" series and contained ten delightfully creepy haunted house stories by Robert D. San Souci, with wash illustrations by Kelly Murphy and Antoine Revoy.

"Presented" by R.L. Stine, *Fear: 13 Stories of Suspense and Horror* contained original stories by Meg Cabot, Heather Brewer, F. Paul Wilson, Heather Graham and others.

As its title indicated, *Zombies vs. Unicorns* contained twelve original stories about either zombies (edited by Justine Larbalestier) or unicorns (edited by Holly Black). Garth Nix, Margo Lanagan and Scott Westerfield were amongst the authors featured in this YA anthology, which grew from an online debate.

*Eternal: More Love Stories with Bite* edited by P.C. Cast and Leah Wilson contained six original paranormal YA romance stories by Lili St Crow, Nancy Holder, Rachel Caine and others, with an Introduction by Cast.

Stephen King's latest collection, *Full Dark, No Stars*, contained four new novellas ("1922", "Big Driver", "Fair Extension" and "A Good Marriage") dealing with retribution, with an Afterword by the author. A four-page extract from "Big Driver" was published in the November 12 edition of *Entertainment Weekly* magazine.

Kelley Armstrong's *Tales of the Otherworld* collected eight stories (one original) set in the author's world of werewolves, vampires and witches. The reprints were originally published on Armstrong's website.

\*　　\*　　\*

Claiming once again to "redefine" the limits of imaginative fiction, *Stories* was billed as a "groundbreaking" anthology of *All-New Tales* edited by Neil Gaiman and Al Sarrantonio. It featured twenty-seven stories by such Big Names as Roddy Doyle, Joyce Carol Oates, Joanne Harris, Walter Mosley, Richard Adams, Lawrence Block, Chuck Palahniuk and Jeffery Deaver, amongst others, along with more traditional genre contributors like Michael Marshall Smith, Joe R. Lansdale, Peter Straub, Diana Wynne Jones, Gene Wolfe (whose name was misspelled in the author notes), Jonathan Carroll, Tim Powers (whose story was inadvertently left out of the uncorrected proof copies), Michael Moorcock, Elizabeth Hand, Joe Hill and the two editors.

One of the best anthologies of the year was *Haunted Legends* edited by Ellen Datlow and Nick Mamatas, which contained twenty original stories inspired by local legends and ghost stories from around the world. Contributors included Richard Bowes, Steven Pirie, Caitlín R. Kiernan, Jeffrey Ford, Gary A. Braunbeck, Stephen Dedman, Laird Barron, Pat Cadigan, Ramsey Campbell and Joe R. Lansdale. Only Mamatas provided an Introduction.

Edited by Christopher Golden, *The New Dead* (aka *Zombies*) collected nineteen original stories about the walking dead by Joe Hill, Joe R. Lansdale, Tad Williams, John Connolly, Tim Lebbon, Mike Carey, David Wellington, Kelley Armstrong and others. A 250-copy signed edition was issued by Subterranean Press.

Originally published in electronic format, *Hungry for Your Love* was an anthology of twenty-one zombie romance stories edited by Lori Perkins. Contributors included Michael Marshall Smith and Brian Keene.

*The Book of the Living Dead* edited by John Richard Stephens contained twenty-seven classic tales of the reanimated dead by H.P. Lovecraft, Edgar Allan Poe, Jack London and others.

*Werewolves and Shapeshifters: Encounters with the Beast Within* edited by John Skipp contained thirty-five stories (nearly half of them original) by Neil Gaiman, Joe R. Lansdale, Angela Carter and others.

Edited by James Lowder, *Curse of the Full Moon* was an anthology of nineteen werewolf stories (one original) and a poem. Contributors included Neil Gaiman, Jonathan Carroll,

Michael Moorcock, Ursula K. Le Guin, Harlan Ellison, Gene Wolfe and Peter S. Beagle.

*Visitants: Stories of Fallen Angels & Heavenly Hosts* edited with an Introduction by Stephen Jones contained twenty-seven stories (thirteen original) by Neil Gaiman, Jay Lake, Jane Yolen, Arthur Machen, Sarah Pinborough, Lisa Tuttle, Graham Masterton, Robert Shearman, Michael Marshall Smith, Ramsey Campbell, Peter Crowther, Robert Silverberg, Christopher Fowler and others.

Even more than the sometimes inappropriate story introductions, the main problem with editor Jonathan Oliver's anthology *The End of the Line: New Horror Stories Set on and Around the Underground, the Subway, the Metro and Other Places Deep Below* was that many of the contributions were too similar to each other. Featuring nineteen tales (one reprint), the impressive line-up of contributors included John L. Probert, Nicholas Royle, Simon Bestwick, Conrad Williams, Pat Cadigan, Adam L.G. Nevill, Mark Morris, Stephen Volk, Ramsey Campbell, Michael Marshall Smith, James Lovegrove, Gary McMahon, Joel Lane and Christopher Fowler.

*Blood Lite II: Overbite* was the second in the series of humorous horror anthologies presented by the Horror Writers Association and edited by Kevin J. Anderson. It featured thirty-one original tales by Heather Graham, Scott Nicholson, Don D'Ammassa, L.A. Banks, Edward Bryant, Sharyn McCrumb, Nancy Kilpatrick, Nina Kiriki Hoffman, Steve Rasnic Tem, Kelley Armstrong and others.

Edited with a short Introduction by Charlaine Harris and Toni L.P. Kelner, *Death's Excellent Vacation* was an original anthology of thirteen paranormal romance stories by Jeff Abbott, L.A. Banks, Christopher Golden, Lilith Saintcrow and others, including a new "Sookie Stackhouse" tale by co-editor Harris.

*Dark and Stormy Knights* edited by P.N. Elrod contained nine stories about supernatural heroes by Jim Butcher, Carrie Vaughn and the editor.

Edited with an Introduction by Carol Sterling, *More Stories from the Twilight Zone* was an all-new collection of nineteen stories (one reprint) written in the vein of the late Rod Serling's classic TV series.

Edited with an Introduction by Trisha Telep, *The Mammoth Book of Paranormal Romance 2* included seventeen original stories. Darrell Schweitzer and Martin H. Greenberg teamed up to edit *Cthulhu's Reign*, an anthology of fifteen Lovecraftian stories set after the return of the Old Ones, and *Full Moon City*, which featured fifteen stories about werewolves.

Greenberg also collaborated with various co-editors to turn out such anthologies as *Vampires in Love* (with Rosalind M. Greenberg), *Fangs for the Mammaries* (with Esther Friesner), *Louisiana Vampires* (with Lawrence Schimel) and *A Girl's Guide to Guns and Monsters* (with Kerrie Hughes).

The second volume of Ellen Datlow's *The Best Horror of the Year* from Night Shade Books contained seventeen stories (including three from her own anthology *Poe*) along with the editor's summation of the year and the usual "Honorable Mentions" (now expanded online).

Prime Books debuted its own series with *The Year's Best Dark Fantasy & Horror 2010*, edited by Paula Guran and containing thirty-nine stories, while the twenty-first volume of *The Mammoth Book of Best New Horror* edited by Stephen Jones contained nineteen stories and novellas, along with a substantial look at the preceding year in horror, a Necrology and list of useful addresses.

Michael Marshall Smith's "What Happens When You Wake Up in the Night" was the only story that appeared in all three "Year's Best" horror anthologies. Norman Prentiss' "In the Porches of My Ears" turned up in two of them, and Ramsey Campbell, Gemma Files, John Langan, Reggie Oliver and Barbara Roden were each represented in two out of the three volumes, but with different stories.

Jones also compiled *The Mammoth Book of the Best of Best New Horror: A Twenty-Year Celebration*, which collected one story from each year of the series' two decades by Brian Lumley, Michael Marshall Smith, Harlan Ellison, Neil Gaiman, Peter Straub, Kim Newman, Joe Hill, Lisa Tuttle, Clive Barker, Stephen King and others, with an Introduction by Ramsey Campbell and extensive commentary about the history of the title by the editor.

\*     \*     \*

With more electronic books than hardcovers reportedly now being sold in the US, Amazon promised to undercut the price of print editions and rival electronic readers and, for the first time, the company also opened a virtual e-bookstore in the UK.

However, for two weeks at the end of January, all the electronic titles published by Macmillan were pulled from Amazon's virtual bookshelves after the publisher claimed that the price being charged for its e-books was too low and could damage hardcover sales. Unsurprisingly, HarperCollins and Hachette supported Macmillan's position.

Apple's iPad tablet computer, launched in January, aimed to "save" the book and magazine industry with its iBook store and revolutionary touchscreen technology for buying and reading electronically. More than 7.5 million were sold in the first six months.

Amazon's new Kindle e-book reader was launched around the world at the end of July. Costing between £109 and £149 (between $139 and $189), it was the size of a paperback and could wirelessly download new titles online from a catalogue of more than 400,000 books.

In November it was the turn of Samsung and Google to launch their Galaxy Tab "Android" media player. Although it was small enough to fit into a jacket pocket and could download thousands of apps from Google's online store, the Tab was more expensive than the iPad.

Google also launched its own Google eBookstore in December, which claimed to offer the "world's largest selection of e-books". Google's three million titles could be read on almost all digital devices except for Amazon's popular Kindle.

Cemetery Dance Publications offered free e-book and audio-book downloads of Brian James' novella *The Painted Darkness* almost four months before the hardcover edition was published. The electronic version, which was only available for a limited time, also included exclusive bonus material, including an Afterword and interview with the author, a new interview with Ray Bradbury and a special feature where Bradbury, Stephen King, William Peter Blatty, Michael Marshall Smith, Douglas Clegg and others shared their thoughts on the future of e-book publishing. More than 10,000 people downloaded the book in the first two weeks, which resulted in CD doubling the first printing. The hardcover edition included an exclusive Introduction by Brian Keene and interior illustrations by Jill Bauman, and a signed, limited edition sold out within twenty-four hours following the publicity generated by the free e-book.

In July, the Syfy channel rebranded its online Sci Fi Wire site to "Blastr" (*sigh*). Scott Edelman remained as editor.

*The Zombie Survival Scanner* from Crown Publishing Group's digital division was a free iPhone app based on Max Brooks' *The Zombie Survival Guide*. It allowed people with too much free time to scan their friends' zombie infection rate.

In July, the first nineteen issues of Joss Whedon's *Buffy the Vampire Slayer: Season Eight* from Dark Horse became available for download as animated "motion comics" on iTunes. The series was subsequently released on DVD.

*Bare Souls: Tales of Love, Sex and Death* was a collection of twelve erotic slipstream stories by Marcelle Perks, published as an e-book by Xcite Books. The volume's two previously unpublished stories were collaborations with Kevin Mullins.

Just in time for Halloween, the Internet Movie Database launched its IMDb Horror Section devoted to the latest news, lists, trailers and photos.

Publisher Roy Robbins continued to put out a number of handsome titles under his Bad Moon Books print-on-demand (PoD) and e-book imprint, many of them in special signed editions.

The last Hollywood film crew decided to shoot the last Hollywood movie in a post-nuclear America in John Skipp and Cody Goodfellow's satirical short novel *The Day Before*.

Gene O'Neill's novella *Jade* was set in the author's post-apocalyptic California and featured an Introduction by Michael McBride and colour plates by Steven Gilberts. It was available in an edition of 150 signed and numbered paperback copies and twenty-six lettered hardcovers.

*Lord of the Lash and Our Lady of the Boogaloo* was the second novella in Weston Ochse's "Vampire Outlaw Trilogy", and a cult attempted to open a gateway to another world on Halloween in Benjamin Kane Ethridge's novel *Black & Orange*.

A young woman witnessed something terrible that shaped her

life in Paul Melnicek's novella *The Watching*, while a couple learned that no good deed went unpunished in Erik Williams' backwoods horror *Blood Spring*. Both books were nicely illustrated by Jill Bauman.

*Mischief Night* was a Halloween novella by Paul Melniczek, illustrated by Caroline O'Neal, as was Lisa Morton's *The Samhanach*, with artwork by Frank Walls. Don D'Ammassa's pulp novella *Wings Over Manhattan* involved a private detective pitted against a supernatural evil.

Containing two novellas featuring senior "Monster Wrangler" J.D. Enron and available in a special signed edition limited to 100 numbered copies and twenty-six lettered, *Monster Town/ The Butcher of Box Hill* by "Logan Savile" (Steven Savile and Brian M. Logan) was packaged like a hardcover Ace Double.

*Blood & Gristle* contained twenty stories (one reprint) by Michael Louis Calvillo, while *Little Things* collected twenty-three stories (four original) by John R. Little with an Introduction by Mort Castle.

Lisa Mannetti's *51 Fiendish Ways to Leave Your Lover* listed various macabre methods of ending a relationship. Glenn Chadbourne supplied the black and white illustrations, and there was a poetic Introduction from P.D. Cacek.

Published as a print-on-demand edition by Bad Moon Books, *Dark Matters* collected forty-nine poems (six original) by Bruce Boston, illustrated by Daniele Serra.

Selected by Charles Black, *The Black Book of Horror* reached its sixth and seventh trade paperback volumes from Mortbury Press. Containing fifteen and seventeen original stories, respectively, the contents of each volume varied wildly between subtlety and the worst excesses of *The Pan Book of Horror Stories*, with contributions from, amongst others, John Llewellyn Probert, Simon Kurt Unsworth, Steve Lockley, R.B. Russell, Paul Finch, Gary Fry, Craig Herbertson, Reggie Oliver, David A. Riley, Anna Taborska, Mark Samuels, Joel Lane, Steve Rasnic Tem, Claude Lalumière, Tony Richards and a particularly unpleasant tale from Stephen Volk.

Available as an attractive hardcover from Mythos Books, Matt Cardin's *Dark Awakenings* collected seven stories (one original and two revised and expanded) and three academic papers (two original and another significantly revised) exploring the intersection between horror and religion.

From Hippocampus Press, *Wait for Thunder: Stories for a Stormy Night* contained twenty-seven stories (two original) by Donald R. Burleson, while *Sin & Ashes* collected forty-nine stories and poems (forty-three original) by Joseph S. Pulver, Sr. with an Introduction by Laird Barron.

Hippocampus also published *The Tindalos Cycle* edited by Robert M. Price, an anthology of twenty-seven Lovecraftian stories (three original) inspired by the classic story by Frank Belknap Long, who was represented with six tales, along with contributions from Robert Bloch, Lin Carter and Peter Cannon, amongst others.

As part of the imprint's "Lovecraft's Library" series, *The Shadowy Thing* was a reprint of H.B. Drake's 1925 novel *The Remedy*.

*From the Cauldron*, containing almost 100 poems by Fred Phillips, was the latest volume in the "Hippocampus Press Poetry Library" series. It featured a cover illustration by Howard Wandrei.

*Lord Ruthven Begins* from Black Coat Press was Frank J. Wood's translation of the 1865 play *Douglas the Vampyre* by Jules Dornay, with an historical Introduction by Jean-Marc Lofficier.

Introduced by Jack Dann and available from Australia's Ticonderoga Publications in PoD trade paperback and limited hardcover editions, *The Girl with No Hands and Other Tales* collected sixteen stories (three original) and an Afterword by Angela Slatter.

Slatter was also one of the contributors to *Scary Kisses*, an anthology of fourteen original paranormal romance stories edited by Liz Grzyb. *Belong* edited by Russell B. Farr brought together twenty-three new tales about people searching for a place to call "home".

Also from Ticonderoga, *Dead Sea Fruit* was a hefty retrospective collection of twenty-seven stories (two original) by Kaaron Warren, with an Introduction by Lucius Shepard and story notes by the author.

Kenneth Goldman's novella *Desirée* from Damnation Books

was about a woman whose love was deadly, while a woman seeking vengeance wanted to become a vampire in David Burton's *Blood Justice* from By Light Unseen Media.

*Vipers* was the second book in the "Veins Cycle" by Lawrence C. Connolly, available from Fantasist Enterprises.

*Mansfield Park and Mummies* was another tiresome Jane Austen mash-up, this time by Vera Nazarian, available as a print-on-demand edition from Norilana Books.

A female police detective uncovered murder and government conspiracies in a San Antonio in the grip of a deadly flu epidemic in *Quarantined* by Texas homicide detective Joe McKinney, published by Canadian PoD imprint Lachesis Publishing.

*Pallid Light: The Walking Dead* was a zombie novel by William Jones, from PoD publisher Elder Signs Press. From the same imprint, *The Best of All Flesh* collected twenty-two stories originally published in editor James Lowder's three *Books of Flesh* anthologies.

There were more zombies in T.W. Brown's *Dead: The Ugly Truth* and *Zomblog*, both from MayDecember Publications. Brown also edited the anthology *Eye Witness: Zombie* for the same PoD imprint.

"Conceived and edited" by Robert Essig, *Through the Eyes of the Undead* from Library of the Living Dead contained thirty-one zombie stories and a poem by writers you've probably never heard of. It was difficult to tell if they were all original, because there was no copyright information anywhere in the book, while the running heads only listed the title and editor and not the individual stories or authors.

*Dark Dimensions*, published in trade paperback by Fairwood Press/Darkwood Press, collected fourteen stories (two original) by William F. Nolan, with a Preface by the author and an Introduction by Jason V. Brock.

*Strange Men in Pinstripe Suits and Other Curious Things* from Strange Publications collected twenty-four stories (ten original) by Cate Gardner with an Introduction by Nathaniel Lambert.

*Beneath the Surface of Things* from New Jersey's Bards and Sages Publishing collected twenty-five short horror stories (sixteen original) by Kevin Wallis, along with an Introduction by A.J. Brown.

*As the Worm Turns* from new PoD imprint Blue Room Publishing contained twenty-two stories (fifteen reprints) by Brian Rosenberger.

Jeremy C. Shipp's collection, *Fungus of the Heart*, contained thirteen stories (six reprints). It was available as a PoD hardcover and trade paperback from Raw Dog Screaming Press.

Available from the grandly titled Library of Horror Press, *Unbound and Other Tales* collected nine stories (six original) by David Dunwoody.

*Animythical Tales* was the debut short story collection from Canadian writer Sarah Totten, available from Fantastic Books with an Introduction by Forrest Aguirre. It contained nine reprint short stories and an original novelette.

From Skullvines Press, *In Sickness: Stories from a Very Dark Place* written by the husband-and-wife team of L.L. Soares and Laura Cooney contained five stories (two original) by Cooney and six (one original) by Soares, along with a new collaboration.

*Dark Faith* was a PoD anthology of twenty-six original stories and five poems edited by Maurice Broaddus and Jerry Gordon for Apex Publications. Contributors included Jay Lake, Brian Keene and Tom Piccirilli.

Editor Jennifer Brozek's *Close Encounters of the Urban Kind* from the same imprint contained twenty tales, while *The Blackness Within: Stories of the Pagan God Moccus* edited by Gill Ainsworth contained thirteen original tales and some recipes centred around the Celtic god of fecundity.

Edited by Tim Lieder for Dybbuk Press, *She Nailed a Stake Through His Head: Tales of Biblical Terror* was a PoD anthology of nine stories (five original).

Available from Static Movement, *Something in the Doorway: A Haunted Anthology* edited and introduced by Gregory Miller contained twenty-two original stories.

Making its debut from BearManor Media, the first volume of *And Now the Nightmare Begins: The Horror Zine* edited by Jeani Rector was a spin-off from the e-zine, featuring twenty stories (one reprint) and fifty-two poems by Ramsey Campbell, Simon Clark, Terry Grimwood, Trevor Denyer, Gary William Crawford, Joe R. Lansdale and Scott Urban, amongst others.

The illustrated PoD trade paperback also included two additional stories by the editor.

The second issue of the PoD magazine *Shock Totem: Curious Tales of the Macabre and Twisted* edited by K. Allen Wood for Shock Totem Publications ("Established in 2009"), featured nine stories by Kurt Newton and others, along with an interview with James Newman and book and film reviews.

The eighth issue of the online *Irish Journal of Gothic and Horror Studies* edited by Elizabeth McCarthy and Bernice M. Murphy included articles on Lesbian Gothic, the *Nightmare on Elm Street* film series, and the short fiction of China Miéville, along with book and media reviews.

In Ramsey Campbell's latest novel, *The Seven Days of Cain*, from PS Publishing, a British photographer began receiving e-mails from an international serial killer who was somehow connected to an event that linked them ten years previously.

Gary Fry's debut novel from PS, *The House of Canted Steps*, was about a haunted family home, while an author with a fear of clowns moved to a rural area where all was not as it seemed in Terry Dowling's first novel, *Clowns at Midnight*.

A recovering heroin addict was haunted by a mysterious and terrible figure from his past in Rio Youers' *End Times*, and a young boy was given a glimpse of his own future in Rick Hautala's short novel *Reunion*, which came with an Afterword by F. Paul Wilson.

*What Will Come After* was a collection of nine superior zombie stories (one original) by Scott Edelman, while *Literary Remains* collected ten often oblique supernatural stories by R.B. Russell (three reprints).

Edited by Stephen Jones, *Darkness Mist & Shadow: The Collected Macabre Tales of Basil Copper* collected all the author's macabre and supernatural fiction (sixty-one stories and novellas) in two hefty volumes. Featuring introductions by the editor (#1) and Kim Newman (#2), the books boasted covers by Stephen E. Fabian and interior art by Randy Broecker, Dave Carson, Les Edwards, Bob Eggleton, Gary Gianni and Allen Koszowski. The two volumes were also available in a 200-copy deluxe slipcased edition signed by the author, editor and artists (£95.00).

Also edited with an Introduction by editor Jones and illustrated by Randy Broecker, *Pelican Cay & Other Disquieting Tales* collected seven stories and novellas (three original) by David Case. The 200-copy deluxe traycased edition (£60.00) contained two extra variant story drafts and was signed by all the contributors, including cover artist Les Edwards.

The eighteen stories (four original) in Garry Kilworth's collection *Tales from the Fragrant Harbour: Short Stories of Hong Kong and the Far East* were divided equally between mainstream tales ("Once-Told Tales") and those featuring the supernatural ("Twice-Told Tales").

*Long After Midnight* was a collection of twenty-two stories by Ray Bradbury from PS, with an Introduction by Ramsey Campbell. The book was available as 500 unsigned hardcovers, 200 slipcased hardcovers signed by the author, and 100 deluxe cased sets signed by both Bradbury and Campbell that included a hand-corrected story that was not included in the other editions (£95.00).

*Ventriloquism* was a collection of thirty-two eclectic short stories by Catherynne M. Valente, and *Counting Tadpoles* collected twenty reprint stories by reclusive author Uncle River.

Scott William Carter's *A Web of Black Widows* was PS Showcase #7 and contained six stories (four original) and an Introduction by the author.

Most novels and collections from PS were available in 500 trade hardcover editions and 100 signed editions.

Published as part of PS Publishing's handsome novella series, Terry Lamsley's *R.I.P.* was about survival after death, while a dead private investigator found himself trying to solve his own murder in Scott Nicholson's hardboiled ghost novella *Transparent Lovers*.

Stephen King's 1977 story *One For the Road*, a sequel-of-sorts to *'Salem's Lot*, was issued by PS as a delightful landscape picture book, featuring eighteen full-colour illustrations by James Hannah. It was available in hardcover as both a 100-copy slipcased edition signed by the artist (£175.00) and a 500-copy unsigned edition (£75.00).

Unlike the previous year's disappointing *Lovecraft Unbound* anthology, most of the twenty-one stories (two reprints) in *Black*

*Wings: New Tales of Lovecraftian Horror* edited by S.T. Joshi
still managed to transcend their eldritch themes while continuing
to remain true to the spirit and imagination of their inspiration.
Aside from a few fan pieces, some of the best work in the book
came from Caitlín R. Kiernan, Michael Shea, Nicholas Royle,
Brian Stableford, Ramsey Campbell, Norman Partridge and
Michael Marshall Smith.

*Darkness on the Edge: Tales Inspired by the Songs of Bruce
Springsteen* was edited and introduced by Harrison Howe and
contained nineteen stories based on The Boss' work by Elizabeth
Massie, Gary A. Braunbeck, Tom Piccirilli, Sarah Langan,
Jeffrey Thomas, T.M. Wright, James A. Moore, Nancy
Kilpatrick and others.

Edited with an Introduction by Allen Ashley, *Catastrophia*
was an anthology of eighteen original stories about the end of
the world (as we know it) by Andrew Hook, Simon Clark, Brian
W. Aldiss and others.

Volume 22/23 of the "Postscripts Anthology" series, *The
Company He Keeps*, was titled after the lead story by Lucius
Shepard. As usual edited by Peter Crowther and Nick Gevers,
the hardcover featured thirty-one original horror, fantasy and SF
stories by John Grant, Joel Lane, Don Webb, Quentin S. Crisp,
Rio Youers, Steve Rasnic Tem, Rhys Hughes, Darrell Schweitzer
and Holly Phillips, amongst others.

PS also issued a special edition of *Brighton Shock! The
Souvenir Book of the World Horror Convention 2010* edited by
Stephen Jones. Featuring fiction, articles and art by and about
the event's Guests of Honour, the 400-plus page hardcover also
included an entire original anthology of seaside horror (*Wish
You* Weren't *Here*), with fiction and poetry by H.P. Lovecraft,
M.R. James, Ramsey Campbell, Brian Lumley, Robert Shearman,
Joel Lane, Christopher Fowler, Michael Marshall Smith, Sarah
Pinborough, Kim Newman, Tim Lebbon and others. Limited to
100 numbered and slipcased copies, it was signed by no fewer
than thirty-three contributors (£95.00).

*Insinuations* from PS Publishing was a slim autobiography by
Australia-based speculative writer Jack Dann. There was a
100-copy limited hardcover available signed by the author.

From Cemetery Dance Publications, Stephen King's *Blockade*

*Billy* was a supernaturally themed baseball novella set in the late 1950s, in which the enigmatic title character mysteriously led a small-town team of losers towards a potential pennant victory. Illustrated by Alex McVey, the first 10,000 deluxe copies included a William "Blockade Billy" Blakely baseball card, while a signed limited edition was published by Lonely Road Books. The trade hardcover edition from Scribner also included the story "Mortality".

*The Secretary of Dreams Volume Two* was an oversized hardcover from CD that collected six reprint stories by King, profusely illustrated in black and white by Glenn Chadbourne. It was available in a slipcased gift edition of 5,000 copies ($75.00) and a leatherbound, signed traycased edition of 750 copies ($300.00).

Ronald Kelly's novel *Hell Hollow* was set in rural Tennessee and was also available in a 1,000-copy signed, lettered and traycased edition ($175.00).

*Last Exit for the Lost* was a hefty hardcover collection of Tim Lebbon's short fiction from Cemetery Dance. Limited to 1,500 signed copies, the book contained nineteen stories (two original) and an Introduction by Joe R. Lansdale.

Equally as big was *Occasional Demons*, which contained thirty stories (two original) by Rick Hautala, every one illustrated by Glenn Chadbourne. The deluxe hardcover was limited to 750 signed copies.

*Johnny Halloween* collected seven stories (including a new "Dark Harvest" tale) by Norman Partridge and was limited to a signed edition of 1,500 copies.

*Futile Efforts* was another huge collection of seventeen stories (one original) by Tom Piccirilli, each with an Introduction by a different author, including Gerard Houarner, Edward Lee, Jack Ketchum, Tom Monteleone, T.M. Wright, Tim Lebbon, Gary Braunbeck, Brian Keene, Ed Gorman, Simon Clark, Michael Laimo and Christopher Golden. The book also collected forty-five poems and was available in a 1,000-copy signed edition.

T.M. Wright's *Bone Soup* collected thirteen stories (three original), twenty poems (seven original) and a revised version of the 2003 novel *Cold House*. Illustrated by the author, this included an Introduction by Jack Ketchum and was also available in a signed edition limited to 750 copies and a lettered traycased edition ($175.00).

Jill Bauman illustrated Peter Straub's 1999 novella *Pork Pie Hat*, which was issued by CD in a trade edition, a signed edition of 350 copies ($50.00), and a traycased lettered edition of fifty-two copies ($200.00).

Limited to 750 signed and numbered copies apiece, Cemetery Dance's hardcover Novella series continued with Volume #19: *Invisible Fences* by Norman Prentiss, in which a cautious man discovered that his parents' often-gruesome warnings might possibly hold some truth. Keith Minnion supplied the interior artwork.

Volume #20 was Greg F. Gifune's *Catching Hell*, which was set in the summer of 1983 and concerned three young actors who found themselves trapped in the demonic rural community of Boxer Hills. Jill Bauman contributed the cover and interior illustrations.

*The Corpse King* by Tim Curran was #21 in the attractive series and told the story of a couple of 18th-century resurrection-ists who discovered that they were not the worst thing haunting graveyards and mortuaries. Keith Minnion again produced the interior art.

From Subterranean Press, *Mister Slaughter* was the third volume in Robert McCammon's series set in pre-Revolutionary America that began with *Speaks the Nightbird* and *The Queen of Bedlam*. This time gay detective Matthew Corbett was on the trail of escaped serial killer Tyranthus Slaughter, who lived up to his name. It was also available in a 274-copy signed edition and a lettered edition of twenty-six copies ($500).

Issued by the same imprint, *The Wolf's Hour* contained McCammon's 1989 World War II werewolf novel and a new novella, illustrated by Vincent Chong. This was issued as a 750-copy signed edition and a twenty-six copy traycased leather-bound edition ($250.00).

*Necroscope: The Plague-Bearer* was the latest "Lost Years" novella featuring Brian Lumley's hero Harry Keogh, who had to save a pack of Scottish werewolves from a vampire-engineered plague that could destroy them. As usual, Bob Eggleton supplied the cover art and interior illustrations for the Subterranean Press hardcover, which was also available in a special signed edition limited to 250 numbered copies.

*The Evil of Pemberley House* was a mix of Gothic horror and pulp fiction by Philip Jose Farmer and Win Scott Eckert. Along with the trade hardcover, it was also published by Subterranean in a 200-copy edition signed by Eckert along with a bonus chapbook.

*Deadman's Road* collected the 1986 novel *Dead in the West* and four stories (one original) featuring Joe R. Lansdale's Weird Western character, the Reverend Jedidiah Mercer, illustrated by Glenn Chadbourne.

*The Juniper Tree and Other Blue Rose Stories* by Peter Straub reprinted the novellas "Blue Rose", "The Juniper Tree", "Bunny is Good Bread" and "The Ghost Village", featuring characters and settings from the novels *Koko*, *Mystery* and *The Throat*. The book also included an interview with the author by publisher Bill Sheehan.

*Strange Wonders: A Collection of Rare Fritz Leiber Works* edited with an Introduction by Benjamin Szumskyj contained various unpublished or uncollected fiction drafts and fragments, early stories, articles and poetry by one of the genre's top names. The book was also available in a 150-copy leatherbound edition.

Originally announced by Hill House but never published by that apparently now defunct imprint, Subterranean teamed up with PS Publishing to produce a new edition of Ray Bradbury's *The Martian Chronicles* containing forty-nine stories (twenty-seven from the original 1950 edition), an essay, two screenplays, two Introductions and Afterwords by Richard Matheson, Joe Hill, Marc Scott Zicree and John Scalzi. Edward Miller (Les Edwards) contributed five colour plates. The book was available in a 500-copy limited edition ($300.00) and a twenty-six copy lettered edition ($600.00).

Also from Subterranean, *A Pleasure to Burn* contained sixteen stories related to *Fahrenheit 451* by Ray Bradbury, who celebrated his ninetieth birthday in August, with the city of Los Angeles hosting a week of Bradbury-themed celebrations.

The imprint also issued the third revised printing of Thomas Ligotti's 1985 collection *Songs of a Dead Dreamer*, containing definitive versions of the twenty stories. A leatherbound, signed edition of 250 copies was also available.

Caitlín R. Kiernan's *The Ammonite Violin & Others* was a new collection of twenty stories originally available to subscribers of the author's monthly online publication, *Sirenia Digest*, featuring "weirdly fantastical dark erotica". A signed, leatherbound edition came with a bonus chapbook.

*Amberjack: Tales of Fear and Wonder* collected stories and songs about the eponymous time-traveller by Australian writer Terry Dowling, while *Lesser Demons* contained ten stories by Norman Partridge. The 250-copy signed and numbered edition included a bonus chapbook.

*The Great Bazaar and Other Stories* was a companion volume to Peter V. Brett's dark fantasy novel *The Warded Man* (aka *The Painted Man*) that included a deleted chapter and scenes, along with a dictionary of terms.

*The Adventures of the Princess and Mr Whiffle: The Thing Beneath the Bed* was a not-suitable-for-children storybook from Subterranean Press, written by Pat Rothfuss and illustrated in black and white by Nate Taylor.

*Matheson Uncollected: Volume Two* from Gauntlet Press collected nine short stories (one original) by Richard Matheson, along with the opening chapters of three uncompleted novels and an unfilmed 1985 screenplay for *What Dreams May Come*.

Also from Gauntlet, *The Fall of the House of Usher/Usher II* was an edition of the two stories by Edgar Allan Poe and Ray Bradbury, heavily illustrated by Allois. It was published in an edition of 250 copies signed by the artist, fifty signed by both Bradbury and Allois ($100.00), and a fifty-two copy traycased and lettered edition ($200.00) signed by both.

Not only was Angela Slatter's *Sourdough and Other Stories* one of the most impressive debut collections of recent years, but the book created by Tartarus Press was a work of art in itself. The volume contained sixteen grim fairy tales (twelve original) by the Australian writer, along with an Introduction by Robert Shearman and an Afterword by Jeff VanderMeer.

As the title indicated, *The Collected Connoisseur* brought together all twenty-three previously published tales of the eponymous psychic detective by Mark Valentine and John Howard, and Tartarus also reissued Robert Aickman's 1968 collection of eight "strange stories", *Sub Rosa*, in a handsomely produced hardcover edition, limited to 350 copies and with a new Introduction by R.B. Russell.

From Canada's Ash-Tree Press, *Stranger in the House: The Collected Short Supernatural Fiction: Volume One* chronologically collected twenty-five stories by Lisa Tuttle with an Introduction by Stephen Jones. It was the first volume in a series that will eventually gather together the author's own selection of stories.

*Pieces of Midnight* was an impressive collection of eighteen stories (eight original) by Gary McMahon with an Introduction by Steve Duffy, and *Lost Places* contained eighteen tales (fourteen original) by Simon Kurt Unsworth, with an Introduction by Barbara Roden and story notes by the author. A special paperback edition was produced for World Horror Convention 2010. All Ash-Tree Press hardcovers were limited to 400 copies apiece.

Published by Irish imprint The Swan River Press in a slim but attractive hardcover edition of just 200 copies, *The Old Knowledge & Other Strange Tales* collected eight of Rosalie Parker's (mostly) genteel supernatural stories (three reprints). Glen Cavaliero supplied the Introduction.

*Riding the Bullet* from Lonely Road Books contained Stephen King's 2000 online novella and Mick Garris' screenplay for his barely seen 2004 movie adaptation. Printed in two colours, the book also featured illustrations by Bernie Wrightson and a wraparound cover by Alan M. Clark, along with numerous photos, storyboards and notes from the film. It was available in a 3,000-copy slipcased "collector's gift" edition ($75.00), a traycased limited edition of 500 copies signed by Garris and Wrightson ($250.00) and a fifty-two copy traycased edition ($750.00) additionally signed by King. Both signed editions sold out prior to publication.

A group of teenage film-makers in 1977 discovered that Willis H. O'Brien used an undead necromancer to help create a new form of animation in 1931 in David Herter's *October Dark* from Earthling Publications. It was available in a 500-copy signed edition and a slipcased lettered edition of just fifteen copies ($300.00).

From MonkeyBrain Books, *Mysteries of the Diogenes Club* collected five novellas (one original) by Kim Newman about the secretive intelligence and law enforcement agency originally created by Sherlock Holmes' smarter brother, Mycroft.

Although the eleventh volume of TTA Press' "Crimewave" series of trade paperback anthologies was entitled *Ghosts*, there was not as much horror content as you would expect in the fourteen stories by Nina Allan, Christopher Fowler, Cody Goodfellow, Steve Rasnic Tem, Joel Lane and others.

The same could not be said for *The Harm* by Gary McMahon, a slim little paperback published as part of the TTA Press Novella series, which dealt with the tricky topic of child abuse.

Limited to 300 signed copies, *In Concert* from Centipede Press collected twenty-one collaborations (one original) by Steve Rasnic Tem and Melanie Tem. The book featured a wraparound cover by Salvador Dalí, endpapers by Max Ernst, and was illustrated with original wood engravings by Howie Michels and colour plates by Marc Chagall.

Edited by Stephen Haffner, *The Early Kuttner Volume One: Terror in the House* was the first of two volumes from Haffner Press collecting the early short fiction of Henry Kuttner. It contained forty stories from 1936 to 1939 along with a Foreword by Richard Matheson and an Introduction by Garyn G. Roberts. There was also a limited slipcased edition for $150.00.

From Romanian small press imprint Ex Occidente Press came Mark Samuels' *The Man Who Collected Machen & Other Stories*, which was limited to 200 copies and contained eleven tales (eight original) and a reprint essay.

D.P. Watt's collection of nineteen stories, *An Emporium of Automata*, and Marvick Louis' novel *The Star Ushak* were both limited to 150 hardcover copies apiece. Insole Colin's *Oblivion's Poppy* from the imprint's Passport Levante line was available in a run of just 100 hand-numbered copies.

Publisher Dan Ghetu announced that Ex Occidente Press was to close in April 2011, saying his work would be done by then. The imprint had recently suffered some criticism over shipping problems.

In June, publisher Dave Barnett announced that he was closing Necro Publications, citing the downturn in the economy and health problems. Necro was a major promoter of Edward Lee's work, amongst others.

*Never Again*, from Gray Friar Press, was yet another sometimes questionable "charity anthology" with profits (after the publisher had recouped printing and distribution costs) being split between three human rights charities. Edited by Allyson Bird and Joel Lane, the book featured twenty-three stories (twelve reprints) supposedly protesting against racism and fascism, although these were not the only themes addressed by the authors represented. The reprint material by such writers as Lisa Tuttle, Joe R. Lansdale, Robert Shearman, Stephen Volk and Ramsey Campbell was notably superior to the original contributions.

*One Monster is Not Enough* was a collection of eight novellas and novelettes by Paul Finch, available as a 100-copy signed hardcover from the same imprint.

From Night Shade Books, *The Loving Dead* by Amelia Beamer was a comedy novel in which the zombie disease was sexually transmitted.

Compiled by Jonathan Strahan and the late Charles N. Brown, *Fritz Leiber: Selected Stories* from the same imprint was a large retrospective volume of seventeen stories with an Introduction by Neil Gaiman, while *Occultation* collected nine stories (three original) by Laird Barron with an Introduction by Michael Shea.

Edited with notes by Scott Connors and Ron Hilger, *The Collected Fantasies of Clark Ashton Smith Volume 5: The Last Hieroglyph* collected twenty-nine stories by the classic pulp author, including alternate and deleted material. Richard A. Lupoff contributed the Introduction to this final volume in the superior series.

Probably the best zombie anthology in an overcrowded year was *The Living Dead 2*, editor John Joseph Adams' substantial follow-up to his best-selling 2008 compilation *The Living Dead*, also published by Night Shade. This time, out of the forty-four featured stories, just over half were original, including those by Kelley Armstrong, Max Brooks, Cherie Priest, Simon R. Green, Robert Kirkman, David Wellington, and John Skipp and Cody Goodfellow, amongst others.

Edited by Tim Pratt, *Sympathy for the Devil* contained thirty-five Satanic stories by Neil Gaiman, Robert Bloch, Kelly Link,

John Collier, Holly Black, China Miéville, Theodore Sturgeon, Michael Chabon, Charles de Lint, Stephen King and others, along with an excerpt from Dante's *Inferno*.

Also published by Night Shade, editor Ellen Datlow's *Tails of Wonder and Imagination* was an attractive reprint anthology of forty feline stories from Neil Gaiman, Michael Marshall Smith, Kelly Link, Tanith Lee, Reggie Oliver, Stephen King, Nicholas Royle, Susanna Clarke and many others.

*What I Didn't See and Other Stories* was a hardcover collection by Karen Joy Fowler from Small Beer Press. It contained twelve stories (one original). The same imprint introduced English readers to the work of celebrated French author Georges-Olivier Châteaureynaud with the twenty-three reprint tales found in *A Life on Paper: Stories*. Brian Evenson supplied the Foreword.

Unashamedly channelling the spirit of Ray Bradbury's *Something Wicked This Way Comes*, William Ollie's novel *Sideshow* from Joe Morey's increasingly ambitious Dark Regions Press involved two thirteen-year-old boys and the secrets they discovered when Hannibal Cobb's dark carnival came to their town.

Jeffrey Thomas' *The Fall of Hades* was the latest volume in the author's ongoing "Hades" sequence, while Jim Gavin's *Hard Boiled Vampire Killers* was about a pair of losers who hunted the undead on the mean streets of Atlanta. Brian Knight supplied the Introduction.

Seventy-four years after he was lashed to a wooden cross and abandoned to God's judgement by the inhabitants of a small Iowa backwoods community, the thing that used to be Reverend Joshua Miller still waited for release in Gord Rollo's novel *Valley of the Scarecrow*.

Written and illustrated by Gabrielle Faust, *Regret* was about a man who literally became his own inner demon and subsequently crossed paths with the other minions of Hell. John Palisano contributed the Introduction.

When a young deputy sheriff moved from the big city to a small mountain community, he did not expect to encounter a man from the past and the monstrous god he worshipped in *Lord of the Mountain* by William Ollie.

As always, Dark Regions Press continued to support short horror fiction with a raft of attractive collections.

Jeffrey Thomas' *Nocturnal Emissions* contained eight stories (three original) and thirteen poems, while Scottish writer Daniel McGachey's *Sherlock Holmes: The Impossible Cases* presented four "recently discovered" stories featuring Holmes and Watson, along with various introductions and story notes.

*Going Back* brought together eighteen reprint stories by Tony Richards, while *Wine and Rank Poison* was a collection of ten stories (seven original) and a novel excerpt by Allyson Bird, with an Introduction by Joe R. Lansdale.

Rick Hautala supplied the Introduction to Harry Shannon's bumper collection *A Host of Shadows: A Short Story Collection*, which featured twenty-five very recent tales (five original), along with story notes.

Paul Melniczek had two new collections out under the imprint: *A Haunted Halloween* contained eleven stories (five original) and an Afterword by the publisher, while *Monsters* collected eight stories (six original).

The fifth volume in Dark Regions' "New Voices of Horror" series was *Do-Overs and Detours*, which collected fifteen stories (four original) by Steve Vernon with an Introduction by Richard Chizmar.

Published two years after the original edition from Humdrumming Ltd, *Beneath the Surface* was a revised and expanded edition of Simon Strantzas' debut collection that contained a different mix of fourteen stories (one original), along with a Foreword by Matt Cardin and an Afterword by the author.

*Charnel Wine: Memento Mori Edition* was a reprint of the 2004 collection by Richard Gavin, featuring twenty-three stories and vignettes (plus five more original to this edition) and a new Foreword by the author.

The first volume in Dark Regions Press' Novella series was Harry Shannon's zombie story *Pain*, in which the remaining inhabitants of a small mountain town defended themselves against a virus-infected horde of the living dead.

*The Mad and the Macabre* contained two serial-killer novellas by Jeff Strand and Michael McBride.

Under Dark Regions Press' Ghost House imprint, *Quill &*

*Candle* collected seventeen original supernatural stories by Scott Thomas set in the New England of the late eighteenth and early nineteenth centuries, while the ubiquitous Tony Richards also had *Our Lady of the Shadows*, another collection, out under the Ghost House banner. The trade paperback contained twelve stories (four original). Both titles were illustrated by Erin Wells.

Most Dark Regions/Ghost House titles were published as signed trade paperback editions.

Written between 1964 and 1970, *Rules of Duel* from Telos Publishing was a previously unpublished "collaboration" between Graham Masterton and William S. Burroughs, with original Introductions by both writers. Telos also reissued Masterton's 1977 novel *The Djinn* in a new edition, with an exclusive introduction by the author.

From the same imprint, *Humpty's Bones* by Simon Clark contained the original title novella, along with a new short story.

Edited by Ian Whates and Ian Watson for NewCon Press, *Shoes, Ships & Cadavers: Tales from North Londonshire* contained twelve multi-genre stories set in Northampton, with an Introduction by Alan Moore. There was a signed, limited edition of just fifty copies.

Also edited by Whates under the same imprint, *The Bitten Word* was an anthology of seventeen vampire stories (one reprint) by Simon Clark, Kelley Armstrong, Sarah Singleton, Gary McMahon, Andrew Hook, Storm Constantine, John Kaiine, Chaz Brenchley, Nancy Kilpatrick, Freda Warrington, Tanith Lee, Jon Courtney Grimwood and Ian Watson, amongst others, including the editor. There was also a special signed hardcover edition limited to 150 numbered copies.

Edited by Nancy Kilpatrick with a brief Foreword by Dacre Stoker, *Evolve: Vampire Stories of the New Undead* published by Edge Science Fiction and Fantasy was yet another vampire anthology. It contained twenty-three original stories and a poem by such Canadian authors as Kelley Armstrong, Tanya Huff, Gemma Files, Bev Vincent, Steve Vernon, Rio Youers, Rebecca Bradley and Claude Lalumière. Unfortunately, someone should have checked the editor's historical Introduction a bit more carefully.

The fourteenth volume in the long-running *Tesseracts* series from the same Canadian publisher was co-edited by John Robert Colombo and Brett Alexander Savory and featured twenty "strange Canadian stories" and several poems by David Nickle, Claude Lalumière, Sandra Kasturi, Robert J. Sawyer and others.

From associated imprint Absolute XPress, *Rigor Amortis* was an anthology of thirty-four original zombie erotica tales and one poem edited by Jaym Gates and Erika Holt.

*A Book of Tongues* from Canada's ChiZine Publications was the first novel by Gemma Files and introduced "Hexslinger" Asher Rook, a former preacher-turned-magician who used his small black Bible to battle supernatural evil in the Wild West.

*The Thief of Broken Toys* was a nicely produced novella by Tim Lebbon from ChiZine, about a man who was struggling to come to terms with a family tragedy. A signed, limited hardcover that was only available through pre-order included an additional story.

*Darkness: Two Decades of Modern Horror* from San Francisco's Tachyon Publications reprinted twenty-five stories from 1984–2005 by Stephen King, Clive Barker, Peter Straub, Neil Gaiman, Joyce Carol Oates, Lucius Shepard, Poppy Z. Brite, Edward Bryant, Elizabeth Hand and others, with a Foreword by Stefan Dziemianowicz and an Introduction by editor Ellen Datlow.

*The Best of Joe R. Lansdale* from the same publisher contained sixteen stories with an autobiographical Introduction by the author.

Published by Underland Press as a trade paperback omnibus, *The Complete Drive-in* contained all three of Joe R. Lansdale's novels in the series, along with an Introduction by film director Don Coscarelli and a selection of colour art by Nickita Knatz for a movie version that was never made.

New British independent imprint Chômu Press launched its list with Quentin S. Crisp's *Remember You're a One-Ball!*, a macabre coming-of-age novel in which a teacher recalled the strange world of his childhood.

The publisher followed it with Reggie Oliver's debut novel, *The Dracula Papers Part One: The Scholar's Tale*, about the early life of Transylvanian Prince Vladimir, and *I Wonder What*

*Human Flesh Tastes Like*, Justin Isis' debut collection of stories set in contemporary Japan, with an Introduction by Crisp.

Connie Corcoran Wilson's debut collection, *Hellfire and Damnation*, was inspired by Dante's nine circles of Hell. The trade paperback from Sam's Dot Publishing came with an Introduction by William F. Nolan, along with effusive cover quotes by Scott Edelman, Gary A. Braunbeck and Lisa Mannetti.

A family was forced to weed a patch of land to prevent monsters growing in Dave Zeltserman's *The Caretaker of Lorne Field*, from Overlook Press.

Available as an attractive (if not particularly well-edited) hardcover from Obverse Books with an Introduction by Nicholas Royale and an Afterword by John L. Probert, the stories (one reprint) in Johnny Mains' *With Deepest Sympathy: Fourteen Tales of the Odd and Twisted* would not have been out of place in the old *The Pan Book of Horror Stories*.

Most of the contributions to *Back from the Dead: The Legacy of The Pan Book of Horror Stories* also lived up to the quality of the anthology's inspiration. The first title from independent imprint Noose & Gibbet Publishing, the hardcover featured five reprints and sixteen new stories by such original contributors to the Pan series as Christopher Fowler, Tony Richards, John Burke, Basil Copper, David A. Riley, John Ware, Nicholas Royle, Harry E. Turner and Conrad Hill, along with a Foreword by Shaun Hutson, an historical essay by David A. Sutton and an extremely candid profile of *Pan Book of Horror* founder Herbert van Thal by editor Johnny Mains.

Edited with a brief Introduction by Mark Harding, *Music For Another World: Strange Fiction on the Theme of Music* from Scotland's Mutation Press contained nineteen original stories by Cyril Simsa, Andrew Hook, Neil Williamson and others.

Small press publishers Pendragon Press, Screaming Dreams and Atomic Fez teamed up to produce a special CD-ROM sampler/beermat for FantasyCon 2010 which featured excerpts and covers from a number of imprints' titles.

Paul Finch's Christmas novella *Sparrowhawk* from Pendragon Press was subtitled *A Victorian Ghost Story* and set during the coldest winter in living memory to grip London. Terry Grimwood's novella *The Places Between*, also from Pendragon, was about one woman's journey of self-discovery, while *Feral Companions* from the same imprint contained two novellas, one apiece by Simon Maginn and Gary Fry. The hardcover was limited to 300 copies, with the first 100 numbered and signed by the authors.

Paul Kane's novel *The Gemini Factor*, from Screaming Dreams, was a supernatural whodunit about a serial killer that only murdered twins and took their body parts. The trade paperback came with an Introduction by Peter Atkins and cover quotes from Peter James, Clive Barker, Kelley Armstrong and Peter Straub.

*Against the Darkness* collected the first eleven cases (six original) of John Llewellyn Probert's paranormal investigators Mr Massene Henderson and Miss Samantha Jephcott, and *Songs from Spider Street* collected twenty-five new and reprint stories by Mark Howard Jones and came with cover quotes from both Ray Bradbury and D.F. Lewis.

Also from Screaming Dreams, *Yuppieville* was a slim horror novella by Tony Richards about a new Nevada community where those who didn't fit in were forced to leave . . . permanently.

Set after "The Terror" had changed animals into the dominant species on the planet overnight, *The Terror and the Tortoiseshell* was the first "Benji Spriteman Mystery" by John Travis, a hardboiled crime mystery featuring a six-foot tall, suit-wearing cat detective. It was issued by Canada's Atomic Fez Publishing as a jacketless hardcover and e-book.

Described by its author as "the maddest thing I've ever written", Rhys Hughes' comic novel *Twisthorn Bellow* involved the explosive golem of the title attempting to prevent the French from taking over the afterlife. It was published in trade paperback and e-book by Atomic Fez and came with a cover quote by Mike Mignola.

*Wicked Delights: A Selection of Stories* from the same imprint collected eighteen stories (seven original) by the busy John Llewellyn Probert, who also contributed an Introduction and story notes. James Cooper's *The Beautful Red* contained twelve stories (five original), along with a Foreword by Christopher Fowler.

Edited by Jeff Connor and published by graphics imprint

IDW, *Classics Mutilated: CTRL-ALT-LIT* contained thirteen original literary "mash-ups" featuring Cthulhu, Billy the Kid, Frankenstein, Edgar Allan Poe, Dr Moreau, Sid Vicious and many others in stories by Kristine Kathryn Rusch, Marc Laidlaw, Mark Morris, Nancy Collins, Thomas Tessier, Rio Youers and others. Mike Dubisch supplied the illustrations.

Joe R. Lansdale's contribution to the anthology, the Mark Twain and H.P. Lovecraft-inspired novella "Dread Island", was issued in a series of four different limited editions – as a 500-copy trade paperback, available at conventions; a 400-copy signed hardcover, and a 100-copy signed and numbered leather-bound edition offered exclusively through the publisher's website. A fourth, "retailer only" edition, was also available to certain key accounts.

From Prime Books, *Zombies: The Recent Dead* edited by Paula Guran contained twenty-two reprint stories from the 21st century and an Introduction by David J. Schow, while Ekaterina Sedia edited *Running with the Pack*, an anthology of twenty-two werewolf stories (nine reprints) from the same imprint.

Edited by Selina Rosen for Yard Dog Press, *A Bubba in Time Saves None!* contained twenty-four humorous zombie stories.

World Fantasy Award-winning Welsh imprint Sarob Press closed in 2007 when owner Robert Morgan moved to northern France. He started up again in 2010 with *Seven Ghosts and One Other*, the second collection of eight M.R. Jamesian stories by C.E. Ward, a follow-up to the author's previous collection, *Vengeful Ghosts*. The hardcover was limited to 200 copies and included illustrations by Paul Lowe and an Afterword by the author.

Edited by educators Todd James Pierce and Jarret Keene, *Dead Neon: Tales of Near-Future Las Vegas* from University of Nevada Press featured fourteen imaginative tales set in or around Sin City by K.W Jeter and others.

Cutting Block Press from Texas published Volume 4 of *Horror Library*, a trade paperback anthology edited and introduced by R.J. Cavender and Boyd E. Harris containing twenty-eight stories by Nate Kenyon, Bentley Little, Hank Schwaeble, Jeff Strand, Tim Waggoner, Gerard Houarner and others.

Robert M. Price edited and supplied the Introduction to *The*

*Yith Cycle* for Chaosium, which included John Taine's 1924 novel *The Purple Sapphire* and thirteen Lovecraftian stories about the Great Race and time travel.

*Sprawl* from Twelfth Planet Press was an anthology edited by Alisa Krasnostein that featured eighteen original fantasy stories about an alternative suburban Australia by Sean Williams, Thoraiya Dyer, Angela Slatter, Anna Tambour, Cat Sparks and others.

Also from Australia, *Macabre: A Journey Through Australia's Darkest Fears* was an anthology edited by Angela Challis and Dr Marty Young from Brimstone Press. Split into three sections – "Classics (1836–1979)", "Modern Masters (1980–2000)" and "The New Era (2000– )" – the book contained thirty-eight stories (fifteen original) by Guy Boothby, Terry Dowling, Robert Hood, Sean Williams, Stephen Dedman, Rick Kennett, Kyla Ward and others, along with an Introduction by Dr Young and a timeline of Australian horror fiction.

*Null Immortalis* was the tenth and final volume in the *Nemonymous* series of original anthologies secretly edited by D.F. Lewis. As a result, the bylines of all twenty-six contributors – including Andrew Hook, Joel Lane, Gary Fry, Mike Chinn, Joseph S. Pulver Sr, Reggie Oliver, Mark Valentine and Steve Rasnic Tem – appeared for the first time in the same volume as their stories.

*Raw Terror: An Anthology of Horror Stories* edited by Ian Hunter featured twelve original stories by Adam Nevill, Mike Chinn and others.

Self-published by Kurt Mitchell, the six original stories in *Scratched from Dreams: A Small Collection of Stories* were illustrated by Randy Broecker, Gary Gianni, Tom Gianni, Scott Gustafson, Douglas Klauba and the author himself.

Not content with publishing more genre titles in the year than most mass-market imprints, or launching a new line of illustrated books, Peter and Nicky Crowther's PS Publishing also added a new poetry imprint to its burgeoning portfolio: Stanza Press was launched at the World Horror Convention 2010 with five handsome hardcover volumes.

Edited by Jo Fletcher, *Off the Coastal Path: Dark Poems of the Seaside* contained thirty new and reprint poems by Clark Ashton Smith, Donald Sidney-Fryer, Ray Bradbury, Tanith Lee, H.P. Lovecraft, Neil Gaiman, Brian Lumley, Ursula K. Le Guin, Joel Lane, Weldon Kees, William Hope Hodgson, T.M. Wright, John Gordon and many others. The book was illustrated with six appropriately spooky full-colour paintings by Ben Baldwin.

Compiled and with introductions by Stephen Jones, *The Complete Poems from Weird Tales* series comprised three slim volumes: *Hallowe'en in the Suburb & Others* by H.P. Lovecraft, *The Singer in the Mist & Others* by Robert E. Howard and *Song of the Necromancer & Others* by Clark Ashton Smith, with artwork by Virgil Finlay, Gary Gianni and Smith, respectively.

Also from Stanza, *Not Quite Atlantis: A Selection of Poems* was a retrospective collection of thirty-six poems by Donald Sidney-Fryer, with a Foreword by the poet and art by Les Edwards.

Edited with an Introduction by Al Sarrantonio, *Halloween: New Poems* was an attractive, oversized hardcover from Cemetery Dance Publications containing forty-one original poems by Steve Rasnic Tem, Elizabeth Massie, T.M. Wright, Melanie Tem, Tom Piccirilli, Joe R. Lansdale, Tom Disch, Peter Crowther and many others, including the editor. Keith Minnion supplied the illustrations.

Australia's P'rea Press collected more than seventy of Richard L. Tierney's poems in the hardcover *Savage Menace and Other Poems of Horror*, with a Preface by S.T. Joshi. Arranged and edited by Charles ("Danny") Lovecraft and covering a span of nearly fifty years, more than a third of the poems were previously unpublished.

From the same imprint, Leigh Blackmore's *Spores from Sharnoth and Other Madness* was a revised and expanded chapbook of a 2008 collection of mostly Lovecraft-inspired verse. Limited to just fifty signed and numbered copies, S.T. Joshi once again supplied the Foreword.

Published as a trade paperback by Anomalous Press, *Diary of a Gentleman Diabolist* collected seventy-eight quite short prose poems by Robin Spriggs, with an Introduction by publisher J.P. Fortner.

Available from Yard Dog Press, Robin Wayne Bailey's

*Zombies in Oz and Other Undead Musings* collected sixteen zombie poems that were mostly parodies of more famous works.

Nicholas Royle's chapbook imprint Nightjar Press continued with Mark Valentine's literary tale of creeping unease, *A Revelation of Cormorants*, along with Joel Lane's *Black Country*, Alison Moore's *When the Door Closed, It Was Dark*, and *The Beautiful Room* by R.B. Russell. Print runs ranged from 200 to 300 signed copies of each booklet.

Produced for the World Horror Convention in Brighton to publicise Scott Edelman's collection *What Will Come After: The Complete Zombie Stories*, PS Publishing's thin chapbook *No More Mr Nice Guy* contained an additional short-short zombie story by the author.

*The Render of the Veils* was another chapbook sampler from PS, designed to promote the imprint's forthcoming revised edition of Ramsey Campbell's Lovecraftian collection *The Inhabitant of the Lake & Less Welcome Tenants*. Besides the title story, the booklet featured a new Introduction by the author and an illustration by Randy Broecker.

*The Red House* was a coming-of-age haunted house novella by David J. Thacker, published by Pendragon Press.

Published by Gothic Press, *Monsters and Victims* was an unpleasant serial killer novella written from two different points of view by Charlie Bondhus. From the same imprint, *Akin to Poetry: Observations on Some Strange Tales of Robert Aickman* was a chapbook containing eight revised essays about the author by Philip Challinor, along with a Bibliography of the works discussed.

Published by Tartarus Press for the Halifax Ghost Story Festival, held over Halloween, *The Inner Room* was a handsome chapbook limited to just 200 copies that reprinted Robert Aickman's titular "strange story" from the imprint's reissue of the author's 1968 collection *Sub Rosa*. The booklet also included a brief biography of Aickman by R.B. Russell and a Bibliography of the author's work.

Peter Atkins and Glen Hirshberg's *The Rolling Darkness Review 2010: Curtain Call* played two dates in Canada and another pair in Hollywood at the end of October. The musical/

literary show featured the final performances of two ageing thespians and, as usual, Earthling Publications produced the attractive tie-in chapbook, which also included a story by James K. Moran.

*The Magazine of Fantasy & Science Fiction* embraced its new bi-monthly schedule with six substantive volumes packed with new fiction, reviews and columns. Some of the contributors included Dean Whitlock (the cleverly titled "Nanosferatu"), John Langan, Albert E. Cowdrey, Elizabeth Bourne, Aaron Schutz ("Dr Death vs. the Vampire"), Ian R. MacLeod, Fred Chappell, Richard Matheson (a nice new *Twilight Zone*-type story), Michael Swanwick, David Gerrold, Terry Bisson, Bruce Sterling, Alan Dean Foster and John Kessel.

John Eggeling, Rick Norwood, Bud Webster, David Langford, the late F. Gwynplaine MacIntyre and Paul Di Filippo all contributed to *F&SF*'s "Curiosities" column, which continued to look at obscure or ignored books.

Britain's best magazine of horror, Andy Cox's *Black Static*, produced six full-colour issues featuring fiction by Simon Kurt Unsworth, Lynda E. Rucker, Suzanne Palmer, John Shirley, Nicholas Royle, Steve Rasnic Tem, Joel Lane, Simon Clark, Lavie Tidhar, Paul Meloy and Sarah Pinborough, and Norman Prentiss, along with interviews with Alexandra Sokoloff, Sarah Pinborough, John Connolly, Adam Nevill and Stephen Jones, and the usual columns from Peter Tennant, Christopher Fowler, Stephen Volk and Mike O'Driscoll. Although Tony Lee's excellent DVD reviews sometimes threatened to overwhelm the other contents, *Black Static* remained the UK's leading all-round title dedicated to the genre.

The magazine's companion title, *Interzone*, also turned out six full-colour issues featuring stories by Jay Lake, Lavie Tidhar, Steve Rasnic Tem and Nina Allan, and interviews with Gene Wolfe, Connie Willis, Jeff VanderMeer and Jason Sanford, who had a special issue devoted to his work.

The two issues of Richard Chizmar's *Cemetery Dance* featured fiction by Al Sarrantonio, Thomas Tessier, Elizabeth Massie, Simon Clark, Peter Crowther, David B. Silva, Bentley Little (who was the subject of a special issue), Stephen King (an excerpt from

*Blockade Billy*), Douglas Clegg, Simon Strantzas and Shaun Jeffrey, amongst others, along with the usual columns from Bev Vincent, Ed Gorman, Rick Hautala, Thomas F. Monteleone, Michael Marano, Don D'Auria, Ellen Datlow, Robert Morrish, Mark Sieber, Brian James Freeman, Scott Allie and Wayne Edwards. Interviewees included Sarrantonio, Crowther, Little, Freeman, Ronald Kelly, Ken Eulo, Steve Vernon and games producer Paul Mackman.

*Weird Tales* also only managed two themed issues in 2010, one of those being a "Steampunk Spectacular" and the other devoted to "Uncanny Beauty". Authors included Jay Lake, Catherynne M. Valente and Ian R. MacLeod, while there were interviews with Jesse Bullington and Cherie Priest, an article about pulp illustrator Margaret Brundage, and some truly terrible poetry.

Having taken over *Realms of Fantasy* from Sovereign Media in 2009 and published six issues since, new publisher Warren Lapine sent out an open letter in May asking readers to support the title by renewing subscriptions. However, in October Lapine announced that he was closing the magazine, along with another title, *Dreams of Decadence*, due to the "terrible economic climate". A month later, small press imprint Damnation Books purchased *Realms of Fantasy*, retaining the editorial staff.

The March issue of *Something Wicked* included fiction, reviews and a column by John Connolly. Two months later, editor Joe Vaz announced that he was putting the South African publication on hiatus for the rest of the year while he re-evaluated "the feasibility of the magazine and how to take it into the future".

Canada's excellent *Rue Morgue* put out eleven full-colour issues during the year, including its 100th edition in May. Along with all the usual reviews, news and features, there were interviews with R.L. Stine, Philip Nutman, Ray Russell of Tartarus Press, Joe Morey of Dark Regions Press, Peter Crowther of PS Publishing, Bill Warren, Marcus Hearn, Carol Serling, the late Paul Naschy, Christopher Lee, George A. Romero, Joe Dante, Roger Corman, Ted V. Mikels, Frank Darabont and Guillermo del Toro, amongst many others.

Following a Chapter-11 bankruptcy, a warehouse fire and its

acquisition by a series of new owners, the veteran horror film magazine *Fangoria* apparently began the year with some financial and management problems that led to the temporary closure of its website. Meanwhile, in his editorial in *Shock Cinema* #38, Steven Puchalski claimed that he was owed nearly $1,000 in unpaid fees.

That same issue of *Shock Cinema* included interviews with director Gordon Hessler and actors Ed Lauter and Jim Kelly.

In July, new publisher Phil Kim re-launched *Famous Monsters of Filmland* with issue #251, featuring four variant covers by Basil Gogos, Richard Corben, William Stout and an exclusive 2010 FM convention cover by Vince Evans. The following issue also featured variant covers of *The Walking Dead* (in black and white or colour) and *Island of Lost Souls*. In December it was announced that the magazine would move up from quarterly publication to bi-monthly, and that the title's late founder, Forrest J Ackerman, would be added to the masthead as the new honorary editor-in-chief.

Meanwhile, in August a group of UK horror fans launched *Shock Horror*, a bi-monthly independent magazine devoted to all forms of horror entertainment and culture. The first three issues included features on Vincent Price, Christopher Lee and Rob Zombie.

*Video WatcHDog: The Perfectionist's Guide to Fantastic Video* began the year by thankfully returning to a bi-monthly schedule and featuring Kim Newman's incisive and entertaining appraisals of the first two seasons of *The Avengers* on DVD and Dean Martin's series of "Matt Helm" sci-spy films. Although the twentieth anniversary issue featured yet another monstrous thirty-four page reappraisal of the career of Hispanic hack director Jess Franco by obsessive editor Tim Lucas, and another issue was mostly given over to the subject of Italian sound dubbing, there were also much more interesting (and relative) pieces on the *Universal Cult Horror Collection* (again by Newman), *Planet of the Apes*, the *Karloff & Lugosi Horror Classics* collection, D. DeAngelo's discredited *Creature from the Black Lagoon* book (by David J. Schow) and Lex Barker's *Tarzan* films.

*SFX*'s bumper 132-page "Special Horror Edition" in February came in an illustrated card envelope with two free horror lapel badges, three pub-themed movie beermats and a double-sided John Carpenter poster. The magazine itself included articles on *The Pan Book of Horror Stories* and the history of horror comics, recommendations of obscure films and books by some well-known names, interviews with Joe Hill, Rick Baker and Breck Eisner, plus a new short story by Simon Clark. Unfortunately, after the outcry the previous year over the lack of women represented in the British Fantasy Society's collection of author interviews, it was pointed out to the publishers of *SFX* that, despite it being published in "Women in Horror Recognition Month" (whatever that was!), there were almost no women represented in the magazine. Once again the story was picked up by the *Guardian* online and various blogging sites.

On a more positive note, Terry Pratchett guest-edited the July edition of *SFX*, and the magazine celebrated its 200th issue in October.

Not to be outdone, the November issue of *Total Film* included a feature on Hammer Films, an interview with John Carpenter, and "The Definitive 25 Greatest Horror Movies Ever Made" (*The Texas Chain Saw Massacre* was #1).

The May issue of *Book and Magazine Collector* included an article by Richard Dalby on collecting werewolf books. Just in time for Halloween, the October edition featured Dalby's guide to the top twenty-five occult and psychic detectives (with some mouth-watering first edition covers), along with Andrew Thomas' look at ghost-hunter books and a lengthy profile of author Thomas M. Disch by Graham Andrews. Unfortunately, after twenty-six years, the magazine closed down at Christmas with issue #328.

Meanwhile, *Publishers Weekly* and its associated website were saved from closure when they were purchased by a company headed by the title's former publisher, George Slowik.

As part of its series of *The Greatest Films of All Time* supplements, the *Guardian* newspaper published *Sci-Fi & Fantasy* in October. A panel of UK experts (including Anne Billson, Philip French and Mark Kermode) came up with a list of twenty-five titles that included *Pan's Labyrinth* (24), *Edward Scissorhands* (21), *King Kong* (10), *The Wizard of Oz* (5) and *Alien* (4). The top three titles were *Blade Runner* (3), *Metropolis* (2) and *2001: A Space Odyssey*.

Stephen King's list of "The Best TV of 2010" in *Entertainment Weekly* included *The Walking Dead* (2), *The Event* (4), *Dexter* (6) and *SpongeBob SquarePants* (8). He also devoted entries in his "The Pop of King" column to the Most Obnoxious TV Commercial Ever and the decline of singer/songwriter Harry Nilsson, while in July the magazine celebrated its twentieth anniversary with "The Wit and Wisdom of Stephen King", a highlight of the author's columns since 2003.

Ably edited by Liza Groen Trombi after the unexpected death of founder Charles N. Brown in 2009, *Locus* included interviews with John Crowley, Charles Coleman Finlay, Samuel R. Delany and Barry M. Malzberg. The September issue was a "Steampunk" special, and the magazine also featured roundtable discussions on "Poe & the Fantastic" with Peter Straub, Ellen Datlow, Gary K. Wolfe and Brian Evenson, and a fascinating discussion about "Pulp Fiction" between Robert Silverberg, Richard A. Lupoff and Frank M. Robinson.

The first issue of Michael Kelly's annual paperback magazine *Shadows & Tall Trees* from Canada's Undertow Publications contained stories by Joel Lane, Adam Golaski, Sandra Kasturi, Simon Strantzas, Geordie Williams Flantz and Nicholas Royle, along with book and film reviews by the editor.

David Longhorn published two attractive editions of *Supernatural Tales* with fiction by Michael Kelly, Richard Gavin, Michael Chislett and others, along with short articles on "neglected authors" Ambrose Bierce and Sir Charles Birkin and the usual book reviews by divers hands.

R. Scott McCoy's Stygian Publications put out four perfect-bound print editions of *Necrotic Tissue: The Horror Writers' Magazine*. The quarterly PoD title included fiction by Jeff Strand and David Dunwoody, and an interview with Joe R. Lansdale. The Halloween edition included advice on being a writer by Graham Masterton, Brian Keene, Sarah Pinborough, Ellen Datlow, Nate Kenyon, Kim Newman, Peter Straub, Paul Kane, T.M. Wright and others.

The four issues of Adam Bradley's *Morpheus Tales* featured

fiction by Ray Garton, Joseph D'Lacey, Andrew Hook and others, along with some excellent interior illustrations by Mark Anthony Crittenden and Douglas Draper, Jr.

Ireland's *Albedo One* produced its usual two issues under a raft of editors. The large-format magazine included stories by Bruce McAllister, Mike Resnick and Uncle River, interviews with Resnick and James Gunn, and the ever-popular book reviews.

The three issues of Hildy Silverman's *Space and Time: The Magazine of Fantasy, Horror, and Science Fiction* featured fiction and poetry by Josepha Sherman, F. Gwynplaine MacIntyre, Darrell Schweitzer, Richard Harland and Bruce Boston, along with an interview with Frederick Pohl.

The fourteenth edition of John O'Neill's beautifully designed *Black Gate: Adventures in Fantasy Literature* was a massive double issue that included an article by Rich Horton on "Modern Reprints of Classic Fantasy" along with the fiction, poetry and reviews.

Edited by Debbie Moorhouse, the sixth paperback issue of *GUD: Greatest Uncommon Denominator Magazine* featured fiction and poetry by Lavie Tidhar and others.

There were two new issues of Small Beer Press' slipstream 'zine *Lady Churchill's Rosebud Wristlet*, edited by Gavin J. Grant, Kelly Link et al. and featuring fiction, poetry and articles.

Justin Marriott's excellent *The Paperback Fanatic* changed its format to a smaller but much more attractive size. Boasting full-colour cover reproductions throughout, the four issues published during the year included interviews with Shaun Hutson, Graham Masterton and Warren Murphy; fascinating articles about Roger Elwood and Laser Books, early Pinnacle titles, Edgar Rice Burroughs at Ace Books, Four Square SF, Pyramid's "Fu Manchu" titles, Karl Edward Wagner's "Kane" books, Guy N. Smith, post-apocalyptic men's SF adventure and Robert A. Lowndes' *Magazine of Horror*, etc., along with a lively letters column in every issue.

#1 Creature fan David J. Schow squeezed out another rare issue of his occasional fanzine, *The Black Lagoon Bugle*. Issue #24 featured news and updates about America's Favourite Amphibian.

*The New York Review of Science Fiction* included an

interview with poet Donald Sidney-Fryer, articles about the supernatural fiction of Elizabeth Walter and Marjorie Bowen by Mike Barrett, and "An Annotated Bibliography on Vampire Media".

Following the tradition of the late and lamented *All Hallows*, *The Silent Companion* was the annual fiction magazine of A Ghostly Company. Boasting front and back cover art by veteran illustrator Alan Hunter, the nicely produced publication contained seven traditional supernatural stories.

The Spring issue of *Machenalia: The Newsletter of The Friends of Arthur Machen* included the usual news, book reviews and articles, including an extensive piece celebrating the 140th anniversary in 2009 of the birth of Algernon Blackwood.

The September 2009 edition of the British Fantasy Society's *Prism* newsletter was belatedly distributed to the membership early in the new year. Although the news and reviews were a bit out of date, the much-delayed issue still contained some fine columns by Ramsey Campbell, Eric Brown and Mark Morris.

The periodical went back to basics under new editor David A. Riley, who had previously co-edited the magazine in the mid-1970s and managed to put out three new issues in 2010. Along with the usual features, Campbell and Morris stayed on as columnists, joined by John Llewellyn Probert, and there were interviews with Johnny Mains, Shaun Jeffrey, Charles Black and Joe Hill.

The BFS also produced two new volumes of *Dark Horizons*, featuring fiction, poetry and articles (including interviews with Simon Bestwick, Brian Stableford, Mark Charan, Aliette de Bodard and Allen Ashley, along with fascinating pieces on the history of Arkham House and the Ballantine Adult Fantasy series by Mike Barrett), plus an edition of *New Horizons* containing more fan fiction.

*Dog Tales* was the second volume of Phil and Sarah Stokes' impressively researched *Memory, Prophecy and Fantasy: The Works and Worlds of Clive Barker*. Once again limited to just 250 hardcover copies, the in-depth study covered Barker's early theatrical projects and was illustrated with numerous photos, posters and concept drawings, many of them in colour.

*Lilja's Library: The World of Stephen King* was a collection of interviews and non-fiction material from Hans-Ake Lilja's website, much of it updated, along with new material. A fifty-two copy signed, lettered and traycased edition was also available ($250.00).

*The Dream World of H.P. Lovecraft: His Life, His Demons, His Universe* from Llewellyn was a biography by occult scholar Donald Tyson that concentrated on the author's more esoteric influences.

*Unrepentant: A Celebration of the Writings of Harlan Ellison®* was a slim hardcover that celebrated the author's appearance at his "last" convention, MadCon 2010 in Madison, Wisconsin. Edited and packaged by Robert T. Garcia in an edition of just 300 copies (100 of which were signed by Ellison), the book contained fiction, essays, art and a bibliography, along with a comic strip by Neil Gaiman.

Illustrated with numerous photos, Sam Weller's *Listen to the Echoes: The Ray Bradbury Interviews* included a Foreword by Black Francis.

Donald Sturrock's family-sanctioned *Storyteller: The Life of Roald Dahl* included an account of the biographer's first visit to the home of the often-difficult author. The book was abridged for a five-part reading by Julian Rhind-Tutt on BBC Radio 4 in September, with Ian McDiarmid as the voice of Dahl.

For those for whom *The Twilight Saga: Eclipse: The Official Illustrated Movie Companion* was not enough, then there was always *The Twilight Mystique: Critical Essays on the Novels and Films* from McFarland & Company, Inc., in which editors Amy M. Clarke and Marijane Osborn collected twelve essays about Stephenie Meyer's series. Edited by Michelle Pan, *Bella Should Have Dumped Edward: Controversial Views and Debates on the Twilight Series* collected comments from an online fan site devoted to Meyer's anaemic vampire books.

From BenBella Books, *Ardeur: 14 Writers on the Anita Blake, Vampire Hunter Series* was edited by Laurell K. Hamilton and Leah Wilson and included fourteen essays by Nick Mamatas, Lilith Saintcrow and others.

*The Fledgling Handbook 101* by P.C. Cast and Kim Doner purported to be a guidebook given to new vampires in the "House of Night" series by P.C. and Kristin Cast.

From McFarland, Deborah Painter's *Forry: The Life of Forrest J Ackerman* looked at the life and career of the legendary sci-fi and horror fan, editor and agent, with a Foreword by Joe Moe.

Edited by S.T. Joshi for Hippocampus Press, *A Weird Writer in Our Midst: Early Criticism of H.P. Lovecraft* was a fascinating compilation of articles and criticism about the writer up to about 1955. From the same PoD publisher, *Ten Years of Hippocampus Press 2000–2010* was a useful annotated bibliography compiled by founders Derrick Hussey and S.T. Joshi, along with David E. Schultz.

In *The Conspiracy Against the Human Race: A Contrivance of Horror* from the same imprint, Thomas Ligotti questioned what it means to be human. Ray Brassier supplied the Introduction.

Also edited by S.T. Joshi, *Encyclopedia of the Vampire: The Living Dead in Myth, Legend, and Popular Culture* from Greenwood was a handy reference guide with contributions from Richard Bleiler, Matt Cardin, Gary William Crawford, Stefan Dziemianowicz, Paula Guran, Melissa Mia Hall, Stephen Jones, John Langan, Barbara Roden, Christopher Roden, Darrell Schweitzer, Brian Stableford, Bev Vincent and many others.

*The Vampire Book: The Encyclopedia of the Undead, Third Edition* was a revised and updated version of J. Gordon Melton's guide to the undead in books, movies and mythology. Martin V. Ricardo contributed the Introduction.

In *The English Ghost: Spectres Through Time*, Peter Ackroyd chronicled a wide range of historical hauntings, including that of the infamous Borley Rectory, which mysteriously burned down in 1939.

Edited by Maria del Pilar Blanco and Esther Peeren, *Popular Ghosts: The Haunted Spaces of Everyday Culture* from Continuum featured twenty-two critical essays about ghosts in the media and popular culture.

Published by McFarland & Company, Inc., *Gothic Realities: The Impact of Horror Fiction on Modern Culture* contained eight critical essays and a Selected Bibliography by L. Andrew Cooper. The scope of the book ranged from Gothic literature to torture porn.

In *Voices in the Dark: Interviews with Horror Movie Writers, Directors and Actors* from the same imprint, Paul

Kane and Marie O'Regan interviewed twenty-five people working in the horror genre, including Clive Barker, Neil Gaiman, James Herbert, Joe Hill, Sarah Pinborough, John Carpenter, Rob Zombie and Ron Perlman. Anne Billson supplied the Foreword.

From University Press of Kentucky, *The Philosophy of Horror* edited by Thomas Fahy contained fourteen essays, while *Zombies, Vampires, and Philosophy: New Life for the Undead* edited by Richard Greene and K. Silem Mohammad for Carus Publishing/Open Court contained twenty-one essays.

The latest volume in *A Brief History* series from Robinson/Running Press was *Vampires* by M.J. Trow. Somewhat oddly, the book was split into two sections, with the first part looking at vampires in mythology and modern culture and the (longer) second part devoted solely to Vlad the Impaler.

A depressing trend in comedy non-fiction guides included *The Vampire Survival Guide: How to Fight, and Win, Against the Undead* by Scott Bowen, and *The Zen of Zombie: Better Living Through the Undead* by Scott Kenemore.

*When Werewolves Attack: A Field Guide to Dispatching Ravenous Flesh-Ripping Beasts* by Del Howison looked at lycanthropic lore, while *The Complete Idiot's Guide to Werewolves* by Nathan Robert Brown included a chapter about literary lycanthropes. *The Complete Idiot's Guide to Zombies* was written by the same author.

From Severed Press, *The Official Zombie Handbook (UK)* by Sean T. Page was an oversized guide along the same lines, giving advice and instructions on how to survive a zombie invasion of Britain.

*Dr Dale's Zombie Dictionary: The A-Z Guide to Staying Alive* by "Dr Dale Seslick" (Ben Muir) was a spin-off of the comedy stage show *How to Survive a Zombie Apocalypse*, which was voted Best Comedy Show 2010 by Buxton Fringe.

PS Publishing launched its new PS Art Books imprint with *Tomorrow Revisited: A Celebration of the Life and Art of Frank Hampson* by Alistair Crompton. The oversized hardcover not only served as a fascinating biography of the comics artist best remembered for his *Dan Dare* strip in *Eagle*, but was also crammed with full-colour reproductions taken from the original artwork, preliminary sketches and hundreds of photographs.

*The Art of Drew Struzan* from Titan Books collected the stunning movie poster roughs and finished paintings of the American artist (*Raiders of the Lost Ark*, *Back to the Future* etc.), along with extremely candid commentary by Struzan, an Introduction and "Outroduction" by David J. Schow, and a lively Foreword by movie director Frank Darabont.

*The Addams Family: An Evilution* was a huge collection of *New Yorker* cartoonist Charles Addams' macabre drawings.

*The Horror! The Horror!: Comic Books the Government Didn't Want You to Read* by Jim Trombetta was an illustrated look at the history of pre-Code comics in America, including the infamous EC line. The book came with a DVD featuring an anti-comics TV documentary from the period directed by Irvin Kirschner (*The Empire Strikes Back*).

From Hieronymous Press, *Into the Land of Shadows* was a large format reprinting of the *Prince Valiant* Sunday newspaper strip by writer Mark Schultz and artist Gary Gianni involving monsters, wizards and a race of subterranean little people.

As usual edited by Cathy and Arnie Fenner, *Spectrum 17: The Best in Contemporary Fantastic Art* from Underwood Books reprinted the work of more than 300 artists, including a profile of the late Al Williamson, who was named recipient of the 2010 Spectrum Grand Master Award for artistic achievement.

From the same imprint, *Sword's Edge: Paintings Inspired by the Works of Robert E. Howard* contained more than twenty full-colour paintings by Spanish artist [Manuel Peréz Clemente] Sanjulian, edited by the Fenners and Manuel Aud.

Edited by publisher Tim Underwood himself, *Savage Art: 20th Century Genre & the Artists That Defined It* showcased a variety of pulp magazine covers by Virgil Finlay, J. Allen St John, Norman Saunders, Frank R. Paul and others. Frank M. Robinson supplied the Introduction.

From Non-Stop Press, *Outermost: The Art + Life of Jack Gaughan* was a biography written by Luis Ortiz that contained numerous illustrations by the prolific Hugo-winning book and magazine artist, along with an intimate Introduction by his widow, Phoebe Adams Gaughan.

*H.J. Ward* from The Illustrated Press was a biography/art book of the pulp artist by David Saunders that also included a checklist of covers.

Meanwhile, at a Heritage art and illustration auction in August, the original Hugh J. Ward cover painting for the August 1936 issue of *Spicy Mystery* smashed the record set by a pulp magazine cover, realising a sale price of $143,400 (with premium). Also in the sale, a Norman Saunders cover for the May 1951 *Marvel Stories* went for $50,787 and a Margaret Brundage cover for the January 1936 *Weird Tales* sold for $37,343.

Following on from a previous lawsuit in 2002, Neil Gaiman accused one-time collaborator Todd McFarlane in June of changing the names of some of the supporting characters they co-created for the comic series *Spawn* to prevent Gaiman sharing in any residual profits. Gaiman subsequently won his case in court.

The first two volumes of Stephen King's *The Stand*, *Captain Trips* and *American Nightmare*, were released in January by Marvel, while King teamed up with comics writer Scott Snyder and artist Rafael Albuquerque for the first five issues of Vertigo's *American Vampire*.

*Locke & Key 2: Head Games* from Subterranean Press included the Lovecraftian graphic sequence written by Joe Hill and illustrated by Gabriel Rodriguez, along with bonus material by Hill. It was also available in a 250-copy signed edition ($250.00) and a lettered edition of twenty-six copies ($500.00) with added art and dust-jacket by Vincent Chong.

The first volume of a two-part graphic adaptation of Stephenie Meyer's *Twilight: The Graphic Novel*, adapted and illustrated by Korean artist Young Kim, had a 350,000-copy first printing from Hachette/Yen Press in the US.

Nicely illustrated by *Buffy the Vampire Slayer* artist Cliff Richards in black and white, *Pride and Prejudice and Zombies* from Del Rey was a black and white graphic novel adaptation by British writer Tony Lee of the *New York Times* best-seller by Jane Austen and Seth Grahame-Smith.

From Moonstone Books, *Kolchak: The Night Stalker: The*

*Lovecraftian Damnation* written by C.J. Henderson and illustrated by Robert Hack pitted the unorthodox reporter against Lovecraft's fishy Deep Ones.

A woman discovered a mysteriously disappearing library that contained everything she had ever read in *The Night Bookmobile* by Audrey Niffenegger.

Scripted by Gary Gerani and illustrated by Stuart Sayger, *Bram Stoker's Death Ship* from IDW was based around the "Demeter", the ship that transported Count Dracula from Transylvania to England.

Joe R. Lansdale and John L. Lansdale co-scripted *Robert Bloch's Yours Truly, Jack the Ripper* for the same imprint, with art by Kevin Colden.

Based on the character created by Robert E. Howard, *The Chronicles of Solomon Kane* from Dark Horse collected stories from *Marvel Premier* and *The Sword of Solomon Kane* adapted by Roy Thomas and Ralph Macchio. Artists included Al Williamson, Mike Mignola and Howard Chaykin. Thomas also teamed up with artist Barry Windsor-Smith for *The Barry Windsor-Smith Conan Archives Volume 1* from the same publisher, which collected the first eleven volumes of Marvel Comics' *Conan the Barbarian*.

*Zombie Terrors* from Asylum Press was the first volume in an annual Halloween graphic anthology series intended for mature readers.

Irish comics imprint Atomic Diner published the horror graphic novel *Róisín Dubh: From the Grave*, written by Maura McHugh and illustrated by Stephen Daly.

In February, a rare issue of *Action Comics* No.1 (1938), the first comic book to feature Superman, sold via an online auction site between two private sellers for a reported $1 million, beating all previous records.

Less than a week later, a copy of *Detective Comics* No.27 (1939), featuring the first appearance of the Batman, sold for $1,075,500. However, that record was beaten late the following month when another copy of the first issue of *Action Comics* changed hands for $1.5 million, almost five times what it had been worth just a year earlier.

\*     \*     \*

Ramsey Campbell wrote the novelisation of Michael J. Bassett's underrated version of *Solomon Kane*, based on the character created by Robert E. Howard.

Jonathan Maberry novelised the new version of Universal's *The Wolfman*, while Alexander Irvine adapted *Iron Man 2* to book form.

T.T. Sutherland's *Alice in Wonderland* was a novelisation of the Tim Burton film, which was a sequel to Lewis Carroll's book.

*Being Human: Bad Blood* by James Goss, *Being Human: Chasers* by Mark Michalowski and *Being Human: The Road* by Simon Guerrier were all based on the cult BBC TV series.

Joe Schreiber's *Supernatural: The Unholy Cause* was also based on The CW series.

The first two books in a packaged trilogy, *The Vampire Diaries: Stefan's Diaries Volume 1: Origins* and *2: Bloodlust*, were anonymously written young adult tie-ins to the book and TV series, credited to L.J. Smith, Kevin Williamson and Julie Plec.

BBC Books' continuing series of tie-ins featuring the eleventh Doctor continued with *Doctor Who: Night of the Humans* by David Llewellyn and *Doctor Who: Apollo 23* by Justin Richards.

Aaron Rosenberg's *Stargate Atlantis: Hunt and Run*, Chris Wraight's *Stargate Atlantis: Dead End* and *Stargate Atlantis: Homecoming* by Jo Graham and Melissa Scott were all based on a cancelled TV series, as was *Stargate SG-1: The Power Behind the Throne* by Steven Savile.

Sheriff Jack Carter investigated the swapping of people and objects from other places in the TV tie-in *Eureka: Substitution Method*, while the townsfolk discovered that they had better keep their thoughts to themselves in *Eureka: Brain Box Blues*, both by Cris Ramsey.

Nancy Holder's *Saving Grace: Tough Love* was based on the TNT angel/cop TV series.

*30 Days of Night: Fear of the Dark* by Tim Lebbon was set in the world of the graphic novels, while *Dead Space: Martyr* by B.K. Evenson was based on the best-selling Electronic Arts video game series.

*Warhammer: Bloodborn* by Nathan Long was the first volume in the "Ulrika the Vampire" series, set in the world of the role-playing game. The same author's *Warhammer: Zombieslayer* was the twelfth book in the "Gotrek & Felix" series, also based on the game.

Easily the most attractive movie-related book of the year was *The Art of Hammer: Posters from the Archive of Hammer Films*, compiled by Marcus Hearn for Titan Books. The large-sized hardcover included almost 300 full-colour posters from around the world.

Following multiple accusations of plagiarism, McFarland & Co. withdrew all copies of D. DeAngelo's *Features from the Black Lagoon: The Film, its Sequels, the Spinoffs and Memorabilia* after little more than a month.

*Keep Watching the Skies: American Science Fiction Movies of the Fifties: The 21st Century Edition* was the second revised and expanded edition of Bill Warren's seminal 1982 study, published by McFarland with a Foreword by Howard Waldrop.

*Richard Matheson on Screen: A History of the Filmed Works* was an excellent study of the author's cinematic work from McFarland. Written by Matthew R. Bradley, with a brief Foreword by Matheson himself, the book also featured some nicely selected stills plus an impressive Bibliography and Index.

In *The Literary Monster on Film: Five Nineteenth Century British Novels and Their Cinematic Adaptations*, also from McFarland, author Abigail Burnham Bloom explored the various film versions of *Frankenstein*, *Dracula*, *Strange Case of Dr Jekyll and Mr Hyde*, *She* and *The Island of Dr Moreau*.

From Telos Publishing, *Silver Scream: 40 Classic Horror Movies Volume Two 1941–1951* featured numerous reviews by Steven Warren Hill, profusely illustrated with fascinating stills.

Also from Telos, Richard Molesworth's *Wiped! Doctor Who's Missing Episodes* chronicled the story of how the BBC controversially destroyed more than 250 episodes of the TV show and how more than 100 programmes are still missing.

*Eclipse: The Complete Illustrated Movie Companion* was a guide to the third film in the *Twilight* series by Mark Cotta Vaz.

Also obviously intended to cash in on the release of the latest *Twilight* movie, the clumsily titled *Vampire Lovers: Screen's Seductive Creatures of the Night: A Book of Undead Pin-Ups* from Plexus Publishing was a heavily illustrated trade paperback that looked at memorable vampires from *Angel* to *The Vampire Lovers*, with better-than-it-deserved text by Gavin Baddeley.

From the same publisher, Steven Savile's *Fantastic TV: 50 Years of Cult Fantasy and Science Fiction* was an oddly selective guide through various small-screen series which was bulked out with a round robin interview between creators and writers Joe Ahearne, Adrian Hodges, Kenneth Johnson, Stephen Volk, Andrew Cartmel, Keith DeCandido, Paul Cornell and Kevin J. Anderson.

In *Six Cult Films from the Sixties: The Inside Stories by Writer/Director Ib Melchior* from BearManor Media, the ninety-three-year-old screenwriter revealed the histories behind his movies *The Angry Red Planet*, *The Time Travellers*, *Reptilicus*, *Journey to the Seventh Planet*, *Robinson Crusoe on Mars* and *Planet of the Vampires*. Visual effects designer Robert Skotak supplied the Introduction.

*Size Matters: The Extraordinary Life and Career of Warwick Davis* was a depreciating autobiography by the diminutive two-foot, eleven-inch British actor from the *Star Wars*, *Leprechaun* and *Harry Potter* film series.

In a shock announcement in July, Britain's new coalition government announced that it was abolishing the profit-making UK Film Council as part of its drastic cost-cutting measures. The decision by Culture Secretary Jeremy Hunt, who was advised by *Stardust* and *Kick-Ass* director Matthew Vaughn, was greeted with outrage by most UK film-makers and others in the arts.

That same month, Switzerland's Justice Ministry denied a request to extradite Roman Polanski to the US for sentencing on child-sex charges dating back thirty-three years. The *Rosemary's Baby* director had been under house arrest since being seized by Swiss authorities while on his way from his home in France to a film festival in the country the previous September.

A survey conducted by Professor Joanne Cantor of Wisconsin University found that watching horror films could lead to life-long fears, such as being frightened to go into the shower after seeing *Psycho*. This latest piece of "No s**t Sherlock" research found that the five most frightening films were *Jaws*, *Psycho*, *It* (based on the Stephen King novel), *A Nightmare on Elm Street* and *Poltergeist*.

2010 was once again all about sequels, remakes and reboots at the box office.

Despite its ongoing conflicts between fit-looking vampires and buff werewolves, David Slade's *The Twilight Saga: Eclipse* dropped all pretence at being a horror film as vampire Edward (Robert Pattinson) and werewolf Jacob (Taylor Lautner) vied for the limited affections of the expressionless Bella (Kristen Stewart). After taking a record-breaking gross of more than $30 million with its midnight launch at over 4,000 movie theatres (including IMAX) at the end of June, this third film in the series only earned $82.5 million over the four-day Fourth of July weekend, which fell short of industry expectations and was less than the previous film, *New Moon*, took during its opening in November 2009.

An open letter to Universal from a *Twilight* fan accused the studio of ripping off Stephenie Meyer's 2006 novel *New Moon* for its version of *The Wolfman*, which of course was a remake of the 1941 movie of (nearly) the same name. Bless.

With its release date repeatedly pushed back for re-edits since 2009, *The Wolfman* actually turned out to be much better than expected. Benicio Del Toro did a commendable job channelling the spirit of Lon Chaney, Jr's Lawrence Talbot, while director Joe Johnston created a sumptuous background to a refreshingly faithful homage to the classic monster movies. Despite that, the film dropped nearly 69 per cent at the US box office in its second week.

The unrated DVD of *The Wolfman* featured a "director's cut" containing an extra sixteen minutes of footage plus five extended and deleted scenes, including a sequence with an uncredited Max von Sydow, which explained how Talbot acquired his wolf-head cane.

Audiences for John Favreau's bombastic sequel *Iron Man 2* reportedly dropped 30 per cent over its opening weekend, although the film still managed a three-day gross of $133.6 million and surpassed the original's worldwide earnings. This time Robert Downey, Jr's millionaire superhero battled Russian villain "Whiplash" (Mickey Rourke).

In October, the Walt Disney Company confirmed that the studio would be taking control of a number of Marvel Studios' upcoming movie releases after buying the company in 2009.

Jackie Earle Haley was given the thankless task of taking over the role of "Freddy Krueger" in *A Nightmare on Elm Street*, Samuel Bayer's pointless reboot of the 1984 Wes Craven original. After debuting at #1 with $32.9 million, the film had one of the year's biggest second-week falls at the US box office.

Matt Reeves' *Let Me In* marked the welcome return of Hammer Films with a surprisingly successful re-imagining of the 2008 Swedish film, *Let the Right One In*, based on the novel by John Ajvide Lindqvist. This time the ageless vampire girl was played by the superb Chloë Grace Moretz, while Richard Jenkins gave a creepily sympathetic performance as her ageing guardian.

In June the teaser trailer for Tod Williams' *Paranormal Activity 2* was pulled from a number of cinemas in Texas after complaints that it was too scary. The $3 million sequel used a family's home video surveillance system to show how the sister of the girl from the first film was targeted by a demon. The film enjoyed the horror genre's biggest opening weekend ever in the US, grossing $40.7 million.

Edward Furlong and Linnea Quigley were in *Night of the Demons*, a remake of the 1987 Halloween horror movie.

The always-excellent Timothy Olyphant starred in Breck Eisner's *The Crazies*, an impressive remake of the 1973 George A. Romero thriller in which the inhabitants of a small Iowa town went homicidal as a result of toxic exposure.

Based on a 1994 screenplay by producer Robert Rodriguez, *Predators* was another unnecessary sequel starring an unlikely Adrien Brody, Laurence Fishburne and Danny Trejo battling the dreadlocked aliens on a jungle planet.

*Nanny McPhee & The Big Bang* (aka *Nanny McPhee Returns*) was to *Bedknobs and Broomsticks* what the original *Nanny McPhee* (2005) was to *Mary Poppins*, as Emma Thompson's slightly creepy child-minder helped a 1940s family keep their farm. The sequel's impressive supporting cast included Maggie Gyllenhaal, Rhys Ifans, Maggie Smith, Ralph Fiennes and a blink-and-you'd-miss-him Ewan McGregor.

Loosely based on Jonathan Swift's satirical novel, even Jack

Black and a cast of British character players couldn't save yet
another remake of *Gulliver's Travels* from flopping at the box
office.

Perhaps the year's most unlikely remake was *I Spit on Your
Grave*, based on Meir Zarchi's 1978 cult classic about a woman
(Sarah Butler) taking gruesome revenge on the men who gang-
raped her.

After the success of James Cameron's *Avatar*, the other big
movie story of the year was 3-D.

Despite suffering from some hastily converted 3-D, Warner
Bros.' big-budget remake of the 1981 *Clash of the Titans* starring Sam Worthington went straight to #1 in the US with a gross
of $63.9 million. Liam Neeson and Ralph Fiennes played
Olympian gods.

Alexandree Aja's *Piranha 3D* was the second remake of Joe
Dante's clever and entertaining 1978 movie about carnivorous
fish attacking a group of kids on spring break. A solid cast that
included Richard Dreyfuss, Ving Rhames, Elisabeth Shue,
Christopher Lloyd, Eli Roth, Jerry O'Connell, Kelly Brook and
porn star Riley Steele tried their best not to end up as fish-food.

Veterans Bruce Dern and Dick Miller turned up in Dante's
own "family-friendly" 3-D horror movie, *The Hole*, in which
three children discovered a gateway to Hell.

Despite outrage from cinema chains that Disney was planning
to cut the release time from movie screen to DVD for Tim
Burton's marvellous version of *Alice in Wonderland*, the 3-D
fantasy opened in America with a record-breaking weekend
gross of $116.3 million, making it the highest-grossing March
release of all time, the biggest non-sequel release, the biggest
IMAX opening, and also the biggest 3-D opening – beating out
*Avatar*, which had previously held the record. Horror veterans,
and Burton favourites, Christopher Lee and Michael Gough
both contributed voice performances.

Meanwhile, a partially restored version of the first known film
adaptation of *Alice in Wonderland* was shown before the Tim
Burton version at London's IMAX theatre. Made in 1903 by
cinema pioneers Percy Stow and Cecil Hepworth at studios in
Walton-on-Thames, Surrey, at the time it was the most expensive and longest (twelve minutes) British film ever made.

Contestants on VH1's *Scream Queens 2* competed for a chance to appear in *Saw 3D*, the seventh and supposedly final instalment in the franchise, which was about a writer (Sean Patrick Flanery) selling a fake book about his experience as one of Jigsaw's victims. Tobin Bell and Cary Elwes returned to the series and, even though the movie wasn't screened for critics on either side of the Atlantic, it topped the US charts over Halloween with an opening gross of $24.2 million.

Despite having a new distributor and being released in digital 3-D, Michael Apted's *The Chronicles of Narnia: The Voyage of the Dawn Treader*, the third in the series based on the books by C.S. Lewis, failed to find an audience. This time, Pevensie siblings Lucy (Georgia Henley) and Edmund (Skandar Keynes) sailed in search of the Seven Lost Lords with their obnoxious cousin Eustace (Will Poulter).

Star Milla Jovovich's husband Paul W.S. Anderson returned to direct the 3-D sequel *Resident Evil: Afterlife*, the disappointing fourth entry in the zombie franchise based on the popular video game series.

Wes Craven's *My Soul to Take* also did not open well, despite being released in 3-D.

*Tron: Legacy* was a belated sequel to the 1982 Disney movie. Sam (Garrett Hedlund) entered a 3-D digital world to find his lost father Flynn (a CGI-enhanced Jeff Bridges, the star of the original).

Despite terrible reviews, M. Night Shyamalan's fantasy *The Last Airbender*, based on the Nickelodeon cartoon series and released in last-minute 3-D, did much better than predicted. 12-year-old Noah Ringer played a young boy who could control the elements.

Disney/Pixar's superior 3-D sequel *Toy Story 3* took $110.3 million during its opening weekend in June, and went on to break numerous records, including becoming the highest-grossing animated film of all time just two months later.

Although it took a huge amount of money and stayed at #1 for three weeks, the 3-D *Shrek Forever After*, the fourth and supposedly last in the franchise, was the weakest performer in the series to date as it recycled the plot from *It's a Wonderful Life*.

Will Ferrell voiced the big blue-headed alien supervillain who had a change of heart in DreamWorks' 3-D *Megamind*, which also featured the voice talents of Brad Pitt and Tina Fey, while Steve Carell was the voice of the master villain planning to steal the moon in the 3-D *Despicable Me*, who also had a change of heart after he adopted three cute siblings. Julie Andrews voiced the protagonist's pushy mother.

Based on Kathryn Lasky's novels, a pair of owlets became embroiled in an epic war between good and evil in Zack Snyder's 3-D *Legend of the Guardians: The Owls of Ga'Hoole*, featuring the voices of Helen Mirren and Geoffrey Rush.

During the mid-1950s and early 1980s 3-D booms, the process lasted for just a couple of years before the novelty wore off. With many more films due to be released in the process in 2011, and 3-D TV being hailed as the Next Big Thing in home entertainment, it will be interesting to see if the fad will last longer this time.

Warner Bros. decided not to release *Harry Potter and the Deathly Hallows – Part 1*, the seventh and penultimate entry in the mega-franchise, in 3-D. However, this was only because the studio apparently could not convert to the process in time for the film's release in November.

Despite only being released "flat", the *Potter* sequel took $125 million during its opening weekend in America, and the film broke records in the UK, where its £18.3 million opening was the biggest ever weekend total, beating the James Bond film *Quantum of Solace*. It also set individual records in Britain for receipts on the Friday, Saturday and Sunday, with Saturday's £6.6 million being the highest for a single day. David Yates' dark and doom-laden penultimate episode set the tone for the final showdown between Harry Potter (Daniel Radcliffe) and the evil Voldemort (Ralph Fiennes), and featured David Legeno as the Dark Lord's werewolf agent, Fenrir Greyback.

Michael J. Bassett's "origin" story of *Solomon Kane* was the best cinema adaptation of Robert E. Howard's work to date. James Purefoy gave a terrific performance as the grim Puritan swashbuckler battling the supernatural, and he was ably supported by a cast that included Max von Sydow, Pete Postlethwaite, Alice Krige, Mackenzie Crook and Jason Flemying.

Delayed from the previous October, Martin Scorsese's over-long and painfully obvious *Shutter Island* played like a Monogram "B" movie as Leonardo DiCaprio's troubled US marshal investigated a missing inmate at Ben Kingsley's creepy Gothic island asylum.

Christopher Nolan's mind-bending *Inception*, in which DiCaprio could enter people's dreams and steal their secrets, took $62.8 million over its opening weekend in the US. In the UK the film opened with a £5.9 million take, making it the actor's best ever opening in that country – even ahead of *Titanic*.

Adrien Brody's second genre film of the year was Vincenzo Natali's superior *Splice*, in which a pair of genetic-engineering scientists (Brody and Sarah Polley, whose characters are named after those in *Bride of Frankenstein*) created a monstrously beautiful hybrid creature (Delphine Chanéac).

A mix of *The Red Shoes* and a Dario Argento *giallo* movie, Darren Aronofsky's psychological thriller *Black Swan* was a surprise hit. It starred Natalie Portman and Mila Kunis as rival ballerinas in a new version of *Swan Lake*.

John Landis' *Burke & Hare*, starring Simon Pegg and Andy Serkis as the bumbling 19th-century bodysnatchers, was an unfortunate attempt to recreate an Ealing comedy. With an impressive British supporting cast that included Tom Wilkinson, Tim Curry, Jessica Hynes, a wasted Christopher Lee, Ronnie Corbett, Paul Whitehouse, Hugh Bonneville, Jenny Agutter and John Woodvine, it should have been much better than it was.

Sean Bean's grim 14th-century knight led a band of mercenaries into a village supernaturally spared from the plague in Christopher Smith's low-budget but atmospheric *Black Death*.

Ethan Hawke's vampire haematologist tried to save a future world dominated by the undead in Michael and Peter Spierig's *Daybreakers*. Originally shot in 2007, it also featured Sam Neill as the head of a ruthless corporation that harvested humans, and Willem Dafoe as the leader of a band of human rebels.

*Vampires Suck* from Jason Friedberg and Aaron Seltzer was a lame send-up of the equally lame *Twilight* movies, while a group of horny college kids found themselves evading Romanian vampires in another spoof, *Transylmania*, which was filmed back in 2007.

Renée Zellweger and Bradley Cooper starred in Christian Alvart's long-delayed *Case 39*, which was also filmed in 2007. It finally received a US release in October after opening overseas first.

Starring Geoffrey Rush, Kate Bosworth and Jang Dong Gun, the long-delayed *The Warrior's Way* was a 1900s-set martial arts fantasy in which the inhabitants of a decaying ghost town rebelled against Danny Huston's tyrannical Colonel. After the studio decided not to preview it, the movie registered one of the year's worst openings at the US box office before going on to lose just over 69 per cent of its audience in its second week.

In *Shelter*, Julianne Moore's forensic psychiatrist discovered that all the multiple personalities inside her new patient (Jonathan Rhys Meyers) were murder victims, including her own husband.

Produced by M. Night Shyamalan, *Devil* had a group of five strangers trapped in an elevator, one of them being Satan himself.

Produced by Eli Roth, *The Last Exorcism* was another "found footage" pseudo-documentary. Made for $1.8 million, it grossed $20.4 million in its first week at the US box office.

*The Collector* was originally developed as a prequel to the *Saw* franchise before it was reworked into the first in a new torture porn franchise, and a group of college bullies found themselves on the receiving end of their victims' brutal revenge in *The Final*.

Three young snowboarders were trapped overnight on a ski lift surrounded by a pack of wolves in Adam Green's *Frozen*, while deformed serial killer "Hatchetface" was back in the same writer-director's *Hatchet II*, which received a limited theatrical release.

Zac Efron's cemetery caretaker played baseball with his dead younger brother in *The Death and Life of Charlie St. Cloud*, and Matt Damon starred as a reluctant psychic in director Clint Eastwood's serious supernatural drama *Hereafter*.

A serial-killer mother (Shabana Azmi) was followed around by her ghostly victims in Gurinder Chadha's British comedy *It's a Wonderful Afterlife*.

William Shakespeare's sorcerer Prospero was changed to a sorceress, "Prospera" (Helen Mirren), in Julie Taymor's re-imagined version of *The Tempest*, which also featured Russell

Brand, Tom Conti, Alan Cumming, Alfred Molina and Djimon Hounsou as Caliban.

As usual, a number of micro-budget British horror films were barely released theatrically before quickly turning up on DVD.

A group of British computer hackers released more than they bargained for when they attempted to unlock the Vatican's "Bible Code" in *The 7th Dimension*, and eight would-be executives had eighty minutes to answer a question and win a job with a mysterious corporation in the British-made *Exam*.

A container washed up near a village in northern England on Christmas Eve caused madness and murder in the surprisingly short *Salvage*, something was killing livestock in rural Wales in *Splintered*, and a trio of cursed female witches preyed on four businessmen on a team-building exercise in the low-budget British film *The Scar Crow*.

Two lonely British exorcists (Ed Gaughan and Andrew Buckley) removed the proverbial skeletons from people's homes in Nick Whitfield's acclaimed low-budget feature debut *Skeletons*.

An upwardly mobile professional (Josie Ho) was prepared to kill to get her *Dream Home* in the Hong Kong slasher, and Elana Anaya's distraught mother returned to the remote island where her five-year-old son disappeared in the Spanish-made *Hierro*.

In *Rare Exports: A Christmas Tale*, an evil Santa Claus was unwittingly released by a team of archaeologists from his Finnish ice prison, while crooked cops and Gallic gangsters teamed up to battle zombie hordes in a deserted tower block in the French-made *The Horde*.

Dieter Laser's mad German scientist stitched his three victims together end-to-end to create *The Human Centipede (First Sequence)* from Dutch writer/director Tom Six.

Ciarán Hinds played a windowed father who found himself involved in a literary love triangle in the low-key ghost story *The Eclipse*, shot in Ireland.

Also filmed in Ireland, *Spiderhole* was about four young art students who squatted in a spider-infested house in London that was already inhabited by a mad surgeon.

Shot on a shoestring by British director Gareth Edwards,

*Monsters* featured a photojournalist (Scoot McNairy) accompanying his boss' spoiled daughter (Whitney Able) through a Mexico "infected" with giant Lovecraftian alien creatures.

Also made for peanuts (well, $10 million), Colin and Greg Strause's *Skyline* starred Eric Balfour in another alien-invasion plot.

A renegade angel (Paul Bettany) and a group of strangers trapped inside a diner owned by Dennis Quaid took a stand against God's Apocalypse in *Legion*, while the apocalypse had already occurred in the Hughes Bothers' *The Book of Eli* starring Denzel Washington as an enigmatic wanderer protecting a Bible from Gary Oldman's crazy town leader.

Viggo Mortensen starred as a father leading his son (Kodi Smit-McPhee) through a post-apocalyptic wilderness in John Hillcoat's adaptation of Cormac McCarthy's acclaimed 2006 novel *The Road*.

When near-future organ collector Jude Law couldn't keep up the payments on his artificial heart, his partner (Forrest Whitaker) was sent to recover it in *Repo Men*.

In *Mr Nobody*, the world's last dying man (Jared Leto) looked back on three stages of his life from the year 2092.

*Hot Tub Time Machine* was a lot more fun than it had any right to be as John Cusack and his three friends took a trip back to 1986. Chevy Chase turned up as the mysterious "Repairman".

Based on the video game, Disney's *Prince of Persia: The Sands of Time* from director Mike Newell was a *Thief of Bagdad* for the 21st century as a bickering Prince (a pumped-up Jake Gyllenhaal) and Princess (Gemma Arterton, straight from the *Clash of the Titans* remake) attempted to stop Ben Kingsley's scheming pretender to the throne from going back in time and changing the past. Alfred Molina stole every scene he was in as a comedy bandit chief.

A teen (Logan Lerman) discovered he was a powerful Olympian demi-god who had been framed for stealing Zeus' lightning bolt in Chris Columbus' *Percy Jackson & the Olympians: The Lightning Thief* (aka *Percy Jackson & the Lightning Thief*), based on the YA books by Rick Riorden. The supporting cast included the busy Sean Bean as Zeus, Pierce Brosnan, Steve Coogan (as Hades), Rosario Dawson, Joe Pantoliano and Uma Thurman as a sexy Medusa.

Disney's *The Sorcerer's Apprentice*, a live-action fantasy starring Nicholas Cage and inspired by the animated Mickey Mouse segment in *Fantasia*, opened to a dismal $17.6 million, despite costing an estimated $150 million to make.

Cage was also in Matthew Vaughn's ultra-violent but hugely enjoyable superhero fantasy *Kick-Ass*, based on the comic book by Mark Millar and John S. Romita, Jr, which topped the US charts with an opening gross of $19.8 million. Aaron Johnson was the teen geek who dressed up as a masked hero only to discover that the marvellous Chloë Grace Moretz's pint-sized avenger was much deadlier than he could ever imagine being.

Based on a Canadian comic book series, Edgar Wright's *Scott Pilgrim vs. the World* was set inside the video-game-saturated minds of three geeky friends.

After the failure of 2009's *Jennifer's Body*, it seemed that actress Megan Fox's name was once again not enough to open a movie when Jimmy Hayward's barely feature-length supernatural Western *Jonah Hex*, based on the DC Comics character (played by Josh Brolin), debuted at #7 in June with just $5.4 million in takings before dropping nearly 70 per cent in its second week.

Based on the best-selling YA book by Alice Sebold, Peter Jackson's adaptation of *The Lovely Bones* starred Saoirse Ronan as a missing fourteen-year-old girl trying to contact her parents (Rachel Weisz and Mark Wahlberg) from a Technicolor afterlife after being raped and murdered by her creepy neighbour (Stanley Tucci).

Dwayne "The Rock" Johnson starred as a minor-league hockey player sentenced to become the titular *Tooth Fairy* as a punishment for crushing a child's hopes. The impressive supporting cast included Ashley Judd, Stephen Merchant, Seth MacFarlane, Julie Andrews and an uncredited Billy Crystal.

Freddie Highmore's Arthur returned to the cartoon kingdom at the bottom of his Granny's garden in Luc Besson's sequel *Arthur and the Great Adventure*, featuring the voice talents of musicians Will i Am, Snoop Dogg and Lou Reed.

Although Disney's hand-drawn re-imagining of *The Princess and the Frog* flopped earlier in the year, *Tangled*, the studio's revisionist version of the "Rapunzel" fairy tale, finally knocked the latest *Harry Potter* off the top of the US box office in early December.

Benefiting from strong word-of-mouth, DreamWorks Animation's 3-D animated *How to Train Your Dragon* returned to the top of the US charts five weeks after it opened.

*Tales from Earthsea* was an *anime* version of the books by Ursula K. Le Guin, directed by Hayao Miyazaki's son, Goro, and featuring the voice talents of Timothy Dalton and Willem Dafoe.

Dan Aykroyd and singer Justin Timberlake voiced Yogi Bear and his friend Boo Boo, respectively, in the animated 3-D comedy *Yogi Bear*, based on the 1960s Hanna-Barbera TV cartoon series.

A sequel to the 2007 film, *Alvin and the Chipmunks: The Squeakquel* depressingly took more than $200 million at the US box office and over £20 million in Britain, with the soundtrack even reaching #6 in the UK album charts!

There were more animated funny animals in *Alpha and Omega*, *Animals Unlimited*, *Marmaduke*, *Space Chimps 2* and the 3-D *Cats & Dogs: The Revenge of Kitty Galore*.

In America, *Toy Story 3* was the top-grossing film of 2010, with a take of $415 million, followed at some distance by *Alice in Wonderland* (#2), *Iron Man 2* (#3), *The Twilight Saga: Eclipse* (#4) and *Inception* (#5). The remainder of the Top 10 included the children's films *Harry Potter and the Deathly Hallows – Part 1* (#6), *Despicable Me* (#7), *Shrek Forever After* (#8) and *How to Train Your Dragon* (#9).

Robert Zemeckis' *Back to the Future* was re-released theatrically in a new digital version to celebrate the film's twenty-fifth anniversary, and a restored version of Fritz Lang's classic *Metropolis* (1927) was reissued in cinemas with an extra twenty-five minutes of found footage. When the movie was shown on TCM, it was followed by an hour-long Argentina programme about how the missing material was discovered in Buenos Aires.

In October, an overexcited local newspaper claimed that workmen refurbishing a Glasgow cinema had discovered a "lost" reel from *King Kong* (1933) hidden behind a partition wall in a projection booth. Sadly, it turned out not to be the missing "Spider Pit" sequence.

\*     \*     \*

In September, the American operation of video-and-games rental store chain Blockbuster filed for Chapter-11 bankruptcy protection with debts of $1.46 billion (£932 million).

James Cameron's overrated *Avatar*, which became the biggest-grossing film of all time in January (beating the same director's *Titanic*), was released in April on Blu-ray in an attempt to boost sales of the struggling high-definition format. A record 1.5 million copies were sold on the first day, although the 3-D film was only initially released in a "flat" version and there were problems playing it on some machines because of the disc's updated security software. A three-disc boxed set "Collector's Edition" of the film released later in the year included a three-hour extended cut of *Avatar*, plus more than forty-five minutes of deleted footage and a making-of documentary.

A group of soldiers battled zombies on a remote island in *Survival of the Dead*, the sixth in George A. Romero's series about the walking dead.

Writer and director Ti West tried unsuccessfully to have his name removed from *Cabin Fever 2: Spring Fever* after it was re-shot and edited by the producers.

David DeCoteau directed *Puppet Master: Axis of Evil*, the tenth entry in the series started by producer Charles Band in 1989. This time the action was set during World War II.

In *After.Life*, Christina Ricci awakened after a car accident to discover that she was a prisoner of Liam Neeson's creepy funeral director, who insisted that she was actually dead.

Edgar Frog (Corey Feldman) teamed up with a best-selling author (Tanit Phoenix) to hunt down a powerful vampire in *Lost Boys: The Thirst*, which was filmed in South Africa and included clips featuring the late Corey Haim. *30 Days of Night: Dark Days* was another direct-to-DVD vampire sequel.

A struggling rock band became involved with vampires in the Canadian comedy *Suck*, featuring appearances by Alice Cooper, Moby, Henry Rollins, Iggy Pop and Malcolm McDowell as "Eddie Van Helsing".

When terrorists threatened to detonate a nuclear weapon in *Universal Soldier: Regeneration*, decommissioned cyborg Luc Deveraux (Jean-Claude Van Damme) was reactivated and pitted against an old adversary (Dolph Lundgren, returning from the first film).

Isabella Calthorpe was among those trapped by a werewolf in an isolated old dark house in the British-made *13hrs*.

In Carlos Brook's contrived horror thriller *Burning Bright*, a teenage girl (Briana Evigan) and her autistic younger brother found themselves trapped in a hurricane-ravaged house with a hungry Bengal tiger.

A remake of the 1970 British psychological thriller scripted by Brian Clemens and Terry Nation, *And Soon the Darkness* moved the original's location from France to Argentina (where it was filmed).

The Australian-made *The Loved Ones* was about a high-school senior who was kidnapped and tortured by the girl he didn't invite to the prom, while a teenager searched for his missing brother amongst the undead in the South Korean/Japanese production *Higanjima: Escape from Vampire Island*.

When Dario Argento's serial-killer thriller *Giallo* was released directly to DVD in the US in October, star Adrien Brody sued the film-makers, claiming that he had not been fully paid and that, contractually, the 2009 movie could not be released without his permission. The lawsuit blocking the movie's release was quickly settled.

*Thriller: The Complete Series* from Image Entertainment finally collected all sixty-seven episodes of the superior 1960s Boris Karloff-hosted TV series on a fourteen-disc box set that included audio commentaries from cast and crew, rare episode previews and extensive stills galleries.

Mark Harmon voiced Superman in the direct-to-DVD animated movie *Justice League: Crisis on Two Earths*.

*Family Guy Presents It's a Trap!* was the disappointing third instalment in the animated *Star Wars*-inspired trilogy. Carrie Fisher was one of the guest voices, along with Patrick Stewart and Michael Dorn from *Star Trek: The Next Generation*.

Richard Donner's *The Goonies* celebrated its twenty-fifth anniversary with new DVD and Blu-ray transfers, packed with such extras as deleted scenes, storyboards and a commentary track featuring the director and his now grown-up stars. The *Back to the Future: 25th Anniversary Trilogy* boxed set also included plenty of bonus material, including long-lost clips of Eric Stoltz as the *original* Marty McFly.

*True: A XXX Parody* was a hardcore spoof of the vampire show *True Blood* from New Sensations starring Ashlynn Brooke and Misty Stone. Actress Anna Paquin admitted on an American late-night talk show that she bought copies of the porno DVD as a wrap gift for cast and crew on the HBO TV series.

In September, The Irish Film Classification Office (IFCO) banned the DVD release of Meir Zarchi's *I Spit on Your Grave* (1978) for "depicting acts of gross violence and cruelty towards humans". The film was still issued in an "Ultimate Collector's Edition" in the UK.

The Syfy channel continued to churn out low-budget monster movies, horror films, science fiction adventures and natural disasters at an alarming rate.

In one of his last roles, David Carradine played an evil industrialist in Syfy's terrible *Dinocroc vs. Supergator*. Directed by Jim Wynorski under a pseudonym, Roger Corman was executive producer.

Corman not only produced *Dinoshark* starring Eric Balfour, but also gave himself a supporting role, and he also turned up in an uncredited cameo in his *Sharktopus* starring Eric Roberts.

Former 1980s pop singer Tiffany was amongst those trying to prevent a mutant strain of giant fish from eating their way to Florida in *Mega Piranha*, and Colin Ferguson's game warden learned that his young son should not feed the crocodiles in *Lake Placid 3*, which also featured Yancy Butler and Michael Ironside.

Sean Patrick Flanery's treasure hunter discovered that experimental oil drilling had awakened the legendary *Mongolian Death Worm*, while the desecration of a mystical Indian burial ground by Robert Picardo's evil industrialist led to the release of a mythical monster in the entertaining *Monsterwolf*.

In *Red: Werewolf Hunter*, also from Syfy, Kavan Smith discovered that his fiancée (Felicia Day) was a modern-day descendant of Little Red Riding Hood who tracked down lycanthropes.

A rural hamlet was visited every Halloween by a child-stealing creature in *Goblin* starring Gil Bellows, and TV ghost hunters

Charisma Carpenter and Corin Nemec investigated a haunted *House of Bones*.

An archaeological team awakened a bloodthirsty half-plant half-animal creature in *Mandrake*, while a West Virginian urban legend took revenge on five childhood friends who covered up an accidental murder in *Mothman*.

Luke Goss was the new king trying to save his kingdom from evil witch-queen Sarah Douglas and her army of sorceresses in *Witchville*, which was filmed in China.

Sean Bean was among the survivors of a post-apocalyptic world battling mutated zombies in the South African-filmed *The Lost Future*, and yet another bunch of TV genre actors attempted to prevent ancient technology from destroying the Earth in the fun *Stonehenge Apocalypse*.

A group of scientists tried to stop the Earth being destroyed by a rogue comet in *Quantum Apocalypse*, and Michael Trucco and Kari Matchett attempted to prevent San Francisco being obliterated by rogue meteorites in *Meteor Storm*.

Michael Shanks was amongst those caught in a super-chilled *Arctic Blast*, and Brendan Fehr and Victor Garber attempted to survive a deadly *Ice Quake*.

Kevin Sorbo played a homicide detective on a parallel Earth investigating a series of magical murders in the enjoyable pilot *Paradox*, based on a comic book by Christos N. Gage.

Having previously attempted to bring Philip Jose Farmer's novels to TV in 2003, Syfy took another shot at adapting *Riverworld* as a two-part mini-series, this time featuring Tahmoh Penikett and Alan Cumming.

Based on the masked comic character created by Lee Falk, the Syfy mini-series *The Phantom* starred Ryan Carnes as "The Ghost That Walks" battling Isabella Rossellini's mind-controlling villain.

The unfortunately titled *Terry Pratchett's Going Postal* was Sky's third TV film based on the author's popular "Discworld" series of novels. A likeable Richard Coyle starred as conman Moist von Lipwig, who was forced to reopen Ankh-Morpork's moribund mail system aided by an army of Golems and the grumpy Adora Belle Dearheart (the wonderful Claire Foy).

*Doctor Who* writer Steven Moffat co-created (with Mark

Gatiss) *Sherlock*, three TV movies for the BBC that re-imagined Sir Arthur Conan Doyle's consulting detective in contemporary London. Benedict Cumberbatch played the charismatic Holmes, who teamed up with former soldier Dr John Watson (Martin Freeman, supplying the series' heart and soul) to solve a trio of baffling mysteries. The first and third episodes worked best, with Una Stubbs as an eccentric Mrs Hudson, Gatiss himself as a sinister Mycroft and Andrew Scott as a very modern Moriarty.

The ever-busy Mark Gatiss also scripted and starred as a fussy Professor Cavor, the eccentric inventor of the anti-gravity substance "cavorite", in the BBC's feature-length adaptation of H.G. Wells' 1901 novel *The First Men in the Moon*. Unfortunately, an illogical 1969 framing story and some unconvincing CGI effects meant that it wasn't nearly as good as the 1964 Ray Harryhausen movie.

MTV's *My Super Psycho Sweet 16 Part 2* was a disappointing sequel to the previous year's Halloween reality slasher.

Catherine Bell returned for the third time as Cassandra "Cassie" Nightingale, who was preparing to get married at Christmas in Hallmark's *The Good Witch's Gift*. In the same network's *The Santa Incident*, Ione Skye helped Santa (James Cosmo) after he was shot out of the sky by a Homeland Security agent's heat-seeking missile, and R.D. Reid's Santa was accidentally sent out a day early and ended up with amnesia in *The Night Before the Night Before Christmas*.

ABC's *Christmas Cupid* was yet another rom-com reworking of Charles Dickens' *A Christmas Carol*.

A super-intelligent family was recruited to a secret scientific project in NBC's *The Jensen Project*, and a family inherited a castle in Romania in Nickelodeon's *The Boy Who Cried Werewolf*, which starred Brooke Shields as the mysterious "Madame Varcolac".

Cartoon Network's live-action *Scooby-Doo! Curse of the Lake Monster* featured guest appearances by Richard Moll, Nichelle Nichols, Marion Ross and genre veteran Michael Berryman.

In Disney's New Zealand-shot TV movie *Avalon High*, based on the novel by Meg Cabot, a young girl (Britt Robertson) discovered that the pupils at her new school were teenage re-incarnations of King Arthur's court.

2010 was the year that technology finally caught up with science fiction as 3-D television sets became the Next Big Thing, mostly due to the phenomenal increase in 3-D movies being released by the major studios. At the beginning of October, Britain's Sky subscription network launched the country's first 3-D HD channel, however, it remains to be seen if the boom will endure, or whether the public will simply tire of the technology as they have in the past.

In April, the UK's Sci-Fi Channel followed its American counterpart and rebranded itself under the less-generic name of "Syfy".

With writer Steven Moffat on board as the new show-runner, David Tennant's manic *Doctor Who* was quickly forgotten with the introduction of 27-year-old Matt Smith as the latest incarnation of the BBC's Time Lord.

Teaming up with enigmatic and feisty sidekick Amy Pond (Karen Gillan), the couple careered through thirteen episodes involving World War II Daleks, vampires (actually fishy aliens) in 16th-century Venice and a tormented Vincent van Gogh (the excellent Tony Curran).

Alex Kingston's enigmatic River Song was back for an *Aliens*-inspired story involving the Weeping Angels (not used to such good effect this time), before returning for the two-part season finale which cleverly connected all the preceding episodes in a convoluted cross-time conundrum that involved many past foes and even incorporated the original UK transmission date! Guest writers included Toby Whithouse, Simon Nye and Richard Curtis.

As usual, the much-hyped Christmas special was disappointing as the Doctor tried to convince a Scrooge-like tyrant (Michael Gambon) to change his ways to save a crashing space liner in Steven Moffat's lazy reworking of *A Christmas Carol*, which co-starred Welsh mezzo-soprano Katherine Jenkins.

However, despite the popularity of Smith in the role, the average viewing figures for *Doctor Who* dropped 1.2 million, although more people were watching the show on BBC iPlayer and other on-demand media.

The fourth season of the BBC's spin-off series for children, *The Sarah Jane Adventures*, kicked off with Sarah Jane's boring alien son Luke (Tommy Knight) being shipped off to university in Oxford with the irritating K-9, freeing the intrepid reporter (Elisabeth Sladen) and her more interesting two teenage companions to continue battling various alien menaces.

Matt Smith's new Doctor turned up in a two-part episode written by Russell T. Davies that also featured Jon Pertwee's 1971–73 companion Jo Grant (Katy Manning), and the trio were sent back in time to the Tower of London in 1554, a haunted house in Victorian times, and the English coast during World War II before Luke returned to save the day in the season finale.

Also from the BBC at Christmas, *Whistle and I'll Come to You* starred John Hurt in director Andy de Emmony's dull and pointless reworking of M.R. James' classic ghost story. Writer Neil Cross seemed mistakenly to believe that he could improve upon the original by updating it and introducing his own character motivation, while the production not only shortened the original title, but also banished James' name to the end credits.

Frank Darabont's gruesome six-part limited series for AMC, *The Walking Dead*, based on the Image Comics series created by writer Robert Kirkman and artist Tony Moore, should have been retitled "The Talking Dead". Less exposition and more excitement was needed as Texas sheriff Rick Grimes (British actor Andrew Lincoln) woke up from a coma only to discover that the world had been overrun by nasty-looking cannibal zombies and even the Centers for Disease Control in Atlanta couldn't help him or his dwindling band of survivors. Although the series was picked up for a second season, in December Darabont let go of the show's entire team of writers.

Loosely based on Stephen King's 2005 mystery novel *The Colorado Kid*, Syfy's thirteen-part *Haven* involved FBI agent Audrey Parker (the likeable Emily Rose) being sent to the small coastal town of Haven, Maine, where every week somebody exhibited a different supernatural power as we learned more about the mystery of the agent's own missing past.

King himself had a cameo as a character named "Bachman" (get it?) in the FX biker series *Sons of Anarchy*.

The gripping sixth season of *Supernatural* continued with episodes in which brothers Sam (Jared Padalecki) and Dean (Jensen Ackles) travelled back to 1978 to save their parents from an angel assassin, confronted flesh-eating zombies raised by Death, travelled to Heaven after being shot, and teamed up with a double-dealing demon named Crowley (the excellent Mark A. Sheppard) to avert the coming apocalypse. Unfortunately, after a marvellous build-up over the past two years, the climactic confrontation with Lucifer (Mark Pellegrino), like so many other season finales in 2010, turned out to be a huge disappointment, despite the apparent death of a major character. The show celebrated its 100th episode in April.

The third season of HBO's *True Blood* kicked off with vampire Bill Compton (Stephen Moyer) being kidnapped from a restaurant just as he had proposed to Sookie (Anna Paquin). After discovering that his abductors were werewolves working for the Vampire King of Mississippi (Denis O'Hare), Sookie set off in pursuit with a lycanthropic bodyguard (Joe Manganiello). However, when the blood-drenched rescue attempt resulted in Bill uncontrollably biting Sookie, she had a glimpse into her mysterious origin, which involved dancing around a bottomless pool in a diaphanous gown. Stars Paquin and Moyer were married in August.

The first season of The CW's wimpy *The Vampire Diaries* ended in death and destruction as an undead Jonathan Gilbert (David Anders) went on a violent rampage during the Founder's Day celebrations in the town of Mystic Falls. Season Two opened with the return of evil vampire Katherine (sulky Nina Dobrev), who happened to be the spitting image of Elena (also Dobrev), while Tyler Lockwood (Michael Trevino) learned about his family's werewolf curse.

A new police chief (Frank Grillo) discovered that his gated community was home to vampires, werewolves and other supernatural creatures in ABC's *The Gates*.

Robin Dunne's Dr Will Zimmerman returned from death after convincing Kali to halt her waves of destruction in the opening episode of the third season of Syfy's *Sanctuary*. Meanwhile, werewolf Henry (Ryan Robbins) infiltrated a clinic filled with patients just like him, and Amanda Tapping's Dr

Helen Magnus encountered a time-hopping Jekyll and Hyde who agreed to lead the team to a hidden city beneath the Earth.

When Peter Bishop (Joshua Jackson) disappeared after learning that he had been abducted from an alternate reality by his scientist father in Fox's *Fringe*, Walter Bishop (John Noble) told a drug-fuelled story set in a fictional *noir* milieu that included several songs! Leonard Nimoy returned as William Bell for the two-part second season finale, as Peter and Walter returned home from the parallel universe with the wrong Olivia (Anna Troy).

In early May, the nineteenth episode of ABC-TV's *FlashForward* scripted by Robert J. Sawyer (who wrote the original novel), pulled in an audience of just 4.75 million, setting a new low for the series. It was no surprise that the show was cancelled after just three more episodes, putting an end to the producers' proposed five-year story arc despite an apparently desperate attempt to continue the show's underlying conspiracy theory. In the unresolved ending, the convoluted time-line was re-set, Mark Benford (Joseph Fiennes) disappeared during the next blackout, and there was an enigmatic coda set in 2015.

The much-hyped, two-and-a-half-hour final episode of ABC's always-pointless *Lost* in May jumped confusingly back and forth between the same characters on the island and in Los Angeles, until they finally realised after six seasons that they were all dead. The end. Thank God.

Another show that will not be missed was NBC's over-hyped and underwhelming *Heroes*, whose fourth and final season only averaged 6.5 million viewers (a whopping drop of 8 million since its first season). The season finale managed to attract a measly audience of 4.4 million.

The dull *Battlestar Galactica* prequel *Caprica* starred Eric Stoltz and Esai Morales and chronicled the origin of the Cylons. The second half of Season One returned to Syfy in September, but it wasn't like anybody cared any more.

Despite its annoying non-linear structure and being yet another attempt to create a "Big Event" TV show with a bewildering cast and and too many plot strands, NBC's *The Event* began promisingly enough with its various US government and alien visitor conspiracies. However, average audiences soon dropped to 7.8 million and in November the show was put on a three-month hiatus after just ten episodes.

Following the murder of his wife by another serial killer, Dexter Morgan (Michael C. Hall) teamed up with a crime victim (Julia Stiles) in the fifth series of the Showtime Network's *Dexter*. Guest stars included Peter Weller and Johnny Lee Miller.

After five seasons and more than 100 episodes, Melinda Gordon (Jennifer Love Hewitt) finally confronted the dark forces that had been terrorising her family when CBS-TV's *Ghost Whisperer* came to an end with an audience share of 6.65 million at the end of May.

The seventh season of *Medium* featured an "arms of Orlac" episode, although CBS cut the number of shows it ordered.

Brooke Elliott returned as possessed attorney Jane Bingum in a second season of Lifetime's body-swap drama *Drop Dead Diva*, while in the second season of *Being Erica* on SOAPnet the time-travelling heroine (Erin Karpluk) had a new therapist.

Making up for its disappointing second series, the third and final season of *Ashes to Ashes* from the BBC was back on form as it concentrated on the relationship between DCI Gene Hunt (Philip Glenister) and time-travelling cop Alex Drake (Keeley Hawes) in 1983 and the mystery surrounding the death of Sam Tyler (from *Life on Mars*). Unfortunately, the ridiculous final episode ruined everything that had gone before as Hunt turned out to be some kind of ghostly guardian angel for policemen and the odious DCI Jim Keats (Daniel Mays) was revealed to be the Devil coveting everyone's souls.

Definitely shaking off its sitcom roots, the much darker second season of the BBC's excellent *Being Human* found house-sharing ghost Annie (Lenora Crichlow), werewolf George (Russell Tovey) and vampire Mitchell (Aidan Turner) being hunted by a crazed scientist (Donald Sumpter) who intended to "cure" them of their supernatural afflictions – at *any* cost.

Created by stars Steve Pemberton and Reece Shearsmith (of *The League of Gentlemen*), the BBC's *Psychoville Halloween Special* featured four nasty tales based around the dilapidated ruins of the old Ravenhill psychiatric hospital. Eileen Atkins, Dawn French and Imelda Staunton guest-starred.

The second series of the BBC's post-apocalyptic *Survivors*

limped through another six episodes as the dull bunch of characters discovered a secret pharmaceutical laboratory that could have been the cause of the outbreak. Thankfully, a third series looked highly unlikely.

Based on the two novels by Douglas Adams, the BBC's hour-long pilot *Dirk Gently* starred engaging comedian Stephen Mangan as the quirky "holistic" detective who investigated a missing cat and a case of time-travel by studying the fundamental interconnectedness of all things.

Echo (Eliza Dushku) could access all her personalities in the second and final season of the Fox Network's *Dollhouse*, which ended with an episode set in a dystopian future where the surviving Dollhouse staff battled murderous mind-wiped zombies while trying to find a safe haven for the remnants of mankind.

In the third and fourth seasons of NBC's struggling *Chuck*, the hapless store clerk-turned-spy (Zachary Levi) learned to control his new-found powers and discovered a family secret from his late father (Scott Bakula). Meanwhile, former James Bond actor Timothy Dalton guest-starred as a MI6 agent looking after Chuck's secret agent mother (Linda Hamilton), and other high-profile guests included Vinnie Jones, Armand Assante, Angie Harmon, Robert Patrick, Fred Willard, Swoosie Kurtz, Udo Kier, Christopher Lloyd, Harry Dean Stanton, Dolph Lundgren, Lou Ferrigno, Nicole Richie, Morgan Fairchild, Robert Englund and Richard Chamberlain.

After her terrific turn in *Terry Pratchett's Going Postal*, Claire Foy had a more thankless role as a disturbed junior doctor in the BBC's *Pulse*, a derivative hospital-set pilot featuring sinister surgeons and parasitical research experiments, written by Paul Cornell.

Even worse was *The Deep*, a five-part mini-series from the BBC. Without even the saving grace of being so bad that it was funny, Minnie Driver's overly emotional submarine captain and her intrepid crew of research scientists (including James Nesbitt and Goran Visnijic) found themselves trapped beneath the Arctic ice with a bunch of crazed Russians, an overheating nuclear reactor and a new species of lava-bug.

In Syfy's *Warehouse 13*, agents Pete Lattimer (Eddie McClintock) and Myka Bering (Joanne Kelly) found themselves involved with a new villain, a *female* H.G. Wells (British actress Jaime Murray), who sent the pair back to 1961 in her time machine. Guest stars included genre TV veterans Lindsay Wagner, Tia Carrere, Rene Auberjonois and Armin Shimerman. The second season finale attracted 2.4 million viewers, the show's biggest audience to date.

In the fourth season opener of Syfy's *Eureka* (aka *A Town Called Eureka*), the main cast members were accidentally transported back to 1947. Upon their return, they discovered that their reality had been subtly changed, as James Callis joined the cast as a scientist from the past. Meanwhile, an experiment turned the personnel of Global Dynamics into rage-filled zombies in an unusually dark episode before the series went on hiatus after just nine episodes.

During the year, both shows also featured fun crossover episodes, when Eureka's Douglas Fargo (Neil Grayston) ended up being trapped inside Warehouse 13 by a sentient computer program, and Claudia Donovan (Allison Scagliotti) turned up to help investigate a series of mysterious materialisations in the town of Eureka.

The two-part opener of the third season of the BBC's *Merlin* saw sorceress siblings Morgana (Katie McGrath) and Morgause (Emilia Fox) using giant scorpions to try to kill the boy wizard (Colin Morgan) and attacking Camelot with an horde of reanimated skeletons. The superb double-episode finale saw the scheming Morgana finally installed upon the throne of Camelot by an army of immortal warriors.

In a two-part episode of *Smallville* that owed more than a nod to Alan Moore's *Watchmen*, some of the surviving members of the Golden Age Justice Society of America (including Hawkman, Stargirl and Doctor Fate) came out of retirement to team up with a nascent Justice League to battle a new conspiracy involving Pam Grier's clandestine Checkmate agent.

In other episodes of The CW show, Clark (Tom Welling) teamed up again with sexy magician Zantanna (Serinda Swan) to find a cursed comic book, and Martha Kent (Annette O'Toole) made a surprise reappearance before Clark defeated the evil Major Zod (Callum Blue) and his army of super-powered Kandorians. The tenth and final season saw the return of Clark's dead stepfather Jonathan Kent (John Schneider), Supergirl Kara (Laura Vandervoort), Brainiac 5 (James Marsters), General Sam Lane (Michael Ironside), Lucy Lane (Peyton List), the late Ella Lane (Teri Hatcher), Jor-El (Julian Sands), Lara-El (Helen Slater), Aquaman (Alan Ritchson), an alternate-world Lionel Luthor (John Glover) and the Justice League.

The second season of Channel 4's *Misfits*, about a group of British teen tearaways with superpowers, featured "ghosts", time-travel and plenty of adolescent angst. A Christmas special/season finale found the group exchanging their powers in return for a "normal" life.

ABC-TV's *No Ordinary Family* was *Heroes* for housewives. After surviving a plane crash in the Amazon, a dysfunctional suburban family discovered that they had each developed a different superpower. Then they didn't stop whining about it.

Syfy's dull reboot of *V* ended with discord spreading amongst the alien Visitors as the scheming Anna (Morena Baccarin) finally ramped up her secret plans to invade the Earth.

The first season of the network's equally dull *SGU Stargate Universe* concluded with a two-part episode in which the starship "Destiny" was invaded by troops of the Lucian Alliance, under the command of the ruthless Commander Kiva (British actress Rhona Mitra). After all that got sorted out, the second season continued the saga of the reluctant space travellers as the show hurtled towards its inevitable cancellation.

Alex (Selena Gomez) discovered that her new English boyfriend Mason (Gregg Sulkin) was actually a werewolf in the third season of Disney's popular children's sitcom *Wizards of Waverly Place*.

When the Farley family moved to Eastern Europe, they found themselves surrounded by vampires, werewolves and zombies in Nickelodeon's British-made teen sitcom *Summer in Transylvania*.

Self-obsessed crime author Rick Castle (Nathan Fillion) and homicide detective Kate Beckett (Stana Katic) found themselves investigating the apparent curse of an Aztec Mummy's tomb in the second season of ABC's lightweight mystery series *Castle*, which could just as well be called *Murder He Wrote*. Season Three included the prerequisite psychic, possible time-travelling killer and apparent alien abduction episodes.

Shawn (James Roday) and Gus (Dulé Hill) investigated a murder on a haunted-house ride that appeared to be committed by the ghost of a man killed there thirteen years before in the USA Network's *Psych*.

19th-century Canadian police inspector William Murdoch (Yannick Bisson) investigated a suspicious death at an apparently cursed and haunted manor in a third season episode of *Murdoch Mysteries*.

The third series of the BBC's *The Armstrong & Miller Show* featured a series of sketches featuring comedians Alexander Armstrong and Ben Miller playing a pair of out-of-touch vampires complaining about the modern world.

Original stars Meat Loaf and Barry Bostwick briefly guest-starred on a Halloween episode of Fox's seriously overrated *Glee* that paid tribute to the *The Rocky Horror Picture Show*. Unfortunately, the result was a horribly homogenised version of the 1975 cult movie.

Fans of Granada Television's never-ending soap opera *Coronation Street* were a little surprised in early November by the return of Vera Duckworth (Elizabeth Dawn) to the show. The character had been dead for nearly three years and apparently returned to guide her husband Jack (Bill Tarmey) into the hereafter.

Harlan Ellison voiced himself and Jeffrey Combs was author "H.P. Hatecraft" in an episode of Cartoon Network's new animated series *Scooby-Doo! Mystery Incorporated* entitled "The Shrieking Madness".

In *The Simpsons Treehouse of Horror XXI* special on the Fox Network, Bart and Milhouse played a possessed board game, Homer and Marge rescued a potentially homicidal castaway (voiced by Hugh Laurie) and, in a *Twilight* spoof, Lisa ran away with romantic vampire Edmund (voiced by *Harry Potter*'s Daniel Radcliffe) to his father's Dracula-la Land.

The original Justice Society of America – The Flash, Hourman, Hawkman, Dr, Mid-Nite and Wildcat – teamed up with the Caped Crusader for an episode of the Cartoon Network's *Batman: The Brave and the Bold*. In another episode of the show, Batman (Diedrich Bader) travelled back in time and met his father and the Phantom Stranger, voiced by previous Batmans Adam West and Kevin Conroy, respectively.

And while Aquaman rescued Batman from the Penguin in another episode of the series, over on Nickelodeon's *SpongeBob SquarePants* in February the porous pair were transported "Back to the Past", where they met superhero duo "Mermaidman" and "Barnacleboy" (voiced by former Batman and Robin, Adam West and Burt Ward). Additionally, *McHale's Navy* veterans Ernest Borgnine and Tim Conway voiced the older versions of the same characters.

Comedy Central revived *Futurama* in time for the show's 100th episode (featuring a guest appearance by Devo) and a three-story Christmas special.

Peter Griffin and his pals attempted to track down the source of the world's funniest dirty joke in an episode of the Fox Network's *Family Guy*, based on a story by Richard Matheson, and the show passed its 150th episode in May.

Based on the venerable satirical magazine, the Cartoon Network's *Mad* featured a segment called "Zombi", about Bambi's mother coming back as a you-know-what . . .

Over on Adult Swim, Zac Efron voiced Anakin Skywalker in *Robot Chicken*'s *Star Wars Episode III*, which attempted to tell the entire saga in just an hour. Meanwhile, the third season of *Star Wars: The Clone Wars* aired on the Cartoon Network.

Hanna-Barbera's *The Flintstones* celebrated its fiftieth anniversary at the end of September.

In the BBC's *The History of Horror with Mark Gatiss*, the actor-writer took a personal look at the history of the horror film in three one-hour episodes covering the Universal cycle from the silent era to the 1940s; Hammer Films, its rivals and Roger Corman's Edgar Allan Poe series, and the birth of modern American horror in the 1970s. Gatiss proved to be an enthusiastic host, and highlights included some well-chosen clips and newsreel footage, along with interviews with such uncommon commentators as centenarians Carla Laemmle and Gloria Stuart, Donnie Dunagan, Sara Karloff, Anthony Hinds, Jimmy Sangster, Roy Ward Baker, Barbara Steele, David Warner, Barbara Shelley and Piers Haggard. The series was supported with a film season on BBC 4.

Author Max Brooks was amongst those interviewed in the National Geographic channel's hour-long documentary *Zombies: The Truth*.

Taking a look at vampires in popular culture, the BBC 3 documentary *Vampires: Why They Bite* was a pointless rehash hosted by pop "historian" Lisa Hilton and featured contributions from Charlaine Harris, Toby Whithouse and others.

Scottish crime author Denise Mina hosted the BBC's *Edgar Allan Poe: Love, Death and Women*, which used dramatisations to look at the life and work of the author through his relationships with three different women.

*Weird Tales* returned with three new episodes to BBC Radio 4 in January. Hosted by horror hoarder "Lovecraft" (Stephen Hogan), the three stories involved a stalker from beyond the grave, a Celtic goddess with powers over life and death, and the secret of a family's new home.

*Fantastic Journeys* on BBC Radio 7 in May featured half-hour dramatisations of stories by Arthur Machen ("The White People"), H.G. Wells ("The Door in the Wall"), James P. Blaylock and Tim Powers ("Fifty Cents"), Kelly Link ("The Faery Handbag") and Peter F. Hamilton ("If at First").

Written and narrated by Paul Evans, *The Ditch* was a creepy episode of Radio 4's *Afternoon Play* in which a natural history sound recordist discovered something nasty in the aural landscape of a remote fenland area. In the same slot, Sebastian Baczkiewicz's four-part *Pilgrim* concerned the exploits of the eponymous character (Paul Hilton), cursed with immortality and doomed to walk between the human world and the world of faerie.

The fifteen-minute *Woman's Hour Drama* slot featured a five-part adaptation of Joan Lindsay's novel *Picnic at Hanging Rock*, while Melissa Murray's ninety-minute play *Perpetual Light*, broadcast on BBC Radio 3, was set in the near future, when a dead man's avatar was uploaded into a virtual memorial site.

Based on the book by Simon Brett, dipsomaniac actor-turned-sleuth Charles Paris (Bill Nighy) landed a role in a low-budget vampire movie whose co-star (Martine McCutcheon) found herself involved in blackmail and murder in Radio 4's four-part *A Charles Paris Mystery: Cast in Order of Disappearance*.

Over five days in late November, the same station's *Book at Bedtime* slot presented *A Night with a Vampire*. For fifteen minutes a night, former Doctor Who David Tennant read extracts from French Benedictine Antoine Calmet's 1746 anthropological study *The Phantom World* along with "The Family of the Vourdalak" by Alexei Tolstoy, "The Horla" by Guy de Maupassant, "Luella Miller" by Mary E. Wilkins Freeman and "Clarimonde" by Théophile Gautier.

Having exhausted Sir Arthur Conan Doyle's original canon of stories, Clive Merrison and Andrew Sachs teamed up for the seventy-fifth time as Sherlock Holmes and Doctor Watson for a brand new story written by Bert Coules. The two-part *The Further Adventures of Sherlock Holmes: The Marlbourne Point Mystery* was set in a disused lighthouse on a remote stretch of the Kent coast. James Laurenson turned up as Sherlock's older brother Mycroft.

Paula Wilcox starred in a new two-part adaptation of Mary Norton's children's classic *The Borrowers* on Radio 4, while Radio 7 broadcast a two-part dramatisation of George MacDonald's *At the Back of the North Wind* featuring Juliet Stevenson and Joss Ackland.

Over Christmas, *Ghost Stories of Walter de la Mare* on Radio 7 featured Richard E. Grant reading "All Hallows", Toby Jones reading "Seaton's Aunt", Kenneth Cranham reading "Crewe", Anthony Head reading "A Recluse" and Julian Wadham reading "The Almond Tree".

Presenter Rory McGrath looked at Horace Walpole's seminal 1764 Gothic novel in Radio 4's *A Guided Tour of the Castle of Otranto*, while in *Grand Guignol*, Sheila McClennon revisited the site of the 1890s Parisian horror theatre whose name became synonymous with the gruesome and the gory.

Radio 4's *Afternoon Play* presented *Peter Lorre v Peter Lorre* in May, Michael Butt's forty-five-minute dramatisation of the real-life court case about Eugene Weingand, who tried to bill himself as "Peter Lorre, Jr" even though he was not related to the film star. Stephen Greif portrayed Lorre.

*Vincent Price and the Horror of the English Bloodbeast* was an episode of *The Saturday Play* written by Matthew Broughton that looked behind the scenes at the making of the 1967 British movie *Witchfinder General*. Nickolas Grace played Price, supported by Kenneth Cranham as producer Tony Tenser and Blake Ritson as maverick director Michael Reeves.

Ian McKellen portrayed the eponymous villain in a new adaptation of Ian Fleming's 1959 novel *Goldfinger* for the same Saturday slot. The star cast included Toby Stephens as James Bond, John Standing as M, Rosamund Pike as Pussy Galore, along with Ian Ogilvy, Alistair McGowan, Hector Elizondo. Tim Pigott-Smith and director Martin Jarvis.

Narrated by Toby Jones, *Tom, Michael and George* looked at the making of Michael Powell's controversial movie *Peeping Tom* and "glamour" photographer/film-maker George Harrison Marks' involvement in the 1960 production. Among the contributors were Shirley Anne Field and Michael Winner.

The ever-busy Mark Gatiss re-teamed with Reece Shearsmith, Jeremy Dyson and Steve Pemberton for the first time in five years for Radio 4's pre-Halloween special *The League of Gentlemen's Ghost Chase*, in which they investigated the reputedly supernatural history of a 12th-century Gloucestershire inn, built on top of a pagan burial ground.

Despite most of the UK media doing little more than pay lip-service to Halloween, BBC Radio 7 went to town with a full day of genre-related material. This included various episodes of *Weird Tales* and *Fear on Four*, readings of Charles Dickens' *The Signal-Man* (by Emlyn Williams) and Robert Forrest's *The Voyage of the Demeter*, dramatisations of *Faust* (with the ubiquitous Gatiss again), Oscar Wilde's *The Picture of Dorian Gray* (with Ian McDiarmid), Henry James' *The Turn of the Screw* (with Rosemary Leach), Mary Shelley's *Frankenstein* (with John Wood), Loren D. Estleman's *Sherlock Holmes v Dracula* and Richard Matheson's *The Twilight Zone: Nightmare at 20,000 Feet*, along with Alan Dein's half-hour documentary *You're Entering the Twilight Zone*, a profile of the show's creator Rod Serling.

The station repeated its commitment to the genre on Christmas Day, with dramatisations of C.S. Lewis' *The Magician's Nephew* and *The Lion, the Witch and the Wardrobe*, Stephen Sheridan's M.R. James parody *The Teeth of Abbot Thomas*, four five-minute episodes of *The Scarifyers*, the ten-minute drama *The Curse of the Cult of Thoth*, Ian McDiarmid reading J. Sheridan Le Fanu's "Schalken the Painter", a *Twilight Zone* adaptation of Jerome Bixby's "It's a Good Life" and a repeat of Alan Dein's *Twilight Zone* documentary from Halloween.

From the UK's Big Finish Productions, the audio drama *Dark Shadows: The Night Whispers* marked the return of Jonathan Frid to the role of Barnabas Collins, with John Karlan reprising his role as the former vampire's reluctant servant Willie Loomis from the 1966–71 TV soap opera. As an added bonus for fans, the CD also featured Barbara Steele as a new character to the series.

Online audio site Cast Macabre featured a free podcast of Barbara Roden's story "Out and Back", included in the previous volume of this anthology.

Established in 2006, Pseudopod.org broadcast readings of new and previously published horror stories on a weekly basis to an audience of around 8,000 listeners.

Although credited to Andrew Lloyd-Webber and Ben Elton, the original plot of the follow-up to the £6 million stage musical of *The Phantom of the Opera*, *Love Never Dies*, which opened at London's Adelphi Theatre in March, was actually created by best-selling author Frederick Forsyth almost a decade earlier. In late November, the show was closed down for four days while it was completely overhauled due to negative criticism and plummeting box-office figures ahead of the production's premiere in Australia.

Meanwhile, the original UK production of *The Phantom* passed 10,000 performances at Her Majesty's Theatre in London.

With music composed by Bono and the Edge of U2 and featuring more than forty cast members, *Spider-Man: Turn off the Dark* was the most expensive show ever staged on Broadway. However, after a stuntman playing Spider-Man fell thirty feet during a preview performance in December, the $65 million musical had its official opening night pushed back a month to February, and then March 2011. It was the latest in a string of problems that had plagued the "jinxed" show, which was critically lambasted by some reviewers, including *The New York Times*, who described it as "beyond repair".

Nathan Lane and Bebe Neuwirth were perfectly cast as Gomez and Morticia in the Broadway musical *The Addams Family*, based on the cartoons by Charles Addams.

Three decades after he first played the character, Paul Reubens revived his most endearing creation on the Broadway stage in *The Pee-wee Herman Show*.

The 2008 Will Ferrell movie *Elf* was turned into a Broadway musical for Christmas. Sebastian Arcelus was the naïve human raised as one of Santa's not-so-little helpers.

An unusual campaign to promote the December revival of Jeff Wayne's musical version of *War of the Worlds*, featuring Jason Donovan, Atomic Kitten's Liz McClarnon and *The X Factor*'s Rhydian, involved the residents of London's Primrose Hill area waking up one morning in September to a number of crushed cars in the street, alien "footprints", and a mocked-up police sign directing them to the show's website. In H.G. Wells' original novel, Primrose Hill served as the base for the Martian invasion.

John Gordon Sinclair was the actor under the bandages in a revival of Ken Hill's 1991 "music hall" adaptation of Wells' *The Invisible Man* at the Menier Chocolate Factory in London. Objects moved around the stage apparently of their own accord thanks to illusionist Paul Kleve.

Written and directed by Andy Nyman and *The League of Gentlemen*'s Jeremy Dyson, *Ghost Stories* was a portmanteau of three tales linked by Nyman's professor of parapsychology. The play enjoyed a limited engagement at the Duke of York's Theatre in London's West End following a successful run at the Lyric Hammersmith.

*Terror 2010*, which ran at London's Southwark Playhouse (a vault under London Bridge station) in October, featured four short plays about "Death and Resurrection". It included three world premiers by Mark Ravenhill, Neil LaBute and April de Angelis, plus an adaptation of H.P. Lovecraft's "Herbert West: Re-animator" by William Ewart. Despite the inclusion of a zombie belly dancer, the reviewers were not kind.

Better received was *Grand Guignol*, which played to sell-out audiences towards the end of the year at London's Etcetera Theatre. A three-part performance from Tom Richards and Stewart Pringle's company Theatre of the Damned, the show was inspired by the 19th-century Parisian original and reportedly caused one audience member to faint in the first act.

Originally starring Jeremy Brett and Edward Hardwicke in

the late 1980s, Jeremy Paul's psychological stage play *The Secret of Sherlock Holmes* was revived at London's Duchess Theatre in July. This time Peter Egan played the great detective and Robert Daws was Dr Watson.

*Room on the Broom* was a new London stage production based on the best-selling children's book by Julia Donaldson and Alex Scheffler (creators of *The Gruffalo*).

Celebrating its subject's ninetieth birthday in June, "Ray Harryhausen: Myths & Legends: The Exhibition" showcased many of the special-effects wizard's original stop-motion models at the London Film Museum. Meanwhile, John Landis hosted a BFI/Bafta tribute to the animator at BFI Southbank that included video tributes from Steven Spielberg, James Cameron and Nick Park.

That same month, The Wizarding World of Harry Potter theme park opened at the Universal Islands of Adventure in Orlando, Florida. The twenty-acre attraction cost $200 million and was launched by actors Daniel Radcliffe, Rupert Grint and Michael Gambon, along with author J.K. Rowling. For $79.00 (adults)/$69.00 (children) admission, fans could buy everything Hogwarts – from a magic wand for $28.95 to a Firebolt broomstick for $300.00.

In July, a digital poster advertising the "Bloody Mary: Killer Queen" exhibit at the London Dungeon tourist attraction was banned from the city's Underground stations by the Advertising Standards Authority after complaints from four passengers who claimed that the animated ads could frighten or distress children.

Two years after the first event was held, the second *Doctor Who* Prom took place at a Tardis-themed Albert Hall in London at the end of July. Series stars Karen Gillan and Matt Smith hosted the evening, with the BBC National Orchestra of Wales performing Murray Gold's musical compositions while various Cybermen, Silurians, Judoons and Daleks paraded across the stage.

All these and many other of the Time Lord's nemeses were also featured in *Doctor Who Live: The Monsters Are Coming!*, the first-ever *Doctor Who* touring stage show, developed with executive producer Steve Moffat. The event visited nine cities in the UK, starting at London's Wembley Arena in early October and finishing in Belfast a month later. Along with flashy special effects, the show starred Nigel Planer as an inter-galactic show-man and included new videos scenes featuring Matt Smith as the Doctor projected on a fifty-foot screen.

Strawberry Hill, the baroque West London home of Gothic novelist Horace Walpole (*The Castle of Otranto*), was reopened to the public in October following a £9 million restoration.

The hand-written first draft of Mary Shelley's novel *Frankenstein: or, the Modern Prometheus* was part of an exhibition entitled "Shelley's Ghost: Reshaping the Image of a Literary Family", which opened in early December at the Bodleian Libraries in Oxford. The exhibition also included other manuscripts, memorabilia, rare books and a previously unseen portrait of the author. The collection was set to transfer to the New York Public Library in 2011.

Microsoft's Kinect device, launched in November, used cameras, sensors and microphones to track a person's movements, thus allowing them to play games hands-free. The system was designed to work with existing Xbox consoles.

In Capcom's video game *Dead Rising 2* players were contestants in a TV game show battling zombies in a Las Vegas-like city. Meanwhile, Bethesda Softworks' *Fallout: New Vegas* was a post-apocalyptic game set in the Nevada resort with characters voiced by Ron Perlman, Kris Kristofferson, Danny Trejo and Matthew Perry.

*Dead Nation* was a budget-priced zombie shooter available for download-only.

Having taken a reported five years to develop, *Alan Wake* was divided into six episodes in which the eponymous best-selling horror writer used light to destroy the game's monsters, "The Taken".

*Darksiders* concerned a conflict between the forces of Heaven and Hell that led to the destruction of humanity. As War, one of the Four Horseman of the Apocalypse, the player had to discover what caused the Apocalypse.

A witch used her hair to battle her enemies in *Bayonetta*, while PC players had to elude radioactive mutants in the exclusion zone around Chernobyl in the oddly-titled *S.T.A.L.K.E.R.: Call of Pripyat*.

*Prince of Persia: The Forgotten Sands* was a follow-up game to *The Sands of Time*, which makers Ubisoft hoped would benefit from the release of the movie starring Jake Gyllenhaal.

Robert Downey, Jr and Don Cheadle voiced their movie characters in the *Iron Man 2* interactive game, which used a new story expanded from the film franchise.

*Alien vs Predator* made a belated return to the games market in February. Set on a jungle planet being exploited by the Weyland-Yutani Corporation, players could experience the game from the point of view of an Alien, Predator or cannon-fodder space marine.

Matt Smith's Doctor and new sidekick Karen Gillan were digitally recreated for *Doctor Who: The Adventure Games*, a series of four original "interactive episodes" available to download for free.

Walt Disney's first-ever creation, "Oswald the Lucky Rabbit", which he lost in a contract dispute with Universal Studios in 1928, returned as the warden of a warped version of Disneyland full of forgotten characters in Junction Point's *Epic Mickey* game for the Wii console.

A twelve-inch limited edition action figure of Christopher Lee as the Creature in Hammer's *The Curse of Frankenstein* was the first in a new series custom designed by Distinctive Dummies. A glow-in-the-dark version was also available.

In a desperate attempt to tie in with the now-cancelled TV show, each *Ghost Whisperer* Cup and Saucer ($65.00 online) featured a "haunted" set from the 1940s or 1950s that came with a certificate of authenticity, its own unique history, and a special message from Jennifer Love Hewitt's character Melinda.

For those who take their "Lovecraft" seriously, for $220.00 a company called Necronomicox offered a hand-crafted two-colour Mythos Art sex toy for women that preferred their Deep Ones to come in sculptured silicone.

At the end of November, an obscure church group in the UK demanded that supermarket chain Tesco withdrew its "sinful"

*Twilight* advent calendar from sale as it claimed that mixing religion and vampires was "deeply offensive" to Christians.

In February, London auction house Bonham's hosted a sale of props from the BBC's *Doctor Who*. A 1988 Dalek sold for £15,600 while a black Dalek from a 1985 episode went for £20,400. Other sale items included a steel panel from the Tardis, a 1988 Cyberman (£4,080), David Tennant's blue shirt (£1,260) and a waitress outfit, boots and bloomers worn by Kylie Minogue in the 2007 Christmas special (£3,120).

Four months later, a fan paid more than £10,800 at the same Knightbridge auction house for a Tardis used in the Christopher Eccleston series. An exhibition prop of the Tardis sold for £900 and a 1967 Cyberman helmet went for £7,800. Two Daleks from the 1960s sold for £4,800 apiece.

The Lone Ranger's original mask and gloves from *The Lone Ranger and the City of Gold*, along with Tonto's original headband, were put up for auction in March. They had been hidden away for fifty years and were sold by a woman who had won them in a competition.

That same month, a rare American insert poster for the 1926 Fritz Lang movie *Metropolis* sold at auction in Dallas, Texas, for $47,800, while an oversized 1933 Swedish poster for *King Kong* went for $28,680.

An Alberta, Canada, man who discovered a horde of vintage movie posters being used as insulation in a recently purchased 1912 house, put around forty of them up for auction in July. In fact, the house contained more than 350 posters and title lobby cards dating back to the silent era. Amongst the titles represented were a title lobby card for *The Mysterious Dr Fu Manchu* (1929), which realised just over $1,000, and a rare rotogravure one-sheet poster for Tod Browning's *The 13th Chair* (1929), which sold for nearly $3,000.

For the first time in its history, the World Horror Convention was held in England in 2010. Over March 25–28, almost 600 horror fans from all around the world attended the event in the Victorian seaside town of Brighton.

Tanith Lee and David Case were the Author Guests of Honour, Les Edwards and Dave Carson were the Artist Guests of Honour, and Hugh Lamb was the Editor Guest of Honour. James Herbert was the Special Guest of Honour, Ingrid Pitt was Special Media Guest, and Jo Fletcher served as Mistress of Ceremonies.

Brian Lumley and William F. Nolan had earlier been announced as winners of Horror Writers Association Lifetime Achievement Awards. As Nolan was unable to attend, Dennis Etchison was there as the HWA Special Guest.

At the awards ceremony, held at a banquet on Brighton Pier on the Saturday evening, James Herbert was the recipient of the WHC Grand Master Award, while Basil Copper received the convention's new Lifetime Achievement Award.

The 2009 HWA Bram Stoker Awards were also presented the same evening. Superior Achievement in Poetry went to Lucy A. Snyder's *Chimeric Machines* (Creative Guy) and the Non-Fiction award went to *Writers Workshop of Horror* by Michael Knost.

Gene O'Neill's *A Taste of Tenderloin* won for Fiction Collection, and the Anthology award went to *He is Legend: An Anthology Celebrating Richard Matheson* edited by Christopher Conlon.

Norman Prentiss' "In the Porches of My Ears" (from *PostScripts* #18) picked up the award for Superior Achievement in Short Fiction, Lisa Morton's *The Lucid Dreaming* won for Long Fiction, and the First Novel Award went to *Damnable* by Hank Schwaeble. Sarah Langan's *Audrey's Door* was recognised for Superior Achievement in a Novel.

Ray Russell and Rosalie Parker's Tartarus Press won the Specialty Press Award, the Richard Laymon President's Award went to Vince Liaguno, and Kathy Ptacek was given the Silver Hammer Award for her HWA volunteer work.

The British Fantasy Society's FantasyCon 2010 was held in Nottingham over September 17–19 with Guests of Honour Garry Kilworth, Bryan Talbot and Lisa Tuttle, Special Guest Peter F. Hamilton, and James Barclay as Master of Ceremonies.

In a whole raft of awards, *Let the Right One In* was voted Best Film and *Doctor Who* won Best Television. *Murky Depths* was awarded Best Magazine/Periodical and *Ansible* picked up Best Non-Fiction. *What Ever Happened to the Caped Crusader?*

won Best Comic/Graphic Novel, and The PS Publishing Small Press Award went to Telos Publishing.

Vincent Chong was voted Best Artist, Robert Shearman's *Love Songs for the Shy and Cynical* collected Best Collection, and *The Mammoth Book of Best New Horror Volume Twenty* won Best Anthology.

The Best Short Fiction Award went to Michael Marshall Smith's "What Happens When You Wake Up in the Night", Sarah Pinborough's *The Language of Dying* was presented with Best Novella and the August Derleth Award for Best Novel was given to *One* by Conrad Williams.

The Sydney J. Bounds Award for Best Newcomer was won by Karri Sperring for *Living with Ghosts*, and the British Fantasy Society's Special Karl Edward Wagner Award went to the late Robert Holdstock.

The thirty-sixth World Fantasy Convention was held in Columbus, Ohio, over October 28–31. Dedicated to "A Celebration of Whimsical Fantasy", writers Dennis L. McKiernan and Esther M. Friesner, editor David G. Hartwell and artist Darrell K. Sweet were the Guests of Honor (apparently you had to have a middle initial to qualify!).

Presented at the usual Sunday banquet, World Fantasy Awards were given to Susan Marie Groppi for *Strange Horizons* (Special Award, Non-Professional), anthology editor Jonathan Strahan (Special Award, Professional), and Charles Vess (Artist).

The Collection Award was a tie between *There Once Lived a Woman Who Tried to Kill Her Neighbor's Baby: Scary Fairy Tales* by Ludmilla Petrushevskaya and *The Best of Gene Wolfe*, while *American Fantastic Tales: Terror and the Uncanny: From Poe to the Pulps: From the 1940s to Now* edited by Peter Straub picked up the Anthology Award.

Karen Joy Fowler's "The Pelican Bar" (from *Eclipse Three*) won Short Fiction, Margo Lanagan's "Sea-Hearts" (from $X^6$ ) won Novella, and China Miéville's *The City & The City* was the recipient of the Novel Award.

Life Achievement Awards were previously announced for Brian Lumley, Terry Pratchett and Peter Straub.

Held over the same Halloween weekend, the Halifax Ghost Story Festival included talks and readings by Jeremy Dyson, G.P.

Taylor, Mark Morris, Stephen Volk and legendary BBC producer/
director Lawrence Gordon Clark, amongst others.

There is no doubt that the way books are published is changing.
As indicated in the above summary, e-books are beginning to take
off in a huge way now that a variety of electronic reading plat-
forms have become available, while the single-author collection
has all but disappeared from the lists of mass-market publishers.

Also, few would disagree that far too many titles are still being
published for an ever-decreasing audience (most major publishers recorded a fall in sales of up to 20 per cent in 2010).

However, perhaps the biggest change in recent years is the
domination of our genre by books variably described as
"paranormal romance", "urban fantasy" or "steampunk". In
the case of the latter two appellations, these labels once belonged
to well-respected sub-genres of imaginative fiction, much in the
same way that vampires, werewolves and other creatures of the
night were once figures of fear and wonder. Of course, since the
start of the boom in so-called "paranormal romances" several
years ago now, these iconic tropes of horror have now been
reduced to romantic stereotypes, mindless action heroines or
teenage fantasies aimed at a totally undiscerning readership.

Written mostly by hacks who have no knowledge or interest
in the horror genre, and churned out so quickly that they often
have to use multiple pseudonyms to meet an admittedly voracious audience of mostly middle-aged or teenage women, the
majority of these "horror-lite" books do nothing for our genre
beyond diluting its impact and clogging up the bookshelves with
identical-looking volumes that accentuate the romantic aspects
of these formerly monstrous metaphors for our greatest fears.

In a recent newspaper interview, Neil Gaiman is quoted as
saying: "I will be glad when the glut is over. Maybe they will be
scary again . . . Maybe it's time for this to play out and go away.
It's good sometimes to leave the field fallow. I think some of this
stuff is being over-farmed."

He's obviously correct, but you cannot blame the publishers
– they are in business to make money, and if this is the kind of
stuff that sells at the moment, then they will continue to pump it
out. And you cannot really blame the readers either – although I

doubt that many of them would ever think of picking up a real horror novel (other than maybe the odd title by King or Koontz); they will continue buy these kinds of books until the next marketing fad comes along ("literary mash-ups" anybody?).

However, I *can* blame people like the Horror Writers Association for embracing this dissolution of the genre by putting their name to such books as the *Blood Light* anthologies in the sole pursuit of recognition and royalties, or the publishers of *Weird Tales* for reducing a once venerable and influential magazine to the level of fan drivel.

Over the past couple of years I have cut back significantly on the amount of coverage I give "paranormal romance" titles and similar books in these volumes. I will obviously continue to support well-written and thoughtful fiction, but the majority of these works have no place in a publication devoted to the *Best New Horror*. The sooner our industry realises this, then the sooner its practitioners and publishers will move on to exploit another literary genre, allowing us once again to reclaim ours for the scary and disturbing fiction that is its true legacy.

The Editor
May, 2011

# SCOTT EDELMAN

## What Will Come After

SCOTT EDELMAN HAS PUBLISHED more than seventy-five short stories in magazines such as *The Twilight Zone*, *Absolute Magnitude*, *Science Fiction Review* and *Fantasy Book*, and in many anthologies, including *The Solaris Book of New Science Fiction*, *Crossroads*, *MetaHorror*, *Once Upon a Galaxy*, *Moon Shots*, *Mars Probes* and *Forbidden Planets*. New short stories are forthcoming in *Why New Yorkers Smoke*, *PostScripts*, *Space and Time* and other publications.

*What Will Come After*, a collection of his zombie fiction, and *What We Still Talk About*, a collection of his science fiction stories, were both published in 2010, and hc has appeared in two previous volumes of *The Mammoth Book of Best New Horror*. He has been a Bram Stoker Award finalist five times, in the categories of both Short Story and Long Fiction.

Additionally, Edelman has worked for the Syfy channel for more than a decade, where he's currently employed as the editor of *Blastr*. He was the founding editor of *Science Fiction Age*, which he edited during its entire eight-year run, and has been a four-time Hugo Award finalist for Best Editor.

"When Peter Crowther agreed to collect my many zombie short stories for publication by PS Publishing," recalls the author, "he asked only one thing of me – that I write a new piece of fiction for the volume to entice readers who might already be familiar with my undead *oeuvre*. Which I, of course, immediately agreed to do.

"But having already pushed the zombie envelope as far as I thought it could go with the story I'd written most recently at the time, 'Almost the Last Story by Almost the Last Man', and wanting to make the new story truly special, I realised that there was only one place to go. I had to get personal. *Very personal.*

"And so, I wrote a story in which *I* was the protagonist, and looked ahead to what would happen after my own death . . . and rebirth. It was an emotionally difficult story to write, but what I didn't realise was that it would become even more emotionally difficult for me as time went by.

"What I should have known when writing 'What Will Come After' was that it would become more difficult for me to reread as time went on. You see, because the story is about me, it is also about the people I love. Even though within the story, many of them are dead, at the time I wrote the tale, they were all alive – and I *still* had trouble not losing it at the ending during a public reading.

"It's been a rough couple of years since I wrote this story, and when I next read it aloud, one of those loved ones had died, and my voice cracked and I had trouble keeping it together during the section that mentioned that death. Now yet another relative is gone, and I had difficulty even proofing this for publication. And there are other relatives still alive, but they, too, will go someday . . .

"So I appear to have set myself up for many more difficult emotional experiences in the future. But it was, of course, worth it. I only hope that when you read the story that follows, some small part of that love bleeds through from me to you . . ."

I AM ALREADY AWARE of certain events surrounding my coming death – which, if I'm reading the signs correctly, is not that far off – as surely as if they'd already occurred and I am merely remembering them.

*I will not really begin to live until after I die.* I will not be alone in that. It will be that way for many, as if what had up until then been the entirety of human existence had suddenly instead become its prologue. Death – though not dying, which will remain as painful, frightening, and mysterious as ever – will have lost its finality. We won't understand why. There'll be no explanation, at least none which will be found acceptable to us. That's just the way it will be one sudden morning, when we will all wake to a world in which death has become only temporary. Some of us will take it to be the vengeance of God, while others will place the blame on the hubris of science. But the finger-pointing of billions will not alter our new situation. Life, for lack of a better word, will go on, and what will come after will more often than not be far more interesting than what had come before. Because how many of us, if tasked to speak the truth, could ever say that we fully used what we had been given in the first place?

*Long before everything changes, I will have already seen the script for my desired death acted out by others.* It won't, however, have been an end capable of rehearsal. It's a scenario I will have hoped for, but which I, which we, will be denied. I will not be as lucky as the ninety-year-old woman, married for sixty-seven years, who had a stroke, or her husband, also ninety, who then phoned 911. I have already read about their ends, now, even as I write these words, long before the world's rebirth, long before I'll need to fear the transformation. As the emergency crew bundled up that elderly woman to rush her to the hospital, the stress from the flurry of activity, from seeing his wife limp and unmoving, caused her husband to have a stroke as well. Neither of the pair ever regained consciousness. They died within days of each other. If I could choose a manner in which to leave this world, it would be that one, my wife and I taken from the world at once, neither of us suffering extended solitude, never alone for long. Those few minutes apart would be an eternity enough. My wife and I have talked about that, hoped for that, and will continue to hope, even after everything changes. But who among us gets to choose the time and place of his or her death? Especially when the world becomes the way the world will henceforth be forever.

*I will die in my own home.* Even though I will have sickened, I will not have sought help as once I might have. The world will no longer contain enough help to go around, not for all the frail and faltering, not once people have changed into predators. Besides, places which used to be symbols of safety will have become too suspect to act as havens. Hospitals, for example, will have become far too dangerous by then for any sane person to visit, what with the undead coming back to life, and though those institutions will uneasily live on, struggling to be more than just a feeding ground as patients become hunters, they will never be safe again, no matter what precautions are taken. Neither will malls, movie theatres, sports arenas, convention centres, schools, or any other businesses at which the public had previously gathered in so carefree a manner. For humans, stepping out of one's sphere of solitude will become a rarity. We will adapt to telecommuting not only in our jobs, but in our personal lives as well. In love, in family, and in marriage, too, the long distance will become commonplace. Our race's slow march to solitude will increase to a breakneck speed.

*I will die alone.* My wife and I will have separated, not the way married couples do when disaffected, but for our own safety, since we will both know what would inevitably happen to her if I were to die by her side, or to me, should she predecease me while I remained within her reach. Neither of us will want to chance that risk of being the first to go, and since the only other way to eliminate that possibility would be a suicide pact, one which we will not trust ourselves to properly effectuate in order to avoid the anticipated horrors, we will, as we sense our individual ends approaching, know that we have to part. I will remain in our home in West Virginia, while she will move to her mother's home in Maryland, which will, at that time, have been empty. Her mother will have been the lucky one, avoiding with impeccable timing what will someday occur. Our parting will be emotional, as we have been together since we were children. At least, that's the way it's always seemed. I will not share the details of that separation here; some things should remain private. The exodus from our home will not be easy for her, as any journey in that future time will have its dangers, but still, it will be safer for her to be a state away rather than here, remaining beside me while we counted down the days, wondering which of us would be the first to fall only to then rise up into a frenzy. Neither one of us will want to shuffle off to what should have been a long sleep with the other still alive beside us, only to have that sleep interrupted, to wake and then begin to feast on the one we love. A solitary death, as painful as that would be, would be preferable.

*I will die in my own bed.* It will bear no relation to the end I had expected. I will have always assumed that I would be attacked and eaten by a bear that wandered over from Sleepy Creek, or else find myself flying through the windshield of my Jeep at dusk after hitting a deer. Or, if I was to be lucky enough to have a death less violent than that, I expected it to be out in the garden. I would clutch my chest – perhaps among the bamboo, the spot which brings me the most happiness – and fall to my knees, tottering a moment before my face hits the earth. But it will prove to be none of those. I know this. I will have tucked into my own bed, which will have suddenly grown to the size of a continent. I will have patted the place where my wife's shape could still be felt, and then fallen into a deep sleep. I will be dreaming of her, missing her, acting out within my mind a scenario in which she is still beside me, in which we are forever young, and in which the nightmare we faced had been replaced by a desired dream, when something will burst in my brain. All bodily functions will stop, but only for a little while . . . then some of them will start up again. Some, but not all, and I, like so many others, will be reborn.

*I will not suffer from Alzheimer's, but I will look at my world as if I did.* When I rise again, in that most miraculous way, I will stare blankly at my surroundings. I will look at the bookshelves filled with people and worlds I had loved, populated by universes created by others and then carefully collected by me, and I will not remember any of them. On other shelves, I will see the books and magazines filled with words I had written and not know that they had ever been mine. I do not even think that books and magazines will any longer register as meaningful objects. They will just be the random static of a world I will no longer be capable of hearing. I will look at the paintings on the walls, many of them created by my own father, and not recognise them, or remember him. I will look at the photographs also hanging there, and see only strangers. Perhaps I will not even be capable of that, of categorising human beings. Perhaps I will only see those photographs as advertisements for feasts which will be beyond my reach. My conscious mind will be gone, and I will be nothing but a moving tropism, a thing of urges alone. Eventually, once my desire manifests, it will only have one true destination.

*I will not immediately be hungry.* This will not surprise me, however, as I will be beyond surprise. I will have assumed, based on many news reports I watched to fulfil my final days – which will prove to be as inaccurate on this matter as they proved to be during my lifetime on so much else – that I would leap up instantly ravenous, and feel caged by the four walls surrounding me. I will have imagined that I would instantly stumble wildly about, lusting for a living target on which to feed. But instead, my waking will be slow, with the birthing of my body first long before my desire, and so, at the start of my second chapter, I will move calmly through the house. That will perhaps be a side effect of the fact that my wife and I had arranged events so that I would be reborn alone. If she would still have been at my side, perhaps her scent would have roused my hunger immediately. But I will never have a chance to learn if that is so, to contrast those two possibilities. One rebirth is the most any of us can expect in our lifetimes.

*I will not be as favourably situated as I would have been had I never left New York.* In the rural location I have chosen, the pickings will be slim, while back in the city of my birth, the possibilities would have been infinite. Candidates to feed upon would have been easily found. But because I have remained here, I will stumble about the house, bouncing off the walls – literally, for once, rather than metaphorically – unable to sense a scent, not understanding how to turn a doorknob in order to get outside and begin whatever journey it is I will be destined to make. As I do those things, I will spot the skittish movement of a deer in the yard, and will mistake its blur for the motion of an escaping human. I will crash through one of the glass doors at the back of our house, an action which, though freeing me from the confines of this home I love, will serve only to frighten the animal away. That loss will not make me sad, or angry, or give rise to any other disappointed feelings, for, separate from the fact that I will be beyond those emotions, I will understand, in a place beyond consciousness, as the creature speeds off, that it had not been human, and I will know, with an awareness beyond intelligence, that only human flesh will henceforth be able to feed my hunger.

*I will not be killed so quickly as I would have thought.* What neighbours I should have had will be gone. Their houses will be abandoned, the doors left ajar. Inside the nearest homes, the ones I will mindlessly enter, will be such total emptiness as to signal that the previous occupants assumed they would never be reclaimed. But I will not be able to interpret that, nor will I any longer have the slightest idea where those neighbours could have gone. If I could have breached the barrier between my far future self and the most recent future former self, that living self of mere days before, I would have asked and learned this – that some of Earth's survivors will have banded together and fled, seeking safety at the government compounds, while others will have gone even more deeply into the woods, seeking to hide high on mountains which they will feel the undead will not be able to climb. Still others, even more fearful of what they are sure is to come, will kill themselves in such ways they feel will prevent return. (At least, that is what they will hope. And in some cases, they will be correct. But not in all.) I will not know any of this, nor will I be able to realise how I am benefiting from those actions, for these disparate decisions of others will keep me alive my first few days of life after death. I am unmolested in my aimless wandering, instead of becoming the immediate object of target practice as I would have been had my neighbours not scattered, or if I had remained in that distant city of my birth.

*I will not be helped by any of the research I will have done.* I will not even remember having done it. But even if I had somehow managed to retain all of the supposed facts of the undead, that knowledge would not have helped. Yes, I will need no sleep, but what good will knowing that do me? And I had once known, but was no longer aware, that the only way for this new self to die would be by a shot through the head, one which would sever the brainstem, but once reborn, this would not help me either, not to live and not to die. And I will not need to be told to seek the living, for finding flesh will be paramount. The knowledge of that will be embedded within me, and I will have no need of instruction from my late, living self to tell me so. I will have no need of knowing because I will be busy *being*. But there is one fact which my former study had not revealed that I would have found fascinating, if only I could reach back to pass it on. One thing I will not have known, and therefore I could not have told myself, is that having been reborn, I will head directly for *her*. For my wife. For my love. She whom I sent away. So I will have forgotten what will have come before, and all I will know is – I must head for her.

*I will not think of my parents.* I will have been thinking about them often during those final days leading up to my death, which will mean that they will be paramount among the many things of which I will not be thinking then, of which I will no longer be able to think. I will have been glad that they had left this world before the uprising will have begun, because the worrying I will have done about them before they died in their normal, though still sad and tragic ways, will be as nothing when compared to the fears added to the menu of our anxiety once death was no longer an option. The world, once everything changed, will have become a place in which we no longer wrestled with letting go as our loved ones were taken, but instead were horrified at the thought that to be merciful, we might have to take part in their final erasure from the Earth. We will have become more than mere bystanders to the deaths of our parents, children, and friends. We will have been forced to become reluctant participants. Some will try to reject that by instead choosing to engineer their own deaths, but it will not always work. Those five stages of grief which had been hammered into us – denial, anger, bargaining, and so on – had a new more horrible stage grafted on to the end, one which I will have been spared having to endure, at least as far as my parents were concerned. As I will be pulled in the direction of Maryland, shambling closer toward the scent of my wife, I will not be conscious of any of this. The world will be made up of only two families then, the living and the living dead, and as I will be part of the latter group, I will not be concerned with the intricate social constructs of the former. When those I've left behind come to mind at all, it will only serve to enflame me toward one ravenous purpose.

*The ability to swim will have been stripped from me.* By the time I reach the spot at which a bridge once crossed over to Maryland, that span will no longer exist. My former living self would have recognised the signs that the bridge's destruction had been deliberate, but the me which will eventually be all that remains will not, will not remember the explosions that had occurred and which I had heard and noted the month before I died, nor will recall my inability then to interpret them. Gunfire in my neck of the woods is common, but I'd never before heard explosions of that magnitude, and had no idea what they could have meant. Whether this action will have been taken to keep the undead from crossing to Maryland from West Virginia or to West Virginia from Maryland, I will not know, or even be able to contemplate, or care. I will arrive at what remains of the bridge and continue walking, out onto bent struts and then beyond, until there is nothing but open air beneath me, and I will fall forward, tumbling into the icy Potomac River below. I will not bother to flail my arms as I drop, and I will emit no sound. Once I hit the water, I will sink, for the dead do not float, but it will not matter. I will keep putting one foot in front of the other, the river bottom no less foreign than the roadway. I will occasionally clamber over rocks, making a slow and clumsy progress, until I reach the other shore. My head will rise slowly out of the water. I will pause there for a moment, still submerged from the neck down, waiting for a sign, waiting until I sense my wife again. Only once she registers will I continue on.

*My first kill will be made in confusion.* As I move closer to dry land and come up out of the water, I will startle a fisherman, who, as he backs violently away from me once he discovers what I am and what I am not, will slip and crack his skull amid the wet rocks. I will, at first, not know quite what to make of his contortions as he twitches there briefly, then stills. I will be momentarily frozen, driven to kill, yet at the same time unable to tell whether the prize of that kill has been taken from me, for I may only feast upon living flesh. I will have a hunger, and I will have known even before that hunger became mine how that hunger would manifest, and how I was meant to assuage it. Somehow, even though I will know so little, I will know that. Since I can only get what I need from those who still breathe, from those who have not yet become like me, when I fall to my knees, I will be uncertain as to what comes next. It won't be until I surge onward uncontrollably, biting through the man's abdomen, and until I then pull back, his intestines in my teeth still pulsing, his blood continuing to flow against my face, that I will realise, as a flower realises that it has been watered, that I will not have been too late.

*As I travel, my life will pass before me, but it will not be a life I am able to recognise.* Moving on from the river's edge, on from my first feast, I will amble slowly across Maryland, heading back to her. Even though the undead will have but one intention for the living in this particular instance, I will not know toward what end. I will pass through places infused with meaning, but I will be walled up beyond the reach of that meaning. I know now that I will not, in my peregrinations, revisit all of the places which were the settings for the pivotal plot points of my life, as most of those will have occurred in New York, before the age of thirty, but still, there will be enough settings overflowing with emotion to have made me weep, if only I will have been capable of remembering them. But I will not. I will not even know this, and that will be in actuality a more devastating loss than the initial loss of life itself. As I move across the map, here will be the office in which a diabetic boss raged while waving his fingers in my face, with my only response being a shoving of my hands into my pockets to avoid slugging him. There will be the park at which my wife and I passed several contemplative hours one afternoon deciding whether to make an offer on our first home. Here will be the highway entrance ramp at which the car ahead of me swerved and then flipped, narrowly missing me, almost creating a world in which this story could not be written and the future I am relating will not be played out. There will be the restaurant at which my wife and son and I had shared many joyful and voracious dim sum lunches. I will also pass through settings I will not want to remember, places the future absence of same from my memory will not be so much a theft as a gift, proving it possible that death, even in that odd, unwelcome guise, will still possess its benefits. All will be gone, all gone. The wise and the foolish, the transcendental and the cringeworthy, the shameful and uplifted, it will be as if they had never happened. And if I will no longer be able to bring them back, did they?

*I will be alone, but I will not be lonely.* The country roads, highways and suburban streets across which I will shamble will be strangely deserted, only I will not know that then. I will have no past, and so be incapable of comparisons. I will not know that my path had ever been any different, and so will not know enough to ask myself the question, "Where is everybody?" Nor would I have the consciousness necessary to theorise an answer. I will not know then what I know now, what I learned in my last few living days, that many killed themselves in ways designed to discourage an undead outcome, others fled far from urban or even suburban areas in search of more sparsely populated, and therefore hopefully more protected, places, while others barricaded themselves in basements, believing that what they were enduring was not the end times, but something that would pass, something survivable, something endurable, something temporary. (After all, even holocausts pass, and even jihads end; but not this.) Those upon whom I do feed along my journey to my wife will not be any of those. My only meals will be made up of the confused, the uncertain, and the uncaring. I will gorge myself only on those who have given up, or gone mad. But I will neither notice nor care about the psychological makeup of my meals. Their flesh satisfies, and that will be enough.

*Others of my kind will be invisible to me.* As we stagger alone together across a landscape which for the most part seems entirely ours, at times escaping collisions by inches, at times careening off each other like pinballs, we will be on different journeys, so their presence will be meaningless to me. I might as well be the last animated creature in the world. I see that now, but then, later, I will not be able to make comparisons to the way I had lived before, to know whether my previous passages across that landscape had been similar or different. I will just, in answer to the call, a call I had been preparing for since I'd first met my wife, keep putting one foot in front of the other. But even though the feet upon which I move propel me with machinelike efficiency, they do not, however, go unscathed.

*I will not remain whole, and I will not care about the parts which go missing.* Occasionally, my attempts at feeding will not go smoothly, and someone will retaliate successfully, lashing out before they inevitably go down, gouging me, or severing a finger, or hacking off a chunk of flesh. But even if I will notice the loss the moment it occurs, I will not care that it occurred, and soon be unable to remember that I was anything else but. The undead will not be haunted by the lingering of phantom limbs which tormented the living. Loss will no longer scar us in that way. As I have already shared, there will be only one injury which could possibly end my journey, and none of those left for me to eviscerate – none save one – will have the presence of mind to either remember it or act upon it. Except for the effect on my balance which will be caused by the results of certain of these attacks, it will be as if they'd never occurred.

*I will not be aware of the passage of time.* I will live in a kind of eternal present, neither caring about the regrets of yesterday nor the worries of tomorrow. There will be only one day for me, and that will be whatever day I occupy. I will move continuously, having no need of sleep or even rest, which is something I will not have expected, since books and films which tried to imagine what I would become always told us that the undead would only rove during night-time hours. But I will never lay myself down. I will not even count each transition from day to night to day again. Though I will be heading toward a goal, and in some subconscious place be aware of the end to my story, I will not be actively measuring my progress, any more than a mountain measures its progress as it is thrust skyward by the shifting of tectonic plates. If my task will take forever, I will not mind, both because I am beyond the minding of anything, and also because I, barring a misstep which will allow a human the upper hand, will actually have forever in which to accomplish it.

*I will encounter my son, though when that moment occurs, he will be the only one of us aware that he is my son.* We will meet not because I will have gone looking for him – that will not be a part of my plan, if the restless urge that motivates me can even be said to be a plan – but because he will have come hunting for me. Which means that during one of those future days, as I will be moving slowly forward in search of her, sensing the growth of my wife's presence in my stilled heart and my shuttered brain, I will be tackled from behind and thrown to the ground. I will retaliate explosively, reacting to that collision with sudden, violent movements, but I will not be surprised, as I will be incapable of surprise. When I am allowed to stand once more, and begin to move toward this person to feed, the attack as forgotten as if it had never occurred, I will discover that I can only move in his direction so far, and no more, for I have been chained. I will stumble as I reach for this man who knows he is my son, because a loop around my ankle will extend tautly to a nearby telephone pole, tripping me. "I knew you would come looking for us," he will say. "I knew you would be like that." I will not understand either his words or his meaning. Speech, both the uttering of it and the understanding of it, will be gone. I will only know that this person is preventing me from reaching my destination, a goal beyond thought, beyond life and death. I will struggle wildly to break free, but it will avail me nothing, as my son will have planned well, and I will succeed only in wrapping myself tightly against the telephone pole, much like a dog that has run in circles around the tree to which he has been tethered. My son will watch me as I struggle without success, and he will smile. He will be glad that I will finally experience what it means to be trapped, not understanding that I am beyond the understanding of it. "Stay right there," he will say, laughing. "I will see you later." And then he will leave me there, where I will remain circling first in one direction, then the other, freedom and the object of my desire both apparently stripped from me.

\*     \*     \*

*I will gnaw off my foot.* There will be no other way to go on. I will have hurled myself repeatedly against my tethering, but I will not have the strength to shatter my restraint. Flesh will never be able to conquer steel, not even when that flesh is of the undead kind. I will sense the intended purpose of this chain, that it was designed to keep me from my wife, and I will realise quickly that it fulfils its function far too well. And so there will be no other way. After having orbited the pole dozens of times – maybe even hundreds of times, for the numbering of things is another concept which will be beyond me – to no end, I will finally sit, and raise the fettered ankle to my mouth, and begin to chew. But unlike with my other feedings, no satiation of hunger will be found there. There will be no reward for this act of autocannibalism other than the restoration of my freedom. When I will continue on, it will be with a lopsided shamble, for I will be limping from my loss. I will move slowly, but I will still move, and that is all that will matter. Nothing will be able to stop me from achieving my intended reunion, not when I have come so far, and will be so close.

*I will find her.* I will have no doubt then that it will happen because there will no longer be any doubt to me, only determination, and I have no doubts now as I write these words, because, even through a thing such as this, I know that my wife and I are meant to be together, and because we are meant to be together, we *will* be together. Our story can end no other way. That final meeting will occur before our son can find me again. He will not be beside her when I at last stumble toward her with a ragged gait, so he will at that moment probably be back at the telephone pole where he will have bound me, staring down in horror at what I will have left behind. My wife will be in the front yard of the house which had once belonged to her mother, and her back will at first be turned to me. As I approach her, it will not be with the kind of hunger you'd expect. It will be a hunger of a different species. I know that now, that one kind of hunger, even in the end times, can still triumph over the other. I will see, during my final approach, that she carries a gun. I will also see that, as she turns and notices my presence, she does not immediately aim it at me as a stranger would. She instead will merely cradle it against her chest. Her expression will not be one of horror, though based upon the damaged countenance I will present to her, it should be. The gaze from anyone else certainly would be. There will be tears in her eyes. I will be driven to my knees before her at the sight of them. I will not be capable of knowing then, as I pause in adoration, but I know right at this moment, what I would do if our roles had been reversed and I had been placed in her position, if I had been the one waiting and she had been the one to come back to me as I will be. The choice would seem inescapable; that is, there will be no choice. But as our lives, or rather, her life and my undeath, will play out, that decision will end up being hers. I will know, even though I will be beyond knowing, even though the electrical impulses in my brain slog instead of race, even though the functioning of my body's cells will have faded, exactly what she will do, and so I will take no further action, and simply wait there, bowed before her, even though I will be overcome by a hunger greater than I will have ever known.

*The last time I will see my wife on this Earth, it will be over a shotgun barrel.* She will raise her weapon, and will point it at me, but I will ignore it, and instead fix my gaze upon her eyes. I will have returned to where I am meant to be, with the woman for whom I was intended, am intended, will be intended. She will take a single step toward me, the gun shaking slightly in her trembling hands, and then her grip will become steady, and she will fire. And as my brain turns to a fine mist, and my shackled undead consciousness is set free, I will be aware in my final moments of the inevitable second shot, as she brings our story to its inevitable and loving conclusion.

# MICHAEL MARSHALL SMITH

## Substitutions

MICHAEL MARSHALL SMITH IS a novelist and screenwriter. Under this name he has published seventy short stories and three novels – *Only Forward*, *Spares* and *One of Us* – winning the Philip K. Dick Award, International Horror Guild Award, August Derleth, and the Prix Bob Morane in France. He has also won the British Fantasy Award for Best Short Fiction four times, more than any other author.

Writing as "Michael Marshall", he has also published five international best-selling thrillers, including *The Straw Men*, *The Intruders*, *Bad Things* and, most recently, *Killer Move*. *The Intruders* is currently under series development with BBC TV.

He is currently involved in screenwriting projects that include a television pilot set in New York and an animated horror movie for children. The author lives in North London with his wife, son, and two cats.

As Smith recalls: "This story came about in the simplest way, the way I always enjoy most – something happening in real life that makes you think 'What if?'

"Our household gets a lot of its food via an online delivery service, and one day when I was unpacking what had just been dropped at our house I gradually realised there was something . . . not quite right about the contents of the bags.

"There's two things that are strange about that experience.

The first is that – given that every household is likely to buy at least some things in common – you don't realise straight away that you've been given the wrong shopping. You don't immediately think 'This is wrong', more like . . . 'This is weird'. The second is how personal it is, gaining accidental access to this very tangible evocation of some other family's life. You can't help but wonder about the people the food was really destined for.

"In real life, I just called up the delivery guy and got it sorted out: but in fiction, you might tackle things slightly differently . . ."

HALFWAY THROUGH UNPACKING THE second red bag I turned to my wife – who was busily engaged in pecking out an email on her Blackberry – and said something encouraging about the bag's contents.

"Well, you know," she said, not really paying attention. "I do try."

I went back to taking items out and laying them on the counter, which is my way. Because I work from home, it's always me who unpacks the grocery shopping when it's delivered: Helen's presence this morning was unusual, and a function of a meeting that had been put back an hour (the subject of the terse email currently being written). Rather than standing with the fridge door open and putting items directly into it, I put everything on the counter first, so I can sort through it and get a sense of what's there, before then stowing everything neatly in the fridge, organised by type/nature/potential meal groupings, as a kind of Phase Two of the unloading operation.

The contents of the bags – red ones for stuff that needs refrigeration, purple for freezer goods, green for everything else – is never entirely predictable. My wife has control of the online ordering process, which she conducts either from her laptop or, *in extremis*, her phone. While I've not personally specified the order, however, its contents are seldom much of a surprise. There's an established pattern. We have cats, so there'll be two large bags of litter – it's precisely being able to avoid hoicking that kind of thing off supermarket shelves, into a trolley and across a busy car park which makes online grocery shopping such a boon. There will be a few green bags containing bottled water, sacks for the rubbish bins, toilet rolls and paper towel, cleaning materials, tins of store cupboard staples (baked beans, tuna, tinned tomatoes), a box of Diet Coke for me (which Helen tolerates on the condition that I never let it anywhere near our son), that kind of thing. There will be one, or at the most two, purple bags holding frozen beans, frozen peas, frozen organic fish cakes for the kid, and so on. We never buy enough frozen to fill more than one purple carrier, but sometimes they split it between a couple, presumably for some logistical reason. Helen views this as both a waste of resources and a threat to the environment, and has sent at least two emails to the company about it. I don't mind much as we use the bags for clearing out the cats' litter tray, and I'd rather have spares on hand than risk running out.

Then there's the red bags, the main event. The red bags represent the daily news of food consumption – in contrast to the contextual magazine articles of the green bags, or the long-term forecasts of the purple. In the red bags will be the Greek yoghurt, blueberries and strawberries Helen uses to make her morning smoothie; a variety of vegetables and salad materials; some free-range and organic chicken fillets (I never used to be clear on the difference between the non-identical twin joys of organic and free range, but eleven years of marriage has made me better informed); some extra-sharp cheddar (Helen favours cheese that tastes as though it wants your tongue to be sad), and a few other bits and pieces.

The individual items may vary a little from week to week, but basically, that's what gets brought to our door most Wednesday mornings. Once in a while there may be substitutions in the delivery (when the supermarket has run out of a specified item, and one judged to be of near equivalence is provided instead): these have to be carefully checked, as Helen's idea of similarity of goods differs somewhat from the supermarket's. Otherwise, you could set your watch by our shopping, if you'll pardon the mixed metaphor – and this continuity of content is why I'd turned to Helen when I was halfway through the second red bag. Yes, there'd been spring onions and a set of red, green and yellow peppers – standard weekly fare. But there were also two packs of brightly-coloured and fun-filled children's yoghurts and a block of much milder cheddar of the kind Oscar and I tend to prefer, plus a family pack of deadly-looking chocolate desserts. Not to mention a six-pack of thick and juicy-looking steaks, and large variety pack of further Italian cured meats holding five different types of salami.

"Yum," I said.

I was genuinely pleased, and a little touched. Normally I source this kind of stuff – on the few occasions when I treat myself – from the deli or mini-market which are both about ten minutes' walk away from the house (in opposite directions, sadly). Seeing it come into the house via the more socially condoned route of the supermarket delivery was strangely affecting.

"Hmm?" Helen said. She was nearing the end of her email. I could tell because the speed of her typing increases markedly as she approaches the point when she can fire her missive off into space.

She jabbed SEND and finally looked up properly. "What's that you said?"

"Good shop. Unusual. But I like it."

She smiled, glad that I was happy, but then frowned. "What the hell's that?"

I looked where she was pointing. "Yoghurts."

She grabbed the pack and stared with evident distaste at the ingredient list. "I didn't order those. Obviously. Or *that*." Now she was pointing at the pile of salamis and meats. "And the cheese is wrong. Oh, bloody *hell*."

And with that, she was gone.

I waited, becalmed in the kitchen, to see what would unfold. A quick look in the other bags – the greens and purples – didn't explain much. They all contained exactly the kind of thing we tended to order.

Five minutes later I heard the sound of two pairs of footsteps coming down the stairs. Helen re-entered the kitchen followed by the man who'd delivered the shopping. He was carrying three red bags and looked mildly cowed.

"What it is, right," he muttered, defensively, "Is the checking system. I've told management about it before. There are flaws. In the checking system."

"I'm sure it can't be helped," Helen said, cheerfully, and turned to me. "Bottom line is that all the bags are correct except for the red ones, which both belong to someone else."

When I'd put all the items from the counter back into the bags I'd taken them out of, an exchange took place. Their red bags, for ours. The delivery guy apologised five more times – somehow making it clear, without recourse to words, that he was apologising for the system as a whole, rather than any failure on his part – and trudged off back up the stairs.

"I'll let him out," Helen said, darting forward to give me a peck on the cheek. "Got to go anyway. You're alright unpacking all this, yes?"

"Of course," I said. "I always manage somehow."

And off she went. It only took a few minutes to unpack the low-fat yoghurts, sharp cheese, salad materials and free-range and organic chicken breasts.

A funny thing happened, however. When I broke off from work late morning to go down to the kitchen to make a cup of tea, I lingered at the fridge for a moment after getting the milk out, and I found myself thinking:

*What if that* had *been our food*?

I wasn't expressing discontent. We eat well. I personally don't have much of a fix on what eating healthily involves (beyond the fact it evidently requires ingesting more fruit and vegetables per day than feels entirely natural), and so it's a good thing that Helen does. If there's anything that I want which doesn't arrive at our door through the effortless magic of supermarket delivery, there's nothing to stop me going out and buying it myself. It's not as if the fridge or cupboards have been programmed to reject non-acceptable items, or set off a siren and contact the diet police when confronted with off-topic foodstuffs.

It was more that I got a sudden and strangely wistful glimpse of another life – and of another woman.

I was being assumptive, of course. It was entirely possible that the contents of the red bags I'd originally unpacked had been selected by the male of some nearby household. It didn't feel that way, however. It seemed easier to believe that somewhere nearby was another household rather like ours. A man, a woman, and a child (or perhaps two, we're unusual in having stopped at one). All of the people in this family would be different to us, of course, but for the moment it was the idea of the woman which stuck in my head.

I wondered what she'd look like. What kind of things made her laugh. How, too, she'd managed to miss out on the health propaganda constantly pushed at the middle classes (she *had* to be middle class, most people in our neighbourhood are, and *everyone* who orders online from our particular supermarket has to be, it's the law) – or what had empowered her to ignore it.

We get steak every now and then, of course – but it would never be in the company of all the other meats and rich foods. One dose of weapons-grade animal fats per week is quite risky enough for this household, thank you. We live a moderate, evenly balanced life when it comes to food (and, really, when it comes to everything else). The shopping I'd seen, however foolishly, conjured the idea of a household which sailed a different sea – and of a different kind of woman steering the ship.

I was just a little intrigued, that's all.

A couple of days later, I was still intrigued. You'd be right in suspecting this speaks of a life in which excitement levels are low. I edit, from home. Technical manuals are my bread and butter, leavened with the occasional longer piece of IT journalism. I'm good at it, fast and accurate, and for the most part enjoy my work. Perhaps "enjoy" isn't quite the right word (putting my editing hat on for a moment): let's say instead that I'm content that it's my profession, am well paid and always busy, and feel no strong desire to be doing anything else, either in general or particular.

But nobody's going to be making an action movie of my life any day soon.

And that's perhaps why, sometimes, little ideas will get into my head and stick around for longer than they might in the mind of someone who has more pressing or varied (or viscerally compelling) things to deal with on a day-to-day basis.

I was still thinking about this other woman.

This different girl.

Not in a salacious way – how could I be? I had no idea what she looked like, or what kind of person she was (beyond that spoken of by her supermarket choices). That's the key word, I think – difference. Like any man who's been in a relationship for a long time (and doubtless a lot of women too, I've never asked), every once in a while you beguile a few minutes in fantasy. Sometimes these are sexual, of course, but often it's something more subtle which catches your internal eye. I've never felt the urge to be unfaithful to Helen – even now that our sex life has dropped to the distant background hum of the long-term married – and that's partly because, having thought the thing through, I've come to believe that such fantasies are generally not about other people, but about yourself. What's *really* going on, if you spend a few minutes dreaming about living in a scuzzy urban bedsit with a (much younger) tattooed barmaid/suicide doll, or cruising some sunny, fuzzy life with a languid French female chef? These women aren't real, of course, and so the attraction cannot be bedded in them. They don't exist. Doubtless these and all other alternate lifestyles would come to feel everyday and stale after a while, too, and so I suspect the appeal of such daydreams actually lies in the shifted perception of yourself that these nebulous lives would enshrine.

You'd see yourself differently, and so would other people, and that's what your mind is really playing with: a different you, in a different now.

Perhaps that insight speaks merely of a lack of courage (or testosterone); nonetheless, the idea of this nearby woman kept cropping up in my mind. Perhaps there was also a creative part of my mind seeking voice. I don't edit fiction, and have never tried to write any either. I enjoy working with words, helping to corral them into neat and meaningful pens like so many conceptual sheep, but I've discovered in myself neither the urge nor the ability to seek to make them evoke people or situations which are not "true". With this imaginary woman, however – not actually imaginary of course, unless it *was* a man, it was more a case of her being "unknown" – I found myself trying to picture her, her house, and her life. I guess it's that thing which happens sometimes in airports and on trains, when you're confronted with evidence of other real people leading presumably real lives, and you wonder where everyone's going, and why: wonder why the person in the seat opposite is reading that particular book, and who they'll be meeting at the other end of the journey you're, for the moment, sharing.

With so little to go on, my mind was trying to fill in the gaps, tell me a story. It was a bit of fun, I suppose, a way of going beyond the walls of the home office in which I spend all my days.

I'm sure I wouldn't have tried to take it further, if it hadn't been for the man from the supermarket.

A week to the day after the first delivery, he appeared on the doorstep again. This was a little unusual. Not there being another order – Helen considerately books the deliveries into the same time slot every week, so they don't disrupt my working patterns – but it being the same man. In the several years we've been getting our groceries this way, I'm not sure I've ever encountered the same person twice, or at least not soon enough that I've recognised them from a previous delivery.

But here this one was again.

"Morning," he said, standing there like a scruffy Christmas tree, laden with bags of things to eat or clean or wipe surfaces or bottoms with. "Downstairs, right?"

I stood aside to let him pass, and saw there were a couple more crates full of bags on the path outside.

That meant I had a few minutes to think, which I suddenly found I was doing.

I held the door open while he came up, re-ladened himself, and tramped back downstairs again. By the time he trudged up the stairs once more, I had a plan.

"Right then," he said, digging into a pocket and pulling out a piece of paper. He glanced at it, then thrust it in my direction. "That's your lot. Everything's there. No substitutions."

Before he could go, however, I held up my hand.

"Hang on," I said, brightly. "You remember last week? The thing with the red bags?"

He frowned, and then his face cleared. "Oh yeah. That was you, right? Got the wrong red bags, I know. I've spoken to Head Office about it, don't worry."

"It's not that," I said. "Hang on here a sec, if you don't mind?"

I quickly trotted downstairs, opened one of the kitchen cupboards and pulled out something more-or-less at random. A tin of corned beef – perfect.

Back up in the hallway, I held it out to the delivery guy.

"I think this should have gone back into the other person's bags," I said. "I'm not sure, but my wife says she didn't order it."

The man took the can from me and peered at it unhappily. "Hmm," he said. "Thought most of the delivery goods was company branded. But it could be. Could be."

"Sorry about this," I said. "Didn't notice until you were gone. I . . . I don't suppose you remember where the other customer lived?"

"Oh yeah," he said. "As it happens, I do. Vans in this area only cover a square mile each day, if that. And I had to go through the bags with her, see, in case there was a problem with it, what with you already unpacking it here."

"Great," I said. His use of the word "her" had not been lost on me.

"Didn't say nothing about something being missing, though," he said, doubtfully. He looked down at the tin again without enthusiasm, sensing it represented a major diversion from standard practices, which could only bring problems into his life. I looked at it too.

"Hang on," he said, as a thought struck him. He gave the tin to me. "Be right back."

I waited on the doorstep as he picked up the crates on the path and carried them back to his van. A couple of minutes later he reappeared, looking more optimistic.

"Sorted," he said. "As it happens, she's next but one on my list. I'll take it, see if it's hers."

I handed the corned beef back to him again, thinking quickly. *I'm going to need my house keys. Oh, and some shoes.*

"Don't worry about bringing it back, if it's not," I said, to hold him there while I levered my feet into a pair of slip-ons which always live in the hallway.

This confused him, however. "But if it's *not* hers, then . . . I can't just . . ."

"It's just I've got to go out for a while," I said. "Tell you what – if it's not hers, then just bring it back, leave it on the step, okay?"

I could see him thinking this was a bit of a pain in the neck – especially over a single tin of canned meat – but then realising that my solution meant less disruption and paperwork than the likely alternatives.

"Done," he said, and walked off down the path.

I trotted to my study, grabbed the house keys from my shelf, and then back to the front door. I slipped out onto the step and locked up, listening hard.

When I heard the sliding slam of a van door, I walked cautiously down the path – making it to the pavement in time to see the delivery vehicle pull away.

There followed half an hour of slightly ludicrous cloak and daggery, as I tried to keep up with the supermarket van without being seen. The streets in our neighbourhood are full of houses exactly like ours – slightly bigger-than-usual Victorian terraces. Many of the streets curve, however, and two intersections out of three are blocked with wide metal gates, to stop people using the area as a rat route between the bigger thoroughfares which border it. The delivery driver had to take very circuitous routes to go relatively short distances, and bends in the street meant that – were I not careful – it would have been easy for him to spot me in his side mirrors. Assuming he'd been looking, of course, which he wouldn't be – but it's hard to remind yourself of that when you're engaged in quite so silly an enterprise.

Keeping as far back as I could without risking losing him, I followed the vehicle as it traced a route which eventually led to it pulling up outside a house six or seven streets away from our house. Once he'd parked I faded back forty yards, and leaned on a tree. He'd said the stop that I was interested in was not this one, but the next, and I judged him to be a person who'd use language in a precise (albeit not especially educated) way. He wouldn't have said "next but one" if he meant this house, so all I had to do was wait it out.

Whoever lived here was either catering for a party, or simply ate a lot, all the time. It took the guy nearly fifteen minutes to drag all the red, green and purple bags up the path and into the house – where a plump grey-haired man imperiously directed their distribution indoors.

This gave me plenty of time to realise I was being absolutely ridiculous. At one point I even decided to just walk away, but my feet evidently didn't get the message, and when he eventually climbed back into the van and started the engine, I felt my heart given a strange double thump.

She would be next.

I don't know if the delivery driver had suddenly realised he was behind schedule, but the next section of following was a lot tougher. The van lurched from the curb as though he'd stamped on the pedal, and he steered through the streets at a far brisker pace than before. I was soon having to trot to keep up – all the while trying not to get *too* close on his tail. I don't exercise very often (something I take recurrent low-level flak from Helen over), and before long I was panting hard.

Thankfully, it was only a few more minutes before I saw the van indicating, and then saw it abruptly swerve over to the curb again. The funny thing was, we were now only about three streets from my house. We were on, in fact, the very road I walked every morning when I strolled out to the deli to buy a latté to carry back to my desk – a key pillar in my attempts to develop something approaching a "life-style".

I waited (again, taking cover behind a handy tree) while the delivery man got out, slid open the van's side door, and got inside. He emerged a few minutes later carrying only three bags. They were all red, which I found interesting. No frozen food. No household materials. Just stuff to go straight in the fridge – and probably meats and charcuterie and cheeses that were a pleasure to eat, rather than foods that came on as if they were part of a work-out.

There were only two front paths that made sense from where he'd parked, and I banked on the one on the right – sidling up the street to the next tree, in the hope of getting a better view. I was right. The man plodded up the right-most path toward a house which, in almost every particular, was functionally identical to the one in which Helen and Oscar and I lived. A three-storey

Victorian house, the lowest level a half-basement slightly below the height of the street, behind a very small and sloping "garden". I was confident this lower floor would hold a kitchen and family room and small utility area, just as ours did – though of course I couldn't see this from my position across the street.

The man had the bags looped around his wrist, enabling him to reach up and ring the doorbell with that hand. After perhaps a minute, I saw the door open. I caught a glimpse of long, brown hair . . .

And then a sodding lorry trundled into view, completely obscuring the other side of the street.

I'd been so focused on watching the house that I hadn't seen or even heard the vehicle's approach. It ground to a halt right in front of me, and the driver turned the engine off. A gangly youth hopped down out of it immediately, busily consulting a furniture note and scanning the numbers of the houses on the side of the street where I was standing.

I moved quickly to the left, but I was too late. The supermarket delivery man was coming back down the path, and the door to the house was shut again.

"*Bollocks*," I said, without meaning to.

I said it loudly enough that the delivery man looked up, however. It took a second for him to recognise me, but then he grinned.

"You was right," he called across the street. "Was hers after all. Cheers, mate. Job done."

And with that he climbed back into his van. I turned and walked quickly in the other direction, thinking I might as well go to the deli and get a coffee.

Maybe they could put something in it that stopped middle-aged men being utter, *utter* morons.

That evening Helen had an assignation with two of her old university friends. This is one of the few occasions these days when she tends to let her hair down and drink too much wine, so I made her a snack before she went out. After she'd gone, and Oscar had been encouraged up to bed (or at least to hang out in his bedroom, rather than lurking downstairs watching reality television), I found myself becalmed in the kitchen.

I'd got almost none of my work done that afternoon. Once the feelings of toe-curling embarrassment had faded – okay, so the supermarket guy had seen me on the street, but he'd had no way of knowing what I was doing there, no reason to suspect I was up to anything untoward – I'd found myself all the more intrigued.

There was the matter of the corned beef, for a start. I knew damn well that there had been no error over it. I'd bought it myself, a month or two back, from the mini-market. I like some corned beef in a sandwich every now and then, with lettuce and a good slather of horseradish cut with mayonnaise. I'd fully assumed that the tin would make its way back to me. And yet, when presented with it, the woman had decided to claim it as her own.

I found this curious, and even a little exciting. I knew that had Helen been in a similar situation she would have done nothing of the sort, even if the item in question had been totally healthy and certified GM-negative. This other woman had been given the chance to scoop up a freebie, however, and had said "Yes please".

Then there was her hair.

It was infuriating that I hadn't been given the chance to get a proper look at her, but in a way, just the hair had been enough. Helen is blonde, you see. Really it's a kind of very light brown, of course, but the diligent attentions of stylists keep it mid-blonde. A trivial difference, but a difference all the same.

Trivial, too, was the geographical distance. The woman lived just three streets away. She paid the same rates, received cheery missives from the same local council, and would use – probably on a more frequent basis than us – the services of the same take-away food emporiums. If she went into the centre of London, she'd use the same tube station. If it rained on our back garden, it would be raining on hers. The air I breathed stood at least some chance of making it, a little later, into her lungs.

This realisation did nothing to puncture the bubble which had started to grow in my head over the previous week. I can't stress strongly enough that this was not a matter of desire, however nebulous. It was just interesting to me. Fascinating, perhaps.

Difference doesn't have to be very great to hold the

imagination, after all. Much is made of men who run off with secretaries twenty years younger than their wives, or women who ditch their City-stalwart husbands to get funky with their dreadlocked Yoga teacher. Most affairs and marital breakages, however, do not follow this pattern. Helen and I knew four couples whose relationships had clattered into the wall of mid-life crisis, and all amounted to basically the same thing. Two men and two women had (in each case temporarily) set aside their partner for someone who was remarkably similar to them. In one case – that of my old friend Paul – the woman he'd been having a semi-passionate liaison with for nine months turned out to be *so* similar to his wife that I'd been baffled on the sole occasion I'd met her (Paul soon after having had the sense to go back to Angela and the children, tail between his legs). Even Paul had once referred to the other woman by the wrong name during the evening, which went down about as well as you'd expect.

And this makes sense. Difference is difference, whether it be big or small, and it may even be that the smaller differences feel the most enticing. Most people do not want (and would not even be capable of) throwing aside a lifetime of preference and predilection and taste. You are who you are, and you like what you like. Short of being able to have their partner manifest a different body once in a while (which is clearly impossible), many seem to opt for a very similar body that just happens to have a slightly different person inside. A person of the same class and general type, but just different enough to trigger feelings of newness, to enable the sensation of experiencing something novel – to wake up, for a spell, the slumbering person inside.

Difference fades quickly, however, whereas love and the warmth of long association do not, which is why so many end up sloping right back to where they started out.

Most people don't end up in liaisons with barmaids or artists or other exotics. They get busy with friends and co-workers, people living in the same tree. They don't actually want difference from the outside world.

They want it within themselves.

I realised, after mulling it over in the quiet, tidy kitchen for nearly an hour, that I wanted to be someone different too, however briefly.

So I went upstairs, told my son that I was popping out to post a letter, and went out into the night.

It was after nine by then, and dark. Autumnal, too, which I've always found the most invigorating time of year. I suppose it's distant memories of changes in the school or university year, falling leaves as an augur of moving to new levels and states of being within one's life.

I didn't walk the most direct route to the house, instead taking a long way round, strolling as casually as I could along the deserted mid-evening pavements, between lamps shedding yellow light.

I was feeling . . . something. Feeling silly, yes, but engaged, too. This wasn't editing. This wasn't ferrying Oscar to and from school. This wasn't listening to Helen talk about her work. The only person involved in this was me.

Eventually I found myself approaching the street in question, via another that met it at right angles. When I emerged from this I glanced up and down the road, scoping it out from a different perspective to it merely being part of the route to my morning latté purveyor.

The road ended – or was interrupted – by one of the traffic-calming gates, and so was extremely quiet. There'd be very little reason for anyone to choose it unless they lived in one of the houses I could see.

I stood on the opposite side of the street and looked at the house where the woman lived, about twenty yards away. A single light shone in the upper storey, doubtless a bedroom. A wider glow from the level beneath the street, however, suggested life going on down there.

My heart was beating rapidly now, and far more heavily than usual. My body as well as my mind seemed aware of this break in usual patterns of behaviour, that its owner was jumping the tracks, doing something new.

I crossed the street. When I reached the other side I kept going, slowly, walking right past the house. As I did so I glanced down and to my right.

A single window was visible in the wall of the basement level, an open blind partially obscuring the top half. In the four seconds or so that it took me to walk past the house, I saw a large green rug on dark floorboards, and caught a glimpse of a painting on one wall. No people, and most specifically, not her.

I continued walking, right the way up to the gate across the road. Waited there a few moments, and then walked back the same way.

This time – emboldened by the continued lack of human occupancy – I got a better look at the painting. It showed a small fishing village, or something of the sort, on a rocky coast. The style was rough, even from that distance, and I got the sense that the artist had not been trying to evoke the joys of waterfront living. The village did not look like somewhere you'd deliberately go on holiday, that's for sure.

Then I was past the house again.

I couldn't just keep doing this, I realised. Sooner or later someone in one of the other houses would spot a man pacing up and down this short section of street, and decide to be neighbourly – which in this day and age means calling the police.

I had an idea, and took my mobile out of my trouser pocket. I flipped it open, put it to my ear, and wandered a little way further down the street.

If anyone saw me, I believed, I'd just be one of those other people you notice once in a while – some man engaged in some other, different life, talking to someone whose identity they'd never know, about matters which would remain similarly oblique. It would be enough cover for a few minutes, I thought.

I arranged it so that my meandering path – I even stepped off into the empty road for a spell, just to accentuate how little my surroundings meant to me, so engaged was I with my telephone call – gradually took me back toward the house. After about five minutes of this I stepped back up onto the curb, about level with the house's front path.

I stopped then, taken aback.

Someone had been in the lower room I could see through the window. She'd only been visible for a second – and I knew it was her, because I'd glimpsed the same long, brown hair from that morning – starting out in the middle of the room, and then walking out the door.

Was she going to come back? Why would she have come into

what was presumably a living room, then left again? Was she fetching something from the room – a book or magazine – and now settling down in a kitchen I couldn't see? Or was she intending to spend the evening in the living room instead, and returning to the kitchen for something she'd forgotten, to bring back with her?

I kept the phone to my ear, and turned in a slow circle. Walked a few yards up the street, with a slow, casual, leg-swinging gait, and then back again.

I'd gone past the point of feeling stupid now. I just wanted to see. When I got back to the pavement, I caught my breath.

The woman was back.

More than that, she was sitting down. Not on the sofa – one corner of which I could just make out in the corner of the window – but right in the middle of the rug. She had her back to me. Her hair was thick, and hung to the middle of her back. It was very different in more than colour to Helen's, who'd switched to a shorter and more-convenient-for-the-mornings style a few years back.

The woman seemed to be bent over slightly, as if reading something laid out on the floor in front of her. I really, really wanted to know what it was. Was it perhaps *The Guardian*, choice of all right-thinking people (and knee-jerk liberals) in this part of North London?

Or might it be something else, some periodical I'd never read, or even heard of? A book I might come to love?

I took another cautious step forward, barely remembering to keep up the pretence with the mobile phone still in my hand.

With my slightly-changed angle I could now see her elbows, one poking out from either side of her chest. They seemed in a rather high position for someone managing reading matter, but it was hard to tell.

My scalp and the back of my neck were itching with nervousness by now. I cast a quick glance either way up the street, just to check no one was coming. The pavements on both sides remained empty, distanced pools of lamplight falling on silence and emptiness.

When I looked back, the woman had altered her position slightly, and I saw something new. I thought at first it must be whatever she was reading, but then realised first that it couldn't be, and soon after, what I was actually seeing. A plastic bag.

A red plastic bag.

Who unpacks their shopping in the living room? Other people do, I guess – and perhaps it was this connection to the very first inkling I'd had of this woman's existence (the temporary arrival of her food in the kitchen of my own house, in the very same kind of bag) that caused me to walk forward another step.

I should have looked where I was going, but I did not. My foot collided with an empty Coke can lying near the low wall at the front of the woman's property. It careered across the remaining space with a harsh scraping noise, before clattering into the wall with a smack.

I froze, staring down at her window.

The woman wrenched around, turning about the waist to glare up through her window.

I saw the red plastic bag lying on the rug in front of her, its contents spread in a semi-circle. She was not holding a newspaper or magazine or book. In one hand she held half of a thick, red steak. The other hand was up to her mouth, and had evidently been engaged in pushing raw minced beef into it when she turned.

The lower half of her face was smeared with blood. Her eyes were wide, and either her pupils were unusually large, or her irises were also pitch black. Her hair started perhaps an inch or two further back than anyone's I had ever seen, and there was something about her temples that was wrong, misshapen, excessive.

We stared at each other for perhaps two seconds. A gobbet of partially chewed meat fell out of her mouth, down onto her dress. I heard her say something, or snarl it. I have no idea what it might have been, and this was not merely because of the distance or muting caused by the glass of the window. It simply did not sound like any language I've ever heard. Her mouth opened far too wide in the process, too, further accentuating the strange, bulged shape of her temples.

I took a couple of huge, jerky steps backward, nearly falling over in the process. I caught one last glimpse of her face, howling something at me.

There were too many vowels in what she said, and they were in an unkind order.

I heard another sound, from up the street, and turned jerkily, saw two people approaching, from the next corner, perhaps fifty yards away. They were passing underneath one of the lamps. One was taller than the other. The shorter of the two seemed to be wearing a long dress, almost Edwardian in style. The man – assuming that's what he was – had a pronounced stoop.

In silhouette against the lamp light, both their heads were clearly too wide across the top.

I ran.

I ran away home.

I have not seen that supermarket man again. I'm sure I will eventually, but he'll doubtless have forgotten the corned beef incident by then. Out there in the real world, it was hardly that big a deal.

Otherwise, everything is the same. Helen and I continue to enjoy a friendly, affectionate relationship, sharing our lives with a son who shows no real sign yet of turning into an adolescent monster. I work in my study, taking the collections of words that people send me and making small adjustments to them, changing something here and there, checking everything is in order and putting a part of myself into the text by introducing just a little bit of difference.

The only real alteration in my patterns is that I no longer walk down a certain street to get my habitual morning latté. Instead I head in the other direction, and buy one from the mini-market instead. It's nowhere near as good, and I guess soon I'll go back to the deli, though I shall take a different route from the one which had previously been my custom.

A couple of weeks ago I was unpacking the bags from our weekly shop, and discovered a large variety pack of sliced meats. I let out a strangled sound, dropping the package to the floor. Helen happened to be in the kitchen at the time, and took this to be a joke – me expressing mock surprise at her having (on a whim) clicked a button online and thus causing all these naughty meats to arrive as a treat for the husband who, in her own and many ways, she loves.

I found a smile for her, and the next day when she was at

work I wrapped the package in a plastic bag and disposed of it in a bin half a mile from our house. There's a lot you can do with chicken, and even more with vegetables.

Meanwhile, we seem to be making love a little more often. I'm not really sure why.

# MARK VALENTINE

## A Revelation of Cormorants

MARK VALENTINE LIVES IN North Yorkshire with his wife Jo and their cat Percy.

He is the author of biographies of Arthur Machen and the fantasist "Sarban". His series of tales about an occult detective, with John Howard, were assembled as *The Collected Connoisseur* from Tartarus Press in 2010, and his short stories have been collected recently in *The Nightfarers*, *The Mascarons of the Late Empire* and *The Peacock Escritoire*.

He edited the Wordsworth anthology *The Werewolf Pack* and also edits *Wormwood*, a journal of the fantastic and supernatural in literature.

"'A Revelation of Cormorants' first appeared in the excellent series of chapbooks published by Nicholas Royle's Nightjar Press," explains Valentine, "and I first encountered the dark grace of the cormorant while visiting Galloway with Jo."

CORMORANT, FROM THE LATIN for "sea-raven". The Tudors saw the bird as a symbol for gluttony: Shakespeare refers to hungry Time as a cormorant. It may have gained this reputation because of its proficiency at catching fish. Milton, however, invested the bird with a dark glamour: he likened Lucifer sitting in the Tree of Life to a cormorant, no doubt because of the bird's habit of standing with its black wings spread out to dry. The satanic image stuck. The occultist and poet Ludovic Horne wrote of his "Cormorant days/dark and sleek". The atheist essayist Llewelyn Powys refers to the birds as "satanic saints" in Parian niches on the chalk cliffs of Dorset, but he celebrated them too as manifesting the ecstasy of the moment, as they plunge into the sea after the silver-scaled fish of their dreams. Conan Doyle alludes to an untold Sherlock Holmes case of "The Lighthouse Keeper and the Trained Cormorant". Isherwood cites them in a nonsense poem. Folklore about them is much barer than the literary record.

Crow. A 15th century Northern ballad tells of a Crow King who rules by magic. The title may involve a punning reference to the "croaking" of the birds. Scott records a Northumberland superstition which counted crows' caws for purposes of divination. As carrion birds they were associated with gallows and gibbets. Ted Hughes . . .

William Utter put down his pen upon his labours at *A Flock of Myths: the Legends, Lore and Literature of the Birds of Britain*, and rubbed his eyes, transferring some of the black ink from his fingers to his eyelids and giving them a bruised, shadowed look. This had the effect of accentuating the length and angularity of his face, which a disobliging acquaintance had once compared to a coffin-lid, with a brass-plaque brow. Utter was in fact quite proud of his brow, which he felt was of the sort once described as "lofty". His hair had shrunk from it some years ago, leaving certainly a bare plate upon which Utter would sometimes write with frowns.

He had taken white-walled Watchman's Cottage, on the sea at a little haven in Galloway, for a quarter of the year, to write, or rather (he supposed he should say) compile this book, a commissioned work, which was really a gathering of greater men's titbits, as if he were a tame bird being fed by hand. Contented: perhaps; replete, but unfree. He had been asked to do it, he knew, only because he was a competent cataloguer of facts who could be relied upon to deliver to deadlines. He longed for the time when he would have reached whatever bird it was that began with "Z". Zanzibar finch? But that was a long way off, as he worked now through the "Cs".

He sighed heavily and the exhalation blew the white slips of paper containing his carefully garnered quotations into the air, where they fluttered for a moment before returning to the surface, in disarray. He muttered to himself and got up impatiently. They could stay like that. Even after just the few days of his stay, settling in, putting everything in proper order, getting in provisions, he felt the need already for some time away from the study lamp.

The only person he had seen to talk to since his arrival was Mr Stair, the caretaker of the cottage, who had let him in and explained its (fairly basic) facilities. Utter had at first wondered if he might undertake a little original research with his new acquaintance. Having established, via a series of cautious pleasantries, that Mr Stair was a local man and had lived in the little fishing harbour most of his life, Utter had mentioned in passing the book he was intending to work on. Then he asked, as he hoped conversationally, if Mr Stair knew of any local sayings about birds. This attempted foray into folklore fieldwork had not proved a marked success.

Mr Stair had lived up to the sound of his name, giving Utter a sombre glare. Then he had run his long fingers through his jackdaw hair – black streaked with silver – and slowly found his way to what proved to be quite a long speech, for him, in that it contained more than one sentence.

"There would be some, I suppose," he had conceded. "But myself I give them no heed. You would be better, I'd suggest, just watching what they do. That's the way, I find, to learn about their habits."

He said this as if he imagined that the visitor really wanted to find out about the local bird-life rather than learning what it was people said about birds, but Utter decided not to pursue the distinction. Politely he had let the conversation run in the direction the caretaker had taken it. He had asked where on the shore might be best for watching the widest range of birds. Mr Stair had regarded him as if this was not a question he was minded to answer. But at length he had said: "If it's the seabirds you are after, I would go over by the White Strand. But watch for the tides, mind. They come in fast there."

Now Utter turned over this piece of advice in his mind, like a gull examining a piece of litter for its edibility. As he gazed out of the window to the long grey skies and the hissing ripple of the murky waves, he admitted to himself that he already felt jaded: and now his quotations were all upset. A walk among the rocks on the shore would do him good. He might, indeed, observe some of the birds, as Mr Stair had suggested, though what quite he would be looking for he was not so sure. He supposed there would be crows, and cormorants, and there might be some glimmer of a point of interest about them that he could work into the entries he was writing. He looked at the illustrations of these two birds, and a few others, in a pocket guide he had bought, and got their shapes roughly fixed in his mind.

Then, picking up a raincoat, the notebook containing his work so far from "Albatross" to "Crow", and a black umbrella, he left the cottage. As he pulled the door to, his strips of other men's sayings rose up once again for a brief flight above the desk.

Often in Galloway the land only dwindles down to the shore, slowly descending in peterings-out of rocks and last gasps of grassy tussocks. But, following the caretaker's directions, the pensive editor found that the path to White Strand rose from the cove where he was staying to higher ground, and he was walking among heather and dying bracken upon a sheep track above the sea. There was a keenness in the air, the way was lonely, and the calling of the seabirds (which ones he did not exactly know) was sharp and plaintive. The great grey clouds all at once struck him as like closed eyelids, and he frowned at the thought that he was now inventing his own quotations, which would not do at all. But perhaps, he reassured himself, he had merely remembered the image from some more notable source.

After a half an hour's quiet walking upon this ridge, Utter judged that he must have reached the region Mr Stair had described. And indeed down below the sands did seem to have a finer, creamier look to them than their tawnier counterparts of earlier in his wandering. Not white exactly, despite their name: more a wan yellow, they stretched, it seemed to him, like a palimpsest, a piece of wrinkled, blurred papyrus. And those grey rocks: they were surely the residue of ancient writings, all but unreadable now, the characters of some lost language. If one gazed long enough, Utter thought to himself, perhaps the script might be deciphered and the pale pages of the sands would yield up their secrets. And then the sturdier part of himself intruded and made his fingers clutch his raincoat more closely about him so that its flaps did not rise in the wind like fawn wings and carry him soaring off the cliff-top. Puckered up inside his mackintosh, and perched carefully upon a mossy rock, he let the fresh wind buffet him about a bit while he looked to see what birds there might be.

He could only just see over the green lip of the cliff but it was enough for him to descry after a while the flights of birds busy about the shore. Gulls, jackdaws, curlews, he thought he could make out and distinguish. And then – yes, surely: that serrated dark shape, that long neck and the angular form of the wings: they must be the cormorants whose quotability he had just this morning been exploring. They would emerge from the shadow of the sheer tower of rock that he was sitting upon, soar down to the shore, and then launch themselves into the sea to graze for fish. These glides upon the unseen currents of the bright air, followed by a gentle descent, soon had a fascination for him, as if he were watching an elaborate ritual or piece of theatre, and he found (despite himself) that he was drawn into an eager absorption in the birds' activities.

After a while he began to feel the chill of his exposed perch upon the cold rock and also the pull of seeing the birds at closer quarters. He saw that there was a worn, winding path from the headland to the beach, a narrow channel between the heather and the tall grasses. Carefully, stolidly, he began to follow this down. The wind died about him as he did so, and a greater silence fell for a while, cut only by the cawing and croaking of the birds. The way was not easy: he had to place his boots firmly and sometimes cling on to whatever lay to hand in the undergrowth. Once or twice this proved to be a crop of spiny gorse and his fingers received a sharp tingle followed by a seeping of blood. He cursed and sucked at his maimed hand, but he was not dissuaded and continued to lumber down.

He reached the shoreline at last and from the final ledge of the path gave a little ungainly leap upon the sand, leaving a scuffed imprint. It came to him then as he made his way across the little inlet that, seen from above, if there had been another Utter watching this one, he would look as if he was writing upon the parchment of the shore. There was a quotation, he knew, one of those sonorous Victorian ones no doubt, perpetrated by men with a level stare, yes, and a lofty brow, and a preponderance of whiskers, about footprints in the sands of time. He knew it because it had always seemed to him an absurdly mixed metaphor. The sands of time, surely, are those that run through an hourglass, showing our moments as they run away. But you can't put footprints in those sands: they are forever running on and, moreover, are generally encased in a glass funnel. But perhaps he was being too literal: as well as too literary. The thought was pursued by another, about the moving finger that writ and having writ moved on; and from the high vantage he had just quitted, he supposed he must seem like just such a scribbling digit.

He took a deep breath of the quickening salt breezes and looked all about him. The birds, disturbed by his presence, set up a more clamorous calling, which echoed away at last as he stood still, clutching his umbrella, and they became more used to his presence. He craned back his neck and looked up to the defile he had just negotiated. The cliffs rose as a great looming shadow, but they were cut by vertical gashes into nearly separated columns, so that the effect was like looking at the spines of a vast case of dark basalt books. There was even gilt tooling upon these volumes, made by clusterings of ochreous moss, and perhaps their titles might be read by discerning the imprints and indentations left by the narrow hollows and niches in the rock. And then Utter saw how right the Powys fellow had been: for in many of these hollows he could make out the forms of cormorants, with their black loop of neck and long beak and their upright, inquisitive stance. Even as he observed them in delight, one dropped from its niche and landed on the rocks, looking inquisitively about, before suddenly, with a supple twist, taking to the shadowy sea.

He walked further into the bay and settled himself once more upon a rock, this one grey and salt-crusted and festooned at its base with black bladder-wrack. White Strand was certainly a favourite habitation of seabirds, and their calling, and the crash of the waves upon the shore, set up a constant background noise like a wireless broadcast from some great station in the clouds. The cormorants were here in great assembly too: not only sheltering in the hollows of the steep cliff-side, but strutting on the shore and standing thoughtfully upon rocks further from him. They were roosting, perhaps, or resting, pausing before one of their fish-seeking dives; or holding out their wings to dry in that Luciferian posture old Milton had evoked; or pecking at their undersides; or simply regarding with their keen dark eyes the world as they found it; a world, he supposed, consisting chiefly of winds, waves, sea-currents, enemies and prey. A world simplified, but also stark and dangerous: where, as Powys had supposed, the bird might take an instinctive pleasure in its own being, in the craft of its fish-catching rituals, in the thrust of the air upon its pinions and the burst of the sea upon its sleek face.

Utter felt a sea fret waft about him, drew his raincoat more closely over his torso, and clung to the bamboo handle of his umbrella. But he did not abandon his study of the cormorants. He felt he could watch for hours their descents, their sea-dippings and their wing-dryings, their apparent glinting-eyed meditations upon what to do next. There always seemed something new to notice. You might think, if put to describing them, that their plumage was black, and there was nothing more to be said. But he soon found this was not wholly true. Beneath the sheen of their scaly cloak of black, there was another hue, a subtle tint of malachite when the light was full on them, a hard green mineral gleam only seen at certain angles.

Then what of their wings? We speak, he thought, of birds' wings as if they were all alike, but he could now see that those of the cormorant had indeed something archangelic, and heraldic, about them. The way they were raised by the bird made them seem like shields of silver held in readiness by a knight's squire for a great tournament.

All the time he watched them he stayed still upon his rock regardless of the lappings of saltwater that found their way around him in little thrusting rivulets. And after a while it was as if the birds became almost used to him, and came to regard him as just an odd outcrop of rock. They began to land and to rest quite close by him and he was able to see their fine malachite-black cloaks, and their mythic wings at the closest possible quarters. He became entranced too by their gaze. One great old cormorant stood on the next rock to him, in its tilt-headed attitude, with its long hook of neck, and glared at him from its black eye with its rim of silver. He could not free himself from regarding the dark grace and the saturnine stare of the bird: he saw now exactly why those writers wanted to make it a myth or a metaphor, for it seemed to belong to some other, plutonic dimension, some strange black gulf of a different time. He looked long upon the preening, prying bird while a wild roar grew around him, as if indeed he were on the brink of entering some other plane of existence.

And when he stirred at last from this reverie, he found that the little foaming streams around his rock had been fortified by a greater advance of the waves, and, gazing more widely, that in fact the sea had burst in upon the shore in great grey drives. He had better get back. He saw that he would have to hop from rock to rock if he were not to get his feet wet. Balancing himself with his umbrella like some seashore Blondin, he began to wobble from one rock to another; and then found that there were no more left, and he was not yet on what could be called the shore; indeed, that there was not very much at all that might now be called shore, for the sea was upon it all. He looked for where his cliff path was: but he could not make it out; and he realised that even if he did, he could not get to it, because the sea between where he was, and where it might be, was now surging in strong currents. Annoyed with himself, he teetered back to where he had been and began to wade through the still traversable tide, feeling its cold claws clutch at his feet, tugging at him. He pushed on as hard as he could toward the base of the rock face but found that the pull of the tide became greater almost at each heavy tread. At last, thoroughly wet and worn out, he made ground on a flat rim of rocks immediately in the lee of the cliff.

He turned and saw the waves pound towards him. He looked down and saw the salt encrustations and the marine weeds even upon the rocks where he stood. These, too, then would be engulfed, and he did not know with what force: he must go further up. Perhaps there might be another path, a way across the face of the rock: it was steep, certainly, but he could make out hand-holds and boot-hollows. Possibly people had been up that way before. He took hold firmly of a chunk of rock and hoisted himself up, then looked about for another and made a diagonal line across the bleak surface. The sea crashed below him and made a greedy sucking noise at the base of the cliff. He scraped his hands and knees as he scrambled further up.

And then his burst of resolution gave way. No obvious places to grip presented themselves to his view. It still seemed a very long way up the cliff and the dim track he had hoped for was no longer apparent. Yet the sea was still roaring against the rocks and thrusting its pale tentacles of spray up towards him: it might only take one really big wave to dash him away. He inched very gingerly onwards until he felt he could go no further. He thrust himself in a sudden imploring hug against the cliff, as if its very nearness made him more secure. And then he tried to think.

But absurdly, all he called to mind was a questionnaire he had been sent the year before, in preparation for giving a radio interview about one of his books. Amongst the many trivial and vulgar questions was one which had asked when he had come nearest to death. He had been tempted to answer on the form: "While doing this: by boredom", but supposed that the answer would not be original. In fact, the question might be better than it seemed; for it had perplexed him. In his forty-four years he did not know that he had ever been close to that highest risk of all. Well, perhaps now he was: now, if he survived, he could certainly quote this experience. He even began, to distract himself and delay taking any decision about inching further up the severe rock face, to compose how he would now word his answer: "Questing for cormorants, I . . ."

But that supposed, of course, that he would live to tell the tale. A sudden fevered surge of fear leapt up in him and his whitened fingers clung even more tenaciously to the little rims of the rock face. A cloud cleared the sun and he saw outlined in a film of light every crevice, every crack, each striation and scratch upon the adamantine surface. It was like looking at a strange map. But the effect, so far from giving him a sure route, was that of casting him into despondency. There simply were not sufficient wide enough and secure enough hand-holds for him to claw at, still less sockets or ledges where he might rest his feet. And even if he did succeed in negotiating the hazardous way, he could not deny that at the very top of the climb there appeared to be a great overhang, thrusting out from the vertical column he was on, so that he would have to work his way at an acute angle over and around it. A very seasoned climber, with all the right impedimenta, might manage it; he knew that he could not.

Very, very slowly he manoeuvred his feet upon the bare outcrop and cautiously turned his body around, keeping his gaze at first straight ahead. Don't look down, he told himself, don't look now. He pushed his palms against the merest hint of pillars on either side of him, and his raincoat unfurled its fawn wings. There was nothing further he could do. There was no question of descending again, for he could not trust himself to do it: and there was no hope of ascending all that terrible way he had seen illumined around him. He would have to wait until somebody came. Perhaps the caretaker might at length wonder that he had not seen him all day, and, remembering their conversation, set out to search for him. He clung to that dim hope as to the rock, with a forlorn desperation.

At intervals he gave a hoarse cry in case there should be anyone passing above: and he was answered by calls quite like his own, coarse and shrill, from the seabirds he had disturbed.

The day darkened: he could see he would soon be benighted here; in the gloom it would be harder to keep his balance; harder to stay awake. It already seemed many hours he had been here and he was very tired. Inevitably after a while he started to imagine, though he knew he must not, what it would be like when – if – he could hold on no longer and he dropped into the churning waters. Could he even then contrive a graceful dive, or would he simply flop? Would he strike his head on a rock, and end things insensible? Or struggle and gasp against the force of the waters until his breath gave out?

In the last of the light he thought he saw a dark flicker of movement come to rest in the next niche of rock to his. There was a sense as of a supple sliver of shape: and a rank, fishy stench. A single bead of black light seemed to stare at him. He remained perfectly still. They were all wrong, really, he reflected, those great men. The cormorant was not after all an embodied vice, not a devil, a dandy or a pagan saint: it was, like his days, like all our days, a living dark question mark, a plunge from the edge of existence into the silvery glinting silence of the future. Yes, that was it. Furtively, with extreme care, he removed his palms from their place of steadying, and then righted himself, reached into the pocket of his raincoat, and took out his notebook and pen. After the entry on the cormorant, he wrote, slowly, gently, "Myself, I have come to the conclusion . . ."

# GARRY KILWORTH

## Out Back

GARRY KILWORTH HAS BEEN a full-time writer of imaginative fiction now for nearly forty years and has had more than eighty books published.

He believes the short story is his forté and is happiest when employing that form. His most recent publications include *Moby Jack and Other Tall Tales* and *Tales from the Fragrant Harbour*, two collections of short stories from PS Publishing. His novel *Attica* attracted the attention of Johnny Depp, whose film company Infinitum Nihil (under the Warner Bros umbrella) will shortly be making a movie of that book.

The author also writes under the name "Richard Argent" and has recently published an historical fantasy, *Winter's Knight*, available from Little, Brown Books.

"'Out Back' was written for a group of friends," Kilworth recalls, "who appear as characters in the story under their initials, as I do myself. Those who know me well will recognise the protagonists.

"Iken is a real village on the edge of the marshes behind Snape Maltings in Suffolk. Two years ago I wandered along the periphery of the reed beds which stretch down towards the coast as a green and golden sea, the waves created by the winds that blow across the flatlands. Looking at the church that sits on a knoll above the marshes I thought, 'This is a perfect setting for a horror story.' And so . . ."

THE COTTAGE WAS EVERYTHING that R. had expected it to be: remote, comfortable and unfussy. He had a book to finish. Ten-thousand words. The other ninety thousand had been difficult. This last tenth seemed impossible. His plot had become derailed. He was unable to see his way through the smoke and coke dust of a mythical railway track that should stretch ahead. Yes, the characters were there, good and solid. Indeed, the story's engine was strong and had shunted yet forward and forward, with only one or two sharp halts. But six weeks ago he met the bumpers. R. was now stuck in a deserted station, his progress blocked.

So, he had come out here, beyond the real marsh country of Snape, where Benjamin Brittan had built his concert hall out of derelict malting houses. The village, some few miles back down a dusty track, was called Iken: an old Anglo-Saxon cluster of dwellings whose only claim to any sort of fame was its church, in which yard Aberdeen Angus cattle roamed, keeping the grass short around the graves. It had been a difficult place to get to, this Iken hamlet, but it might be worth the journey. Here there were no distractions, as there had been in London, especially now S. was working at home. They got in each other's way, entangled mentally if not physically, and R. was sure with his mind freed from traffic noise, neighbourhood noise, postmen, plumbers, random religious sects knocking on the door and various other infuriating interruptions, he would be able to grasp the vision of his novel's final destination.

"Well H., here we are," he said to the squirming bundle in his arms. He put the cat down on the stone flags of the kitchen floor. "Just you and me for a whole month."

H. was in a bad mood, as any cat plucked from his familiar home and whisked out to the end of nowhere had a right to be.

"You'll like it here," R. said, filling a plastic bowl with water from the ancient brass tap. "Out back looks like a jungle. You like jungles. You can hunt to your heart's content here, old chap. Bring in a mouse or two. A rabbit? Perhaps even a deer. Think you're up to a deer? Those muntjacs are not so big. Just go for the jugular."

H. looked with disgust at the bowl of water.

R., large and lately somewhat ungainly, ambled to the kitchen window to stare out. There was nothing resembling a garden at the back of the cottage. A lagoon of rugged-looking turf rolled away from the back door for about twenty feet and then suddenly the landscape leapt up into a wild sea of unkempt gorse bushes and batches of stinging nettles tall as ships' masts. There were also tall ferns, some gone to bracken, and thistles crowding the gaps. Like R.'s book, the view had no visible end. The dark green shrubbery tumbled over and over itself in waves which seemed to go beyond the horizon. It was a bleak scene. One could get just as lost out there as in the plot of a novel.

"S. would soon get stuck into that lot," he murmured. "She'd sickle the lot down to three inches."

He then wondered about the legitimacy of turning a noun into a verb to give his image more effect. Yes, why not?

A knock on the front door jerked him out of his word mode. He opened it to find the estate agent who had rented him the cottage.

"You didn't sign all the documents," said the harassed-looking woman. "Would you mind?" She waved some papers under his nose.

R. let her in and motioned her towards a rickety-looking walnut table in the front room. He found a pen amongst his luggage and signed the two documents the woman placed before him. Then he asked her if she wanted a drink of some kind. A cup of tea?

"No thanks, I have to get back. It's quite a trek out here, isn't it? I had to walk that narrow footpath from the road in these."

R. glanced down with her to see medium-heeled shoes that were now covered in mud.

"I know. I had to carry two suitcases and a cat."

She smiled. "You could have let the cat walk."

"H. would have bolted. In fact the suitcases would have run away too, if I'd put them down. This place is a bit weird for Londoners like H. and me."

"It's a bit weird for the locals too," she replied, taking his cue, "and of course the last . . ." She stopped, abruptly.

R.'s invisible antennae quivered. "Last?"

"Nothing – I – I was thinking of something else. Oh well, back to the grind. Sorry about the intrusion. I know you wanted peace and quiet. I'm sure you'll get that, once I've gone. Goodbye."

They shook hands and she left. Last? Last *time*? Last *person*? Last *waltz*? What? Who knew how that sentence ended? R. shrugged. He had more important puzzles to solve. One was ten thousand words long. He set about unpacking his bags and making himself comfortable just as evening came on. It was September. The darkness came in like fine black dust and settled on the cottage and surroundings. He switched on the light but could see no others out there. He was alone with a grumpy feline beast and nine-tenths of a novel. That was the way it had been planned, so he could congratulate himself on a job well done, rather than succumb to this sinking feeling.

He went to the back door and held it open.

"Off you go, H. See you in the morning."

H., a slim grey cat with black tiger stripes along his flanks, stared out into the gloaming. He stood for a long time, peering into a slow twilight that was draping shadows like dust-covers over the bushes. Something out there seemed to be worrying the animal. R. went and stood by the cat and stared out with him, seeing nothing but the gloom of an early-autumnal evening descending upon a wasteland. Then H. turned away, walked to the front door, and looked up to be let out.

"Oh, your majesty doesn't want to use the tradesman's entrance, eh? Well bugger off out the front then. It makes no difference to me, mate."

R. let H. out, then went to make himself some tea before settling down before a coal fire to think. This is what he had come out here to do, to *think*. Those who did no creative writing did not know how important it was to simply clear away the mind-clutter and let one's thoughts roam, where they were free to bump into all sorts of interesting other thoughts, one of which might be the key to the solving the ending of a novel. Other folk – wives, girlfriends, mums, dads, tax inspectors – they failed to understand that *thinking* was work. It was the hardest work a writer had to do. G. understood that. His other writer friends understood it. Actually punching the words onto paper was child's play next to thinking through the story, even a story without a coherent narrative that flowed chronologically. R.'s books never did that of course. They were enigmatic voyages through a misty otherworld where strange men met supernatural beasts, and women whirled paradoxes like gladiators' nets over both sets of creatures.

For the first week at the cottage, R. did nothing more than open his mind. It was essential that he allowed his imagination this free space in order that there was room for ideas to come sailing in from wherever it was that ideas were harboured. R. was one of those writers who did not like to think too deeply about the source of his genius, afraid that rooting it out might cause it to dry up. He continued to try to interest H. in going out back, into that wasteland beyond, thinking the cat would enjoy hunting such a fruitful-looking jungle. H. was having none of it though. He stood in the doorway and stared out, clearly uneasy with what was out there. Perhaps he could smell a rogue cat, a feral tom? Ferals, R. knew, could be quite dangerous creatures having wild untamed natures.

Finally, one evening R. became impatient with H. and gave him a little nudge with his foot, then shut the door. H. whined, long and loud. R. went and made himself a drink, ignoring his cat, thinking it would be good for H. to get over his prejudices. Even if there was a feral out there, surely H. could handle himself? He was a tough cat, a little tiger when he wanted to be. R. knew that H. had taken on foxes before now. H. had to face his fears the same as R., who had come to Iken carrying a whole sheath of them.

The next morning R. woke early. He immediately felt guilty. Fancy forcing H. to do something which clearly worried him! R. went downstairs and opened the back door, expecting to find an indignant, perhaps dew-coated H., waiting to be let in. There was no H., no cat in sight. That in itself was not unusual. H. came and went when it suited him. If he had found good hunting out there amongst the tall weeds and spiky gorse, then he would have fed himself and perhaps be looking to punish his master. R. left the door open, a saucer of milk just inside, and went to write. He had actually started writing at last and while the muse was on him, he had little thought for anything else. S. telephoned halfway through the morning and asked after both of them, but R. failed to mention the missing H. The signal was not good and her voice kept fading away. R. did not like making explanations into the ether.

Lunch time came. Still no cat. R. wandered out back for the first time, calling H.'s name. "H.! H.! Come on H., stop messing about." But no cat parted the tall grasses and came trotting to R.'s feet. Just a whisper of wind through the weeds and a sort of dead-air silence beyond. "You bugger – I know you're out there," cried R., beginning to get annoyed with his pet. "If I have to come in there and get you . . ." But the gorse bushes looked formidable. A cat could squeeze under them, but not a great lumbering R.

Evening. Still no H.

Morning again. The doorway was empty.

R. was now seriously worried. This was strange territory for his cat and perhaps H. was lost? What should he do? Start putting up notices on telephone poles? Who ever came out here, to this god-forsaken area of the marshes? Only mad-capped ramblers. R. had seen one or two of these, but not many. If he saw any more he would mention H. to them. Tell them to keep an eye open for a tiger-striped cat. And what would S. say? It was a bugger, that was certain.

The next day R. dressed himself in thick jeans, gloves, coat and walking boots. He was going in. He had to search for H. Leaving the back door to the cottage wide open, he crossed the uneven sods of turf to the edge of the gorse, hesitated, then entered. All the while he called H.'s name, using a walking stick to part the spiny fronds of the gorse, looking for traces of his pet.

Nothing. What he found were old carcasses, littering the whole area. Nothing to do with H., he was sure. They looked like the fur- and hair-covered skeletons of rabbits and foxes or dogs, with some large birds among them, hard flesh still stuck to the bones of many of them. Hell, what had killed these creatures? R.'s heart was beating fast now. It was hot and dusty out here, where old cobwebs formed nets between the bushes and the air was as still as death. Perhaps his initial thoughts on the wasteland had been correct? A feral tom? But surely even a big un-neutered tom could not kill a fox or dog? Something bigger then? A wild hound of some kind? Or a big cat escaped from a zoo? Something pretty savage lived in these shrubs. H. had been right all along.

Then, a few more paces, and R. found him. Or half of him.

H.'s fur was unmistakable. That tiger stripe on the corpse could not be anything else. Just the head was gone. The rest was covered in green flies that feasted on flesh that was already crusted and hard.

"Oh shit!" R. cried. "Oh fuck. Poor H."

What a horrible end for a lovely cat. And R. knew it was partially his fault. If he had taken notice of H.'s instincts, H.'s intuition, the cat might still be alive. Why hadn't he just left well enough alone and allowed H. his foibles? No, he had to be the big master-of-the-house and know everything about everything.

R. stared around him. What in hell's name was out here? What demon of a beast had killed his little cat? His first thought was to get a shotgun and bait a trap for the creature. It wouldn't bring H. back, but it would give R. some satisfaction. Bring the murderer to justice. But R. was a city dweller. After some thought he admitted to himself that he knew nothing about shotguns, how to get them, whether one needed a licence, nothing. In the end he knew that would not happen. But a club of some sort? A heavy club. Put something tempting out in the back yard and wait. If the creature came and it was small enough, R. could then destroy it. He was a big man and could handle a club all right. Of course, if the beast was some huge hound of hell, then such action was not on. At least he would know what was out here and could call the authorities, get them to catch it.

R. went back to the house, leaving H.'s remains to the maggots and flies in the dead zone of the wasteland. He intended to tell S. that H. had simply wandered off and got lost. No point in distressing her unnecessarily.

Once indoors he defrosted some pork chops in the microwave and left them in the back garden on an upturned dustbin lid. There were some golf clubs in a cupboard under the stairs. R. selected a heavy iron, wondering whether he could actually use this weapon on a live animal. But he was still smouldering with anger over his H. and he felt that rage could drive him to such action. Kill his cat? Whatever was out back was going to get some of its own, in spades.

Evening came. Twilight. That time when shadows lengthen and seem to move of their own accord. R. stood awkwardly by the rear window, looking out. It would have been better if he could stand in the open doorway, but the creature would undoubtedly get his scent and fail to come near the bait. Perhaps he should have poisoned the meat, just in case he couldn't deal the mortal blow? But then, what if some innocent creature came and ate the chops? Someone's runaway Golden Retriever, or little white Westie? R. couldn't risk such a thing. It had to be the golf club round the head. Split the bastard's skull with the iron.

He waited until well into the night.

Nothing came.

In the morning there was a knock on the door.

*Oh please, not S.,* R. thought.

Thankfully, it wasn't S. It was a man with a white collar worn the wrong way around. A vicar. R. let him in, having had no human contact for more than a week he was eager to talk to someone.

"Not evangelising," apologised the vicar, "just saw your light during the evenings and thought to give you a neighbourly social call. I'm Iken church – you can see the tower sticking up over that corner of the marsh. The Rectory is just beyond. Oh, tea please. How are you getting on? Are you here permanently, or just for the summer?"

They sat and drank tea, while R. answered the questions, and then asked a few of his own.

Finally, he confessed to the man of the cloth.

"My pet's been killed," he said. "Out back."

The vicar looked suitably shocked.

"Any idea who did it?"

"Who? I rather think *what.* There's some sort of beast out there, I'm sure of it. The area is covered with bones of all kinds. Why, the whole scene is . . ." R. had a sudden and chilling thought. *He hadn't noticed any skulls. Plenty of legbones, spines, pelvises, but no skulls. H.'s head had been missing. Eaten? A HEAD? What sort of beast eats only the heads of other beasts?*

"Are you all right?"

"Eh?" replied R. "Oh, yes. Tell me, did the last occupant of this cottage have any pets?"

The vicar looked uncomfortable.

"Not that I know of."

"You don't happen to have his – or her – phone number do you? I could give them a ring and have a chat."

"No – no, I don't. Wouldn't do any good." The vicar cleared his throat and put down the mug of tea he was holding. "You see the last person who lived here, simply disappeared one night. A Welsh gentleman. Never saw him at the church. Chapel, I expect. A writer like yourself, came out here to get away from the noise of the city just like you. Vanished. No one knows why. I'm told he never contacted the estate agent again."

"Skipping rent?"

"Apparently his rent had been paid in advance."

"He didn't go out back, did he?" said R., jokingly.

The vicar failed to be amused. "I'm fairly new here. I'm sure I don't know the details, but I do know that Mr E. took none of his possessions with him. It was indeed as if he had simply walked out of the door wearing what he stood up in."

The hairs on R.'s neck stood on end.

"Which door? Front or back?"

"No one knows. Both doors were found open. He simply – vanished. The police were called, of course. They searched the house, the surrounds, even dredged the marshes. No trace of Mr E. was ever found." The vicar sighed. "You hear of these cases, someone goes out for a newspaper and never returns. Never to be seen again by loved ones and those who know them. The brain is a delicate instrument. Something tips it this way or that, and the owner wanders off not knowing who he is, where he lives, or where he's going. It's my belief Mr E. is probably now one of those poor creatures you see in city centres wearing a beard, rags and smelling of alcohol."

The vicar left half-an-hour later, but he told R. that the pork chops probably would not work.

"You need warm-blooded bait. You know, a live rabbit or something. Dead meat is often ignored by wild beasts. They sense a trap. They're very wily creatures with sharp instincts for survival."

R. sat down after the vicar had left. He considered what the man had left him as a parting suggestion. A live creature? No, he couldn't do it. It would mean buying an animal at a pet shop and leaving it out, like a sacrificial goat, to be decapitated. It wasn't fair. It wasn't right. What he should do, now rather than later, was pack his bags and leave this unholy place before something

else happened. Something a little more terrible. Where was Mr
E.? Was his skeleton out back somewhere, perhaps at the bottom
of some boggy sinkhole, minus its skull? How very strange. R.
tried to think of some animal that might want to eat another
animal's head and could not come up with any answer.

The next village was seven miles away. R. decided to walk
there along the marsh-edge footpaths. He would not need to go
out back to do this. There was a well-defined walker's path at
the front. He would have a pub lunch, perhaps talk to one or
two of the locals and try to gauge their reaction to his experiences, then come back and call a taxi to take him to the nearest
railway station. It seemed a sensible plan. Perhaps the death of
poor old H. had unbalanced the situation in his mind somewhat?
Maybe a walk would clear his head and help him to see things in
perspective? After all, the evidence for a single assassin being
responsible for all those rotting carcasses was very thin. It could
be that all those dead remains had been the result of foxes or
badgers, or some other natural carnivorous beast.

As he stepped out along the track, painfully aware that his
right foot was not in prime condition since he had suffered
unwelcome visits from gout ever since he'd started spending
every New Year in G.'s place in Spain (oh, that Andalucian red
wine!), he carefully considered his last thought. *Natural.* Why
had he used that word? *Natural* carnivorous beast. An unusual
adjective in the context. Was there some idea deep in his subconscious, perhaps even deeper in his id, that there was something
*unnatural* about H.'s death? Something preternatural? A head-
hunting ghoul? R. searched his encyclopaedic mind for a
supernatural being that bit off the heads of living things. He
could think of none.

A partridge clattered out of a bush startling him as he skirted
a dark woodland grown to weakness in the centre. He shook
himself, physically, and told himself to get a grip. What the hell
was he doing, seriously considering something out of folklore,
myth or the spirit world. He *wrote* about such stuff, he didn't
*experience* it. Fact was fact, fiction was fiction. He'd been too
long on his own. He needed to get back to the sensible and practical company of S. She would put his feet back on the ground
and very soon the world would cease to tilt.

The Wild Boar pub turned out to be virtually empty. Apparently there was a carnival on in Lowestoft and everyone had gone there for the day. The only other occupant of the bar was an elderly farm labourer who drank half pints of warm bitter. R. bought the old boy one or two halves, but got nothing out of him regarding the cottage and its surrounds. It turned out the man, in his eighties, had never been more than five miles from his own back door. He had never been to Iken, let alone Lowestoft, which accounted for his presence in the Wild Boar on a day when village excitement was at fever pitch. The barman was an Australian youth in his early twenties and was "just passing through the county of Suffolk, mate". They talked cricket for a while, with the Aussie making disparaging remarks about the English team, while R., being English, made polite remarks about the Baggie Greens.

Before he left though, there was a shock to come. As he waved goodbye to the old boy, the Suffolk yokel called to him, "By the by, did they ever find that young fellah who went a-missin' from Iken?" He pronounced the word "find" as "fyund" making it a double-syllabled word. The local accent tended to do that.

"You mean the Welshman, Mr E.?" R. said.

"No, no, weren't no Welshman. Went by the name of R.K. Just disappeared into the mist, so's I bin told."

A sort of electric tingling went through R.'s skull.

"Are you sure it wasn't Mr E.?"

"Positive. Doctor told me. Doctor Williams didn't ever tell lies, lad, he were a good Christian soul. Seven year ago, now, it were. An' I may now be goin' on a bit, but the noddle's still workin'." He tapped the side of his heavy grey head. "I never heard of no Mr E."

"Shit!" murmured R., under his breath, realising that the old boy was talking about an earlier incident which had probably happened before the Iken vicar took over his church. For some reason the news of Mr E.'s later disappearance had not reached the farm labourer. Perhaps Dr Williams, bearer of news beyond the pale of the Wild Boar and confines, no longer resided in the vicinity? (Or something worse.) *Was* a good Christian soul? Perhaps the doctor himself was dead?

R. moaned, "Oh, holy shit."

The walk back to Iken was blisteringly hot despite the month, not improving R.'s mood as he tried to cover the ground at an Olympian pace. As R. approached the cottage he could see something white and fluttering pinned to the front door. It was a note. When he ripped it off and read it, R.'s sweat turned cold and clammy. It was from a friend, a good friend, a writer like himself. *Couldn't get an answer,* read the note. *You're obviously out somewhere. Had a look along the marshes, then went out back to see if you're there. If you return before me, go out back and give me a shout. G.*

R.'s hands shook as he read the note over and over again.

He then opened the front door with the old iron key and rushed to the back of the house, opening the back door.

"G!" he called. "Are you out there? G?"

No answer.

"This is stupid," R. said to himself. "What am I getting so worked up about? I'll just go out there and find him."

He strode purposefully into the wasteland out back, calling G's name every few yards. When he reached the shallow gully where H.'s body had lain, he stumbled over something and almost fell full length into a patch of nettles. At first he gave a strangled cry, thinking it was a dead animal, but it turned out to be a rotten log. Just a lump of wood. He sat up, his head aching, and stared around him. Evening was coming on now: the gloaming settling in. Shadows slid like fat black snakes along the ground, between the gorse bushes. R. realised he hadn't drunk anything since the pub, four hours ago. He felt giddy and sick. Alcohol dried a man out. He actually needed fluid. Water, preferably. Climbing to his feet he stared ahead, seeing something on the far side of a hump. It wasn't clear in the dying light, but the shape suggested a body.

A human corpse? He peered hard. Surely not? But it had to be. However, the contours were strangely misshapen. What was it? Yes – yes. There was no head, not even a neck. Surely that slick-looking black patch of shadow was a pool of blood? *Some creature with enormous strength had physically torn G.'s head from his shoulders.* R. let out a terrible scream and began running, back towards the cottage. He could sense something behind him, in the tall grasses, watching him intently. A monster was out there, its hot breath fouling the afternoon air. R. felt he had escaped a horrible death by the merest split second. Had he not turned and run when he did, he felt sure his headless corpse would lay beside that of G.'s, their blood staining the dirt together.

R. reached the cottage and ran inside, slamming the back door behind him. He leaned against it, gasping for breath. Shit. That was G. back there, headless. Poor bastard. Poor sodding bastard. What the hell had done that? What manifestation of evil was out there ripping the heads from the shoulders of the living? A werewolf? Did werewolves do that? There was indeed a moon, if not full. Vampires simply drank the blood of their victims: they didn't bury their faces in gore. What else was there of that ilk? Banshees. R. had no idea what banshees did. Or was it just *one* Banshee, like the Grim Reaper? You couldn't have two Grim Reapers, could you? Two harbingers of death. Well then, perhaps a wild man, the Green Man, the wodwo of Ted Hughes' poem? He knew how to kill a werewolf and a vampire. How did you kill a wodwo?

"It knows I'm here," he croaked. "It knows I'm in here."

He felt dreadfully thirsty and went to the brass kitchen tap serving that big white square chipped enamel basin, and drank the running water. Then he stuck his head under, to cool it, hoping the cold water would help clear his thoughts and give him the ability to think through his problem clearly. Water cascaded over his brow, soaking what was left of his hair, washing away the sweat and the dust of the last few hours.

"*Are you in there?*"

R.'s body jerked upright sharply with shock. He struck his head on the spout of the brass tap. Silently, he slid to the floor, unconscious. There were various dreams of the telescope kind, where events fold into one another and make no sense whatsoever. R. woke on the floor to find G. standing over him with a wet sponge. R.'s face was running with cold water and he spluttered as it entered his nose and mouth.

"You're drowning me," he protested.

"Sorry," said G., "but that's a horrible crescent moon cut you've got there from the edge of the tap."

R. touched his forehead and felt the bloody indentation.

"Ow, that hurts."

"It looks as if it does."

A memory came shooting through R.'s pain.

"Wait a minute . . . you're . . . you were . . . that is, I thought you were dead."

"Dead?" G. looked shocked.

"You left a note to say you were going out back."

R. sat up and felt his wound again.

G. said, "I did, but I couldn't get past the gorse bushes, so I turned around and went to the church instead."

"But I saw – that is, I thought I saw . . ."

G. made him a cup of coffee and they sat on an over-stuffed sofa and talked. R. told him everything that had happened since he'd been at the cottage. G. listened thoughtfully, before saying, "So you thought that was my headless body, lying out back?"

"Yes."

"Now then," said G., thoughtfully, "let's go over this carefully. First H. was killed. There's no doubting that. You saw the headless carcass. Then you heard about Mr E., who went missing and this was tied in with another missing person from this very same village – but not necessarily from this address? Right?"

R. nodded.

"Okay, fine. H. is dead. But that doesn't mean Mr E. is also a headless corpse, now does it? And this second missing person – R.K. – why, he simply went missing from the village. I would say you've been on your own too long. You've started tying things together that just don't go – like a fishing line and wharf rope. My guess is your brain is feverish and throwing out all sorts of images, all kinds of scenarios. Dammit, you're a creative writer for God's sake. A *fantasy* writer. We both are. I know if I spent a few weeks in this place I'd be imagining things too. Listen, that *body* you saw out back. My guess is it was made of bits of old branches, rocks and shadows. Believe me."

"You – you think so?"

R.'s head was pounding.

"Listen man, you've just lost your pet cat – in a horrific way. I'd be devastated if it was me. And I bet you haven't told S. yet? Am I right?"

"Right."

G. glanced towards the window. "Look," he said, "there's a moon out there. Almost as clear as daylight. Let's you and I go out back and find your so-called headless body, and I'll prove it to you. Are you on?"

"Not really. My head hurts."

"Aspirin, paracetamol, we'll soon sort that out. The main thing is for you to get some good rest tonight. How can you sleep properly believing what you believe at the moment? There's *nothing* out there. Take my word for it. I'm the sane one here. You're the loopy bugger. We've got to unloop you, man, before you go to bed."

R. gathered his courage and finally nodded. "All right."

"Good. Now you just stay behind me. If there's any ghoulies or ghosties out there, they'll get me first."

That was some comfort to R.

"I guess so."

"Here we go then."

They left the cottage and went out back, R. pointing out the path he had made through the gorse bushes. It was cool and eerie outside and despite what G. had told R. the visitor felt a little spooked by the place. It wasn't a *happy* land out back, that much was certain. No doubt it had been left wild too long. Who knew how long? Maybe years, maybe a decade, perhaps even a century? After all, why would anyone go there, except to look for a lost cat? It had a – what was it – yes, a pre-Christian feel to it. Pagan? Something of that nature. One of those areas which had been left well enough alone to be able to retain its ancient spirits. But that did not mean, G. reminded himself, that there was anything out here that could harm a modern man. By no means.

"Are we near yet?" he asked R.

"There," came R.'s voice, from some way back. "Out there in front of you."

G. looked down. There was a dip in the landscape, then a shallow rise. He was standing on the edge of the hollow. About ten yards away, below him, he could see a strange lumpy shape, half-hidden in the moonshades, camouflaged as it were by a confluence of darkness and light. It seemed out of place, not quite part of the natural scene. Was it a trick of the mind?

Perhaps it was indeed composed of bits of tree, pieces of stone, shards of shadow? Perhaps. It was so difficult to tell being as it was in amongst the shrubs and weeds of the wasteland. The more he stared at it, the more the mound looked as if it were somehow unnatural in the setting. Not a part of the landscape but placed there.

From behind R. made a noise clearing his throat.

The shape seemed to stir at the sound. A ripple, a quiver went over its pale broad surface. Then something quite horrible happened. It actually sat up. Two arms appeared on the sides of the lump. A shock wave went through G.'s body. What had risen from the ground appeared to be the torso of a headless man. This had to be a trick. Someone was pulling strings, or working some sort of mechanism. Headless bodies do not lift themselves up of their own accord. G. looked around, wildly, hoping to see some grinning local, hoping to hear giggling in the bushes, hoping that what he was witnessing was a fool's joke.

The next moment he almost swallowed his tongue.

R. let out a frightened and frightening scream.

A monstrous figure rose from its sitting position in front of the two writers. It was taller than they were, much taller, despite the fact that there was no head on its shoulders. It was a man, or would have been had its facial features not been on its chest. The creature was naked, its skin covered in strange markings or tattoos which the scholar in G. thought he recognised as runes. The mouth in the abdomen opened in a kind of angry sneer to reveal rows of square white teeth. The chest-eyes widened as it stared at the two writers. The look was at first focused on G.'s facial features. Then its eyes switched to R., intently studying that globe-shaped appendage on the other man's shoulders.

"What the fuck is it?" said G., shuddering with both disgust and terror.

"Blemmyae," replied the quietly hysterical voice of R. from behind him. "I remember seeing pictures of Blemmyes in a Medieval bestiary when I was researching one of my books. Ugly bastard, isn't it? Do you – do you think it envies us our heads? Or maybe it sees them as nature's abominations and wants to help us, by removing them?"

On hearing speech the Blemmyae began to croon shrilly, from

somewhere in the back of its abdomen. The sound was that of a vesper spilling from the mouth of a castrato. It rose in volume gradually, until it cut through the evening. The creature rolled those horrible dark lidless eyes, one either side of its sternum. Its long narrow nose, in the parting between the ribs, was dribbling thick mucus down its torso and matting the hairy regions below its mouth. This foul demonic-looking being had a face on its chest, but where was its brain? Did it indeed have one? Perhaps a brain where its heart should be?

"It's singing. Is that a good sign? I don't know what that means. What shall we do, R.?" croaked G. from his dry throat. "Any ideas?"

"Only one," cried R. "*Run!*"

Both men turned at once and began crashing through the gorse bushes, ignoring the shredding of their shins on the long wicked thorns, falling more than once and piercing their hands and faces, as well as their legs. Gasping for breath, sick with fear, G. almost overtook R. on the straight race to the back door of the cottage. However R. held his head start jealously, even though he was half-dead with fright. Not once did either man look back to see whether they were being chased. They had written many a story themselves, each of them, where the victims were running for their lives and the monster was close on their heels.

A welcome rectangle of light grew ever nearer.

Thank God, each of them thought, as they scrambled through briar, thorn and nettle, thank God we left the back door of the cottage open.

They almost made it.

# ALBERT E. COWDREY

## Fort Clay, Louisiana: A Tragical History

BORN AND BROUGHT UP in New Orleans, Albert E. Cowdrey was educated at Tulane and Johns Hopkins universities, and worked for twenty-five years as a military historian, mostly in and around Washington, D.C.

He is possibly the only writer to receive awards from both the American Historical Association and the World Fantasy Convention. Fifty of his stories have appeared or soon will appear in print, as well as one novel, *Crux*.

"'Fort Clay . . .' had its genesis long ago in picnics and snake-collecting expeditions to the defences originally built to protect New Orleans from the British fleet," explains Cowdrey. "(By the time they were completed, the Battle of New Orleans was over – the Brits didn't come back, but the Yanks did.)

"Fort Jackson, Fort St Philip and Fort Pike were as close to castles as I could get – grand places, shadowy and creepy and cool even in the hottest weather, beloved of serpents and the small boys who pursued them. Later, as a researcher for the Interior Department, I worked at Baltimore's Fort McHenry – where the British fleet did come, provoking Francis Scott Key to write 'The Star-Spangled Banner' – and studied Fort Sumter in Charleston harbour, where the Civil War began.

"It seemed only right to think about deeds of blood in such appropriate places, about the intersection of past and present, and about drowned men who emerge from lapping waters to take a hand in the affairs of the living. And so this tale took form."

"WELL, DOC!" CRIED SAFFRON, throwing open the door of her little Bywater studio to the tall, thin old man who stood on the stoop, blinking in the light. "Come in out of the rain!"

Mumbling apologies, Corman handed over his streaming black umbrella and shed his antique London Fog. Saffron took only a minute or two to get him seated amid the clutter of lights, tripods, strobes, reflectors, and other photographic equipment that filled the room. She'd already made tea, and pressed a chipped mug of fragrant oolong into the Doc's surprisingly big hands. The hands were the kind of detail she noticed. *He may be a scholarly scarecrow now,* she thought, *but sometime in his long life he's done manual labour.*

Then it was time to make him a present of her book, *A Lost World* – one of the ten free copies her publisher had sent her. Saffron had all the usual artistic mixture of arrogance and butter-flies, and wondered: what if he hates it? Watching him begin to leaf through the pictures, pausing to scan the text, she reminded herself of her agent's last letter modestly comparing her to Annie Leibovitz, Diane Arbus, Margaret Bourke-White, Dorothea Lange – not *quite* to Ansel Adams, but then she'd never worked in Yosemite.

She was smiling at her own egotism, a bit mocking, a bit tense, when Dr Corman began muttering under his breath. "Remarkable," he said. "Quite remarkable!"

Saffron relaxed. He liked it too. Everybody needed to like it. The *world* needed to like it. She smiled at the old scarecrow with real affection, and when he asked for an inscription, she picked up a felt-tip pen and wrote, "To Dr Quentin Corman, without whom this book might never have existed at all."

Strange now to think that she'd hardly noticed him the first time they met – if you could call it meeting.

He'd been standing behind the desk in the Chief Ranger's office at Chalmette on the field of the Battle of New Orleans, as silent and almost as thin as the flagstaff. Meanwhile the well-barbered bureaucrat in his uniform, with his Smokey the Bear hat hanging from a rack, gave Saffron her instructions.

"We're about to lose Fort Clay, Ms Genève, so we want to document it while it's still here. That's what the contract you've signed is about. We want a thorough pictorial record. We don't want *art*," he said, pronouncing the last word as if it soiled his palate.

She made a noncommittal noise, figuring that once alone on Île du Sable, she'd do what she damn well pleased. Didn't this guy realise that two of her Katrina pictures had appeared in *Vanity Fair*? Sure, she was young, still struggling, she needed the job and expected to do competent work. But on her own terms. She certainly didn't expect Smokey to send Dr Corman along to watch her.

But that was exactly what he did. Under orders, she met Corman at Pilot Town just above the Passes of the Mississippi, and during their two-hour boat trip on a Corps of Engineers lighter he lectured on his specialty. He was a National Park Service historian, an expert on 19th-century fortifications, and like most experts wanted to share everything he knew about the old brick forts that ringed the Atlantic and Gulf coastlines – why they'd been built, and when, and by whom.

*Old farts like old forts,* thought Saffron sourly, deciding, as they bucked and rolled through choppy brown water between the jetties of Pass à Loutre and headed out into the open Gulf, that Corman knew more about less than anybody she'd ever met. Even after the boat dropped them on the island, he went on and on, like a cricket that gets into your house in autumn. Still chirping, he led her through an impressive arched gateway and up a flight of weedy brick steps.

"Fort Clay," he admitted, "had rather an uneventful history. Yet I've made a special study of it."

*Figures,* she thought, taking her new Macron ZX-300 digital camera (9 megapixels, 10x Zeiss optical zoom) out of its carrying pouch. While she hungered for fame, Corman seemed to have an inverted lust for celebrity. The less important something was, the better he liked it. He was a moth drawn to obscurity instead of light.

"In the forty years it was in service," he nattered on, "the garrison never heard a shot fired in anger. In 1870 it was decommissioned and stood abandoned until a group of enthusiasts (myself included) managed to get it on the National Register. The Park Service restored it, and it became a popular destination for boaters who stopped off to sunbathe and swim and picnic. And, I suppose, to satisfy their morbid curiosity."

"Can we get started now?" asked Saffron. But the last phrase had caught her ear, and she added unwillingly, "Morbid curiosity about what?"

"Why, the one truly sensational event of the fort's history – Sergeant Schulz and his men and their sad fate."

"Sad fate," she muttered, wondering how many archaic clichés Corman kept in his arsenal.

"*Very* sad. Sad and shocking. I wrote the official brochure telling the story. First came the yellow fever, and then the hurricane, and then the poor fellows were beheaded by a madman. Would you like to begin with the casemates, Ms Genève, or would you rather photograph the gun emplacements *en barbette* first?"

Barbette guns turned out to be the ones that stood on the open parapet, nothing above them but empty sky. "*So* vulnerable to plunging fire," sighed Corman. "Almost suicide to service them if there'd ever been a heavy bombardment. Many men joined the heavy artillery hoping to stay safe. Some of them got a nasty surprise."

Unfortunately, the big guns – the Columbiads and Dahlgrens and Parrotts, as Corman called them – had long since been removed and melted down for use in other wars. A few stones and bits of rusty iron were all that remained, so Saffron dutifully documented the lack of anything to document.

"Maybe we'd better do the casemates," she suggested. "By the way, what are casemates?"

"I'll show you."

He led her down another flight of brick steps ("Be careful, Ms Genève, even routine maintenance has been discontinued") into a vast chamber he called Casemate One. Instantly all her artistic instincts awakened. Massive brick arches rose and met in a vaulted ceiling from which hung pale finger-long stalactites. Light came in through a wide gun port. She peered through it, and caught her breath.

The Ranger had told her that the next hurricane would probably sink Île du Sable beneath the waves. But that was only *knowledge*. Now she actually saw the rolling blue Gulf of Mexico lapping at the bricks, while by some trick of perspective the distant horizon already seemed higher than her head.

"It really is about to go under," she murmured in awe. "The coast really is washing away."

Corman nodded soberly. "A crew will be out tomorrow to put up warning signs. The Coast Guard is notifying boaters not to come ashore. Oh – please watch the snake."

Saffron froze, then looked where he was pointing. Not a yard from her right foot, a water moccasin big enough to fill a wash-tub lay coiled against one wall, tongue flickering.

"You should have worn boots," said Corman reprovingly, looking down at her Nikes. "Well, go ahead – take your pictures. We don't have all day. The engineer boat will pick us up at three."

Saffron used her flash to shoot Casemate One from every angle she could imagine. Then she followed Corman through a series of low-vaulted passages leading to Casemates Two, Three, Four and Five. By the time they'd completed a circuit of the pentagonal fort, her irritation had given way to an awestruck sense that maybe, just maybe, this potboiler of a job could turn into something important for her career.

Even as she worked and watched for snakes, another part of her multi-track mind began to wonder if some of the images she was capturing might be manipulated into art photos, whether the Park Service liked it or not. She began to dream of publishing a coffee-table book, a collection of dramatic black-and-white photographs, something like Clarence John Laughlin's *Ghosts Along the Mississippi*. Something wildly romantic, befitting an American castle that was also part of a vanishing world.

Digital technology enabled you to do just about anything with images, she reflected. And what she couldn't do herself with her ImageMaker program, the techs at her favourite photo lab could do for her. If the Park Service threatened to sue her on the grounds that her work belonged to them, she'd argue that only the basic documentary images were theirs. Once transfigured into art, they'd be her own.

Casemate Five differed from the others in having a kind of anteroom, a dank chamber sunk deep into one wall, with rusty, disintegrating iron bars. "The guardhouse," explained Corman. "Be sure and document it."

Normally kept for misbehaving soldiers, it once had held a celebrated captive, the accused murderer Gabriel Letourneau, known as the Headsman. Corman shook his own head and clucked over it.

"Even back then, the casemates flooded in a hurricane. Sergeant Schulz was too compassionate to let Letourneau drown like a rat. And just look what happened!"

They were back to Sergeant Schulz and his men and their sad fate. Only now, with her book in mind, Saffron wanted a story to provide a lively text, and asked, "What *did* happen?"

"Let's go up to the Parade, and I'll tell you."

The Parade turned out to be nothing but the weedy open space inside the walls. Saffron could see that buildings once had stood here – brick foundation piers remained – and Corman paced off the outlines of the barracks, the cookhouse, the officers' quarters, the long-sealed powder magazine, and the latrine ("called a *sink* by the Victorians. Hence our expression, 'He has a mind like a sink'").

Reluctantly, she was coming to appreciate his scholarship. Love compelled respect, and Corman loved his topic, bizarre and narrow though it might be. They sat down on adjacent piers of the barracks, and he began to fill her in about Fort Clay's last and most dangerous captive. After New Orleans fell to the federal fleet, he explained, the fort had served as a prison for obstreperous Rebels, male and female. But by 1864 it had lost even that function – either the captives had been set free, shipped off to camps in the North, or expelled into the Confederacy. With soldiers dying like flies in the battles for Atlanta and Richmond, the garrison had been stripped down to a skeleton crew, without even an officer to command them.

So there they were, two miles from the marshy coastline,

sixteen men with little to do but swim, fish, and perform routine maintenance. They rotated the job of cooking; a private who'd worked as a hospital orderly attended to bruises and upset stomachs; a corporal named Quant from upstate New York's Burnt-Over District – once famous for its hellfire religion – acted as part-time chaplain and gave rousing sermons every Sunday.

The NCO in charge was First Sergeant Abram Schulz. Corman described him as a typical bluecoat, bearded like most, wearing the red chevrons of the artillery on his sleeve and crossed gold cannons on his kepi. He was twenty-six, an Ohio merchant's son and by no means an ignorant man. After his death, copies of Dickens and Thackeray were found in his quarters, as well as a stack of technical manuals and a textbook of basic French reflecting his years on occupation duty in New Orleans.

Compared to the bloodbaths in Virginia and Georgia, Schulz and his men had lucked into incredibly easy duty. But also tedious. As if to relieve their boredom, in August the monthly supply boat arrived and Letourneau stepped onto the fort's floating dock with shackles jingling, followed by a member of the provost marshal's guard carrying an internment order and a drawn pistol. The garrison crowded around to stare at the big, rangy man with the tangled beard and hair and the unexpectedly gentle, submissive manner. (He even addressed privates as "*m'sieu*.") After he'd been locked up, they all found reasons to visit Casemate Five to gape and stare at him some more, as if he were a dangerous animal caged in Barnum's circus. In fact, some wit borrowed a phrase from the great showman and posted a hand-lettered sign over his cell that read THE ORIGINAL GORILLA.

Month-old copies of the *Picayune* with details of his crime found a fascinated audience. Decapitated corpses had been showing up for the past two years. With fingerprinting yet to be invented, record-keeping primitive, and a vast drifting population of refugees created by the war, none of them had been firmly identified. Letourneau was arrested after his landlady, noticing a bad smell, checked the slum room he inhabited and found a woman's head in a cupboard. Subsequently, a patrol sent by the provost marshal discovered under the bed a cane knife – a wicked-looking bolo-like tool made for cutting sugarcane.

At this point the evidence looked so firm that carpenters began bidding for the job of building the gallows. But then the case started to unravel. With the crude forensics of the time, there was no way to determine if the carefully cleaned and oiled cane knife actually was the murder weapon. Letourneau had a good reason for owning it, for he lived by doing odd jobs that included clearing weeds and brush – in fact, he'd been employed for that purpose by the military government itself. As for the head, he claimed he'd found it among the weeds near the levee and brought it home as a curiosity, an alibi so bizarre that it might even be true.

All his life Letourneau had been known as a "natural," meaning a half-wit. He was also a pack rat. His room yielded an amazing collection of useless objects – glass beads, ballast stones, dried beetles, a brass telegrapher's key, the skull of a horse, some cypress knees, Indian arrowheads, even a small meteorite – that lent a kind of loony credence to his story. Despite his physical strength and mental problems, he had no police record and no reputation for violence. The few people who knew him treated him with a mixture of compassion and contempt. Worst of all, from the viewpoint of execution buffs who were eagerly awaiting the hanging, another headless body was discovered while Letourneau was locked up in Parish Prison.

The provost marshal decided to hold him, pending further investigation. Fort Clay was secure and almost empty. And so the disaster began to take form.

"But now, Ms Geneve," said Corman, showing a Schcherazade-like ability to interrupt himself at critical moments, "I really think we ought to document the external walls. Work before play, you know, and when it's all done and all the pictures are locked up in the brain of your little camera, I'll finish the story for you."

Actually, their hour-long hike around the fort's perimeter proved more interesting than Saffron had expected.

The place was ruinous, and for that reason picturesque. At two spots, sinking foundations had caused huge cracks to open in the walls, and she made sure that her camera caught the crooked daggers of pale sky thrusting down through the bricks.

Barbed wire hadn't been invented when the fort was built, so rows of sharp wooden spikes – Corman called them the *abatis* – still projected from the dunes, dry and grey and worm-eaten like driftwood. She took a series of pictures through the spikes to suggest both the fort's original warlike purpose and its present hopeless decay.

Meanwhile Corman chattered about life in the 1860s, which he knew in detail. He explained the problems of supplying the fort in bad weather, of securing fresh water for the garrison in the absence of natural springs, of keeping the men healthy so close to the malarial coast. There'd been other problems, he recalled, in the days when Fort Clay was used as a prison both for Rebel sympathisers and common criminals. Along with forty or so men, a dozen women had been jailed, charged with a variety of crimes great and small – spying, prostitution, insulting the flag, emptying chamber pots on the heads of Union soldiers. Keeping them secure from rape among a crowd of unwillingly celibate males had not been easy.

"Bathing was a problem," he mused. "The men skinny-dipped by the roster on the Gulf side of the fort, women on the land side. While the ladies were washing, guards were posted with orders to turn their backs and not to peek. I *don't* think those orders were always obeyed," he added, with a dry little chuckle.

That gave Saffron another idea. How about taking some nude photos in her studio, and having the geniuses at the lab transform them into ghostly images against the grim, looming walls of the fort? A little nudity never hurt anything. And how about a bit of softcore porn as well? With all those randy males around, surely the jailed hookers found *some* way to ply their trade, prison or no prison. She could fabricate some sex scenes, pale forms suggesting the repressed passions of men and women locked up under a discipline that made captives of the soldiers as well as the prisoners.

*Ghosts Along the Mississippi* was fine as a model. But her book would be a lot more saleable if she put a bit of Robert Mapplethorpe into it as well.

The afternoon was advancing and the sunlight hot when she and Corman wended back through the vaulted gateway into the Parade. She was tired and sweaty, and the walls shut off the breeze from the Gulf. In her bag, along with two more cameras and some extra lenses and filters, she'd brought a couple of small Evian bottles. She gave one to Corman and downed the other herself. Sharing the water completed their transformation from strangers into companions, even collaborators.

"You were saying that the men actually welcomed the Headsman's arrival as a break in the routine," she reminded him.

"Yes. And just a few days later came another."

A dot appeared on the southern horizon and turned into a steamship called the *Floradora* – an old-fashioned side-wheeler that had survived into the age of the screw propeller. It tied up to the floating dock, and the soldiers who were off duty began to swap tobacco and gossip with the crew. Sergeant Schulz politely invited the captain into the officers' quarters he'd commandeered for himself and Corporal Quant, and poured him a glass of whiskey he'd commandeered too.

The ship had come from Habana (as it was spelled then) and the captain had a bit of disquieting news to report: when they left the harbour, hurricane flags had been flying on the walls of Moro Castle. Schulz duly noted this information, then asked if yellow fever had broken out in Cuba, as it usually did during the summer. The captain said no, not to his knowledge, then swallowed his whiskey at a gulp and said he must be getting his ship underway. Something furtive in his manner roused the sergeant's suspicion, so he accompanied him to the dock and cast a sharp eye over the *Floradora*'s crewmen. All he could see appeared lively and healthy enough.

Yet when the ship arrived at the Head of Passes, an army medical inspector descended to the lower deck and found a sailor lying in his hammock, parchment coloured, burning with fever and bringing up black vomit – Yellow Jack's classic symptom. The *Floradora* was immediately quarantined and the sick man removed to an isolation ward. Of course Schulz had no way of knowing about that, or whether a few mosquitoes might have fluttered ashore during the *Floradora*'s brief stay at Île du Sable. And wouldn't have cared anyway, for as yet nobody on earth knew how the fever spread.

Corman based his vivid account of these happenings on a log that Schulz kept, with a meticulous day-to-day and even hour-to-hour record of events at Fort Clay. Wrapped in oilcloth and locked in a metal dispatch box, the log had survived the catastrophe and ended up in the National Archives, along with the other records of the Department of the Gulf. So Corman knew that during the next few days, the weather had been sunlit but oppressively hot and still. And then the Gulf began to change. Long ripples running up from the south slowly grew into waves, then into rollers. By the end of the week, breakers were pounding the dock and chewing at the coarse sea grass that anchored the dunes. The sky to the south turned from the dull sheen of pewter to the blue-black of gunmetal.

Sure now that the storm was heading his way, Schulz set his men to work, blocking the cannon ports with wooden barriers braced by logs wedged against the carriages of the big guns. They covered the muzzles and plugged the firing vents, then went to work on the fort itself – barring the main gate, moving their carbines and swords from the underground magazine to the barracks' upper floor, closing and nailing the shutters on the windows of the barracks and the officers' quarters. Since the wooden cistern that supplied them drinking water might be toppled by the wind, Schulz had the men fill barrels with water, muscle them into the barracks, and store them between their bunks. He couldn't have known that *Aedes aegypti*, the mosquito that spreads yellow fever, is a domestic sort of creature and likes nothing better than to breed in artificial containers close to its blood source. For all his forethought and common sense, he'd created a nursery for Yellow Jack right where his men slept.

On the Sunday before the storm, with breakers smashing against the south and south-east walls of the fort, salt spray leaping higher than the parapet, and the wind moaning, Schulz ordered the American flag taken down before it was torn apart, and summoned his fifteen men to a service of prayer and supplication. They met in Casemate Five, with Letourneau watching from his cell. Corporal Quant delivered a rousing sermon asking God to spare them, like Jonah, from the wind and waves – and also (with a glance at Letourneau) from the terror that walketh about in darkness. They sang Old Hundred and the Doxology, and the men's strong voices resounded from the shadowy arches and set echoes careening around the whole circuit of the fort, with the final *Amen* returning in ghostly fashion again and again for a full minute after they fell silent.

Then from his cell, the prisoner in a deep sonorous bass began to chant the *Dies Irae*. Perhaps he'd learned the sounds like a parrot in church, with no idea what the words meant. But the sergeant had had a bit of Latin flogged into him at a Catholic school in Cincinnati, and he admitted that the chant filled him with dread. When his men asked him what the loony was singing, he muttered that he didn't know, fearing to reveal that the words meant *Day of Wrath*.

Saffron sat with the bag of equipment at her feet, the empty Evian bottle in her hand, her mouth half open and her eyes distant. *I have to do the book,* she thought. *This is too good to pass up – I have to do the book.*

Schulz (Corman continued) had become fascinated with the Headsman. That night he and Quant went down to Casemate Five, carrying pistols, a lighted candle, and a loaf of bread. Letourneau was pathetically grateful for the extra rations and even more for the company. Schulz sat down on an empty powder keg, Quant leaned against the wall, and in the glow of the candle the three began to talk in a gumbo of languages – French, English, bits of Creole. Quant did much of the translating, for while Schulz knew textbook French, the corporal had a better command of the language of the streets – where learned, the sergeant preferred not to speculate. Bunking with Quant had taught him that his chaplain knew some surprising things about the seamy underside of New Orleans life.

The Headsman's story was part of that seamy side. He'd never known his father, and his mother Madeleine had been a woman of the town. She'd cared for him as best she could until he was ten, when her latest pimp drove him out. He became what Victorians called a street Arab, a ragged homeless boy who survived by cadging tips, committing petty crimes, and renting his body to whoever wanted it. He was a "hobbledehoy" or teenager when he learned that Madeleine had died and was to be buried in Potter's Field on the marshy edge of the *cypriere*, the great cypress swamp. Letourneau brought to the burial two ballast stones he'd taken from the levee, and when the pine box was in the ground he set them on it to prevent it floating to the surface, as the coffins of the poor so often did in rainstorms. The sexton then filled the hole, and Letourneau tipped him a dime, which was all he had. The man bit it, looked at him suspiciously, and walked away without a word, carrying his shovel.

The next few years contained nothing but work and sleep, interrupted by rare bouts of drunkenness in barrel-houses or pleasure in cheap brothels. Not life at all, really. One wet afternoon Letourneau walked to the Third District levee to decide if he wanted to drown himself or not. He brought along a bottle of cheap wine and his cane knife, which he'd used that morning, chopping weeds to earn the price of the wine. He sat down on a wooden bollard in the rain, and spent the next hour drinking and looking at the river and wondering if he had the courage to jump in.

"I never thought of killing anybody but myself," he insisted, and the man seemed so dim and passive and detached from reality that Schulz almost believed him.

Letourneau had a bellyful of wine when, no more than ten feet away, a head bobbed to the surface of the river. Raindrops dimpled the water all around it, as if little fish were feeding. At first he believed the head must belong to a drunk who'd fallen in and drowned. But then it rose above the surface and looked at him *avec les yeux blancs d'une statue,* with the white eyes of a statue. The head was perfectly bald, lacking even eyebrows and eyelashes, and its skin was the colour of a bruise.

The drowned man stood up and stretched out a hand for help. Letourneau thought, *I've never been this drunk before,* but still he rose and leaned down and took the hand. It was cold and the fingers and palm were wrinkled and white, as if the man had been in water for a long time. The nails curled like fishhooks. When the fellow was safe ashore, he spent some time rearranging his sodden rags of clothing, which smelled like river mud. Then he began to speak *"comme Allemand."*

"Like a *German*?" demanded Schulz indignantly.

Letourneau answered, "Yes, in his throat, you know? And his voice bubbled up, as if he was still full of water."

At this point the candle flared and went out. Letourneau kept talking, his words distilling out of the darkness, with the muted sounds of the stormy Gulf as background. The drowned man was a Yankee seaman named Morrow, who'd been serving on Farragut's flagship *Hartford* when he was blown overboard during a battle upriver at Port Hudson. Like many sailors he couldn't swim, and for a few minutes threshed his limbs helplessly, like a crab being boiled. Then the cold river water sluiced into his lungs and turned to fire. He was only twenty, and the last thing he felt was an overwhelming rage that he had to perish with his life unlived.

Perhaps his rage was what saved him from dying completely. Anyway, he awoke far down in the murky river, tumbling seaward with the current while an immense shadowy fish – a giant river cat, maybe – nibbled at his bare feet. He kicked it away, and discovered that he didn't need to breathe any longer. He was a corpse, and yet could move and even think. Could Letourneau, he asked, possibly understand that?

Letourneau could. "I've always been like that," he said.

"You feel alone, do you?"

"Yes."

"I can help you find a companion. Come with me. And bring your blade."

They walked together into the riverside slums, where water gushed from clay pipes and the gutters whirled rubbish away like millraces. Soon they spotted a woman, clearly a "hooker" – a streetwalker in the slang of the time – who'd taken refuge in a doorway while waiting for the rain to pass. She was holding a wad of newspapers she'd been using as an umbrella and she peered short-sightedly into the street. Morrow took the cane knife from Letourneau's hand and backed against the nearest wall.

"Call her over," he whispered. "She's hungry, I can feel it, so she'll come out, rain or no rain."

Letourneau did as he was told – Letourneau *always* did as he was told. The woman stared at him, then lifted the newspapers over her head and stepped into the street. Coming up behind her, Morrow swung the blade with his right hand and with his left caught her head before it hit the ground. He picked up the sodden paper, wrapped the head in it, and gave the bundle to Letourneau, along with the cane knife.

"The soul lives in the brain," he explained. "When you take

the head, you take the soul with you. I've done it often. Of course the brain doesn't last long, and when it decays the soul escapes. But then you can always take another."

The rain began to slacken, and Morrow said he had to go back to the river, explaining that if he dried out he'd die for good. "I wish I could come ashore oftener. I get lonesome down there with nothing but the mud and the fishes. Then I want somebody I can talk to, if only for a little while. Maybe I'll see you again."

Letourneau walked home in a dream. In his room he carefully dried the cane knife and oiled it to prevent rust. Then he unwrapped the woman's head and put it into a cupboard, because he didn't know what else to do with it. He hung his sodden clothes outside on the rickety gallery that ran past his room, got into bed, and pulled up the tattered coverlet. He was lying there, shivering, when the head began to sing.

The voice was a little weak, but sweet, like his mother's when he was a young child. Back in those days, when she brought a customer home she'd take Gabriel out of the bed and lay him on the floor, wrapped in a quilt. After the man had finished and gone away, she'd bring him back into the bed, which still smelled of the stranger, and sing him lullabies until he fell asleep.

Letourneau thought the woman in the cupboard must have a nice soul, because instead of bawdy songs she sang sweet old ballads like "Green Grow the Rushes" and "I Dreamt I Dwelt in Marble Halls." He went to sleep and slept longer and more peacefully than he had in many years. The next night had been the same, and the next. Then the head fell silent. He ought to have buried it, but couldn't bear to part with it, and that was why he'd been arrested and wound up in Fort Clay. He'd never seen the drowned man again, and hadn't told the provost marshal about him, because he knew he wouldn't be believed.

Then, saying he was feeling tired, he told the soldiers good night. He wished them pleasant dreams.

All of this Schulz wrote down, and had Quant sign the record as witness. For a while they drank together, back in their quarters, listening to the rising wind outside, and arguing about their prisoner. Schulz thought him a dangerous lunatic, but believed that sixteen strong and well-armed men had no reason to fear him. But Quant said the Headsman had caught the eye of a devil who would follow him wherever he went. After the corporal fell asleep, Schulz recorded his comment, adding that his roommate also believed in ghosts, witches, and salamanders, and was, all in all, the strangest preacher he'd ever met.

"In my long life," Corman went on, after a moment of silence, "I've often noticed a peculiar tendency of disasters to follow one another, like sheep trailing the bellwether. Next morning, when Schulz checked the barracks, he found that the rest of the flock had begun to arrive."

Three soldiers complained of fever. At first Schulz diagnosed malaria, a common affliction at the time, distressing but not usually fatal, and dosed them with quinine. That afternoon, just as the storm was arriving in full force, two more fell sick. Schulz and Quant now abandoned the officers' quarters and moved in with their men. By nightfall the situation had become truly grim – the old wooden barracks shaking and shuddering in a gale that may have reached a hundred miles an hour, the five patients either burning with fever or shaking with cold, teeth rattling in their heads like dice.

Schulz was also concerned about his prisoner. The man was his responsibility, and he had to save him if only for the gallows. Fighting the wind at every step, the sergeant struggled back down into Casemate Five, accompanied by Quant carrying a lantern. They found Gabriel Letourneau standing to his knees in water that had seeped through the barriers and gazing at them with the dumb supplication of a caged animal. Schulz ordered him to extend his hands between the bars, manacled them, and only then opened the cell door. Bent double, the three men fought their way back to the barracks through horizontal rain that stung like birdshot. When a gust almost bowled Quant over, Letourneau grabbed him by the arm and pulled him upright again.

Once inside, Schulz added leg irons to the prisoner's manacles, leaving thirty inches of chain between his ankles so that he could shuffle around. He considered cuffing Letourneau's hands behind his back, but that would have left him helpless, forcing the soldiers to feed him, give him water, and even help him use the so-called honey bucket. Since they already had plenty to do, between nursing their sick comrades and trying to keep the barracks from coming apart, he left the prisoner's hands in front, manacled but still usable.

Toward midnight the wind dropped suddenly. The eye of the storm was passing overhead. Schulz ventured outside into an eerie dead calm. He climbed the wall by the light of a serene half-moon at the summit of the sky, and gazed with astonishment at the pale encircling clouds of the eyewall. Later on, Île du Sable received a second punch, the wind now rising from the north-west, but this round was much less violent, and by dawn the hurricane had passed inland, where it soon dispersed in gusts of torrential rain.

But as the weather improved, the patients grew worse. Even to the untrained eye of a Yankee artillery sergeant, their disease clearly was not malaria, for instead of coming and going the fever was continuous, unrelenting.

Hoping for sight of a relief ship, he splashed his way back to the wall. The Parade was ankle deep, and the rising sun shone every-where on water, nothing but water. The storm tide was running high, and for the time being Île du Sable had disappeared under the Gulf, only the walls of Fort Clay standing free. The floating dock had broken its moorings and become a raft, bucking and rolling its way northward toward a shoreline that no longer existed.

Schulz realised that the garrison was stuck for days, maybe a week or longer, until somebody ashore remembered them and sent a rescue boat with an engine powerful enough to make headway against the sea. Until then, they had to survive on what they had – barrels of drinking water, tin canisters of hardtack, sacks of cornmeal, and slabs of salt beef and bacon sealed in casks. Food would have to be cooked on the parapet, using dry wood torn from the barracks' inner walls.

By the Wednesday following the storm, eight men were sick of the fever, one already moribund, and the others (including Letourneau) were taken up day and night with the tasks of nurs-ing. The Headsman was both strong and gentle with the sick, holding down delirious patients without hurting them, giving water a spoonful at a time to those who could still drink, and cleaning up their filth without complaint. But if men were merciful, nature was not. The storm tide had ripped open the gun ports, and the casemates had flooded to their roofs. Water spurted up from below and covered the Parade to a depth of three feet – foul water too, for the contents of the latrine floated out. The powder magazine was under water, the officers' quarters had lost its roof, and the other buildings had simply disappeared.

Water entered the first floor of the barracks, forcing the decreasing number of men who were still well to carry everything – sick comrades, bedding, water barrels, food – to the sweltering second floor, which was already crowded with heaps of supplies and racks of weapons. Even after they knocked open all the shutters, the searing tropical heat exhausted the healthy and hastened the sick toward death. At night, some men waded through the stew of salt water, mud, and excrement to the wall and slept up there between the barbette guns. But that was dangerous too, because so many snakes had found refuge in the same place.

Then, just when life had become all but unbearable, the Gulf began to recede. Île du Sable emerged from its bath smaller than before and with its outline changed, but with its dunes largely intact, secured by the roots of the coarse sea grass. The sky clouded up and a breeze blew from the north that was almost cool. Rain pattered down, the temperature dropped twenty degrees in as many minutes, and sick men and well alike breathed deep and gave thanks to God for sending them relief.

"And it's just at this point," said Corman, glancing at his watch, "that the sergeant's log ends. So there are things we'll never know for sure. We do know that among the weapons stored on the second floor of the barracks were sixteen broadswords of the type the army traditionally issued to artillerymen – in case, I suppose, they were attacked by a Roman legion. Each sword had a double-edged blade twenty-six inches long. Nobody had ever been able to find a practical use for them, except to carve meat for the mess. Gabriel Letourneau, however, had a use for one of them – or so it seems.

"When a rescue party at last reached the island, two weeks after the storm, only he remained alive. Eight men were dead of fever, dead and stinking. Sergeant Schulz in the barracks, and three men lying on the barbette had all been beheaded. The heads were never found. The last four members of the garrison must have tried to swim ashore, preferring to drown rather than face whatever was happening in Fort Clay. Three bodies were later found entangled in the nets of fishermen and shrimpers. Though badly bitten by sharks, they still had their heads. Perhaps the last man of the sixteen survived. A strong swimmer, if lucky, *could* have made it to shore. Nobody knows."

"That corporal – what was his name—?"

"Quant."

"Yes. Did they find him?"

"They found a headless body wearing a blouse with corporal's stripes," said Corman carefully. "On that basis, he was pronounced dead."

"And Letourneau?"

"He was sitting quietly on a barbette gun – a twenty-four pounder Dahlgren – chewing a hardtack cracker. He absolutely denied having anything to do with the murders, especially that of the sergeant, whom he described as a very nice man – *très gentil, très sympathique*. He claimed that a drowned man with blue skin and white eyes had come into the barracks during a rainstorm and killed Schulz, but spared him *en souvenir du passé* – for old times' sake. When the man left, carrying the head, Letourneau took the keys to his shackles from Schulz's body and freed himself. He found the other dead men lying on the wall.

"Understandably, he was not believed. The soldiers took the Headsman back to New Orleans in cuffs and leg irons, kicking and pummelling him the whole way because they were angry over their comrades' deaths. He endured silently, like a beaten animal, but stuck to his tale so tenaciously that the provost marshal, instead of hanging him, committed him to an asylum. Like most such places at that time, the asylum was a pesthouse, and the Headsman soon died of either typhoid or typhus – even good doctors had trouble with differential diagnosis back then.

"Of course," Corman added apologetically as the whistle of the engineer boat shrilled in the distance, "that's an unsatisfactory conclusion. But so often history *is* unsatisfactory, Ms Genève. Sometimes its wildest adventures end in mid-air."

Now, on this rainy evening in December, a year and a half after their jaunt to Fort Clay, she inhaled the fragrance of the oolong along with the incense of Dr Corman's praise. Either he loved her book or he was a very good liar.

"It's a transfiguration," he told her, shaking his head. "You've turned that old heap of decay into a vision of life and lust and war, and how they all pass away, leaving nothing behind but ruins and sand and silence. But these—" he tapped the pictures "—also show what art can do to save something from the wreckage. To make transience immortal."

Saffron almost purred with pleasure. Showing her work always made her feel like some sort of carnival freak, exhibiting the most private parts of her spirit to strangers. Yet until she did, she never really knew whether her work was any good or not – whether it communicated, or just sat there.

"I'm not sure Schulz would have understood," mused Corman. "Wonderful man – brave, smart, sensitive. But underneath, very much the stolid, conventional Midwesterner. That made him a good soldier, but for a creature of enthusiasm like Quant, sometimes rather a dull companion."

"You could tell all that from the logbook?" asked Saffron, smiling. "It must read like *War and Peace*."

"I'm afraid I fibbed about that. Schulz's log is actually quite dry – facts, figures, that sort of thing. I only use the copy I made of it at the Archives to refresh my memory."

Saffron stared at him, sitting there, tall and skinny, the cup invisible in his big workman's hands. And old. He was *very* old.

"Souls are fascinating things," he went on. "I admit that at first I thought you quite a superficial young woman. Watching you at work, I sensed something more. Now I know I was right the second time. There's more to you than meets the eye, Ms Genève. There are depths in you I want to explore."

The rain murmured at the window. A soft knock sounded at the door. Saffron didn't even hear it. *Corporal Quant*, she thought, *who delivered sermons and believed in devils*.

The knocking resumed, so loud now that she jumped. Corman finished his tea, set the cup aside, and turned to look at the door.

"The Headsman," she gabbled, desperate now to distract him. To distract *it*, whatever *it* was. "What about Gabriel Letourneau?"

"He was never anything but the – what's the cant phrase? The 'fall guy'. Maybe that's out of date, too. I find it so hard to keep up with slang, the way it's always changing. Letourneau was just one of *les abaissés du monde*, the downtrodden of the earth. Morrow liked him, but then Morrow's rather a primitive character himself. He tried to kill *me*."

He chuckled. "Can you imagine that? Afterward he became a good servant. He helped me get ashore. Water's really become his element . . . Aren't you going to answer the door, Ms Genève?"

A barrage of knocks sounded, making the old door jump against its frame. Corman shook his head. "Poor devil. Always afraid the rain might end. Quite a phobia with him . . . Well?"

She sat holding her pictures, the physical embodiment of her soul. At least, when she was gone, they would last. Wouldn't they?

"If you won't open it," said Corman, "then I'll have to," and he rose, tall and shadowy, set down the cup, and shambled to the door.

# BRIAN HODGE

## Just Outside Our Windows, Deep Inside Our Walls

BRIAN HODGE LIVES IN Boulder, Colorado, once again ranked by the Gallup-Healthways Well-Being Index as the #1 Happiest City in America, no thanks to his own efforts.

He also dabbles in music, sound design and photography, loves everything about organic gardening except the thieving squirrels, and thrice weekly trains in Krav Maga and Brazilian Jiu Jitsu, which are of no use at all against the squirrels.

Hodge is the author of ten novels, around 100 short stories, novelettes and novellas, and four book-length collections. His first collection, *The Convulsion Factory*, was chosen by critic Stanley Wiater as one of the 113 best books of modern horror. The capstone of his second collection, the novella "As Above, So Below", was selected for inclusion in the massive *Century's Best Horror* anthology.

His most recent title is his latest collection, *Picking the Bones*, from Cemetery Dance Publications. Another recent big project has been converting his back-list titles into various e-book formats.

"I hardly ever write extended fragments of things and then leave them indefinitely," the author reveals, "but that's how 'Just Outside Our Windows, Deep Inside Our Walls' got started.

"I first wrote the part about the fantasised magic show, plus the earliest bit about Roni moving in, after rereading a Thomas Ligotti collection. It may not be apparent to anyone else, but some flavour of his lingered in me for a little while and wanted to come out, and the magic show was the result.

"Then it sat idle for three years or so before I knew what more to do with it. Maybe because I had to forget about how it had begun and get back to being myself again."

SOMEWHERE IN OUR EARLY teen years it's inevitable that our parents become sources of great embarrassment to us, held accountable for everything they are and aren't, could've been or should never be.

Before things can get to that stage, though, it sometimes goes the other direction. We realise, even if we can't articulate it with the same sharpness with which we sense it, that once the bloom is off the earliest years of childhood, we stand revealed as something our parents are mortified to have created.

I always knew a lot more about the latter than the former.

It was spring when she moved into the house next door. It must have been spring, because my window was open, and, directly across from it, so was hers, and had been for at least a day, as though the neighbours were expecting her and had to flush the stale winter air out of the room or maybe the entire uppermost floor.

Everything there was to know about life on the third floor, I understood it inside and out by this point, and had for over two years.

I knew she was there to stay because she sang. Not at first, though. At first there was just bumping and thudding, the sounds of luggage and boxes, and three voices, their words too faint to make out, but only two were familiar. I knew the sounds of my neighbours. This new female voice sounded higher and younger than the other, entirely unfamiliar, although for all that, it seemed to me that she sounded just as tired.

She only sang later, when she thought she was alone.

Whatever the words were, it wasn't a happy-sounding song, not the kind of song you might hear sung by a group of people crowded around my parents' grand piano downstairs and someone who knew how to play it. I listened awhile, then dropped to the floor and crept like a spy toward the window until I was underneath it, careful not to make any noise because she still had no way to know I was there, and I didn't want her to until I'd had a chance for a closer listen and to figure out what she was up to. In the way her voice started and stopped and started again, as though she were pausing between each line or two, the song seemed to require effort. It made me think of a song sung in tribute of someone who has died, only not in a way that sounded, in my word at the time, *churchy*.

I popped up into the window only when she seemed to have quit, not so much finishing the song as abandoning it, and called to her across the space between our houses: "What's that you were singing?"

Until now, all I'd seen of her was a silhouette, a thin shape moving around in a room and beyond the reach of the sun. But now she came to the window and smacked her elbows down onto the sill and scowled across at me. Her straight brown hair swept past both wrists as if to whisk her agitation at me, and one hand darted up to grab the bottom of the window and flexed as though she were going to slam it down, but then she kept looking at me and stopped herself, although when she spoke she sounded no less furious.

"Have you been there the whole time?"

"I was here first," I said. "I've always been here first."

"Well . . . you should *announce* yourself, is what you should do." She told me this as if she suspected she might be speaking to an idiot. She looked very much older to me, twelve or maybe as old as thirteen, and this hurt deeply, because it meant she must have been very worldly and knowledgeable when it came to idiots. "It's the *polite* thing to do."

I told her I was sorry, then asked about the song again.

"I'm sure it wouldn't mean anything to you. I'm sure you don't speak the language."

"What language?"

"The language the song's in." Now she sounded convinced beyond all doubt of my idiocy. Then her scowl lifted and she appeared to relent in her harsher appraisals. "It's not from here." After another moment, "It's not *for* here."

"Oh," I said, as if this made sense to me. "Then what are *you* doing here?"

She seemed not to have heard me even though I knew she had, and I started to feel bad for asking it at all. While at first I'd found her not very nice to look at, I began to wonder if I wasn't wrong, because now it seemed I'd only been misled by a trick of light and her annoyance. I wondered, too, if she might jump from the window, or lean forward and let herself fall. In that other world three floors down, the neighbours' house was ringed with square slabs of stone to walk on. Nobody could survive a fall like that.

"I draw," I told her, volunteering a distraction to save her life. "Want to see?"

I'd sneaked up some old ones, at least, even if I couldn't make new ones.

"Later, maybe," she said, and pulled away. Like before, her hand went to the bottom of the window, lingering a few moments, but as she moved back into the room she again left it open.

That night after the lights were out I lay in my bed and imagined her doing the same. I fought to stay awake as long as I could in case there were other songs to hear, or a repeat performance of the first one. Barring that, it seemed possible that she might cry instead, because that's what I'd done the first night they'd moved me up here, but just before I fell asleep I wondered if the reason I hadn't heard anything from her was because she was lying in the dark listening for some sound out of me.

The distant future I imagined for myself must have been inspired by something I'd seen on TV, which helped assure me that it was possible to turn my fascinations into a life that could take me far away, where I would be loved by thousands. For what will become obvious reasons, I wanted to be a magician.

I would spend many hours planning what my stage show would be like, and soon grew bored with the idea that I would merely escape from deadly traps and make elephants disappear. This admission seemed to unlock something deep inside, an openness to possibilities that would be mine alone to explore.

While I don't believe they came while I was asleep, they were more than just flights of imagination. I began to experience long afternoons of waking dreams in which I would take stage assistants, full of smiles and trust and with no thought of doing anything other than surrendering to my will, and I would lock them into cabinets. The blades would come next, whirring and rasping through the cabinets and cutting them into four, five, even six sections, which I would separate with a flourish before moving on to the next. It would take a while, because my audience and I could never be satisfied with my rendering just one assistant into pieces. That would only be the same old trick.

Once the assistants were in pieces and scattered around the stage, smiling and waving and tapping their feet from the separate remnants of the cabinets, I would begin to reassemble them, although never the same way they'd been. They were meant for better things. I would start simply, swapping an assistant's arms for his legs, and vice versa, or grafting her grinning head onto the middle of her body. Then, after I had basked in the applause for that trick, I would combine the parts of one assistant with those of another, and finally give one or two several more parts than they'd started with, creating human spiders, which would leave others armless and legless, to wriggle across the stage like caterpillar prey.

But the waking dreams of my performance would always end with the assistants dancing like puppets on the stage to prove to the audience how happy they were with their new bodies, and that whatever dramas had played out a few minutes earlier were just theatrics. And so everyone could go home safe and secure in the knowledge that sometimes harm was nothing more than an illusion.

Her name was Roni, I found out a couple days later, which was short for Veronica, and by now short for Ronnie, too. She claimed that there had been a time, lasting for years, when she wanted to be a boy, and so *Ronnie* was how she had insisted on signing her name, writing it over and over when she was alone, just her and a pen and a piece of paper, and she didn't have to tell me why.

But while I understood the business with the paper, I didn't understand why she would need to in the first place. Why would she want to be a boy? I had to ask her this many times before she gave me any kind of an answer.

"You're a boy," she said from her window. "What have you killed?"

Bugs, I told her. And fish, because I remembered catching some once with a grandfather, and we hadn't thrown them back, so I supposed that had to count. And a couple of birds, when I had gotten to play with the pellet rifle a friend had been given for his birthday. Those were all I could remember. Except for the other times. But it seemed like those shouldn't count, because to really do something like that you have to mean it.

Roni seemed to be hoping for more, but before I could make up anything else, some stupid meaningless thing that wouldn't scare her away from the window forever, she asked me another question. "Wasn't it easier to do it because you're a boy than it would've been if you weren't?"

"I don't know," I told her, because I had no experience being a girl. Although, yes, I could imagine them being more squeamish about murderous activities. "I guess so. Probably."

"Well, there you go."

I was glad then that I wasn't a girl, because it seemed that they talked in riddles. Then again, if I *were* a girl, maybe I would have understood everything she was telling me by not coming right out and saying it.

"I heard about something in school," she said.

I nodded, and sort of remembered what that was like.

She pointed to her right, beyond the front of the houses and toward the park that our block faced. It was bright green in there now, and people were finally going there again the way they used to, little specks of colour on the paths and between the trees, and every so often, when the air was just right, a laugh would carry over, and wished I knew what was so funny.

"What I heard was that back in the winter, after Thanksgiving, three different people, on three different days, were found with their heads off," Roni said. "It wasn't any girl who did that. She wouldn't even think to do it."

"She wouldn't?" By now I was just comfortable enough with Roni to think I might be able to get away with challenging her a little. "Who says?"

"Well, she might *think* it. But she'd never *do* it."

"Why not?"

"We don't have the hands for it, for one thing." She craned her neck forward, angling to see as much of the room behind me as she could. "You've got windows in there, don't you, that look out the front? And you don't go to my school and you never seem to leave. So . . . did you see anything?"

For a moment I was suspicious. Maybe the police had sent her, and the next-door neighbours weren't really her aunt and uncle. Maybe she hadn't really come to stay with them until further notice because of . . . well, she hadn't actually said anything about why. But I didn't believe this. If the police had sent her, they would have sent her with a better lie that she could actually tell. I knew that much from TV.

"If I did see something," I said, "what would you want to know about it?"

She turned serious, thinking, as if she hadn't planned this far. Then she knew. "Most people would want to know why there wasn't any blood. But what I'd rather know is if the person who did it ran away, or just walked, like it was any other day."

This was very weird to me. "What would that matter?"

Her face became a riddle then, and she knew it, and seemed to like it that way.

"Maybe he didn't do either," I said. "Walk *or* run."

She burst out laughing. "Well, he didn't fly!"

I realised then how much more I liked her when she laughed. I never got to see anyone laugh any more, only hear it, and not very often, only when I was lucky. After three days this was the first time she'd laughed, too, but it didn't seem likely to happen again any time soon. I remembered school, and how it could be bad enough at the start of the year, and she was getting here toward the end of a school year, and that couldn't have been easy.

So I told her maybe she wouldn't have to go to the new school if she didn't want to, that I had a governess who came most days and, if Roni wanted, she could listen at the window. The idea met with instant disdain – not because it was a bad idea, just that the offer was meaningless.

"What's she going to teach you that I don't already know?"

*       *       *

I began to wish the spring away . . . that summer would hurry up and arrive, so the schools would lock their doors and I wouldn't have to wait for late afternoons. While the waiting didn't get any easier, at least as spring went on the days got longer, with more light filling the space between the houses. Even though we could lean in the windows and talk to each other any time of the night, it was better when I could see her, because otherwise she wouldn't seem as real. She'd tell me what they were trying to teach her at school, and I'd tell her what the governess was trying to teach me, and there didn't ever seem to be much in common, and eventually I realised something was missing.

"What about art class?" I asked. "Don't you ever go to art?"

"Of course not. It's middle school."

The way she said this made it sound horrible.

"Don't you miss it? Art class?"

"I guess. I don't know." She sounded as if nobody had ever told her that she *could* miss it.

"Could you do me a favour anyway? Could you bring back some paper for me? And pencils or something?" Crayons or coloured markers seemed too much to ask for at this stage, but if this first part went well, I could get to those later.

"What kind of kid doesn't have paper and pencils of his own? Everybody has those." Roni appeared not to believe me, and who could blame her. "You say you have a governess. How do you do your lessons, then? How do you do your math problems?"

"I do them in front of her. I just don't get to keep the paper and pencils. They make her take everything away when she leaves."

Roni realised I was serious, and froze for a moment with her mouth half open and one eye half shut. No one would ever make up a thing like this. "Why?" she said, as if she'd never heard of anything so ridiculous.

"Because I draw."

"Only you and a billion other grade school lower life-forms. So?"

I shut my eyes for a moment and sighed, and when I opened them, I think maybe, just for an instant, she saw someone else she'd never realised lived here.

"Are you going to help me or not?"

"I never said I wouldn't, did I?" She blinked a few times, startled. "I've already got all the pencils I can ever use in this lifetime. You can have a couple of those." She briefly disappeared from the window. "Knock yourself out."

She took aim and sent them flipping end-over-end, across the space and through my window. Two bright yellow pencils lying on the rug, with no one to take them away. At first I didn't dare touch them. I just wanted to look at them.

"Are you okay?" she called. "I didn't sink one in your eye, did I?"

I turned back around and remembered to thank her. Saying thank you is very important, especially when you're a prisoner.

"I've got a notebook here you can have, too. Just let me rip a few pages out first."

It was tempting. But no.

"I'd rather have blank paper. Totally blank." I'd waited this long. I could wait another day. "I hate lines."

"And speaking of lines, did you ever hear the one about beggars and choosers? That's a good one."

"I still hate lines."

She nodded, getting it. "They really don't let you have paper and writing utensils of your own. They really don't."

I shook my head no.

"What about toilet paper?" She was smirking. But she wasn't serious, although at first I thought she was, and she laughed. "Let me see what I can come up with," she said, and seemed to take a new satisfaction in it now. Something wrong to do, a law to break, and if she was lucky she might even get to steal, and it must have been then that everything changed between us, and each of us didn't just have a neighbour to pass the time with, but maybe the closest thing either of us could find to a friend.

She came through a couple days later, way beyond anything I believed I could hope for. I'd been thinking she would bring, at best, a few dirty sheets of unwanted paper with shoe prints on them. Instead, that evening, she popped up in her window, grinning, and when I couldn't stand it anymore she held up an unopened package of copier paper.

"Five hundred sheets. I got it from a teacher's supply closet," Roni said. "Are you ever gonna owe me big time. Like maybe for the rest of eternity."

Except then we had to deal with the problem of transferring it from her room to mine. Throwing pencils was one thing. For this, she didn't trust her arm. *I* didn't trust her arm.

"Why can't I just bring it over under my clothes?" she said. "What are your parents going to do, search me?"

No, I told her. She'd never get through. I never had visitors, except for the governess, and there were locks. Besides, the paper may have come from downstairs, but it belonged to the upstairs world now. It could never go downstairs again.

But I had a dart gun, the kind with the suction cup tips. And I had string. And Roni found some rope, a little thicker than twine, that she could tie to the string I shot over. And a wicker basket her aunt no longer used in the garden, whose handle she could slip the rope through. By the time it got dark, I'd used the string to pull the rope back, first one end and then the other, and we'd looped it around our bed frames, like pulleys. I tied the ends together with one of the best knots I remembered from scouting, when they still used to let me go out, and then all we had to do was keep the handle from slipping along the rope and we could pull it back and forth, from room to room, all we wanted.

That's how she sent me the paper.

It took me even longer to touch this than it did the pencils. I knew I'd be up half the night, finding the best possible hiding place for it. Nobody could know. Nobody could *ever* know. If they found this, I'd never have a window again, just walls.

"Hey," she called over after the sky had gone dark, and she hadn't seen any sign of me for a while. "You have to tell me why. What did you do? Draw a bunch of dirty pictures once and it fried their brains?"

I leaned on the sill for a long time. In her window, she was a silhouette, a mystery lit from behind, and if I'd been a little older then, I might have wanted to draw every single strand of hair that cut the light into ribbons. She'd done the kindest thing for me that anyone ever had, and we'd never even been in the same room, or closer than twelve feet.

"Sometimes I draw things and they come true," I told her. Because she'd asked, and I had no one else to tell and couldn't imagine a day when I ever would. "Sometimes I draw things and it makes them happen. Or makes them change."

She didn't say a word. *Liar* . . . I might've expected that. Might've even hoped for it. The longer the silence, the more I wished she'd just make fun of me. My fingers hung onto the windowsill the way bird claws hold branches.

"You're not going to go away now, are you? You'll still come to the window?"

"It depends," she said.

"On what?"

"How does it work? Do you just draw anything, and whatever happens, happens? Or do you have to want it to, first?"

"I think I have to mean for it to. Even if I don't know that at the time."

And even if I *wanted* it to happen, sometimes nothing did. Otherwise, the park would've been full of T-Rexes and a brontosaurus herd. Which had made me think I was limited to working with what was there already, not making something out of nothing.

"Interesting," she said. "Listen. They tell me I'm going to have to have braces starting next year. The last thing I want is a big shiny metal mouth. If I gave you a really good look at them, do you think you could fix my teeth?"

I've always wondered what her dentist would have said if he'd ever gotten a chance to see her teeth again.

It wasn't a hard thing to do, and I was able to get a closer look at her mouth than she expected, because I had a telescope, all the better to see everything on the earth and sky I was missing. Roni stood in her window and smiled a wide, crazy smile, and I let it fill the telescope's eyepiece, and first drew her teeth the way they were, how the ones around the side tilted in and one in the front overlapped the other. Then I concentrated really hard and started changing the lines a little at a time. Twice she said it hurt, but didn't want to stop.

After we were done, it took a while before she came back from the bathroom mirror. But she said I'd done a good job.

It wasn't the first time I'd fixed something, and I was better at it by now than I was before, when I was smaller and my fingers didn't move as well, and this was all new to me, and something my parents didn't understand. All I'd done until that time was little things around the house, like switch the arms and legs on a dancing figure that spun around on top of my mother's music box. They never suspected, not until the night they had a party, for Christmas, I think, and they marched me around to all the guests, and had me show off things I'd drawn so everyone could see what a great artist they had here.

One of the guests asked me to draw his portrait.

So I did.

Except I drew him the way I wanted him, because I didn't like him. He was loud and his breath stank and he spit when he talked and it hurt my ears to be around him, so first I drew his ugly flapping mouth, and then I smeared it out, and his eyes, too, to stop him from looking at me the way he was starting to.

That changed the party in a hurry.

My parents figured things out, finally, and made me put him back together again, but I was scared by then, and didn't draw as well, and it was the first time I'd tried to make anything the way it was before. A few days later, when I was eavesdropping on my parents as they argued about what to do with me, I heard them say the man was going to be having surgeries for years.

So it was good to help Roni.

But there wasn't much else that needed changing, so the rest of the time I just drew without any other reason behind it, mostly other places I would rather be, if only I knew how to get there.

The school year ended for everyone but me, and summer got hotter. Whenever I wasn't having lessons and Roni wasn't somewhere else, we lived at our open windows, so our top floors got warmer, too, and we wore the windowsills smooth with our elbows.

Plus we'd never taken down the rope.

"Do you think we should?" I asked one night.

"No. Definitely not," she said. "They never paid any attention to what's going on over their heads before, so why would they start now?"

So we used the basket to pass stuff back and forth, like books and magazines and comics and music and other things we liked, plus things we made. I sent her drawings, some to keep, and she sent me some stories she was working on, not only to read but for me to draw pictures for them.

She admitted they were all set in the place where the songs came from.

Roni had never stopped singing after that first night. I was glad of it, and by now she didn't seem to mind if I heard or not. I still didn't understand the language, and she wouldn't tell me what the words meant, but I began imagining what they must've been about from the sound of them. And from her stories, which I did understand. These were mostly about girls who killed trolls and ogres, or held them captive forever, or held them captive awhile and then killed them. At first I felt sorry for them, because as a fellow prisoner I knew what they were going through, but then I realised each one of them had done something terrible to the girls, so it was probably for the best when the princesses and peasants and warrior girls started by cutting off the monsters' hands.

Then, one evening, when the sky was soft and purple and fireflies flickered close to the ground, she peered at me with her head cocked at a curious tilt. "It was you, wasn't it?" she said. "Those people in the park, in the winter. You did that, didn't you?"

I'd been waiting for this for weeks. "I didn't mean to. It was an accident."

"Three different times it was an accident?" She laughed the way you laugh when you don't believe something, but didn't sound mad. She hadn't known them, so what was it to her if their heads had come off. "How did you do it without paper?"

I asked if she ever had known what it was like to want to do something so bad, only not be able to, that you thought you were going to explode. She didn't have to think about it. Well, that was me without paper. Until I'd noticed a layer of frost on the inside of the windows overlooking the park.

"All I did was look through the glass and use my fingernail to scratch an outline around them." And then flick my fingernail across their necks. "I didn't mean anything. The first time I didn't even know it would happen."

She looked confused. "When I first asked you how it worked, you told me you *did* have to mean it."

Right. I had. So maybe I was mad at the people for being able to be out while it was snowing and I had to stay inside. Maybe I'd done it the second time to make sure the first was really my fault. Maybe a third time just because I could. Mostly I remembered the way they fell, first one part and then the other, straight down into the snow without any sound.

"Is it something you'll always be able to do?"

"I guess so," I told her. "But I heard my parents talking once and they were wondering if I might grow out of it someday."

She nodded, very solemn, very serious. "I have to think about this."

"Are you mad at me?"

But she was already gone from the window. I still heard her voice, though, and it gave me hope: "I'll never tell on you, if that's what you mean."

Later that night I was awakened by the basket clunking at the window. I turned on a light, the only light burning in the whole world, and got out of bed to see what she'd sent me. It was a picture, Roni and two boys, one obviously older and one who looked younger, plus a woman and a man. Roni wasn't smiling, at least not so you could see her teeth and whether any of them were crooked or not, and I sort of remembered what it was like, having to pretend to smile that way.

Her voice was a whisper now, floating like a mist across the space between our rooms.

"If someone was going to come over, and I told you what time, and you knew who to look for, and you saw him, could you do it then?" she said. "The trick with the head?"

I rubbed my eyes and looked at the picture some more. "Who to?"

She made a sound I'd never heard. "Don't make me say it."

A little later I turned out the light because maybe it would be easier on her that way, and I listened to her breathe and leaned in the window in the moonlight so she could see I would stay there for as long as it took.

"The one in the middle," she finally said.

*        *        *

It was early August when I heard her crying. I didn't even know she did that, because she seemed very much older to me, twelve or maybe as old as thirteen, and I thought nothing could get to her that bad anymore.

I suppose I'd always been afraid that all of this would only be for the summer, or a year, anything but forever, that it was too good to last. I'd made a friend and so had she, and as far as I knew, no one else in the downstairs world was even aware of it, and this was just the way we liked it. But tomorrow she would be going away again. They would be coming to pick her up and take her home again.

"Nothing will change there," she told me. "They say it will this time, but I know it won't."

It was a long time before I understood what she really meant by that. At the time, all I knew was that it meant a lot to her, meant *everything* to her.

"You could come over here," I said. "I'll hide you."

She laughed through her tears. It had been a long time since I'd heard it, the you're-such-an-idiot laugh. "You don't think your parents will notice me down there looking for the keys?"

"That's not how I mean. Just come across. Like we did with the paper and everything else."

"On the rope? It'll never hold me."

It could. I was very sure of this. I told her how it could.

I didn't mean for this to make her cry even harder, but it did.

I stayed awake the rest of that night, pinching myself whenever I got sleepy, in case Roni changed her mind. It was kind of fun, because I hardly ever got to see the sunrise, and now I had a reason, something important to do for once.

"Okay," she said when the sky was first beginning to go pink and orange. "I think I trust you."

We started with her legs.

Had I ever drawn anything this carefully before? Never. Never in my whole life.

She tied each one to the rope by the ankle, and once I'd pulled them across I unfastened them and rested them side-by-side on my bed, toes up, the way they'd be if she were lying there whole, and I never knew she had a birthmark the size of a quarter on one thigh.

Now we had to start planning more carefully, because once we did the first arm, she wouldn't be able to tie things very well with just one hand, so she had to start tying parts of herself to the line ahead of time. The last thing she did was lean over to one side with her head in the basket and wait for me to take care of the rest.

After I had all her parts laid out in place I thought of my assistants, my human spiders, and how happy we made the audience and how loudly it clapped for us. I really wanted to try it, except Roni hadn't agreed to this, and probably wouldn't like it, and I could see how impatiently her head was staring at me from the pillow.

So I just drew her back together again like normal.

"What did it feel like?" I wanted to know. "Did it hurt?"

"Not much." She thought awhile longer. "Cold, though. It felt cold." She looked around at all the space I had, a whole floor to myself. "This is nice. This is really, really nice."

We cut the rope and pulled all of it over, then cut it into little pieces so she would never have to go across again. Some of the pieces we threw out the window, down to the ground and up on the roof, and the rest we hid. I knew where to hide anything.

I knew where to hide her when they brought breakfast up, and we shared it even though it wasn't enough for two of us. I knew where to hide her when the governess came, so she could listen without being heard. I just wasn't sure where to hide her if anyone really came looking. And they would, I was sure of it. It wouldn't matter that there were locks on the door at the bottom of the stairs. They'd still come looking. Because they knew there was something different about me.

But for as long as it lasted, it was the best day of my life.

In between the fun stuff, we kept watch at the window, and listened, and late in the day a car stopped in front of the house next door. People got out and I recognised them from the photo she'd sent me, including the one in the middle.

I held up paper and a pencil. "Do you still want me to? The trick with the head?"

We watched them walk closer, and I was glad all over again that I wasn't a girl, because I couldn't ever imagine myself looking that confused over a simple question.

"No," she finally whispered. "I couldn't really do that."

I sort of remembered what that was like.

It was less than an hour before they came, but before then we heard people calling outside and watched them troop over to the park and back again. Eventually the doorbell rang downstairs, big bonging chimes you could hear all the way up here.

It was time.

And I knew where to hide her now. It could work. I was very sure of this. I told her how it could, and this time she didn't cry.

I drew myself first, getting everything just right because this was the trick that mattered most of all. Then I waited while we looked at each other, because I knew now that I loved her, even if I didn't know as what, and there was nothing more to say, just listening for the voices and footsteps to get closer, until the keys began to click in the door, and Roni closed her eyes and nodded.

Back to the paper, concentrating very hard, blocking out everything else.

I drew her inside me.

And when I looked up again she was gone.

That was a long time ago, in a house I hardly remember, except for every square inch of the top floor, and the views. The house isn't standing anymore.

But we'd pulled it off, waiting there innocent while they looked for her. It wasn't as if they had to tear the place apart. Even with an entire third floor to search, there are only so many places something the size of a person can hide. I think they were a little afraid of me by this time, too. There's what you know, and what you suspect, and what you don't know, and they realised what they didn't know was the biggest part of it, and so they must have decided it would be safer not to grill me too hard.

Inside, I could feel her moving, but later on she went to sleep, the way you can sleep when you're with someone you trust.

We waited a long time, weeks and then months, for the search and suspicions to die down.

"Aren't you ready to come out now?" I'd ask every so often.

"Just a little longer," she'd tell me. "This is nice. This is really, really nice."

Never in a hurry. So I asked less and less often.

Until there was no point asking anymore.

Of all the things my parents were wrong about when it came to me, why did they have to be right about this one: that the thing with the paper was something I'd grow out of someday. I don't even know when it happened. It just did, and while whatever I put down on paper looked better than ever, it just sat there doing nothing, empty and lifeless and inert.

By now I must have gone through forests of trees, trying to remember what it was like, to recapture what once seemed so easy, so I could draw her back out of me again. But the results are always the same. One more crumpled wad of paper, one more curl of ash.

Yet still, she's close, so close I can almost touch her.

But now her voice comes from so far away.

# MARK MORRIS

## Fallen Boys

MARK MORRIS BECAME A full-time writer in 1988 on the Enterprise Allowance Scheme, and a year later saw the release of his first novel, *Toady*. He has since published a further sixteen novels, among which are *Stitch*, *The Immaculate*, *The Secret of Anatomy*, *Fiddleback*, *The Deluge* and four books in the popular *Doctor Who* series.

His short stories, novellas, articles and reviews have appeared in a wide variety of anthologies and magazines, and he edited *Cinema Macabre*, a book of fifty horror movie essays by genre luminaries, for which he won the 2007 British Fantasy Award.

His most recent work includes a novella entitled *It Sustains* for Earthling Publications, a *Torchwood* novel entitled *Bay of the Dead*, several *Doctor Who* audios for Big Finish Productions, a follow-up volume to *Cinema Macabre* entitled *Cinema Futura*, and a new short story collection, *Long Shadows, Nightmare Light*.

"Porthellion Quay, which features in this story, is a real place – only the name is different," says Morris. "My family and I spent a lovely, sunny day there one summer a few years ago during a Cornish holiday.

"I love Cornwall not only because it's breathtakingly beautiful, but also because it is wild and rugged and desolate, and because past echoes and ancient legends seem to seep out of the very rock. It's a landscape which lends itself perfectly to the kinds of ghost stories I love, of which it seems there are far too few these days – stories which are not cosy and comforting and familiar, but which are dark and insidious, and evoke a crawling sense of dread."

W HEN THE CHILD SCREAMED, Tess Morton felt guilty for having to repress the urge to snap at it. She was aware that it wasn't Matthew Bellings who should be punished, but his tormentors, and yet the boy's cry of pain or distress was so *whiny* that it grated on her nerves.

The reason she felt little compassion for the child was because she knew it took almost nothing to provoke a wail of complaint from him. Matthew would cry out whenever someone barged into him in the school corridor; whenever a football was kicked towards him in the playground; whenever a classmate flicked a paper pellet at him, or snatched a text book out of his hand, or pushed in front of him in the lunch queue. Indeed, the merest slight would cause Matthew's red-cheeked, strangely wizened face to crumple, his mouth to twist open and that familiar, toe-curling bleat to emerge.

Tess liked children; she truly did. Unlike many of her more world-weary colleagues, she was still young enough, and optimistic enough, to regard teaching as a noble and worthwhile profession. She looked back on her own school days fondly, and regarded many of her former teachers with great affection. And as such she liked the idea of feeding and enthusing young minds, of equipping her pupils for the trials of life that would inevitably lie ahead.

All of which made her feel doubly bad for the way she felt about Matthew. He wasn't a naughty boy. He wasn't disruptive or snide or cruel. He was just . . . unlikeable.

Physically, he was stick-thin and uncoordinated. When he ran his limbs resembled a collection of slender twigs loosely bound together. He had no real friends, and as far as Tess could tell had made no particular efforts to acquire any. Breaks and lunchtimes he could most commonly be found in the library, cowering behind an open book, as if hiding from pursuers. He was the sort of child whose parents – of whom Tess had only ever met his nervous, bird-like mother – did him no favours whatsoever. Whereas the other boys carried rucksacks or sports bags, Matthew had been provided with a satchel of gleaming, conker-brown leather. Additionally, his shoes were too shiny, his trousers too short, and his old-fashioned crew cut gave him the look of a child actor in a wartime drama series.

For a while Tess had taken pity on the boy. She had put herself out, spent extra time with him, in an effort to prise him from his shell. Matthew, however, had remained not only unresponsive, but so sulky and ungrateful that in the end she had given up. She still felt a bit ashamed of abandoning the cause, but she consoled herself with the thought that at least she wasn't as downright hostile towards Matthew as some of her colleagues. The other teacher on this year eight field trip, for instance, Yvonne Harrison, who most of the kids loved for her friendliness and good humour, frequently referred to Matthew Bellings as "that snivelling little shit".

Turning now, Tess saw that Jason Hayes, his back to her, was hopping from foot to foot, waving his arm in the air. Her immediate thought was that Jason had snatched something of Matthew's and was taunting him, holding whatever-it-was out of reach. Then she saw Jason lunge forward, lowering his arm in a thrusting motion, which made Matthew squeal again. Some of the other children, especially the girls, squealed too, though there was laughter in *their* voices.

"Eew, you are *so* gross!" one of the girls (Tess thought it might be Francesca Parks) shrieked delightedly.

Muttering at the child behind her to halt, Tess strode towards the knot of pupils at the back of the queue. "*What* is going on here?"

Jason Hayes looked over his shoulder guiltily, and then flicked his arm, tossing away whatever he'd been holding. Because of the other kids milling around, Tess couldn't tell what it was, though she got the impression of something black and ragged sailing over the edge of the metal walkway and disappearing into the scrubby bushes below.

"Nothing, miss," Jason said innocently, turning to face her.

"Nothing," Tess repeated. "Do you honestly think I'm stupid, Jason?"

Jason was a sporty, thick-set boy with spiky hair. Often cheeky and excitable, but essentially a good kid.

"No, miss. No way."

"I'm very glad to hear it. So perhaps you'd like to tell me what you were doing to Matthew?"

Tess still couldn't see the smaller boy. It was as if the other children were purposely shielding him from view.

"Nothing, miss," Jason said again, and then added quickly, "I was just showing him something."

Tess sighed inwardly. She knew that to get to the heart of the onion you had to patiently peel away the layers one by one. "I see. And *what* were you showing him?"

"Just something I found, miss."

Tess stared at him silently for a moment, and then very deliberately said, "Do you *want* to go on the Mine Railway, Jason?"

"Yes, miss."

"Because it's no skin off my nose to take you back to the coach. For all I care, you can sit there for the rest of the afternoon, writing an essay on how important it is to be a positive representative of the school. Would you like that?"

"No, miss."

Francesca Parks, a precocious thirteen-year-old with a pierced navel, shrilled, "You can't do that, miss."

"Can't I, Francesca?" Tess said coolly. "And why's that?"

"You can't leave Jace on his own. It's against the law."

"He wouldn't be on his own," Tess said. "Mr Jakes would be there."

Mr Jakes was the school coach driver. He was a scrawny man in his early sixties who always stank of cigarettes. He had a collapsed cavern of a mouth and bad teeth.

Francesca's eyes, still bearing the trace of the eyeliner she applied every afternoon the instant she stepped out of the school gates, widened. "You can't leave him with that old perv."

Tess stared at her unblinkingly. "I beg your pardon?"

Francesca's eyelids flickered and she bowed her head. "Sorry, miss," she mumbled.

"I don't want to hear another word from you, Francesca. Not one. Do you understand me?"

Francesca's head jerked in a single, sullen nod.

Tess paused just long enough to allow her words to sink in and then she focused on Jason again. "Now, Jason," she said, "I want you to tell me exactly what you were tormenting Matthew with, and I want the truth. This is your one and only chance to explain. Don't blow it."

Jason braced himself. "It was a bird, miss."

"A bird?"

He nodded. "I found a bird on the path back there, miss. A dead one. It was a bit manky."

Tess could guess what had happened. Jason had picked up the bird, waved it in Matthew's general direction, and Matthew, as ever, had overreacted. It wasn't much more than boyish high jinks, but Matthew's response – and the fact that Jason must have known from experience exactly how his classmate *would* respond – meant that she couldn't be seen to condone his behaviour.

Curtly she said, "What did I tell you before getting on the coach today, Jason?"

"You told us we were representing the school and we had to be on our best behaviour, miss," he replied dutifully.

"Correct," said Tess. "And would you say you've adhered to those stipulations?"

"No, miss."

"No," she confirmed. "You've let us all down, haven't you?"

"Yes, miss. Sorry, miss."

"I appreciate the apology," Tess said, "but it's not me you should be apologising to."

"No, miss."

Raising her voice, Tess said, "Step forward please, Matthew."

The gaggle of Jason's classmates, who had been hovering in the background, now half-turned, shuffling aside to create an aisle. Revealed at the end of the aisle, crouching against the chain-link fence which enclosed the metal walkway leading to the mine entrance, was Matthew Bellings.

Tess immediately saw that Matthew was trembling and that he had something dark on one cheek. She wondered whether the incident had been more serious than she had thought. Surely Jason hadn't *punched* Matthew, knocked him down, bruised his face? Despite the antipathy that the other children felt towards the boy, she couldn't believe that any of them would actually resort to violence. As Matthew shakily straightened up, Tess saw one of the girls – Charlotte McDonald – silently hold something out to him. Something small and white. A tissue. And immediately Tess realised what was really on Matthew's face.

It wasn't a bruise. It was blood.

It wasn't his own blood, though; she was sure of that. His face wasn't cut or swollen, and the blood was too thin and brownish to be fresh. As Tess looked at Matthew staring at the tissue but not taking it, her brain made another connection.

It wasn't human blood. It was the bird's blood. Jason must have swung the dead and rotting creature – whether intentionally or not – right into Matthew's face. The thought of it made her feel a little sick.

However, the fact that Matthew was doing nothing to help himself, that instead of taking the proffered tissue and cleaning himself up he was simply cowering against the fence, elicited in Tess a wave not only of revulsion, but of an almost contemptuous irritation towards the boy. Marching forward, she snatched the tissue from Charlotte's hand and brusquely applied it to Matthew's cheek. Matthew was so surprised that he half-twisted away, releasing another of his plaintive squeals.

"Oh, for God's sake," Tess muttered, "don't be a baby."

Instantly she knew she'd overstepped the mark, shown too much of her true feelings. She was aware of shrewd eyes on her, could almost hear the identical thoughts forming in half-a-dozen thirteen-year-old heads: *Miss doesn't like him either.*

"Jason," she snapped, trying to make amends, "didn't you have something to say?"

"Er . . . yeah. Sorry, Matthew," Jason said, but there was a smugness in his voice that left Tess in no doubt that the damage had already been done. Despite his behaviour, Jason *knew* he was still the popular choice, even with his teacher, and that could only mean more trouble for Matthew further down the line.

"Everything okay?"

Tess turned briskly and straightened up. Her friend and head of department, Yvonne, older and more experienced by five years, was standing behind her. Yvonne had returned from collecting their pre-booked group ticket from the kiosk at the foot of the walkway.

"Just a little incident with a dead bird," Tess said. "All sorted now."

She glanced at Matthew, who stared resentfully back at her. The boy still had a faint brown stain on his red cheek. If she had been his mother she would have spat on the tissue and rubbed it until it was gone.

"I don't want to know," Yvonne said jovially. She was a large, rosy-faced woman with a mass of red hair. Raising her voice, she looked up and down the queue and called, "Right you lot, nice, straight line. No pushing or shoving. Who's looking forward to a terrifying plunge into the centre of the earth?"

Most of the kids cheered and raised their hands. A few of the girls looked gleefully terrified.

"Excellent!" Yvonne said. "Come on then."

For the next few minutes, Tess and Yvonne busied themselves handing out yellow hard hats and getting the children settled into the wooden seats of the open-sided train which would transport them underground. Aside from the bird incident, it had been a good day. Even the weather had held up, though the clouds were gathering now and a few spots of rain were beginning to patter on the plastic canopy of the walkway overhead.

They were at Porthellion Quay, a tin mining museum and visitor centre surrounded on three sides by towering Cornish cliffs. The museum was a sprawling affair, set in two hundred acres of hilly countryside, and consisting of a long-abandoned (though beautifully preserved) mining village, and a small quayside and docks beside the fast-flowing River Tam. The children had been given a tour of the village and assay office, had had a lesson in the Victorian school (after first dressing up in period costume, much to their embarrassment and hilarity), had made rope on the 'rope walk', and had enjoyed a picnic lunch down by the quayside. Now it was the highlight of the trip – a journey on a rickety narrow-gauge railway into the tin mine itself.

"Everybody wearing their hard hats?" asked the driver, a grizzled, wiry man dressed in blue overalls and an old miner's helmet with a lamp on the front.

Tess glanced at Francesca. She was the only one who had protested about the headgear, but even she was now perched sullenly in her seat, the strap tightly fastened beneath her chin.

"All ready, Mr Hardacre!" shouted Yvonne, looking around and raising her eyebrows in gleeful anticipation.

"Let's be off then," Mr Hardacre called.

He gave an unnecessary double-blast on the whistle, which made several of the children jump, and then, to a smattering of cheers, the train chugged jerkily forward.

Tess settled back, enjoying the rattling motion and the feel of wind on her face. She knew that the train cut leisurely through half a mile of woodland before plunging downhill into the mine itself, and she half-closed her eyes, relishing the sensation of light flickering across her vision as it forced its way through the gaps in the passing trees and bushes.

Raising his voice above the noise of the train, Mr Hardacre began to deliver what was obviously a well-rehearsed spiel, providing them with various facts about mining and the mine itself. Tess listened as he told them how arsenic was a by-product of tin smelting, and how one of the often lethal jobs given to women and children was scraping the condensed arsenic off the walls of the calciners, which drew toxic fumes up from the smelting houses.

She phased out when he started to quote facts and figures relating to ore production and the length and depth of the mine's various shafts, and only knew that the mine entrance was coming up when several of the children sitting near the front of the train began to whoop. Opening her eyes, Tess saw the glinting thread of track, like a long zip, disappearing into the centre of an approaching black arch. Dazzled by the flickering sunlight, the arch seemed to her to be not quite there; it was like an absence of reality into which they were being inexorably drawn, its edges fuzzy, its heart of darkness utterly impenetrable.

She blinked fully awake just in time to be swallowed by blackness. A palpable ripple of fearful excitement ran through the group at the sudden claustrophobic chill emanating from the rocky walls, and at the way the light from Mr Hardacre's lamp slithered and fractured across the tunnel's myriad planes and surfaces. Tess swallowed to ease the sudden pressure in her head, but even after the silent pop in her eardrums the previously guttural rumble of the train's engine sounded thick and muffled. She imagined the thick, dusty air clogging her throat and had to make a conscious effort not to cough. After a couple of minutes of travelling downhill, Mr Hardacre eased back on the brake and brought the train to a grinding halt.

He gestured towards a tableau on their left. Illuminated by the light of a number of ersatz Davy lamps, fuelled not by oil but by electricity, was a family of mannequins. There was a father, a mother, a boy and a girl, all dressed in the drab clothes of a typical mid-nineteenth century mining family. The father's shiny, chipped face was streaked with black paint, evidently intended to represent subterranean grime. Like Mr Hardacre, he wore a mining helmet and was resting a pickaxe on his shoulder.

"They're well creepy," Tess heard one of the girls whisper. She glanced in the direction of the voice and placed a finger to her lips, though she couldn't disagree.

The wide, painted eyes of the family seemed to stare blankly at the newly arrived group. The little girl was missing a chunk of plaster from the centre of her face, which gave the impression that some hideous skin disease had eaten away her nose and part of her mouth.

Mr Hardacre told them about life underground, about how the father would toil away for ten or twelve hours at a time in stifling conditions, while the children would sit waiting, often in pitch darkness, looking after his food and matches and whatever else he might bring down the mine with him. Meanwhile the women – if they weren't scraping arsenic off the walls of the calciners – would be at home, cleaning and washing and cooking the Cornish pasties that their husbands ate every day.

"Any questions?" Mr Hardacre asked finally.

For a long moment there was silence, and then Simon Lawson tentatively raised a hand.

"Is the mine haunted?"

The shadows occupying the wrinkles in Mr Hardacre's face deepened as he frowned. "Haunted?"

"Yes . . . I mean . . . well, people must have died down here. Accidents and that. So I just wondered whether there were any, like, stories or legends or anything . . ."

Tess glanced at the boy, but in the gloom he was nothing but a hunched shadow.

"Ghosts, eh?" Mr Hardacre said, and this time he smiled, the shadows flocking to his widening mouth. "Well, I don't know about that, but have you come across the story of the fallen boy on your travels today?"

There was a general shaking of heads.

"There's a bench with a plaque on it outside the sweet shop," Mr Hardacre said. "It's dedicated to Michael Rowan, who died at the age of thirteen on March 16, 1865. Did anyone see that?"

A few hands went up, though Tess herself had not noticed the plaque.

"Well, there's a strange little story associated with him," Mr Hardcastle said. "Not a ghost story exactly, but still . . . sad. And a bit creepy.

"The mine, as I told you earlier, was founded in 1832. However there's a secondary shaft, which we'll see in a few minutes, which was created in 1865. The reason for this was that after thirty years of mining, the seams on this level were all but exhausted. It was decided, therefore, to mine deeper – and so the secondary shaft was created, in the hope that further seams would be discovered on a lower level.

"One of the most prominent miners at that time – he was a sort of manager, answerable directly to the mine owner – was a man called William Rowan. By all accounts, Rowan was not popular. He was a bear of a man, and something of a bully, and he had a son, Michael, who was apparently much the same.

"One of the victims of Michael's bullying was a young lad called Luke Pellant. The story goes that Michael chased Luke into the mine one night and that in the darkness Michael ended up losing his way and falling down the secondary shaft. It was just a big hole in the ground at that point, and back in those days there were no safety barriers or anything like that. Anyway, when Luke told everyone what had happened, a rescue operation was mounted, but of course it was too late – the lad had fallen eighty feet or so onto solid rock and was pretty much smashed to pieces.

"Although Luke claimed that Michael had fallen, Michael's father, William Rowan, didn't believe him. He accused Luke of pushing his son down the shaft, of murdering him, and he swore he'd see the boy brought to trial and punished. The general view, however, was that Michael's death had been nothing but the result of a terrible accident, and one that he had brought on himself. When nothing came of Rowan's campaign to see Luke brought to justice, Rowan was furious.

"A few weeks later, Luke disappeared, and it seems that although Rowan was initially suspected of having had something to do with it, Rowan himself put it about that the boy had fled out of guilt or shame for what he had done. In any event, nothing ever came of the incident – until about twenty years ago, when they were excavating the ground down by the quayside to lay the foundations for the information centre. During the excavation some bones were found – an almost entire skeleton, in fact – which tests revealed were about a hundred and fifty years old, and were those of a boy somewhere between the ages of ten and fifteen." Mr Hardacre shrugged. "It's never been proven, but the general consensus is that William Rowan abducted and killed Luke Pellant and buried his remains down by the river. Of course, the Rowan family, who are still quite prominent in the area, refuse to accept it, and had the bench erected as a sort of . . . well, a sort of statement of defiance, I suppose."

"Are there any members of the Pellant family still about?" Tess asked.

Mr Hardacre shook his head. "Not that I know of. Not in these parts anyway."

"So the bad kid gets remembered and the good one gets forgotten," one of the girls piped up. "That is *so* not fair."

Mr Hardacre shrugged. "I don't think it makes much difference after all this time. Although if it's any consolation, Michael Rowan, despite the commemorative bench, is not regarded fondly around these parts. The locals call him the 'fallen boy', not only because he fell down the shaft, but also because, in their eyes, he – and his father – had fallen from grace."

"So does Michael Rowan's ghost haunt the mine then?" Simon Lawson asked.

Mr Hardacre smiled. "Not that I know of. Shall we carry on?"

He started the train up again and they went deeper, the engine creaking and grinding as they chugged downhill. The tunnel became narrower, the walls more jagged and uneven, and Tess had to suppress a wave of claustrophobia when she looked up at the black ceiling and got the impression that it was crushing down on them, closing them in.

She was relieved several minutes later when the tunnel abruptly widened and they found themselves in a natural arena-like cavern, the walls and ceiling sloping away on all sides, giving a sudden disorientating sense of space. Once again, Mr Hardacre eased back on the brake and the engine groaned to a halt.

"Right," he said, "who fancies a bit of mining?"

This time the response was not quite as enthusiastic. Tess and Yvonne ushered the children out of the train and ordered them to follow Mr Hardacre, who led them across to what looked like a huge, squared-off well, surrounded by a metre-high wall. The shaft of the 'well', a raft-sized square of impenetrable blackness, had been overlaid with a sheet of thick but rusty wire mesh.

"This is the secondary shaft I was telling you about," he said.

"The one that the boy fell down?" one of the girls asked.

"That's right. This shaft has been unused since the mine closed a hundred years ago. Even before then it was prone to floods and cave-ins."

"Are there any plans to open the shaft up again?" asked Yvonne.

Hardacre shook his head. "It would cost too much money. And there's nothing to see down there that you can't see up here." He raised a finger. "Now, remember I told you that children often used to sit down here for hours in the darkness, waiting for their fathers to finish work? Well, when I said darkness, I *meant* darkness. I was talking about the kind we don't usually experience in this modern age. The kind where you literally can't see your hand in front of your face. How many of you want to know what that kind of darkness is like?"

Tess glanced around. Most of the hands were going up, though some of the children looked nervous.

"All right then," Mr Hardacre said. "But when the lights go off, I want you all to stand absolutely still. We don't want any accidents. Okay?"

There was a murmur of assent.

Mr Hardacre crossed to a chunky plastic box on the wall, which had once been white but was now grimed and smeared with black fingerprints. The box had a single switch in its centre, and thick black wires snaked out of the top of it, leading to the ceiling of the tunnel, along the length of which, Tess noticed, were a series of dimly illuminated light bulbs. Mr Hardacre switched off the lamp on his miner's helmet and then looked around at the group and smiled, evidently relishing the moment.

"Ready?" he said, and before anyone could answer he pressed his finger down on the switch.

There was a loud click, like a bone snapping, and the world vanished. Around her, Tess heard a brief, shrill chorus of alarmed squeals, which then seemed to abruptly cut off, leaving a silence and a darkness that felt skin-tight, constrictive. For a few seconds Tess was convinced that she could no longer move; she felt her throat closing up, her chest tightening. She couldn't shake the notion that she was all at once utterly alone. With an effort she raised her hand in front of her face, but she couldn't see it, she couldn't see anything.

She didn't realise she was holding her breath, waiting for something to happen, until she heard a scuffle of movement to her left. Then, for the third time in twenty minutes, Matthew Bellings cried out, his familiar, teeth-grating mewl of protest echoing jaggedly in the confined space. Immediately the light clicked back on and the world was restored. Blinking, somewhat dazed, Tess looked around her.

The children were standing in little groups, all except for Matthew. He was standing alone, in their midst but isolated. Tess focused on him, and her heart gave a sudden lurch. Matthew's face was scored with streaks of blackness. It was as if the darkness had not allowed him fully to return, as if it had eaten part of him away.

But of course that was nonsense. The black streaks were not darkness; they were simply dirt. Clearly someone had stepped up behind Matthew when the lights were out and had smeared begrimed hands across his cheeks. The question was—

"Who did this?" Yvonne snapped, stepping forward.

Tess's colleague was quivering with rage, pointing at Matthew but sweeping her burning gaze around the rest of the class. The children stared back at her silently or looked down at the floor.

"What did Mr Hardacre tell you?" she continued. And when again she was met with silence, she shouted, "Well?"

"He told us to stand still so there wouldn't be any accidents, miss," replied Julie Steele, whose dark fringe half-obscured her chubby face.

"Yes he did, Julie. So why did one of you decide to be an idiot and do the exact opposite?"

Again, silence. Angrily Yvonne said, "Right, well there's only one way to resolve this. Everyone hold out your hands."

There was a shuffling, a collective glancing around, and then hands appeared, palms up, for inspection. Tess looked from one pair to the next, her gaze skittering. As far as she could see, they were all white, unsullied.

But not all the children had complied with Yvonne's instructions. At the back of the largest group, partly concealed by their classmates, were two crouching, whispering figures. They appeared to be facing each other, holding hands. And then Tess realised that they were not *holding* hands, but that one was *cleaning* the hands of the other.

"You two," she shouted, pointing, striding across.

Two guilty heads snapped up. Beneath the yellow bulbs of their hard hats, Tess recognised the faces of Jason Hayes and Francesca Parks.

Yvonne had joined her now. With her curly red hair streaming from beneath her own hard hat, she looked faintly ridiculous, but no one was laughing.

"Come here!" she hissed, her furiously sibilant voice echoing around the cavern.

Jason and Francesca shuffled forward. Francesca was holding a begrimed Wet Wipe.

"Jason Hayes, show me your hands," Yvonne ordered.

Jason hesitated, but the expression on his face was almost resigned. Slowly he turned over his hands, revealing his palms. Despite Francesca's ministrations they were still mostly black.

And so, a split-second later, was everything else.

Just as they had a couple of minutes before, the lights in the tunnel suddenly went out. This time, caught unawares, the screams from some of the children were louder, edged with panic. There was shuffling movement and someone called out; from the sounds they made, either they or someone else appeared to stumble and fall. Yvonne's furious voice rose above the melee:

"Everyone just *stand still!* Mr Hardacre, what's going on?"

Tess heard the click-click, click-click of their guide testing the light switch.

"Must be a power cut," he said. "Hang on a sec."

There was a smaller click and suddenly a thin beam of white light cut through the blackness. It was the lamp on Mr Hardacre's helmet. The beam bobbed and shivered, playing across the walls and the faces of the children as he moved his head.

"No need to panic," he said. "We'll just get back on the train. I'll soon have us out of here."

"Miss?" said a voice in the darkness.

Tess turned, but the children were little more than shadowy shapes.

"What is it?" she asked.

"Jason's gone, miss," the voice said, and now Tess recognised it as belonging to Francesca Parks. "He's not here."

"What do you mean – *gone*?" snapped Yvonne.

"I don't know, miss," said Francesca. "He was standing right next to me. But when the light came back on, he'd . . . disappeared."

Yvonne huffed. "Oh, this is ridiculous. What is that little idiot playing at?"

"Matthew Bellings has gone too, miss," one of the boys said.

Tess felt as though the situation was spiralling out of control. "What?" she said. "Are you sure?"

"Yes, miss. He was right there." A shadowy shape raised an arm, pointing at the spot where Matthew had been standing a few seconds before.

"Matthew?" Tess called, looking around. "Jason?"

There was no response. Tess and Yvonne looked at each other. Tess saw a flicker of fear in her colleague's eyes.

"Let's get the other children on the train," Yvonne said. "Count them to make sure we haven't lost anyone else."

They did it as quickly as the darkness would allow, while Mr Hardacre did a quick recce of the tunnels leading off from the central cavern, shining his helmet-mounted light down each one and calling the boys' names.

Finally he returned, shaking his head. "I'll put a call through to the main office," he said. "Find out what—"

"*Listen*," said Tess.

"What—" Yvonne began, but Tess held up a hand for silence. "I heard something . . . There it is again!"

They all listened now. From somewhere ahead of them and to their left came a scraping, a shuffling, as if someone or something was emerging from a burrow, scrabbling towards the light. Mr Hardacre walked slowly forwards, placing his feet with care on the uneven ground, the beam of light from his helmet sweeping across the cavern walls.

Several of the children gasped as something suddenly tumbled out of one of the side tunnels. Tess saw white hands clawing at the ground, eyes flashing as a face turned towards them.

"Matthew!" she shouted and ran forward, ignoring Mr Hardacre's warning about minding her footing.

Matthew was on his hands and knees, shivering with fear, his eyes wide and staring. His face was black with dirt. His mouth was hanging open, and as Tess approached him a string of drool fell from his lips and spattered on the ground.

She dropped to her knees, gathered him up in her arms. He flinched and then relaxed, clutching at her as though craving her warmth.

"Matthew," she said softly. "What happened? Do you know where Jason is?"

Matthew looked up at her. He was clearly dazed, confused.

"He called me Michael," he whispered.

"Who did?" asked Tess. "Jason, you mean?"

Matthew shook his head. "He called me Michael. He thought . . . he said . . ."

Suddenly his face crumpled and he began to sob.

As Tess hugged him tight, trying to comfort him, Hardacre slipped past her, into the tunnel. Yvonne, bringing up the rear, panting a little, crouched down beside her. Before Yvonne could say anything, Tess gently transferred Matthew into her colleague's arms and muttered, "Look after him."

She stood up shakily. She could still see the white light from Hardacre's lamp shimmering across the walls of the side tunnel – and then he turned a corner and all at once they were plunged into blackness again.

Tess stepped forward, feeling her way into the tunnel. She moved sideways, crab-like, her hands sliding along the rocky walls, her feet probing ahead. With every step she couldn't help but imagine a precipice in front of her, a gaping abyss. She told herself she was being foolish, but she couldn't shake the idea from her mind.

Then she rounded a corner and suddenly saw thin slivers of ice-white light limning the jags and crevices of the tunnel ahead.

"Mr Hardacre, wait!" she called and hurried towards him.

She flinched as he turned towards her, the light from his lamp flashing across her vision, blinding her.

"What are you doing here?" he said almost angrily. "You should have stayed in the cavern with the children."

"Yvonne's with them," Tess said. "Jason is one of my pupils. I couldn't just wait around in the darkness, doing nothing."

Hardacre made an exasperated sound, but he said, "Come on then. But be careful."

They moved on down the tunnel, Hardacre leading the way, his lamplight sliding across the glossy walls. Down here the world was stark and primal. A world of rock and silence, of harsh white and deep black, nothing in between.

"How deep does this tunnel go?" Tess whispered.

Hardacre's shoulders hunched in a shrug. "A mile maybe."

"Will it—" Tess began, but then she stopped.

There was a figure crouching in the tunnel ahead.

It was on its haunches, bent forward, its back to them. It was naked, its forehead resting against the rocky wall. It reminded Tess of a child playing hide-and-seek, counting to a hundred before standing up and shouting, "Coming, ready or not."

Hardacre had halted too. Tess stepped up beside him.

"Jason?" she said.

The figure didn't respond. Tess slipped by Hardacre, moving towards it.

"Be careful, miss," Hardacre said.

"It's all right," Tess replied, though her stomach was crawling with nerves. "There's nothing to be frightened of."

She was within arm's reach of the figure now. She could see the nubs of its vertebrae, the white skin streaked blackly with grime.

"Jason," she said again, and reached out to touch the figure's shoulder. It was freezing cold.

Unbalanced by her touch, the figure rocked backwards. It tumbled over like a turtle on to its back, still in a crouching position, its hands crossed in front of its belly, its knees drawn up.

When she saw what had been done to Jason's face, Tess screamed. She screamed and screamed, the sound echoing off the walls. Forever afterwards she would see the image in her mind. She would see black dirt spilling from the gaping cavern of Jason's mouth and tumbling from his empty eye sockets like thick dark tears.

# SIMON KURT UNSWORTH

## The Lemon in the Pool

SIMON KURT UNSWORTH WRITES when he's not working, spending time with his family, cooking, walking the dogs, watching suspect movies, eating pizza or lazing about.

His stories have appeared in the Ash-Tree Press anthologies *At Ease with the Dead*, *Exotic Gothic 3* and *Shades of Darkness*, as well as in *Lovecraft Unbound*, *Gaslight Grotesque*, *The Sixth Black Book of Horror*, *Never Again* and *Black Static* magazine. His story "The Church on the Island" was nominated for a World Fantasy Award, and was reprinted in *The Mammoth Book of Best New Horror Volume Nineteen* and *The Mammoth Book of the Best of Best New Horror*.

His first collection, *Lost Places*, was published by Ash-Tree in 2010, and his collections *Quiet Houses* and *Strange Gateways* are due from Dark Continents and PS Publishing, respectively.

"In the summer of 2009, I went on holiday with my family – the extended version. As well as my wife and son, Wendy and Ben, there were my parents, my sister and her husband, and my mother-in-law all sharing a villa in Moreira, Spain.

"One of the delights of the holiday was having a private pool, and seeing Ben enjoy himself in the water, where over the course of seven days he learned to swim. Perhaps even more fun was seeing his joy when things started to appear in the pool on a daily basis – a tomato, a lemon, two courgettes, three green chillies.

"I have no idea where they came from, but I suspect that children in a neighbouring villa were playing a joke on us and Ben loved it. It got to be one of the most exciting things about the holiday, waiting to see what would appear that day. After the appearance of the courgettes, my sister said, 'This'll find its way into one of Simon's stories,' and everyone laughed and someone (I think my mum) said, 'Even he couldn't write a story about this.'

"Mum, if it was you that said that, this story is entirely your fault."

O N THE THIRD AFTERNOON, it was a lemon.
        The first day, it had been a tomato, half-battered and sunk to the bottom of the pool, and on the second a courgette which floated and bobbed merrily on the wavelets by the filter intake, and Helen had laughed. The tomato, she first assumed, had been dropped by a bird; it was small and the damage to it could have been caused by the fall but the courgette was flawless, its green skin mottled and undamaged.

Thinking about it then, she reasoned that it must be an odd sort of joke. Oblique and impenetrable unless you were its perpetrator, certainly, and not something that she understood, it was the kind of joke that children carried out, young children like the ones from the villa up the hill. By the time the lemon appeared, also floating like a reflection of the sun at noon, she was sure of it.

Helen's rented villa was built into the side of a hill. Below her, if she peered over the wall at the end of the garden, she could see the roofs of the shops that lined the road around the base of the hill, and to either side were villas inhabited by retired couples. Neither had grandchildren that visited as far as she knew, which only left the villa behind her, up the slope.

Standing by her pool, holding the lemon (still warm from bobbing at the surface of the water in the afternoon's heat), she looked up at it. Her back wall was high, over fifteen feet, and it obscured most of the villa's lower floor, but she could still see the upper storey. No one moved on the balconies or behind the windows, and she could not hear the children playing.

She put the lemon in the kitchen, next to the courgette. It was full and bright, and Helen thought she might cut it into slices for her evening gin and tonic. She hadn't thrown either of them away because it seemed a shame to waste them and, although she didn't find the mysterious appearance of fruit and vegetables particularly funny, she was slightly touched by the effort the children were going to.

Every day for three days now, they must have waited until she went in for her siesta and then thrown things into her pool. Or, if they weren't throwing them, they were sneaking in and placing them in the water. Either way, it showed a strange commitment that she liked. It was, she thought, nice to be the focus of someone's attention again, however gentle and odd that attention might be.

On the fourth day it was green peppers, large and emerald, the type she had thought were overlarge chillies when she first arrived in Spain. She fished them out and turned to the villa up the hill, waving at it even though she could see no one. She hoped she might hear the laughter of hidden children, and intended for her wave to show that she was enjoying the joke, but she received no response. The villa's white walls and glittering windows reflected the afternoon sunlight back at her, sending glints across the pool's surface and catching the splashes on the tiled poolside. Shielding her eyes helped block the brightness; she kept looking at the villa, tracing around its whitewashed walls and shaded verandas with vision that was bleached by the glare, but still she saw no movement. The building remained blank and stolid.

Helen put the peppers with the courgette and lemon, still untouched in her kitchen. She hadn't wanted to slice the fruit in the end, partly because she felt that cutting it up would be in some way rude or dismissive of the joke that the children were taking such care over, and partly because of the way it felt. Mostly because of the way it felt, actually. When she picked up the lemon the previous evening, it hadn't felt very right, not at all. It was still bright, its yellow skin gleaming and slightly waxy, but it was soft and pulpy when she squeezed it and she wondered if its time in the pool had affected it in some way. It felt mushy, somehow. Rotten inside. In the end, she found another lemon and used that, having a couple of drinks on her veranda and enjoying the cooling day's end as the pool chuckled to itself in the slight breeze.

On the fifth day, the joke started to wear a little thin. Helen came out after her afternoon rest (*Siesta*, she told herself, *it's a siesta and everyone does it*) to find that the pool was covered with a floating scum of redcurrants, a myriad little spheres dancing in the splintering gleam of the sun. Like the courgette, lemon and peppers, the redcurrants were undamaged and looked juicily ripe, but there were so *many* of them. They covered most of the surface, a slick that tinged the pool a deep and lustrous pink as the light glittered off them and down into the water.

It took Helen almost half an hour to clear them all, scooping them out with the net she usually used to clear dead insects and leaves from the surface of the water before they were drawn into the filter. By the time she finished, she had filled a large metal bucket with the fruit and it was almost too heavy to lift, so that she had to tug it to make it move and then drag it tilted onto its lower rim, shrieking and leaving a white track behind it. Hauling it across to the kitchen so that she could put the fruit into bags, she looked once more at the villa up the hill, hoping that the children would see her, see that her face no longer showed amusement. Apart from anything, it was a waste of fruit because she couldn't possibly eat all these redcurrants, and she had left her jam-making days behind her when she left the grey drear of England and moved to Moreira.

Day six, and the joke collapsed in on itself completely.

Emerging from the cool shade of the villa when the sun had moved around far enough to lose some of its glaring power, Helen found two large fruit floating in the pool. They were the size of melons, but it was impossible to tell what they actually were; they were disintegrating and rotten. Strings of yellowing, slimy flesh trailed from the fruit, whose dark skin was mottled green and brown. The water around the two floating things was hazy and opaque, coloured like stale urine with the fruits' juices. Even as Helen watched, tendrils of pulpy flesh drifted from two globes, along with things that looked like seeds, performing somnambulant spirals as they sank to the pool's bottom. Once there, they joined more of the yellowing tendrils, like shed snake-skin, all of them drifting in currents that made them dip and rise in a low harmony. It looked like they were dancing.

Helen tried to fish the large pieces of fruit out with the net but they broke apart as she pulled them to the side, the green skin flapping like a torn flag and the insides escaping and floating back towards the centre of the pool, spreading in the eddies created by the net's movement and the breeze that tickled at the water's surface.

"Shit," muttered Helen. There was no way that she could get it all out with the net; it was dissolving as she watched, breaking into tiny fibrous pieces and giving the surrounding water a pale yellow corona as though it were haloed by corruption. It smelled too, a sharp, scraping odour that itched in her nose. The whole of the pool was fouled with it, and she needed to run a full back-wash filter cycle before she could use it again.

As Helen went to the pool controls, she looked up at the hill-side villa and glared, wondering if the children could see her and tell how angry she was. She only ever had to run a full filter cycle once every few weeks normally; apart from bugs and a floating layer of sun cream, the pool stayed generally clean and she could freshen it by hand and with a little water turbulence from the jets once a day. Between the net and the pool's own filter, she had little to do to maintain the water and could, instead, just enjoy it. She had only run the full cycle 6 days ago, and now she had to do it again, and it annoyed her. It wasn't funny.

As the jets circulated the water in the pool, pushing the debris towards the filters, Helen fished out the larger pieces as best she could. Most of it had sunk and she had to reach deep with the net to catch it, and it was hard work; the water was heavy against the mesh, pushing the pieces into a swirling dance around the pole and making her arms ache as she dug and chased. She couldn't reach the middle of the pool very easily from the side, but she didn't want to get into the water. It might have made things easier, but the smell of the fruit hovered, viscous and unpleasant, and if that was how it smelled, it would surely feel worse. She didn't like the idea that, unseen, tiny particles of it would be brushing against her, clammy against her skin, worming their way below her costume, tangling themselves in her pubic hair, getting inside her, into her mouth, her throat, her nose. Her stomach. No, whatever this rotten fruit was, she wanted as little contact with it as possible.

The last thing Helen had to do was clean the filters themselves; she had removed all of the larger pieces from the water and had regulated the level of chlorine, testing and adding until the water was back to something approaching normal and safe. In the hours that it had taken her, the water in the pool had been cycled through the filtration system, which meant she now had to remove and clean the meshes themselves. It was never a particularly pleasant job, cleaning away the broken bodies of insects and scraping off the scum of dirt and grease that collected across the fine nylon netting but today it was awful. The filters were clogged with torn and pulpy flesh and with a thick, clinging slime that stank. Seeds clustered in the slime, nestling against dead insects whose bodies looked wrong somehow, half-formed and dissolving as though the slime was corrosive. Helen didn't want to touch it.

She found a pair of old rubber gloves in the kitchen, and a wooden spoon that she no longer used, and began to scrape the filters clean. Each time she dragged the spoon through the muck, she uncovered new things, little treasures given up like dinosaur bones from tar pits. A large grasshopper, its wings almost gone and its face weirdly distorted; a clump of leaves, soaked down to a dark blob like melting toffee; a single cranberry, ripe and apparently unmarked but softer than it should have been, shifting between her fingers like jelly as Helen squeezed it; a larger piece of fruit that smelled like fermenting star fruit. She put it all into the bucket along with the pieces she had managed to strain from the pool, where it settled in viscid puddles. The smell from the bucket as it baked in the heat was overpowering, like ammonia or bleach.

By the time Helen finished, the bucket was full and heavy and getting it to the villa was difficult. She didn't want to slop its contents on her as she walked, so she ended up dragging it, stretched out, her back aching and her muscles singing in protest. This wasn't what she had thought she'd be doing when she retired, she reflected, looking again at the villa up the hill. All those years of drudgery in the office, all the meetings and reports and filing, all the late nights in the office completing the work for bosses, and the lonely nights at home, all the insincere greetings and hollow works' parties, they were the bedrock on which her villa was built. Somewhere hot and private, where she could rest, read and never, ever be at anyone else's beck and call again, that was the plan. Not this.

"Shit," she muttered again, and carried on dragging the bucket towards the bin.

The next day, it was meat.

One of the pieces looked like a haunch; the other was a ragged mess of redly-gleaming flesh and white bone that she couldn't identify. Furious, she swung at them with her net, watching in dismay as both chunks broke into smaller pieces even as she drew them from the pool, watching as the water tinged pink around them and knowing that she would have to run a full filter cycle again. Like the fruit, the meat smelled, a corrupted, sour scent of bile and decay, and as it dried in the heat its surface mottled to a patched and bruised grey. It had looked fresh in the water, certainly, but the way the flesh sloughed off the bone as it lay in her net convinced Helen that it was old, kitchen waste or something scavenged from the bins behind the supermarket.

Using the net to keep the meat away from her, she went to the gate, intending to go to the villa up the hill and complain, but she stopped before going out onto the road. She had no proof, only suspicions, and besides, even if she was right, the likelihood was she would be dismissed as a foolish, raving woman, going senile in the heat. *Meat?* they would say. *Our children? No, not our children. You must be mistaken.*

As the filter cycle ran, Helen sat in the shade drinking juice and wondering about her options. The sound of the pumps was calming, like hearing the distant hum of bees. She could go to the villa in person, she thought. Not carrying a net of meat and not in her swimming costume, definitely, but still go, explain politely and rationally that it had been amusing at first but that it wasn't amusing now, that it was a waste of her time having to keep cleaning her pool. The problem was, she knew, she had no proof. She had never seen the children throw anything, never seen them looking at her over their wall or heard them laughing. *And besides*, she thought, *how likely is it that this is the work of young children? The fruit, maybe, but meat?* No. It didn't seem likely.

Then what? Tell the police? Again, no. Moreira was a tourist town, so she wouldn't be dismissed entirely because they relied on tourism and had to make sure they listened when tourists complained, but they wouldn't take her seriously. It wasn't exactly a major crime. "Excuse me, officer," said Helen quietly to herself, "someone appears to have thrown a courgette into my pool, and then a lemon, and then redcurrants and then some meat. No, I don't want it stopped, I just wondered if you could find out who it was and ask them for an onion and rice and some pastry as well. I was hoping to make a risotto and then a fruit pie to follow." She sighed and sipped her drink. It was so stupid.

The filters were clogged with meat, greying and semi-liquid, and Helen wore the gloves again to clean them. There were more pieces of fruit in the mesh as well, tiny fragments of something that looked like it might once have been orange segments and more of the yellowing slimy residue that wrapped itself around her gloved fingers and stank like raw shit. At the bottom edge of one of the filter screens she tugged loose a long, thin piece of meat. It stretched out before snapping free and she had the impression that it was covered in tiny suckers like an octopus' tentacle. It curled around itself in the palm of her hand, disintegrating as she tried to unwrap it so that she could look more closely and releasing an oily, bitter smell. Finally she dropped it in the bucket with the other pieces of flesh and slime; whoever it was was dropping pieces of octopus in her pool now. Fine. Brilliant. Fucking *wonderful*. And Helen, kneeling by her pool in the day's dying sun began, very quietly and calmly, to weep.

The next day, Helen didn't go inside for her usual siesta. Instead, she set herself up at a table in the shade, where she could read and keep an eye on the pool. She brought a huge jug of juice, clinking with ice cubes, several magazines and a book she had been intending to start for a while. Let them, whoever *them* was, try to throw things into her pool now. Perhaps, if she did this for several days and stopped them having their fun, they would grow bored. Helen no longer thought it was the children in the villa; the addition of meat had made it feel nastier, one of the pranks of youth rather than childhood. Expats were, she knew, not always popular and she was particularly vulnerable. Older, female and on her own, she must have seemed like a perfect target.

"Well, fuck you," she said loudly, pouring herself her first glass of juice, using the language she would never have used back home but which she had secretly always loved. "Fuck you all."

Even though she sat and read through the hottest part of the day, the sweat gathering in a thin slather across her skin despite the shade, Helen saw nothing. Several times, she rose and walked to the edge of the pool, peering into its blue waters in case she had missed something falling or being thrown in, but the water remained clear and clean. She managed to read her magazines, but the book proved too dense for her to cope with when she came up against the impenetrable wall of unbroken black text and heat and sun and her mind moving far more slowly than she would have liked it to. Instead, she finished the juice, the ice cubes long since melted into nothing, and was almost dozing when she heard the noise.

It was like a bath emptying, she thought as she jerked her head up from the table. Or, more accurately, it was like the sound air made as it broke the surface as water emptied away, a sort of deep, bass rumble that seemed to have no end and no real beginning. She went to the poolside, not sure what to expect, and found that the surface was choppy and broken. Fat bubbles rose from under the water, emerging in gross mushroom domes that burst and splashed. Watching the agitation, Helen smelled something sulphurous and dank and corpulent that bloomed with every new bubbleburst and then faded as the water calmed, dissipating like the scent of a match after it had been extinguished, until nothing of it remained but a sour memory and the itch of it in her nose.

When the water finally settled, Helen checked the pool carefully. She thought at first that it was empty but then saw, floating near the bottom of the deeper end, something small and black.

"Another piece of fruit?" she asked herself aloud, and then the black thing shifted sluggishly. Helen watched as it unfurled, stretching out until it was a few inches long. It jerked and then moved through the water before slowing and stopping, finally drifting to the bottom like a half-furled parachute. She picked up the net and trawled for it but couldn't reach; the bottom of the net passed over the top of the thing, making it drift towards the centre of the pool in lazy, curling arcs. She tried to use the net to create updrafts in the water to bring the thing within grabbing distance but it remained stubbornly low and out of reach. Not liking the way it hung there like a tiny black shadow intruding into her clean, clear pool, Helen took her sarong off and slipped into the water.

Diving down, Helen remembered with something almost like surprise how much she enjoyed being in the water, and why she had been so insistent about finding a villa with a pool for her retirement. These last days had taken away the joy of it, replacing it with dull irritation and a tension in her chest whenever she thought about the pool, and it was nice to rediscover pleasure once more in the water's cooling embrace.

She swam around the pool's floor until her breath gave out, looking for the thing and not finding it but not really minding. Surfacing, she released the stale air from her lungs and drew in a fresh breath. It was sweet and warm, and she liked the taste of it in her mouth. Turning onto her back, she floated for a while without moving, feeling the light against her face and her closed eyes and enjoying its warmth. This was why she had come here; the lightness of the air and the caressing weight of the heat, the way her skin seemed to open when the sun hit it and the smell of olives and oranges and the sea, all of it making a world as delicate and far removed from her lumpen, leaden old home as could be. There were no commuter journeys here, no weekends trapped inside by rain and boredom, no layers of clothing to deal with unexpected rain or cold snaps, no dismissive bosses or condescending work colleagues, no pitying looks in shops when she bought only enough food for one, no endless days of drudgery and repetition, only lightness and exhilaration and enjoyment.

And no one was going to spoil it for her.

Turning, she dived again, this time making a more precise search for the small, dark thing. She found it in the corner of the pool, not quite sunk to the bottom. Without her goggles on she couldn't see it clearly, grabbing it and rising to the surface rather than trying to work out what it was whilst underwater. It felt warm and soft, rubbery and smooth. An olive, she wondered? A ball of some sort? Emerging and making her way to the side, she shook water from her eyes and looked at the thing in her hand.

It might have been an octopus or a squid, it was hard to be sure. It had tentacles, to be sure, seven of them and a ragged stump where an eighth might have been and two smaller, almost vestigial nubbins above them. Above these limbs was a bulbous body, looking and feeling like a ripe and boneless fruit in her hand. It was only two inches long and out of the water it was an iridescent black, sparkling with colours that prickled over its surface and faded as she watched.

Even as she held it, it deflated somehow, its little bulb body collapsing in on itself. Black liquid like coagulated ink spattered out from between the tentacles and slicked across her fingers. It was warm and sticky and smelled of fish that had been left to rot in the heat and light and closeness.

Helen gagged, spat, gagged again and then dropped the thing onto the side of the pool, far enough away so that it wouldn't drip back into the water; she had no desire to clean the pool for a third time. She moved away from it before climbing out, not wanting to be near it, still feeling the bitter swirl of bile in her throat and stomach and unsure whether she was going to vomit or not. The smell of it still clung to her, the tepid clamminess of the liquid on her hand making her want to scream or cry again. She was so angry, and terribly sad at the same time. Whoever was doing this, and however they were doing it, this was *horrible*. The octopus thing, some local fish she assumed, had done nothing wrong except be unable to survive outside of saltwater and had been sacrificed for the sake of what she now thought of as a campaign of harassment. Well, no more.

She washed her hands in the outside shower, went inside and got as far as picking up the phone to call the police before stopping. What, really, could she say to them? Really? The only time she had called them previously, when someone had tried to force a window one afternoon as she slept, had not been a good experience. The young policeman had listened to her concerns and looked at the scratched window lock and asked bored-sounding questions, but seemed more interested in letting his eyes crawl up and down her chest, making her wish she had put on something more covering than a sarong and swimsuit before he had arrived. He had told her, in halting English, that he would file a report and that she should not worry, and left and she never heard from him again.

How would they treat her if she tried to report this, she wondered. Not well, she thought. They would, she imagined, see her as a silly old woman, come here to escape the casual cruelties of life and to die in peace but unable to stop seeing ghosts in the shadows of every corner. She was too easy to dismiss, neither rich enough nor well known enough to demand attention, another incomer who didn't speak the language and who didn't belong. She replaced the phone in the cradle without dialling. This was supposed to be her safe place, and she did not want to open herself to ridicule within its walls. She went to clean the mess of the dead thing up.

The next day, she had a new idea. At the time she normally went back into the villa to escape the harshest of the afternoon sunlight, she instead slathered herself with the strongest sun cream she possessed and lowered herself into the pool. If whoever it was threw or dropped something in the pool today, fruit or beast, she would know. She would see it. *See if they dare*, she thought, and out loud said, "See if you dare, you little bastards."

Helen floated. She could swim well, but she enjoyed more letting the water support her, take her where it wanted to go. It was as though a huge hand was holding from below, cupping her buttocks and back and shoulders with the gentlest touch she had experienced in a long and not always easy life. In the water she wasn't old or young, she was neither spinster nor maid, she wasn't retired or working, she wasn't a collection of aches and pains, she wasn't even female, she was just *Helen*. Helen, who had learned to like her own company but sometimes would have liked to share it, Helen who could cook but rarely did, Helen who read books and wanted to write one but knew she never would. Just Helen, whole and complete and real.

There was something in the water with her.

It was something about the way the water moved, the way it rose and dropped again in a gentle swell, scooping her and then letting her down, that gave it away. Something large had passed below her; impossible, but it had happened.

She rolled onto her front, more surprised than anything else, and dipped her face into the water. Her vision blurred, her eyes wanting to shut, treading water and seeing little but the fizzing blue of the water pressed against her pupils. She held it as long as possible, turning around and peering as best she could all around the pool. Nothing.

Only, the pool looked deeper, *felt* deeper than it should be, the water chilled suddenly as though she had somehow floated far out into a place where the sun no longer had the strength to reach and reflect back from the tiled floor.

Impossible.

Helen raised her head, convinced that she'd spooked herself but not knowing how, and as she shook her face free from her wet hair, a shadow moved in front of her. It was under the water, large and dark and swift, moving around from her front to her rear. Circling her. Instinctively, she stopped swimming; there was something predatory and cold about the shape that made her imagine teeth and black eyes and mouths that stretched wide and gaping. As slowly as she could, Helen turned, letting the currents take her towards the poolside.

It wasn't there.

Or rather, it was, but it wasn't where it should be. The pool was only forty feet long and about twenty wide, but now the side looked as though it were a hundred yards or more away.

The water was chilling further, darkening down to a slate grey and beyond, to the roiling near-black of storm clouds in leaden skies. The surface of the water was choppier now, wavelets breaking over her face and sending questing fingers into her nose and mouth, making her choke and cough.

She could not see the shadow now, the water opaque and dark, but the moving thing was still there. Helen could sense it, feel the current buffet her as it circled, the play of the water stronger and stronger around her legs and belly as whatever it was drew closer. A haze gathered above the water like a heat flicker but denser, distorting the now-distant lip of the poolside, and she wondered for a brief, fractured moment if she had put too much chlorine in the water before dismissing the thought.

This wasn't a hallucination brought on by too many chemicals, nor too vivid an imagination. This was no longer her pool; it was somewhere she did not recognise, somewhere vast and chill, and then something bumped against her foot.

The bump itself was not hard, but it was rough like sandpaper and it tore at her skin and she screamed and started to swim. All thoughts of motionlessness, of remaining a floating thing and not attracting attention were gone. The water rose and fell, knocking her, as the dark shape passed underneath her, close enough for her to make out scales and eyes like slick black plates and a fin curved like a sickle and then she was swimming with wild, thrashed strokes.

She choked as she swam, water that tasted flat and stagnant filling her mouth and a smell of sour, flat bile burning in her nostrils. She didn't know whether the smell was her own fear or the haze above the water, and didn't care. The only thing that mattered was to reach the side.

It was behind her. She knew it, could feel the water drive her forward as something pushed a bow-wave ahead of itself, the curl of it gathering behind her head and threatening to overwhelm her. She kicked her legs, urging her body on, pulling at the water with hands that felt numb and clumsy, sure she could feel lips kiss at her toes, teeth nip at her ankles. The side was still so far away, shrinking away from her rather than coming closer, the water bucking now, the air leached of colour and metallic-tasting, her hair draggling into her eyes and her body weighted and slow. She choked again, spitting out foul water, and struck out, trying to reach further, pull harder.

Trying to swim faster.

The thing in the water came at her from behind. Something banged into her legs and pushed her up, lifting her out of the water. Helen shrieked, kicking back and feeling her feet strike something rubbery and soft, going into a frenzy as the something clamped heavily around her calves and kicking even harder. Her left foot shifted within a writhing, sucking thing and she shrieked again, still rising from the water as she was pushed from below, water in her mouth and burning her nose. Her other foot scraped against a gelid mass and she kicked as best she could, feeling like her legs were wrapped in a heavy rubber sheet that constricted them and stole their strength. Her toes pushed against something that was warm and pulsed and she pushed, *pushed,* and then she felt it burst and her legs were suddenly enveloped in slimy warmth.

The thing that had hold of her bucked, thrashed her further out of the water and she felt something like pulsing plastic ropes grip at her thighs and then she banged into the side of the pool and was gripping at the smooth tile surface and climbing. The thing gripping her legs pulled and she slammed down into the hard poolside and started to slip back into the water, the ropes around her thighs tightening and the sucking about her legs increasing. She screamed and spat, tensing her arms and pulling and kicking and dragging and then, with a noise like a tooth pulling from a rotten gum, she slithered out of the water, skin scraping against the edge of the wall. She flailed, pulling at the tiled floor and thrashing with her legs so that it could not grab her again and she heaved, heaved with everything she had, and she was out.

Helen collapsed on the floor, gasping and weeping. Sunlight played across her face, warming her skin. She opened her eyes into a bright sky, wincing as the light lanced into them. She squinted and rolled over, rising to her hands and knees and looking out across the pool. It was twenty feet wide, and forty long, the water clear and blue and its surface, apart from the rapidly settling evidence of her own exit from it, was smooth and unbroken. There was nothing in its depths.

Nothing? No. There was a shadow at its centre, a darker smear that dwindled as she watched, shrinking in upon itself until nothing remained except the tiniest patch of shade which broke apart into droplets and dispersed. It was like watching ink escaping from a bottle in reverse and she had the sense of something closing. Those droplets, though, were still there in the water even though she could not see them; it wasn't completely closed, was still open the tiniest invisible fraction somewhere in the pool.

Helen spat; the taste of the water was still in her mouth, rich and bitter and foetid. Was she going mad? Unexplained tastes were a symptom of brain tumours, she remembered. Was that it? Was she ill?

No. The stain from the dead thing yesterday was still clear on the poolside; she could see it from where she knelt. Looking down at herself, she saw scratches across her legs, stark against her pale skin. Her thighs were marked with abrasions that curled around in spirals, rising from her knees to just below her crotch. A slick of some darker liquid like grey oil covered her up to her knees and under it, her skin prickled.

She stood, unsteady but determined, and went to the outdoor shower. Turning it as hot as she could bear, she let the water flow over her, filling her mouth and swilling it around, spitting to clear the taste. It did not clear the slime on her legs until she rubbed at it and then it fell away in clumps, slithering down the drain like jelly. Helen cried as she scrubbed at her skin, the sick wash of old adrenaline and spent fear making her shake. When she vomited, thin strings of bile spattering from her mouth and disappearing down the drain with the pallid jelly, she hardly noticed.

Later, Helen brought her old photo albums out to the table and leafed through them. Even though they were mostly colour, they appeared black and white to her, fragments of a life that had died the moment she stepped out from the plane in Alicante, collected her luggage and walked to the hire car office. Who were these people, she wondered. People in office clothes, in jeans, in gardens and on beaches, in winter, in summer, smiling and drinking and walking and posing, all of them forgotten by her and who almost certainly didn't remember her. When were they taken, these endless photos of men and women, smiling and blank and unknown? She didn't know. None of the photographs showed her in the villa; she had no friends here to take her photograph, no one to share this place with.

No one to tell about the pool.

She didn't know what was happening in the water, or why, but she knew that it was real. She had seen it, smelled it. Felt it. She looked down at her photographs again and suddenly wished that she was home, not the home she had tried to make here but the dismal home she had left behind. In one of the photographs, she was smiling at the camera and wearing a heavy woollen hat. Had she still got that hat? She couldn't remember but suspected she had thrown it away, thinking she would never need it because she was moving somewhere hot. She was hit by a terrible sadness, wishing that she still had the hat, that things were different, that they were back to normal and dull and boring and grey and cold. Back to *safe*.

The pool glittered in front of her, blue and calm in the Moreira sun.

# THANA NIVEAU

## The Pier

THANA NIVEAU LIVES IN the Victorian seaside town of Clevedon, where she shares her life with fellow writer John Llewellyn Probert, in a Gothic library filled with arcane books and curiosities.

Her short fiction has appeared in *The Seventh Black Book of Horror* and *The Eighth Black Book of Horror*, *Delicate Toxins* and the charity anthology *Never Again,* as well as the final issue of *Necrotic Tissue*. Her Jack the Ripper *giallo*, "From Hell to Eternity", won first place in the Whitechapel Society's short story contest and appears in an e-book collection of the same name.

"The pier exists," explains the author, "and yes, it is decorated with strange plaques and cryptic memorials, although none are quite as morbid as I've invented.

"It's mostly Clevedon Pier, which is where the story was born. I was reading the plaques one day and a couple of the quirkier ones made me wonder. What if they weren't written by the living to remember the dead at all, but were instead a channel for voices from somewhere else?

"Somerset is the original Wicker Man country, after all. It's a place rich in pagan tradition and many of its strange rituals are lost to time. Or are they?"

THE SEA WAS FLAT and grey, mirroring the leaden sky, yet offering no reflection of the Victorian pier that marched into the water on spindly legs. The charred remains of the central pagoda gave little hint of the pier's former grandeur. Jagged bits of timber lay scattered across the pierhead where frock-coated gentlemen and wasp-waisted ladies once strolled. Alan glanced at the informational sign showing a sepia photograph of the pier in its heyday. It was hard to believe that this was the same place.

Across the channel he could see the mountains of South Wales and to the south, Cornwall. A ferry was said to have once run tourists across to Cardiff, but the docking platform collapsed in a storm and had never been repaired.

A derelict hotel crouched on the rock face beside the pier. Alan could just make out enough faded letters on its façade to supply the rest of the name: The Majestic Hotel. It was one of those ostentatious gothic palaces that would have been decorated with plundered Egyptian artefacts and overseen by an army of servants. Now it was just a hulking ruin held together by scaffolding and protected by razorwire.

"The ticket office is shut," said Claudia, panting as though she'd exerted herself in going to look, "and there's nothing in the gift shop."

"I didn't want postcards," Alan said with a trace of annoyance. "I wanted to go out on the pier."

She gave him a flat look. "I mean there's *nothing* in the gift shop. It's empty. Deserted. Like this eyesore." She gestured dismissively.

"It's not deserted. Look, there are fishermen on the promenade."

"Well, I don't like it. It doesn't look safe."

He rolled his eyes. "It looks perfectly safe. There'd be 'Keep Out' signs if it wasn't."

"But the fire—"

"It's not on fire *now*, is it? Come on, I want to see."

Without waiting for her he walked out onto the pier. The boards were warped but they looked sturdy enough. Not bad at all considering the damage salt and the sea could do. Below him the water was silky smooth but peering down through the slats threatened to make him dizzy.

"It must have been nice once," Claudia said.

"I think it's nice now."

"It's depressing. Like that rotting hotel over there. Probably crawling with rats and God knows what else."

Alan bit his tongue. There was no point in starting the tired old "eye of the beholder" argument. She'd never been able to appreciate the strange beauty of graveyards or abandoned buildings. Junky antique shops made her nervous and she couldn't stand the smell of old books.

He'd spent the past few days suffering in silence. His shrill in-laws had kept him constantly on edge with their paranoid *Daily Mail* rants about immigrants and foreigners. A week was more than anyone should be expected to endure his wife's family and he'd congratulated himself on making it through without killing one or all of them.

"How could they let it fall into disrepair like this?" Claudia continued. She had clearly inherited her parents' need to find someone to blame.

He sighed. "I'm sure *they* didn't do it on purpose."

"Are you going to patronise me all day? Because if so—"

"I'm not patronising you," he said carefully, trying hard to mean it. "You're just so . . . unadventurous." It was the kindest word he could manage.

"But it's old and ugly. Why can't we look at country houses and museums like normal people? Why do we always have to go slumming in places that ought to be condemned?"

"'Always'? Hey, we go to plenty of places you like. And they're always heaving with tourists and families with screaming babies. Isn't it nice to get off the beaten path once in a while? See something with real character?"

"I just don't like this place, Alan. It gives me the creeps."

He was about to tell her she didn't have to stay when he noticed the plaques. All along the promenade were little brass memorials, set into the wood of the decking and the railing.

OUR DEAREST ISABELLA, TAKEN TOO SOON

GRANDPA GEORGE, GONE FISHING

TOO MUCH OF WATER HAST THOU, POOR OPHELIA

"Look at these," he said.

But Claudia had already spotted them and was eyeing them with disapproval.

MY BELOVED JOHN, LOST AT SEA, HOME AT LAST
ANNA, YOU GOT THERE FIRST
HOW DOES IT FEEL NOW, DARLING?
Claudia grimaced. "Is this for real?"

"They're just commemorative plaques."

She advanced several uncertain steps, shaking her head in response to what she read. "There's something not right about them. I mean, look at this: 'You reap what you sow'. What the hell kind of memorial is that?"

Alan chuckled at the one he'd just found. "'If you can read this, you're next'."

"Ugh! That's in such bad taste."

"Not as bad as this one: '''Go on, push her in'."

"Alan, that's not funny."

"Don't blame me. I didn't write it."

"No, but you obviously don't see anything wrong with it."

"As a matter of fact, I don't. It makes a refreshing change from that clichéd 'in the arms of the angels' crap."

"Well, I think it's horrible."

"You think everything is horrible," he muttered. No matter where they went it seemed she was determined to have a lousy time. And to make sure he did too.

DO IT, YOU KNOW YOU WANT TO
The plaques were certainly unusual. Did the town just have a weird sense of humour? He read as he walked, fascinated by the universally morbid tone.

"Alan?" Claudia had stopped a few paces behind him.

"What is it now?"

"Haven't you noticed something?"

"Noticed what?"

"They're all memorials."

"Yeah, so?"

She stared at him as though waiting for him to catch on. He shrugged, oblivious to whatever it was she'd spotted that he hadn't.

"No birthdays or wedding anniversaries. No 'World's Best Mum'. No 'Happy Retirement'. They're all about death."

They'd only come about a quarter of the way down the pier but Alan estimated he'd seen at least a hundred plaques so far.

And she was right. Some were more cryptic than others but they all shared a single theme.

FOR BILLY, WHO LOVED THIS PIER. NOW YOU'LL NEVER LEAVE

"Yeah, I suppose that is a bit strange."

Claudia wrapped her arms around herself, though it wasn't remotely chilly. "I don't like this at all."

"So you keep saying."

"I mean it. It gives me a bad feeling and I don't want to stay here. We're leaving now."

Alan squared up to her like a gunslinger. "No sweetie, *you're* leaving; I'm staying here."

Her eyes flashed as her mouth worked at forming a retort. "Fine," she said at last through clenched teeth. "I'm going back to the hotel. I'm going to order room service and a bottle of their most overpriced wine. I'm sure you won't mind. *Sweetie.*" She smiled icily and then stalked away, her pointy-toed heels clacking on the boards.

"Fine," Alan growled to himself. At least now he could enjoy the pier on his own. As Claudia's retreating figure dwindled and finally disappeared from sight, he felt all the unpleasantness of the past week vanish with her. All that was left was peace. Waves whispered beneath him, a low ambient hiss like voices on a radio station just out of range.

YOU LOST HER

He glanced up nervously, half expecting the voices from within the plaques to manifest themselves behind him. He wasn't surprised they had spooked Claudia, but now even he was finding them unsettling.

A fisherman stood halfway down the promenade, peering over the railing. He'd anchored a hefty fishing rod against the planking and its line disappeared into the water at a sharp angle. He looked up as Alan drew near, his weathered cap shading an equally weathered face.

"Nice day for it," Alan said with a friendly nod towards the fishing gear.

The man simply stared in response, the unwelcoming expression of a local confronted by an odious tourist.

Alan had hoped to engage him, to ask about the plaques, but

his companion's unfriendliness intimidated him. He smiled nervously and cleared his throat before finding his voice again.

"Hey, listen, I'm sorry if I'm disturbing you. I couldn't help but notice the rather odd character of the memorials out here."

Again he was met with cold silence. After a week of his in-laws' strident opinions he wasn't sure how to handle the silent treatment.

For several seconds he felt sure the man would just continue to stare. But at last he broke eye contact and looked Alan up and down before parting his lips with an unpleasant smack. "Odd," the man echoed.

Alan wasn't sure if it was a question or an agreement. He added hopefully, "I wondered if maybe there was some local story behind them?"

The man nodded thoughtfully and a humourless smile made his lips curl slightly. Then he turned his attention back to his fishing line with a grunt. Clearly the interview was over.

Alan's face burned at the wordless rebuke. He backed away and then continued along the pier.

WE WANTED WHAT WAS INSIDE

IT WAS OURS

The plaques seemed to be getting weirder and weirder the further he went. He felt like he should have reached the end of the pier by now but when he looked up he saw he was only little more than halfway along. The pierhead and its charred centre was still some distance yet.

Beneath him the water sloshed gently against the legs of the pier, soothing, hypnotic. He could imagine drifting asleep to the sound. A yawn overtook him and he shook himself. The argument with Claudia must have exhausted the little strength her family hadn't sapped from him. His spurned wife had had the right idea, though: a good meal and some wine was just what he needed too. He'd make it up to her after she'd had a chance to cool off. No doubt the week had been taxing for her as well.

ALAN AND CLAUDIA

His breath caught in his throat and he stood gaping at the little plaque. It was several minutes before he got hold of himself. It was an astonishing coincidence, but just that – coincidence. Their names weren't exactly unique. Still, he felt unable to move on.

He dug his phone out of his back pocket and set it to camera mode. Framing the inscription in the phone's window he pressed the button and saved the image. Then he sent it to Claudia. *You won't believe this*, he texted.

Then he saw the adjacent plaque. SHE DESERVES IT. And beside that: IT WON'T HURT.

A chill raced along his spine and he almost dropped the phone. He was too unnerved to photograph the inscriptions, but he wanted confirmation of what he was seeing. He spied another fisherman near the end of the pier and Alan made his way there, determined to find out what was going on.

"Excuse me," he said brazenly, "but what can you tell me about these plaques?"

This man was even older than the first and looked so frail Alan marvelled that he'd managed to carry all his gear this far out along the pier. He blinked so long at the intrusion Alan wondered if the man was deaf or blind. But then his eyes fixed on Alan and he shrugged. "What's there to tell?" he said at last. "They remember."

This struck Alan as deliberately unhelpful. "They remember? Remember what?"

But he simply nodded as though Alan had answered his own question. Were the old timers just senile?

Spurred by a sense of inexplicable urgency Alan pressed on. "I really want to know about these plaques. I've never seen anything like them before. It's almost like they're alive. Reading my mind. Like someone's talking to me through them." He laughed. "I know that sounds crazy."

Something like fear shone for a moment in the old man's eyes. Then he looked away, out towards the sea. "No one reads those things," he said hoarsely.

"What do you mean? My wife and I were just reading them."

"Your wife?"

"She didn't stay. They upset her so she left."

Alan took the pensive silence for approval of Claudia's decision. But enough was enough. He was losing his patience. Angrily, he seized the man's coat. "Tell me what this is about!"

The man continued to stare out across the waves, his expression unreadable. Finally, he leaned in close and whispered "Those messages aren't for you."

"What are you talking about? Who are they for?"

The man shook his head fiercely. "If you're seeing strange things in those plaques I'd advise you to turn around and go back the way you came."

"But I—"

"Go!" With that he tore free of Alan's grip and turned his back, keeping his eyes fixed on the water.

Alan backed away, staring in bewilderment. It was some local sport, that's all, a game they played on outsiders. The pier clearly wouldn't last another hundred years. Probably not even another ten. Why not decorate it with cryptic messages to confound tourists until it fell to pieces?

"Crazy old geezer," he muttered, turning away. The ruined pagoda beckoned and he made for it in earnest, determined to get there without reading any more of the plaques.

Soon it was only a few yards away but his eyelids felt heavy again and he suppressed another yawn. Baffled by his sudden weariness he scrubbed at his face, producing starbursts behind his eyes. His cheeks felt like sandpaper. Had he forgotten to shave that morning? When he opened his eyes again tombstones slithered in his vision, rising and falling softly in the mud. Each time he blinked it took real effort to open his eyes.

A sharp pain in his hand brought him back to himself and he stared at the splinter embedded in his palm. He was standing on the bottom rung of the railing, his left hand bracing against the top plank. The ashen expanse before him was the sea, his graveyard only waves. Startled, he pulled the splinter out and backed away, bewildered and disoriented. Behind him on the pier the old man was still looking out over the water, his back to Alan. Of the first man there was no sign at all. If Alan had fallen in, no one would have seen.

His back prickled with sweat and he dug out his phone. Claudia hadn't responded to his text so she probably had her phone turned off. When a polite computer voice confirmed that, he rang off. What was there to tell her anyway? That he'd fallen asleep on his feet and nearly done a header off the pier? He sure as hell couldn't tell her the plaques were talking to him.

The time display on the phone surprised him and he double-checked it against his watch. Although the sky had darkened considerably, that couldn't possibly be right. When had he sent that text with the photo? He scrolled through the menu and blinked uncomprehendingly at it. He'd been on the pier for nearly six hours.

YOU BELONG HERE

Alan forced himself towards the middle of the promenade, trying to get as far away from the railing as he could. He was nearly at the end of the pier and he felt a wild sense of victory, as though he'd been swimming against the current to reach a goal. When he finally arrived at the blackened pierhead he was exhausted. His legs ached as though he'd walked miles.

It might have been a bonfire that had gone out. Crooked trestles encircled the remains, bound at intervals by torn yellow tape. The low sun turned the debris into a mass of writhing shadows and for a moment Alan was convinced that the burnt and broken timber was trying to reassemble itself. That would explain the faint clacking sound he heard. But there was no breeze. The strips of tape hung limp as flags. The sea was dead calm.

He peered into the rubble and a flash of pale grey caught his eye. Something *was* moving in there. Birds picking at crumbs? But while he remembered seagulls wheeling in the sky that morning, he hadn't seen or heard any since stepping out onto the pier.

He moved closer, squinting into the darkness. There was the smell of charred wood and the sea, along with something else, something rotten. He could just discern a few small pale shards, jutting like brambles from the ruins. It couldn't possibly be the bed of oysters it resembled, the shells broken open to relinquish the scattering of pearls at his feet. Even as his fingers closed around the tiny misshapen object, Alan knew it wasn't a pearl. He dropped the tooth and staggered back with a cry. His eyes soon found the lumps and hollows of a skull, then another.

The clacking was growing louder. Alan stared hard into the shadows, straining to see in the growing darkness. He fumbled for his phone again and used its display as a torch, bathing the ruins in a sickly greenish glow. Shadows leapt as he passed the light over the debris. Staring faces rose to meet the glow, their mouths stretched far too wide, their eyes glinting with a light of their own. The phone clattered to his feet as he understood at last what he was seeing. The pagoda had never been made of timber at all.

His gaze fell on a series of memorials at the base of the ruins.

I WASN'T READY

CAN YOU FEEL ME?

I'M STILL HERE

The words spun in his head and he stumbled away from the plaques. He felt dizzy, spinning out of control and unable to find solid ground. Wind rushed in his ears and coalesced into a chorus of voices both menacing and alluring. Determined to resist the pull of the ruins, he turned away only to see the pier stretching on impossibly long, far away from the shore. And it was no longer deserted. Hundreds of people lined the promenade, gazing coldly at him.

Behind him the bones crackled like flames while the silent masses watched him. Even if he had the strength to run, he'd never get past them all or survive the distance to the shore. The dizziness passed with the realisation and he sank to his knees on the planks. Shadows bloomed around him like a spreading stain, engulfing him. He didn't want to see what form they were taking behind him.

As he closed his eyes and waited to join the others, he knew the voices had lied. It *did* hurt. He only hoped it wouldn't be forever.

# ROBERT SHEARMAN

## Featherweight

ROBERT SHEARMAN IS AN award-winning writer for stage, television and radio. He was resident playwright at the Northcott Theatre in Exeter, and regular writer for Alan Ayckbourn at the Stephen Joseph Theatre in Scarborough. He is the winner of the Sunday Times Playwriting Award, the Sophie Winter Memorial Trust Award and the Guinness Award for Ingenuity in association with the Royal National Theatre. Many of his plays are collected in *Caustic Comedies*, published by Big Finish Productions.

For BBC Radio he is a regular contributor to the *Afternoon Play* slot, produced by Martin Jarvis, and his series *The Chain Gang* has won two Sony Awards. However, he is probably best known for his work on *Doctor Who*, bringing the Daleks back to the screen in the BAFTA-winning first series of the revival in an episode nominated for a Hugo Award.

Shearman's first collection of short stories, *Tiny Deaths*, was published by Comma Press in 2007. It won the World Fantasy Award for Best Collection, and was also short-listed for the Edge Hill Short Story Prize and nominated for the Frank O'Connor International Short Story Prize. One of the stories from it was selected by the National Library Board of Singapore as part of the annual Read! Singapore campaign.

His second collection, *Love Songs for the Shy and Cynical*, published by Big Finish, won the British Fantasy Award and the Edge Hill Readers' Prize, and was joint winner of the Shirley

Jackson Award. The story that follows also appears in his third collection, *Everyone's Just So So Special*, again published by Big Finish.

"I don't like writing at home much," admits the author. "Home is a place for sleeping and eating and watching afternoon game shows on TV. There are too many distractions. So, years ago, I decided I'd only write first drafts in art galleries.

"And the best of them all is the National Gallery, in London, a pigeon's throw from Nelson's Column. I can walk around there with my notebook, thinking up stories – and if I get bored, there are lots of expensive pictures to look at. Perfect.

"A lot of those paintings, however, have angels in them. They're all over the place, wings raised, halos gleaming – perching on clouds, blowing trumpets, hovering around the Virgin Mary as if they're her strange naked childlike bodyguards. And I began to notice. That, whenever the writing is going well, the angels seemed happy, and would smile at me. And whenever the words weren't coming out right, when I felt sluggish, when I thought I'd rather take off and get myself a beer, they'd start to glare.

"I wrote this story in the National Gallery. Accompanied by a lot of glaring angels. Enjoy."

H E THOUGHT AT FIRST that she was dead. And that was terrible, of course – but what shocked him most was how dispassionate that made him feel. There was no anguish, no horror, he should be crying but clearly no tears were fighting to get out – and instead all there was was this almost sick fascination. He'd never seen a corpse before. His mother had asked if he'd wanted to see his grandfather, all laid out for the funeral, and he was only twelve, and he really really didn't – and his father said that was okay, it was probably best Harry remembered Grandad the way he had been, funny and full of life, better not to spoil the memory – and Harry had quickly agreed, yes, that was the reason – but it wasn't that at all, it was a bloody dead body, and he worried that if he got too close it might wake up and say hello.

And now here there *was* a corpse, and it was less than three feet away, in the passenger seat beside him. And it was his *wife*, for God's sake, someone he knew so well – or, at least, better than anyone else in the world could, he could say that at least. And her head was twisted oddly, he'd never seen her quite at that angle before and she looked like someone he'd never really known at all, he'd never seen her face in a profile where her nose looked quite that enormous. And there was all the blood, of course. He wondered whether the tears were starting to come after all, he could sense a pricking at his eyes, and he thought it'd be such a *relief* if he could feel grief or shock or hysteria or something . . . when she swivelled that neck a little towards him, and out from a mouth thick with that blood came "Hello".

He was so astonished that for a moment he didn't reply, just goggled at her. She frowned.

"There's a funny taste in my mouth," she said.

"The blood," he suggested.

"What's that, darling?"

"There's a lot of blood," he said.

"Oh," she said. "Yes, that would make sense. Oh dear. I don't feel I'm in any pain, though. Are you in any pain?"

"No," he said. "I don't think so. I haven't tried to . . . move much, I . . ." He struggled for words. "I didn't get round to trying, actually. Actually, I thought you were dead."

"And I can't see very well either," she said.

"Oh," he said.

She blinked. Then blinked again. "No, won't go away. It's all very red."

"That'll be the blood," he said. "Again."

"Oh yes," she said. "Of course, the blood." She thought for a moment. "I'd wipe my eyes, but I can't seem to move my arms at all. I have still got arms, haven't I, darling?"

"I think so. I can see the right one, in any case."

"That's good. I do wonder, shouldn't I be a little more scared than this?"

"I was trying to work that out too. Why I wasn't more scared. Especially when I thought you were dead."

"Right . . . ?"

"And I concluded. That it was probably the shock."

"That could be it." She nodded, and that enormous nose nodded too, and so did the twisted neck, there they were, all nodding, it looked grotesque – "Still. All that blood! I must look a sight!"

She did, but he didn't care, Harry was just so relieved she was all right after all, and he didn't want to tell her that her little spate of nodding seemed to have left her head somewhat back to front. She yawned. "Well," she said. "I think I might take a little nap."

He wasn't sure that was a good idea, he thought that he should probably persuade her to stay awake. But she yawned again, and look! – she was perfectly all right, wasn't she, there was no pain, there was a lot of *blood*, yes, but no pain. "Just a little nap," she said. "I'll be with you again in a bit." She frowned. "Could you scratch my back for me, darling? It's itchy."

"I can't move."

"Oh, right. Okay. It's itchy, though. I'm allergic to feathers."

"To what, darling?"

"To feathers," she said. "The feathers are tickling me." And she nodded off.

His first plan had been to take her back to Venice. Venice had been where they'd honeymooned. And he thought that would be so romantic, one year on exactly, to return to Venice for their first anniversary. They could do everything they had before – hold hands in St Mark's Square, hold hands on board the *vaporetti*, toast each other with champagne in one of those restaurants by the Rialto. He was excited by the idea, and he was going to keep it a secret from Esther, surprise her on the day with plane tickets – but he *never* kept secrets from Esther, they told each other everything, it would just have seemed weird.

And thank God he had told her, as it turned out. Because she said that although it was a lovely idea, and yes, it *was* very romantic, she didn't want to go back to Venice at all. Truth to tell, she'd found it a bit smelly, and very crowded, and *very* expensive; they'd done it once, why not see somewhere else? He felt a little hurt at first – hadn't she enjoyed the honeymoon then? She'd never said she hadn't at the time – and she reassured him, she'd *adored* the honeymoon. But not because of Venice, because of him, she'd adore any holiday anywhere, so long as he was part of the package. He liked that. She had a knack for saying the right thing, smoothing everything over.

Indeed, in one year of marriage they'd never yet had an argument.

He sometimes wondered whether this was some kind of a record. He wanted to ask all his other married friends, how often do you argue, do you even argue at all? – just to see whether what he'd got with Esther was something really special. But he never did, he didn't want to rub anyone's noses in how happy he was, and besides, he didn't have the sorts of friends he could be that personal with. He didn't need to, he had Esther. Both he and Esther had developed a way in which they'd avoid confrontation – if a conversation was taking a wrong turning, Esther would usually send it on a detour without any apparent effort.

Yes, he could find her irritating at times, and he was certain then that she must find him irritating too – and they could both give the odd warning growl if either were tired or stressed – but they'd never had anything close to a full-blown row. That was something to be proud of. He called her his little diplomat! He said that she should be employed by the UN, she'd soon sort out all these conflicts they heard about on the news! And she'd laugh, and say that he clearly hadn't seen what she was like in the shop, she could really snap at some of those customers sometimes – she was only perfect around *him*.

And he'd seen evidence of that, hadn't he? For example – on their wedding morning, when he wanted to see her, and all the bridesmaids were telling him not to go into the bedroom, "*Don't*, Harry, she's in a filthy temper!" – but he went in anyway, and there she was in her dress, she was so beautiful, and she just *beamed* at him, and kissed him, and told him that she loved him, oh, how she loved him. She wasn't angry. She wasn't ever going to be angry with him. And that night they'd flown off to Venice, and they'd had a wonderful time.

So, not Venice then. (Maybe some other year. She nodded at that, said, "Maybe.") Where else should they spend their anniversary then? Esther suggested Scotland. Harry didn't much like the sound of that, it didn't sound particularly romantic, especially not compared to Venice. But she managed to persuade him. How about a holiday where they properly *explored* some-where? Just took the car, and *drove* – a different hotel each night, free and easy, and whenever they wanted they could stop off at a little pub, or go for a ramble on the moors, or pop into a stately home? It'd be an adventure. The Watkins family had put their footprints in Italy, she said, and now they could leave them all over the Highlands! That did sound rather fun. He didn't want it to be *too* free and easy, mind you, they might end up with nowhere to stay for the night – but he did a lot of homework, booked them into seven different places in seven different parts of Scotland. The most they'd ever have to drive between them was eighty miles, he was sure they could manage that, and he showed her an itinerary he'd marked out on his atlas. She kissed him and told him how clever he was.

And especially for the holiday he decided to buy a Sat Nav. He'd always rather fancied one, but couldn't justify it before – he knew his drive into work so well he could have done it with his eyes closed. He tried out the gadget, he put in the postcode of his office, and let it direct him there. It wasn't the route he'd have chosen, he was quite certain it was better to avoid the ring road altogether, but he loved that Sat Nav voice, so gentle and yet so authoritative: "You have reached your destination," it'd say, and they'd chosen a funny way of getting there, but yes, they certainly had – and all told to him in a voice good enough to be off the telly. The first day of the holiday he set in the postcode to their first Scottish hotel; he packed the car with the suitcases; Esther sat in beside him on the passenger seat, smiled, and said, "Let's go."

"The Watkinses are going to leave their footprints all over the Highlands!" he announced, and laughed.

"Happy anniversary," said Esther. "I love you."

On the fourth day they stayed at their fourth stately home of the holiday a little too long, maybe; it was in the middle of nowhere, and their next hotel was also in the middle of nowhere, but it was in a completely different middle of nowhere. It was already getting dark, and there weren't many streetlights on those empty roads. Esther got a little drowsy, and said she was going to take a nap. And the Sat Nav man hadn't said anything for a good fifteen minutes, so Harry knew he *must* be going in the right direction, and maybe Esther sleeping was making him a little drowsy too – but suddenly he realised that the smoothness of the road beneath him had gone, this was grass and field and *bushes*, for God's sake, and they were going down, and it was quite steep, and he kept thinking that they had to stop soon surely, he hadn't realised they were so high up in the first place! – and there were now branches whipping past the windows, and actual trees, and the car wasn't slowing down at all, and it only dawned on him then that they might really be in trouble. He had time to say "Esther," because stupidly he thought she might want to be awake to see all this, and then the mass of branches got denser still, and then there was sound, and he hadn't thought there'd been sound before, but suddenly there was an awful lot of it. He was flung forward towards the steering wheel, and then the seatbelt flung him right back where he had come from – and that was when he heard a snap, but he wasn't sure if it came from him, or from Esther, or just from the branches outside. And it was dark, but not yet dark enough that he couldn't see Esther still hadn't woken up, and that there was all that blood.

The front of the car had buckled. The Sat Nav said, "Turn around when possible." Still clinging on to the crushed dashboard. Just the once, then it gave up the ghost.

He couldn't feel his legs. They were trapped under the dashboard. He hoped that was the reason. He tried to open the door, pushed against it hard, and the pain of the attempt nearly made him pass out. The door had been staved in. It was wrecked. He thought about the seatbelt. The pain that reaching it would cause. Later. He'd do that later. Getting out the cell phone from his inside jacket pocket – not even the coat pocket, he'd have to bend his arm and get into the coat first and *then* into the jacket . . . Later, later. Once the pain had stopped. Please, God, then.

Harry wished they'd gone to Venice. He was sure Venice had its own dangers. He supposed tourists were always drowning themselves in gondola-related accidents. But there were no roads to drive off in Venice.

He was woken by the sound of tapping at the window.

It wasn't so much the tapping that startled him. He'd assumed they'd be rescued sooner or later – it was true, they hadn't come off a main road, but someone would drive along it sooner or later, wouldn't they? It was on the *Sat Nav route*, for God's sake.

What startled him was the realisation he'd been asleep in the first place. The last thing he remembered was his misgivings about letting Esther nod off. And some valiant decision he'd made that whatever happened *he* wouldn't nod off, he'd watch over her, stand guard over her – *sit* guard over her, he'd protect her as best he could. As best he could when he himself couldn't move, when he hadn't yet dared worry about what damage might have been done to him. What if he'd broken his legs? (What if he'd broken his spine?) And as soon as these thoughts swam into his head, he batted them out again – or at least buried them beneath the guilt (some valiant effort to protect Esther that had been, falling asleep like that!) and the relief that someone was there and he wouldn't need to feel guilt much longer. Someone was out there, tapping away at the window.

"Hey!" he called out. "Yes, we're in here! Yes, we're all right!" Though he didn't really know about that last bit.

It was now pitch black. He couldn't see Esther at all. He couldn't see whether she was even breathing. "It's all right, darling," he told her. "They've found us. We're safe now." Not thinking about that strange twisted neck she'd had, not about spines.

Another tattoo against the glass – *tap, tap, tap*. And he strained his head in the direction of the window, and it hurt, and he thought he heard something pop. But there was no one to be seen. Just a mass of branches, and the overwhelming night. Clearly the tapping was at the passenger window behind him.

It then occurred to him, in a flash of warm fear, that it was *so* dark that maybe their rescuer couldn't see in. That for all his tapping he might think the car was empty. That he might just give up tapping altogether, and disappear into the blackness. "We're in here!" he called out, louder. "We can't move! Don't go! Don't go!"

He knew immediately that he shouldn't have said don't go, have tempted fate like that. Because that's when the tapping stopped. "No!" he shouted. "Come back!" But there was no more; he heard something that might have been a giggle, and that was it.

Maybe there hadn't been tapping at all. Maybe it was just the branches in the wind.

Maybe he was sleeping through the whole thing.

No, he decided forcefully, and he even said it out loud, "No." There had been a *rhythm* to the tapping; it had been someone trying to get his attention. And he wasn't asleep, he was in too much pain for that. His neck still screamed at him because of the strain of turning to the window. He chose to disregard the giggling.

The window tapper had gone to get help. He'd found the car, and couldn't do anything by himself. And quite right too, this tapper wasn't a doctor, was he? He could now picture who this tapper was, some sort of farmer probably, a Scottish farmer out walking his dog – and good for him, he wasn't trying to be heroic, he was going to call the *experts* in, if he'd tried to pull them out of the car without knowing what he was about he might have done more harm than good. Especially if there *was* something wrong with the spine (forget about the spine). Good for you, farmer, thought Harry, you very sensible Scotsman, you. Before too long there'd be an ambulance, and stretchers, and safety. If Harry closed his eyes now, and blocked out the pain – he could do it, it was just a matter of not *thinking* about it – if he went back to sleep, he wouldn't have to wait so long for them to arrive.

So he closed his eyes, and drifted away. And dreamed about farmers. And why farmers would giggle so shrilly like that.

The next time he opened his eyes there was sunlight. And Esther was awake, and staring straight at him.

He flinched at that. And then winced at his flinching, it sent a tremor of pain right through him. He was glad to see she was alive, of course. And conscious was a bonus. He just hadn't expected the full ugly reality of it.

He could now see her neck properly. And that in its contorted position all the wrinkles had all bunched up tight against each other, thick and wormy; it looked a little as if she were wearing an Elizabethan ruff. And there was blood, so much of it. It had dried now. He supposed that was a good sign, that the flow had been staunched somehow, that it wasn't still pumping out all over the Mini Metro. The dried blood cracked around her mouth and chin as she spoke.

"Good morning," she said.

"Good morning," he replied, and then automatically, ridiculously, "did you sleep well?"

She smirked at this, treated it as a deliberate joke. "Well, I'm sure the hotel would have been nicer."

"Yes," he said. And then, still being ridiculous, "I think we *nearly* got there, though. The Sat Nav said we were about three miles off."

She didn't smirk this time. "I'm hungry," she said.

"We'll get out of this soon," he said.

"All right."

"Are you in pain?" he asked.

"No," she said. "Just the itching. The itching is horrible. You know."

"Yes," he said, although he didn't. "I'm in a fair amount of pain," he added, almost as an afterthought. "I don't think I can move."

"Not much point bothering with that hotel now," said Esther. "I say we move right on to the next, put it down as a bad lot."

He smiled. "Yes, all right."

"And I don't think we'll be doing a stately home today. Not like this. Besides, I think I've had my fill of stately homes. They're just houses, aren't they, with better furniture in? I don't care about any of that. I don't need better furniture, so long as I have you. Our own house, as simple as it might be, does me fine, darling. With you in it, darling."

"Yes," he said. "Darling, you do know we've been in a car crash. Don't you?" (And that you're covered in blood.)

"Of course I do," she said, and she sounded a bit testy. "I'm itchy, aren't I? I'm itching all over. The feathers." And then she smiled at him, a confrontation neatly avoided. Everything smoothed over. "You couldn't scratch my back, could you, darling? Really, the itching is *terrible.*"

"No," he reminded her. "I can't move, can I?"

"Oh yes," she said.

"And I'm in pain."

"You said," she snapped, and she stuck out her bottom lip in something of a sulk. He wished she hadn't, it distorted her face all the more.

"I'm really sorry about all this," he said. "Driving us off the road. Getting us into all this. Ruining the holiday."

"Oh, darling," she said, and the lip was back in, and the sulk was gone. "I'm sure it wasn't your fault."

"I don't know what happened."

"I'm sure the holiday isn't ruined."

Harry laughed. "Well, it's not going too well! The car's a write-off!" He didn't like laughing. He stopped. "I'll get you out of this. I promise." He decided he wouldn't tell Esther about the rescue attempt, just in case it wasn't real, he couldn't entirely be sure what had actually happened back there in the pitch black. But he couldn't keep anything from Esther, it'd have been wrong, it'd have felt wrong. "Help is on its way. I saw a farmer last night. He went to get an ambulance."

If the Scottish farmer *were* real, then he wouldn't ever need to bend his arm to reach his cell phone. The thought of his cell phone suddenly made him sick with fear. His arm would snap. His arm would snap right off.

"A farmer?" she asked.

"A Scottish farmer," he said. "With a dog," he added.

"Oh."

They didn't say anything for a while. He smiled at her, she smiled at him. He felt a little embarrassed doing this after a minute or two – which was absurd, she was his wife, he shouldn't feel awkward around his wife. After a little while her eyes wandered away, began looking through him, behind him, for something which might be more interesting – and he was stung by that, just a little, as if he'd been dismissed somehow. And he was just about to turn his head away from her anyway, no matter how much it hurt, when he saw her suddenly shudder.

"The itch," she said. "Oh God!" And she tried to rub herself against the back of the seat, but she couldn't really do it, she could barely move. The most she could do was spasm a bit. Like a broken puppet trying to jerk itself into life – she looked pathetic, he actually wanted to laugh at the sight of her writhing there, he nearly did, and yet he felt such a pang of sympathy for her, his heart went out to her at that moment like no other. On her face was such childlike despair, *help me*, it said. And then: "Can't you scratch my fucking back?" she screamed. "What fucking use are you?"

He didn't think he'd ever heard her swear before. Not serious swears. Not "fucking". No. No, he hadn't. "Frigging" a few times. That was it. Oh dear. Oh dear.

She breathed heavily, glaring at him. "Sorry," she said at last. But she didn't seem sorry. And then she closed her eyes.

And at last he could turn from her, without guilt, he *hadn't* looked away, he hadn't given up on her, in spite of everything he was still watching over her. And then he saw what Esther had been looking at behind his shoulder all that time.

Oddly enough, it wasn't the wings that caught his attention at first. Because you'd have thought the wings were the strangest thing. But no, it was the face, just the face. So round, so *perfectly* round, no, like a sphere, the head a complete sphere. You could have cut off that head and played football with it. And there was no blemish to the face, it was like this had come straight from the factory, newly minted, and every other face you had ever seen was like a crude copy of it, some cheap hack knock-off. The eyes were bright and large and very very deep, the nose a cute little pug. The cheeks were full and fat and fleshy, all puffed out.

But then Harry's eyes, of course, *were* drawn to the wings. There was only so long he could deny they were there. Large and white and jutting out of the shoulder blades. They gave occasional little flaps, as the perfect child bobbed about idly outside the car window. Creamy pale skin, a shock of bright yellow hair, and a bright yellow halo hovering above it – there was nothing to keep it there, it tilted independently of the head, sometimes at a rather rakish angle – it looked like someone had hammered a dinner tray into the skull with invisible nails. Little toes. Little fingers. Babies' fingers. And (because, yes, Harry did steal a look) there was nothing between the legs at all, the child's genitals had been smoothed out like it was a naked Action Man toy.

The little child smiled amiably at him. Then raised a knuckle. And tapped three times against the glass.

"What are you?" – which Harry knew was a pointless question, it was pretty bloody obvious what it was – and even the cherub rolled his eyes at that, but then smiled back as if to say, just kidding, no offence, no hard feelings.

The child seemed to imitate Harry's expressions, maybe he was sending him up a little – he'd put his head to one side like he did, he'd frown just the same, blink in astonishment, the whole parade. When Harry put his face close to the window it hurt, but he did it anyway – and the child put its head as close as it could too. There was just a sheet of glass between them. They could have puckered up, they could almost have kissed had they wanted! And at one point it seemed to Harry the child *did* pucker up those lips, but no, it was just taking in a breath, like a sigh, a hiss. "Can you understand me? Can you hear what I'm saying?" The child blinked in astonishment again, fluttered its wings a bit. "Can you get help?" And what did he expect, that it'd find a phone box and ring the emergency services, that it'd fly into the nearest police station? "Are you here to watch over us?"

And then the cherub opened its mouth. And it wasn't a sigh, it *was* a hiss. Hot breath stained the glass; Harry recoiled from it. And the teeth were so sharp, and there were so many, how could so many teeth fit into such a small mouth? And hiding such a dainty tongue too, just a little tongue, a *baby's* tongue. The child attacked the window, it gnawed on the glass with its fangs. Desperately, hungrily, the wings now flapping wild. It couldn't break through. It glared, those bright eyes now blazing with fury, and the hissing became seething, and then it was gone – with a screech it had flown away.

There was a scratch left streaked across the pane.

Harry sat back, hard, his heart thumping. It didn't hurt to do so. There *was* pain, but it was something distant now, his body had other things to worry about. And whilst it was still confused, before it could catch up – and before he could change his mind – he was lifting his arm, he was bending it, and *twisting it back on itself* (and it didn't snap, not at all), he was going for his coat, pulling at the zip, pulling it down hard, he was reaching inside the coat, reaching inside the jacket inside the coat, reaching inside the pocket inside the jacket inside the – and he had it, his fingers were brushing it, his fingers were gripping it, the phone, the cell phone.

By the time he pulled it out his body had woken up to what he was trying to do. Oh no, it said, not allowed, and told him off with a flush of hot agony – but he was having none of that, not now. The phone was turned off. Of course it was. He stabbed at the pin number, got it right second time. "Come on, come on," he said. The phone gave a merry little tune as it lit up. He just hoped there was enough battery power.

There was enough battery power. What it didn't have was any network coverage. Not this far out in the Highlands! Not in one of the many middles of nowhere that Scotland seemed to offer. The signal bar was down to zero.

"No, "he insisted, "no." And the body really didn't want him to do this, it was telling him it was a *very* bad idea, but Harry began to wave the phone about, trying to pick up any signal he could. By the time a bar showed, he was raising the phone above his head, and he was crying.

He stabbed at 999. The phone was too far away for him to hear whether there was any response. "Hello!" he shouted. "There's been a car crash! We've crashed the car. Help us! We're in . . . I don't know where we are. We're in Scotland. Scotland! Find us! Help!" And his arm was shaking with the pain, and he couldn't hold on any longer, and he dropped it, it clattered behind his seat to the floor. And at last he allowed himself a scream as he lowered his arm, and that scream felt good.

The scream didn't wake Esther. That was a good thing. At least she was sleeping soundly.

For a few minutes he let himself believe his message had been heard. That he'd held on to a signal for long enough. That the police had taken notice if he had. That they'd be able to track his position from the few seconds he'd given them. And then he just cried again, because really, why the hell shouldn't he?

He was interrupted by a voice. "Turn around when possible." His heart thumped again, and then he realised it was the Sat Nav. It was that nice man from the Sat Nav, the one who spoke well enough for telly. The display had lit up, and there was some attempt at finding a road, but they weren't on a road, were they? And the Sat Nav was confused, poor thing, it couldn't work out what on earth was going on. "Turn around when possible," the Sat Nav suggested again.

Harry had to laugh, really. He spoke to the Sat Nav. It made him feel better to speak to someone. "I thought I'd heard the last of you!"

And then the Sat Nav said, "Daddy."

And nothing else. Not for a while.

\*      \*      \*

For the rest of the day he didn't see anything else of the child. He didn't see much else of Esther either; once in a while she seemed to surface from a sleep, and he'd ask her if she were all right. And sometimes she'd glare at him, and sometimes she'd smile kindly, and most often she wouldn't seem to know who he was at all. And he'd doze fitfully. At one point he jerked bolt upright in the night when he thought he heard tapping against the window – "No, go away!" – but he decided this time it really was the wind, because it soon stopped. Yes, the wind. Or the branches. Or a Scottish farmer this time, who can tell? Who can tell?

In the morning he woke to find, once again, Esther was looking straight at him. She was smiling. This was one of her smiling times.

"Good morning!" she said.

"Good morning," he replied. "How are you feeling?"

"I feel hungry," she said.

"I'm sure," he said. "We haven't eaten in ages."

She nodded at that.

Harry said, "The last time would have been at that stately home. You know, we had the cream tea. You gave me one of your scones."

She nodded at that.

Harry said, "I bet you regret that now. Eh? Giving me one of your scones!"

She nodded at that. Grinned.

"The itching's stopped," she declared. "Do you know, there was a time back there that I really thought it might drive me *mad*. Really, utterly loop the loop. But it's stopped now. Everything's okay."

"That's nice," he said. "I'm going to get you out of here, I promise."

"I don't care about that any more," she said. "I'm very comfortable, thanks." She grinned again. He saw how puffed her cheeks were. He supposed her face had been bruised; he supposed there was a lot of dried blood in the mouth, distorting her features like that. "In fact," she said, "I feel as light as a feather."

"You're feeling all right?"

She nodded at that.

"Can you open the door?" he asked. She looked at him stupidly. "The door on your side. Can you open it? I can't open mine."

She shrugged, turned a little to the left, pulled at the handle. The door swung open. The air outside was cold and delicious.

"Can you go and get help?" he asked. She turned back to him, frowned. "I can't move," he said. "I can't get out. Can you get out?"

"Why would I want to do that?" she asked.

He didn't know what to say. She tilted her head to one side, waiting for an answer.

"Because you're hungry," he said.

She considered this. Then tutted. "I'm sure I'll find something in here," she said. "If I put my mind to it." And she reached for the door, reached right outside for it, then slammed it shut. And as she did so, Harry saw how his wife's back bulged. That there was a lump underneath her blouse, and it was moving, it *rippled*. And he saw where some of it had pushed a hole through the blouse, and he saw white, he saw feathers.

"Still a bit of growing to do, but the itching has stopped," she said. "But don't you worry about me, *I'll* be fine." She grinned again, and there were lots of teeth, there were too many teeth, weren't there? And then she yawned, and then she went back to sleep.

She didn't stir, not for hours. Not until the child came back. "Daddy," said the Sat Nav, and it wasn't a child's voice, it was still the cultured man, calm and collected, as if he were about to navigate Harry over a roundabout. And there was the cherub! – all smiles, all teeth, his temper tantrum forgotten, bobbing about the window, even waving at Harry as if greeting an old friend. And, indeed, he'd brought friends with him, a whole party of them! Lots of little cherubs, it was impossible to tell how many, they would keep on bobbing so! – a dozen, maybe two dozen, who knows? And each of them had the same perfect face, the same spherical head, the same halos listing off the same gleaming hair. Tapping at the window for play, beating on the roof, beating at the door – laughing, mostly laughing, they wanted to get in but this was a game, they liked a challenge! *Mostly* laughing, though there was the odd shriek of frustration, the odd hiss, lots more scratches on the glass.

One little cherub did something very bad-tempered with the radio aerial. Another little cherub punched an identical brother in the face in a dispute over the rear-view mirror. They scampered all over the car, but there was no way in. It all reminded Harry of monkeys at a safari park. He'd never taken Esther to a safari park. He never would now. "Daddy Daddy," said the Sat Nav. "Daddy Daddy," it kept on saying, emotionless, even cold – and the little children danced merrily outside.

"Oh, aren't they beautiful!" cooed Esther. She reached for the door. "Shall we let them in?"

"Please," said Harry. "Please. Don't."

"No. All right." And she closed her eyes again. "Just leaves more for me," she said.

For the first few days he was very hungry. Then one day he found he wasn't hungry at all. He doubted that was a good thing.

He understood that the cherubs were hungry too. Most of them had flown away, they'd decided that they weren't going to get into this particular sardine tin – but there were always one or two about, tapping away, ever more forlorn. Once in a while a cherub would turn to Harry, and pull its most innocent face, eyes all wide and Disney-dewed, it'd look so *sad*. It'd beg, it'd rub its naked belly with its baby fingers, and it'd cry. "Daddy," the Sat Nav would say at such moments. But however winning their performance, the cherubs still looked fat and oily, and their puffy cheeks were glowing.

Harry supposed they probably were starving to death. But not before he would.

One day Harry woke up to find Esther was on top of him. "Good morning," she said to him, brightly. It should have been agony she was there, but she was as light as air, as light as a feather.

Her face was so very close to his, it was her hot breath that had roused him. Now unfurled, the wings stretched the breadth of the entire car. Her halo was grazing the roof. The wings twitched a little as she smiled down at him and bared her teeth.

"I love you," she said.

"I know you do."

"I want you to know that."

"I do know it."

"Do you love me too?"

"Yes," he said.

And she brought that head towards his – that now spherical head, he could still recognise Esther in the features, but this was probably Esther as a child, as a darling baby girl – she brought down that head, and he couldn't move from it, she could do whatever she wanted. She opened her mouth. She kissed the tip of his nose.

She sighed. "I'm so sorry, darling," she said.

"I'm sorry too."

"All the things we could have done together," she said. "All the places we could have been. Where would we have gone, darling?"

"I was thinking of Venice," said Harry. "We'd probably have gone back there one day."

"Yes," said Esther doubtfully.

"And we never saw Paris. Paris is lovely. We could have gone up the Eiffel Tower. And that's just Europe. We could have gone to America too."

"I didn't need to go anywhere," Esther told him. "You know that, don't you? I'd have been just as happy at home, so long as you were there with me."

"I know," he said.

"There's so much I wanted to share with you," she said. "My whole life. My whole life. When I was working at the shop, if anything funny happened during the day, I'd store it up to tell you. I'd just think, I can share that now. Share it with my *hubby*. And we've been robbed. We were given one year. Just one year. And I wanted *forever*."

"Safari parks," remembered Harry.

"What?"

"We never did a safari park either."

"I love you," she said.

"I know," he said.

Her eyes watered, they were all wide and Disney-dewed. "I want you to remember me the right way," she said. "Not covered with blood. Not mangled in a car crash. Remember me the way I was. Funny, I hope. Full of life. I don't want you to spoil the memory."

"Yes."

"I want you to move on. Live your life without me. Have the courage to do that."

"Yes. You're going to kill me, aren't you?"

She didn't deny it. "All the things we could have done together. All the children we could have had." And she gestured towards the single cherub now bobbing weakly against the window. "All the children."

"Our children," said Harry.

"Heaven is *filled* with our unborn children," said Esther. "Yours and mine. Yours and mine. Darling. Didn't you know that?" And her wings quivered at the thought.

She bent her head towards him again – but not yet, still not yet, another kiss, that's all, a loving kiss. "It won't be so bad," she said. "I promise. It itches at first, it itches like hell. But it stops. And then you'll be as light as air. As light as feathers."

She folded her wings with a tight snap. "I'm still getting used to that," she smiled. And she climbed off him, and sprawled back in her seat. The neck twisted, the limbs every which way – really, so ungainly. And she went to sleep. She'd taken to sleeping with her eyes open. Harry really wished she wouldn't, it gave him the creeps.

Another set of tappings at the window. Harry looked around in irritation. There was the last cherub. Mewling at him, rubbing his belly. Harry liked to think it was the same cherub that he'd first seen, that it had been loyal to him somehow. But of course, there was really no way to tell. Tapping again, begging. So hungry. "Daddy," said the Sat Nav.

"My son," said Harry.

"Daddy."

"My son."

Harry wound down the window a little way. And immediately the little boy got excited, started scrabbling through the gap with his fingers. "Just a minute," said Harry, and he laughed even – and he gave the handle another turn, and the effort made him wince with the pain, but what was that, he was used to that. "Easy does it," he said to the hungry child. "Easy does it." And he stuck his hand out of the car.

The first instinct of his baby son was not to bite, it was to nuzzle. It rubbed its face against Harry's hand, and it even purred, it was something like a purr. It was a good five seconds at least before it sank its fangs into flesh.

And then Harry had his hand around its throat. The cherub gave a little gulp of surprise. "Daddy?" asked the Sat Nav. It blinked with astonishment, just as it had echoed Harry's own expressions when they'd first met, and Harry thought, I taught him that, *I taught my little boy*. And he squeezed hard. The fat little cheeks bulged even fatter, it looked as if the whole head was now a balloon about to pop. And then he pulled that little child to him as fast as he could – banging his head against the glass, *thump, thump, thump,* and the pain in his arm was appalling, but that was good, he *liked* the pain, he wanted it – *thump* one more time, and there was a crack, something broke, and the Sat Nav said "Daddy," so calm, so matter-of-fact – and then never spoke again.

He wound the window down further. He pulled in his broken baby boy.

He discovered that its entire back was covered with the same feathers that made up the wings. So for the next half-hour he had to pluck it.

The first bite was the hardest. Then it all got a lot easier.

"Darling," he said to Esther, but she wouldn't wake up. "Darling, I've got dinner for you." He hated the way she slept with her eyes open, just staring out sightless like that. And it wasn't her face any more, it was the face of a cherub, of their dead son. "Please, you must eat this," he said, and put a little of the creamy white meat between her lips; it just fell out on to her chin. "Please," he said again, and this time it worked, it stayed in, she didn't wake up, but it stayed in, she was eating, that was the main thing.

He kissed her then, on the lips. And he tasted what would have been. And yes, they would have gone to a safari park, and no, they wouldn't have gone back to Venice, she'd have talked him out of it, but yes, America would have been all right. And yes, they would have had rows, real rows, once in a while, but that would have been okay, the marriage would have survived, it would all have been okay. And yes, children, yes.

When he pulled his lips from hers she'd been given her old

face back. He was so relieved he felt like crying. Then he realised he already was.

The meat had revived him. Raw as it was, it was the best he had ever tasted. He could do anything. Nothing could stop him now.

He forced his legs free from under the dashboard, it hurt a lot. And then he undid his seatbelt, and that hurt too. He climbed his way to Esther's door, he had to climb over Esther, "Sorry, darling," he said, as he accidentally kicked her head. He opened the door. He fell outside. He took in breaths of air.

"I'm not leaving you," he said to Esther. "I can see the life we're going to have together." And yes, her head was on a bit funny, but he could live with that. And she had wings, but he could pluck them. He could pluck them as he had his son's.

He probably had some broken bones, he'd have to find out. So he shouldn't have been able to pick up his wife in his arms. But her wings helped, she was so light.

And it was carrying Esther that he made his way up the embankment, up through the bushes and brambles, up towards the road. And it was easy, it was as if he were floating – he was with the woman he loved, and he always would be, he'd never let her go, and she was so light, she was as light as feathers, she was as light as air.

# JOEL LANE

## Black Country

JOEL LANE LIVES IN Birmingham, England, and works as a journalist. His contributions to the supernatural horror genre includes three collections of short stories, *The Earth Wire*, *The Lost District* and *The Terrible Changes*; a novella, *The Witnesses are Gone*, and a chapbook, *Black Country*. He has also written two mainstream novels, *From Blue to Black* and *The Blue Mask*, and three collections of poetry, *The Edge of the Screen*, *Trouble in the Heartland* and *The Autumn Myth*. Forthcoming projects include a short booklet of crime stories, *Do Not Pass Go*.

Lane has also edited an anthology of subterranean horror stories, *Beneath the Ground*, co-edited (with Steve Bishop) the crime fiction anthology *Birmingham Noir*, and co-edited (with Allyson Bird) an anthology of anti-fascist and anti-racist stories in the weird and speculative fiction genres, *Never Again*.

"'Black Country' is one of a sequence of weird crime stories set in the West Midlands that I've been working on for years," says the author. "A collection of them is forthcoming with the title *Where Furnaces Burn*. 'Black Country' is also a sequel to my earlier story 'The Lost District', which describes another narrator's experience of Clayheath.

"I'd like to thank The Nightingales and Gul Y. Davis, whose words influenced this story. It was originally published as a chapbook by Nightjar Press, with an enigmatic cover illustration by Birmingham photographer Trav28."

And time would prove the weapon
His crime would be to breathe the air
He would stain the sheets of the Black Country
            —*The Nightingales*

C LAYHEATH, THE TOWN I was born in, is no longer on the
  map. We moved to Walsall when I was nine, and I never felt
like going back. I vaguely knew that it had become a district, and
that its boundaries had changed. Then it just ceased to exist as a
distinct place, so that by the early 1990s it had been absorbed
into the Black Country landscape somewhere between Netherton
and Lye. The mixture of redevelopment and dereliction had
gradually erased it. Even local people I knew seemed to disagree
about where it was. Perhaps they weren't local enough.

In the late 1990s, my superintendent at the Acocks Green
station passed on to me some case notes about an outbreak of
juvenile crime in a part of Dudley. Perhaps he thought the
stranger aspects of the case would interest me; I was already
getting a reputation as the Fox Mulder of the West Midlands
police force. A mention of the waste ground near the swimming
baths struck a chord in my memory, and I found a couple of the
streets named in the report in the A–Z map. Another street
wasn't there, however, and it was hard to relate the map to the
place I half-remembered. Perhaps it only sounded like Clayheath
because I wanted it to.

*Something's got into the children* was the best the DS at the
Netherton station could manage by way of an explanation, while
the only adult witness to any of the crimes had offered the
comment "Must be something in the water round here making
them yampy." To which the helpful DS had appended a note:
*This means insane, unpredictable or violent.* I remembered the
word from my childhood – in fact, it had probably been applied
to me on a few occasions. I couldn't remember much about those
days, which was fine by me.

To start with, the local primary school had reported a series of
unexplained injuries to children: facial bruises, a dislocated arm,
a broken finger. The children claimed nothing had happened:
they'd fallen asleep in bed or on the bus, and woken up having

somehow hurt themselves. The school nurse had reported the injuries to the police, who'd made discreet enquiries and learned nothing. The possibility of parental abuse didn't explain the pattern of similar injuries in children from around the area. One eight-year-old girl had offered the confusing comment: "They all hate me, the others, it was all of them. All of them in one." Asked to draw her attacker, she'd gone on drawing one face over another until the image was impossible to make out. She'd been referred for psychiatric assessment.

The local toyshop had been broken into via a back window, too small for a normal adult. The cat burglar had escaped before the police could respond to the automatic alarm, taking a random sample of items: toy soldiers, plastic musical instruments, model aircraft, dinosaurs, monsters. A newsagent had been burgled by the unusual process of making a narrow gap in the felt roof, perhaps over several nights. All that had gone was a shelf of comics. Someone had smashed the front window of a hairdresser's simply in order to spray black paint over a displayed photo of a cute smiling child. The discarded spray-can had the small fingerprints of several individuals, all apparently children.

The name Clayheath didn't appear in the report, but one of the episodes detailed brought back strong images of place for me. Someone had gone into the swimming baths early on a Sunday morning and dropped a litter of new-born kittens into the water. Around the same time, their mother had been garrotted and hung from a fence at the back of the waste ground nearby. She was the pet of a local family, and had been missing for a week. The murdered cat was seen and reported by a teenage couple on the Sunday evening. During the day, children had been playing football on the same patch of waste ground. They hadn't bothered to tell anyone about the cat. An autopsy found four small metal objects in the cat's throat: a car, a boot, an iron and a dog, playing pieces from a Monopoly board.

Finally, the same primary school that had seen an epidemic of injuries to pupils was broken into in the early hours of a Monday morning. All the pieces of children's artwork on the walls had been viciously slashed with a knife. All the mirrors in the school toilets had been smashed. The caretaker, who'd come into the school at seven a.m., claimed to have seen a "scraggy-looking" child of nine or so, moving so fast his face was a blur. "Shaking like he was in a fit, all over, had to keep moving not to collapse. And laughing, or pretending to laugh, like when a kid's trying to upset another kid. There must have been a few of them because the laughing was everywhere." The caretaker had since been dismissed for drinking at work, which cast some doubt over the reliability of his account.

I contacted the Netherton station and offered to help out with the investigation, telling them I knew the school and other local places from my own childhood, and might be able to shed some light on what was happening. They agreed to put me up in a local hotel for a couple of days while I looked around. But the more I thought about going back to Clayheath, the less it appealed to me. It felt like going back to nothing – not in a neutral way, but in a way that might suck me back in and draw the life out of me. The night I was packing up, I asked Elaine whether she thought losing memories could actually change the past. She looked into my eyes and said: "You should charge yourself rent."

Driving to Netherton, I decided to stop off in the area I'd identified as having been part of Clayheath. From the expressway, I could see old factories and terraced streets that reminded me of my childhood. I wondered how much of the past was waiting for me to rediscover it. All I could think of was my own recurring dream of another life in which I was a musician, travelling from one country to another, staying in ancient hotels and meeting beautiful, unattainable women. I found the street where the school was, but it wasn't my school: it was a small, flattened building not unlike a secure unit. The houses had been replaced by tower blocks and prefabs, while the high street had become a shopping mall. The location of the swimming baths eluded me. I ended up in Netherton an hour late, confused and tired.

DS Richards, a thin man who seemed vaguely ill at ease, took me for lunch at the local pub. "No one seems to know what's going on," he said. "It must be a bunch of kids, or maybe a few teenagers who aren't quite the full shilling. You get the feeling they're doing it to make a point. To get attention. Maybe they think it's a joke. We catch them, they'll find out how funny it is."

"The place has really changed since I was a kid," I said. "I'm not even sure it *is* the right place. What happened to the old school?"

"They shut it down twenty years ago, the building's gone now. Not enough children. The old town was just dying off. It was called Clayheath in those days. Local people never seemed to be well, probably toxic waste or something. The population fell. It just became . . . well, what you see. A grid reference."

"It must be difficult living with that sense of a lost community."

"For the older people, yeah. Not the kids, they take it for granted."

I swallowed a mouthful of black coffee. It tasted of nothing. "When I offered to help out, I thought I could find where local kids are hiding. Getting up to things. I was that kind of kid too. But I'm not sure those places still exist."

"Do you want to give us a statement?" Richards asked, then winked. "Only joking, our kid. Don't look like that. You never know, there might be something we've missed. Local team aren't exactly the FBI, you know.

"It's a shitty place to live. I don't blame you for leaving. But don't start feeling sorry for the little fuckers that are doing these things. What's important is stopping them before something worse happens."

The Netherton hotel was quiet and inexpensive, which is what you need for undercover work. A couple of sales reps were talking market access in the bar. Alone in my cell-like room, I pocketed a book of matches (I didn't smoke any more, but the memory of 1970s power cuts stayed with me) and switched on the TV to catch the local news. More firms going out of business, more violence on the streets of Dudley; but nothing about juvenile crime. I switched off the set and at once, as if looking through a window into a darkened room, saw my parents sitting on opposite sides of the living-room table, not speaking. And then the narrow bed where I'd curled up with a pillow over my head, night after night, hoping they wouldn't start. Not knowing what to do when they did. The relief I'd felt when my father got a job that took him away from home most of the week. Then discovering that my parents saved up all their resentments for the weekend. The shouting, the bitter silences, the hours of quiet crying, the times when it became violent. The years of it.

I'd suffered from nightmares and broken sleep, been put on a medication that I'd discovered only quite recently to have been a tricyclic antidepressant known for its side-effects. Yes, I'd got up to stuff. Nothing that would make a play on BBC2, but enough to hide my childhood beyond the view of everyday memory. I'd stolen from shops and other kids, defaced library books and posters, smeared my own shit on the walls of toilet cubicles. In family photos, I used to pull faces and pretend I had a stomach-ache. Throughout junior school and the first year of secondary school, I was a disruptive, friendless, arrogant little sod. My parents knew it, and felt it was their duty to keep telling me. If they ever glimpsed the hopelessness behind it, they didn't let on. Eventually puberty gripped me and I turned quiet.

Despite being effectively on duty, I went down into the bar and had a pint of real ale. The two reps were swapping accounts of their one-night stands. It still sounded like they were talking about market access. I was grateful for their voices, which covered up the silence in my head. Maybe that's why heavy metal is so popular in the Black Country. Either that or it evokes some collective memory of the generations of factory work.

A leaflet pinned to the wall of the bar caught my eye: a blues night at a local pub. The date was tonight. That could be a chance to relax after visiting what had been Clayheath. But I'd better get a move on. I drained my pint and went out into the narrow street, the case notes in a vinyl folder under my arm. Richards had told me the number of the bus from here to the swimming baths. He'd also given me a file of press cuttings that I'd flicked through, noticing a photo of the newsagent who'd been robbed. I recognised him.

Perhaps if there'd been more of the old Clayheath still in place, I would have gone on reliving the past. But there was hardly anything I recognised. The swimming baths, badly in need of renovation. The viaduct and the old railway it carried. The grey canal below street level. The derelict brickworks. These were relics, surviving only because there was no profit in removing them. They had lost the town that gave them a purpose. The expressway that cut through the area brought people to the shopping mall and took them away to whatever jobs they had. The tower blocks and prefabricated housing units didn't look like anyone's permanent homes, though no doubt they were. I tried, and failed, to visualise the district as it had been. No memories of any kind came back to me.

With some difficulty, I found the newsagent where the comics had been stolen. The man behind the counter had grey stubble on his head and jowls. He looked too old to be still working. Was this the same shopkeeper, perhaps even the same corner shop? If so, should I apologise for stealing his Sherbet Fountains three decades ago? This probably wasn't the right time. I looked around: stacked copies of *Auto Trader*; bags of loose tobacco; discounted end-of-line food packages; specialist porn. I bought a copy of the local *Express and Star* and let him see my ID card. "Sorry to hear about the break-in," I said. "Any trouble since?"

He shook his head. "I don't let any kids in here now without an adult. Sometimes I can hear them outside, laughing. Waiting to sneak in when my back's turned. I've seed them hiding between the houses. Watching. Bring back the cane, that's what I say. And in public." His thin hands were trembling above the counter. I gave him my phone number and asked him to get in touch if he had any worries. Somehow I felt I owed him.

As the streets grew dark, I walked back to Netherton. One question troubled me: why had none of the stolen goods come to light? Local parents would surely be watching their children for anything suspicious. You'd expect a black market with a fairly visible audit trail. Children were no good at secrets. The more blurred and indistinct the buildings became, the more they resembled my state of mind.

Back at the hotel, I ordered a plate of sandwiches and settled down with the press clippings. The only story more recent than the case notes was a mother who'd turned in her nine-year-old son. The police had questioned him for several hours, but released him saying he knew nothing about the crimes. His mother wasn't convinced. "He's a liar and a thief," she'd told the local paper. "He'd cheat at solitaire. His father's a villain."

Before going out I phoned Elaine to check that she and our daughter Julia were okay. She said Julia still wasn't eating much. "Do you think she's being bullied in school?" I said that might be part of it, and I'd try to have a chat with her when I got home. "Remind her who you are," Elaine said. I didn't rise to it. After I'd put the phone down, I wondered if my habit of avoiding any kind of conflict in the home was making silence a family member, giving it a place at the table, and if that might be as harmful as arguments. Then I decided what I needed was a drink.

The pub with the blues night was just around the corner. It was an open-mic session. Feeling only half awake, I firkled in my weekend bag until I found the small harmonica that travelled everywhere with me. I'd bought it in Stourbridge a few days after leaving home, back in the early 1970s. Hadn't played in front of an audience for twenty years. I wiped it with a tissue, checked it still worked. The first note took my breath away, literally.

The next couple of hours passed in a bittersweet haze of whisky, acoustic blues and second-hand smoke. Twenty or so people in a small function room with a coal-effect gas fire – predominantly middle-aged men, with a few women and youngsters. Nearly all musicians. I played a couple of Sonny Boy Williamson songs, though my harp skills were painfully inadequate. The highlight was when a young woman with red hair sang "God Bless the Child". At the end, most of us joined in a medley of Leadbelly songs. I felt uneasy singing about racist police officers, but sometimes unease is good for you.

When I left the pub, the cold night air filled my lungs like a cry. I was far more drunk than I'd meant to get. Something was drifting at the back of my mind, impossible to focus on: the image of a hollow face like a dried-out ulcer. I let myself into the hotel and climbed the stairs as quietly as possible. My tiny room seemed to intensify the face of loneliness in my mind. I dropped the harmonica on the bedside table, stripped down to my boxer shorts and climbed under the duvet. But I couldn't get to sleep until I'd curled up on my side, arms crossed over my chest, head thrust deep into the pillows.

I was standing at the edge of the school playground, watching the other kids play some arcane game I didn't understand. No one came near me. Then I heard laughter through the railings, and turned round. A gang of street brats, not wearing any school uniform. Some of them reached out for me. I ran towards them, jumped the railings without effort, landed hard on my knees, got up and ran with them away from the school, down the grey street, into the park. Dead leaves were falling around us like flakes of skin. Their hands brushed my arms and head as we ran, caresses that were nearly blows. The wind tore their laughter to shreds.

At the back of the park was a chain-link fence with gaps we struggled through into the waste ground. Our feet sank in the muddy grass, but we kept running. Fireweed smeared our clothes with its whitish feathery seeds. The children's faces were pale in the moonlight, but their eyes were black hollows. When I slowed down, they dragged me with them. Finally we broke through a line of ragged trees into a valley where a brick embankment supported the railway line. A train was approaching, black against the moth-eaten grey clouds.

Set into the embankment was a tiny house: a railwayman's cottage. The windows were bricked up. But there was a narrow passage to one side, and a dead tree with a branch close to a window where some bricks had been removed. One by one we climbed the tree, helping each other up, and squeezed through into the lightless room. The children were all around me now, their thin bodies pressed together, and they'd stopped laughing.

I rose slowly from the depths of sleep, still curled up on the bed. The sense of being trapped stayed with me for minutes. I could see a faint smear of moonlight on the curtain. My eyes were wet, but my mouth felt so dry it was a struggle to breathe. I pushed myself off the bed and began to dress slowly, in the dark. Then I reached out to the bedside table and felt until my hand gripped the harmonica.

Outside, it was raining softly. There was no traffic in the streets, though I could see lights moving on the expressway in the distance. I let the dream guide me the couple of miles to where Clayheath had been. Old buildings and roadways were clinging to the new ones like flaps of peeled-off skin. It was cold. I was still drunk, and more asleep than awake. Cats or seagulls were crying somewhere in the night. Soon I passed the derelict school, and walked on through the park. The smell of decay almost made me pass out. More than nature was rotting. The chain-link fence had mostly fallen apart, and I staggered over the marshy ground to the line of bare, distorted trees. My ankles were heavy with mud. My own breath was a rusty wheeze in my ears, a bad harmonica solo.

The railwayman's cottage was still there, unchanged. I pulled myself up onto the dead branch. The gap in the bricked-up window was only large enough for a child. But somehow I forced myself through, tearing my shirt. I was alone in the dark room. There was no sound of laughter. I reached for the book of matches, tore one off and struck it. Then lit another as the contents of the den slowly revealed themselves to me. Every inch of space on the rotting shelves and floorboards was covered with stolen things: dog-eared books, flaking comics, model soldiers and aircraft, soft toys, bars of chocolate, Coke cans, sticks of liquorice. All of it carefully, neatly arrayed, to be gloated over and sampled through the long nights. A secret hoard.

The half-moon passed across the window. Soon it would be daylight. I was sobering up. He was here, I knew, but he wouldn't show himself to me. There was only one way to bring him out. I grabbed a handful of comics with shiny covers, crumpled them and used a third match to set fire to them. A bird screamed with laughter out among the trees. I dropped my harmonica into the burning heap of paper. The fire spread up the wall, caught the dry curtain. I forced myself back out the window and fell to the stony ground, jarring my ankle. The window breathed out a gust of black smoke. I leaned against the tree, biting my lip against the pain. Something was moving inside the house, like a squirrel trapped in a nest.

There was a sound of falling bricks. Flame licked the darkness outside the window. Then a thin figure leapt onto the tree branch and fell, curled up on himself. I caught him as he tried to get away. Felt the cold and absence of him in my arms. Looked down into his blurred face as his skin creased like a thumbprint, like an image in a sketchbook rubbed out and redrawn. I was in there somewhere. I held him close as his breath faded, as his face broke apart from the inside, until I was holding something blackened and flaky like a rose of ashes.

# ANGELA SLATTER

## Lavender and Lychgates

ANGELA SLATTER IS THE author of two short story collections, *Sourdough and Other Stories* from Tartarus Press (UK), and the Aurealis Award-winning *The Girl with No Hands & Other Tales* from Ticonderoga Publications (Australia), both published in 2010.

Her short stories have appeared in anthologies such as Jack Dann's *Dreaming Again*, Tartarus Press' *Strange Tales II* and *III*, and Twelfth Planet Press' *2012*, along with journals such as *Lady Churchill's Rosebud Wristlet* and *Shimmer*. Her work has had several "Honourable Mentions" in the Datlow, Link and Grant *Year's Best Fantasy and Horror* series and in Datlow's more recent *Best Horror of the Year* anthologies.

She has been short-listed five times for Australia's *Aurealis Award* in the Best Fantasy Short Story category, and twice in the Best Collection category. She is also a graduate of Clarion South 2009 and the Tin House Summer Writers Workshop 2006.

Forthcoming is another collection of short stories, *Midnight and Moonshine*, a collaboration with friend and writing-partner-in-crime, Lisa L. Hannett, which will be published by Ticonderoga.

"'Lavender and Lychgates' is the second last story in *Sourdough and Other Stories*," recalls Slatter. "I had ideas I wanted to continue to explore – consequences of actions in an earlier story in the collection – and I had a picture in my head of a young girl in a graveyard.

"Many years ago, a friend had told me a garbled tale of lilacs and lychgates, the details of which I cannot remember. I managed to garble it even more, and I couldn't get the words 'lavender and lychgates' out of my head, nor the image of shadows swirling in the apex of a lychgate roof above the heads of people passing out underneath. I also wondered what happens when you hang onto a memory too tightly."

M Y MOTHER'S HAIR CATCHES the last rays of the afternoon sun and burns. My own is darker, like my father's, but in some lights you can see echoes of Emmeline's bright fire buried deep.

She leans over the grave, brushing leaves, dirt and other wind-blown detritus away from the grey granite slab. A rosebush has been trained over the stone cross, and its white blooms are still tightly curled, with just the edges of the petals beginning to unfurl. Thomas Austen has rested here for fifteen years. Today would have been my brother's birthday.

To our right is one wall of the Cathedral, its length interrupted by impressive stained-glass windows that filter light and drop colours onto the worshippers within. My father, Grandma Tildy and my twin brothers, Henry and Jacoby, are among them, listening to the intoning of the mass. I can hear the service and the hymns as a kind of murmur through the thick stones. Emmeline has refused to set foot in there since Thomas's untimely demise. I used to attend, too, but only until I was three or so, when I made plain my preference for my mother's company over one of the hard-cushioned pews. Peregrine gave up arguing about it long ago, so I've been perched on the edge of Micah Bartleby's tomb, weaving a wreath. I braid in lengths of lavender to add colour. I put the finished item beside my mother and tap her on the shoulder to draw her attention.

"Thank you, sweetheart," she says, voice musical. Her face is smooth and her skin pale; only the flame-shaped streak of white at her widow's peak shows that she's older than you might think. Her figure remains trim and she still catches my father's eye. "Don't go too far, Rosie."

She says this every time even though she knows the graveyard is my playground. When I was smaller, Emmeline would not let me wander on my own. She knew – knows – that things waited in the shadows, bright-eyed and hungry-souled. Now I am older she worries less for I'm aware of the dangers. Besides, the dark residents here want only to steal *little* children – they are easier to carry away, sweeter to the taste. She believes I am safe. I drop a kiss on the top of her head, feel how warm the sun has made her hair. She smells of strawberries.

I take my usual route, starting at Hepsibah Ballantyne, ages dead and her weeping angel tilted so far that it looks drunk and about to fall over. Under my carefully laced boots crunch the pieces of quartz making up the paths, so white it looks like a twisted spine. Beneath are miles and miles of catacombs, spreading out far beyond the aboveground boundaries of the graveyard. This city is built upon bones.

The cemetery devours three sides of Lodellan Cathedral, only the front entrance is free, its portico facing as it does the major city square. High stone walls run around the perimeter of the churchyard, various randomly located gates offer ingress and egress. The main entrance is a wooden lychgate, which acts as the threshold to the home of those-who-went-before.

No rolling acres of peaceful grass for our dead, but instead a labyrinth, a riotous mix of flora and stone, life and death. There are trees, mainly yew, some oak, lots of thick bushes and shrubs making this place a hide-and-seek haven. It's quite hard, in parts, to see more than a few feet in front of you. You never know if the path will run out or lead over a patch of ground that looks deceptively firm, but is in fact as soft and friable as a snowdrift. You may find yourself knee-deep in crumbling dirt, your ankles caught in an ancient ribcage or, worse, twenty feet down with no one to haul you back into the air and light.

I am safe from these dangers at least, for I recognise the signs, the way the unreliable earth seems to breathe, just barely.

You might think perhaps that becoming dust would level all citizens, make social competitions null and void, but no. Even here folk vie for status. Inside the Cathedral, in the walls and under the floor, is where our royalty rests – the finest location to wait out the living until the last trumpet sounds. Where my mother sits is the territory of the merchant classes, those able to afford a better kind of headstone and a fully weighted slab to cover the spots where the dearly departed repose.

Further on, the poorer folk have simple graves with tiny white wooden crosses that wind and rain and time will decimate. Occasionally there is nothing more than a large rock to mark that someone lies beneath. In some places sets of small copper bells are hung from overhanging branches – their tinkling plaint seems to sing "remember me, remember me".

Over by the northern wall, in the eastern corner, there are the pits into which the destitute and lost are piled and no one can recognise one body from another. These three excavations are used like fields: two lie fallow while one is planted for a period of two years. Lodellan does not want her dead restless, so over the unused depressions lavender is grown, a sea of purple amongst the varying greens, browns and greys. These plants are meant to cleanse spirits and keep the evil eye at bay, but rumour suggests they are woefully inadequate to the task.

In the western corner are the tombs proper, made from marble rather than granite, these great mausoleums rise over the important (but not royal) dead. Prime ministers and other essential political figures; beloved mistresses sorely missed by rich men; those self-same rich men in neighbouring sepulchres, mouldering beside their ill-contented wives, bones mingling in a way they never had whilst they breathed; *parvenus* whose wealth opened doors that would otherwise have remained firmly shut; and families of fine and old name, whose resting places reflected their status in life.

My father's family has one of the largest and most elaborate of these, but he is banned from resting there – as are we. Even after all the scandal with his first wife and the kerfuffle when he set up sinful house with my mother, Peregrine had his own money. His parents saw no point, therefore, in depriving him of an inheritance and left him their considerable fortunes when they died. What they *did* refuse him was the right to be buried with them. They seemed to think this would upset him most, which caused Peregrine to comment on more than one occasion that it was proof they really had no idea at all.

Once upon a time I liked to play with my dolls in the covered porch that fronts the Austen mausoleum, imagining these grandparents I'd never met. But now I'm older, I don't trouble with dolls anymore, nor do I concern myself with grands who didn't care enough to see me when they lived. I feel myself poised for I know not what; that I stand on a brink. Grandma Tildy tells me this is natural for my age. So I simply wait, impatiently. I walk up the mould-streaked white marble steps and sit, staring into the tangled green of the cemetery.

Across the way a veil of jasmine hangs from a low yew branch, and something else besides. Something shining and shivering in the breeze: a necklace. I leave my spot and move closer to examine it without touching. There's little finesse in its making, the blue stones with which it is set are roughly cut and older than old. The whole thing looks pretty, but raw. I know not to take it. Corpse-wights set traps for the unwary. There are things here the wise do not touch. Should you find something, a toy, a stray gift that seems lost, do not pick it up thinking to return it for chances are its owner is *already* contemplating you from the shadows. There are fetishes, too, made of twigs and flowers, which catch the eye, but nettles folded within will bite. Even the lovely copper bells may be a trick, for many's the time no one will admit to hanging them.

There's a rustle in the boughs above me and I see a face, wrinkled and sallow, with yellowed buck teeth, the brightest green eyes and hair that is, in the very few parts that are not white, as fiery as Emmeline's. The creature seems a "not-quite" – part human, part something else. Troll? My heart stops for a few beats as I stare up at the funny little visage; its gnarled hands hold the leaves back so it may peer at me clearly. Then it tries a smile, a shy strangely lovely expression, which I cannot help but return. I do not think this being is associated with the shiny temptation on the branch below it.

"Rosie! Rosamund!" My mother's shout reaches me. I back away and race through the bone orchard, my feet sure.

Emmeline is standing, stretching her arms up to the sky. In her hand is her sun bonnet, which she wears less than she should, its ribbons fluttering. She smiles to see me. "Afternoon service will be finished soon."

I'm almost there when my foot catches on a tree root I could swear was not in existence a moment before and I fall towards my brother's grave. My hands hit the rough-polished granite and while one stays put, merely jarring the wrist, the right one skids across the surface, catching on the letters of his name. I feel the skin peel from my palm and let out a squeal of shock and pain. A slew of hide and a scarlet stain mar the stone. The ring my mother gave me, silver vines and flowers all entwined, is embedded into the flesh of my finger and I think I feel it grind against bone. I knock my knees against the sharp edge of the slab, too, ensuring impressive bruises in spite of the padding of my petticoats and skirt.

I may be almost an adult, but for all that I wail like a child while Emmeline fusses about with her lacy handkerchief.

"Oh, oh, oh, my girl! Come along home, we'll get those seen too. Your grandma will have something we can put on that." She helps me up and dabs at the seeping blood while I howl. My abused flesh stings and burns as we pass out under the lychgate. Shadows crowd above us in the angles of its ornate roof.

As we hobble away, I remember that I forgot to whisper good wishes to my brother.

My father has streaks of grey at his temples and furrows on his forehead. He says it's because he is given to thinking deeply. Peregrine looks tired and gives me a weary smile as I kiss his cheek and go to my place at the table. The breakfast room is painted a warm lemon and the curtains are pulled back so as to catch all the natural light.

There is a sideboard loaded with food, but no sign of servants. Cook and her girl set out our meals, but neither Emmeline nor Tildy could get used to being waited upon. "No point pretending we're better than we are," they said. I think Peregrine, only child of aged and proper parents, loves the chaos of this household. When he was growing up, he told me once, *everything* had a place, including him. Heaven forbid he should stick a toe out of line. "Your mother," he said, "rescued me from the tyranny of order."

"Bad sleep?" I ask, refilling his cup and pouring tea for myself.

"Emmeline was restless, so neither of us slept well. Or rather, she slept but didn't rest." He stifles a yawn. "She kept kneading the covers and the mattress as if she would change their shape. I suppose I should be grateful it wasn't me."

I, too, feel tired. Last night Tildy painstakingly cleaned the wounds and smeared them with a salve that reeked of lavender, before applying bandages. The three drops of Valerian she put in my milk ensured I slept without pain, but my slumber was fraught with dreams of mud and dirt closing over me, sucking the moisture from my skin and turning me into a cold dry husk. "She's still abed?"

"Preparing the boys," he grins. My parents take turns-about rousting Henry and Jacoby. It's not that they are hard to wake, it's that getting two nine-year-olds washed and dressed in the morning is a challenge. No one parent should have to deal with that every day. My younger brothers are wild but not bad, and Grandma Tildy (a twin herself) says they will calm down in a year or two. It should be noted, however, that she no longer takes the morning shift.

"And you didn't think to take her turn after she's had such an awful night?" I ask primly. My father throws up his hands in defence.

"It just so happens that I *did* offer, and it just so happens that your mother refused, Miss Bossy Boots," he grins and butters a piece of toast, then continues, "And shouldn't *you* be getting ready?"

It's a Monday and that means the pain of four hours at Miss Peach's Academy for Accomplished Young Ladies. When I got too old for governesses, Peregrine insisted I be equipped with an education suitable for a young woman of Lodellan's *Quality*. He said there was no need for me to become the wife of a rich man and even if I chose not to join *society*, I should at least know how to behave. Forewarned and forearmed, if you will.

Grandma agreed with the sentiment in principle, but she said I should have a trade, just in case life took me in a different direction. After all, today's heiress is just as easily tomorrow's guttersnipe – Emmeline's path upward might very well be a slippery slope downward for me. Peregrine replied there was enough time for me to learn a trade after a few years of becoming *accomplished*.

Tildy got that look she sometimes gets and took me to the bakery anyway. It's run now by Kezia and Sissy, the 'prentices she took on when Emmeline stopped baking. My Uncles, George and Artor, married them, so when Grandma finally admitted her hands no longer had the strength for the work, the business stayed in the family. Tildy concedes with gloomy pride that everything seems to be running smoothly without her.

She tried to teach me how to make the fancy bread for which she and her daughter had been famous. Alas, even though I was most willing, I showed very quickly that I had no talent at all. I think Tildy was more disappointed than she let on, but she shrugged it off.

When Emmeline, who'd been apathetic at best about Peregrine's plan, heard about my first attempt at a trade, she was not happy with her mother. My fate at Miss Peach's was sealed.

The door to the breakfast room is flung open and the twins fly in, clean and dressed, but no less frenetic for it. They aim themselves at the platter of bacon, from which I have already taken more rashers than is considered proper for a delicate young lady. Emmeline follows them, dark circles under her eyes, a tired smile on her lips. She stands in front of the sideboard, contemplating the breakfast options with something like confusion. Peregrine, rising, steers her to sit down while I put a mix of munchables onto a plate for her. She gives us a look that says *I'm quite capable of doing this for myself, you know*, but eats what she's been given and asks, "How is your hand, Rosie?"

I display the offending limb: apart from a few pale scars there is no trace of yesterday's injury. Tildy, at a loose end when her baking days ended, started brewing things instead – not beer, although she's a dab hand at wheat beer. She took lessons from an old friend who used to do her best business after the *real* doctors had paid their expensive visits to patients. My grandma takes a particular pride in the things she can now do with herbs and mixtures, ointments and potions.

Emmeline nods. "Your grandmother will be pleased with herself."

With the twins safely delivered to the hands of their schoolmaster (private tutors do not last too long with them), I continue towards Miss Peach's. A few streets away, I can hear the noise from the market at Busynothings Alley, siren-song subtle but strong. Any absence from school will be reported (as I know from bitter experience), so it's hardly worth the trouble. Lateness, however, although frowned upon, isn't generally met with anything more than a tut-tut from the principal's pursed lips.

I hesitate at the corner of Gisborne Street and Whortleberry Lane and contemplate my options.

Today is needlework. Tuesday is charity day, when we all troop down to the kitchen and make meals for the *less fortunate* (but I have a theory that all those dinners end up on Miss Peach's very own table). Wednesday is painting. Thursday is healthy outdoor activities: walking to a park and sitting under trees to protect our complexions. Friday is deportment. The older girls have extra classes to learn beauty and styling techniques, how to manage households and how to best have and raise children. Apparently, accomplished young ladies don't need to know anything else. Trifles such as literature, science, history, maths and geography are taught to me by Peregrine, or I pick them up by my own reading in our impressive library at home.

I think of needlework and how many times I am likely to prick my fingers, how much blood I am likely to spill on the fine sampler fabric. I *am* early, and I also know that while forty-five minutes is counted as "absent", thirty minutes is merely "late". My decision is thus almost made for me.

Whortleberry Lane is where books are born.

There are three tiny printeries, which never seem to lack for business. Two specialist paper-makers inhabit long, thin shops and will create a paper for whatever purpose you require: invitations, thank you cards, sympathy cards, sketch sheets, even the special black-edged paper for the desks of those in mourning. Three bookbinders have premises in the Lane and they will cover your books, fix old and ill ones or make you your very own journals and diaries for writing, stamping your initials on the cover in gold or silver flake. An ink-maker has strange, ill-ventilated little rooms in which it can be hard to breathe. And then there are the bookstores proper where you might find all manner of ordinary and extraordinary tomes.

My favourite of these is run by the pretty Misses Arbuthnot, two sisters who will find you any book you care to ask for, or may suggest something you just might like – should you be in the mood for a suggestion. The place, although very neat, has crooked staircases and leaning bookshelves and the smell of old knowledge embedded in the walls. Some days Tildy asks me to request the Misses Arbuthnot to find her a particular book. Invariably I will bring it home wrapped in brown paper with string tied tightly about to keep the busybodies out. She's a good library in her rooms, does Grandma.

Today, the younger Miss Arbuthnot (the one with the blonde curls) is minding the store. She gives a smile when she sees me slip in, but otherwise goes on with her inventory. The newly arrived books are in small wooden crates, some with the lids already jemmied off, presumably with the small lady-like crowbar lying on the counter. As I go past, I can see some of them have their spines marked with a fine golden "M". The younger Miss A subtly moves her body to obscure my view and the message is clear: *too young for these ones*.

I take the first flight of stairs, then the second, then the third and am puffing, just a little, by the time I reach what should by rights be an attic. There were customers on the lower floors, but this one is empty, the aisles between the shelves all deserted as far as I can see as I scamper up one, down the next to check. This level exists in a kind of clever *déshabillé*, seemingly disorganised unless you know the system. These are the books *about* books. They are arranged in what might be called Birth, Life, Death – the making of, caring for and disposal of books too injured to go on.

This is my favourite place.

Carabhille's *Birth of the Book* waits just where I left it. I hide it away on a lower shelf, out of its ostensible order so no one else might buy it before me. Moneyed family or no, I still have to earn my pocket money and nothing by Carabhille is cheap. It will be another good month before I can make an offer. This one has a tooled leather cover in blood-red, the lettering on its spine and front is silvered. Open it and you find a hand-illuminated manuscript in brilliant colours with gold leaf highlights; no woodcuts, no moveable type. The frontispiece depicts a great tree from which hangs strange fruit: more books, each one tiny and beautifully detailed. The edges of the pages are rough – hand-cut by their first owner, whoever that may have been. The book smells old. It's weighty and I feel as if I'm *holding* knowledge.

"How's your hand?"A voice asks. It's a pleasant enough voice, not quite broken, but I still shout in fright. I turn around and see a tall, handsome-looking lad, dark-haired, pale-skinned, green-eyed.

"What?" Strictly speaking, I know it should be "Pardon?" but he's taken me by surprise.

"Your hand. I saw you leave the churchyard yesterday with your hand all bloody. I wondered if you were all right?"

I'd not seen him, nor anyone else, but then I suppose I was not at my most attentive.

"Oh," I say. "Fine." I show him. He looks impressed and gives a low whistle.

"Someone's clever."

"My grandma."

"Not your mother?"

"No, not yet. Maybe one day she'll ask Tildy to teach her."

"What's she do now, your mama?"

"Paints."

"Houses?"

"Portraits. Pictures of rich people and their unattractive children," I say and poke out my tongue like a brat. My manners, thus far, have not been up to scratch, so why change tack now?

"Naughty," he says. Before I can reply there's a scuttling at his feet. A fox comes out of the shadows of the shelving and weaves about his boots. He seems to think there's nothing unusual about this. It spits out a bark and gives me a long measuring look. I crouch down and offer my hand, hoping it will let me stroke its pretty red fur. It moves toward me as if it will, but then tries to nip my outstretched fingers and runs away, back into the shadows.

"Not very friendly."

"Picky things, foxes."

I look up and find the boy is gone. I wander between the shelves, searching for him but he's nowhere in evidence. I put the Carabhille back in its hiding place and make my way down the stairs, a little shaken. I check each of the floors to see if he made it down before me, but there's no sign. He must still be hiding upstairs, in some spot I don't know – although I cannot imagine where that might be.

Outside the sun is very bright and blinds me for a moment so I don't see who grabs me by the arm and gives me a bit of a shake. When my eyes adjust I find my father, his handsome face dark with an anger he so seldom experiences he doesn't seem to know how to wear it. Luckily I bit back those swear words I'm not supposed to know.

"What do you have to say for yourself?"

"I was just . . . I was only . . . I was late, not absent." In truth, I'm too perplexed to be afraid of Peregrine's temper, and I also know he never can maintain a rage for very long. Sure enough, I'm rewarded by the clearing of his expression the same way a strong wind blows away storm clouds. "And anyway, what are you doing here?"

"Collecting a book for your grandmother about the uses and tasteful arrangement of lilacs." He pulls a face. "How much do you hate that school?"

"It bores me rigid, Papa, you know that." I lean my head against his shoulder. He smells like aftershave and wool. "The instruction is mindless and I fear my brain will atrophy if I'm left there much longer."

He snorts. Peregrine is especially bad at being authoritarian. "Then, my Rose, what *do* you want to do?"

"Well," I say slowly as if I haven't been thinking about it. "I do believe Grandma was right when she said I should learn a trade."

"It won't be baking, my heart."

"Yes, I think we all know that even if it weren't for Mother's objections, I have absolutely no talent in that direction anyway." I sigh unconvincingly. "But what I would like to try, Father dear, is bookbinding."

"Bookbinding?" He looks startled as if this would never have occurred to him in a hundred years – and truly it would not. It's only been in my head for a couple of months.

"I'm sure someone will take me on – if not as a proper 'prentice, then at least someone will teach me, surely?"

"There's a Mistress Kidston who is a bookbinder of great repute – she's in the one at the end of the Lane," he says, considering. "She's repaired books for me before, made my diaries and ledgers. I think she would be appropriate."

I love that my father knows this. He wouldn't have me 'prenticed to some smelly old man. I also love that my father doesn't insist on me becoming a lady too fine to tie my own laces or pour my own milk. I love that he's given up on my young ladies' education as a bad joke.

"This, of course, is on the condition that you promise to attend better to your 'prentice studies than you have thus far to your young ladies' studies. And you will confess to your mother what you've done. And what agreement you've forced me into." He rolls his eyes upward like a saint being martyred.

"Cowardly cat," I scorn, but hug him hard. "We have an accord, sir."

"I suppose there's no point in sending you off to – what is it today?"

"Needlework."

"Oh, messy. Now, come on home. May as well get into trouble sooner rather than later."

In a week, I will start my 'prenticeship. Emmeline met my announcement with an amicable and rather relieved "Thank Heaven". Grandma grumbled but accepted it. Henry and Jacoby looked at me with a new respect, for a while at least. Now it's time to gather all the accoutrements for my new trade.

Peregrine has ordered all the tools from a man Mistress Kidston recommended. Had it been up to my father, each and every instrument would have been hand-made and carved with my initials, but I think he sensed the pain of embarrassment this would cause me. I must admit my excitement as the craftsman listed all the things I would need: the nippers, the *frottoir*, the paring and lifting and skife knives, the polishing irons and the ever-so-elegant spokeshave, but to turn up on my first day like a princess with her own engraved tools was a little too much.

Tildy has taken it upon herself to organise the uniform part of my requirements. Miss Lucy's tiny *modiste*'s is set below street level, but bright in spite of it. The full fronted glass of the shop draws in light, and the artfully-made gas lamps are all alight and cast a golden glow over the white and green rooms.

"I'd prefer overalls, you know," I grumble, flapping at the outfit being pinned on me. It's calico, a practical fabric and hardwearing and perfectly suited to a 'prentice. What's not practical are the skirts, which are almost as voluminous as those of a party dress; the pockets are good, though, and deep.

Lucy Pye, tiny silver spikes held precariously in her mouth and stuck in the silken cushion on her wrist, puffs up at me, mumbling about *little misses*.

"I know," sighs Grandma. "But it's enough you're being allowed to be a 'prentice instead of going to that fancy school, isn't it?"

I grudgingly admit it is.

"Can't expect to dress like a boy too, my Rose. Now go and change. We'll pick these up in two days, Miss Pye."

I go behind the curtains into the cramped dressing room and strip off the frock, careful to avoid the pins. I can hear the whine of the seamstress as she talks at Tildy.

"No point, if you ask me, in your young miss to be 'prenticing. What's she need that for? Got money and a fancy home; no doubt her father'll find her a husband to look after her. Why does she need a trade?"

"That's enough out of you, Lucy Pye, keep your fingers to stitching and your lips from flapping and making a breeze," says Tildy mildly. "My granddaughter won't depend on chance in her life – she's smart enough to know the only person she can rely on to look after her is herself. That makes her smarter than most people I know. I never relied on anyone, nor did *you* so don't go looking down on my Rosamund for not being a lazy brainless girl with nothing in her head but sequins and beads."

"Might have been nice," snipes Lucy, "to have the choice, though. Do you really think I'd have spent all these years sewing if there'd been some useful man around to take care of me?"

"Take care of yourself. Can't ever be sure when a man's going to die or change." I hear the clink of coins on the glass top of the counter. "Be thankful you've only yourself to rely on."

I struggle back into my own frock and do up the buttons on the front of the bodice, cursing every one of them. I tidy my hair and step out. Grandma Tildy stands and nods to a chastened seamstress. "We'll see you Friday, Miss Pye."

We walk out the white door that looks like a wedding cake, then take the steps leading to the street. You can tell it's a good neighbourhood because crevices like this don't smell like cats' pee.

"Honestly, Lucy Pye and her opinions everyone's got to hear!" Tildy clicks her tongue in annoyance. "Now, a few years back there was a seamstress who sewed like an angel, you've never seen such dresses for all that she worked in the Golden Lily. Gentle as a doe and never said a mean word about anyone. She's one I miss."

"What happened to her?"

"Moved away," says Tildy shortly, and I recognise the tone she gets when she realises she's started telling a story she doesn't want to give you the end of. I'm about to start pricking at her to ease out more information when a tall shape appears a few paces ahead of us in the gathering afternoon. I see him only briefly; he gives a sharp-toothed smile and then slides into an alleyway. I think I see a flash of dark red at his heels.

I turn to Tildy, whose hand convulses on my arm. Her face is stricken-white.

"Who is that, Rosie? That boy?"

"I don't know, Grandma. I met him a few days ago at the bookshop."

I can feel her shaking and worry that she will fall. "Come away, Rosamund, we must get home."

"Tildy, are you all right? Do you need to sit down?" There's a tea shop not far down the street.

She shakes her head. "No, love. We just need to get home."

Tildy insists we cross the road even though it takes us out of our way – but it also keeps us away from the mouth of the alley, which is black, toothless. "Rosie, promise me you'll stay away from him if you see him again."

"Why? I barely know him, Grandma." I protest, not about the ban on him, but the idea she seems to have about my connection with the nameless boy.

"Let's just get home, Rosie."

I heard from some of the girls at Miss Peach's how their grandparents went soft in the head, but with my fierce grandmother it seems unlikely. Still she's frail and afraid and I've never seen her like that before. It frightens me.

She spends much of our walk looking back over her shoulder as if we might be followed.

Emmeline has gone to bed early, troubled by a headache.

After dinner, I leave Tildy and Peregrine to talk and take the boys upstairs.

When they are washed, sleepy and in their pyjamas (the ones with the feet in them), I agree to read them a story. They always choose the one about the Robber Bridegroom because, they say, the clever girl wins. So I give them the tale and only when they are drifting off do they let slip a disturbing fact.

"Met your boyfriend today, Rosie-rose," singsongs Henry as I pull the covers up to his chin.

"Boyfriend!" chimes Jacoby, who holds tight around my neck before I tuck him in too.

"I've not got a boyfriend, as you both know." I kiss two warm, shiny foreheads.

"He said he knew you," mumbles Henry. "He was waiting outside the gates of our school and talked to us."

"What'd he look like?" I ask the drowsing children. Jacoby mutters that he is tall and dark-haired, which tells me very little, but makes me cold. There's no further news to be had from the twins, both are asleep and even if I had the heart to wake them I doubt I'd get much more information.

I look in on my mother. Her nightgown has ridden up as she's tossed and turned in distressed sleep, her hair is damp and sweat beads her brow. Beneath her lids, her eyes dart here and there, searching for something. Her hands clutch and clench. I wipe her forehead and cover her with the sheet lest she take a chill.

Peregrine and Tildy are talking still, and I can hear their voices raised. This is unusual in and of itself.

I creep down the stairs, careful to avoid the ones I know will protest my weight.

"I know what I saw, Peregrine. I saw him look at Rosamund and I *saw* him true." Tildy's voice is hard with urgency. "He's a cold lad."

"Oh, Tildy. Don't be ridiculous. I don't believe in any of that nonsense." But Peregrine's tone is more bravado than truth and Grandma hits back at him with undiluted scorn.

"You don't believe! How can you say that? You of all people, when you know what Emmeline did! You know what's *possible.*"

What Emmeline did. Why my mother no longer bakes. Her power and its consequences, her revenge and how awful it was. What Emmeline did.

I don't pay attention to his reply for there is a shifting of the air behind me and my mother walks past me. Her eyes are still closed and she moves toward the other stairs that lead down to the kitchen.

I stick my head in the door of the dining room and beckon my arguing relatives.

They follow and by the time we get to the stone-vaulted basement kitchen Emmeline is a whirl of white nightgown and red and white hair. Her eyes are closed, but she moves with graceful assurance around the room and finds everything she needs. Emmeline begins to make the bread mixture she's not dipped her hands into since before I was born. On my mother's face is an expression which plainly says that she does this against her will. She mouths "no, no, no" but her hands keep mixing, mixing, then she dumps the dough out onto the tabletop and begins to knead it angrily. I am frozen, unsure of what to do; Peregrine and Tildy watch with a kind of fascinated horror that pins them to the spot.

Emmeline makes no recognisable shape. I think her mind resists even in sleep, and whatever has pulled her from her bed has failed. When at last she stands, unmoving, her head low and her tears dripping into the leftover flour on the bench, then I put my arms around her. She doesn't start or cry out. I talk to her in a low voice and Peregrine and Tildy do the same. We walk her out of the kitchen, up the stairs and back into her own bed. We do not wash Emmeline's hands for fear the touch of water might wake her, so we gently try to pick off the remains of any dough, and hope she will not remember this night's venture.

The day is miserable, grey and dull. It has been raining constantly, monstrous great drops of moisture hit the windows with a savage sound and pour down the panes like small violent rivers.

Emmeline retreated to her bed again soon after breakfast. We none of us have spoken about her nightly excursion and she senses something is wrong and it makes her short with us, as if she knows we are not telling her something important. That we are treating her as if she's a child. She pleads weariness and a headache and no one doubts it. Tildy gives her a tincture of Valerian. In return, I do not tell my father what the boys said last night about the slender young man. I do not wish to worry him, although I'm certain Tildy would be happy to crow a victory over that piece of information.

The twins have been bickering since early this morning and by the afternoon it has worn thin. Peregrine has, uncharacteristically, lost his temper and sent them to their room. This caused no end of uncomprehending distress and many tears. My father maintained his rage long enough for the boys to disappear up the stairs, pathetic sobs wafting down behind them as they slowly closed their door as if waiting for the reprieve that did not come.

I give my father a severe look and he has difficulty meeting my eyes. The trouble with being so easy-going is that people start acting as though you've no right to a bad mood. It is unfair but unavoidable.

"Oh, all right!" he huffs and makes his way up the curved staircase, his boots thudding with displeasure on every step. The boys will think themselves in line for a hiding now. I smother a grin, and Tildy stomps out of the front parlour. Her temper is no better than anyone else's in the house at the moment.

"Shouldn't you be doing something?" she demands. Idle hands and all that. I sigh.

I try to look saintly and put-upon. "Saturday, Grandma, and even the worst of the wicked get a day off."

"You little . . ." she trails off so I never hear what she thinks of me. Her eyes dart past my shoulder and out one of the front windows. I turn and follow her gaze.

Through the decoratively etched glass panes on either side of the front door I can see the youth, impervious to rain or so it seems. I fling open the door and make to go out, but Tildy grabs my arm and pulls me back. She charges past me and I can feel her fear like a cold breath coming off her skin. She's terrified but she will protect me no matter what.

"Who are you?" she yells. "What do you want?"

I see his mouth curl up at one corner, part contempt, part fondness, as if he knows her better than she might ever think; as if he won't do her harm because he's terribly, irrationally, mysteriously fond of her.

But then she slips on the soaked stone steps and falls like a sack of potatoes down our long front stairs. The expression on the boy's face is one of distress in the moment when he's still there. I look to my grandmother, flick my eyes back up and he's gone yet again.

The rain is *cold* and hard against my skin as I kneel down beside my grandmother.

"Tildy! Tildy, are you all right?" I'm too scared to move her. Did she hit her head? Did I hear bones crack? Is there blood anywhere? Will she be all right?

At first there is a silence, a lack of response that makes my heart contract to the size of a pin. And then the sound of salvation, the most beautiful noise in the world: Tildy cursing up a blue storm.

Peregrine has heard the commotion. He looks impressed at the range of his mother-in-law's profanity. Indeed, there are things I'd like to write down – one never knows when one will need a decent curse.

"Can you get up, Tildy?" My father speaks to her as if she is better beloved than his own mother – which she is.

"Everything aches and it will be worse tomorrow." She moans, lying still. I try to feel for any broken bones. She tolerates it for a moment, then brushes my hands away. "Enough, child."

"I'll send for the doctor," says my father, and puts his hands under one of Tildy's arms, and gestures for me to do the same.

"Never mind that. I'll go and see my friend – she'll have something will dull the pain better than any of those sawbones will come up with."

"She's on the other side of town."

"A walk will do me good." She's being stubborn. She doesn't want to go out alone, doesn't want to encounter the cold lad again.

"Take her in the carriage, Papa. It won't take you more than an hour. I'll keep an eye on things."

There is no more debate when Tildy gives in and admits that

although nothing's broken, she is not in a state to walk the streets and she will need some kind of treatment to ease her aches.

They climb into the carriage, Peregrine's driver at the reins, just as the afternoon bruises into night.

I ask cook to throw together a light supper. I go upstairs to check on the twins and find them both asleep, curled beneath their beds as if they hid there after Peregrine's tirade. Dark, damp curls are infested with dust-bunnies.

I open the door to my own room and immediately something feels wrong. The carpet underfoot squelches, saturated as if someone dripping wet paused there. On the cream coverlet of my bed I can see paw prints, large but fine, in a mud that may be almost as red as their owner's fur. The prints trek across the wide expanse of the mattress, then show a leap onto the small stool with its covering of cream and gold brocade, then a slight skid across the glossy painted surface of the duchess.

I go through my trinkets, the shiny things in the small cut-crystal bowls, all the bits of jewellery I've been given over the years by my parents and Tildy. The only piece missing is the ring twisted out of true by my fall and still stained by my blood. Given mother to daughter and then again, as I expected to do to my own daughter in turn.

There's the sound of a door opening somewhere in the house. At first I think it my father and grandmother, but realise it's too soon and the tenor was surreptitious, sneaky. I go out to the corridor and peer over the railings into the entry hall.

The front door is wide open.

I thought it too soon for Peregrine and Tildy to return; now I know it is too late.

I take the curved staircase at a dangerous pace, careful not to fall. In the drying shallow puddle on the stoop I can see the outline of two smallish feet as if imprinted there by the moon-light. At the end of our street, seemingly so far away, I see a flash of white and know it for my mother. I slam the door behind me and run into the road, my shoes slapping against the cold wet cobbles. Sometimes I almost slip, slide along, then regain my balance.

Always just in front of me, always just at the end of the next street is the flickering flag, leading me on. I cannot believe she moves so fast.

At last I gain our destination – I should have known it all along. The graveyard is lit in part by the lambent light from the portico of the Cathedral. The Archbishop's wolf-hounds strain as if against leashes; they cannot leave the bounds of their building. Then there are the corpse candles dancing around the graves, I follow the grim path to where more of them helpfully serve to illuminate my mother's grisly task.

Emmeline kneels in the muddy mess of the bone pit. She is scooping up great hunks of mud with her cupped hands, gathering it to her as if it is an injured child she can put back together. When she has enough, when it clumps together like clay – do I see it *move* in the moonlight? Shuddering with breath? – then she begins to mould it as she once fashioned loaves of bread. When she finds a bone, she sets it aside – will she find a use for it later?

The boy watches her, sitting cross-legged on a grave so old that the elements have removed any trace of the name of its occupant. His expression is fond and unhealthy all at the same time. I step as quietly as I can but the quartz is no friend to me this eve. I know these ways, these paths, but then, I suppose, so does he. This is as much his playground as it ever was mine – more.

"Hello, Rosie." He doesn't even bother to look at me as I creep along. I give up all pretence and stand next to him, watching as the captive sleeper sculpts the graveyard mud. I take steps towards her, but he holds up his thin hand – I notice for the first time its port-wine birth mark, a match for the one my father bears. On his finger, loose and worn wispy by age, is my silver ring. "Uh-uh. It's not safe for anyone to wake her but me now. Besides, my mummy's got work to do."

"What's she doing?"

"Building a body. Of course it will be just a shell to start with, but once it's tempered with your blood, sister-dear, it will be a vessel fit for me." He smiles. "And when I settle my soul inside, I will walk out under the lychgate, Rosamund, and I will have everything you stole."

"I didn't steal anything from you." I want to turn and run, but I will not leave Emmeline behind.

"Oh, yes you did, my life and my place here. You stole my mother."

"She's *our* mother, Thomas."

"*Mine*!" When he yells his face elongates, the rims of his eyes seem to dry out and crack, his mouth opens to ridiculous size and his tongue, red and sharp, is split like a serpent's. The moment passes and he's a handsome youth once more, rather like my father in looks. *Our* father.

He calms and continues. "I should have been first, but you sat in my place. You took her." He sighs lovingly, his eyes moist upon my mother. "But she remembers me. That's what kept me here, you know. Her memory is true. She really just wanted me, never you. Just me."

I am silent and he continues, "I must thank you, though, that taste of blood and flesh you gave me for my birthday was just the thing I needed. Of course it's the very least you can offer, little thief."

"Have you spent all these years thinking that?"

"*She* told me."

"Emmeline?" I ask, my heart breaking. Surely not my mother. Surely not my Emmeline.

"No, *her*." He jerks his chin towards a tree and next to it sits the fox, now unnaturally large as if it may change its size at will. As the moon shifts and clouds obscure part of the silver disk, there seems to be a woman in the animal's place, with neat dark hair and sharp features, watching spitefully as my beautiful mother drudges in filth. The moon's face clears and once more there is merely a fox. "She has been my friend all these years."

"What's her name, Thomas?"

"Sylvia."

"Do you know who she was? What lies has she told you?"

"The dead don't tell each other lies," he sniffs, but it's unconvincing and I feel I can go on.

"She was Father's wife. She's the one who killed you."

There's a sharp bark from the fox. I can't tell if it's a protest or a laugh.

"You're lying. You'll say anything to stop me living."

"Thomas, if you wake Emmeline and ask her, she'll tell you. You trust her, don't you? You trust *your* mother."

"If I wake her she won't finish."

"Yes, she will, if I'm lying! She'll want to show you – she'll want you back, you're her first-born." *Oh please, oh please, oh please let it be a lie!* I need to know as much as he does, how true our mother's heart is.

He's reluctant. I wonder that the fox-bride doesn't take on her human body, yell at me, stop my dissident tongue, but perhaps she can't. Perhaps this is her punishment, that she can only flicker between one form and another, never able to hold onto a woman's shape, try though she might; never able to speak with more than the bark of a fox and in a tongue only the dead can understand.

"Wake Emmeline, Thomas. Wake her. If I lie, then what's to lose? If I lie then why should your friend object to me being found out?" Above the fox I can see something stirring the leaves of the tree, ever-so-subtly, ever-so-quietly that not even Sylvia notices.

Thomas doesn't see either. He shifts his attention to our mother and calls out softly. "Mother? Oh, Mother-mine, wake up."

Emmeline blinks and shakes her head. She takes in her hands and the black marks on her nightgown and the dark stains of clay and mud streaking up her forearms. Thomas stands over her and helps her up. None of the muck on her rubs off on him, as if his substance will not allow anything to stick.

Emmeline looks at me, her eyes confused, her expression pleading. *Oh, please explain, my Rosamund.* How to do so? How to say it without angering this frightful spirit?

"Emmeline." I'm wary of calling her *Mother* in front of so jealous a brother. "Emmeline, this is Thomas, your first-born. He has a question for you. He has been waiting for so long to come back to us – to *you*."

Her eyes flash and I hope I see understanding there. Emmeline and her talented hands, Emmeline and her strong will; Emmeline who did what she did all those years ago. My mother is clever and quick.

"Mother, how did I die? How was I lost to you?"

She flicks a look at me and I give a barely perceptible nod. I have known this story as long as I can remember, heard it at Tildy's knee before Emmeline could stop her. Heard it so I might know who my mother was and how special she was, what she could and would do to protect her family.

"Your father's first wife cursed me."

Thomas howls as if stuck with a knife and the fox barks sharp enough to hurt my ears. She makes to disappear into the shadows but a dark lumpen shape drops from the boughs above and scoops her up, holding tight as tight can be so she can neither nip nor struggle. The hands are gnarled but very strong and they wrap around the animal's throat with an astonishing speed and begin to squeeze. One moment it is a fox, the next a young woman with a thin neck, the next a fox again; one barks, the other cries out; in the end both are silent. A limp red carcass dangles in my strange friend's grip.

Now there is Thomas to deal with.

He looks so stricken and already he seems . . . thinner. I think I can see through him to the faint outlines of gravestones. He has been held here by belief and memory, and now his foundation has been shaken to its core, shown to be false.

I feel sorry for my brother.

He shakes where he stands. The mud at his feet seems to suck up at him. "Mother," he whimpers. "Don't you want me back?"

"I never really had you, lovely boy. I miss you, Thomas, I truly do."

"Wouldn't you rather me, though? Me, not her? I was the one you were supposed to have."

"But I do not love Rosamund less. She did not take anything from you, she did not replace you. You must understand, Thomas, that I would not have you instead of her. You were taken from me so long ago. I grieve every day, but I know I cannot have you back."

"You don't mean that," he screams. The mud is now most certainly sucking at his lower limbs but he does not seem to notice. Emmeline smiles and nods.

"Yes, I do, my darling boy. I love you but I will not exchange my *rosa mundi* for you. And I will not forgive you if you harm your sister." She reaches out to put a gentle hand on his chest. Her palm meets something not quite solid, sinking further into his flesh than it should.

"Mother," he whimpers and he weeps. "Don't you love me?"

"Ah, so much, so much. Yes. And I will miss you forever."

He sinks to his knees, suddenly weak. Emmeline kneels beside him and cradles him against her. I *can* see through him, now, to the ground beneath. She strokes his face but her fingers begin to dip beneath the skin as he loses solidity, loses his form.

Thomas wanted nothing more than to be loved, to have his chance with our family. He had only a child's selfish desire for something with no idea that there are some things we cannot have. This night, I understand my brother. One day I may weep for him and one day I may forgive him. Until then I give him what I can. I sit next to him and hold his rapidly fading hand. He looks at me with moon-washed eyes; I'm not sure he can see me anymore.

Robbed of his power, of Emmeline's yearning memory, he becomes shadow and recollection, nothing more. In a few more beats of the night, he is gone and there are only Emmeline and I and our strange ally.

We rise and move towards the creature, who is hunched and wizened. It's dressed in rags that were once proper clothes. The fox's corpse is rotting now, quite rapidly, and the not-quite-human-not-quite-troll throws the body as far away as it can.

I notice that Emmeline's green eyes more or less match those of the weird human-ish thing. It – she, it is obviously a she – gives a shy smile and a curiously graceful curtsey. My silver ring, which fell into the mud when my brother's hand dissolved, is cold in my palm. I hold it out to her. She looks pleased and slips it onto one enlarged knuckle and pushes with determination until it pops over and dangles around the thin digit. With a nod of thanks, she turns to the yew tree once again and climbs swiftly, her large feet and hands finding holds not obvious to the eye.

"Who is she?" I ask.

Emmeline shakes her head. "My father had varied tastes, Rosie. I think the hair and eyes tell a story."

She holds me close and there is no place nicer or kinder than in my mother's arms. I think of Thomas, deprived of this, a cold lad his whole life. I hope the last memory of our mother holding him sustains him in his final sleep. I hope he will not be forever alone in the dark.

# JOE R. LANSDALE

## Christmas with the Dead

JOE R. LANSDALE LIVES in East Texas with his wife, Karen. The author of over thirty novels and two hundred short stories and articles, he is the recipient of numerous awards, including the British Fantasy Award, the Edgar, seven Bram Stoker Awards, Italy's Grinzani Cavour Prize, and many others. In 2007 he received the Grand Master Award from the World Horror Convention.

His novella *Bubba Ho-tep* was filmed in 2002 by producer/ director Don Coscarelli, starring Bruce Campbell and Ossie Davis, while his story "Incident On and Off a Mountain Road" became the first episode of Showtime Networks' *Masters of Horror* series, from the same director.

Lansdale's most recent novel is *Devil Red*, the latest in his best-selling series of quirky crime novels featuring mismatched investigators Hap Collins and Leonard Pine, which includes such titles as *Savage Season*, *Mucho Mojo*, *The Two-Bear Mambo*, *Bad Chili*, *Rumble Tumble*, *Captains Outrageous* and *Vanilla Ride*.

"I wrote 'Christmas with the Dead' simply because I wanted to write a holiday horror story," Lansdale admits. "This was the result.

"Currently it is in pre-production to be filmed in June. That's right – Christmas in June, an alteration in the screenplay written by my son, Keith, based on the story. As a film, this looks to be a hoot."

IT WAS A FOOLISH thing to do, and Calvin had not bothered with it the last two years, not since the death of his wife and daughter, but this year, this late morning, the loneliness and the monotony led him to it. He decided quite suddenly, having kept fairly good record on the calendar, that tomorrow was Christmas Eve, and zombies be damned. The Christmas lights and decorations were going up.

He went into the garage to look for the lights. He could hear the zombies sniffing around outside the garage door. The door was down and locked tight, and on top of that, though the zombies could grab and bite you, they weren't terribly strong most of the time, so the door was secure. The windows inside were boarded over, the doors were locked, and double locked, and boarded. The back yard the dead owned, but the windows and doors were boarded really well there, so he was shut in tight and safe.

Prowling through the holiday ornaments, he found immediately the large plastic Santa, and three long strings of lights.

He managed all of the strings of lights into his living room. He plugged the wires into the extension cord that was hooked up to the generator he had put in the kitchen, and discovered most of the lights were as dead as the proverbial dodo bird. Many were broken from him having ripped the whole thing off the house in anger two years back.

He sat for a moment, then went to the little refrigerator he had replaced the big one with – used less energy – and pulled a bottled coffee out, twisted off the cap, and walked over to the living-room window.

Unlike the garage on the side of the house, or the back yard, he had fenced the front yard off with deeply buried iron bars to which he had attached chicken wire, overlapped with barb wire. The fence rose to a height of eight feet. The gate, also eight feet tall, was made of the same. He seldom used it. He mostly went out and back in through the garage. There was no fence there. When he went out, they were waiting.

More often than not, he was able to run over and crush a few before hitting the door device, closing the garage behind him. On the way back, he rammed a few more, and with the touch of a button, sealed himself inside. When they were thin in the yard, he used that time to stack the bodies in his pickup truck, haul them somewhere to dump. It kept the stink down that way. Also, the rotting flesh tended to attract the hungry dead. The less he made them feel at home, the better.

Today, looking through the gaps between the boards nailed over the window, he could see the zombies beyond the fence. They were pulling at the wire, but it was firm and they were weak. He had discovered, strangely, that as it grew darker, they grew stronger. Nothing spectacular, but enough he could notice it. They were definitely faster then. It was as if the day made them sluggish, and the night rejuvenated them; gave them a shot of energy, like maybe the moon was their mistress.

He noticed too, that though there were plenty of them, there were fewer every day. He knew why. He had seen the results, not only around town, but right outside his fence. From time to time they just fell apart.

It was plain old natural disintegration. As time rolled on, their dead and rotten bodies came apart. For some reason, not as fast as was normal, but still, they did indeed break down. Of course, if they bit someone, they would become zombies, fresher ones, but, after the last six months there were few if any people left in town, besides himself. He didn't know how it was outside of town, but he assumed the results were similar. The zombies now, from time to time, turned on one another, eating what flesh they could manage to bite off each other's rotten bones. Dogs, cats, snakes, anything they could get their hands on, had been devastated. It was a new world, and it sucked. And sometimes it chewed.

Back in the garage, Calvin gathered up the six, large, plastic snowmen and the Santa, and pulled them into the house. He plugged them in and happily discovered they lit right up. But the strings of lights were still a problem. He searched the garage, and only found three spare bulbs – green ones – and when he screwed them in, only one worked. If he put up those strings they would be patchy. It wasn't as if anyone but himself would care, but a job worth doing was a job worth doing right, as his dad always said.

He smiled.

Ella, his wife, would have said it wasn't about doing a job

right, it was more about fulfilling his compulsions. She would laugh at him now. Back then a crooked picture on the wall would make him crazy. Now there was nothing neat about the house. It was a fortress. It was a mess. It was a place to stay, but it wasn't a home.

Two years ago it ended being a home when he shot his wife and daughter in the head with the twelve gauge, put their bodies in the dumpster down the street, poured gas on them, and set them on fire.

All atmosphere of home was gone. Now, with him being the most desirable snack in town, just going outside the fence was a dangerous endeavour. And being inside he was as lonely as the guest of honour at a firing squad.

Calvin picked the strapped shotgun off the couch and flung it over his shoulder, adjusted the .38 revolver in his belt, grabbed the old-fashioned tire tool from where it leaned in the corner, and went back to the garage.

He cranked up the truck, which he always backed in, and using the automatic garage opener, pressed it.

He had worked hard on the mechanism so that it would rise quickly and smoothly, and today was no exception. It yawned wide like a mouth opening. Three zombies, one he recognised faintly as Marilyn Paulson, a girl he had dated in high school, were standing outside. She had been his first love, his first sexual partner, and now half of her face dangled like a wash cloth on a clothesline. Her hair was falling out, and her eyes were set far back in her head, like dark marbles in crawfish holes.

The two others were men. One was reasonably fresh, but Calvin didn't recognise him. The other was his next door neighbour, Phil Tooney. Phil looked close to just falling apart, and so was his nose.

As Calvin roared the big four-seater pickup out of the garage, he hit Marilyn with the bumper and she went under, the wing mirror clipped Phil and sent him winding. He glanced in the rearview as he hit the garage mechanism, was pleased to see the door go down before the standing zombie could get inside. From time to time they got in when he left or returned, and he had to seal them in, get out and fight or shoot them. It was a major annoyance, knowing you had that waiting for you when you got back from town.

The last thing he saw as he drove away was the remaining zombie eating a mashed Marilyn as she squirmed on the driveway; he had shattered her legs with the truck. She was unable to rise or fight back. The way its teeth bit into her, the skin stretched, it looked as if it was trying to pull old bubble gum loose from the sidewalk.

Another glance in the mirror showed him Phil was back on his feet. He and the other zombie got into it then, fighting over the writhing meal on the cement. And then Calvin turned the truck along Seal Street, out of their view, and rolled on toward town.

Driving, he glanced at all the Christmas decorations. The lights strung on houses, no longer lit. The yard decorations, most of them knocked over: Baby Jesus flung south from an overturned manger, a deflated blow-up Santa Claus in a sleigh with hooked-up reindeer, now laying like a puddle of lumpy paint spills in the high grass of a yard fronting a house with an open door.

As he drove, Calvin glanced at the dumpster by the side of the road. The one where he had put the bodies of his wife and daughter and burned them. It was, as far as he was concerned, their tomb.

One morning, driving into town for supplies, a morning like this, he had seen zombies in the dumpster, chewing at bones, strings of flesh. It had driven him crazy. He had pulled over right then and there and shotgunned them, blowing off two heads, and crushing in two others with the butt of the twelve gauge. Then, he had pulled the tire tool from his belt and beat their corpses to pieces. It had been easy, as they were rotten and ragged and almost gone. It was the brain being destroyed that stopped them, either that or their own timely disintegration, which with the destruction of the brain caused the rot to accelerate. But even with them down for the count, he kept whacking at them, screaming and crying as he did.

He swallowed as he drove by. Had he not been napping after a hard day's work, waiting on dinner, then he too would have been like Ella and Tina. He wasn't sure which was worse, becoming one of them, not knowing anything or anyone anymore, being eternally hungry, or surviving, losing his wife and daughter and having to remember them every day.

Mud Creek's Super Saver parking lot was full of cars and bones and wind-blown shopping carts. A few zombies were wandering about. Some were gnawing the bones of the dead. A little child was down on her knees in the centre of the lot gnawing on the head of a kitten.

As he drove up close to the Super Saver's side door, he got out quickly, with his key ready, the truck locked, the shotgun on his shoulder, and the tire tool in his belt.

He had, days after it all came down, finished off the walking dead in the Super Market with his shotgun, and pulled their bodies out for the ones outside to feast on. While this went on, he found the electronic lock for the sliding plasti-glass doors, and he located the common doors at side and back, and found their keys. With the store sealed, he knew he could come in the smaller doors whenever he wanted, shop for canned and dried goods. The electricity was still working then, but in time, he feared it might go out. So he decided the best way to go was to start with the meats and fresh vegetables. They lasted for about six weeks. And then, for whatever reason, the electricity died.

It may have been attrition of power, or a terrific storm, though not nearly as terrific as the one Ella and Tina had described. The one that had changed things. But something killed the electricity. He managed to get a lot of meat out before then, and he tossed a lot away to keep it from rotting in the store, making the place stink.

By then, he had a freezer and the smaller refrigerator both hooked to gas generators he had taken from the store. And by siphoning gas from cars, he had been able to keep it running. He also worked out a way to maintain electricity by supplanting the gas-powered generators with car batteries that he wired up and used until they died. Then he got others, fresh ones from the car parts house. He didn't know how long that supply would last. Someday he feared he would be completely in the dark when night fell. So, he made a point of picking up candles each time he went to the store. He had hundreds of them now, big fat ones, and plenty of matches.

The weather was cool, so he decided on canned chilli and crackers. There was plenty of food in the store, as most of the town had seen the storm and been affected by it, and had immediately gone into zombie mode. For them, it was no more cheese and crackers, salads with dressing on the side, now it was hot, fresh meat and cold dead meat, rotting on the bone.

As he cruised the aisle, he saw a rack with bags of jerky on it. He hadn't had jerky in ages. He grabbed bags of it and threw them in the cart. He found a twelve pack of bottled beer and put that in the cart.

He was there for about six hours. Just wandering. Thinking. He used the restrooms, which still flushed. He had the same luxury at his house, and he could have waited, but the whole trip, the food, walking the aisles, using the toilet, it was akin to a vacation.

After a while he went to the section of the store that contained the decorations. He filled another basket with strings of lights, and even located a medium-sized plastic Christmas tree. Three baskets were eventually filled, one with the plastic tree precariously balanced on top. He found a Santa hat, said, "What the hell," and put it on.

He pushed all three baskets near the door he had come in. He slung the shotgun off his shoulder, and took a deep breath. He hated this part. You never knew what was behind the door. The automatic doors would have been better in this regard, as they were hard plastic and you could see through them, but the problem was if you went out that way, you left the automatic door working, and they could come and go inside as they pleased. He liked the store to be his sanctuary, just like the pawnshop down town, the huge car parts store, and a number of other places he had rigged with locks and hidden weapons.

He stuck the key in the door and heard it snick. He opened it quickly. They weren't right at the door, but they were all around his truck. He got behind one of the baskets and pushed it out, leaving the door behind him open. It was chancy, as one of them might slip inside unseen, even be waiting a week or two later when he came back, but it was a chance he had to take.

Pushing the basket hard, he rushed out into the lot and to the back of the truck. He had to pause to open up with the shotgun.

He dropped four of them, then realised he was out of fire-power. For the first time in ages, he had forgotten to check the loads in the gun; his last trek out, a trip to the pawnshop, had used most of them, and he hadn't reloaded.

He couldn't believe it. He was slipping. And you couldn't slip. Not in this world.

He pulled the .38 revolver and popped off a shot, missed. Two were closing. He stuck the revolver back in his belt, grabbed a handful of goodies from the basket and tossed them in the back of the pickup. When he looked up, four were closing, and down the way, stumbling over the parking lot, were more of them. A lot of them. In that moment, all he could think was: at least they're slow.

He pulled the .38 again, but one of them came out of nowhere, grabbed him by the throat. He whacked at the arm with his revolver, snapped it off at the shoulder, leaving the hand still gripping him. The zombie, minus an arm, lunged toward him, snapping its teeth, filling the air with its foul stench.

At close range he didn't miss with the revolver, got Armless right between the eyes. He jerked the arm free of his neck, moved forward quickly, and using the pistol as a club, which for him was more precise, he knocked two down, crushing one's skull, and finishing off the other with a close skull shot. A careful shot dropped another.

He looked to see how fast the other zombies were coming.

Not that fast. They were just halfway across the lot.

There was one more dead near the front of his truck. It had circled the vehicle while he was fighting the others. He hadn't even seen where it came from. He watched it as he finished unloading the car. When it was close, he shot it at near point-blank range, causing its rotten skull to explode like a pumpkin, spewing what appeared to be boiled, dirty oatmeal all over the side of his truck and the parking lot.

Darting back inside, he managed to push one cart out, and then shove the other after it. He grabbed the handles of the carts, one in each hand, and guided them to the back of the truck. The zombies were near now. One of them, for some reason, was holding his hand high above his head, as if in greeting. Calvin was tempted to wave.

Calvin tossed everything in the back of the truck, was dismayed to hear a bulb or two from his string of bulbs pop. The last thing he tossed in back was the Christmas tree.

He was behind the wheel and backing around even before the zombies arrived. He drove toward them, hit two and crunched them down.

As if it mattered, as he wheeled out of the lot, he tossed up his hand in a one finger salute.

"They were so pretty," Ella had said about the lightning flashes.

She had awakened him as he lay snoozing on the couch.

"They were red and yellow and green and blue and all kinds of colours," Tina said. "Come on, daddy, come see."

By the time he was there, the strange lightning storm was gone. There was only the rain. It had come out of nowhere, caused by who knew what. Even the rain came and went quickly; a storm that covered the earth briefly, flashed lights, spit rain, and departed.

When the rain stopped, the people who had observed the coloured lightning died, just keeled over. Ella and Tina among them, dropped over right in the living room on Christmas Eve, just before presents were to be opened.

It made no sense. But that's what happened.

Then, even as he tried to revive them, they rose.

Immediately, he knew they weren't right. It didn't take a wizard to realise that. They came at him, snarling, long strings of mucus flipping from their mouths like rabid dog saliva. They tried to bite him. He pushed them back, he called their names, he yelled, he pleaded, but still they came, biting and snapping. He stuck a couch cushion in Ella's mouth. She grabbed it and ripped it. Stuffing flew like a snowstorm. And he ran.

He hid in the bedroom, locked the door, not wanting to hurt them. He heard the others, his neighbours, outside, roaming around the house. He looked out the window. There were people all over the back yard, fighting with one another, some of them living, trying to survive, going down beneath teeth and nails. People like him, who for some reason had not seen the weird storm. But the rest were dead. Like his wife and daughter. The lights of the storm had stuck something behind their eyes that killed them and brought them back – dead, but walking, and hungry.

Ella and Tina pounded on his bedroom door with the intensity of a drum solo. *Bam, bam, bam, bam, bam, bam.* He sat on the bed for an hour, his hands over his ears, tears streaming down his face, listening to his family banging at the door, hearing the world outside coming apart.

He took a deep breath, got the shotgun out of the closet, made sure it was loaded, opened the bedroom door.

It was funny, but he could still remember thinking as they went through the doorway, here's my gift to you. Merry Christmas, family. I love you.

And then two shots.

Later, when things had settled, he had managed, even in the midst of a zombie take-over, to take their bodies to the dumpster, pour gas on them, and dispose of them as best he could. Months later, from time to time, he would awaken, the smell of their burning flesh and the odour of gasoline in his nostrils.

Later, one post at a time, fighting off zombies as he worked, he built his compound to keep them out, to give him a yard, a bit of normalcy.

Calvin looked in the rearview mirror. His forehead was beaded with sweat. He was still wearing the Santa hat. The snowball on its tip had fallen onto the side of his face. He flipped it back, kept driving.

He was almost home when he saw the dog and saw them chasing it. The dog was skinny, near starved, black and white spotted, probably some kind of hound mix. It was running all out, and as it was nearing dark, the pace of the zombies had picked up. By deep nightfall, they would be able to move much faster. That dog was dead meat.

The dog cut out into the road in front of him, and he braked. Of the four zombies chasing the dog, only one of them stopped to look at him. The other three ran on.

Calvin said, "Eat bumper," gassed the truck into the zombie who had stopped to stare, knocking it under the pickup. He could hear it dragging underneath as he drove. The other zombies were chasing the dog down the street, gaining on it; it ran with its tongue hanging long.

The dog swerved off the road and jetted between houses. The zombies ran after it. Calvin started to let it go. It wasn't his problem. But, as if without thought, he wheeled the truck off the road and across a yard. He caught one of the zombies, a fat slow one that had most likely been fat and slow in life. He bounced the truck over it and bore down on the other two.

One heard the motor, turned to look, and was scooped under the bumper so fast it looked like a magic act disappearance. The other didn't seem to notice him at all. It was so intent on its canine lunch. Calvin hit it with the truck, knocked it against the side of a house, pinned it there, gassed the truck until it snapped in two and the house warped under the pressure.

Calvin backed off, fearing he might have damaged the engine. But the truck still ran.

He looked. The dog was standing between two houses, panting, its pink tongue hanging out of its mouth like a bright power tie.

Opening the door, Calvin called to the dog. The dog didn't move, but its ears sprang up.

"Come on, boy . . . girl. Come on, doggie."

The dog didn't move.

Calvin looked over his shoulders. Zombies were starting to appear everywhere. They were far enough away he could make an escape, but close enough to be concerned.

And then he saw the plastic Christmas tree had been knocked out of the back of the pickup. He ran over and picked it up and tossed it in the bed. He looked at the dog.

"It's now are never, pup," Calvin said. "Come on. I'm not one of them."

It appeared the dog understood completely. It came toward him, tail wagging. Calvin bent down, carefully extended his hand toward it. He patted it on the head. Its tail went crazy. The dog had a collar on. There was a little aluminium tag in the shape of a bone around its neck. He took it between thumb and forefinger. The dog's name was stencilled on it: BUFFY.

Looking back at the zombies coming across the yard in near formation, Calvin spoke to the dog, "Come on, Buffy. Go with me."

He stepped back, one hand on the open door. The dog sprang past him, into the seat. Calvin climbed in, backed around, and they were out of there, slamming zombies right and left as the truck broke their lines.

As he neared his house, the sun was starting to dip. The sky was as purple as a hammered plum. Behind him, in the mirror, he could see zombies coming from all over, between houses, out of houses, down the road, moving swiftly.

He gave the truck gas, and then a tire blew.

The truck's rear end skidded hard left, almost spun, but Calvin fought the wheel and righted it. It bumped along, and he was forced to slow it down to what seemed like a near crawl. In the rearview, he could see the dead gaining; a sea of teeth and putrid faces. He glanced at the dog. It was staring out the back window as well, a look of concern on its face.

"I shouldn't have stopped for you," Calvin said, and in an instant he thought: If I opened the door and kicked you out, that might slow them down. They might stop and fight over a hot lunch.

It was a fleeting thought.

"You go, I go," Calvin said, as if he had owned the dog for years, as if it were a part of his family.

He kept driving, bumping the pickup along.

When he arrived at his house, he didn't have time to back as usual. He hit the garage remote and drove the truck inside. When he got out, Buffy clambering out behind him, the zombies were in the garage, maybe ten of them, others in the near distance were moving faster and faster toward him.

Calvin touched the remote, closed the garage door, trapping himself and the dog inside with those ten, but keeping the others out. He tossed the remote on the hood of the pickup, pulled the pistol and used what ammunition was left. A few of them were hit in the head and dropped. He jammed the empty pistol in his belt, pulled the tire iron free, began to swing it, cracking heads with the blows.

He heard growling and ripping, turned to see Buffy had taken one down and was tearing its throat out, pulling its near rotten head off its shoulders.

"Good dog, Buffy," Calvin yelled, and swung the iron. "Sic 'em."

They came over the roof of the truck, one of them, a woman, leaped on him and knocked him face down, sent his tire iron flying. She went rolling into the wall, but was up quickly and moving toward him.

He knew this was it. He sensed another close on him, and then another, and then he heard the dog bark, growl. Calvin managed to turn his head slightly as Buffy leaped and hit the one above him, knocking her down. It wasn't much, but it allowed Calvin to scramble to his feet, start swinging the tire iron. Left and right he swung it, with all his might.

They came for him, closer. He backed up, Buffy beside him, their asses against the wall, the zombies in front of them. There were three of the dead left. They came like bullets. Calvin breathed hard. He grabbed the tire iron off the garage floor, swung it as quickly and as firmly as he could manage, dodging in between them, not making a kill shot, just knocking them aside, finally dashing for the truck with Buffy at his heels. Calvin and Buffy jumped inside, and Calvin slammed the door and locked it. The zombies slammed against the door and the window, but it held.

Calvin got a box of .38 shells out of the glove box, pulled the revolver from his belt and loaded it. He took a deep breath. He looked out the driver's side window where one of the zombies, maybe male, maybe female, too far gone to tell, tried to chew the glass.

When he had driven inside, he had inadvertently killed the engine. He reached and twisted the key, started it up. Then he pushed back against Buffy, until they were as close to the other door as possible. Then he used his toe to roll down the glass where the zombie gnashed. As the window dropped, its head dipped inward and its teeth snapped at the air. The revolver barked, knocking a hole in the zombie's head, spurting a gusher of goo, causing it to spin and drop as if practising a ballet move.

Another showed its face at the open window, and got the same reception. A .38 slug.

Calvin twisted in his seat and looked at the other window. Nothing. Where was the last one? He eased to the middle, pulling the dog beside him. As he held the dog, he could feel it shivering. Damn, what a dog. Terrified, and still a fighter. No quitter was she.

A hand darted through the open window, tried to grab him, snatched off his Santa hat. He spun around to shoot. The zombie arm struck the pistol, sent it flying. It grabbed him. It had him now, and this one, fresher than the others, was strong. It pulled him toward the window, toward snapping, jagged teeth.

Buffy leaped. It was a tight fit between Calvin and the window, but the starved dog made it, hit the zombie full in the face and slammed it backwards. Buffy fell out the window after it.

Calvin found the pistol, jumped out of the car. The creature had grabbed Buffy by the throat, had spun her around on her back, and was hastily dropping its head for the bite.

Calvin fired. The gun took off the top of the thing's head. It let go of Buffy. It stood up, stared at him, made two quick steps toward him, and dropped. The dog charged to Calvin's side, growling.

"It's all right, girl. It's all right. You done good. Damn, you done good."

Calvin got the tire iron and went around and carefully bashed in all the heads of the zombies, just for insurance. Tomorrow, he'd change the tire on the truck, probably blown out from running over zombies. He'd put his spare on it, the doughnut tire, drive to the tire store and find four brand new ones and put them on. Tomorrow he'd get rid of the zombies' bodies. Tomorrow he'd do a lot of things.

But not tonight.

He found the Santa hat and put it back on.

Tonight, he had other plans.

First he gave Buffy a package of jerky. She ate like the starving animal she was. He got a bowl out of the shelf and filled it with water.

"From now on, that's your bowl, girl. Tomorrow . . . Maybe the next day, I'll find you some canned dog food at the store."

He got another bowl and opened a can of chilli and poured it into it. He was most likely overfeeding her. She'd probably throw it up. But that was all right. He would clean it up, and tomorrow they'd start over, more carefully. But tonight, Buffy had earned a special treat.

He went out and got the tree out of the truck and put it up and put ornaments on it from two years back. Ornaments he had left on the floor after throwing the old dead and dried tree over the fence. This plastic one was smaller, but it would last, year after year.

He sat down under the tree and found the presents he had for his wife and child. He pushed them aside, leaving them wrapped. He opened those they had given him two Christmases ago. He liked all of them. The socks. The underwear. The ties he would never wear. DVDs of movies he loved, and would watch, sitting on the couch with Buffy, who he would soon make fat.

He sat for a long time and looked at his presents and cried.

Using the porch light for illumination, inside the fenced-in yard, he set about putting up the decorations. Outside the fence the zombies grabbed at it, and rattled it, and tugged, but it held. It was a good fence. A damn good fence. He believed in that tediously built fence. And the zombies weren't good climbers. They got off the ground, it was like some of whatever made them animated slid out of them in invisible floods. It was as if they gained their living dead status from the earth itself.

It was a long job, and when he finished climbing the ladder, stapling up the lights, making sure the Santa and snowmen were in their places, he went inside and plugged it all in.

When he came outside, the yard was lit in colours of red and blue and green. The Santa and the snowmen glowed as if they had swallowed lightning.

Buffy stood beside him, wagging her tail as they examined the handiwork.

Then Calvin realised something. It had grown very quiet. The fence was no longer being shaken or pulled. He turned quickly toward where the zombies stood outside the fence. They weren't holding onto the wire anymore. They weren't moaning. They weren't doing anything except looking, heads lifted toward the lights.

Out there in the shadows, the lights barely touching them with a fringe of colour, they looked like happy and surprised children.

"They like it," Calvin said, and looked down at Buffy.

She looked up at him, wagging her tail.

"Merry Christmas, dog."

When he glanced up, he saw a strange thing. One of the zombies, a woman, a barefoot woman wearing shorts and a T-shirt, a young woman, maybe even a nice-looking woman not so long ago, lifted her arm and pointed at the lights and smiled with dark, rotting teeth. Then there came a sound from all of them, like a contented sigh.

"I'll be damn," Calvin said. "They like it."

He thought: I will win. I will wait them out. They will all fall apart someday soon. But tonight, they are here with us, to share the lights. They are our company. He got a beer from inside, came back out and pulled up a lawn chair and sat down. Buffy lay down beside him. He was tempted to give those poor sonofabitches outside the wire a few strips of jerky. Instead, he sipped his beer.

A tear ran down his face as he yelled toward the dead.

"Merry Christmas, you monsters. Merry Christmas to all of you, and to all a good night."

# KIRSTYN McDERMOTT

## We All Fall Down

KIRSTYN MCDERMOTT WAS BORN in Newcastle, Australia, on Halloween – an auspicious date which perhaps accounts for her life-long attraction to all things dark and mysterious.

She has published short fiction in a wide variety of magazines and anthologies, including *Aurealis*, *Scenes from the Second Storey*, *Macabre*, *Southerly*, *Island*, *GUD* and *Southern Blood*.

Her debut novel, *Madigan Mine*, was published by Picador Australia in 2010. Her second, *Perfections*, is due for release in 2012. McDermott's work has been nominated for Bram Stoker and Australian Shadows Awards, and has been the recent recipient of Aurealis, Ditmar and Chronos Awards.

She lives in Melbourne with her husband and fellow scribbler, Jason Nahrung.

"I carried the bones of this story around for quite a few years before I finally stumbled upon its beating heart," explains the author. "In my head was the image of a doll house, huge and not quite right, and a woman searching desperately for something concealed inside. But I could never work a story around it that didn't seem twee. Doll houses, you know?

"But then Emma and Holly appeared – trapped within their own fractured, futile relationship – and everything just, well, *fell* together. Beautifully. Awfully. And now I have a doll house story. Of a kind."

"NO WAY, NOT AGAIN you're not," Holly snaps, leaning forward to switch off the radio before Wham even gets past their second jitterbug. "What's that, the hundredth time they've played that piece of crap song today?"

Emma shrugs. "It's been in the charts for weeks, I guess they have to play it."

"Yeah, well I don't have to listen to it." Pissy little voice getting pissier by the minute, and Emma keeps her eyes on the road. Cyclone Holly brewing ever since the cassette player chewed up her mix tape an hour ago, but Emma doesn't want to fight. Not this weekend. Not *their* weekend.

"Check the glove-box," she suggests. "There should be a couple tapes in there. Velvet Underground maybe, and—"

Holly snorts. "Fuck Lou Reed."

"Or we can just talk." Another snort, served with extra derision, and Emma leaves it alone. Less than an hour and they'll be at Buchan anyway, though with the sun already an hour past setting it'll be too late to go up to the caves tonight. They hadn't even left Melbourne until after four – Holly not being able to find first her boots, then her keys – and it's ended up being a longer drive than either of them predicted while studying maps on the kitchen bench. Somehow, this is Emma's fault, along with the Corolla's dodgy cassette player and the fact that Holly has left her camera back at the flat. She only hopes the motel is as good as it looks in the tourist guide. Hell, clean sheets and high-pressure hot water will do. With Holly coaxed into the shower, few are the wonders a pair of soap-slicked hands cannot work.

"What are you grinning about?"

"Huh?" Emma shakes her head. "Nothing much, just thinking how good a hot shower's gonna feel tonight."

"If they even *have* hot water out here. Fricken Hicksville."

"Hol, come on. Stop looking for problems."

"Don't have to look very far, do I?"

Emma sighs and sneaks a sideways glance at the girl in the passenger seat. Even in the post-twilight haze she can see the crease drawn deep at the corner of her mouth, the strand of long brown hair winding, unwinding and winding again round her index finger, tight enough to stop blood. Fair warnings for foul weather, and Emma feels the angry spark of tears behind her eyes. God damn it to hell, nothing ever seems to go right these days; the rift widening between them for weeks and every attempt to bridge it proving futile. Holly is falling away, faster than Emma can run to catch her, and she hasn't the faintest idea why.

What has she done? What hasn't she done?

And if the girl is planning to leave her, why doesn't she just bloody well get it over and done with instead of scattering this daily minefield of eggshells for Emma to tiptoe over? Damn it, why doesn't—

"Em! Fuck!"

She's already seen the animal by the time Holly screams, but it's still a fraction of a second too late and her stomach rolls as she wrenches the wheel to the left, riding the brakes as the car skids off the road and into the shoulder. Gravel crunches, sliding sharp beneath the wheels, and the kangaroo seems to almost turn in mid-air, a balletic turbo-charged leap to clear the bonnet and in its place a looming, shadow-thick shape that Emma barely registers as a telegraph pole before the car slams into it. Sickening metallic crunch louder than the blood beating in her ears, the seatbelt jerking tight against her collarbone, throwing her back against the seat with a sharp whiplash jolt, and throughout it all the flow of time slower than honey poured out on a cold winter morning.

Beside her, Holly starts to cry.

"Holly? Baby, are you okay?" The girl has her face in her hands, breathworn sobs hitching her shoulders in sharp, spastic rhythms, and when Emma touches her thigh she whimpers. Soft, kicked-puppy whimper and then she's fumbling with the door handle, half-climbing, half-falling onto the road, with a wet-dark shadow on her cheek that makes Emma sick to see. Calling for the girl to wait, to please just *wait*, as her own seatbelt refuses to unbuckle and her masochistic brain flashes up every Hollywood post-crash explosion she's ever witnessed. *Damn it, Holly, help me*. Then the belt slips loose at last and she clambers out, panting in the chill night air.

*Fresh* night air. No stink of leaking petrol, no greasy smell of smoke.

Holly is standing in front of the car, what's left of the front of the car, skinny arms crossed over her chest. The headlights are still shining, albeit askew, and Emma can see the blood on the girl's face. Dark red smear like the worst kind of raspberry birth-mark, and she swallows the panic that threatens to rise. "Holly, are you hurt? How badly are you hurt?"

The girl shakes her head. "I'm fine."

"But you're . . ." Emma limps around the car, a dull pain throbbing in her right knee. "You're bleeding, baby. A lot."

Holly pushes Emma's hand away. Sniffs and wipes at her face with the back of her wrist. "Just a bloody nose, I must have bashed it."

"You sure, 'cause it looks—"

"What the fuck *was* that, Em?"

"A kangaroo, I think."

"I *know* it was a kangaroo, I mean what the fuck were you doing? Why weren't you paying attention to the road instead of . . . of . . . of whatever it was you were doing? You could have *killed* me, Em. Don't you fucking realise that?"

Emma bites her lip, reaches out, but the girl pushes her away. Hard. Pushes her away and lands a series of savage kicks on the crumpled radiator grill, as though she could hope to outdo the telegraph pole in the damage stakes. "Look. At. This. Shit."

"Holly, calm down."

"*You* calm down." Crying again, her voice hoarse and broken.

Emma says nothing, because nothing will help, just grabs the girl and pulls her close. Holly such a tiny thing, little more than skin and bone and sharp, furious elbows, and Emma holds her until she stops struggling, holds her tighter than she ever has, than she ever might again, and makes soft, soothing noises into her hair. *It's okay*, she whispers when the girl finally gives up, burns out, and sags exhausted against her. *It's okay, we're okay, we're okay, we're okay*. Over and over and over again, until she's no longer talking about the accident.

Until it no longer feels like so much of a lie.

There isn't a clear path up the hill, not one that is lighted at least, and Emma swears loudly as she trips for the third time. Her knee is really hurting now, little darts of pain marking every step, but she isn't about to beg for a rest break.

"Em?" Holly's voice falls down through the darkness. "You all right?"

"Yeah," she grunts. "Just tripped on something."

A sigh, short and sharp, edged with frustration. "Come on, almost there."

Which seems about right, looking up. Close enough to the house to make out the striped curtains hanging on each side of the lighted window, the shapes of furniture within. No movement inside, though, and Emma lets out a breath she hadn't realised she'd been holding. If no one is home after all, if they've walked up this damn hill for nothing . . .

"Em?"

"Coming." One foot in front of the other, never mind the pain, never mind the fact that they probably would have been picked up by a passing motorist by now if they'd just waited by the car. Once Holly noticed the light on the hill – *Come on, Em, we can use their phone* – that was that. The girl refuses to wait for anything if she can help it, if there is something she can be *doing* instead. Even if the alternative ends up costing more in time and effort, for Holly anything is always better than standing still.

It's one of the things Emma loves about her. Most of the time.

There's a yellowish porch light shining by the time they reach the house, so maybe someone's heard them coming and rolled out the welcome, or maybe she just didn't notice it before. No bell or knocker, so Holly thumps three times on the front door with the flat of her fist. Loud enough to raise the dead but there's no response from inside the house, no footsteps or floorboard creak, and Emma opens her mouth to say something she probably shouldn't, how Holly better be prepared to *carry* her back down that fucking hill now but—

"Shhh," Holly says, tilting her head. "Listen."

So Emma does. Closes her eyes and even holds her breath for a couple seconds, trying to pluck a sound from beyond the ratchety, rhythmic buzz of the cicadas which seem to have colonised the surrounding trees in near plague proportions, but there's nothing. Nothing whatsoever until she opens her eyes again to see Holly with her cheek pressed close against the front door, her lips slightly parted, and even then it's not something that she *hears* exactly. More like feels, or senses.

Something standing motionless on the other side of that door, its lean-long face turned in precisely the same manner as Holly's, with two slim inches of hardwood the only thing between them.

Emma doesn't think, just grabs the girl's arm and jerks her backwards. Away from the door, away from whatever it is that's waiting on the other side – "Let's go, Holly!" – and she's still tugging on her when the door swings abruptly open, and both of them shriek in sudden fright.

All *three* of them, actually: Emma, Holly and the plump, middle-aged woman who stands before them with one hand on the doorjamb and the other fluttering at her throat like a pale, panic-struck bird.

Holly is the first to recover. "Sorry, we didn't mean to scare you."

"That's all right." The woman forces a dry, cracked chuckle which says otherwise. "Seems I scared the two of you just as badly."

Emma doubts that as well. The woman has lowered her hand, but her fingers still tremble at her side, and her face is ashen. It's the face of a woman who lives alone, who has no one to come running from the back of the house should she cry out again. A woman who is already regretting the decision to open her door that night, and who might just slam it shut again at any second.

"I'm Emma Vargus," she says quickly. "This is my friend, Holly Davidson." Nudging Holly with her elbow to ward off the scowl that's already forming at her use of that word – that *friend* word – 'cause now is damn sure not the time for flag-waving, and for once the girl steps into line, switches gears and produces a smile that would put the sun to shame. When the woman makes no attempt to offer her own name, Emma presses on, rushing to explain about the accident and the long walk up the hill and how bloody glad, excuse her language, they are that someone was home and how much gladder they'll be if they could just make a quick phone call to the RACV and get a tow-truck organised.

"Or you could call for us," she finishes. "If that's easier."

"Are you hurt?" the woman asks.

"No, I don't think so, not really. My knee's a bit sore and Holly had a nosebleed for a while, but I think we're okay." Emma grins, hopes it looks less psychotic than it feels. "I mean, we managed to walk up your hill without keeling over."

The woman nods – satisfied, decisive – and steps back from the doorway. "The mozzies will eat you alive if you stand out there all night." A strange half-smile shadows her lips. "There's no getting rid of them, once they have a taste."

Holly is scowling as she stalks back into the living room where Emma has been studying an unframed painting of two little girls sitting on a merry-go-round. It's the old-fashioned kind, with prancing horses and gold-spiralled posts, and one of the children seems to be half-climbing, half-falling from her saddle as she reaches for something off-camera. The other girl clutches the hem of her friend's bright red sundress, her mouth a round splotch of paint the colour of maraschino cherries. The execution is clumsy, the expression on the young faces ambiguous, and the rolling white eye of the closest horse gives Emma the creeps.

"Useless!" Holly says.

Emma turns to face her. "What did they say?"

"Nothing, I was disconnected three times."

"You didn't get through at all?"

"Yeah, I think I just said that," Holly snaps.

As though it's Emma's fault the damn RACV have a dodgy phone line. But then everything seems to be Emma's fault these days.

Behind them, the woman who finally introduced herself as Mrs Jacoby clears her throat. "If I can make a suggestion?" She is less nervous now, obviously no longer afraid that her unexpected guests might be about to slit her throat and make off with the family silver. "Why don't you both stay the night and try again in the morning? If you still can't reach anyone then, I can drive you into town myself."

Emma looks at Holly, who shrugs, noncommittal. Those two vertical frown-lines between her eyebrows have deepened, and her lips are drawn tight. It's obvious she's going to leave all the decision making to Emma from this point on – all the better for apportioning blame later – and anger flares hot and sudden in her guts. Fine, what-the-fuck-ever. "That'd be great, Mrs Jacoby," she says, forcing a smile. "I mean, if it's not putting you to too much trouble."

"Not at all. I always keep the spare room made up." The

woman's gaze flicks between them as she runs a hand through her short, silvery-grey hair. "It's a double bed; I hope you girls won't mind sharing?"

Emma, this time refusing Holly even the briefest of glances, barely skips a beat. "I'm sure we'll manage."

Mrs Jacoby smiles – that queer, slim twist of the lips – and Emma wonders if perhaps she isn't in on the joke after all.

Rubbing her shower-damp hair with one of Mrs Jacoby's fluffy green towels, Emma closes the bedroom door quietly behind her. "All yours," she says, and then, "Jesus, Hol, you *still* mucking about with that thing?"

The doll house is huge. A massive Victorian, its base covering almost the entire surface of the table upon which it has been set up, easily a metre square and maybe more, and inside there are three separate storeys, plus some extra little rooms in the attic. Holly is poking about inside these now, standing on tip-toes to lift out and examine pieces of scale replica furniture from the very back corners.

"It's amazing, Em. You need to come look at this." She holds up what appears to be a tiny steamer trunk, then slips a finger-nail beneath the lid and pops it open. Inside is a small square of tartan cloth, about the size of a matchbox, folded into quarters like an old woollen blanket packed away for the winter. "Fricken details, huh?"

"Yeah, but I don't think you should be playing with it."

"Why not?"

"'Cause it's probably worth more than my car." Emma pictures her Corolla's intimate new friend, the telegraph pole, and grimaces. "Definitely, now."

"She wouldn't have it here if she didn't want people to touch it."

"Hol, this is her *spare room*. How many houseguests do you think that lady actually gets? Just be careful, okay?"

Holly's eyes narrow, the frown lines returning to furrow her brow. "I'm not five years old, you know."

*Sometimes I fucking wonder.* But Emma bites her tongue. She's tired – more than tired, damn near *exhausted*, caught deep in a post-adrenaline crash – and she doesn't want to fight. Not now, not here in this house with Mrs Jacoby right down the hall, blankets pulled up to her chin as she wonders just what it is that two young l-e-s-b-i-a-n-s get up to when the lights go out. Emma steps out of her jeans, modestly donned for the brief trip from bathroom to here, and slips an arm around Holly's waist.

"Have a shower and come to bed, baby." She squeezes the girl's hip. "Please?"

"I don't feel like doing anything." Holly doesn't look up from the little red *chaise longue* she's turning over and over in her hands.

Emma sighs. "Neither do I." Her arm drops to her side. "To be honest, I don't think the bed does either. Creaky old thing sounds worse than the one at your gran's. Remember when we stayed over that time?"

"Yeah," Holly says with a smile. "She couldn't even look at me at breakfast."

"Baby, things we did, *I* couldn't look at you at breakfast!"

Grinning now, Holly returns the little *chaise* to the doll house. "There's a secret room or something under the staircase, I think. See those seams in the wall?"

"Come on, let's just get some sleep."

"Help me find the catch first. Don't you want to know what's in there?"

"Just leave the stupid house alone and come to bed!" Not meaning to raise her voice, but the sound of Holly's fingernails scrabbling around in the stairwell sparked a tight, queasy feeling in her guts which needed to be quelled.

Holly isn't smiling anymore, and that feels even worse.

"I'm sorry, Hol. It's been a real shitty day and I'm tired."

The girl says nothing, merely turns her shoulder and retrieves a small wooden cabinet from the doll house. It has a glass-fronted door that opens and closes on tiny brass hinges, and Holly spends a second or two doing just that.

"Okay, fine." One pissy little straw too many and Emma stalks over to the bed, pulls back the musty, seldom-used sheets. "Do whatever you want, as always."

"Fuck you, Em," Holly hisses. "I wish I could!"

"Fuck you right back, baby." Emma curls her bare legs to her chest and pulls a pillow over her head to block out the overhead light. Faintly, she thinks she hears Holly starting to cry. Soft, muffled sounds that tear at her heart, tear at her resolve, and *fuck you, Holly*, she says to herself, for herself. *Fucking crybaby. You know where to find me once you're done.*

It's dark, new moon dark, and the grass is slippery-wet beneath her feet, even though she doesn't think it has rained for a long time. Up ahead, Holly calls out again, calls out her name and something else that Emma can't make out above the cicada song that rises and falls like slow-drawn breath. *Holly? Hol, wait up*, she shouts but her voice is lost to the night and to the insects, and so she just starts running again.

She doesn't want to open the door, doesn't want to even touch that tar-black wood, but her hand is already on the knob, fingers grasping, wrist turning, and she holds her breath as it swings away from her. *Look at this*, Holly is saying, *you need to look at this*. Kneeling by the doll house which seems bigger now, or maybe Holly is smaller, Holly in a pretty red sundress that Emma has never seen before – *never? never ever?* – Holly kneeling with her palm outstretched and on it, something small and yellow and crumpled. A toy car, matchbox size, and, *That's not right*, Emma says, *it's doesn't fit, it's too small. See, Holly, it's only as big as the steamer trunk*. But the girl just smiles. *You need to look harder.*

Because it *is* the steamer trunk and Holly pops the lid again, pulls out that little scrap of tartan and unfolds it. Unfolds it again and again and again, that shonky old magician's trick, the blanket growing bigger, heavier, and Emma has to grab one end to keep it off the floor. The wool so rough against her cheek, dry as old dust, as she pulls it up over her shoulders, tucks herself in like a good little girl sitting here in the corner beneath the sloping attic ceiling, and watches Holly play with the doll house on the other side of the room. *Do you know where you are? Em, do you know?*

Running, still running, breath painful as broken glass in her lungs, and all around her the damn cicadas continue fill the air with their manic, buzzing chorus. It can't be more than a dozen steps away, that huge Victorian house with its porch light shining the way home, not more than half a dozen now and there's Holly waiting for her at the front door, bare arms outstretched and waving. Waving her *away*, warding her off, and *Leave me alone*, the girl shrieks, tears streaming dark as blood down her face.

*It's not right*, Holly says and turns her back. *You don't fit*. She's right, the doll house is too small, way too small for Emma to get more than an arm and a leg inside and only then if she starts smashing down walls. Holly is crying, and Emma reaches out to touch her, to pull her close, because that might quell the ache in her arms, the ache in her heart, only it's not Holly she's holding onto now. *Let me go*, Mrs Jacoby whispers, not even the ghost of a smile left on those thin, pale lips. And Emma begins to scream.

Light, the harsh light of early morning streaming through the curtainless window, and for a few dream-dazzled moments Emma has absolutely no idea where she is. Only when she reaches out a sleepy arm to find the bed empty beside her, empty and cold, does she remember.

"Holly? Baby?"

No answer, no indication that the other side of the bed has been slept in or even sat upon, no trace of Holly at all. Okay, fine, so the girl stayed pissed with her and crashed somewhere else. Downstairs maybe, sprawled on Mrs Jacoby's red *chaise longue* like some absinthe-soaked poetess and—

No, that's wrong. The red *chaise* isn't downstairs, it's in the doll house. But even that thought is wrong, because there *is* no downstairs. Not in *this* house, not in the *real* house.

Emma shakes her head, rubs at her eyes until stars begin to spark behind her lids. Too many damned dreams, too much time spent chasing her own frightened tail; no wonder she's still exhausted. At least her jeans are where she left them. And, as she pulls them up over her hips, Emma finds herself staring at the doll house, wondering if it's just the daylight that makes it look different this morning.

Because it really does seem smaller, more crowded somehow.

Then she sees the dolls and her breath catches hard in her throat.

There are two of them, about half the length of her hand in height, their tiny porcelain faces painted with such exquisite attention to detail that Emma can even see the familiar smatter of freckles across the nose of the one with the long, brown hair. The one dressed in purple shorts and a white peasant-style blouse far too similar to what Holly was wearing yesterday for coincidence to lay any claim. Definitely not if you count the second doll, the one wearing blue denim jeans and a T-shirt that might once have been black before too many rides round the washing machine rendered it a dirty, charcoal grey.

The doll with short-cropped hair grown back long enough to curl. Frizzy blonde ringlets like those Holly once begged her to leave alone, to let grow out, just to see what they would look like.

*Lil' Orphan Annie with a serious peroxide problem*, Emma joked.

The dolls stare at her, their unblinking gaze the most frightening thing she has ever seen, and Emma has to force herself to snatch each one up in a trembling, white-knuckled fist before she flees the bedroom, expecting all the while to feel the frost-sharp bite of tiny porcelain teeth.

Calling Holly's name as she runs down the hall, bare feet slapping on old floorboards, ridiculously thankful that there still *is* a hall – long and empty and leading straight to the front door – and not a winding Victorian staircase. But no answer, no sign of anyone in the house at all until she reaches the living room and there's Mrs Jacoby standing by the window in a lilac terry-cloth robe, hands wrapped tightly around a steaming mug. Mrs Jacoby who turns now to regard her with a look that Emma doesn't like one bit: disappointment blended with resignation, the look of a parent whose daughter has failed yet another important exam.

"I thought you might be gone," the woman says, and sighs. "I thought, maybe, if I didn't check the room, if I waited . . ."

"Where's Holly?"

"Oh, *she's* gone."

"Gone where?" Emma crosses the room and holds out her

fists, opens them without looking because if she sees those frozen little faces one more time she might start screaming. "What the fuck are these?"

Mrs Jacoby doesn't flinch, merely takes a sip from her mug as she glances at Emma's flattened palms. "Where did you get those things?"

"From the doll house."

"Odd," the woman says. "That one's almost certainly a Greengrocer. The other might have been a Black Prince, perhaps a Black Friday. Hard to tell."

Confused, Emma looks down to see not dolls in her hands but two smaller, stranger shapes, desiccated and almost weightless, their spike-stiff legs sickle-curved to scratch at her skin.

"I think a Prince," says Mrs Jacoby. "We're too far south for Fridays."

Emma cries out, shakes the empty cicada husks to the floor and very nearly stomps them to pieces, has one foot already raised before she stops herself. No desire to feel the crack and split of those things against her bare sole, no desire to touch them again *at all*, and only realises that she's actually backing away from them when her hip bumps against the open door. "What *is* this?" Raising her voice against the immanent threat of tears. "What the fuck is going on?"

But Mrs Jacoby only shakes her head. "You need to ask your *friend*."

"Holly? Where is she?" Nails digging into her palms – *deeper deeper deeper* – because this has to be another of those whacked-out dreams, right? And she just needs to wake herself up, right? *Right?* "Where's Holly?"

"She went to wait by the car."

"Bullshit, why would she do that? Why wouldn't she tell me?"

"Perhaps she'll tell you now." And with that Mrs Jacoby turns away from her, turns to stare out of the window once more, and when she speaks again her voice sounds weary and old. "Just go, Emma. For once, just go."

Amazingly, Holly *is* there. Sitting in the dirt by the rear wheel of the wrecked Corolla, knees drawn up to her chest and head bowed, and Emma almost sobs to see her.

"Holly!"

At the sound of her name, the girl looks up. Shades her eyes with one hand to watch Emma crab-hobble the rest of the way down the dew-slick hill, but doesn't smile or call back a greeting, just sits and waits as though she's been doing it her whole life and doesn't expect to have to stop anytime soon.

"What are you doing here?" Emma asks when she reaches the road. "Why didn't you wake me?"

A shrug, and Holly looks away, looks back down the road from where they'd come the night before. Emma follows her gaze but there's nothing, just empty black-top already starting to simmer in the morning heat, barren brown fields on either side, and above them the sky sprawling vast and cloudless as a faded sheet.

"Get up, Hol. We have to go."

But the girl just shakes her head. "Where? Where are we going, Em?" A grim, razor-thin smile splits her mouth as she whacks the side of the car. "And how we gonna get there?"

She's right, they're pretty much stranded out here. No one and nothing within even the most ambitious of walking distances, just that crazy old woman with her crazy old house, and ten seasons in hell won't get Emma to trek back up there. So they, what, just sit on their butts in the dirt until a car comes by and picks them up? Might as well get moving anyway then, two feet and a heartbeat all that's needed to get them up and away and out of sight of that damn spooky house. Two feet that Emma now remembers are *bare*, her Docs still in the bedroom where she kicked them off last night before her shower, and she swears, punches the car roof, and swears again as pain shoots up her wrist.

Holly is muttering at her feet and for one blood-seared second Emma wants to kick her, takes a deep breath instead. "What did you say, Hol?"

"Look in the front seat," the girl says flatly. "You need to see it."

No, she really doesn't *need* to see anything, certainly not anything that has Holly so cowed, but she's already moving around to the front of the car, wincing because in this light she can see how bad – write-off bad – the damage is to the front end, and it's a damn wonder that—

That—

It flickers, the thing that is – that isn't – that is – in the front seat.

Impossible blacklight flicker that gives Emma a headache, turns her spit to dust, and she blinks, and she squints, and she tries to look at it from the corner of her eye, and still the damn thing isn't there. And is there, still.

"You need to look harder," Holly whispers in her ear and Emma yelps, tries to take a step backwards, several of them, but Holly is behind her, pushing her closer to the crumpled yellow car with its windscreen that isn't shattered so much as caved in, the safety glass cracked and streaked with blood and shit and matted fur from the animal that lies half-in, half-out of the driver's seat. The flickering over and done with now, but Emma would give anything to have it back, to have what is in front of her returned to the realm of what isn't.

The young woman slumps in the passenger seat, bloodied face and bloodied throat and bloodied God knows what else beneath the tartan blanket someone has pulled up over her shoulders. Tucked in like a child on a long drive home, eyes closed and blonde hair smoothed back from her face, as much as unruly curls can be smoothed, but it's wrong. *It's all wrong*, and Emma wants to pull the blanket higher, up and over that waxy, bruise-blemished face because that's what you *do* for dead people, that's what would be *right*, because that woman is—

Is—

Then Holly is tugging at her sleeve, steering her away from the car and over to the side of the road, where Emma stumbles on something sharp and hidden in the long scraggly grass that grows there, and doesn't even try to stop herself from falling.

"Are we?" she whispers. "Did we?"

Holly sinks down beside her. "No," she says, squeezing Emma's shoulder. "No, Em, we didn't." Intensely sweet, the feeling of relief, but it lasts for less than a second before Emma gets her meaning.

*We* didn't.

"I'm so sorry," Holly says. "I tried, I really tried, but there was so much blood and no one drove past, not one fricken car the whole time." Weeping softly as she describes dragging Emma across to the passenger seat, admitting that maybe she shouldn't have moved her at all but the kangaroo was impossible to shift, so heavy, and she couldn't just leave Emma entangled like that. Thick and black, the claws which did all the damage, those powerful hind legs thrashing about in panic and pain after the animal came through the windscreen, and Emma's throat right in their path. Emma's face and arms and chest as well, more blood than Holly had ever seen in her life, and she couldn't stop the spill of it.

She just couldn't stop it.

"The blanket," Emma whispers. "It's from the doll house."

Holly shakes her head. "It's from the boot. My picnic blanket, remember, from when we went up to Mount Dandenong? I left it in your car." She rubs at her bare arms. "You were cold, you kept saying how cold you were, so I went to find a jumper or something and the blanket was right there, too easy, but when I got back . . ."

Emma swallows.

"I didn't know what to do, Em. I just covered you up and waited, and finally this truckie came by in a semi and called the cops on his CB." Holly sniffs and wipes her nose. "He waited with me, too. Pretty nice guy, gave me half his sandwich and some coffee from his thermos. Didn't have to do that, didn't have to wait either, but he did. Nice guy, you know."

"I don't understand, Hol."

Holly sighs. "What?"

"You didn't die?"

"I didn't die."

"So what are you doing here? It doesn't make sense, if you're still alive." Emma thinks about that, and frowns. "Are you still alive?"

"Oh, I'm still alive." Holly rises to her feet, brushes dust and grass from her backside and shades her eyes again as she looks up towards the hill opposite them. "I bought that house almost ten years ago now. Ten years come October."

Emma shakes her head. "Ten years ago you were fourteen."

"Then," Holly says. "Well, *now* I guess. *Here.*"

"Hol, please. Try making some sense."

Holly swings around to face her. "What year is it, Em?"

"Stop fucking around."

"1984, right? The year you died. But up there?" – waving her hand in the direction of the hill and the house that perches upon its crest like a weather-beaten vulture, a house Emma doesn't even want to so much as glimpse again, so she keeps her eyes firmly locked on Holly's and finds that vista only marginally less terrifying – "Up there, it's *years* later. Decades. And it's where I live."

"What, with that Jacoby woman?"

Holly smiles, and that's worse than what Emma saw in the front seat of the Corolla. Possibly worse than anything she has seen anywhere, ever.

"Every time I think you'll realise," the girl tells her. "Every time I think you'll finally catch on, but you never do. Add a good twenty-five years to my age, Em – no, make it a *bad* twenty-five years – cut my hair and turn it grey, throw in some wrinkles, *lots* of wrinkles, plus an extra twenty kilos or so. What do you see then?"

Emma shakes her head. "You can't be her. You can't be her and you *both*. How is that even possible?"

Holly runs her hands through her hair, a gesture of exasperation Emma knows only too well, and she wants to grab those hands, squeeze them tight and never, ever let go. But Holly has already turned her back again, is kicking at the grass with one white-sneakered foot, and Emma is afraid to move because the world now feels so unstable, so insubstantial, that even a misdrawn breath might send it spinning off its axis and into the hungry dark.

"You won't let me leave," Holly says in a small, thin voice. "All these years, I've tried so many things but nothing works. I can be doing the dishes, or watching a movie, or trying to enjoy my honeymoon for godsake, and you just . . . call me back. And I'm here, in that car, and there's nothing I can do. I've tried explaining things to you over and over, showing you, but you never listen. Or you listen, but mustn't remember, because you . . ."

Her voice breaks on that last heavy syllable.

"Holly, baby I—"

"Shut up!" Turning on Emma with flashbright eyes, furious eyes, one skinny finger stabbing right in her face, and Emma obeys instantly. "I bought that damn house because of you. I thought if I was closer to this place, maybe I'd be stronger as well, stronger than you. But it didn't work and now all I can do is set stupid little traps and tripwires and hope that maybe the truth will slip in sideways and wake you the fuck up, or send you on your way, wherever the hell *that* might be. But it never does, every time we end up back here . . ."

*Traps and tripwires.*

Emma closes her eyes. Mrs Jacoby, the carousel painting, the damn doll house she had refused to examine – did she always refuse? always? – and who knew what other subtle hints and whispers Holly kept hidden in plain view up in that house. Because she's right, clever girl: truth wields a razor blade with more finesse than a sledgehammer, and now Emma knows (remembers? relives?) what happened

*—glass and claws and pain and blood and cold—*

what always happens. Every time. How every time she pushes it away, aside, asunder, because she doesn't want to believe, doesn't want

*—blood and cold and dark and fear—*

to die. Doesn't want to die.

And doesn't *ever* want to be alone.

"You know what the worst part is?" Holly is crouching in front of her now, gloss-damp eyes red round the edges. Emma shakes her head mutely, not sure she wants to know, but sure she always has. "We were *over*, Em. That stupid cave trip was *my* idea, you didn't even want to go. You didn't love me anymore, you'd told me that, but I thought if maybe we just went away, just the two of us . . . and now you've swapped it all around inside your head somehow. As if that will fix everything."

Holly picks up Emma's hand, presses it against her cheek. "You don't *love* me, Em. You don't love me, but you *still* won't let me go."

And Emma swallows hard, and nods, and feels the thin cold blade slide between her ribs. "I'm sorry, baby. I'm so sorry."

"You always say that."

"I know, I remember." She studies Holly's face, those gentle curves that she really did love once, those pale blue eyes that could break her heart a million times over and still be able to put it back together. "And I *will* remember, I promise. Next time, okay? Next time it'll be different."

Holly smiles, empty-sad twist of her lips that Emma can't stand to look at.

"You always say that, as well."

No answer she can make which won't taste like a lie, salt and ashes and bitter-cold dirt, so she says nothing. Just sits there with Holly's fingers entwined in her own, watching the slow roll of tears dampen the girl's face as, behind them, the darkness seeps ever closer, ever colder.

"Please," Holly whispers. "Just let go this time. Please, Em?"

And Emma nods, and squeezes Holly's hand, and tries not to think about all the sweet and terrifying ways a person can fall.

# CHRISTOPHER FOWLER

## Oh I Do Like to Be Beside the Seaside

CHRISTOPHER FOWLER WAS BORN in Greenwich, London. He is the award-winning author of thirty novels and ten short story collections, and creator of the "Bryant & May" series of mysteries.

His memoir *Paperboy* won the Green Carnation Award. He has written comedy and drama for the BBC, has a weekly column in the *Independent on Sunday*, is the Crime Reviewer for the *Financial Times*, and has written for such newspapers and magazines as *The Times*, *Telegraph*, *Guardian*, *Daily Mail*, *Time Out*, *Black Static* and many others.

His latest books are a homage to Hammer horror called *Hell Train*, *The Memory of Blood*, and a two-volume collection of twenty-five new stories entitled *Red Gloves*. Forthcoming are two further novels, *Dream World* and *The Invisible Code*.

As Fowler explains: "'. . . Seaside' came about firstly because I was commissioned to write a story for the World Horror Convention souvenir book and, as the event was to take place in Brighton, it seemed logical to set a tale on the South coast of England.

"I had written a fantasy novel, *Calabash*, some years earlier, hinting at the dark madness of such seaside towns, which are the antithesis of their Mediterranean counterparts. I thought of the depressing Morrissey song "Every Day is Like Sunday", which captures the awfulness of English resorts.

"Coincidentally, Kim Newman and I were discussing the inherent creepiness of pantomime dames, and I decided it was time to give vent to my horror of these coastal pleasuredomes. I wish I'd thought to include screaming gangs of hen-nighters as well. And I thought it was a nice touch to have everyone in the story telling the hero to 'fuck off' until he finally does."

T OBY PUSHED THE NAIL deep inside the piece of bread, placed it in his steel catapult and fired it high over the side of the pier. A seagull dropped from the steel-grey cloudscape, its yellow beak agape, and swallowed it.

"Choke, you fucker," Toby yelled. He turned to Harry. "Got any more?"

"That was the last one," said Harry. "We're wasting our time. They can eat broken glass without dying. They've got special stomachs."

"What about barbed wire?"

"Same. My dad's got some rat poison in the shed. He saved it from when he was in the military. They're not allowed to sell it in shops."

"Nah." Toby kicked at the railing until a chip of blue paint came off. "Do you think the pier would burn?"

"The one in Brighton burned."

"Let's get something to eat." He cast a cheated look back at the gull, which had alighted on a post further along the pier. It gave a healthy shriek as he passed. He threw a pebble at it and missed.

The funfair was empty. A boy with a Metallica tattoo across his shoulders was mopping patches of rainwater from the steel plates on the bumper car floor. Everyone teased him because the tattooist had spelled the band's name wrong, with two "T"s and one "L".

"Oi Damon, you wanna be careful, you'll electrocute yourself," Toby called.

"Fuck off," Damon shouted back. "It only works if you touch the ceiling." He raised his metal broom handle and thrashed the mesh above his head, spraying sparks, forgetting he had bare feet. "Fuck!" He hopped back and swung the broom at them.

"What a moron." Toby and Harry laughed together. Damon had ingested so many drugs during his clubbing years that he could barely remember his own name.

They passed Gypsy Rosalee the fortune teller, who was actually a secretary at Cole Bay Co-Operative Funerals, making a bit of money on the side by building sales pitches for lay-away burial plans into the predictions for her elderly clients.

Once Toby had paid to have his palm read, and she had told him he would go to the bad. "You're not satisfied with your lot," she had said, sitting back and folding her arms. "You think you're too good for us. Lads like you always come unstuck."

"You're not a real fortune teller."

"I know enough to recognise someone living under a curse when I see one." She dug out his money and threw it back at him. "Go on, fuck off."

Now he skirted the helter-skelter, where rain had removed so much lubrication from the slide's runners that it was common to see someone getting off their mat halfway down and giving it a push. Ahead was the big dipper that had been closed ever since a pair of toddlers were catapulted into the sea when their carriage braking system failed. Apparently one of them was still in a coma.

He hated the pier even more than he hated the rest of the town.

Cole Bay, population 17,650, former fishing village, was like a hundred other British seaside resorts, a by-word for boredom, a destination that might have amused the Victorians, but was hopelessly outpaced by the expectations of modern day-trippers, who wanted something more than rip-off amusements, a few chip shops, some knackered beach donkeys and a floral clock. By day sour-faced couples huddled in shelters unwrapping sandwiches and opening thermos flasks. By night every teenager in town was out in the back streets, getting pissed and goading their friends into punch-ups. Where the land met the sea, all hopes and ambitions were drawn away by the tide.

Ahead, a bored girl was rolling garish pink spider-webs of

candy floss around a stick. Her name was Michelle, and she had originally planned to work at the fair on Saturdays until she could get away to London, but now she seemed to be on the Pavilion Pier every day. As she blankly swirled the stick, strands of reeking spun sugar flicked onto her bare midriff.

"What the fuck are you lookin' at?" she said, popping a pink bubble of gum at Toby.

"Why do you keep making that shit when you haven't got any customers?" Toby stuck his finger in the tub and allowed sugar to cover it.

"It gets bunged up if I stop. We get flies in it and all sorts. The punters don't notice. I'm not going out with you so don't ask."

"Wasn't going to. You're too old for me, and you're getting fat. Anyway, I thought you were leaving Cole Bay and going to London."

"Changed my mind, didn't I. Went full-time. It's easy work 'cause there's no one here mid-week."

"Boring, though."

"Not as boring as being at school. Which is where you and your mouthy mate are supposed to be."

"Double games period. We bunked off. We're going to see a horror film."

"The living dead thing? You don't need to watch a movie for that, just hang around here. And you ain't gonna pass for eighteen, neither of you."

"The ticket guy goes out with my sister. If he doesn't let us in I'll put the blocks on his chances."

The first fat drops of rain spattered on the pier's floorboards. "Go on then, take your grubby fingers out my tub and fuck off to your film." Michelle tugged at the striped awning of her stall, dismissing them.

They ran back along the pier, past pairs of shuffling pensioners in plastic rain-hoods. They still had an hour to kill before the film started.

The Punch and Judy Man was on the beach packing up his theatre. They called down as they passed. "No show today, Stan?"

"Fucking weather," Stan called back. "I'd make the effort and stay open, but we had a gang of kids in earlier, right tearaways, the little bastards were making fun and chucking stuff. Puppets not good enough for them now there's video games."

"You should try putting in some new material," said Toby.

"I've tried that. Blue jokes, new songs. I had Mr Punch perform a yodelling number, but the last time I tried it I swallowed me swozzel."

They headed up to the promenade, where the old folk sat in hotel greenhouses trying to ripen like tomatoes. The air reeked of doughnut fat and seaside rock. Outside the Lord Nelson, a drunk fat girl in a tiny halter top was sitting on the kerb, stoically attempting to be sick between her spread legs.

Dudley Salterton was sitting on a bench outside the Crow's Nest playhouse, looking more than ever like a tramp. He pulled the withered roll-up from his lips as the boys stopped before him and coughed hard, spitting a green globule onto the pavement.

"You all right, Dudley?" asked Toby. "You got a piece of cigarette paper stuck on your lip."

"Fuck off, will you? I'm on in a minute."

"You're not in the panto, are you? I thought it started ages ago." Toby looked up at the poster for *Aladdin*, which starred someone from Steps and a runner-up from *Big Brother*. Dudley was the resident compère at the Crow's Nest's variety nights, filling the gaps between acts with lame magic tricks and banter he had first used in the years after the war, half-heartedly updated to include jokes about modern TV personalities. Not that his elderly audience cared; they came to catch up with each other, to wave and eat and chat. They came because it was raining, because there was nothing else to do in Cole Bay on a wet Wednesday afternoon, because they were afraid of dying alone.

Dudley was ancient and yellow with nicotine, but vanity required him to dye his hair and eyebrows a peculiar shade of chestnut. He never shaved properly, and had been living in a single room in a bed and breakfast joint on the front ever since his wife killed herself. He smelled of sweat, rolling tobacco and Old Spice.

"I'm doing a guest spot in the second act because their comic got fired for always being pissed during rehearsals. But I told them I'm not doing it Chinese, I'll play it straight, thank you very much. I sing 'Windmills of Your Mind', do some newspaper tearing and balloon animals, let Barnacle Bill tell a couple of off-colour jokes, then I'm off over the Lord Nelson for a pint."

Barnacle Bill was Dudley's ventriloquist's dummy. Quite what he was doing in *Aladdin* was anyone's guess. With its lascivious wink, rolling eyes, peeling lips and dry, startled hair, the dummy tended to have a terrifying effect on children. Lately, Dudley had been dyeing his hair darker and was starting to look more like his dummy than ever. Both had been at their peak of popularity during the war, and were soon to be shut up in boxes.

"What's it like, being in a panto?" Harry asked.

"Fucking awful. Widow Twankey went to prison for child molesting a few years back. How he got the job here I'll never know. Must know someone on the council. It's not right. We have to get children up on stage and make them do a dance. Barnacle Bill shouted at one of them last week and the little fucker pissed himself. I gave his arm a right good pinch as he left the stage. It stinks up there."

"Do you get comps?"

"I wouldn't bother, there's nobody in except a party of spastics from Rhyll, and they're making a hell of a noise. I don't think they're getting any of the jokes. They're probably throwing shit at each other by now."

"You're not supposed to say spastics."

"Who fucking cares down here? It's not exactly the London Palladium, is it?"

"Is there an orchestra?"

"No, Eileen's on the piano and there's a bloke with a drum kit. But he's only got one arm."

"Shark?"

"Thalidomide. There's a wiggly little hand at the end. Gives me the creeps."

Toby and Harry kept walking. They passed the rock shop, where stretches of sickly peppermint folded back and forth on metal spindles like elasticated innards. The window was filled with edible novelty items: giant false teeth, bacon and eggs, an outsized baby's dummy, a bright pink penis. Behind the counter an enormously fat girl in hoop earrings and a tiny skin-tight top stared at them as if she was wondering how they might taste.

At the next corner, four old people stood watching while a fifth attempted to park his car. The car was small and the space was huge, but the driver managed to hit both the vehicle behind and the one in front several times over. The pensioners stood there watching, without offering any advice or help. Finally the car was parked two feet from the kerb and the group crept on, their excitement over.

"You know that Morrissey song, 'Every Day is Like Sunday'?" asked Harry. "Do you think he wrote it about Cole Bay?"

"What, '. . . the coastal town they forgot to close down'? Yeah, probably. How much longer?"

Harry checked his mobile. "Forty-five minutes. Wanna go in the funfair?"

"Not really, but we're here now." They walked in beneath the broken coloured bulbs of the Cole Bay Kursaal and headed for the ghost train. The Kursaal used to be called Funland, but the council changed the name after too many accidents gave the place a bad reputation.

The ghost train's plywood frontage had been painted with crude copies of Scooby-Doo characters, along with some skeletons and demons cribbed from old Marvel comics. From within came a shriek of unoiled metal and a wail like a ghost calling through a hooter. Toby and Harry bypassed the deserted ticket counter – Charleen, the girl who worked there, was around the back having a fag – and flicked on the power as they passed the ride's main junction box.

Jumping into the first narrow carriage, they rolled off, banging through the doors into darkness. An acrid tang of electricity and damp cloth filled their nostrils. The car twisted about on its miniature track, its wheels crackling with errant voltage as they passed a dummy of Dracula that looked more like a leprous orchestra conductor.

"So, are you in?" Toby shouted as they juddered around a day-glo graveyard.

"It's up to you," said Harry, who always followed Toby's instructions. "I guess so. Are we really going to the pictures?"

"No, of course not. Go home and get your stuff, then meet me at the arcade." That was it. Toby's mind was made up. Harry felt a pitch in his stomach, and knew it was real now.

They would run away and leave this miserable cemetery behind for good.

When the ghost train carriage returned to its station at the front of the ride, it was empty.

Harry knew what he had to do. He ran back along the street toward his parents' house. Meanwhile, Toby walked into the Paradise Penny Arcade. He passed the old man who spent his life rhythmically shovelling coins into the Penny Rapids, passed the Skee-Ball slides, the Driving Test, the Flick-A-Ball slots and came up against the creepy Jolly Jack Tar in its wooden case.

The damned thing was a museum piece, and had been giving him nightmares ever since he was a baby. Its skin was just plaster, its rictus smile mere painted wood, but it looked leathery and cancerous, like an embalmed corpse. When a ten-pence piece was inserted, it rocked back and forth squealing with laughter while a crackly organ recording of 'I Do Like to Be Beside the Seaside' played. The sailor grinned and eyed him from the side of its head, as if to say *I know what you're up to.*

He carried on past banks of beeping, squealing money-stealers and jerky out-of-date video games, to the change booth. He knocked on the scratched, filthy glass, startling Winfrey.

"Fuck off, Toby, you nearly gave me a fucking heart attack," Winfrey complained, wiping mustard pickle from his T-shirt. He set down his sandwich and stared blearily through the glass. There was a red spider-web tattooed across his forehead and he had several teeth missing, so that at first glance it looked as if he had fallen through a plate-glass window. "What do you want?"

"What time are you cashing up?"

"My shift ends in twenty minutes, but Michelle can't get here until half-past. You gonna mind the booth for me?"

"What's it worth?"

"I'll give you a quid. If you're gonna hang around, don't fuck up the machines with plastic."

"Yeah, all right. I'm waiting for Harry anyway." He made his way over to a one-arm bandit, watched until Winfrey had turned his back and inserted a coin-shaped piece of plastic into the slot. He waited for the tumblers to trip, then removed it. While he was playing, he checked the railway timetable in his pocket.

He became aware that a gigantic woman was standing beside

him. She looked like something from a seaside postcard. She was wearing a red and white spotted cap the size of a Christmas pudding above a shiny purple wig, a billowing green and yellow gown with metal saucepans fixed over breasts like beach balls, union-jack bloomers and striped leggings. She pursed bee-sting lips and batted her false eyelashes at him. Her doughy face was coated in Belisha beacon-coloured make-up that ended in a line across her wobbly chin.

"I hope you're not trying to cheat the machines, little boy," she said in a bizarre falsetto.

Toby turned to look at her. "Who are you supposed to be?" He took an involuntary step back.

"I'm the Widow. All the little boys and girls come to see me. Haven't you been to see me?" Widow Twankey fluttered and simpered, waggling her padded hips. She had come off stage between numbers to have a couple of ciggies and a few slugs of scotch from her hip flask. "Aladdin's singing his ballad. He'll drag it out for twenty minutes at least. Thinks someone from the telly will spot him and make him a star. Fat fucking chance."

Twankey's voice had dropped to a normal male register now, but still retained an unpleasantly theatrical sibilance. "Show me what you've got in your hand." Pudgy beringed fingers slapped his knuckles. Toby opened his fist to reveal the clear plastic coin.

"Perhaps I should tell old Winfrey what you're up to, stealing his money?"

"No, don't."

"Then come and give your old auntie a kiss."

"You're not my auntie."

"No, but you can fucking pretend for a minute, unless you want Winfrey to call the cops on you." The Widow came close enough for Toby to smell whisky on her breath. She wetly pursed her lips. Toby grimaced and allowed her to plant a kiss on his cheek. As she did so, she slid her hand over the top of his right thigh and the crotch of his jeans.

"You've got some good muscles on you for a young 'un," she hissed, giving his cock a squeeze. "Big for your age. Come and see matron after the show and I'll take you backstage if you like. I keep special presents for my favourite boys and girls back there." The widow gave a slow, exaggerated wink and released him. "Now run along and play."

Harry ran in with the duffel bag and was holding it high. "I've got it," he said excitedly as the pantomime dame sailed past him.

"For Christ's sake stop waving it around." Toby snatched it away and dragged him into the shadows behind the machines, beyond the range of Winfrey's convex ceiling mirrors. He pulled open the bag and checked its contents.

"It belonged to my brother. Do you know how it works?"

"Of course I know. Give me a minute, will you?"

"I brought you something else as well. It's at the bottom."

Toby pulled up a rusty tin and examined the label. It read: GOVERNMENT ISSUE IMPERIAL BRAND RODENT EXTERMINATOR. CAUTION: CONTAINS WARFARIN AND CAUSTIC SODA.

"How old is this?"

"Really old. But it should still work on seagulls. Are we going back on the pier to try it out?"

"No," said Toby. "We're never going back on the pier."

"Never? But I thought we could kill loads of them before we left."

Toby ignored him. He pocketed the items he needed and passed the bag back to Harry. "Come on."

Stepping from the shadows, he made his way over to Winfrey's booth. Winfrey was picking his way through a pile of filthy ten-pound notes that had been softened with over-handling. As soon as he saw the boy he snapped a red rubber band around the bundle and slid it into his bank bag. Winfrey's takings at the arcade weren't high, but his lads sold amphetamines around the town and used him to launder the cash for a cut.

"If you want to get off, I'll cover for you," said Toby.

"Hang on, I haven't finished me tea yet."

Behind them, Harry was banging on the Penny Falls to make the coins slip from the steel shelves. "Oi, you little fucker," Winfrey shouted, fumbling his way out of the booth.

Toby slipped inside and pulled the lid off the rusty tin Harry had brought along. He thrust his hand into the white powder, emptying as much as he could into Winfrey's tea, which reeked of whisky. The powder went everywhere, but he managed to blow it off the counter and wipe the rim of the mug before Winfrey came back.

The cashier grabbed his nylon jacket and pulled it over his shoulders. "Your little pal is going to get into trouble and end up inside, like his brother," he warned. "Fucking rubbish, that whole family."

As Winfrey drank down his tea, Toby watched blankly, wondering if he could taste any difference. Apparently not. He couldn't imagine the cashier had any taste buds left, given the amount he drank. Winfrey drained his mug completely, leaving a rime of white powder around his cracked lips.

Toby retreated to the far side of the arcade, keeping one eye on the booth. "Unbelievable," he muttered, "he can't even taste rat poison. I put half the pot in."

Harry hadn't heard. He had been hypnotised by a two-pound coin that was hovering on the edge of a narrow metal platform in the Coin Cascade machine. Toby craned back at the booth, watching for signs of pain and death.

"Hello Toby."

He whirled around to find Michelle standing beside him.

"I thought you two were off to the flicks?"

"There's still time. You're early."

"I was looking for you. I know you're up to something, both of you."

"I don't know what you mean."

"Don't fuck me about. You're going somewhere. You're getting out."

"Who said that?"

"I hear everything that's going on. Take me with you."

"What?"

"Take me with you. I have to leave this place, Toby. I'm going mental. I can't stay here any longer. I can't even go home because of my folks."

He looked at her bare midriff. "Aren't you cold?"

"I'm trying to get air on it. My belly button ring went septic. Of course I'm not cold. I'm never cold anymore. I'm fucking pregnant."

"I didn't know."

She looked to the sky, blinking. "That's a surprise, everyone else in this shithole town does."

"Who's the father?"

"What am I, psychic? Maybe I should go and ask Gypsy Rosalee?" She shifted her weight to the other foot and looked at him with desperation in her eyes. "So what do you think? Can I come?"

"I can't, Michelle. Especially not if you're pregnant."

"But you and Harry are going."

"I'm not taking Harry with me."

"Does he know that?"

"No. I just decided."

"But you can't leave him behind. He worships you. What's he going to do without you?" She peered over at the booth. "Shit, what's wrong with Winfrey?"

Toby looked around and saw Winfrey's face pressed hard against the glass, as if he was trying to force his way through it. He was drooling and spitting, grinding his forehead.

"Stay here a second," he said, panicked, and ran over to the booth as Harry picked up that something was wrong and followed after him.

Toby knew exactly where to kick the booth door to open it. Winfrey had thrown up over himself, the counter, the till, his paperwork. He must have eaten a couple of pizzas earlier, because everything was red. He clutched feebly at Toby as the boy tore the bank bag from his grip and popped it open. The takings weren't inside.

"Where's the money?" Toby asked.

"My guts are killing me." Winfrey spat again. "Give me a hand outside."

"The takings. They're gone."

"No, I gave 'em to Eddie to bank for me."

"Eddie? Who's Eddie?"

"The Widow. Widow Twankey." He coughed and licked at his lips, wiping up the remains of the powder. Dark blood leaked over his lower teeth, onto his T-shirt. He tried to stand and slipped from his stool. There was a terrible smell. Winfrey had soiled himself.

"What are you doing?" Michelle called. "What's going on?"

But before she could reach them, Toby had grabbed Harry's hand and was dragging him away towards the rear exit.

The boys found themselves in the stinking trash-filled alleyway behind the arcade that was meant to be kept clear in case of fire. "Toby, you're taking me with you, aren't you?" Harry asked anxiously.

"I can't, Harry. You're too young. You'd get us caught."

"I'm only two years younger than you."

"I'm sorry, mate."

"You said I could come with you."

"Listen." Toby stopped in the alley and squeezed his eyes shut, not turning around. "You can't come because I don't want you with me. You're just a kid. You'd be a drag on my style, all right? Go on home."

"But Toby—"

"Look, just fuck off, will you?"

He bit his cheek, waiting and listening, refusing to turn. He heard a whimper like a dog being kicked, followed by footsteps stamping away. Part of his heart went with Harry.

Toby pushed open the unguarded fire door of the Crow's Nest theatre and climbed the concrete steps in darkness. The show had finished – he had seen the clusters of homebound children drifting past the arcade. The building smelled of fresh-cut wood, cheap scent, mildew. He followed the only light source to another short staircase and found himself in the backstage area. Passing between the flats of Wishee Washee's laundry house, he entered an artificial forest that owed more to the Sussex Downs than the China steppes.

"There you are, you little scamp," drawled Widow Twanky. She was sitting on a giant polystyrene toadstool leisurely smoking a cigarette. She wore a hat with a miniature line of union-jack knickers suspended across it. "This is the only time I can bear this fucking place. When the tinies have all fucked off home. It's the screaming that does my head in. It sounds like pigs being slaughtered in here some afternoons."

Toby looked about. A backpack sat beside the widow's stockinged right ankle. The dame was studying the glowing tip of her cigarette. "I suppose you've come for your gift?"

"Why are you still in that outfit?"

"Aladdin's fucking Cinderella in my dressing room. Well, she's the Emperor of China's daughter in this production, but if she thinks she's doing *Cinderella* at Christmas she's another thought coming. The bitch couldn't carry a note in a bucket. Besides . . ." He hitched up his bosom. ". . . I like being in drag. It's a good place to hide."

Twankey rose to his feet. "Christ, my knees are fucking killing me. Come on then, let's go to Ali Baba's cave." She sailed back into a darkened area of the stage.

Toby followed and found himself surrounded by plywood treasure chests filled with gold-painted plastic trinkets, as if the genie's fabled cavern had fallen on hard times and had been reduced to a pound store.

"Winfrey lent us this lot from his arcade. What a load of shit." The dame plonked herself down on a stack of money-bags marked with cartoon dollar signs. "Come here. Want to see what the Widow's got for you?" Twankey pulled him close and began fumbling in her red, white and blue bloomers.

Toby pulled the gun from his pocket, took aim and shot the dame in the balls. It wasn't a very powerful weapon and made hardly any noise, but Twankey released an incredible scream, so Toby made sure to aim the next shot into her mouth, which shut her up.

Her purple wig skewed over her left ear, revealing a sweaty bald pate. She thrashed about on the money-bags, spitting crimson teeth, her pudgy fingers digging into the bloody patch between her legs.

Toby emptied the remainder of the clip into her stomach and face, then snatched up the backpack and checked its contents. The money was inside.

The dame had torn down his union-jack bloomers and was scrabbling blindly at his flopping scarlet cock, as if trying to recover his original identity in his dying moments.

Toby crashed out of the stage door and passed the rear of the arcade. It was raining in hard squalls as he emerged from the end of the alley and dashed across the empty road, heading toward the station. The promenade was completely deserted now, the pier lost behind grey skeins of rain. The only living thing in sight was a single bedraggled donkey on the beach, tethered and facing stupidly into the downpour.

He swung his arm high and threw the gun far into the grey sea.

The train to London was due to leave in just over seven minutes. In London no one would ever find him. There, he could be anyone he wanted to be. He increased his speed but the pavement was dangerously slick, and he did not want to risk a fall. The town would try any old trick to keep him back.

He was getting soaked. Ahead he could just make out an odd figure approaching through the downpour. There was something about it he recognised. It was short and stumpy, and was walking as if it had broken its legs. At first he thought Harry had come after him. But as its appearance became more defined, Toby's thumping heart rose in his chest.

The thing crystallised from within the hammering clouds of rain, and he saw now that it was a truncated sailor the size of a child, dressed in navy blue, its hands flapping uselessly at its sides, its knees rising and falling like a puppet's. The peals of recorded laughter grew louder as it approached. It rocked from side to side and rolled its eyes.

The awful Edwardian seaside song warped and wavered through blasts of wind as it ran faster towards him. The music was distorted and sinister now, less a celebration of holiday pleasure than a Satanists' chant.

The Jolly Jack Tar slammed into Toby, winding him, sending him to his knees. As it threw its arms around his neck, he felt wood through coarse material, then realised that its wooden limbs were held together with wires that were cutting into his skin. He could feel them in its fingertips as it tightened its embrace, digging into his flesh.

The dummy's eyes rolled and its grin widened. It rocked back and forth, knocking against Toby's head with a look that said *I told you so*. It was a museum piece, a doll, nothing more, but how like a living thing it was, filled with ancient seawisdom, preserved and trapped in a glass case for the amusement of others.

Toby rolled over onto his side, the dummy clinging tight, then tighter still. He dropped the bag as its death-grip stopped his breath and the wires from its wooden fingers jabbed into his chest, as if trying to worm their way to his heart.

It bit him with a strangely flat wooden mouth, but bit down hard and would not be dislodged, and he knew that he was destined to fall and remain here beside the seaside, beside the sea.

His last clear sight was across the desolate beach to the tethered donkey standing stoically in the rain, doomed like the rest of them – in the arcades and ticket booths, in the filthy glass cases and crumbling beach shelters – to live out its days at the end of the land.

# MARK SAMUELS

## Losenef Express

MARK SAMUELS IS THE author of four short story collections: *The White Hands and Other Weird Tales*, *Black Altars*, *Glyphotech & Other Macabre Processes* and *The Man Who Collected Machen* (recently reprinted by Chômu Press), as well as the short novel *The Face of Twilight*. "Losenef Express" is the sixth of his tales to have appeared in *The Mammoth Book of Best New Horror*.

About the story, Samuels explains: "I think most fans of horror will recognise at once the late, great American author upon whom the central character of this tale is based (or, perhaps more accurately, filtered through my imagination).

We never met, although I did once catch sight of him across a room at the 1988 World Fantasy Convention in London and, prompted by curiosity, took a hasty, half-obscured photograph.

"A number of my friends knew him well, and I regret I myself never had the chance to do so. Sadly, I only discovered his brilliant work years after his untimely death."

T HE TOWN OF STRASGOL is situated in a corner of Eastern Europe forgotten by all but nationalistic Poles and Ukrainians. Their governments have squabbled over this tiny piece of territory for decades. Since neither claim has received international recognition, and its aged, insular citizens have scarcely any interest in politics, it has been allowed to fall into a

state of decay. Its cobbled streets are mossy. Its mixture of architectural styles, ranging from Neo-Classical to Art Deco, has been
disfigured by the state of near dereliction into which its buildings
have fallen. Windows are sooty, with cracked panes, and once-
elegant balconies now rot on lichen-crusted facades. At night
scarcely half of the street lamps light up, due to either a lack of
sufficient electrical power or their not being kept in a state of
proper repair. In daytime the sky is invariably leaden, and low
thick clouds hang heavy just above Strasgol. The myriad bell
towers and spires of the town disappear upwards into the mist as
if only half-constructed.

What had brought Eddie Charles Knox to the town had been
an incorrigible wanderlust and a desire to escape from his
commitments by retreat into an alcoholic haze. He had been
looking for an unknown quarter of the continent where
Americans were absent; such was his desire to escape from every
trace of their pernicious worldwide influence. His only means of
communication with people in this part of the globe was via the
foreign language phrasebooks he carried with him, and by hand
signals. He wanted nothing more by way of interaction.

Like the buildings of Strasgol, Knox was derelict. Only forty-
eight, he had managed to destroy his liver. With his mottled face,
broken capillaries and beer gut, he had long since ceased to draw
attention from the young women at whom he stared and over
whom he dreamed and wove impossible romantic fantasies as he
sat in the Zacharas Café nursing a glass and a bottle of Jack Daniel's.

Being a true son of Tennessee, he had a thirst for Old No. 7
whiskey. And had done for the last thirty years.

Back in the USA, devotees of supernatural fiction in mass-
market paperback called Eddie Knox the "Berserker of Horror".
His heavy bulk, the flaming mane of red hair and beard, the
mirror shades, had all added to the legend that had grown up
around him. Only the incongruous Harris Tweed jacket with the
worn elbows distorted the overall image. But he couldn't bring
himself to do away with it. Each ink blot, each smear of lipstick,
each booze or ingrained powder stain on the fabric, recalled a
precious memory he did not care to forget. First drafts in long-
hand with his trusty Waterman, drinking alcoholic English
editors under the table at conventions, educating groupie nymphs

in seedy hotel rooms, the acrid tang of cocaine as it hit the sinuses and the back of the throat after being snorted in toilets on first-class transatlantic flights and in stretch limos. Now those glories were of the past and had faded away like ripples, like echoes, like the dying of the light.

Eddie Knox chuckled to himself grimly. He took another swig of Jack Daniel's from his personal shot glass engraved with a Confederate flag and looked around the Zacharas Café. Black humour with your choice of poison, Fortunato? But of course, Knox replied to himself, emptying his glass and making a silent toast; "The South will Rise". Another toast – "to Edgar A. Poe". Not "Allan" and certainly *never* "Allen". America was an igno-rant Yankee Military-Industrial Complex, and traditional southern gentlemen were not required. The bastards had got to Poe in the end. Banged him on the head in Baltimore. Damn the Freemasons!

Knox wished he could drown his sense of self-contempt. Sure, it was delightful to be here in the Zacharas Café, with its inti-mate booths for private intellectual conversation, with its rococo plaster ceiling, its air of 1920s European decadence, pre-war cabaret, and engraved windows of dazzling green glass. But it was dirty money that got him here. And he believed he wasn't even worthy of raising a fellow author's silent toast to the likes of Poe.

Knox felt like a fake. It wasn't his tales of horror that seemed cheap; sure, they were hard to find but when found were never-theless rightly lauded for their authenticity. No, it was the endless novels he'd written detailing the pulp adventures of Mungo the Barbarian and the sexual shenanigans of Mother Superior Lucia Vulva that had paid the bills and that had given respectability to the bank account. Those were what felt like cheating. When he was talking with fellow professionals, he laughed off any other objective than making big bucks. He was only a working writer. Fuck the pretentious snobs amongst us. But when he was alone, the compromise hit him hard. He wanted to be remembered as an artist. Nothing else really mattered in the end. There was no other form of survival after death. In the final analysis, all writ-ers find out this hard truth. Whether or not they admit to it is a different matter.

Knox loved Europe. He adored its sense of history and slow decay. He wanted to be absorbed into its fabric and leave behind every single last trace of the obnoxiously optimistic and bogus "American Dream". He'd lived and fulfilled that dream; and found it as nightmarish as an endlessly repeated TV advert for fast food, as a "you're worth it" fixed smile with oh-so-perfect white teeth. And so he stopped dreaming, and crashed headlong into a sea of reality he couldn't bear, but which suited him better. He preferred to drown quickly than die via a suicide stretched out across years.

He downed another dose of Jack Daniel's from his shot glass and stared across the expanse of the Zacharas Café. It was sparsely occupied. There were one or two eastern European businessmen in sharp suits nursing beers, a couple arguing quietly in a corner, and, behind him, a fat man slouched back into a booth with his face lost in shadow. Knox had turned around once, pricked by the sensation of being watched, and, although he could not make out the man's face clearly enough to tell, he had the distinct impression this person was staring fixedly at him. Maybe, Knox thought, he's one of the natives who hates tourists just as much as I, another tourist, do. The way the lights were arranged in that part of the bar meant the fat man was visible only as a shadowy bulk, except for his gnarled powerful hands. These were resting on the table, in a pool of light cast by a shaded lamp. They were every inch as large and impressive as Knox's own.

After a couple more shots, Knox's agitation increased. He tried to resist the impulse to glance behind him, but it was impossible. Each time he had the impression the fat man was not only staring at him with a malicious contempt, but also with a sneer about his lips. There was no way he could be sure of this, for the shadow over the stranger's face masked it, but he felt certain, on some primal, instinctive level, it was true. Finally, with enough booze in his gut to overcome any sense of restraint, and with his bill settled by the US banknote he left behind, he stood up abruptly, spun round and made directly for the booth containing the fat man in order to confront him.

But the stranger was no longer seated there. The booth was empty.

Knox cast his gaze around and saw the fat man outside, through one of the café windows. He was making his way into the fog and the back of his bulk was only visible for a moment before it was swallowed up entirely.

Knox decided to go after him. Had he been sober, the idea would have seemed ridiculous. Chase after someone in the fog, in a foreign city, for the offence of having apparently stared at you with contempt? But he was not sober. He was drunk. Moreover, he was drunk and he was sick of everything. And the stranger had become a symbol of that "everything" in his mind. Knox did not know what he would do when he confronted the fat man, but he didn't think the outcome would be pleasant. Back in Tennessee, Knox used to shoot snakes on his porch.

Outside, the air was cold, clammy and thick. The shock of it made Knox gasp for breath momentarily. For a second he thought of returning to the café and forgetting about the whole thing. But he pressed on instead, accompanied by the sound of his heels clattering across the slippery cobblestones. He could see only a short distance ahead, and the street lamps burned like spectral pools of light in the gloom. Knox knew he could not have kept pace with a younger, slimmer, fitter man, and it was only the fact that his quarry was as overweight as Knox that made the chase a contest. He had no idea if the stranger even knew he was being followed along the series of narrow alleyways and claustrophobic courtyards, although from the circuitous route taken, it seemed likely.

The streets became a delirium of images, of skeletal trees, arched passageways and tendrils of fog.

Just as Knox had reached the point of breathless collapse and could not continue, he found that the stranger's stamina had also given out only moments before. He saw the fat man's bulk leant up against railings, hunched over and gasping for air. Knox summoned his last reserves of energy and hurled himself towards the fat man before he could land a first blow.

All the hatred, rage and disappointment he had ever felt in life seemed to well up inside him and demanded vengeance upon this individual. Knox could not even bring himself to say anything to the fat man, but found his hands fumbling madly towards the stranger's throat. The fog fortuitously closed in around them in order to hide Knox's crime. The blood seemed to boil in his veins, and he squeezed and squeezed the fat man's fleshly throat, choking him to death. Knox heard a voice, its accent indistinguishable, croak out the words *I waited for you*, or what sounded like them, before a gurgling sound and then final silence.

Impossible that he had not seen his tormentor's – *his victim's* – face. But it was true. And Knox realised that, had the fog not closed in, he would have deliberately avoided looking at it, because he was unaccountably terrified of what he would see. He was grateful to have been spared the sight of the dead stranger's face at the end, since he had pulled out the jack-knife he always carried in his breast pocket, the one with the corkscrew at one end and the blade at the other, and slashed madly at the countenance of the corpse, tearing through flesh and scratching against the bone of the skull. He used the weapon to slice and hack until his hands were dripping, and the cuffs of his Harris Tweed jacket soaked with blood.

But the deed had not been carried out silently. The sounds of the struggle, and of his victim's cries, had been heard. Knox heard the noise of advancing footsteps racing across the cobblestones behind him. There was more than one person closing in. Knox was sure no one could have seen him commit the murder, for the darkness and all-encompassing fog had been his ally, but he had to flee now and flee quickly.

A return to his hotel in order to collect his meagre luggage seemed out of the question, for haste was of the essence, and Knox resolved to make his way to Strasgol Station, which he recalled was close by. He would board the first available train; clean himself up immediately in one of the compartment toilets and travel as far away from the town as he was able. As he stumbled through the narrow alleyways that weaved between the mouldering buildings, he thought to check his wallet. He'd cashed some traveller's cheques yesterday, and had a sudden fear he might have lost it in the struggle with the fat man. Nothing was missing.

Knox heard no sound of pursuit and, after walking for some ten minutes, arrived at the ill-lit and rundown concourse of the train station. A few passengers milled around inside under grimy fluorescent strip lighting, but it was late at night, and, in order to hide the blood on his hands and on the cuffs of his jacket, he stuffed his hands deep into his pockets. The ticket office had closed, and a sign on the notice board indicated that payment should be made to the conductor on the train. Also pinned to the notice board was a timetable. The final service, at eleven fifty, was scheduled to depart in five minutes, and was the express to Losenef.

Knox kept his head down as he joined the other seven passengers who were making their way onto the platform. The train was already waiting for them. It consisted of six coaches painted with olive livery and a driving cab, marked PKP SN-61. The passengers climbed aboard, hauling their luggage into the compartments, and Knox waited until the other seven travellers had chosen seats before he joined the service. He wanted to find a seat where he could not easily be seen by anyone else, at least until he had managed to clean himself up. The very last compartment of the rear coach was completely unoccupied and so Knox chose this one for his purposes, climbing inside only as the platform guard blew his whistle and the train actually began to move.

Once he was seated and the train picked up speed, leaving Strasgol Station behind, he removed his jacket with the bloodied cuffs and rolled up his shirtsleeves in order to conceal the blood that had soaked through. He folded his jacket so that its arms were hidden beneath folds, and nestled the garment under his arm. Then he left his compartment and looked along the narrow, rubbish-strewn corridor that ran along the length of the coach. It was deserted. At the end was the door to the toilet, and Knox was relieved to see, as he approached, that the indicator above the handle was green; it was unoccupied.

The inside was tiny and dirty. There was not even enough room to stretch one's arms out to their full extent. A light bulb had been screwed into a socket on the low ceiling and provided a urine yellow glare by way of illumination. The lid of the squat plastic toilet was down, and for this mercy Knox was grateful, for he could detect the lingering stench of unflushed excrement. Above the crack-webbed washbasin was a round mirror about six inches in diameter. Its surface was coated with a thin layer of silvery-white residue, making it appear to be filled with mist.

Knox turned on the tap above the sink, put the bloodied cuffs of his jacket underneath the dribble of cold running water and rubbed them vigorously with a token sliver of hand soap. After a few minutes of work, the cuffs turned from crimson to pink. No further change seemed likely, and the soap had been used up, so Knox ceased his labours. He looked up from the sink into the recesses of the small mirror.

At first he saw his own haggard face staring back at him, the eyes haunted, but then the image lost focus, and it dissolved into something else. He discerned a smear of red and black, until at last the vision gained form, and Knox stared at the ravaged features of the man whose face he had obliterated with his knife. The mutilated reflection in the mirror gazed back at him with Knox's eyes. Its lipless grinning mouth breathed out a single sentence in a gloating whisper; *I still await.* For one terrifying instant it even seemed to Knox that he had switched bodies with the revenant in the mirror and was looking out from it through a cloud of mist at his own face. He raised his hands and covered his eyes to block out the sight, and when he lowered them, it had vanished. His hands were trembling and his nerves were shredded. He needed a drink to calm himself down. No, he needed much more than that; enough to blot out the night journey until morning came, and he was hundreds of miles away from Strasgol and the scene of the senseless murder he had committed.

He cupped water from the tap in his hands and splashed it across his forehead, his cheeks and his beard. He looked again in the mirror, and to his relief, saw only his own face and the background of the toilet, but nothing more.

He passed along the corridor to the next carriage and found the buffet cabin situated in a small section at the end. The metal shutter in front of the counter was down, and Knox knocked on it, hoping to draw the attention of a recalcitrant railway staff member. The possibility that the buffet was closed on this service was one he did not wish to entertain; such was the desire he had for the relief only alcohol could provide. There had been no initial response to his knocking and so Knox tried again, more forcefully this time, using his fist, until he felt someone tap him on the shoulder. Knox turned and saw the train conductor. This individual was muffled up against the cold and had wrapped a scarf high above his neck and just beneath his nose. He wore a tatty railway-issue greatcoat, with the collar turned up and it seemed, from its condition, the garment had seen many years of service. His dark green cap was pulled down low across his forehead, its brim resting on the top of thick-lensed and impenetrable eyeglasses.

"Ticket, sir?" the conductor said, his voice hollow and his English heavy with an Eastern European inflexion.

Knox rummaged in the pockets of his jacket, turning over loose scraps of paper, until he remembered he had no ticket and had intended to pay his fare on the train.

"I have no ticket," Knox said, "can't I buy one from you now?"

"More money. Two hundred zlotys," he said.

"I see," Knox replied, irked that the conductor had immediately marked him out as an American tourist, and was prepared to take financial advantage accordingly. Still, Knox thought, perhaps the man could be useful.

"How much extra would it cost to get a bottle of something warming to drink from the buffet? How about a discount for US dollars?" he asked, pulling out his wallet from the inner recesses of his tweed jacket with the pinkish cuffs.

"Buffet is closed. No buffet. No drink. Unless you pay maybe," the conductor said, as his head nodded towards the notes Knox had drawn out and held in his hand.

The conductor flashed a set of keys attached to a chain that he drew from the pocket of his greatcoat and rattled them ostentatiously. He unlocked the door of the buffet cabin, disappeared inside and then emerged a few moments later bearing a half litre glass bottle and a plastic cup.

Knox handed over twenty dollars in denominations of five each. He was not at all sure whether this amount would cover both the cost of the ticket and the unknown booze provided by the conductor, but the man looked at the notes, held them up to the lamplight above their heads and grunted something unintelligible Knox took as a sign of satisfaction.

For his part, Knox was busy examining the bottle he'd just purchased. It contained a cloudy green liquid. The label gave no clue, at least in English, as to its contents. It was decorated with an obscure design, something five-pointed and akin to a swastika. Certainly, at least, the legend "85% vol" inspired confidence.

"It's good," the conductor said, as if aware an American would not be familiar with the brand. "It is the Nepenthe drink."

"A brand of absinthe?" Knox asked.

"Better. You drink. Have a good trip." He laughed and then shuffled off, making his way along the length of the corridor, swaying with the motion of the train.

Knox went in the opposite direction, back towards the coach in which he'd boarded the train. He wanted to lose himself in the strange green liquid as quickly as possible and feel it coursing down his throat, filling his stomach with warmth and turning his brains into a soothing grey mush. He noticed that his fellow passengers appeared to be as uninterested in mingling with one another as was he; they sat as far apart from one another as they could, in individual compartments where possible, or at the opposite ends of seating where a compartment was already occupied. They slumped in their places as if they had already travelled for hours and hours. Some were either already drunk or else in a dull confused state between sleep and waking. One could not easily tell which.

He pulled open the door to the unoccupied compartment at the rear where he'd boarded and sat down on the edge of the seat, gazing at the liquid in the bottle finding its level as the train rattled over points on the track. It had a screw top, for which he was grateful; since his hands still trembled to the extent he was not confident about working a cork free with his jack-knife (say rather, he thought, grimly, *murder weapon*). As it was, he still fumbled with the plastic cup whilst pouring out a large measure, and almost spilt its contents. He knocked back the first dose swiftly, coughing as the liquid passed down into his insides. Christ, he thought, what is this stuff? It felt as if someone had kicked him in the head. He leant forward, feeling a wave of nausea, and was momentarily afraid he would vomit. But after the second shot, taken as quickly as the first, all the unpleasant sensations passed and he was overcome with a deadening numbness. He could not feel the ends of his fingers and toes, his anxiety ebbed away, the tide of fear was at last drawing out, and he exhaled what seemed to be an eternal breath. He slumped back into the long seat and nestled the bottle on his lap, watching the green liquid inside tumble like a captured ocean wave.

The darkness outside made it seem, from within, as if the train were stationary. Knox flopped along the length of the seat towards the carriage window and peered out through the glass into the gloom. He saw vague shapes and branches of trees that had not been sufficiently cut back – their sharp ends scraped along the sides and roof of the train.

His eyes refocused and instead of looking through the glass, he now saw his own reflection on the surface of the window. His gaze was filled with hatred. There was a sneer on his lips. Knox was terrified the reflection would reach across the divide and strangle him. He backed away from the sight, afraid of its taking on the appearance of the torn and bloodied revenant he'd seen earlier. He heard a voice in his head, the same voice as before, but this time the words it spoke were different: "*you come closer*," it said, "*you draw close to me*".

Knox pulled down the blinds on all the windows and poured himself another dose of the potent bad medicine. His head was swimming, and he heard the sound of his teeth chattering in his mouth. The compartment around him blurred, the overhead luggage racks, the electric lamps and the advertisements on the walls faded from view and he passed out.

When he awoke it must have been hours later. His watch had stopped, so he had no precise way of telling just how long it had been. But he knew he still travelled by night for it was dark outside; he had lifted the blind a little to see if it were daylight yet. His mouth was dry and his lips were encrusted with the scum of dried saliva.

The half-drunk bottle of booze had wedged itself between the cushions of the long seat. Alongside it was the remains of the plastic cup, crushed by the weight of Knox's body where he had lain slumped after having passed out. The light from the compartment's electric lamps hurt his eyes and so he took out his mirror shades from the glasses case he kept in the breast pocket of his tweed jacket, and put them on. The hangover was so bad he felt he would never recover from it. He took a swig from the bottle, but the taste made the bile rise in his throat. He decided to go in search of the train conductor in order to find out how much further it was to Losenef.

As he passed the compartment adjacent to his own he heard a groaning from within and stopped to look inside. A solitary passenger was sprawled across the floor, face down and motionless. The man was dressed in a badly crumpled light grey suit covered with dark brown stains. He had a foul odour about him, of eggs that had turned rotten. Knox considered, for a moment, ignoring him but then the groan came again and this time it was louder and more prolonged than before. The man in the grey suit had, like Knox, been drinking the green spirit. An empty bottle of it lay just outside his reach.

Knox knelt down, pinching his nose and covering his mouth with one hand to guard against the stench and, with the other, he grabbed the shoulder of the man's jacket and turned his body over.

His face was a grisly ruin. Half of it had been eaten away by the maggots that writhed and burrowed through yellowish flesh. There was nothing at all left of the eyes; only vacant sockets remained. And then the corpse groaned for a third time, a hollow and despairing groan that issued from unimaginable depths of suffering. Something conscious existed within the shell.

Knox backed away, leaving the hideous cadaver face-upright. And still it continued to issue its uncanny cries.

The next compartment along contained a similar horror. The occupant, a woman with long dusty blonde hair, faced the wall with her hands reached out as if clutching at it for support. She made heartrending sobbing and snuffling noises. But she was dead. The skin on her hands was flaking away like paint on a weather-beaten wall, and Knox was glad he was spared the sight of her face, for the malformed sound of sobbing could only emanate from a deformed mouth.

The litany of terror was repeated throughout the whole of the carriage and, so too, throughout the next. All the passengers were dead but not one was silent.

Knox took a deep breath and leant with his back to the wall behind him. He took off his mirror shades, rubbed his eyes with his knuckles, and spat on the floor. This was junk, he thought. He'd written stories worse than this in his time. He didn't believe any of it. He must have bashed his head on something whilst he was sozzled, causing him to hallucinate. He had impacted his skull, affecting the brain, resulting in a wild bout of concussion. The more he thought of it, the more the idea fitted. He was having a psychotic episode. Nothing more. He had killed no one back in Strasgol; he'd only imagined he had. All this business on the train was brought on by a bump to the head. He put his shades back on and grinned. Then he ran his fingers over the entirety of his skull, working through the mass of red hair that covered it. His grin evaporated. There was no damage to his skull.

The train began to slow down and finally drew to a halt amidst a grinding screech. From further along the corridor, out of the buffet cabin, the conductor emerged. He'd removed the long scarf he had wound around the lower half of his face. Now Knox could see why it had been covered up. There was no lower half of his face. Where there should have been a bottom jaw there was instead a gaping bloody hollow. The conductor's voice issued from a vacuum, and without tongue or lips should have been impossible to form. Yet the sound was as real as when he had spoken previously.

"Last stop, sir," the conductor breathed, "Losenef."

What was odd was that, after disembarking from the train, Knox found Losenef to be an exact duplicate of Strasgol and, moreover, he had arrived an hour earlier than he departed. It was only in the Zacharas Café, having spotted the duplicate of himself drinking Jack Daniel's, that he realised the truth. He'd wait a little longer and then try yet again to take his revenge. Eventually, he hoped, he would succeed.

# NORMAN PARTRIDGE

## Lesser Demons

NORMAN PARTRIDGE'S FICTION INCLUDES horror, suspense and the fantastic – "sometimes all in one story," says his friend Joe R. Lansdale. Partridge's novel *Dark Harvest* was chosen by *Publishers Weekly* as one of the "100 Best Books of 2006", and two short story collections appeared in 2010 – *Lesser Demons* from Subterranean Press, and *Johnny Halloween* from Cemetery Dance.

Other work includes the "Jack Baddalach" mysteries, *Saguaro Riptide* and *The Ten-Ounce Siesta*, plus *The Crow: Wicked Prayer*, which was adapted for film. Partridge's compact, thrill-a-minute style has been praised by Stephen King and Peter Straub, and his work has received multiple Bram Stoker Awards.

"I was surprised to receive an invitation for S.T. Joshi's *Black Wings*," reveals Partridge, "an anthology of Lovecraftian fiction. Although I knew S.T. admired my work, I've never quite seen myself as a Mythos writer.

"While I respect H.P. Lovecraft and his contribution to horror, I've never felt that his worldview (or maybe I should say *universe*-view) meshed with mine.

"In the end, that's what made the story work . . . at least for me. I concentrated on my differences with Lovecraft, and approached the material from a place where Jim Thompson would be more comfortable than HPL. And I'm delighted that so many people have enjoyed the tale – it was a lot of fun to write."

Down in the cemetery, the children were laughing.
They had another box open.

They had their axes out. Their knives, too.

I sat in the sheriff's department pickup, parked beneath a willow tree. Ropes of leaves hung before me like green curtains, but those curtains didn't stop the laughter. It climbed the ridge from the hollow below, carrying other noises – shovels biting hard-packed earth, axe blades splitting coffinwood, knives scraping flesh from bone. But the laughter was the worst of it. It spilled over teeth sharpened with files, chewed its way up the ridge, and did its best to strip the hard bark off my spine.

I didn't sit still. I grabbed a gas can from the back of the pickup. I jacked a full clip into my dead deputy's .45, slipped a couple spares into one of the leather pockets on my gun belt and buttoned it down. Then I fed shells into my shotgun and pumped one into the chamber.

I went for a little walk.

Five months before, I stood with my deputy, Roy Barnes, out on County Road 14. We weren't alone. There were others present. Most of them were dead, or something close to it.

I held that same shotgun in my hand. The barrel was hot. The deputy clutched his .45, a ribbon of bitter smoke coiling from the business end. It wasn't a stink you'd breathe if you had a choice, but we didn't have one.

Barnes reloaded, and so did I. The June sun was dropping behind the trees, but the shafts of late-afternoon light slanting through the gaps were as bright as high noon. The light played through black smoke rising from a Chrysler sedan's smouldering engine and white smoke simmering from the hot asphalt piled in the road gang's dump truck.

My gaze settled on the wrecked Chrysler. The deal must have started there. Fifteen or twenty minutes before, the big black car had piled into an old oak at a fork in the county road. Maybe the driver had nodded off, waking just in time to miss a flagman from the work gang. Over-corrected and hit the brakes too late. Said: *Hello tree, goodbye heartbeat.*

Maybe that was the way it happened. Maybe not. Barnes tried to piece it together later on, but in the end it really didn't matter much. What mattered was that the sedan was driven by a man who looked like something dredged up from the bottom of a stagnant pond. What mattered was that something exploded from the Chrysler's trunk after the accident. That thing was the size of a grizzly, but it wasn't a bear. It didn't look like a bear at all. Not unless you'd ever seen one turned inside out, it didn't.

Whatever it was, that skinned monster could move. It unhinged its sizeable jaws and swallowed a man who weighed two-hundred-and-change in one long ratcheting gulp, choking arms and legs and torso down a gullet lined with razor teeth. Sucked the guy into a blue-veined belly that hung from its ribs like a grave-robber's sack and then dragged that belly along fresh asphalt as it chased down the other men, slapping them onto the scorching roadbed and spitting bloody hunks of dead flesh in their faces. Some it let go, slaughtering others like so many chickens tossed live and squawking onto a hot skillet.

It killed four men before we showed up, fresh from handling a fender-bender on the detour route a couple miles up the road. Thanks to my shotgun and Roy Barnes' .45, all that remained of the thing was a red mess with a corpse spilling out of its gutshot belly. As for the men from the work crew, there wasn't much you could say. They were either as dead as that poor bastard who'd ended his life in a monster's stomach, or they were whimpering with blood on their faces, or they were running like hell and halfway back to town. But whatever they were doing didn't make too much difference to me just then.

"What was it, Sheriff?" Barnes asked.

"I don't know."

"You sure it's dead?"

"I don't know that, either. All I know is we'd better stay away from it."

We backed off. The only things that lingered were the afternoon light slanting through the trees, and the smoke from that hot asphalt, and the smoke from the wrecked Chrysler. The light cut swirls through that smoke as it pooled around the dead thing, settling low and misty, as if the something beneath it were trying to swallow a chunk of the world, roadbed and all.

"I feel kind of dizzy," Barnes said.

"Hold on, Roy. You have to."

I grabbed my deputy by the shoulder and spun him around. He was just a kid, really – before this deal, he'd never even had his gun out of its holster while on duty. I'd been doing the job for fifteen years, but I could have clocked a hundred and never seen anything like this. Still, we both knew it wasn't over. We'd seen what we'd seen, we'd done what we'd done, and the only thing left to do was deal with whatever was coming next.

That meant checking out the Chrysler. I brought the shotgun barrel even with it, aiming at the driver's side door as we advanced. The driver's skull had slammed the steering wheel at the point of impact. Black blood smeared across his face, and filed teeth had slashed through his pale lips so that they hung from his gums like leavings you'd bury after gutting a fish. On top of that, words were carved on his face. Some were purpled over with scar tissue and others were still fresh scabs. None of them were words I'd seen before. I didn't know what to make of them.

"Jesus," Barnes said. "Will you look at that."

"Check the back seat, Roy."

Barnes did. There was other stuff there. Torn clothes. Several pairs of handcuffs. Ropes woven with fishhooks. A wrought-iron trident. And in the middle of all that was a cardboard box filled with books.

The deputy pulled one out. It was old. Leathery. As he opened it, the book started to come apart in his hands. Brittle pages fluttered across the road . . .

Something rustled in the open trunk. I pushed past Roy and fired point blank before I even looked. The spare tire exploded. On the other side of the trunk, a clawed hand scrabbled up through a pile of shotgunned clothes. I fired again. Those claws clacked together, and the thing beneath them didn't move again.

Using the shotgun barrel, I shifted the clothes to one side, uncovering a couple of dead kids in a nest of rags and blood. Both of them were handcuffed. The thing I'd killed had chewed its way out of one of their bellies. It had a grinning, wolfish muzzle and a tail like a dozen braided snakes. I slammed the trunk and chambered another shell. I stared down at the trunk, waiting for something else to happen, but nothing did.

Behind me . . . well, that was another story.

The men from the road gang were on the move.

Their boots scuffed over hot asphalt.

They gripped crowbars, and sledgehammers, and one of them even had a machete.

They came towards us with blood on their faces, laughing like children.

The children in the cemetery weren't laughing anymore.

They were gathered around an open grave, eating.

Like always, a couple seconds passed before they noticed me. Then their brains sparked their bodies into motion, and the first one started for me with an axe. I pulled the trigger, and the shotgun turned his spine to jelly, and he went down in sections. The next one I took at longer range, so the blast chewed her over some. Dark blood from a hundred small wounds peppered her dress. Shrieking, she turned tail and ran.

Which gave the third Bloodface a chance to charge me. He was faster than I expected, dodging the first blast, quickly closing the distance. There was barely enough room between the two of us for me to get off another shot, but I managed the job. The blast took off his head. That was that.

Or at least I thought it was. Behind me, something whispered through long grass that hadn't been cut in five months. I whirled, but the barefoot girl's knife was already coming at me. The blade ripped through my coat in a silver blur, slashing my right forearm. A twist of her wrist and she tried to come back for another piece, but I was faster and bashed her forehead with the shotgun butt. Her skull split like a popped blister and she went down hard, cracking the back of her head on a tombstone.

That double-punched her ticket. I sucked a deep breath and held it. Blood reddened the sleeve of my coat as the knife wound began to pump. A couple seconds later I began to think straight, and I got the idea going in my head that I should put down the shotgun and get my belt around my arm. I did that and tightened it good. Wounded, I'd have a walk to get back to the pickup. Then I'd have to find somewhere safe where I could take care of my arm. The pickup wasn't far distance-wise, but it was a steep climb up to the ridgeline. My heart would be pounding double-time the whole way. If I didn't watch it, I'd lose a lot of blood.

But first I had a job to finish. I grabbed the shotgun and moved towards the rifled grave. Even in the bright afternoon sun, the long grass was still damp with morning dew. I noticed that my boots were wet as I stepped over the dead girl. That bothered me, but the girl's corpse didn't. She couldn't bother me now that she was dead.

I left her behind me in the long grass, her body a home for the scarred words she'd carved on her face with the same knife she'd used to butcher the dead and butcher me. All that remained of her was a barbed rictus grin and a pair of dead eyes staring up into the afternoon sun, as if staring at nothing at all. And that's what she was to me – that's what they all were now that they were dead. They were nothing, no matter what they'd done to themselves with knives and files, no matter what they'd done to the living they'd murdered or the dead they'd pried out of burying boxes. They were nothing at all, and I didn't spare them another thought.

Because there were other things to worry about – things like the one that had infected the children with a mouthful of spit-up blood. Sometimes those things came out of graves. Other times they came out of car trunks or meat lockers or off slabs in a morgue. But wherever they came from they were always born of a corpse, and there were corpses here aplenty.

I didn't see anything worrisome down in the open grave. Just stripped bones and tatters of red meat, but it was meat that wasn't moving. That was good. So I took care of things. I rolled the dead Bloodfaces into the grave. I walked back to the cottonwood thicket at the ridge side of the cemetery and grabbed the gas can I'd brought from the pickup. I emptied it into the hole, then tossed the can in, too. I wasn't carrying it back to the truck with a sliced-up arm.

I lit a match and let it fall.

The gas *thupped* alive and the hole growled fire.

Fat sizzled as I turned my back on the grave. Already, other sounds were rising in the hollow. Thick, rasping roars. Branches breaking somewhere in the treeline behind the old funeral home. The sound of something big moving through the timber – something that heard my shotgun bark three times and wasn't afraid of the sound.

Whatever that thing was, I didn't want to see it just now. I disappeared into the cottonwood thicket before it saw me.

Barnes had lived in a converted hunting lodge on the far side of the lake. There weren't any other houses around it, and I hadn't been near the place in months. I'd left some stuff there, including medical supplies we'd scavenged from the local emergency room. If I was lucky, they would still be there.

Thick weeds bristled over the dirt road that led down to Roy's place. That meant no one had been around for a while. Of course, driving down the road would leave a trail, but I didn't have much choice. I'd been cut and needed to do something about it fast. You take chances. Some are large and some are small. Usually, the worries attached to the small ones amount to nothing.

I turned off the pavement. The dirt road was rutted, and I took it easy. My arm ached every time the truck hit a pothole. Finally, I parked under the carport on the east side of the old lodge. Porch steps groaned as I made my way to the door, and I entered behind the squared-off barrel of Barnes' .45.

Inside, nothing was much different than it had been a couple of months before. Barnes' blood-spattered coat hung on a hook by the door. His reading glasses rested on the coffee table. Next to it, a layer of mould floated on top of a cup of coffee he'd never finished. But I didn't care about any of that. I cared about the cabinet we'd stowed in the bathroom down the hall.

Good news. Nothing in the cabinet had been touched. I stripped to the waist, cleaned the knife wound with saline solution from an IV bag, then stopped the bleeding as best I could. The gash wasn't as deep as it might have been. I sewed it up with a hooked surgical needle, bandaged it, and gobbled down twice as many antibiotics as any doctor would have prescribed. That done, I remembered my wet boots. Sitting there on the toilet, I laughed at myself a little bit, because given the circumstances it seemed like a silly thing to worry about. Still, I went to the ground-floor bedroom I'd used during the summer and changed into a dry pair of Wolverines I'd left behind.

Next I went to the kitchen. I popped the top on a can of chilli, found a spoon, and started towards the old dock down by the lake. There was a rusty swing set behind the lodge that had been put up by a previous owner; it shadowed a kid's sandbox. Barnes hadn't had use for either – he wasn't even married – but he'd never bothered to change things around. Why would he? It would have been a lot of work for no good reason.

I stopped and stared at the shadows beneath the swing set, but I didn't stare long. The dock was narrow and more than a little rickety, with a small boathouse bordering one side. I walked past the boathouse and sat on the end of the dock for a while. I ate cold chilli. Cattails whispered beneath a rising breeze. A flock of geese passed overhead, heading south. The sun set, and twilight settled in.

It was quiet. I liked it that way. With Barnes, it was seldom quiet. I guess you'd say he had a curious mind. The deputy liked to talk about things, especially things he didn't understand, like those monsters that crawled out of corpses. Barnes called them lesser demons. He'd read about them in one of those books we found in the wreck. He had ideas about them, too. Barnes talked about those ideas a lot over the summer, but I didn't want to talk about any of it. Talking just made me edgy. So did Barnes' ideas and explanations . . . all those *maybes* and *what ifs*. Barnes was big on those; he'd go on and on about them.

Me, I cared about simpler things. Things anyone could understand. Things you didn't need to discuss, or debate. Like waking up before a razor-throated monster had a chance to swallow me whole. Or not running out of shotgun shells. Or making sure one of those things never spit a dead man's blood in my face, so I wouldn't take a file to my teeth or go digging in a graveyard for food. That's what I'd cared about that summer, and I cared about the same things in the hours after a Bloodfaced lunatic carved me up with a dirty knife.

I finished the chilli. It was getting dark. Getting cold, too, because winter was coming on. I tossed the empty can in the lake and turned back towards the house. The last purple smear of twilight silhouetted the place, and a pair of birds darted into the chimney as I walked up the dock. I wouldn't have seen them if I hadn't looked at that exact moment, and I shook my head. Birds building nests in October? It was just another sign of a world gone nuts.

Inside, I settled on the couch and thought about lighting a fire. I didn't care about the birds – nesting in that chimney was their own bad luck. I'd got myself a chill out at the dock, and there was a cord of oak stacked under the carport. Twenty minutes and I could have a good blaze going. But I was tired, and my arm throbbed like it had grown its own heartbeat. I didn't want to tear the stitches toting a bunch of wood. I just wanted to sleep.

I took some painkillers – more than I should have – and washed them down with Jack Daniel's. After a while, the darkness pulled in close. The bedroom I'd used the summer before was on the ground floor. But I didn't want to be downstairs in case anything came around during the night, especially with a cool liquid fog pumping through my veins. I knew I'd be safer upstairs.

There was only one room upstairs – a big room, kind of like a loft.

It was Barnes' bedroom, and his blood was still on the wall.

I didn't care. I grabbed my shotgun. I climbed the stairs.

Like I said: I was tired.

Besides, I couldn't see Barnes' blood in the dark.

At first, Roy and I stuck to the sheriff's office, which was new enough to have pretty good security. When communication stopped and the whole world took a header, we decided that wasn't a good idea anymore. We started moving around.

My place wasn't an option. It was smack dab in the middle of town. You didn't want to be in town. There were too many blind corners, and too many fences you couldn't see over. Dig in there, and you'd never feel safe no how many bullets you had in your clip. So I burned down the house. It never meant much to me, anyway. It was just a house, and I burned it down mostly because it was mine and I didn't want anyone else rooting around in the stuff I kept there. I never went back after that.

Barnes' place was off the beaten path. Like I said, that made it a good choice. I knew I could get some sleep there. Not too much, if you know what I mean. Every board in the old lodge seemed to creak, and the brush was heavy around the property. If you were a light sleeper – like me – you'd most likely hear anything that was coming your way long before it had a chance to get you.

And I heard every noise that night in Barnes' bedroom. I didn't sleep well at all. Maybe it was my sliced-up arm or those pain-killers mixing with the whiskey and antibiotics – but I tossed and turned for hours. The window was open a crack, and cold air cut through the gap like that barefooted girl's knife. And it seemed I heard another knife scraping somewhere deep in the house, but it must have been those birds in the chimney, scrabbling around in their nest.

Outside, the chained seats on the swing set squealed and squeaked in the wind. Empty, they swung back and forth, back and forth, over cool white sand.

After a couple months, Barnes wasn't doing so well. We'd scavenged a few of the larger summer houses on the other side of the lake, places that belonged to rich couples from down south. We'd even made a few trips into town when things seemed especially quiet. We'd gotten things to the point where we had everything we needed at the lodge. If something came around that needed killing, we killed it. Otherwise, we steered clear of the world.

But Barnes couldn't stop talking about those books he'd snatched from the wrecked Chrysler. He read the damned things every day. Somehow, he thought they had all the answers. I didn't know about that. If there were answers in those books, you'd have one hell of a time pronouncing them. I knew that much.

That wasn't a problem for Barnes. He read those books cover to cover, making notes about those lesser demons, consulting dictionaries and reference books he'd swiped from the library. When he finished, he read them again. After a while, I couldn't stand to look at him sitting there with those reading glasses on his face. I even got sick of the smell of his coffee. So I tried to keep busy. I'd do little things around the lodge, but none of them amounted to much. I chainsawed several oak trees and split the wood. Stacking it near the edge of the property to season would also give us some cover if we ever needed to defend the perimeter, so I did that, too. I even set some traps on the other side of the lodge, but after a while I got sloppy and began to forget where they were. Usually, that happened when I was thinking about something else while I was trying to work. Like Barnes' *maybes* and *what ifs*.

Sometimes I'd get jumpy. I'd hear noises while I was working. Or I'd think I did. I'd start looking for things that weren't there. Sometimes I'd even imagine something so clearly I could almost see it. I knew that was dangerous . . . and maybe a little crazy. So I found something else to do – something that would keep my mind from wandering.

I started going out alone during the day. Sometimes I'd run across a pack of Bloodfaces. Sometimes one of those demons . . . or maybe two. You never saw more than two at a time. They never travelled in packs, and that was lucky for me. I doubted I could have handled more than a couple, and even handling two . . . well, that could be dicey.

But I did it on my own. And I didn't learn about the damn things by reading a book. I learned by reading them. Watching them operate when they didn't know I was there, hunting them down with the shotgun, blowing them apart. That's how I learned – reading tales written in muscle and blood, or told by a wind that carried bitter scent and shadows that fell where they shouldn't.

And you know what? I found out that those demons weren't so different. Not really. I didn't have to think it through much, because when you scratched off the paint and primer and got down to it those things had a spot in the food chain just like you and me. They took what they needed when they needed it, and they did their best to make sure anything below them didn't buck the line.

If there was anything above them – well, I hadn't seen it.

I hoped I never would.

I wouldn't waste time worrying about it until I did.

Come August, there were fewer of those things around. Maybe that meant the world was sorting itself out. Or maybe it just meant that in my little corner I was bucking that food chain hard enough to hacksaw a couple of links.

By that time I'd probably killed fifteen of them. Maybe twenty. During a late summer thunderstorm, I tracked a hoofed Minotaur with centipede dreadlocks to an abandoned barn deep in the hollow. The damn thing surprised me, nearly ripping open my belly with its black horns before I managed to jam a pitchfork through its throat. There was a gigantic worm with a dozen sucking maws; I burned it down to cinders in the water-treatment plant. Beneath the high school football stadium, a couple rat-faced spiders with a web strung across a cement tunnel nearly caught me in their trap, but I left them dying there, gore oozing from their fat bellies drop by thick drop. The bugs had a half-dozen cocooned Bloodfaces for company, all of them nearly sucked dry but still squirming in that web. They screamed like tortured prisoners when I turned my back and left them alive in the darkness.

Yeah. I did my part, all right.

I did my part, and then some.

Certain situations were harder to handle. Like when you ran into other survivors. They'd see you with a gun, and a pickup truck, and a full belly, and they'd want to know how you were pulling it off. They'd push you. Sometimes with questions, some-times with pleas that were on the far side of desperate. I didn't like that. To tell you the truth, it made me feel kind of sick. As soon as they spit their words my way, I'd want to snatch them out of the air and jam them back in their mouths.

Sometimes they'd get the idea, and shut up, and move on. Sometimes they wouldn't. When that happened I had to do something about it. Choice didn't enter in to it. When someone pushed you, you had to push back. That was just the way the world worked – before demons and after.

One day in late September, Barnes climbed out of his easy chair and made a field trip to the wrecked Chrysler. He took those books with him. I was so shocked when he walked out the door that I didn't say a word.

I was kind of surprised when he made it back to the lodge at nightfall. He brought those damn books back with him, too. Then he worked on me for a whole week, trying to get me to go out there. He said he wanted to try something and he needed some backup. I felt like telling him I could have used some backup myself on the days I'd been out dealing with those things while he'd been sitting on his ass reading, but I didn't say it.

Finally I gave in. I don't know why – maybe I figured going back to the beginning would help Barnes get straight with the way things really were.

There was no sun the day we made the trip, if you judged by what you could see. No sky either. Fog hung low over the lake, following the roads running through the hollow like they were dry rivers that needed filling. The pickup burrowed through the fog, tires whispering over wet asphalt, halogen beams cutting through all that dull white and filling pockets of darkness that waited in the trees.

I didn't see anything worrisome in those pockets, but the quiet that hung in the cab was another story. Barnes and I didn't talk. Usually that would have suited me just fine, but not that day. The silence threw me off, and my hands were sweaty on the steering wheel. I can't say why. I only know they stayed that way when we climbed out of the truck on County Road 14.

Nothing much had changed on that patch of road. Corpses still lay on the asphalt – the road gang, and the bear-thing that had swallowed one of them whole before we blew it apart. They'd been chewed over by buzzards and rats and other miserable creatures, and they'd baked guts-and-all onto the road during the summer heat. You would have had a hell of a time scraping them off the asphalt, because nothing that mattered had bothered with them once they were dead.

Barnes didn't care about them, either. He went straight to the old Chrysler and hauled the dead driver from behind the steering wheel. The corpse hit the road like a sack of kindling ready for the flame. It was a sight. Crows must have been at the driver's face, because his fishgut lips were gone. Those scarred words carved on his skin still rode his jerky flesh like wormy bits of gristle, but now they were chiselled with little holes, as if those crows had pecked punctuation.

Barnes grabbed Mr Fishguts by his necktie and dragged him to the spot in the road where the white line should have been but wasn't.

"You ready?" he asked.

"For what?"

"If I've got it figured right, in a few minutes the universe is going to squat down and have itself a bite. It'll be one big chunk of the apple – starting with this thing, finishing with all those others."

"Those books say so?"

"Oh, yeah," Barnes said, "and a whole lot more."

That wasn't any kind of answer, but it put a cork in me. So I did what I was told. I stood guard. Mr Fishguts lay curled up in that busted-up foetal position. Barnes drew a skinning knife from a leather scabbard on his belt and started cutting off the corpse's clothes. I couldn't imagine what the hell he was doing. A minute later, the driver's corpse was naked, razored teeth grinning up at us through his lipless mouth.

Barnes knelt down on that unmarked road. He started to read.

First from the book. Then from Mr Fishguts' skin.

The words sounded like a garbage disposal running backward. I couldn't understand any of them. Barnes' voice started off quiet, just a whisper buried in the fog. Then it grew louder, and louder still. Finally he was barking words, and screaming them, and spitting like a hellfire preacher. You could have heard him a quarter mile away.

That got my heart pounding. I squinted into the fog, which was getting heavier. I couldn't see a damn thing. I couldn't even see those corpses glued to the road anymore. Just me and Barnes and Mr Fishguts, there in a tight circle in the middle of County Road 14.

My heart went trip-hammer, those words thumping in time, the syllables pumping. I tried to calm down, tried to tell myself that the only thing throwing me off was the damn fog. I didn't know what was out there. One of those inside-out grizzlies could have been twenty feet away and I wouldn't have known it. A rat-faced spider could have been stilting along on eight legs, and I wouldn't have seen it until the damn thing was chewing off my face. That Minotaur-thing with the centipede dreadlocks could have charged me at a dead gallop and I wouldn't have heard its hooves on pavement . . . not with Barnes roaring. That was all I heard. His voice filled up the hollow with words written in books and words carved on a dead man's flesh, and standing there blind in that fog I felt like those words were the only things in a very small world, and for a split second I think I understood just how those cocooned Bloodfaces felt while trapped in that rat-spider's web.

And then it was quiet. Barnes had finished reading.

"Wait a minute," he said. "Wait right here."

I did. The deputy walked over to the Chrysler, and I lost sight of him as he rummaged around in the car. His boots whispered over pavement and he was back again. Quickly, he knelt down, rearing back with both hands wrapped around the hilt of that wrought-iron trident we'd found in the car that very first day, burying it in the centre of Mr Fishguts' chest.

Scarred words shredded, and brittle bones caved in, and an awful stink escaped the corpse. I waited for something to happen. The corpse didn't move. I didn't know about anything else. There could have been anything out there, wrapped up in that fog. Anything, coming straight at us. Anything, right on top of us. We wouldn't have seen it all. I was standing there with a shotgun in my hands with no idea where to point it. I could have pointed it anywhere and it wouldn't have made me feel any better. I could have pulled the trigger a hundred times and it wouldn't have mattered. I might as well have tried to shotgun the fog, or the sky, or the whole damn universe.

It had to be the strangest moment of my life.

It lasted a good long time.

Twenty minutes later, the fog began to clear a little. A half-hour later, it wasn't any worse than when we left the lodge. But nothing had happened in the meantime. That was the worst part. I couldn't stop waiting for it. I stood there, staring down at Mr Fishguts' barbed grin, at the trident, at those words carved on the corpse's jerky flesh. I was still standing there when Barnes slammed the driver's door of the pickup. I hadn't even seen him move. I walked over and slipped in beside him, and he started back towards the lodge.

"Relax," he said finally. "It's all over."

That night it was quieter than it had been in a long time, but I couldn't sleep and neither could Barnes. We sat by the fire, waiting for something . . . or nothing. We barely talked at all. About four or five, we finally drifted off.

Around seven, a racket outside jarred me awake. Then there was a scream. I was up in a second. Shotgun in hand, I charged out of the house.

The fog had cleared overnight. I shielded my eyes and stared into the rising sun. A monster hovered over the beach – leathery wings laid over a jutting bone framework, skin clinging to its muscular body in a thin blistery layer, black veins slithering beneath that skin like stitches meant to mate a devil's muscle and flesh. The thing had a girl, her wrist trapped in one clawed talon. She screamed for help when she saw me coming, but the beast understood me better than she did. It grinned through a mouthful of teeth that jutted from its narrow jaws like nails driven by a drunken carpenter, and its gaze tracked the barrel of my gun, which was already swinging up in my grasp, the stock nestling tight against my shoulder as I took aim.

A sound like snapping sheets. A blast of downdraft from those red wings as the monster climbed a hunk of sky, wings spreading wider and driving down once more.

The motion sent the creature five feet higher in the air. The shotgun barrel followed, but not fast enough. Blistered lips stretched wide, and the creature screeched laughter at me like I was some kind of idiot. Quickly, I corrected my aim and fired.

The first shot was low and peppered the girl's naked legs. She screamed as I fired again, aiming higher this time. The thing's left wing wrenched in the socket as the shot found its mark, opening a pocket of holes large enough to strain sunlight. One more reflexive flap and that wing sent a message to the monster's brain. It screeched pain through its hammered mouth and let the girl go, bloody legs and all.

She fell fast. Her anguished scream told me she understood she was already dead, the same way she understood exactly who'd killed her.

She hit the beach hard. I barely heard the sound because the shotgun was louder. I fired twice more, and that monster fell out of the sky like a kite battered by a hurricane, and it twitched some when it hit, but not too much because I moved in fast and finished it from point-blank range.

Barnes came down to the water. He didn't say anything about the dead monster. He wanted to bury the girl, but I knew that wasn't a good idea. She might have one of those things inside her, or a pack of Bloodfaces might catch her scent and come digging for her with a shovel. So we soaked her with gasoline instead, and we soaked the winged demon, too, and we tossed a match and burned down the both of them together.

After that, Barnes went back to the house.

He did the same thing to those books.

A few days later, I decided to check out the town. Things had been pretty quiet . . . so quiet that I was getting jumpy again.

They could have rolled up the streets, and it wouldn't have mattered. To tell the truth, there hadn't been too many folks in town to begin with, and now most of them were either dead or gone. I caught sight of a couple Bloodfaces when I cruised the main street, but they vanished into a manhole before I got close.

I hit a market and grabbed some canned goods and other supplies, but my mind was wandering. I kept thinking about that day in the fog, and that winged harpy on the beach, and my deputy. Since burning those books, he'd barely left his room. I was beginning to think that the whole deal had done him some good. Maybe it was just taking some time for him to get used to the way things were. Mostly, I hoped he'd finally figured out what I'd known all along – that we'd learned everything we really needed to know about the way this world worked the day we blew apart the inside-out grizzly on County Road 14.

I figured that was the way it was, until I drove back to the house.

Until I heard screams down by the lake.

Barnes had one of the Bloodfaces locked up in the boathouse. A woman no more than twenty. He'd stripped her and cuffed her wrists behind a support post. She jerked against the rough wood as Barnes slid the skinning knife across her ribs.

He peeled away a scarred patch of flesh that gleamed in the dusky light, but I didn't say a word. There were enough words in this room already. They were the same words I'd seen in those books, and they rode the crazy woman's skin. A couple dozen of them had been stripped from her body with Roy Barnes' skinning knife. With her own blood, he'd pasted each one to the boathouse wall.

I bit my tongue. I jacked a shell into the shotgun.

Barnes waved me off. "Not now, boss."

Planting the knife high in the post, he got closer to the girl.

Close enough to whisper in her ear. With a red finger, he pointed at the bloody inscription he'd pasted to the wall. "*Read it*," he said, but the woman only growled at him, snapping sharpened teeth so wildly that she shredded her own lips. But she didn't care about spilling her own blood. She probably didn't know she was doing it. She just licked her tattered lips and snapped some more, convinced she could take a hunk out of Barnes.

He didn't like that. He did some things to her, and her growls became screams.

"She'll come around," Barnes said.

"I don't think so, Roy."

"Yeah. She will – this time I figured things out."

"You said that when you read those books."

"But she's a book with a pulse. That's the difference. She's alive. That means she's got a connection – to those lesser demons, and to the things that lord it over them, too. Every one of them's some kind of key. But you can't unlock a gate with a bent-up key, even if it's the one that's supposed to fit. That's why things didn't work with the driver. After he piled up that Chrysler, he was a bent-up key. He lost his pulse. She's still got hers. If she reads the words instead of me – the words she wrote with a knife of her own – it'll all be different."

He'd approached me while he was talking, but I didn't look at him. I couldn't stand to. I looked at the Bloodface instead. She screamed and spit. She wasn't even a woman anymore. She was just a naked, writhing thing that was going to end her days cuffed to a pole out here in the middle of nowhere. To think that she could spit a few words through tattered lips and change a world was crazy, as crazy as thinking that dead thing out on County Road 14 could do the job, as crazy as . . .

"Don't you understand, boss?"

"She digs up graves, Roy. She eats what she finds buried in them. That's all I need to understand."

"You're wrong. She knows . . ."

I raised the shotgun and blew off the Bloodface's head, and then I put another load in her, and another. I blew everything off her skeleton that might have been a nest where a demon could grow. And when I was done with that little job I put a load in that wall, too, and all those scarred words went to hell in a spray of flesh and wood, and when they were gone they left a jagged window on the world outside.

Barnes stood there, the girl's blood all over his coat, the skinning knife gripped in his shaking hand.

I jacked another shell into the shotgun.

"I don't want to have this conversation again," I said.

After Barnes had gone, I unlocked the cuffs and got the Bloodface down. I grabbed her by what was left of her hair and rolled her into the boat. Once the boathouse doors were opened, I yanked the outboard motor cord and was on my way.

I piloted the boat to the boggy section of the lake. Black trees rooted in the water, and Spanish moss hung in tatters from the branches. It was as good a place as any for a grave. I rolled the girl into the water, and she went under with a splash. I thought about Barnes, and the things he said, and those words on the wall. And I wished he could have seen the girl there, sinking in the murk. Yeah, I wished he could have seen that straight-on. Because this was the way the world worked, and the only change coming from this deal was that some catfish were going to eat good tonight.

The afternoon waned, and the evening light came on and faded. I sat there in the boat. I might have stayed until dark, but rain began to fall – at first gently, then hard enough to patter little divots in the calm surface of the lake. That was enough for me. I revved the outboard and headed back to the lodge.

Nothing bothered me along the way, and Roy didn't bother me once I came through the front door. He was upstairs in his room, and he was quiet . . . or trying to be.

But I heard him.

I heard him just fine.

Up there in his room, whispering those garbage-disposal words while he worked them into his own flesh with the skinning knife. That's what he was doing. I was sure of it. I heard his blood pattering on the floorboards the same way that rat-spiders' blood had pattered the cement floor in the football stadium. Sure it was raining outside, but I'd heard rain and I'd heard blood and I knew the difference.

Floorboards squealed as he shifted his weight, and it didn't take much figuring to decide that he was standing in front of his dresser mirror. It went on for an hour and then two, and I listened as the rain poured down. And when Deputy Barnes set his knife on the dresser and tried to sleep, I heard his little mewling complaints. They were much softer than the screams of those cocooned Bloodfaces, but I heard them just the same.

Stairs creaked as I climbed to the first floor in the middle of the night. Barnes came awake when I slapped open the door. A black circle opened on his bloody face where his mouth must have been, but I didn't give him a chance to say a single word.

"I warned you," I said, and then I pulled the trigger.

When it was done, I rolled the deputy in a sheet and dragged him down the stairs. I buried him under the swing set. By then the rain was falling harder. It wasn't until I got Barnes in the hole that I discovered I didn't have much gas in the can I'd gotten from the boathouse. I drenched his body with what there was, but the rain was too much. I couldn't even light a match. So I tossed a road flare in the hole, and it caught for a few minutes and sent up sputters of blue flame, but it didn't do the job the way it needed to be done.

I tried a couple more flares with the same result. By then, Roy was disappearing in the downpour like a hunk of singed meat in a muddy soup. Large river rocks bordered the flowerbeds that surrounded the lodge, and I figured they might do the trick. One by one I tossed them on top of Roy. I did that for an hour, until the rocks were gone. Then I shovelled sand over the whole mess, wet and heavy as fresh cement.

It was hard work.

I wasn't afraid of it.

I did what needed to be done, and later on I slept like the dead.

And now, a month later, I tossed and turned in Barnes' bed, listening to that old swing set squeak and squeal in the wind and in my dreams.

The brittle sound of gunfire wiped all that away. I came off the bed quickly, grabbing Barnes' .45 from the nightstand as I hurried to the window. Morning sunlight streamed through the trees and painted reflections on the glass, but I squinted through them and spotted shadows stretching across the beach below.

Bloodfaces. One with a machete and two with knives, all three of them moving like rabbits flushed by one mean predator.

Two headed for the woods near the edge of the property. A rattling burst of automatic gunfire greeted them, and the Bloodfaces went to meat and gristle in a cloud of red vapour.

More gunfire, and this time I spotted muzzle flash in the treeline, just past the place where I'd stacked a cord of wood the summer before. The Bloodface with the machete saw it, too. He put on the brakes, but there was no place for him to run but the water or the house.

He wasn't stupid. He picked the house, sprinting with everything he had. I grabbed the bottom rail of the window and tossed it up as he passed the swing set, but by the time I got the .45 through the gap he was already on the porch.

I headed for the door, trading the .45 for my shotgun on the way. A quick glance through the side window in the hallway, and I spotted a couple soldiers armed with M4 carbines breaking from the treeline. I didn't have time to worry about them. Turning quickly, I started down the stairs.

What I should have done was take another look through that front window. If I'd done that, I might have noticed the burrowed-up tunnel in the sand over Roy Barnes' grave.

It was hard to move slowly, but I knew I had to keep my head. The staircase was long, and the walls were so tight the shotgun could easily cover the narrow gap below. If you wanted a definition of dangerous ground, that would be the bottom of the staircase. If the Bloodface was close – his back against the near wall, or standing directly beside the stairwell – he'd have a chance to grab the shotgun barrel before I entered the room.

A sharp clatter on the hardwood floor below. Metallic . . . like a machete. I judged the distance and moved quickly, following the shotgun into the room. And there was the Bloodface . . . over by the front door. He'd made it that far, but no further. And it wasn't gunfire that had brought him down. No. Nothing so simple as a bullet had killed him.

I saw the thing that had done the job, instantly remembering the sounds I'd heard during the night – the scrapes and scrabbles I'd mistaken for nesting birds scratching in the chimney. The far wall of the room was plastered with bits of carved skin, each one of them scarred over with words, and each of those words had been skinned from the thing that had burrowed out of Roy Barnes' corpse.

That thing crouched in a patch of sunlight by the open door, naked and raw, exposed muscles alive with fresh slashes that wept red as it leaned over the dead Bloodface. A clawed hand with long nails like skinning knives danced across a throat slashed to the bone. The demon didn't look up from its work as it carved the corpse's flesh with quick, precise strokes. It didn't seem to notice me at all. It wrote one word on the dead kid's throat . . . and then another on his face . . . and then it slashed open the Bloodface's shirt and started a third.

I fired the shotgun and the monster bucked backwards. Its skinning knife nails rasped across the doorframe and dug into the wood. The thing's head snapped up, and it stared at me with a head full of eyes. Thirty eyes, and every one of them was the colour of muddy water. They blinked, and their gaze fell everywhere at once – on the dead Bloodface and on me, and on the words pasted to the wall.

Red lids blinked again as the thing heaved itself away from the door and started towards me.

Another lid snapped opened on its chin, revealing a black hole.

One suck of air and I knew it was a mouth.

I fired at the first syllable. The thing was blasted back, barking and screaming as it caught the doorframe again, all thirty eyes trained on me now, its splattered chest expanding as it drew another breath through that lidded mouth just as the soldiers outside opened fire with their M4s.

Bullets chopped through flesh. The thing's lungs collapsed and a single word died on its tongue. Its heart exploded. An instant later, it wasn't anything more than a corpse spread across a puddle on the living-room floor.

"Hey, Old School," the private said. "Have a drink."

He tossed me a bottle, and I tipped it back. He was looking over my shotgun. "It's mean," he said, "but I don't know. I like some rock 'n' roll when I pull a trigger. All you got with this thing is *rock*."

"You use it right, it does the job."

The kid laughed. "Yeah. That's all that matters, right? Man, you should hear how people talk about this shit back in the Safe Zone. They actually made us watch some lame-ass stuff on the TV before they choppered us out here to the sticks. Scientists talking, ministers talking . . . like we was going to talk these things to death while they was trying to chew on our asses."

"I met a scientist once," the sergeant said. "He had some guy's guts stuck to his face, and he was down on his knees in a lab chewing on a dead janitor's leg. I put a bullet in his head."

Laughter went around the circle. I took one last drink and passed the bottle along with it.

"But, you know what?" the private said. "Who gives a shit, anyway? I mean, really?"

"Well," another kid said. "Some people say you can't fight something you can't understand. And maybe it's that way with these things. I mean, we don't know where they came from. Not really. We don't even know what they *are*."

"Shit, Mendez. Whatever they are, I've cleaned their guts off my boots. That's all I need to know."

"That works today, Q, but I'm talking long term. As in: What about tomorrow, when we go nose-to-nose with their daddy?"

None of the soldiers said anything for a minute. They were too busy trading uncertain glances.

Then the sergeant smiled and shook his head. "You want to be a philosopher, Private Mendez, you can take the point. You'll have lots of time to figure out the answers to any questions you might have while you're up there, and you can share them with the rest of the class if you don't get eaten before nightfall."

The men laughed, rummaging in their gear for MREs. The private handed over my shotgun, then shook my hand. "Jamal Quinlan," he said. "I'm from Detroit."

"John Dalton. I'm the sheriff around here."

It was the first time I'd said my own name in five months.

It gave me a funny feeling. I wasn't sure what it felt like.

Maybe it felt like turning a page.

\*     \*     \*

The sergeant and his men did some mop-up. Mendez took pictures of the lodge, and the bloody words pasted to the living room wall, and that dead thing on the floor. Another private set up some communication equipment and they bounced everything off a satellite so some lieutenant in DC could look at it. I slipped on a headset and talked to him. He wanted to know if I remembered any strangers coming through town back in May, or anything out of the ordinary they might have had with them. Saying *yes* would mean more questions, so I said, "No, sir. I don't."

The soldiers moved north that afternoon. When they were gone, I boxed up food from the pantry and some medical supplies. Then I got a gas can out of the boathouse and dumped it in the living room. I sparked a road flare and tossed it through the doorway on my way out.

The place went up quicker than my house in town. It was older. I carried the box over to the truck, then grabbed that bottle the soldiers had passed around. There were a few swallows left. I carried it down to the dock and looked back just in time to see those birds dart from their nest in the chimney, but I didn't pay them any mind.

I took the boat out on the lake, and I finished the whiskey, and after a while I came back.

Things are getting better now. It's quieter than ever around here since the soldiers came through, and I've got some time to myself. Sometimes I sit and think about the things that might have happened instead of the things that did. Like that very first day, when I spotted that monster in the Chrysler's trunk out on County Road 14 and blasted it with the shotgun – the gas tank might have exploded and splattered me all over the road. Or that day down in the dark under the high school football stadium – those rat-spiders could have trapped me in their web and spent a couple months sucking me dry. Or with Roy Barnes – if he'd never seen those books in the back seat of that old sedan, and if he'd never read a word about lesser demons, where would he be right now?

But there's no sense wondering about things like that, any more than looking for explanations about what happened to Barnes, or me, or anyone else. I might as well ask myself why the thing that crawled out of Barnes looked the way it did or knew what it knew. I could do that and drive myself crazy chasing my own tail, the same way Barnes did with all those *maybes* and *what ifs*.

So I try to look forward. The rules are changing. Soon they'll be back to the way they used to be. Take that soldier. Private Quinlan. A year from now he'll be somewhere else, in a place where he won't do the things he's doing now. He might even have a hard time believing he ever did them. It won't be much different with me.

Maybe I'll have a new house by then. Maybe I'll take off work early on Friday and push around a shopping cart, toss steaks and a couple of six-packs into it. Maybe I'll even do the things I used to do. Wear a badge. Find a new deputy. Sort things out and take care of trouble. People always need someone who can do that.

To tell the truth, that would be okay with me.

That would be just fine.

# STEVE RASNIC TEM

## Telling

STEVE RASNIC TEM'S RECENT stories have appeared in *Asimov's*, *Black Wings II* and the Ellen Datlow anthology *Blood & Other Cravings*. His new novel, *Deadfall Hotel*, will be published by Solaris Books in early 2012, while New Pulp Press will be bringing out a collection of his *noir* short stories, *Ugly Behavior*, later the same year.

"As for the following story," reveals the author, "it began with a dreadful image at the end of a dream. I couldn't remember the other details of that dream, but I was determined to find out where that image might have come from."

B EFORE HE MET MAGGIE, he thought he understood the difference between sense and nonsense. By the end, and he could smell it coming – redolent of fish and sweaty sheets – he could hardly tell the difference between breath and flesh.

They had visited three, four hundred houses for sale. They had driven down every street in the county, every nameless lane. They had done this in late October, with a layer of ice-capped snow on the ground, the wind low but steady enough to scour the back of your throat until you were made inarticulate.

Wayne did not complain, but it was painful, creeping along, enduring the stares of suspicious neighbours, as in the shaded lanes the ice cracked and exploded beneath his tyres. It might have been better if he'd had any idea what she was looking for, but she did not share her criteria. Wayne supposed that was what artists were like. But it exhausted the people who loved them.

In most cases a relatively slow drive-by was sufficient: the house would apparently be in the wrong architectural style, or too tall, or too wide. He wasn't permitted to say anything – he couldn't even hum while he was driving. And now and then she would insist that they step inside, or walk around, or lie on the floor and gaze at the ceiling. Wayne had been unemployed two years, but he did have his real estate license – for once that made him feel useful.

Wayne didn't enjoy any of it. He especially didn't enjoy lying on those dusty floors, looking into those crusty ceilings, inviting dust into his eyes, dust into his mouth, where it tasted aspirin bitter, like all that was left by the end of the day, like the end of life itself.

He had no idea why they were doing it, except Maggie said it was something she needed to do before she could choose the right house. And as much as she annoyed and infuriated him, Wayne adored Maggie, and would do anything she asked.

"This is the one," she said. "Finally, this is the one. I can feel it."

The house was in worse shape than most of the others. Unpainted grey boards pushed through tatters of off-white colour. Inside, the walls were thin as paper. Wayne imagined he could see the colours of the next room bleeding through.

"If you dropped something you'd hear it in every room of the house." As if on cue, vague, hesitant sounds travelled from the other end of the house, or farther.

Maggie hadn't heard, or ignored them. "But that's a good thing, isn't it? Nothing can ever sneak up on you."

The fact that something sneaking up was even a consideration appalled him. "It smells funny in here," he said. "Are you sure you can live in a place that smells funny?"

"They make paint with chemicals that kill the odour."

And that was that. She'd made up her mind. He supposed she didn't care how the place smelled. For him it was as if he'd crawled inside a loaf of old, damp bread. The rich stink filled the nose and spilled over into the mouth. He imagined a sponginess in the wood open to rot, mould, mildew.

Sun glare flashed through the window glass. A suggestion of double-exposed imagery floated across the wall. But when he shifted his head slightly it had gone. Maggie had chosen, and he had to make the best of it. It was her money.

The day after they closed, Wayne had their bedroom ready. By evening they had the appliances arranged in a rudimentary kitchen. He spent a difficult weekend stocking Maggie's new studio with paints, canvases, and a myriad other supplies.

In her studio he watched as she put the finishing touches on a new painting. Maggie never seemed to mind his visits to her workplace – often she invited him. It didn't seem to matter how unfinished a piece might be.

But then she always acted as if he wasn't there. Her focus could be disturbing, the way she stared at the canvas, aggressively applying paint, not even bothering to check her pigments, holding her breath, unable to do anything else until the canvas filled with colour.

It was one of her house paintings. Almost all of her paintings were of houses, at least as long as he'd known her. Those paintings had proved surprisingly popular in the galleries – they were the reason they could afford to buy this house, and pay for everything else. "They work because the right house will remind us of other houses important in our lives," she explained. "They resonate. You look at certain houses, and you can just imagine the lives of the people inside, trapped by those walls, or lovingly embraced. Their experience is also our own."

When Maggie painted it was always an attack upon the canvas. She thickened the acrylic paint until it was the consistency of brilliantly coloured liquid clay. She shovelled the colour onto the surface, then worked quickly to create vegetation, planks, timbers, brick, doors, windows, roofs, sky. He was always surprised when her fury suddenly turned a chaos of swirling thick colour into something recognisable.

But what was even more surprising was that something extraordinarily appealing resulted from this process. These were the prettiest, most intensely welcoming houses he'd ever seen.

"So what do you think?" she asked.

The painting was like all the others, but he could sense subtle differences. "The lines around the door, the porch roof, that window, it's like this house, isn't it?"

"In better days, yes. Or maybe the way it will be, after we finish fixing it up."

"So this place is the model you were looking for?"

"Maybe I've been painting it since the beginning, the spaces, the lines. It's like I was trying to recall it."

"Then you've been here before?"

"No – I'm sure I haven't."

"Maybe with your dad?" It was a risk – her father had always been a sore point.

"No – I don't think so. The house he moved into after the divorce may have been similar. I stayed there summers until I graduated from high school, a few years before his death."

"It would have helped if I'd known what we were looking for."

"I couldn't have put it into words before now. I'm a picture person, not a word person. I had to see it, be inside it, and then start painting it. That's the way I've always found out things about myself. I've never been here, Wayne, but maybe someone like me lived here, or at least nearby. Someone I'm in sympathy with."

"So – living with your dad, that was hard?"

She nodded silently, then the tears began to drop. He started toward her but she held up her hand. "Sorry. I don't know why I get like this. It was a sad time, but you know how kids are. You can't think of much outside yourself. I'm not aware of hating that house, but I don't remember ever actually being in it. I remember saying goodbye to my mom, and starting out on this long bus trip, but I can't remember ever arriving, living with my dad, or anything about his house. I do remember telling my mother I could never go back, and my mother telling me I had to go back."

He listened, but he couldn't take his eyes off the new canvas. There was an out-of-place shadow peeking out of the upstairs front window: faded, sepia-coloured, uninvited.

Maggie worked late into the evening. Early the next morning Wayne left the house so as not to disturb her sleep. It was cold for working outdoors, but he could at least clear some of the dead vegetation out of the back yard.

He removed a large quantity of dead brush before he could see the ground. And even after he'd got rid of the taller plants he'd get the occasional slap, the random clawing from some unseen branch or stalk, like an untrimmed fingernail tracing the skin. Nothing terribly serious, but enough to well the blood.

A blurred shadow loomed beyond the last sweep of netted branches. With his sleeve he brushed a gritty paste of chaff and blood from his face. "Maggie? You're up?" But when his vision cleared no one was there. He exhaled in exasperation. The fogged air hung suspended, as if poised.

As he removed dead flowers, the stray remains of potatoes, an onion or two, he began finding ash spread under everything, and bits of foundation from an old wall. An impatient weight crouched nearby, waiting for him to look up, which he eventually did, and found nothing. That was when he heard Maggie yelling from inside the house.

She was on her hands and knees in her studio. He dropped beside her and laid one hand gently on her back. "What happened?"

She shook her head, ran a finger up and down one of the wide gaps between the floor planks. Extensive sections of the ceiling below were missing, so that he could see most of the living room on the first floor.

"I don't know what time I got to bed last night, but when I woke up I was anxious to get back to the painting. Then as I was picking up the brush I smelled something – I don't know – smoky, but terribly sour as well, like overpowering body odour. I felt threatened, as if the stench might smother me. I looked down, and there was this person standing under me. His clothes were dark, dripping and greasy. And then he shifted, and he was looking at me. Two white, shiny spots staring up at me, but Wayne, no pupils."

It took him minutes to check the house and yard. He rushed in to tell her he'd found nothing. She was still sitting on the floor, shaking. "You say you just woke up. It was probably just a shadow, the light confusing you."

She shook her head. Then Wayne noticed the new painting.

Despite the obscuring strokes of shadow and translucent mist it was still recognisably the same house, but done in a much darker colour palette: greys, burnt umber, deep purple, shades of black and the evening blues. Deepest night. Deepest dream.

"I probably won't be able to sell my usual clients this one."

"Unwelcoming is the word, I guess."

"It terrifies me."

"Then stop working on it."

"I really don't think I can paint anything else until I can finish this one."

It was powerful. A series of vaguely realised trees led you to the front porch, caked in soot, deteriorating under the assault of some oily disease. A gauze of fog hung from the porch roof. But something more: a blurred presence seemed to be arriving out of the darkness from the back of the porch.

"I don't know why we came here."

Wayne grabbed her hand. "It's like you said, houses and people resonate. You're here because of someone who lived here before. You're here because of whatever happened to them."

Every evening Maggie worked on the new painting into the early morning hours. Wayne had never known her to take so long with an individual work – usually she finished them in a couple of days. But she revisited the same areas of canvas again and again, applying additional thin layers of sombre colour, constantly revising lines and shades as she apparently grew closer to her vision.

Each morning when Wayne got up he checked the painting: the blurred figure slightly more resolved, its position slightly shifted on the porch, as if it were pacing. After a few more nights it had left the porch, and was making its way up the sidewalk.

Wayne moved forward on repairs to the house and yard, although concerns over Maggie slowed him. He put a ceiling up in the living room, hoping it might comfort her that she no longer had that god's-eye glimpse into their downstairs. The backyard didn't look so much like a refuse pile anymore. The uncovered foundation proved to extend to all points in the yard – the building it once supported the size of a full house. He also uncovered bits of an old flagstone walk leading back to the alley that ran behind the long row of neighbouring houses.

A night came that Maggie collapsed early, and for once he was the late one up, reading, listening.

At first he thought the breathing he heard might be his own – the book, about secrets and lies and misunderstood identities, had made him tense. But when he put it down and laid his hand on his chest, he realised the rapid panting was more distant – somewhere down the hall and up the stairs. As he made that journey the panting grew louder, and the loudness of it made him think of a dog, the way a dog breathes with his entire body, especially when in pain, heaving and exhaling, unlike people who tend to breathe shallowly from their chests.

The pale little blonde girl lay with her back to him across two steps near the top of the stairs. Her body heaved like an injured dog's. Shadows gathered along her spine: hand-shaped bruises, ending in a crown of yellow curls streaked with dark blood.

Something burned his nostrils – an acrid stench of urine. But he could find no signs of a spreading stain beneath her.

He wanted to say something, but was afraid. And he dared not touch that tender, panting shape. Suddenly coughing violently, she faded into deep shadow, then lit up again with each new intake of breath. What could he do for her? Spying on her in her old distress was some kind of violation, so he slowly crept backwards down the stairs. At the last moment her head jerked up, staring at the door at the top of the stairs. Her body started to slide toward him as she made ready her escape, but he turned and made his way downstairs and to bed.

"Wayne! Wayne, I want to leave!" He awakened with Maggie's face a collapsed moon hanging over him, her fingers clawing his shoulder. "Now! We have to leave! Please, Wayne."

"Of course." He jerked himself from bed, dragging at his pants. "Just let me get a bag."

"No!" she screamed. Shocked, he stumbled backwards onto the bed. "We have to leave! We have to get into the car! Please!"

"Okay, honey. I'm getting my clothes on right now."

She was unsteady on her feet. They stumbled into the hall. Then she cried, "Wait! Wait right here so I'll know where you are." Then she raced away.

Wayne was just outside her open studio door. In the painting the shadow-wrapped figure was almost to the end of the sidewalk, ready to step out of the canvas. The floppy hat was pulled down over his face. That's his house in the yard. That was his poor child on the stairs. They're why we're here.

"Ready! Let's go, Wayne!" She carried a pillow and blanket under one arm, a butcher knife raised in her other hand. He hurried over, pushed down the arm with the knife. "I need the knife! I have to protect myself!" They started down.

She insisted on sitting in the back seat, the pillow in her lap, the blanket over her, the knife ready in her hand. Wayne didn't ask where they were going, just pulled away from the curb.

He knew immediately that things had changed. Roads and houses, fences and fields, rearranged. When he got half-way down their street it ended in a left-hand turn, with nothing ahead where streets used to be but a hayfield studded in bales. He didn't know what else to do but follow the turn.

After a short distance he had to turn again. The road narrowed, the pavement deteriorated. Soon they were on a dirt road, and headed back in the direction of the house. Maggie stared out the window intently.

She must have realised about the same time he did that they were actually in the alley that ran behind their house. But it was dirt now, and the houses faced it. She began rocking the pillow in her lap, making soft soothing sounds. "Did you see the little girl, Wayne? Did you see her? She was just like I used to be. We have to tell someone!"

Before they reached their own house, he realised something large was blocking their view of it. Then he understood the buried foundation had suddenly grown an old dilapidated house.

Maggie started wailing when they saw the hulking dark figure by the edge of the road. Their headlights caught a glimpse of an old see-saw, the pale children teetering there, wide eyes reflecting like cats'.

"Oh, Wayne we have to tell, we have to tell! That poor little girl!"

"We will, honey, we will," he promised, although there was no one left alive to tell.

When the man began lifting his face out from under that floppy brim Maggie was screaming so loudly Wayne couldn't think, and when they'd finally driven past, and made the next turn that would drag them around that house again, Wayne couldn't imagine how they would ever get off that road.

# CAITLÍN R. KIERNAN

## As Red as Red

CAITLÍN R. KIERNAN IS an award-winning, Irish-born author living in Providence, Rhode Island. She has to her credit eight novels, including *Daughters of Hounds*, *The Red Tree* and, forthcoming, *The Drowning Girl: A Memoir*.

Her tales of the fantastic, macabre and science fiction have been collected in *Tales of Pain and Wonder*, *From Weird and Distant Shores*, *To Charles Fort, with Love*, *Alabaster*, *A is for Alien* and, most recently, *The Ammonite Violin and Others*.

In 2012, Subterranean Press will release both her short SF novel, *The Dinosaurs of Mars*, and *Two Worlds and In Between: The Best of Caitlín R. Kiernan (Volume One)*, a comprehensive retrospective of the first eleven years of her work.

"I don't know that 'As Red as Red' had any single source of inspiration," says Kiernan. "It coalesced from numerous experiences and accounts of the supernatural in Rhode Island. Also, I very much wanted to write a non-conventional vampire story which was also (and maybe more so) a werewolf story *and* a ghost story.

"It's also true that I was just coming off having finished *The Red Tree*, and, in some ways, 'As Red as Red' is an extended footnote to that novel. I was still trying to get *The Red Tree* out of my system."

# I

"So, YOU BELIEVE IN vampires?" she asks, then takes another sip of her coffee and looks out at the rain pelting Thames Street beyond the café window. It's been pissing rain for almost an hour, a cold, stinging shower on an overcast afternoon near the end of March, a bitter Newport afternoon that would have been equally at home in January or February. But at least it's not pissing snow.

I put my own cup down – tea, not coffee – and stare across the booth at her for a moment or two before answering. "No," I tell Abby Gladding. "But, quite clearly, those people in Exeter who saw to it that Mercy Brown's body was exhumed, the ones who cut out her heart and burned it, clearly *they* believed in vampires. And that's what I'm studying, the psychology behind that hysteria, behind the superstitions."

"It was so long ago," she replies and smiles. There's no foreshadowing in that smile, not even in hindsight. It surely isn't a predatory smile. There's nothing malevolent, or hungry, or feral in the expression. She just watches the rain and smiles, as though something I've said amuses her.

"Not really," I say, glancing down at my steaming cup. "Not so long ago as people might *like* to think. The Mercy Brown incident, that was in 1892, and the most recent case of purported vampirism in the north-east I've been able to pin down dates from sometime in 1898, a mere hundred and eleven years ago."

Her smile lingers, and she traces a circle in the condensation on the plate-glass window, then traces another circle inside it.

"We're not so far removed from the villagers with their torches and pitchforks, from old Cotton Mather and his bunch. That's what you're saying."

"Well, not exactly, but . . ." and when I trail off, she turns her head towards me, and her blue-grey eyes seem as cold as the low-slung sky above Newport. You could almost freeze to death in eyes like those, I think, and I take another sip of my lukewarm Earl Grey with lemon. Her eyes seem somehow brighter than they should in the dim light of the coffeehouse, so there's your foreshadowing, I suppose, if you're the sort who needs it.

"You're pretty far from Exeter, Ms Howard," she says, and

takes another sip of her coffee. And me, I'm sitting here wishing we were talking about almost anything but Rhode Island vampires and the hysteria of crowds, tuberculosis and the Master's thesis I'd be defending at the end of May. It had been months since I'd had anything even resembling a date, and I didn't want to squander the next half-hour or so talking shop.

"I think I've turned up something interesting," I tell her, because I can't think of any subtle way to steer the conversation in another direction; there are things I'd rather be talking with this mildly waiflike, comely girl than shop. "A case no one's documented before, right here in Newport."

She smiles that smile again.

"I got a tip from a folklorist up at Brown," I say. "Seems like maybe there was an incident here in 1785 or thereabouts. If it checks out, I might be onto the oldest case of suspected vampirism resulting in an exhumation anywhere in New England. So, now I'm trying to verify the rumours. But there's precious little to go on. Chasing vampires, it's not like studying the Salem witch trials, where you have all those court records, the indictments and depositions and what have you. Instead, it's necessary to spend a lot of time sifting and sorting fact from fiction, and, usually, there's not much of either to work with."

She nods, then glances back towards the big window and the rain. "Be a feather in your cap, though. If it's not just a rumour, I mean."

"Yes," I reply. "Yes, it certainly would."

And here, there's an unsettling wave of not-quite *déjà vu*, something closer to dissociation, perhaps, and for a few dizzying seconds I feel as if I'm watching this conversation, a voyeur listening in, or I'm only remembering it, but in no way actually, presently, taking part in it. And, too, the coffeehouse and our talk and the rain outside seem a lot less concrete – less *here and now* – than does the morning before. One day that might as well be the next, and it's raining, either way.

I'm standing alone on Bowen's Wharf, staring out past the masts crowded into the marina at sleek white sailboats skimming over the glittering water, and there's the silhouette of Goat Island, half hidden in the fog. I'm about to turn and walk back up the hill to Washington Square and the library, about to leave the gaudy, Disney-World concessions catering to the tastes of tourists and return to the comforting maze of ancient gabled houses lining winding, narrow streets. And that's when I see her for the first time. She's standing alone near the "seal safari" kiosk, staring at a faded sign, at black-and-white photographs of harbour seals with eyes like the puppies and little girls from those hideous Margaret Keane paintings. She's wearing an old pea coat and shiny green galoshes that look new, but there's nothing on her head, and she doesn't have an umbrella. Her long black hair hangs wet and limp, and when she looks at me, it frames her pale face.

Then it passes, the blip or glitch in my psyche, and I've snapped back, into myself, into *this* present. I'm sitting across the booth from her once more, and the air smells almost oppressively of freshly roasted and freshly ground coffee beans.

"I'm sure it has a lot of secrets, this town," she says, fixing me again with those blue-grey eyes and smiling that irreproachable smile of hers.

"Can't swing a dead cat," I say, and she laughs.

"Well, did it ever work?" Abby asks. "I mean, digging up the dead, desecrating their mortal remains to appease the living. Did it tend to do the trick?"

"No," I reply. "Of course not. But that's beside the point. People do strange things when they're scared."

And there's more, mostly more questions from her about Colonial-Era vampirism, Newport's urban legends, and my research as a folklorist. I'm grateful that she's kind or polite enough not to ask the usual "you mean people get paid for this sort of thing" questions. She tells me a werewolf story dating back to the 1800s, a local priest supposedly locked away in the Portsmouth Poor Asylum after he committed a particularly gruesome murder, how he was spared the gallows because people believed he was a werewolf and so not in control of his actions. She even tells me about seeing his nameless grave in a cemetery up in Middletown, his tombstone bearing the head of a wolf. And I'm polite enough not to tell her that I've heard this one before.

Finally, I notice that it's stopped raining. "I really ought to get back to work," I say, and she nods and suggests that we should have dinner sometime soon. I agree, but we don't set a date. She has my cell number, after all, so we can figure that out later. She also mentions a movie playing at Jane Pickens that she hasn't seen and thinks I might enjoy. I leave her sitting there in the booth, in her pea coat and green galoshes, and she orders another cup of coffee as I'm exiting the café. On the way back to the library, I see a tree filled with noisy, cawing crows, and for some reason it reminds me of Abby Gladding.

## II

That was Monday, and there's nothing the least bit remarkable about Tuesday. I make the commute from Providence to Newport, crossing the West Passage of Narragansett Bay to Conanicut Island, and then the East Passage to Aquidneck Island and Newport. Most of the day is spent at the Redwood Library and Athenaeum on Bellevue, shut away with my newspaper clippings and microfiche, with frail yellowed books that were printed before the Revolutionary War. I wear the white cotton gloves they give me for handling archival materials, and make several pages of hand-written notes, pertaining primarily to the treatment of cases of consumption in Newport during the first two decades of the 18th century.

The library is open late on Tuesdays, and I don't leave until sometime after 7:00 p.m. But nothing I find gets me any nearer to confirming that a corpse believed to have belonged to a vampire was exhumed from the Common Burying Ground in 1785. On the long drive home, I try not to think about the fact that she hasn't called, or my growing suspicion that she likely never will. I have a can of ravioli and a beer for dinner. I half watch something forgettable on television. I take a hot shower and brush my teeth. If there are any dreams – good, bad, or otherwise – they're nothing I recall upon waking. The day is sunny, and not quite as cold, and I do my best to summon a few shoddy scraps of optimism, enough to get me out the door and into the car.

But by the time I reach the library in Newport, I've got a headache, what feels like the beginnings of a migraine, railroad spikes in both my eyes, and I'm wishing I'd stayed in bed. I find a comfortable seat in the Roderick Terry Reading Room, one of the armchairs upholstered with dark green leather, and leave my sunglasses on while I flip through books pulled randomly from the shelf on my right. Novels by William Kennedy and Elia Kazan, familiar, friendly books, but trying to focus on the words only makes my head hurt worse. I return *The Arrangement* to its slot on the shelf, and pick up something called *Thousand Cranes* by a Japanese author, Yasunari Kawbata. I've never heard of him, but the blurb on the back of the dust jacket assures me he was awarded the Nobel Prize for Literature in 1968, and that he was the first Japanese author to receive it.

I don't open the book, but I don't reshelve it, either. It rests there in my lap, and I sit beneath the octagonal skylight with my eyes closed for a while. Five minutes maybe, maybe more, and the only sounds are muffled footsteps, the turning of pages, an old man clearing his throat, a passing police siren, one of the librarians at the front desk whispering a little louder than usual. Or maybe the migraine magnifies her voice and only makes it seem that way. In fact, all these small, unremarkable sounds seem magnified, if only by the quiet of the library.

When I open my eyes, I have to blink a few times to bring the room back into focus. So I don't immediately notice the woman standing outside the window, looking in at me. Or only looking *in*, and I just happen to be in her line of sight. Maybe she's looking at nothing in particular, or at the bronze statue of Pheidippides perched on its wooden pedestal. Perhaps she's looking for someone else, someone who isn't me. The window is on the opposite side of the library from where I'm sitting, forty feet or so away. But even at that distance, I'm almost certain that the pale face and lank black hair belong to Abby Gladding. I raise a hand, half-waving to her, but if she sees me, she doesn't acknowledge having seen me. She just stands there, perfectly still, staring in.

I get to my feet, and the copy of *Thousand Cranes* slides off my lap; the noise the book makes when it hits the floor is enough that a couple of people look up from their magazines and glare at me. I offer them an apologetic gesture – part shrug and part sheepish frown – and they shake their heads, almost in unison, and go back to reading. When I glance at the window again, the black-haired woman is no longer there. Suddenly, my headache is much worse (probably from standing so quickly, I think), and I feel a sudden, dizzying rush of adrenaline. No, it's more than that. I feel afraid. My heart races, and my mouth has gone very dry. Any plans I might have harboured of going outside to see if the woman looking in actually was Abby vanish immediately, and I sit down again. If it was her, I reason, then she'll come inside.

So I wait, and, very slowly, my pulse returns to its normal rhythm, but the adrenaline leaves me feeling jittery, and the pain behind my eyes doesn't get any better. I pick the novel by Yasunari Kawbata up off the floor and place it back upon the shelf. Leaning over makes my head pound even worse, and I'm starting to feel nauseous. I consider going to the restrooms, near the circulation desk, but part of me is still afraid, for whatever reason, and it seems to be the part of me that controls my legs. I stay in the seat and wait for the woman from the window to walk into the Roderick Terry Reading Room. I wait for her to be Abby, and I expect to hear her green galoshes squeaking against the lacquered hardwood. She'll say that she thought about calling, but then figured that I'd be in the library, so of course my phone would be switched off. She'll say something about the weather, and she'll want to know if I'm still up for dinner and the movie. I'll tell her about the migraine, and maybe she'll offer me Excedrin or Tylenol. Our hushed conversation will annoy someone, and he or she will shush us. We'll laugh about it later on.

But Abby doesn't appear, and so I sit for a while, gazing across the wide room at the window, a tree *outside* the window, at the houses lined up neat and tidy along Redwood Street. On Wednesday, the library is open until eight, but I leave as soon as I feel well enough to drive back to Providence.

### III

It's Thursday, and I'm sitting in that same green armchair in the Roderick Terry Reading Room. It's only 11:26 a.m., and already I understand that I've lost the day. I have no days to spare, but already, I know that the research that I should get done today isn't going to happen. Last night was too filled with uneasy dreaming, and this morning I can't concentrate. It's hard to think about anything but the nightmares, and the face of Abby Gladding at the window; her blue eyes, her black hair. And yes, I have grown quite certain that it *was* her face I saw peering in, and that she was peering in *at* me.

She hasn't called (and I didn't get her number, assuming she has one). An hour ago, I walked along the Newport waterfront looking for her, but to no avail. I stood a while beside the "seal safari" kiosk, hoping, irrationally I suppose, that she might turn up. I smoked a cigarette, and stood there in the cold, watching the sunlight on the bay, listening to traffic and the wind and a giggling flock of grey sea gulls. Just before I gave up and made my way back to the library, I noticed dog tracks in a muddy patch of ground near the kiosk. I thought that they seemed unusually large, and I couldn't help but recall the café on Monday and Abby relating the story of the werewolf priest buried in Middletown. But lots of people in Newport have big dogs, and they walk them along the wharf.

I'm sitting in the green leather chair, and there's a manila folder of photocopies and computer printouts in my lap. I've been picking through them, pretending this is work. It isn't. There's nothing in the folder I haven't read five or ten times over, nothing that hasn't been cited by other academics chasing stories of New England vampires. On top of the stack is "The 'Vampires' of Rhode Island", from *Yankee* magazine, October 1970. Beneath that, "They Burned Her Heart . . . Was Mercy Brown a Vampire?" from the *Narragansett Times*, October 25 1979, and from the *Providence Sunday Journal*, also October 1979, "Did They Hear the Vampire Whisper?" So many of these popular pieces have October dates, a testament to journalism's attitude towards the subject, which it clearly views as nothing more than a convenient skeleton to pull from the closet every Halloween, something to dust off and trot out for laughs.

Salem has its witches. Sleepy Hollow its headless Hessian mercenary. And Rhode Island has its consumptive, consuming phantoms – Mercy Brown, Sarah Tillinghast, Nellie Vaughn, Ruth Ellen Rose, and all the rest. Beneath the *Providence Sunday Journal* piece is a black-and-white photograph I took a couple of years ago, Nellie Vaughn's vandalised headstone, with its infamous inscription: I AM WAITING AND WATCHING FOR YOU. I stare at the photograph for a moment or two, and set it aside. Beneath it there's a copy of another October article, "When the Wind Howls and the Trees Moan", also from the *Providence Sunday Journal.* I close the manila folder and try not to stare at the window across the room.

It is only a window, and it only looks out on trees and houses and sunlight.

I open the folder again, and read from a much older article, "The Animistic Vampire in New England" from *American Anthropologist,* published in 1896, only four years after the Mercy Brown incident. I read it silently, to myself, but catch my lips moving:

In New England the vampire superstition is unknown by its proper name. It is believed that consumption is not a physical but spiritual disease, obsession, or visitation; that as long as the body of a dead consumptive relative has blood in its heart it is proof that an occult influence steals from it for death and is at work draining the blood of the living into the heart of the dead and causing his rapid decline.

I close the folder again and return it to its place in my book bag. And then I stand and cross the wide reading room to the window and the alcove where I saw, or only thought I saw, Abby looking in at me. There's a marble bust of Cicero on the window ledge, and I've been staring out at the leafless trees and the brown grass, the sidewalk and the street, for several minutes before I notice the smudges on the pane of glass, only inches from my face. Sometime recently, when the window was wet, a finger traced a circle there, and then traced a circle within that first circle. When the glass dried, these smudges were left behind. And I remember Monday afternoon at the coffeehouse, Abby tracing an identical symbol (if "symbol" is the appropriate word here) in the condensation on the window while we talked and watched the rain.

I press my palm to the glass, which is much colder than I'd expected.

In my dream, I stood at another window, at the end of a long hallway, and looked down at the North Burial Ground. With some difficulty, I opened the window, hoping the air outside would be fresher than the stale air in the hallway. It was, and I thought it smelled faintly of clover and strawberries. And there was music. I saw, then, Abby standing beneath a tree, playing a violin. The music was very beautiful, though very sad, and completely unfamiliar. She drew the bow slowly across the strings, and I realised that somehow the music was shaping the night. There were clouds sailing past above the cemetery, and the chords she drew from the violin changed the shapes of those clouds, and also seemed to dictate the speed at which they moved. The moon was bloated, and shone an unhealthy shade of ivory, and the whole sky writhed like a Van Gogh painting. I wondered why she didn't tell me that she plays the violin.

Behind me, something clattered to the floor, and I looked over my shoulder. But there was only the long hallway, leading off into perfect darkness, leading back the way I'd apparently come. When I turned again to the open window and the cemetery, the music had ceased, and Abby was gone. There was only the tree and row after row of tilted headstones, charcoal-coloured slate, white marble, a few cut from slabs of reddish sandstone mined from Massachusetts or Connecticut. I was reminded of a platoon of drunken soldiers, lined up for a battle they knew they were going to lose.

I have never liked writing my dreams down.

It is late Thursday morning, almost noon, and I pull my hand back from the cold, smudged windowpane. I have to be in Providence for an evening lecture, and I gather my things and leave the Redwood Library and Athenaeum. On the drive back to the city, I do my best to stop thinking about the nightmare, my best not to dwell on what I saw sitting beneath the tree, after the music stopped and Abby Gladding disappeared. My best isn't good enough.


## IV

The lecture goes well, quite a bit better than I'd expected it would, better, probably, than it had a right to, all things considered. "Mercy Brown as Inspiration for Bram Stoker's *Dracula*", presented to the Rhode Island Historical Society, and, somehow, I even manage not to make a fool of myself answering questions afterwards. It helps that I've answered these same questions so many times in the past. For example:

"I'm assuming you've also drawn connections between the Mercy Brown incident and Sheridan Le Fanu's 'Carmilla'"?

"There are similarities, certainly, but so far as I know, no one has been able to demonstrate conclusively that Le Fanu knew of the New England phenomena. And, of course, the publication of 'Carmilla' predates the exhumation of Mercy Brown's body by twenty years."

"Still, he might have known of the earlier cases."

"Certainly. He may well have. However, I have no *evidence* that he did."

But, the entire time, my mind is elsewhere, back across the water in Newport, in that coffeehouse on Thames, and the Redwood Library, and standing in a dream hallway, looking down on my subconscious rendering of the Common Burying Ground. A woman playing a violin beneath a tree. A woman with whom I have only actually spoken once, but about whom I cannot stop thinking.

*It is believed that consumption is not a physical but spiritual disease, obsession, or visitation . . .*

After the lecture, and the questions, after introductions are made and notable, influential hands are shaken, when I can finally slip away without seeming either rude or unprofessional, I spend an hour or so walking alone on College Hill. It's a cold, clear night, and I follow Benevolent Street west to Benefit and turn north. There's comfort in the uneven, buckled bricks of the sidewalk, in the bare limbs of the trees, in all the softly glowing windows. I pause at the granite steps leading up to the front door of what historians call the Stephen Harris House, built in 1764. One hundred and sixty years later, H.P. Lovecraft called this the "Babbitt House" and used it as the setting for an odd tale of lycanthropy and vampirism. I know this huge yellow house well. And I know, too, the four hand-painted signs nailed up on the gatepost, all of them in French. From the sidewalk, by the electric glow of a nearby street lamp, I can only make out the top

half of the third sign in the series; the rest are lost in the gloom
– *Oubliez le Chien*. Forget the Dog.

I start walking again, heading home to my tiny, cluttered
apartment, only a couple of blocks east on Prospect. The side
streets are notoriously steep, and I've been in better shape. I
haven't gone twenty-five yards before I'm winded and have a
nasty stitch in my side. I lean against a stone wall, cursing the
cigarettes and the exercise I can't be bothered with, trying to
catch my breath. The freezing air makes my sinuses and teeth
ache. It burns my throat like whiskey.

And this is when I glimpse a sudden blur from out the corner
of my right eye, hardly *more* than a blur. An impression or the
shadow of something large and black, moving quickly across the
street. It's no more than ten feet away from me, but downhill,
back towards Benefit. By the time I turn to get a better look, it's
gone, and I'm already beginning to doubt I saw anything, except,
possibly, a stray dog.

I linger here a moment, squinting into the darkness and the
yellow-orange sodium-vapour pool of streetlight that the blur
seemed to cross before it disappeared. I want to laugh at myself,
because I can actually feel the prick of goose bumps along my
forearms, and the short, fine hairs at the nape of my neck standing on end. I've blundered into a horror-movie cliché, and I can't
help but be reminded of Val Lewton's *Cat People*, the scene
where Jane Rudolph walks quickly past Central Park, stalked by
a vengeful Simone Simon, only to be rescued at the last possible
moment by the fortuitous arrival of a city bus. But I know there's
no helpful bus coming to intervene on my behalf, and, more
importantly, I understand full fucking well that this night holds
nothing more menacing than what my over-stimulated imagination has put there. I turn away from the streetlight and continue
up the hill towards home. And I do not have to *pretend* that I
don't hear footsteps following me, or the clack of claws on
concrete, because I *don't*. The quick shadow, the peripheral blur,
it was only a moment's misapprehension, no more than a trick of
my exhausted, preoccupied mind, filled with the evening's
morbid banter.

*Oubliez le Chien*.

Fifteen minutes later, I'm locking the front door of my

apartment behind me. I make a hot cup of camomile tea, which I drink standing at the kitchen counter. I'm in bed shortly after ten o'clock. By then, I've managed to completely dismiss whatever I only thought I saw crossing Jenckes Street.

## V

"Open your eyes, Ms Howard," Abby Gladding says, and I do. Her voice does not in any way command me to open my eyes, and it is perfectly clear that I have a choice in the matter. But there's a certain *je ne sais quoi* in the delivery, the inflection and intonation, in the measured conveyance of these four syllables, that makes it impossible for me to keep my eyes closed. It's not yet dawn, but sunrise cannot be very far away, and I am lying in my bed. I cannot say whether I am awake or dreaming, or if possibly I am stranded in some liminal state that is neither one nor the other. I am immediately conscious of an unseen weight bearing down painfully upon my chest, and I am having difficulty breathing.

"I promised that I'd call on you," she says, and, with great effort, I turn my head towards the sound of her voice, my cheek pressing deeply into my pillow. I am aware now that I am all but paralysed, perhaps by the same force pushing down on my chest, and I strain for any glimpse of her. But there's only the bedside table, the clock radio and reading lamp and ashtray, an overcrowded bookcase with sagging shelves, and the floral calico wallpaper that came with the apartment. If I could move my arms, I would switch on the lamp. If I could move, I'd sit up, and maybe I would be able to breathe again.

And then I think that she must surely be singing, though her song has no words. There is no need for mere lyrics, not when texture and timbre, harmony and melody, are sufficient to unmake the mundane artefacts that comprise my bedroom, wiping aside the here and now that belie what I am meant to see, in this fleeting moment. And even as the wall and the bookshelf and the table beside my bed dissolve and fall away, I understand that her music is drawing me deeper into sleep again, though I must have been very nearly awake when she told me to open my eyes. I have no time to worry over apparent contradictions, and

I can't move my head to look away from what she means for me to see.

*There's nothing to be afraid of*, I think, and *No more here than in any bad dream*. But I find the thought carries no conviction whatsoever. It's even less substantial than the dissolving wallpaper and bookcase.

And now I'm looking at the weed-choked shore of a misty pond or swamp, a bog or tidal marsh. The light is so dim it might be dusk, or it might be dawn, or merely an overcast day. There are huge trees bending low near the water, which seems almost perfectly smooth and the green of polished malachite. I hear frogs, hidden among the moss and reeds, the ferns and skunk cabbages, and now the calls of birds form a counterpoint to Abby's voice. Except, seeing her standing ankle-deep in that stagnant green pool, I also see that she isn't singing. The music is coming from the violin braced against her shoulder, from the bow and strings and the movement of her left hand along the fingerboard of the instrument. She has her back to me, but I don't need to see her face to know it's her. Her black hair hangs down almost to her hips. And only now do I realise that she's naked.

Abruptly, she stops playing, and her arms fall to her sides, the violin in her left hand, the bow in her right. The tip of the bow breaks the surface of the pool, and ripples in concentric rings race away from it.

"I wear this rough garment to deceive," she says, and, at that, all the birds and frogs fall silent. "Aren't you the clever girl? Aren't you canny? I would not think appearances would so easily lead you astray. Not for as long as this."

No words escape my rigid, sleeping jaws, but she hears me, all the same, my answer that needs no voice, and she turns to face me. Her eyes are golden, not blue. And in the low light, they briefly flash a bright, iridescent yellow. She smiles, showing me teeth as sharp as razors, and then she quotes from the Gospel of Matthew.

"Inwardly, they were ravening wolves," she says to me, though her tone is not unkind. "You've seen all that you need to see, and probably more, I'd wager." And with this, she turns away again, turning to face the fog shrouding the wide green pool. As I watch, helpless to divert my gaze or even shut my eyes, she lets the violin and bow slip from her hands; they fall into the water with quiet splashes. The bow sinks, though the violin floats. And then she goes down on all fours. She laps at the pool, and her hair has begun to writhe like a nest of serpents.

And now I'm awake, disoriented and my chest aching, gasping for air as if a moment before I was drowning and have only just been pulled to the safety of dry land. The wallpaper is only dingy calico again, and the bookcase is only a bookcase. The clock radio and the lamp and the ashtray sit in their appointed places upon the bedside table.

The sheets are soaked through with sweat, and I'm shivering. I sit up, my back braced against the headboard, and my eyes go to the second-storey window on the other side of the small room. The sun is still down, but it's a little lighter out there than it is in the bedroom. And for a fraction of a moment, clearly silhouetted against that false dawn, I see the head and shoulders of a young woman. I also see the muzzle and alert ears of a wolf, and that golden eyeshine watching me. Then it's gone, she or it, whichever pronoun might best apply. It doesn't seem to matter. Because now I do know exactly what I'm looking for, and I know that I've seen it before, years before I first caught sight of Abby Gladding standing in the rain without an umbrella.

## VI

Friday morning I drive back to Newport, and it doesn't take me long at all to find the grave. It's just a little ways south of the chain-link fence dividing the North Burial Ground from the older Common Burying Ground and Island Cemetery. I turn off Warner Street onto the rutted, unpaved road winding between the indistinct rows of monuments. I find a place that's wide enough to pull over and park. The trees have only just begun to bud, and their bare limbs are stark against a sky so blue-white it hurts my eyes to look directly into it. The grass is mostly still brown from long months of snow and frost, though there are small clumps of new green showing here and there.

The cemetery has been in use since 1640 or so. There are three Colonial-Era governors buried here (one a delegate to the

Continental Congress), along with the founder of Freemasonry in Rhode Island, a signatory to the Declaration of Independence, various Civil-War generals, lighthouse keepers, and hundreds of African slaves stolen from Gambia and Sierra Leone, the Gold and Ivory coasts and brought to Newport in the heyday of whaling and the Rhode Island rum trade. The grave of Abby Gladding is marked by a weathered slate headstone, badly scabbed over with lichen. But, despite the centuries, the shallow inscription is still easy enough to read:

HERE LYETH INTERED Y<sup>e</sup> BODY
OF ABBY MARY GLADDING
DAUGHTER OF SOLOMON GLADDING <sup>esq</sup>
& MARY HIS WYFE WHO
DEPARTED THIS LIFE Y<sup>e</sup> 2<sup>d</sup> DAY OF
SEPT 1785 AGED 22 YEARS
SHE WAS DROWN'D & DEPARTED & SLEEPS
<sup>ZECH 4:1</sup> NEITHER SHALL THEY WEAR
A HAIRY GARMENT TO DECEIVE

Above the inscription, in place of the usual death's head, is a crude carving of a violin. I sit down in the dry, dead grass in front of the marker, and I don't know how long I've been sitting there when I hear crows cawing. I look over my shoulder, and there's a tree back towards Farewell Street filled with the big black birds. They watch me, and I take that as my cue to leave. I know now that I have to go back to the library, that whatever remains of this mystery is waiting for me there. I might find it tucked away in an old journal, a newspaper clipping, or in crumbling church records. I only know I'll find it, because now I have the missing pieces. But there is an odd reluctance to leave the grave of Abby Gladding. There's no fear in me, no shock or stubborn disbelief at what I've discovered or at its impossible ramifications. And some part of me notes the oddness of this, that I am not afraid. I leave her alone in that narrow house, watched over by the wary crows, and go back to my car. Less than fifteen minutes later I'm in the Redwood Library, asking for anything they can find on a Solomon Gladding, and his daughter, Abby.

"Are you sick?" the librarian asks, and I wonder what she sees in my face, in my eyes, to elicit such a question. "Are you feeling well?"

"I'm fine," I assure her. "I was up a little too late last night, that's all. A little too much to drink, most likely."

She nods, and I smile.

"Well, then. I'll see what we might have," she says, and, cutting to the chase, it ends with a short article that appeared in the *Newport Mercury* early in November 1785, hardly more than two months after Abby Gladding's death. It begins, "We hear a ftrange account from laft Thursday evening, the Night of the 3rd of November, of a body difinterred from its Grave and coffin. This most peculiar occurrence was undertaken at the beheft of the father of the deceafed young woman therein buried, a circumftance making the affair even ftranger ftill." What follows is a description of a ritual which will be familiar to anyone who has read of the 1892 Mercy Brown case from Exeter, or the much earlier exhumation of Nancy Young (summer of 1827), or other purported New England "vampires".

In September, Abby Gladding's body was discovered in Newport Harbour by a local fisherman, and it was determined that she had drowned. The body was in an advanced state of decay, leading me to wonder if the date of the headstone is meant to be the date the body was found, not the date of her death. There were persistent rumours that the daughter of Samuel Gladding, a local merchant, had taken her own life. She is said to have been a "child of singular and morbid temperament", who had recently refused a marriage proposal by the eldest son of another Newport merchant, Ebenezer Burrill. There was also back-fence talk that Abby had practised witchcraft in the woods bordering the town, and that she would play her violin (a gift from her mother) to summon "voracious wolves and other such dæmons to do her bidding".

Very shortly after her death, her youngest sister, Susan, suddenly fell ill. This was in October, and the girl was dead before the end of the month. Her symptoms, like those of Mercy Brown's stricken family members, can readily be identified as late-stage tuberculosis. What is peculiar here is that Abby doesn't appear to have suffered any such wasting disease herself, and the speed with which Susan became ill and died is also atypical of consumption. Even as Susan fought for her life, Abby's mother, Mary, fell ill, and it was in hope of saving his wife that Solomon Gladding agreed to the exhumation of his daughter's body. The article in the *Newport Mercury* speculates that he'd learned of this ritual and folk remedy from a Jamaican slave woman.

At sunrise, with the aid of several other men, some apparently family members, the grave was opened, and all present were horrified to see "the body fresh as the day it was confignted to God", her cheeks "flufhed with colour and lufterous". The liver and heart were duly cut out, and both were discovered to contain clotted blood, which Solomon had been told would prove that Abby was rising from her grave each night to steal the blood of her mother and sister. The heart was burned in a fire kindled in the cemetery, the ashes mixed with water, and the mother drank the mixture. The body of Abby was turned facedown in her casket, and an iron stake was driven through her chest, to ensure that the restless spirit would be unable to find its way out of the grave. Nonetheless, according to parish records from Trinity Church, Mary Gladding died before Christmas. Abbey's father fell ill a few months later, and died in August of 1786.

And I find one more thing that I will put down here. Scribbled in sepia ink, in the left-hand margin of the newspaper page containing the account of the exhumation of Abby Gladding is the phrase *Jé-rouge,* or "red eyes", which I've learned is a Haitian term denoting werewolfery and cannibalism. Below that word, in the same spidery hand, is written *As white as snow, as red as red, as green as briers, as black as coal.* There is no date or signature accompanying these notations.

And now it is almost Friday night, and I sit alone on a wooden bench at Bowen's Wharf, not too far from the kiosk advertising daily boat tours to view fat, doe-eyed seals sunning themselves on the rocky beaches ringing Narragansett Bay. I sit here and watch the sun going down, shivering because I left home this morning without my coat. I do not expect to see Abby Gladding, tonight or ever again. But I've come here, anyway, and I may come again tomorrow evening.

I will not include the 1785 disinterment in my thesis, no matter how many feathers it might earn for my cap. I mean never to speak of it again. What I have written here, I suspect I'll destroy it later on. It has only been written for me, and for me alone. If Abby was trying to speak *through* me, to find a larger audience, she'll have to find another mouthpiece. I watch a lobster boat heading out for the night. I light a cigarette, and eye the herring gulls wheeling above the marina.

# RAMSEY CAMPBELL

## With the Angels

RAMSEY CAMPBELL WAS BORN in Liverpool, where he still lives
with his wife Jenny. His first book, a collection of stories entitled
*The Inhabitant of the Lake and Less Welcome Tenants*, was
published by August Derleth's legendary Arkham House imprint
in 1964, since when his novels have included *The Doll Who Ate
His Mother*, *The Face That Must Die*, *The Nameless*, *Incarnate*,
*The Hungry Moon*, *Ancient Images*, *The Count of Eleven*, *The
Long Lost*, *Pact of the Fathers*, *The Darkest Part of the Woods*,
*The Grin of the Dark*, *Thieving Fear*, *Creatures of the Pool*, *The
Seven Days of Cain* and the movie tie-in *Solomon Kane*.

His short fiction has been collected in such volumes as *Demons
by Daylight*, *The Height of the Scream*, *Dark Companions*, *Scared
Stiff*, *Waking Nightmares*, *Cold Print*, *Alone with the Horrors*,
*Ghosts and Grisly Things*, *Told by the Dead*, and *Just Behind
You*. He has also edited a number of anthologies, including *New
Terrors*, *New Tales of the Cthulhu Mythos*, *Fine Frights: Stories
That Scared Me*, *Uncanny Banquet*, *Meddling with Ghosts*, and
*Gathering the Bones: Original Stories from the World's Masters
of Horror* (with Dennis Etchison and Jack Dann).

PS Publishing recently issued the novel *Ghosts Know*, and the
definitive edition of *Inhabitant of the Lake*, which included all
the first drafts of the stories. Forthcoming is another novel, *The
Black Pilgrimage*.

Ramsey Campbell has won multiple World Fantasy Awards,
British Fantasy Awards and Bram Stoker Awards, and is a

recipient of the World Horror Convention Grand Master Award, the Horror Writers Association Lifetime Achievement Award, the Howie Award of the H.P. Lovecraft Film Festival for Lifetime Achievement, and the International Horror Guild's Living Legend Award. A film reviewer for BBC Radio Merseyside since 1969, he is also President of both the British Fantasy Society and the Society of Fantastic Films.

"My fellow clansman Paul Campbell will remember the birth of this tale," he reveals. "At the Dead Dog party after the 2010 World Horror Convention in Brighton, someone was throwing a delighted toddler into the air. I was ambushed by an idea and had to apologise to Paul for rushing away to my room to scribble notes. The result is here."

A S CYNTHIA DROVE BETWEEN the massive mossy posts where the gates used to be, Karen said "Were you little when you lived here, Auntie Jackie?"

"Not as little as I was," Cynthia said.

"That's right," Jacqueline said while the poplars alongside the high walls darkened the car, "I'm even older than your grandmother."

Karen and Valerie giggled and then looked for other amusement. "What's this house called, Brian?" Valerie enquired.

"The Populars," the four-year-old declared and set about punching his sisters almost before they began to laugh.

"Now, you three," Cynthia intervened. "You said you'd show Jackie how good you can be."

No doubt she meant her sister to feel more included. "Can't we play?" said Brian as if Jacqueline were a disapproving bystander.

"I expect you may," Jacqueline said, having glanced at Cynthia. "Just don't get yourselves dirty or do any damage or go anywhere you shouldn't or that's dangerous."

Brian and the eight-year-old twins barely waited for Cynthia to haul two-handed at the brake before they piled out of the Volvo and chased across the forecourt into the weedy garden. "Do try and let them be children," Cynthia murmured.

"I wasn't aware I could change them." Jacqueline managed not to groan while she unbent her stiff limbs and clambered out of the car. "I shouldn't think they would take much notice of me," she said, supporting herself on the hot roof as she turned to the house.

Despite the August sunlight, it seemed darker than its neighbours, not just because of the shadows of the trees, which still put her in mind of a graveyard. More than a century's worth of winds across the moors outside the Yorkshire town had plastered the large house with grime. The windows on the topmost floor were half the size of those on the other two storeys, one reason why she'd striven in her childhood not to think they resembled the eyes of a spider, any more than the porch between the downstairs rooms looked like a voracious vertical mouth. She was far from a child now, and she strode or at any rate limped to the porch, only to have to wait for her sister to bring the keys. As Cynthia thrust one into the first rusty lock the twins scampered over, pursued by their brother. "Throw me up again," he cried.

"Where did he get that from?"

"From being a child, I should think," Cynthia said. "Don't you remember what it was like?"

Jacqueline did, not least because of Brian's demand. She found some breath as she watched the girls take their brother by the arms and swing him into the air. "Again," he cried.

"We're tired now," Karen told him. "We want to see in the house."

"Maybe grandma and auntie will give you a throw if you're good," Valerie said.

"Not just now," Jacqueline said at once.

Cynthia raised her eyebrows high enough to turn her eyes blank as she twisted the second key. The door lumbered inwards a few inches and then baulked. She was trying to nudge the obstruction aside with the door when Brian made for the gap. "Don't," Jacqueline blurted, catching him by the shoulder.

"Good heavens, Jackie, what's the matter now?"

"We don't want the children in there until we know what state it's in, do we?"

"Just see if you can squeeze past and shift whatever's there, Brian."
Jacqueline felt unworthy of consideration. She could only

watch the boy wriggle around the edge of the door and vanish into the gloom. She heard fumbling and rustling, but of course this didn't mean some desiccated presence was at large in the vestibule. Why didn't Brian speak? She was about to prompt him until he called "It's just some old letters and papers."

When he reappeared with several free newspapers that looked as dusty as their news, Cynthia eased the door past him. A handful of brown envelopes contained electricity bills that grew redder as they came up to date, which made Jacqueline wonder "Won't the lights work?"

"I expect so if we really need them." Cynthia advanced into the wide hall beyond the vestibule and poked at the nearest switch. Grit ground inside the mechanism, but the bulbs in the hall chandelier stayed as dull as the mass of crystal teardrops. "Never mind," Cynthia said, having tested every switch in the column on the wall without result. "As I say, we won't need them."

The grimy skylight above the stairwell illuminated the hall enough to show that the dark wallpaper was even hairier than Jacqueline remembered. It had always made her think of the fur of a great spider, and now it was blotchy with damp. The children were already running up the left-hand staircase and across the first-floor landing, under which the chandelier dangled like a spider on a thread. "Don't go out of sight," Cynthia told them, "until we see what's what."

"Chase me." Brian ran down the other stairs, one of which rattled like a lid beneath the heavy carpet. "Chase," he cried and dashed across the hall to race upstairs again.

"Don't keep running up and down unless you want to make me ill," Jacqueline's grandmother would have said. The incessant rumble of footsteps might have presaged a storm on the way to turning the hall even gloomier, so that Jacqueline strode as steadily as she could towards the nearest room. She had to pass one of the hall mirrors, which appeared to show a dark blotch hovering in wait for the children. The shapeless sagging darkness at the top of the grimy oval was a stain, and she needn't have waited to see the children run downstairs out of its reach. "Do you want the mirror?" Cynthia said. "I expect it would clean up."

"I don't know what I want from this house," Jacqueline said.

She mustn't say she would prefer the children not to be in it. She couldn't even suggest sending them outside in case the garden concealed dangers – broken glass, rusty metal, holes in the ground. The children were staying with Cynthia while her son and his partner holidayed in Morocco, but couldn't she have chosen a better time to go through the house before it was put up for sale? She frowned at Cynttia and then followed her into the dining-room.

Although the heavy curtains were tied back from the large windows, the room wasn't much brighter than the hall. It was steeped in the shadows of the poplars, and the tall panes were spotted with earth. A spider's nest of a chandelier loomed above the long table set for an elaborate dinner for six. That had been Cynthia's idea when they'd moved their parents to the rest home; she'd meant to convince any thieves that the house was still occupied, but to Jacqueline it felt like preserving a past that she'd hoped to outgrow. She remembered being made to sit up stiffly at the table, to hold her utensils just so, to cover her lap nicely with her napkin, not to speak or to make the slightest noise with any of her food. Too much of this upbringing had lodged inside her, but was that why she felt uneasy with the children in the house? "Are you taking anything out of here?" Cynthia said.

"There's nothing here for me, Cynthia. You have whatever you want and don't worry about me."

Cynthia gazed at her as they headed for the breakfast room. The chandelier stirred as the children ran above it once again, but Jacqueline told herself that was nothing like her nightmares – at least, not very like. She was unnerved to hear Cynthia exclaim "There it is."

The breakfast room was borrowing light from the large back garden, but not much, since the overgrown expanse lay in the shadow of the house. The weighty table had spread its wings and was attended by six straight-backed ponderous chairs, but Cynthia was holding out her hands to the high chair in the darkest corner of the room. "Do you remember sitting in that?" she apparently hoped. "I think I do."

"I wouldn't," Jacqueline said.

She hadn't needed it to make her feel restricted at the table, where breakfast with her grandparents had been as formal as dinner. "Nothing here either," she declared and limped into the hall.

The mirror on the far side was discoloured too. She glimpsed the children's blurred shapes streaming up into a pendulous darkness and heard the agitated jangle of the chandelier as she made for the lounge. The leather suite looked immovable with age, and only the television went some way towards bringing the room up to date, though the screen was as blank as an uninscribed stone. She remembered having to sit silent for hours while her parents and grandparents listened to the radio for news about the war – her grandmother hadn't liked children out of her sight in the house. The dresser was still full of china she'd been forbidden to venture near, which was grey with dust and the dimness. Cynthia had been allowed to crawl around the room – indulged for being younger or because their grandmother liked babies in the house. "I'll leave you to it," she said as Cynthia followed her in.

She was hoping to find more light in the kitchen, but it didn't show her much that she wanted to see. While the refrigerator was relatively modern, not to mention tall enough for somebody to stand in, it felt out of place. The black iron range still occupied most of one wall, and the old stained marble sink projected from another. Massive cabinets and heavy chests of drawers helped box in the hulking table scored by knives. It used to remind her of an operating table, even though she hadn't thought she would grow up to be a nurse. She was distracted by the children as they ran into the kitchen. "Can we have a drink?" Karen said for all of them.

"May we?" Valerie amended.

"Please." Once she'd been echoed Jacqueline said "I'll find you some glasses. Let the tap run."

When she opened a cupboard she thought for a moment that the stack of plates was covered by a greyish doily. Several objects as long as a baby's fingers but thinner even than their bones flinched out of sight, and she saw the plates were draped with a mass of cobwebs. She slammed the door as Karen used both hands to twist the cold tap. It uttered a dry gurgle rather too reminiscent of sounds she used to hear while working in the geriatric ward, and she wondered if the supply had been turned off.

Then a gout of dark liquid spattered the sink, and a gush of rusty water darkened the marble. As Karen struggled to shut it off Valerie enquired "Did you have to drink that, auntie?"

"I had to put up with a lot you wouldn't be expected to."

"We won't, then. Aren't there any other drinks?"

"And things to eat," Brian said at once.

"I'm sure there's nothing." When the children gazed at her with various degrees of patience Jacqueline opened the refrigerator, trying not to think that the compartments could harbour bodies smaller than Brian's. All she found were a bottle of mouldering milk and half a loaf as hard as a rusk. "I'm afraid you'll have to do without," she said.

How often had her grandmother said that? Supposedly she'd been just as parsimonious before the war. Jacqueline didn't want to sound like her, but when Brian took hold of the handle of a drawer that was level with his head she couldn't help blurting "Stay away from there."

At least she didn't add "We've lost enough children." As the boy stepped back Cynthia hurried into the kitchen. "What are you doing now?"

"We don't want them playing with knives, do we?" Jacqueline said.

"I know you're too sensible, Brian."

Was that aimed just at him? As Cynthia opened the cupboards the children resumed chasing up the stairs. Presumably the creature Jacqueline had glimpsed was staying out of sight, and so were any more like it. When Cynthia made for the hall Jacqueline said "I'll be up in a minute."

Although she didn't linger in the kitchen, she couldn't leave her memories behind. How many children had her grandmother lost that she'd been so afraid of losing any more? By pestering her mother Jacqueline had learned they'd been stillborn, which had reminded her how often her grandmother told her to keep still. More than once today Jacqueline had refrained from saying that to the twins and to Brian in particular. Their clamour seemed to fill the hall and resonate all the way up the house, so that she could have thought the reverberations were shaking the mirrors, disturbing the suspended mass of darkness like a web in which a spider had come to life. "Can we go up to the top now?" Brian said.

"Please don't," Jacqueline called.

It took Cynthia's stare to establish that the boy hadn't been asking Jacqueline. "Why can't we?" Karen protested, and Valerie contributed "We only want to see."

"I'm sure you can," Cynthia said. "Just wait till we're all up there."

Before tramping into the nearest bedroom she gave her sister one more look, and Jacqueline felt as blameworthy as their grandmother used to make her feel. Why couldn't she watch over the children from the hall? She tilted her head back on her shaky neck to gaze up the stairwell. Sometimes her grandfather would raise his eyes ceilingwards as his wife found yet another reason to rebuke Jacqueline, only for the woman to say "If you look like that you'll see where you're going." Presumably she'd meant Heaven, and perhaps she was there now, if there was such a place. Jacqueline imagined her sailing upwards like a husk on a wind; she'd already seemed withered all those years ago, and not just physically either. Was that why Jacqueline had thought the stillbirths must be shrivelled too? They would have ended up like that, but she needn't think about it now, if ever. She glanced towards the children and saw movement above them.

She must have seen the shadows of the treetops – thin shapes that appeared to start out of the corners under the roof before darting back into the gloom. As she tried to grasp how those shadows could reach so far beyond the confines of the skylight, Cynthia peered out of the nearest bedroom. "Jackie, aren't you coming to look?"

Jacqueline couldn't think for all the noise. "If you three will give us some peace for a while," she said louder than she liked. "And stay with us. We don't want you going anywhere that isn't safe."

"You heard your aunt," Cynthia said, sounding unnecessarily like a resentful child.

As Brian trudged after the twins to follow Cynthia into her grandmother's bedroom Jacqueline remembered never being let in there. Later her parents had made it their room – had tried, at any rate. While they'd doubled the size of the bed, the rest of the furniture was still her grandmother's, and she could have fancied that all the swarthy wood was helping the room glower at the intrusion. She couldn't imagine her parents sharing a bed there, let alone performing any activity in it, but she didn't want to think about such things at all. "Not for me," she said and made for the next room.

Not much had changed since it had been her grandfather's, which meant it still seemed to belong to his wife. It felt like her disapproval rendered solid by not just the narrow single bed but the rest of the dark furniture that duplicated hers, having been her choice. She'd disapproved of almost anything related to Jacqueline, not least her husband playing with their granddaughter. Jacqueline avoided glancing up at any restlessness under the roof while she crossed the landing to the other front bedroom. As she gazed at the two single beds that remained since the cot had been disposed of, the children ran to cluster around her in the doorway. "This was your room, wasn't it?" Valerie said.

"Yours and our grandma's," Karen amended.

"No," Jacqueline said, "it was hers and our mother's and father's."

In fact she hadn't been sent to the top floor until Cynthia was born. Their grandfather had told her she was going to stay with the angels, though his wife frowned at the idea. Jacqueline would have found it more appealing if she hadn't already been led to believe that all the stillbirths were living with the angels. She hardly knew why she was continuing to explore the house. Though the cast-iron bath had been replaced by a fibreglass tub as blue as the toilet and sink, she still remembered flinching from the chilly metal. After Cynthia's birth their grandmother had taken over bathing Jacqueline, scrubbing her with such relentless harshness that it had felt like a penance. When it was over at last, her grandfather would do his best to raise her spirits. "Now you're clean enough for the angels," he would say and throw her up in the air.

"If you're good the angels will catch you" – but of course he did, which had always made her wonder what would happen to her if she wasn't good enough. She'd seemed to glimpse that thought in her grandmother's eyes, or had it been a wish? What would have caught her if she'd failed to live up to requirements? As she tried to forget the conclusion she'd reached Brian said "Where did they put you, then?"

"They kept me right up at the top."

"Can we see?"

"Yes, let's," said Valerie, and Karen ran after him as well.

Jacqueline was opening her mouth to delay them when Cynthia said "You'll be going up there now, won't you? You can keep an eye on them."

It was a rebuke for not helping enough with the children, or for interfering too much, or perhaps for Jacqueline's growing nervousness. Anger at her childish fancies sent her stumping halfway up the topmost flight of stairs before she faltered. Clouds had gathered like a lifetime's worth of dust above the skylight, and perhaps that was why the top floor seemed to darken as she climbed towards it, so that all the corners were even harder to distinguish – she could almost have thought the mass of dimness was solidifying. "Where were you, auntie?" Karen said.

"In there," said Jacqueline and hurried to join them outside the nearest room.

It wasn't as vast as she remembered, though certainly large enough to daunt a small child. The ceiling stooped to the front wall, squashing the window, from which the shadows of the poplars seemed to creep up the gloomy incline to acquire more substance under the roof at the back of the room. The grimy window smudged the premature twilight, which had very little to illuminate, since the room was bare of furniture and even of a carpet. "Did you have to sleep on the floor?" Valerie said. "Were you very bad?"

"Of course not," Jacqueline declared. It felt as if her memories had been thrown out – as if she hadn't experienced them – but she knew better. She'd lain on the cramped bed hemmed in by dour furniture and cut off from everyone else in the house by the dark that occupied the stairs. She would have prayed if that mightn't have roused what she dreaded. If the babies were with the angels, mustn't that imply they weren't angels themselves? Being stillbirths needn't mean they would keep still – Jacqueline never could when she was told. Suppose they were what caught you if you weren't good? She'd felt as if she had been sent away from her family for bad behaviour. All too soon she'd heard noises that suggested tiny withered limbs were stirring, and glimpsed movements in the highest corners of the room.

She must have been hearing the poplars and seeing their shadows. As she turned away from the emptied bedroom she caught sight of the room opposite, which was full of items covered with dustsheets. Had she ever known what the sheets concealed? She'd imagined they hid some secret that children weren't supposed to learn, but they'd also reminded her of enormous masses of cobweb. She could have thought the denizens of the webs were liable to crawl out of the dimness, and she was absurdly relieved to see Cynthia coming upstairs. "I'll leave you to it," Jacqueline said. "I'll be waiting down below."

It wasn't only the top floor she wanted to leave behind. She'd remembered what she'd once done to her sister. The war had been over at last, and she'd been trusted to look after Cynthia while the adults planned the future. The sisters had only been allowed to play with their toys in the hall, where Jacqueline had done her best to distract the toddler from straying into any of the rooms they weren't supposed to enter by themselves – in fact, every room. At last she'd grown impatient with her sister's mischief, and in a wicked moment she'd wondered what would catch Cynthia if she tossed her high. As she'd thrown her sister into the air with all her strength she'd realised that she didn't want to know, certainly not at Cynthia's expense – as she'd seen dwarfish shrivelled figures darting out of every corner in the dark above the stairwell and scuttling down to seize their prize. They'd come head first, so that she'd seen their bald scalps wrinkled like walnuts before she glimpsed their hungry withered faces. Then Cynthia had fallen back into her arms, though Jacqueline had barely managed to keep hold of her. Squeezing her eyes shut, she'd hugged her sister until she'd felt able to risk seeing they were alone in the vault of the hall.

There was no use telling herself that she'd taken back her unforgivable wish. She might have injured the toddler even by catching her – she might have broken her frail neck. She ought to have known that, and perhaps she had. Being expected to behave badly had made her act that way, but she felt as if all the nightmares that were stored in the house had festered and gained strength over the years. When she reached the foot of the stairs at last she carried on out of the house.

The poplars stooped to greet her with a wordless murmur.

A wind was rising under the sunless sky. It was gentle on her face – it seemed to promise tenderness she couldn't recall having experienced, certainly not once Cynthia was born. Perhaps it could soothe away her memories, and she was raising her face to it when Brian appeared in the porch. "What are you doing, auntie?"

"Just being by myself."

She thought that was pointed enough until he skipped out of the house. "Is it time now?"

Why couldn't Cynthia have kept him with her? No doubt she thought it was Jacqueline's turn. "Time for what?" Jacqueline couldn't avoid asking.

"You said you'd give me a throw."

She'd said she wouldn't then, not that she would sometime. Just the same, perhaps she could. It might be a way of leaving the house behind and all it represented to her. It would prove she deserved to be trusted with him, as she ought not to have been trusted with little Cynthia. "Come on then," she said.

As soon as she held out her arms he ran and leapt into them. "Careful," she gasped, laughing as she recovered her balance. "Are you ready?" she said and threw the small body into the air.

She was surprised how light he was, or how much strength she had at her disposal. He came down giggling, and she caught him. "Again," he cried.

"Just once more," Jacqueline said. She threw him higher this time, and he giggled louder. Cynthia often said that children kept you young, and Jacqueline thought it was true after all. Brian fell into her arms and she hugged him. "Again," he could hardly beg for giggling.

"Now what did I just say?" Nevertheless she threw him so high that her arms trembled with the effort, and the poplars nodded as if they were approving her accomplishment. She clutched at Brian as he came down with an impact that made her shoulders ache. "Higher," he pleaded almost incoherently. "Higher."

"This really is the last time, Brian." She crouched as if the stooping poplars had pushed her down. Tensing her whole body, she reared up to fling him into the pendulous gloom with all her strength.

For a moment she thought only the wind was reaching for him

as it bowed the trees and dislodged objects from the foliage – leaves that rustled, twigs that scraped and rattled. But the thin shapes weren't falling, they were scurrying head first down the tree-trunks at a speed that seemed to leave time behind. Some of them had no shape they could have lived with, and some might never have had any skin. She saw their shrivelled eyes glimmer eagerly and their toothless mouths gape with an identical infantile hunger. Their combined weight bowed the lowest branches while they extended arms like withered sticks to snatch the child.

In that helpless instant Jacqueline was overwhelmed by a feeling she would never have admitted – a rush of childish glee, of utter irresponsibility. For a moment she was no longer a nurse, not even a retired one as old as some of her patients had been. She shouldn't have put Brian at risk, but now he was beyond saving. Then he fell out of the dark beneath the poplars, in which there was no longer any sign of life, and she made a grab at him. The strength had left her arms, and he struck the hard earth with a thud that put her in mind of the fall of a lid.

"Brian?" she said and bent groaning to him. "Brian," she repeated, apparently loud enough to be audible all the way up the house. She heard her old window rumble open, and Cynthia's cry: "What have you done now?" She heard footsteps thunder down the stairs, and turned away from the small still body beneath the uninhabited trees as her sister dashed out of the porch. Jacqueline had just one thought, but surely it must make a difference. "Nothing caught him," she said.

# RICHARD L. TIERNEY

## Autumn Chill

RICHARD L. TIERNEY LIVES in his house, "The Hermitage", in Mason City, Iowa. He has a degree in entomology from Iowa State University and worked with the US Forestry Service for many years. An editor, poet and critic, his seminal essay "The Derleth Mythos" is considered a cornerstone of modern Lovecraftian criticism.

A great admirer of the writings of Robert E. Howard, Tierney edited *Tigers of the Sea* and *Hawks of Outremer* for publisher Donald M. Grant, completing a few unfinished tales in the process.

His novels include *The Winds of Zar*, the "Bran Mak Morn" pastiche *For the Witch of the Mists* (with David C. Smith), *The House of the Toad*, *The Scroll of Thoth: Simon Magus and the Great Old Ones*, *The Gardens of Lucullus* (with Glenn Rahman), *The Drums of Chaos*, and six "Red Sonja" books (1981–83), also in collaboration with Smith.

Inspired by the work of Edgar Allan Poe, H.P. Lovecraft, Donald Wandrei, Robert E. Howard and Frank Belknap Long, Tierney's poetry has been collected in *Dreams and Damnations*, *The Doom Prophet and One Other*, the Arkham House volume of *Collected Poems*, *Nightmares and Visions*, *The Blob That Gobbled Abdul and Other Poems and Songs* and *Savage Menace and Other Poems of Horror*.

S.T. Joshi has described Tierney as "one of the leading weird poets of his generation."

Howdy, young fellow! what brings you down here
     To this old graveyard in the piney woods?
Not many folks come wandering this way.
Lost, you say? Well, I figured you must be.
This family plot of mine's a right far piece
From any town. But, don't you worry none,
Just keep on this dirt road 'bout two miles more
And it'll bring ye to the Aylesbury Pike.
But why not stop and rest a spell, young sir?
The evening's fair and clear, and I don't get
Much chance to chat and hear the outside news
     From folks like you just passing through.

Yes, yes, I know you can't stay long,
     But bear with me a bit.
I'm a mite lonely here since brother Ned,
My only close kin, recently passed away.
Come on, I'd like to show ye 'round this place,
If you can spare some minutes from your trip.
Good! I won't keep ye long. Come, follow me.
The evening's mild and mellow – aye, and look!
There's bright Orion climbing up the sky.
     See how his jewelled sword-belt gleams!
And here comes Sirius, nipping at his heels!
Just hear that night-breeze starting up to whisper—
Listen to how it makes the dry leaves rattle
     Like skeleton spiders!
A sad and spooky time o' day it is,
The sun gone down behind the piney ridge,
The autumn afterglow a-fading out.

But, look, here's what I wanted you to see—
This ancient graveyard nestled 'midst the trees.
It's old, young sir, older than this Republic,
And 'most all of my kin lie buried here.
Look how those headstones hump up from the moss
With skulls and crossbones carved upon their faces.
     They're centuries old, some of 'em.

But, see that fresh-dug mound and wooden cross?
Poor Ned was buried there a week ago.
Ain't even got a proper headstone yet.
Ned, he was sort of odd and troublesome,
You know, like some of closest kinfolk are,
But I was mighty heartstruck when he up
And died so sudden . . . But, my God! What's *that*?

You seen it too, young fellow, didn't you?
Looked like a 'possum running fast, you say?
    Well, I allow you may be right.
Just let me catch my breath a bit. 'Twas quite
A shock to see that critter scuttling from
Ned's grave. You're right, it must have been a 'possum . . .
Shaking, you say? Well, yes, I guess I am.
Gave me a start, that critter did, and I've
Been brooding some about poor brother Ned.
He'd read these books Great-grandpa'd handed down
Full of strange things most folks don't know about.
Our family goes a long way back, y'know,
And some of them has had the wisdom-gift.
Ned, now, he had it too, I guess, 'cause soon
After he'd studied them old books awhile
The folks he didn't like took sick and died,
Like cousin Henry and old Auntie Liz,
And when he started looking dark at me
I took to sleeping with an axe at hand.
They say a grave can't keep a sorcerer,
But surely if his head's been split in half
He can't—

    My God! That hole above Ned's grave—
It don't look like no 'possum could have dug it,
For look at how the fresh black dirt is mounded
As if it's been pushed *out*! And now, what's *that*—?
A rustling in the weeds, heading this way—
No 'possum goes like that with thin white tendrils
Waving above the grass. No. *No*! It's *Ned*!
His brain's done burrowed up beneath the sod,

Dragging its spinal cord like to a tail,
Waving its nerves like sorcery-poisoned stings.
It's coming for me—see it? *It's his brain!*

No, no, young fellow, don't run off like that,
Don't leave me here to meet that thing alone!
*Come back!*

# JOHN LANGAN

## City of the Dog

JOHN LANGAN LIVES IN upstate New York with his wife and son. He is the author of the novel *House of Windows* and a collection, *Mr Gaunt and Other Uneasy Encounters*.

His stories have appeared in *The Magazine of Fantasy & Science Fiction*, and in such anthologies as *Poe*, *By Blood We Live* and *The Living Dead*. More stories are forthcoming in *Supernatural Noir*, *Ghosts by Gaslight* and *Blood and Other Cravings*.

"This story arose from my desire to see what I could do with the figure of the ghoul," reveals Langan, "and as I've tried to indicate within the narrative, I drew inspiration both from H.P. Lovecraft ('Pickman's Model') and Caitlín R. Kiernan (*Daughter of Hounds*).

"The miserable years in New York State's capital, though, were mine alone."

### I

I THOUGHT IT WAS a dog. From the other side of the lot, that was what it most resembled: down on all fours; hair plastered to its pale, skeletal trunk by the rain that had us hurrying down the sidewalk; head drawn into a snout. It was injured, that much was clear. Even with the rain rinsing its leg, a jagged tear wept fresh blood that caught the headlights of the cars turning onto Central – that had caught my eye, caused me to slow.

Kaitlyn walked on a few paces before noticing that I had

stopped at the edge of the lot where one of the thrift stores we'd plundered for cheap books and cassette tapes had burned to the ground the previous spring. (The space had been cleared soon thereafter, with conflicting reports of a Pizza Hut or Wendy's imminent, but as of mid-November, it was still a gap in the row of tired buildings that lined this stretch of Central Ave.) Arms crossed over the oversized Army greatcoat that was some anonymous Soviet officer's contribution to her wardrobe, my girlfriend hurried back to me. "What is it?"

I pointed. "That dog looks like it's pretty hurt." I stepped onto the lot. The ground squelched under my foot.

"What are you doing?"

"I don't know. I just want to see if he's all right."

"Shouldn't you call the cops? I mean, it could be dangerous. Look at the size of it."

She was right. This was not one of your toy dogs; this was not even a standard-sized mutt. This animal was as large as a wolfhound – larger. It was big as Latka, my Uncle Karl and Aunt Belinda's German Shepherd, had appeared to me when I was seven and terrified of her, and more terrified still of her ability to smell my fear, which my cousins assured me would enrage her. For a moment, my palms were slick, and I felt a surge of lightness at the top of my chest. Then I set to walking across the lot.

Behind me, Kaitlyn made her exasperated noise. I could see her flapping her arms to either side, the way she did when she was annoyed with me.

Puddles sprawled across the lot. I leapt a particularly wide one and landed in a hole that plunged my foot into freezing water past the ankle. "Shit!" My sneaker, sock, and the bottom of my jeans were soaked. There was no time to run back to the apartment to change. It appeared I'd be walking around the QE2 with one sopping sneaker for the rest of the night. I could hear Kaitlyn saying she'd *told* me to wear my boots.

The dog had not fled at my approach, not even when I dunked my foot. Watching me from the corner of its eye, it shuffled forward a couple of steps. The true size of the thing was remarkable; had it raised itself on its hind legs, it would have been as tall as me. There was something about the way it walked, its hips high, its shoulders low, as if it were unused to this pose, that made the image of it standing oddly plausible. Big as the dog was, it didn't seem especially menacing. It was an assemblage of bones over which a deficit of skin had been stretched, so that I could distinguish each of the oddly-shaped vertebrae that formed the arch of its spine. Its fur was pale, patchy; as far as I could see, its tail was gone. Its head was foreshortened, not the kind of elongated, vulpine look you expect with dogs bred big for hunting or fighting; although its ears were pointed, standing straight up, and ran a good part of the way down the side of its skull. I was less interested in its ears, however, than I was its teeth, and whether it was showing them to me. It continued to study me from one eye, but it appeared to be tolerating my presence well enough. Hands out and open in front of me, I stepped closer.

As I did, the thing's smell, diluted, no doubt, by the rain, rolled up into my nostrils. It was the thick, mineral odour of dirt, so dense I coughed and brought a hand to my mouth and nose. The taste of soil and clay coated my tongue. I coughed again, turned my head and spat. "I hope you appreciate this," I said, wiping my mouth. I squinted at the wound on its leg.

A wide patch of the dog's thigh had been scraped clear of hair and skin, pink muscle laid bare. Broader than it was deep, it was the kind of injury that bleeds dramatically and seems to take forever to quiet. While I doubted it was life-threatening, I was sure it was painful. How the dog had come by this wound, I couldn't say. When we were kids, my younger brother had been famous for this sort of scrape, but those had been from wiping out on his bike in the school parking lot. Had this thing been dragged over a stretch of pavement, struck by a car, perhaps, and sent skidding across the road? Whatever the cause, I guessed the rain washing it was probably a good thing, cleaning away the worst debris. I bent for a closer inspection.

And was on my back, the dog's forepaws pressing my chest with irresistible force, its face inches from mine. There wasn't even time for me to be shocked by its speed. Its lips curled away from a rack of yellowed fangs, the canines easily as long as my index finger. Its breath was hot, rank, as if its tongue were rotten in its mouth. I wanted to gag, but didn't dare move. Rain spilled from the thing's cheeks, its jaw, in shining streams onto my neck, my chin. The dog was silent; no growl troubled its throat; but its eyes said that it was ready to tear my windpipe out. They were unlike any eyes I had looked into, irises so pale they might have been white surrounded by sclerae so dark they were practically black, full past the brim with – I wouldn't call it intelligence so much as a kind of undeniable *presence*.

As fast as it had put me down, the thing was gone, fled into the night and the rain. For a few seconds, I stayed where I was, unsure if the dog were planning to return. Once it was clear the thing was not coming back, I pushed myself up from the sodden ground. "Terrific," I said. My wet sneaker was the least of my worries; it had been joined by jeans soaked through to my boxers; not to mention, my jacket had flipped up when I'd fallen, and the back of my shirt was drenched. "So much for the injured dog." Although doing so made me uncomfortably aware of the space between my shoulders, I turned around and plodded across the lot. This time, I didn't worry about the puddles.

That Kaitlyn was nowhere to be found, had not waited to witness my adventure with man's best friend, and most likely had proceeded to the club without me, was the sorry punchline to what had become an unfunny joke. Briefly, I entertained the idea that she might have run down the street in search of help, but a rapid walk the rest of the way to QE2 showed most shops closed, and the couple that were open empty of a short woman bundled into a long, green coat, her red hair tucked under a black beret. At the club's door, under the huge QE2 sign, I contemplated abandoning the night's plans and returning to my apartment on State Street, a trek that would ensure any remaining dry spots on my person received their due saturation. I was sufficiently annoyed with Kaitlyn for the prospect of leaving her to wonder what had become of me to offer a certain appeal composed of roughly equal parts righteous indignation and self-pity. However, there had been a chance we might meet Chris here, and the possibility of her encountering him with me nowhere to be found sent me to the door to pay the cover.

Inside, a cloud of smoke hung low over the crowd, the din of whose combined conversation was sufficient to dull the Smithereens throbbing from the sound system. The club was more full than I would have expected for the main act that Wednesday, a performance poet named Marius Elliott who was accompanied by a five-piece rock band, guitars, bass, keyboards, drums, the whole thing. Marius, who favoured a short black leather jacket and tight black jeans onstage, was an instructor at Columbia-Greene Community College, where he taught Freshman Writing. He was a lousy poet, and a lousy performer, too, but he was the friend of a friend I worked with, and the band was pretty good, enough so that they should have ditched him and found a frontman with more talent. This was Marius's second show at the QE2; I couldn't understand why the owner had booked him after hearing him the first time. While the club did feature poets, they tended toward the edgier end of the literary spectrum, in keeping with the place's reputation as the Capital District's leading showcase for up and coming post-punk bands. (That same friend from work had seen the Chili Peppers play there before they were red hot.) Marius wrote poems about eating breakfast alone, or walking his dog in the woods behind his apartment. Maybe the owner's tastes were more catholic than I knew; maybe he owed someone a favour.

In his low, melancholy voice, the Smithereens' lead told the room about the girl he dreamed of behind the wall of sleep. I couldn't see Kaitlyn. Given the dim light and number of people milling between the stage and bar, not to mention that Kaitlyn was hardly tall, there was no cause for my stomach to squeeze the way it did. Chris wasn't visible, either. Trying not to make too much of the coincidence, I pushed my way through to the bar, where I shouted for a Macallan I couldn't really afford, but that earned me a respectful nod from the bartender's shaven head.

The Scotch flaring on my tongue, I stepped away to begin a protracted circuit of the room in quest of my girlfriend. The crowd was a mix of what looked like Marius's community college students, their blue jeans and sweatshirts as good as uniforms, and the local poetry crowd, split between those affecting different shades of black and those whose brighter colours proclaimed their allegiance to some notion of 1960s counterculture. Here and there, an older man or woman in a professorial jacket struggled not to let the strain of trying to appear comfortable show; Marius's colleagues, I guessed, or professors from SUNY. The air was redolent with the odours of wet denim, cotton, and hair, of burning tobacco and pot, of beer, of sweat.

I exchanged enough nods with enough faces I half-recognised for me not to feel too alone, and traded a few sentences with a girl whose pretty face and hip-length blond hair I remembered but whose name eluded me. The Smithereens finished singing about blood and roses and were replaced by the Screaming Trees, their gravelly-voiced lead uttering the praises of sweet oblivion.

At the end of forty-five minutes that took me to every spot in the club except the Ladies Room, and that left the Macallan a phantom in my glass, I was no closer to locating Kaitlyn. (Or Chris, for that matter, although I was ignoring this.) Once more at the bar, I set the empty glass on its surface and ordered another – a double, this round. A generous swallow of it was almost sufficient to quiet the panic uncoiling in my chest.

I was about to embark on another, rapid circuit of the crowd before the show began when I caught someone staring at me. Out of the corner of my eye, I thought the tall, pale figure was Chris, just arrived. I was so relieved to find him here that I couldn't help myself from smiling as I turned to greet him.

The man I saw was not Chris. He was at a guess two decades older, more, the far side of forty. Everything about his face was long, from the stretch of forehead between his shaggy black hair and shaggy black eyebrows, to the nose that ran from his watery eyes to his narrow mouth, to the lines that grooved the skin from his cheekbones to his jaw, from the edges of his nostrils to the edges of his thin lips. His skin was the colour of watery milk, which the black leather jacket and black T-shirt he wore only emphasised. I want to say that, even for a poet, the guy looked unhealthy, but this was no poet. There are people – the mentally ill, the visionary – who emit cues, some subtle, some less so, that they are not travelling the same road as the rest of us. Standing five feet away from me doing nothing that I could see, this man radiated that sensation; it poured off him like a fever. The moment I had recognised he was not Chris, I had been preparing the usual excuse, "Sorry, thought you were someone else," or words close enough, but the apology died in my mouth, incinerated by the man's presence. The Screaming Trees were saying they'd heard it on the wing that I was going to die. I could not look away from the man's eyes. Their irises were so pale they might have been white, surrounded by sclerae so dark they were practically black. My heart smacked against my chest; my legs trembled madly, all the fear I should have felt lying pinned on my back in that empty lot finally caught up to me. With that thing's teeth at my neck, I hadn't fully grasped how perilous my position had been; now, I was acutely aware of my danger.

Two things happened almost simultaneously. The lights went down for the show, and Chris stood between the man and me, muttering, "Hello," unwrapping his scarf, and asking where Kaitlyn was. The pale man eclipsed, I looked away. When I returned my gaze to where he'd been standing, he was gone. Ignoring Chris's questions, I searched the people standing closest to us. The man was nowhere to be found. What remained of my drink was still in my hand. I finished it, and headed to the bar as Marius Elliott and his band took the stage to a smattering of applause and a couple of screams. Chris followed close behind. I was almost grateful enough for him appearing to buy him a drink; instead, I had another double.

## II

In the late summer of 1991, I moved to Albany. While I swore to my parents I was leaving Poughkeepsie to accept a position as senior bookseller at The Book Nook, an independent bookstore located near SUNY Albany's uptown campus – which was true; I had been offered the job – the actual reason I packed all my worldly belongings into my red Hyundai Excel and drove an hour and a half up the Hudson was Kaitlyn Bertolozzi. I believe my parents knew this.

Yet even then, the August morning I turned left up the on-ramp for the Taconic north and sped towards a freedom I had been increasingly desperate for the past four years of commuting to college – even as I pressed on the radio and heard the opening bass line of Golden Earring's "Twilight Zone", which I turned up until the steering wheel was thumping with it – even as the early-morning cloud cover split to views of blue sky – the sense of relief that weighted my foot on the gas pedal was alloyed with another emotion, with ambivalence.

At this point, Kaitlyn had been living in Albany for a little more than six months. After completing undergrad a semester early, she had moved north to begin a Master's in Teaching English to Speakers of Other Languages at the University Centre. We had continued to speak to one another several times a week, and I had visited her as often as my school and work schedules permitted, which wasn't very much, once a month, if that. It was on the first of those visits, a couple of weeks after Kaitlyn had moved to the tiny apartment her parents had found her, that she introduced me to Christopher Garofalo.

He was not much taller than I was, but the thick, dark brown hair that rose up from his head gave the impression that he had a good few inches on me. His skin was sallow, except for an oblong scar that reached from over his left eyebrow into his hairline. When Kaitlyn and I met him at Bruegger's Bagels, his neck was swaddled in a scarf that he kept on the length of our lunch, despite the café's stifling heat. He shook my hand when he arrived and when he left, and each time, his brown eyes sought out mine. In between, his conversation was sporadic and earnest. Kaitlyn and he had attended the same orientation session at the University for students starting mid-year. Chris was studying to be a geology teacher; after trying to find a living as part of a jazz band, he said, he had decided it was time for a career with more stability.

Once he had departed, I commented on his scarf, which I'd taken as the lingering affectation of a musician; whereupon my girlfriend told me that Chris wore the scarf to cover the scar from a tracheotomy. While my face flushed, she went on to say that he had been in a severe motorcycle accident several years ago, in his early twenties. He hadn't been wearing a helmet, and should have been killed; as it was, he'd spent a week in a coma and had to have a steel plate set in his skull, which was the origin of the scar on his forehead. As a consequence of the trauma, he'd experienced intermittent seizures, which had required months of trial-and-error with different medications and combinations of medications to bring under some semblance of control. He was a sweet guy, Kaitlyn said, who was (understandably) self-conscious about the reminders of his accident. I muttered a platitude and changed the subject.

I wasn't especially concerned about my girlfriend having become friendly with another guy so soon; as long as I had known her, Kaitlyn had numbered more men than women among her friends, just as my circle of friends consisted largely of women. She had always had a weakness for what I called her strays, those people whose quirks of character tended to isolate them from the rest of the pack. Driving home that night, I was if anything reassured at a familiar pattern reasserting itself.

Three weeks to the day later, I listened on the phone as Kaitlyn, her voice hitching, told me she'd slept with Chris. While I'd made the same sort of confession to previous girlfriends, I'd never been on the receiving end of it before. I moved a long way away from myself, down a tunnel at one end of which was the thick yellow receiver pressed to my ear, full of Kaitlyn crying that she was sorry, while the other end plunged into blackness. Dark spots crowded my vision. I hung up on her sobs, then spent five minutes furiously pacing the bedroom that had shrunk to the size of a cage. Everything was wrong; a sinkhole had opened under me, dumping my carefully arranged future into muddy ruin. Before I knew what I was doing, the phone was in my hand and I was dialling Kaitlyn.

The next month was an ordeal of phone calls, two, three, four times a week. After the initial flourish of apologies and recriminations, we veered wildly between forced cheerfulness and poorly concealed resentment. Once Kaitlyn started to say that Chris was very upset about the entire situation, and I told her I wasn't interested in hearing about that fucking freak. Another time, she complained that she was lonely, to which I replied that I was sure she could find company. Rather than slamming the receiver down, she cajoled me, told me not to be that way, she missed me and couldn't wait until she could see me. However, when I at last drove to see her one Thursday afternoon, Kaitlyn was reserved, almost formal. I wanted nothing more than to go straight to bed, to find in her naked body some measure of reassurance that we would recover from this. Kaitlyn demurred, repeatedly, until I left early, in an obvious huff.

Strangely, Kaitlyn's infidelity and its jagged aftermath only increased my desire to move to Albany. Those moments regret and anger weren't gnawing at me, I told myself that, had I been there with her, this never would have happened. I could just about shift the blame for her sleeping with Chris onto us having been apart after so long so close together. There were times I could, not exactly pardon what Chris had done, but understand it. Underwriting my effort to reconcile myself to events was my desire to escape my home. As far as I could tell, my father and mother were no worse than any of my friends' parents – and, in one or two cases, they seemed significantly better – but I was past tired of having to be home by twelve and to call if I were going to be later, of having to play chauffeur to my mother and three younger siblings, of having to watch what I said lest my father and I begin an argument from which I inevitably backed off, because he had suffered a heart attack ten years earlier and I was deeply anxious not to be the cause of a second, fatal one. Although I was their oldest child, my parents had a much harder time easing their hold on me than they did with my siblings. My younger brother was already away at RPI, enrolled in their Bio-Med program, while my sisters enjoyed privileges I still dreamed of. When I had started at SUNY Huguenot, my father had assured me that, if I commuted to college the first year, I could move onto campus my sophomore year; during a subsequent disagreement, he insisted that the deal had been for me to remain home for two years, and then he and my mother would see about me living in a dorm. After that, I didn't raise the issue again, nor did he or my mother.

Albany/Kaitlyn was my opportunity to extricate myself from the life that seemed intent on maintaining my residence under the roof that had sheltered me for the last two decades. Every awkward conversation with Kaitlyn shook my hopes of leaving the bed whose end my feet hung over, while the arguments, aftershocks of that original revelation, that struck us shuddered my dream of Albany to rubble. That I went from the black mood that fell on me after Kaitlyn and I had concluded our latest brittle exchange, when I was convinced I would live and die in Poughkeepsie, to driving to my new apartment and job was a testament to almost brute determination. In the end, I had to leave my parents', which meant I had to do whatever was necessary to slice through the apron strings mummifying me, and if that included working through things with Kaitlyn – if it included making peace with Chris, accepting him as her friend – then that was what I would do.

Not only did I make peace with Chris, he was to be my room-mate. What would have been impossible, inconceivable, a month before became first plausible and then my plan when I failed to find a place I could afford on my own, and the guy with whom Chris had previously been rooming abruptly moved out. Enough time had passed, I told myself. According to Kaitlyn, Chris was a night owl; he and I would hardly see one another. (I didn't dwell on how she knew this.) I decided I would stay there only until I could find another, better place, and then fuck you, Chris.

As it turned out, though, after more than a year, I was still in that apartment on State Street, in what I referred to as student-hell housing. Ours was the lower half of a two-storey house wedged in among other two-storey houses, the majority of them family residences that had been re-purposed for college students. My room was at the rear of the place, off the kitchen, and was entered through a kind of folding door more like what you'd find on a closet. Chris inhabited the front room, next to the combina-tion living room-dining room; between us, there was an empty room opposite the bathroom. For reasons unclear to me, that room had remained unoccupied, though I didn't object to the extra distance from Chris. Kaitlyn had been right: he was up late into the night, sequestered in his room, which he did not invite me into and whose door – a single solid piece of wood some previous tenant had painted dark green – he kept closed. Probably the longest conversation I had with him had come when he'd showed me the basement, whose door, outside mine, was locked by a trio of deadbolts. The stairs down to it bowed perceptibly under my weight, the railing planted a splinter in the base of my thumb. A pair of bare bulbs threw yellow light against the cement walls, the dirt floor. The air was full of dust; I sneezed. Chris showed me the location of the fuse box, how to reset the fuses, the furnace and how to reset it. After I'd been through the procedures for both a couple of times, I pointed to the corner opposite us and said, "What's down there?"

Chris looked at the concrete circle, maybe two and a half feet in diameter, set into the basement floor. A heavy metal bar flaked with rust lay across it; through holes in either end of the bar, thick, heavily-rusted chains ran to rings set into smaller pieces of concrete. He shrugged. "I'm not sure. The landlord told me it used to be a coal cellar, but that doesn't make any sense. Some kind of access to the sewers, maybe."

"In a private residence?"

"Yeah, you're right. I don't know."

When he wasn't in his room, Chris was at SUNY, either in class or at the library. Despite this, I saw him a good deal more than I would have wished, especially when Kaitlyn stayed over, which she did on weekends and occasional weeknights. I would be in the kitchen, preparing dinner, while Kaitlyn sat on the green and yellow couch in the living room, reading for one of her classes, and I would hear Chris's door creak open. By the time I carried Katilyn's plate through to the folding table that served as the dining-room table, Chris would be leaning against the wall across from her, his arms crossed, talking with her about school. Although they stiffened perceptibly as I set Kaitlyn's plate down, they continued their conversation, until I asked Chris if he wanted to join us, there was plenty left, an offer he inevitably refused, politely, claiming he needed to return to his work. During the ensuing meal, Kaitlyn would maintain a constant stream of chatter to which I, preoccupied with what she and Chris had *actually* been discussing, would respond in monosyllables. If the phone rang and Chris happened to answer it, he would linger for a minute or two, talking in a low, pleasant murmur I couldn't decipher before calling to me that it was Kaitlyn. I knew they met for coffee at school every now and again, which seemed to translate into once a week.

Of course the situation was intolerable. Forgiving Chris – believing that what had occurred between him and Kaitlyn was in the past – accepting that they were still friends, but no more than that – all of it had been much easier when I was eighty miles removed from it, when it was a means to the end of me leaving home. As a fact of my daily life, it was a wound that would not heal, whose scab tore free whenever the two of them were in any kind of proximity, whenever Kaitlyn mentioned Chris, or (less frequently) vice-versa. Had I known him before this, had we shared some measure of friendship, there might have been another basis on which I could have dealt with Chris. As it was, my principal picture of him was as the guy who had slept with my girlfriend. No matter that we might share the occasional joke, or that he might join Kaitlyn and me when we went to listen to music at local clubs and bars, and try to point out what the musicians were doing well, or even that he might cover my rent one month I needed to have work done on my car, I could not see past that image, and it tormented me. I was more than half-convinced Kaitlyn wanted to return to him, and her protests that, if she had, she would have already, did little to persuade me otherwise.

One night, after I'd been in Albany six months, in the wake of a fierce argument that ended with Kaitlyn telling me she was tired of doing penance for a mistake she'd made a year ago, then slamming her apartment door in my face, and me speeding home down Western Avenue's wide expanse, I stood outside Chris's room, ready for a confrontation twelve months overdue. I hadn't bothered to remove my coat, and it seemed to weigh heavier, hotter. My chest was heaving, my hands balled into fists so tight my arms shook. The green door was at the far end of a dark tunnel. I could hear the frat boys who lived above us happily shouting back and forth to one another about a professor who was a real dick. I willed Chris to turn the doorknob, to open his door so that he would find me there and I could ask him what it had been like, if she'd pulled her shirt over her head, pushed down her jeans, or if he'd unhooked her bra, slid her panties to her ankles? Had she lain back on the bed, drawing him onto her, and had she uttered that deep groan when he'd slid all the way up into her? Had she told him to fuck her harder, and when she'd ridden him to that opening of her mouth and closing of her eyes, had she slid her hand between them to cup and squeeze his balls, bringing him to a sudden, thunderous climax? A year's worth of scenes I'd kept from my mind's eye cavorted in front of it: Kaitlyn recumbent on her bed, her bare body painted crimson by the red light she'd installed in the bedside lamp; Kaitlyn, lying on top of a hotel room table, wearing only the rings on her fingers, her hands pulling her knees up and out; Kaitlyn with her head hanging down, her arms out in front of her, hands pressed against the shower wall, her legs straight and spread, soapy water sluicing off her back, her ass. In all of these visions and more, it was not I who was pushing in and out of her, it was Chris – he had spliced himself into my memories, turned them into so much cheap porn. Worse, the look I envisioned on Kaitlyn's face said, shouted that she was enjoying these attentions far more than any I'd ever paid her.

While I desperately wanted to cross the remaining distance to Chris's door and smash my fists against it, kick it in, some inner mechanism would not permit me to take that first step. My jaw ached I was clenching my teeth so hard, but I could not convert that energy into forward motion. If Chris appeared, then what would happen, would happen. In the meantime, the best I could do was maintain my post.

Perhaps Kaitlyn had called to warn him, but Chris did not leave his room that night. I stood trembling at his door for the better part of an hour, after which I decided to wait for him on the living-room couch. I had not yet removed my coat, and I was sweltering. The couch was soft. My lids began to droop. I yawned, then yawned again. The room was growing harder to keep in focus. There was a noise – I thought I heard something. The sound of feet, of many feet, seemed to be outside the front window – no, they were underneath me, in the basement. The next thing I knew, I was waking to early morning light. I could have resumed my position outside Chris's door; instead, I retreated to my room. That was the closest I came to facing him.

Had a friend of mine related even part of the same story to me – told me that his girlfriend had cheated on him, or that he couldn't stop thinking about her betrayal, or that he was sharing an apartment with the other guy – my advice would have been simple: leave. You're in a no-win situation; get out of it. I was in possession of sufficient self-knowledge to be aware of this, but was unable to attach that recognition to decisive action. In an obscure way I could perceive but not articulate, this failing was connected to my larger experience of Albany, which had been, to say the least, disappointing. Two weeks into it, I had started having doubts about my job at The Book Nook; after a month, those doubts had solidified. Within two months of starting there, I was actively, though discreetly, searching for another position. However, with the economy mired in recession, jobs were scarce on the ground. None of the local bookstores were hiring full-time. I sank three hundred dollars into the services of a job placement company whose representative interviewed me by phone for an hour and produced a one-page resume whose bland and scanty euphemisms failed to impress me, or any of the positions to which I sent it. I wasted an hour late one Tuesday sitting a test for an insurance position the man who interviewed me told me I was unlikely to get because I didn't know anyone in the area, and so didn't have a list of people I could start selling to. (He was right: they didn't call me.) I lost an entire Saturday shadowing a travelling salesman as he drove to every beauty salon in and around Albany, hawking an assortment of cheap and gaudy plastic wares to middle-aged women whose faces had shown their suspicion the moment he hauled open their doors. That position I could have had if I'd wanted it, but the prospect was so depressing I returned to The Book Nook the following day. When I heard that their pay was surprisingly good and their benefits better, I seriously considered taking the exam that would allow me to apply for a job as a toll collector on the Thruway, going so far as to find out the dates on which and the locations where the test was being offered. But, unable to imagine telling my parents that I had left the job that at least appeared to have something to do with my undergraduate degree in English for one that required no degree at all – unwilling to face what such a change would reveal about my new life away from home – I never went. I continued to work at The Book Nook, using my employee discount to accumulate novels and short story collections I didn't read, and for which I soon ran out of space, so that I had to stack them on my floor, until my room became a kind of improvised labyrinth.

Nor did the wider world appear to be in any better shape. In addition to its reports on the faltering local and national economies, WAMC, the local public radio station, brought news of the disintegration of Yugoslavia into ethnic enclaves whose sole purpose appeared to be the annihilation of one another through the most savage means possible. The fall of the Berlin Wall, the break-up of the Soviet Union and end of the Cold War, which had promised brighter days, an end to the nuclear shadow under which I'd grown up, instead had admitted a host of hatreds and grievances kept at bay but not forgotten, and eager to have their bloody day. On EQX, the alternative station out of Vermont, U2 sang about the end of the world, and the

melodramatic overstatement of those words seemed to summa-
rise my time in Albany.

By that Wednesday night in November, when I fumbled open
the door to the apartment and stumbled in, the Scotches I'd
consumed at the QE2 not done with me yet, I had been living in
a state of ill-defined dread for longer than I could say, months, at
least. I had attempted discussing it with Kaitlyn over dinner the
week before we went to see Marius, but the best I could manage
was to say that it felt as if I were waiting for the other shoe to
drop. "What other shoe?" Kaitlyn had said around a mouthful
of dumpling. "The other shoe to what?"

I'd considered answering, "To you and Chris," but we'd been
having a nice time, and I had been reluctant to spoil it. To be
honest, though there was no doubt she and Chris were part of
the equation, they weren't all of it: there were other integers
involved whose values I could not identify. To reply, "To everything" had seemed too much, so I'd said, "I don't know," and
the conversation had moved on.

Yet when I saw that the apartment was dark, and a check of
my room showed my bed empty, and a call to Kaitlyn's brought
me her answering machine, I knew, with a certainty fuelled by
alcohol and that deep anxiety, that the other shoe had finally
clunked on the floor.

### III

For the next couple of days, I continued to dial Kaitlyn's number,
leaving a series of messages that veered from blasé to reproachful
to angry to conciliatory before cycling back to blasé. I swore that
I was not going to her apartment, a vow I kept for almost three
days, when I used my key to unlock her door Saturday night. I
half-expected the chain to be fastened, Kaitlyn to be inside (and
not alone), but the door swung open on an empty room. The
lights were off. "Kaitlyn?" I called. "Love?"

There was no answer. The apartment was little more than a
studio with ambition; it took all of a minute for me to duck my
head into the bedroom, the bathroom, to determine that Kaitlyn
wasn't there. The answering machine's tally read thirty-one
messages; I pressed Play and listened to my voice ascend and

descend the emotional register. Mixed in among my messages were brief how-are-you's from Kaitlyn's mother, her younger brother, and Chris. When I recognised his voice, I tensed, but he had called to say he had missed her at the show the other night, as well as for coffee the next day, and he hoped everything was okay. After the last message – me, half an hour prior, trying for casual as I said that I was planning to stop by on my way home from work – I ran through the recordings a second time, searching for something, some clue in her mother's, her younger brother's words to where she had spent the last seventy-two hours. That I could hear, there was none. An hour's wait brought neither Kaitlyn nor any additional phone calls, so I left, locking the door behind me.

Two days later, I asked Chris to call Kaitlyn's parents. He was just in from a late-night library session; I had waited for him on the couch. He didn't notice me until he was about to open the door to his room. At my request, he stopped pulling off his gloves and said, "What?"

"I need you to call Kaitlyn's parents for me."

"Why?"

"I want to find out if she's there."

"What do you mean?"

"I haven't seen her since the other night at QE2."

"Maybe she's at her place." He stuffed his gloves in his jacket's pockets, unzipped it.

"I checked there."

"Maybe she didn't want to talk to you."

"No – I have a key. She isn't there. I don't think she has been since Wednesday."

"Of course you do," Chris muttered. "So where is she – at her parents, which is why you want me to call them. Why can't you do it?"

"I don't want to worry them."

Chris stared at me; I could practically hear him thinking, *Or look like the overly possessive boyfriend.* "It's late," he said, "I'm sure—".

"*Please,*" I said. "Please. Look, I know – we – would you just do this for me, please?"

"Fine," he said, although the expression on his face said it was anything but. He hung his jacket on the doorknob and went to the phone.

Kaitlyn's father was still awake. Chris apologised for calling so late but said he was a friend of hers from high school who'd walked through his parents' front door this very minute – his flight had been delayed at O'Hare. He was only in town through tomorrow, and he was hoping to catch up with Kaitlyn, even see her. A pause. Oh, that was right, the last time they had talked, she had told him she was planning to go to Albany. Wow, he guessed it had been a while since they'd spoken. Could her father give him her address, or maybe her phone number? That would be great. Another pause. Chris thanked him, apologised again for the lateness of his call, and wished Kaitlyn's father a good night. "She isn't there," he said once he'd hung up.

"So I gathered."

"The number he gave me is the one for her apartment."

"Okay." I stood from the couch.

"I'm sure everything's all right. Maybe she went to visit a friend."

"Yeah," I said. "A friend."

"Hey—"

"Don't," I said. I started towards my room. "All because I stopped to help a fucking dog . . ."

"What?"

I stopped. "On the way to the club. There was this stray in that lot over on Central – you know, where the thrift store used to be. It looked like it was in rough shape, so I went to have a look at it—"

"What kind of dog?"

"I don't know, a big one. Huge, skinny, like a wolfhound or something."

Chris's brow lowered. "What colour was it?"

"White, I guess. It was missing a lot of fur – no tail, either."

"Its face – did you see its eyes?"

"From about six inches away. Turned out, the thing wasn't that hurt, after all. Pinned me to the ground, stuck its face right in mine. Could've ripped my throat out."

"Its eyes . . ."

"This sounds strange, but its eyes were reversed: the whites were black, and the pupils were, well, they weren't white, exactly, but they were pale—"

"What happened with the dog? Were there any more?"

I shook my head. "It ran off. I don't know where to."

"There wasn't a man with it, was there?"

"Just the dog. What do you mean, a man? Do you know who owns that thing?"

"Nobody owns – never mind. You'd know this guy if you saw him: tall, black hair. He's white, I mean, really, like-a-ghost white. His face is lined, creased."

"Who is he?"

"Don't worry about it. If he wasn't—"

"He was at the club, afterwards. Right before you arrived."

"Are you sure?"

"I was about as far away from him as I am from you."

Now Chris's face was white. "What happened?"

"Nothing. One minute, he was standing there giving me the heebie-jeebies, the next—"

"Shit!" Chris grabbed his jacket from the doorknob. "Get your coat."

"Why?"

"Do you have a flashlight?"

"A flashlight?"

"Never mind, I have a spare." His jacket and gloves on, Chris shouted, "Move!"

"What are you—"

He crossed the room to me in three quick strides. "I know where Kaitlyn is."

"You do?"

He nodded. "I know where she is. I also know that she's in a very great deal of danger. I need you to get your coat, and I need you to get your car keys."

"Kaitlyn's in danger?"

"Yes."

"What – how do you know this?"

"I'll tell you in the car."

## IV

For all that I had been resident in the city for over a year, my knowledge of Albany's geography was at best vague. Aside from a few landmarks such as the QE2 and the Empire State Plaza downtown, my mental map of the place showed a few blocks north and south of my apartment, and spots along the principle east–west avenues, Western, Washington, and Central. I had a better sense of the layout of Dobb's Ferry, Kaitlyn's hometown, to which I'd chauffeured her at least one weekend a month the past twelve. Chris told me to head downtown, to Henry Johnson. Once I'd scraped holes in the frost on the windshield and windows, and set the heater blowing high, I steered us onto Washington and followed it to the junction with Western, but that was as far as I could go before I had to say, "Now what?"

Chris looked up from the canvas bag he was holding open on his lap while he riffled its contents. Whatever was in the bag clinked and rattled; the strong odour of grease filled the car. "Really?" he said. "You don't know how to get to Henry Johnson?"

"I'm not good with street names. I'm more of a visual person."

"Up ahead on the left – look familiar?"

"Actually, no."

"Well, that's where we're going."

"Well okay."

I turned off Western, passed over what I realised was a short bridge across a deep gully. "What's our destination?"

"A place called the Kennel. Heard of it?"

I hadn't.

"It's . . . you'll see when we get there."

We drove past shops whose shutters were down for the night, short brick buildings whose best days belonged to another century. Brownstones rode a steep side street. A man wearing a long winter coat and garbage bags taped to his feet pushed a shopping cart with an old television set canted in it along the sidewalk.

"How far is it?"

"I don't know the exact distance. It should take us about fifteen minutes."

"Enough time for you to tell me how you know Kaitlyn's at the Kennel."

"Not really. Not if you want the full story."

"I'll settle for the Cliff's Notes. Did you take her there?"

"No," he said, as if the suggestion were wildly inappropriate.

"Then how did she find out about it?"

"She didn't – she was brought there."

"Brought? As in, kidnapped?"

Chris nodded.

"How do you know this?"

"Because of the Keeper – the man you saw at the club."

"The scary guy with the weird eyes."

"You noticed his eyes."

"Same as the dog's."

"Yes."

"I don't – how do you know this guy, the what? The Keeper?"

"Ahead, there," Chris said, pointing, "keep to the left."

I did. The cluster of tall buildings that rose over Albany's downtown, the city's effort to imitate its larger sibling at the other end of the Hudson, was behind us, replaced by more modest structures, warehouses guarded by sagging fences, narrow two- and three-storey brick buildings, a chrome-infused diner struggling to pretend the fifties were alive and well. As I drove through these precincts, I had the sense I was seeing the city as it really was, the secret face I had intuited after a year under its gaze. I said, "How do you know him?"

"He . . ." Chris grimaced. "I found out about him."

"What? Is he some kind of, I don't know, a criminal?"

"Not exactly. He's – he's someone who doesn't like to be known."

"Someone . . . all right, how did you find out about him?"

"Left. My accident – did I ever tell you about my accident? I didn't, did I?"

"Kaitlyn filled me in."

"She doesn't know the whole story. Nobody does. I didn't take a corner too fast: one of the *Ghûl* ran in front of me."

"The what? 'Hule'?"

"*Ghûl*. What you saw in that lot the other night."

"Is that the breed?"

Chris laughed. "Yes, that's the breed, all right. It was up towards Saratoga, on Route 9. I was heading home from band practice. It was late, and it was a New Moon, so it was especially dark. The next thing I knew, there was this animal in the road. My first thought was, *It's a wolf.* Then I thought, *That's ridiculous: there are no wolves around here. It must be a coyote.* But I had already seen this wasn't a coyote, either. Whatever it was, it looked awful, so thin it must be starving. I leaned to the left, to veer around it, and it moved in front of me. I tried to tilt the bike the other way, overcompensated, and put it down, hard."

In the distance, the enormous statue of Nipper, the RCA mascot, that crowned one of the buildings closer to the river cocked its head attentively.

"The accident itself, I don't remember. That's a blank. What I do remember is coming to in all kinds of pain and feeling something tugging on my sleeve. My sleeve – I'm sure you heard I wasn't wearing a helmet. I couldn't really see out of my left eye, but with my right, I saw the animal I'd tried to avoid with my right arm in its mouth. My legs were tangled up with the bike, which was a good thing, because this creature was trying to drag me off the road. If it hadn't been for the added weight, it would have succeeded. This wasn't any Lassie rescue, either: the look on its face – it was ravenous. It was going to kill and eat me, and not necessarily in that order.

"Every time the animal yanked my arm, bones ground together throughout my body. White lights burst in front of my eyes. I cried out, although my jaw was broken, which made it more of a moan. I tried to use my left arm to hit the creature, but I'd dislocated that shoulder. Its eyes – those same, reversed eyes you looked into – regarded me the way you or I would a slice of prime rib. I've never been in as much pain as I was lying there; I've also never been as frightened as I was with that animal's teeth beginning to tear through the sleeve of my leather jacket and into the skin beneath. The worst of it was, the creature made absolutely no sound, no growl, nothing."

We passed beneath the Thruway, momentarily surrounded by the whine of tires on pavement.

"Talk about dumb luck, or Divine Providence: just as my legs are starting to ease out from the bike, an eighteen-wheeler rounds the corner. How the driver didn't roll right over me and the animal gripping my arm, I chalk up to his caffeine-enhanced reflexes. I thought that, if I were going to die, at least it wouldn't be as something's dinner. As it was, the truck's front bumper slowed to a stop right over my head. Had it been any other vehicle, my would-be consumer might have stood its ground. The truck, though, was too much for it, and it disappeared.

"When the doctors and cops – not to mention my mother – finally got around to asking me to relate the accident in as much detail as I could, none of them could credit a creature that wasn't a coyote that wasn't a wolf, which caused my crash and then tried to drag me away. I'd suffered severe head trauma, been comatose for five days – that must be where the story had come from. The wounds on my forearm were another result of the accident. Apparently, no one bothered to ask the truck driver what he'd seen.

"For a long time after that night, I wasn't in such great shape. Between the seizures and the different medications for the seizures, I spent weeks at a time in a kind of fog. Some of the meds made me want to sleep; some ruined my concentration; one made everything incredibly funny. But no matter what state I was in, no matter how strange or distant my surroundings seemed, I knew that that animal – that what it had done, what it had tried to do to me – was real."

To the left, the beige box of Albany Memorial Hospital slid by. I said, "Okay, I get that there's a connection between the thing that caused your accident and the one I ran into the other night. And I'm guessing this Keeper guy is involved, too. Maybe you could hurry up and get to the point?"

"I'm trying. Did you know that State Street used to be the site of one of the largest cemeteries in Albany?"

"No."

"Till almost the middle of the 19th century, when the bodies were relocated and the workers found the first tunnels."

"Tunnels?"

"Left again up here. Not too much farther."

To either side of us, trees jostled the shoulder. They opened briefly on the left to a lawn running up to shabby red brick apartments, then closed ranks again.

"So why are these tunnels so important?"

"That concrete slab in the basement, the one that's locked down? What if I told you that opens on a tunnel?"

"I'd still want to know what this has to do with where Kaitlyn is."

"Because she – when we – all right." He took a deep breath. "Even before my doctor found the right combination of anti-seizure meds, I was doing research. I probably know the name of every librarian between Albany and Saratoga. I've talked to anyone who knows anything about local history. I've spent weeks in the archives of the State Museum, the Albany Institute, and three private collections. I've filled four boxes worth of notebooks."

"And?"

"I've recognised connections no one's noticed before. There's an entire – you could call it a secret history, or shadow history, of this entire region, stretching back – you wouldn't believe me if I told you how far. I learned things . . ."

"What things?"

"It doesn't matter. What does is that, somehow, they found out about me."

"The Keeper and his friends."

"At first, I was sure they were coming for me. I put my affairs in order, had a long conversation with my mom that scared her half to death. Then, when they didn't arrive, I started to think that I might be safe, even that I might have been mistaken about them knowing about me."

"But you weren't. Not only were they aware of you, they were watching you, following you. They saw you with Kaitlyn. They figured . . ."

"Yeah."

My heart was pounding in my ears. A torrent of obscenities and reproaches threatened to pour out of my mouth. I choked them down, said, "Shouldn't we go to the cops? If you've gathered as much material on this Keeper as you say you have—"

"It's not like that. The cops wouldn't – if they did believe me, it wouldn't help Kaitlyn."

"I can't see why not. If this guy's holding Kaitlyn, a bunch of cops outside his front door should make him reconsider."

We had arrived at a T-junction. "Left or right?"

"Straight."

"Straight?" I squinted across the road in front of us, to a pair of brick columns that flanked the entrance to a narrow road. A plaque on the column to the right read ALBANY RURAL CEMETERY. I turned to Chris. "What the fuck?"

He withdrew his right hand from the bag on his lap, his fingers curled around the grip of a large automatic handgun whose muzzle he swung towards me. "Once this truck passes, we're going over there." He nodded at the brick columns.

The anger that had been foaming in my chest fell away to a trickle. I turned my gaze to the broad road in front of me, watched a moving van labour up it. The gun weighted the corner of my vision. I wanted to speak, to demand of Chris what the fuck he thought he was doing, but my tongue was dead in my mouth. Besides, I knew what he was doing. Once the van was out of sight, Chris waved the gun and I drove across into the cemetery.

Even in the dark, where I could only see what little my head-lights brought to view, I was aware that the place was big, much bigger than any graveyard I'd been in back home. On both sides of the road, monuments raised themselves like the ruins of some lost civilisation obsessed with its end. A quartet of Doric columns supporting a single beam gave way to a copper-green angel with arms and wings outstretched, which yielded to a grey Roman temple in miniature, which was replaced by a marble woman clutching a marble cross. Between the larger memorials, an assortment of headstones stood as if marking the routes of old streets. A few puddles spread amongst them. Tall trees, their branches bare with the season, loomed beside the road.

As we made our way further into the cemetery, Chris resumed talking. But the gun drew his words into the black circle of its mouth, allowing only random snippets to escape. At some point, he said, "Old Francis was the one who finally put it all together for me. He'd found an Annex to the Kennel during a day-job digging graves. A pair of them came for him that night, and if there hadn't been a couple of decent-sized rocks to hand, they would have had him. But he'd played the Minor Leagues years before, and his right arm remembered how to throw.

Even so, he hopped a freight going west and stayed out there for a long time." At another point, he said, "You have no idea. When the first hunters crossed the land bridge to America, the *Ghûl* trailed them." At still another moment, he said, "Something they do to the meat." That Chris had not dismounted his hobby-horse was clear.

All I could think about was what was going to happen to me once he told me to stop the car. He wouldn't shoot me in it – that would leave too much evidence. Better to walk me someplace else, dispose of me, and ditch the car over in Troy. He didn't want to leave me out in the open, though. Maybe an open grave, shovel in enough dirt to conceal the body? Too dicey: a strong rain could expose his handiwork. One of the mausoleums we passed? Much more likely, especially if you knew the family no longer used it. When he said, "All right: we're here," in front of an elaborate marble porch set into a low hill, I felt an odd surge of satisfaction.

I had the idea this might be my time to act, but Chris had me turn off the engine, leaving on the headlights, and hand him the keys. He exited the car and circled around the front to my side, the automatic pointed at me throughout. Standing far enough away that I couldn't slam my door against him, he urged me out of the car. I wanted – at least, I contemplated refusing him, declaring that if he were going to shoot me, he would have to do it here, I wasn't going to make this any easier for him. I could hear myself defiant, but his shouted, "Now!" brought me out in front of him without a word.

"Over there," he said, pointing the gun at the mausoleum. "It should be open."

That sentence, everything it implied, revived my voice. "Is this where you took Kaitlyn?" I said as I walked towards the door.

"What?"

"I've been trying to figure out how you did it. Did you meet her at the club and whisk her out here? What – did you have a cab waiting? A rental? I can't quite work out the timing of it. Maybe you brought her somewhere else, first? Some place to hold her until you could take her here?"

"You haven't heard a single thing I've been saying, have you?"

"Were you afraid I'd discover it was you? Or was this always your plan, kill the girl you couldn't have and the guy she wouldn't leave?"

"You asshole," Chris said. "I'm doing this for Kaitlyn."

That Kaitlyn might be unharmed, might be in league with Chris, was a possibility I had excluded the second it had occurred to me as I drove into the cemetery, and that I had kept from consideration as we'd wound deeper into its grounds. There would be no reason for her to resort to such an extreme measure; if she wanted to be with Chris, she could be with him. She already had. All the same, his statement was a punch in the gut; my words quavered as I said, "Sure – you tell yourself that."

"Shut up."

"Or what – you'll shoot me?"

"Just open the door."

The mausoleum's entrance was a tall stone rectangle set back between a quartet of pillars that supported a foreshortened portico. On the front of the portico, the name UPTON was bordered by dogs capering on their hind legs. Behind me, there was a click, and a wide circle of light centred on the door. There was no latch that I could see. I put out my right hand and pushed the cold stone. The door swung in easily, spilling the beam of Chris's flashlight inside. The heavy odour of soil packed with clay rode the yellow light out to us. I glanced over my shoulder, but Chris had been reduced to a blinding glare. His voice said, "Go in."

Inside, the mausoleum was considerably smaller than the grandiosity of its exterior would have led you to expect. A pair of stone vaults occupied most of the floor, only a narrow aisle between them. The flashlight roamed over the vaults; according to the lids, Beloved Husband and Father Howard rested to my left, while Devoted Wife and Mother Caitlin took her repose on the right. (The woman's name registered immediately.) Under each name, a relief showed a nude woman reclining on her left side, curled around by a brood of young dogs, a pair of which nursed at her breasts. Beyond the stone cases, the mausoleum was a wall of black. The air seemed slightly warmer than it was outside.

With a clatter, the light tilted up to the ceiling. Chris said, "I put the flashlight on the end of the vault to your left. I want you to take two steps backwards – slowly – reach out, and pick it up." I nodded. "And if you try to blind me with the light, I'll shoot."

When I was holding the bulky flashlight, I directed its beam at the back of the mausoleum. A rounded doorway opened in the centre of a wall on which the head of an enormous dog had been painted in colours dulled by dust and time. Eyes whose white pupils and black sclerae were the size of serving plates glared down at us. The dog's mouth was wide, the door positioned at the top of its throat. A click, and a second light joined mine. "In there," Chris said.

"I was wondering where you were going to do it."

"Shut up."

I stepped through the doorway into a wide, dark space. I swept the light around, saw packed dirt above, below, to either side, darkness ahead. There was easily enough room for me and Chris and a few more besides, though the grey sides appeared to close in in the distance. The air was warmer still, the earth smell cloying. Chris's light traced the contours of the walls, their arch into the ceiling. It appeared we were at one end of a sizeable tunnel. "All right," Chris said.

"Where's Kaitlyn?"

"Shut up."

"Aren't you going to let me see her?"

"Shut up."

"Oh, I get it. This is supposed to be the icing on the cake, isn't it? You bring me to the place you killed my girlfriend, but you shoot me without allowing me to see her." I turned into the glare of Chris's flashlight, which jerked up to my eyes. I didn't care. Tears streaming down my cheeks, I said, "Jesus Christ: what kind of a sick fuck are you?"

Chris stepped forward, his arm extended, and pressed the automatic against my chest. My eyes dazzled, I couldn't see so much as feel the solid steel pushing against my sternum. The odour of soil and clay was interrupted by that of grease and metal, of the eight inches of gun ready to bridge me out of this life. Between clenched teeth, Chris said, "You really are a stupid shit."

"Fuck you."

The pressure on my chest eased, and I thought, *This is it. He's going to shoot me in the head.* My mouth filled with the taste of, not so much regret, as sour pique that this was the manner in which my life had reached its conclusion, beneath the surface of the city of my disappointment, murdered by the broken psychotic who'd spoiled my relationship and fractured what should have been the start of my new life. *It's only a moment*, I thought, *then you'll be with Kaitlyn*. But I didn't believe that. I would be dead, part of the blackness, and that was the most I had to look forward to.

"Here you are."

Not for an instant did I mistake this voice for Chris's. It wasn't only that it was behind me – the instrument itself was unlike any I'd heard, rich and cold, as if the lower depths of the tunnel in whose mouth we stood had been given speech. Ignoring Chris, I spun, my light revealing him, the white man with the shaggy black hair and seamed face who'd held me with his strange eyes in QE2, the man Chris had dubbed "The Keeper". He'd exchanged his black leather jacket for a black trenchcoat in whose pockets his hands rested. Chris's flashlight found that long face, deepened the shadows in its creases. The man did not blink.

Chris said, "You know why I've come."

"Yes?"

"I'm here to offer a trade."

"What do you offer?"

"Him."

"What?" I looked over my shoulder. Chris still held the automatic pointed at me.

"Shut up."

"You're going to trade me for Kaitlyn?"

"Shut up."

"So whatever this guy and his friends – you think – this is your solution?"

"Shut up."

"Jesus! You're even worse than I thought."

"This'll be the best thing you've ever done," Chris said. "I've lived with you long enough to know. It's the best thing you could ever do for her."

I opened my mouth to answer, but the Keeper coughed, and our attentions returned to him. He said, "For?"

"The woman you took six days past."

"A woman?"

"Damn you!" Chris shouted. "You know who I'm talking about, so can we cut the coy routine? In the names of Circë, Cybele, and Atys, in the name of Diana, Mother of Hounds, I offer this man's life for that of the woman you took and hold."

"Let us ask the Hounds," the man said. From the darkness behind him, a trio of the same creatures I'd crossed a vacant lot to help on a rainy night emerged into the glow of our flashlights and slunk towards me. Big as that thing had been, these were bigger, the first and largest as tall at the shoulder as my chin, its companions level with my heart. Each was as skeletally thin as that first one, each patched with the same pale fur. At the sight of them, my mind tilted, all my mental furniture sliding to one side. Everything Chris had said in the past hour tumbled together. Inclining their heads in my direction, the Hounds walked lazily around me, silent except for the scrape of their claws on the tunnel floor. Their white skin slid against their bones, and I thought that I had never seen creatures so frail and so deadly. The leader kept its considerable jaws closed, but its companions left theirs open, one exposing its fangs in a kind of sneer, the other licking its lips with a liver-coloured tongue. Their combined reek, dirt underscored with decay, as if they'd been rolling in the remains of the cemetery's more recent residents, threatened to gag me. I concentrated on breathing through my mouth and remaining calm, on not being afraid, or not that afraid, on not noticing the stains on the things' teeth, on not wondering whether they'd go for my throat or my arms first, on not permitting the panic that was desperate to send me screaming from this place as fast as my legs would carry me from crossing the boundary from emotion to action. The trio completed their circuit of me and returned to the Keeper, assuming positions around him.

"The Hounds are unimpressed."

I could have fainted with relief.

"What do you mean?" Chris said. "In what way is this not a fair trade?"

"The Hounds have their reasons."

"This is bullshit!"

"Do you offer anything else?"

"What I've offered is enough."

The man shrugged, turning away.

"Wait!" Chris said. "There are boxes – in my room, there are four boxes full of the information I've collected about you. Return the woman, and they're yours, all of them."

The man hesitated, as if weighing Chris's proposal. Then, "No," he said, and began to walk back down the tunnel, the things accompanying him.

"Wait!" Chris said. "Stop!"

The man ignored him. Already, he and his companions were at the edge of the flashlights' reach.

"Me!" Chris shouted. "Goddamn you, I offer myself! Is that acceptable to the Hounds?"

The four figures halted. The Keeper said, "Freely made?"

"Yes," Chris said. "A life for a life."

"A life for a life." The man's face, as he revolved towards us, was ghastly with pleasure. "Acceptable."

"What a surprise."

"Leave the light – and the weapon."

Chris's flashlight clicked off. The clatter of it hitting the floor was followed by the thud of the automatic. His shoes scuffed the floor and he was stepping past me. He stopped and looked at me, his eyes wild with what lay ahead. He said, "Aren't you going to stop me? Aren't you going to insist you be the one they take for Kaitlyn?"

"No."

He almost smiled. "You never deserved her."

I had no answer for that.

When he was even with them, the Hounds surrounded him. From the tense of their postures, the curl of their lips from their teeth, I half-expected them to savage him right there. The straightening of Chris's posture said he was anticipating something similar. The Keeper bent his head towards Chris. "It's what you really wanted," he said, nodding at the blackness. One of the smaller things nudged him forward with its head, and the four of them faded down into the dark. For a time, the shuffle of Chris's feet, the scrape of the things' claws, told their progress, then those sounds faded to silence.

His gaze directed after Chris, the Keeper said, "Leave. What's left of him won't be too happy to learn the life he's bartered for was yours."

I didn't argue, didn't ask, *What about Kaitlyn?* I obeyed the man's command and fled that place without another word. In my headlong rush through the mausoleum proper, I ran my left hip into the corner of Howard Upton's vault so hard I gasped and stumbled against his wife's, but although the pain threatened to steal my breath, the image of what might be stepping into the mausoleum after me propelled me forward, out the still-open entrance.

My car was where we'd left it, its headlights undimmed. I fumbled for my wallet and the spare key I kept in the pocket behind my license. As I lowered myself into the driver's seat, my hip screaming in protest, I kept checking the door to the mausoleum, which remained ajar and in which I continued to think I saw shadowy forms about to emerge. The car started immediately, and in my haste to escape the way I'd come, I backed into a tall tombstone that cracked at the base and toppled backwards. I didn't care; I shifted into first and sped out of the cemetery, stealing glances in the rear-view mirror all the way to my apartment.

## V

Despite the bruise on my hip, the increased pain and difficulty moving that sent me to the emergency room the next day with a story about colliding with a doorstep, to learn after an x-ray that I had chipped the bone, I half-expected Chris to walk in the front door as usual the following night. It wasn't that I doubted what had happened – I was in too much discomfort – it was more that I couldn't believe its finality. Not until another week had passed, and the landlord appeared wanting to know where Chris and his rent were (to which I replied that I hadn't seen him for days), did the fact of his . . . I didn't have the word for it: his sacrifice? His abduction? His departure? Call it what you would, only when I was standing at the open door to his room, which was Spartan as a monk's cell, watching the landlord riffle through Chris's desk, did the permanence of his fate settle on me.

The week after that brought a concerned call from Kaitlyn's parents, asking if I'd seen their daughter (to which I replied that I hadn't had any contact with her for weeks). This began a chain of events whose next link was her father driving to Albany to ask a number of people, including me, the last time they'd seen Kaitlyn. Within a couple of days, the police were involved. They interviewed me twice, the first time in a reasonably friendly way, when I was no more than the concerned boyfriend, the second time in a more confrontational and extended session, occasioned by the detective's putting together my disclosure that Kaitlyn and Chris had been briefly involved with the fact that both of those people had gone missing in reasonably close proximity to one another. There wasn't any substantial evidence against me, but I had no doubt Detective Calasso was certain I knew more than I was saying. Kaitlyn's mother shared his suspicion, and during a long phone call before Christmas attempted to convince me to tell her what I knew. I insisted that, sorry as I was to have to say it, I didn't know what had happened to Kaitlyn. I supposed this was literally true.

Not that I hadn't dwelled on the matter each and every day since I'd awakened fully dressed on my futon, my hip pounding, a trail of muddy footprints showing my path from the front door to the refrigerator, the top of which served as a nominal liquor cabinet, to my room, where the bottle of Johnny Walker Black that had plunged me into unconsciousness leaned against my pillows. That Kaitlyn should be at the far end of that dark tunnel, surrounded by those things, the Hounds, the *Ghûl*, was unbelievable, impossible. Yet a second stop at her apartment failed to reveal any change from my previous visit. I sat on the edge of her bed, the lights out, my head fuzzy from the painkiller I'd taken for my hip, and struggled to invent alternative scenarios to the one Chris had narrated. Kaitlyn had met another guy – she was in the midst of an extended fling, a romantic adventure that had carried her out of Albany to Cancun, or Bermuda. She'd suffered a breakdown and had herself committed. She'd undergone a spiritual awakening and joined a convent. But try as I did to embrace them, each invention sounded more unreal than the last, no more than another opiate-facilitated fantasy.

I weighed going after her, myself, returning to the mausoleum suitably armed and equipped and braving the tunnel to retrieve her. I even went so far as to browse a gun store on Route 9, only to discover that the weapons I judged necessary if I were to stand any kind of chance – a shotgun, a minimum of three pistols, boxes of ammunition for each – cost vastly more than my bookstore salary would allow. Trying to buy guns on the street was not a realistic option: I had no idea where to go, how to open any such transaction. On a couple of occasions, I found myself driving north through the city, retracing the path Chris and I had followed to the cemetery. When I realised what I was doing, I turned onto the nearest side street and headed back towards my apartment. Some nights, I unlocked the deadbolts on the basement door and descended the stairs to stand staring down at the cement circle sunk in the floor. The chains securing the bar across it looked rusted right through; with a little effort, I ought to be able to break them, heave the cover up, and . . . I made sure to lock the basement door behind me.

On the morning of February 2, 1993, as the sun was casting its light across the apartment's front window, I stuffed every piece of clothing I owned, all my toiletries, whatever food was in the cupboards over the sink, into a green duffel bag that I struggled out the front door, down the front steps, and through my Hyundai's hatchback. The apartment's door was wide open, the place full of my possessions, but I started the engine, threw the car into gear, and fled Albany. I didn't return home to my parents; I didn't head north or west, either. I wanted the shore, the sea, someplace where the earth was not so deep, so I sped east, along I-90, towards what I thought would be the safety of Cape Cod. I didn't stop for bathroom breaks; I didn't stop until Albany was a ghost in my rear-view mirror and the Atlantic a grey sheet spread in front of me.

All the way to Provincetown, while I pressed the gas pedal as near the floor as I could and maintain control of the car, I kept the radio at full volume, tuned to whatever hard rock station broadcast clearest. Highway to Hell bled into Paranoid became Lock Up the Wolves. Although the doors, the dash thrummed with a bass line that changed only slightly from song to song, and my ears protested another shrieking singer, guitar, none of it was enough to drown out the sound that had drawn me from my bed the previous night and rushed me to the basement door, hands shaking as I unsnapped the deadbolts and turned the doorknob. Some kind of loud noise, a crash, and then Kaitlyn – I had heard her voice echoing below me, calling my name in that low, sing-song tone she used when she wanted to have sex. I had thought I was in a dream, but her words had led me up out of sleep, until the realisation that I was awake and still hearing her had sent me from my room, kicking over several stacks of books on the way. The door open, I switched on the light and saw, at the foot of the stairs, shielding her eyes against the sudden brightness, Kaitlyn, returned to me at last.

At the sight of her there – the emotion that transfixed me was some variety of, *I knew it*. I knew she hadn't really vanished, knew she wasn't lost under the earth. She was wearing the oversized army greatcoat, which was streaked with mud. Her feet were bare and filthy. Her skin was more than pale, as if her time underground had bleached it. Her hair was tangled, clotted with dirt, her mouth flaked with something brown.

I was on the verge of running down the stairs to her when she lowered her hand from her eyes and I saw the white centres, the black sclerae. A wave of dizziness threatened to topple me headlong down the stairs. Kaitlyn smiled at my hesitation, reached over, and pulled open her coat. Underneath, she was naked, her white, white flesh smeared with dirt and clay. She called to me again. "Here I aaa-mmm," she half-sang. "Didn't you miss me? Don't you wanna come play with me?"

A bolt of longing, of desire sudden and intense, pierced me. God help me, I did want her. My Eurydice: I wanted to bury myself in her, and who cared if her eyes were changed, if her flesh bore evidence of activities I did not want to dwell on? I might have, might have crossed the dozen pieces of wood that separated the life to which I clung from that which had forced itself on me, surrender myself to sweet oblivion, had a large, bony shape not stumbled into view behind Kaitlyn. Of the *Ghûl* I had seen previously, none had given so profound an impression of being unaccustomed to walking on all fours. It held its head up too high, as if unused to the position. Its weird eyes were rheumy, its gums raw where its lips drew back from them. It curled around Kaitlyn from behind, dragging its muzzle across her hip before nuzzling between her thighs. She sighed deeply. Eyes lidded, lips parted, she extended her hand towards me while the other pressed the *Ghûl's* head forward.

The thing pulled away long enough to give me a sidelong glance, and it was that gesture that sent me scrambling backwards, grabbing for the door and slamming it shut, throwing myself against it as I snapped the deadbolts. It kept me there while I listened to the stairs creak under the combined weights of Kaitlyn and her companion, who settled themselves on the opposite side of the door so that she could murmur tender obscenities to me while the *Ghûl*'s claws worried the wood. They left with the dawn. Once I was sure they were gone, I ran into my room and began frantically packing.

If the far end of Cape Cod was not as secure a redoubt as I might have thought, hoped, if Martha's Vineyard and Nantucket proved no more isolated, they were preferable to Albany, whose single, outsized skyscraper was an enormous cenotaph marking a necropolis of whose true depths its inhabitants remained unaware. I fled them, over the miles of road and ocean; I am still fleeing them, down the long passage that joins *now* to *then*. That flight has defined my life, is its individual failure and the larger failures of the age in sum. I see the two of them still, down there in the dark, where their wanderings take them along sewers, up into the basements of houses full of sleeping families, under roads and rivers, to familiar cemeteries. Kaitlyn has grown more lean, her hair long. She has traded in her old greatcoat for a newer trenchcoat. The *Ghûl* lopes along beside her, nimble on its feet. It too has become more lean. The scar over its left eye remains.

*For Fiona and for Ellen Datlow, who knows about Albany.*

# KARINA SUMNER-SMITH

## When the Zombies Win

KARINA SUMNER-SMITH IS A Toronto-based author and Nebula Award nominee. Her short fiction has been published in a number of anthologies, including *The Living Dead 2, Children of Magic* and *Ages of Wonder*.

In addition to writing fiction, Karina works as a freelance communications specialist and performs with a local belly-dance troupe.

As she recalls: "In a discussion about the Apocalypse, I joked that someone should write a story set after everyone has been eaten or turned into zombies. What would the zombies eat? What would they do when there's no one left to infect? Then I paused (in that way that writers have), and said, 'You know, that's not a bad idea . . .'

"Once I'd considered the consequences, a total Zombie Apocalypse seemed not horrific, nor comedic, but tragic.

"It's not just that everyone has died, but that we have died and yet continue to stumble through the ruins of our world with no way to understand or acknowledge what's happened, or mourn the loss of everything we once were."

WHEN THE ZOMBIES WIN, they will be slow to realise their success. Word travels slowly on shambling feet.

It will take years to be sure that there aren't still humans hiding in high mountain camps or deep within labyrinthine caverns; that the desert bunkers are empty, the forest retreats fallen; that the ships still afloat bear no breathing passengers.

And then: victory. Yet the zombies will not call out to each other, or cry in relief, or raise their rotting hands in triumph. They will walk unseeing beneath telephone wires and over cell phones, computers, radios. They will pass smouldering rubble without thinking of smoke signals, trip on tattered bed sheets and not consider making flags.

They are zombies; they will only walk and walk and walk, the word spreading step by step across continents and oceans and islands, year by year. And the word, to them, will feel like hunger.

When the zombies win, their quest to eat and infect human flesh will continue unabated. They will have known only gorging, only feasting; they will not understand the world as anything other than a screaming buffet on the run.

Yet there will be only silence and vacant rooms where once there was food, and the zombies, in their slow and stumbling way, will be surprised. Stomachs once perpetually distended will feel empty and curve inward towards their spines, the strength of even animated corpses beginning to fail without fuel. They will look about, cloudy eyes staring, and they will groan, unbreathing lungs wheezing as they try to push out enough air to ask slowly, hungrily, *"Brains?"*

But there will be no one left to find. Only each other.

Zombies, they will learn, do not taste good.

When the zombies win, they will become restless. There is little to do when one is dead.

Their old pastimes – their favourite pastimes – will hold no satisfaction. They will shamble down streets, arms outstretched as they groan and wail, yet inspire no fear. Together they will pound on doors, beat on windows with decaying hands until the glass shatters, hide in rivers and lakes, stumble after cars on the highway. But the cars will all be stopped, forever in park; the breaking glass will elicit no screams; and no swimmer's hands or feet will break the water's surface to be grabbed. When the doors burst open there will be no one cowering behind.

There will be no people to stalk, no food to eat, no homes to build, no deaths to die. Lost and aimless they will turn as if seeking a leader's guidance, and find none. With zombies, the only leader is the one who happens to be walking first.

So they will walk alone, all of them alone, with no destinations, only the need to keep putting one unsteady foot in front of the other, over and over without end. The world is a big place to wander, even when inhabited only by the dead.

When the zombies win, they will not think of the future. There will be no next generation of zombies, no newborn zombie children held in rotting arms. The zombies will not find comfort in each other, will not rediscover concepts like friendship or companionship, will not remember sympathy or empathy or kindness. They will not learn or dream, or even know that they cannot.

They will build no buildings, fix no cars, write no histories, sing no songs. They will not fall in love. For zombies, there is only an endless today – this moment, this place, this step, this need, this hunger, this hunger unrelenting.

And the streets will begin to crumble, and windows break, and buildings fall. Cities will burn and flood, towns be reclaimed by grassland and forest, desert and ocean.

The human world will go to pieces, decaying to nothing as empty eyes stare.

When the zombies win, they will not fear. They will not laugh or rejoice, they will not regret, they will not mourn. And the world will turn and turn, seasons burning and freezing across the landscape, the sun flashing through the sky, and they will continue.

When the zombies win, they will not stop. They will still moan and cry and whisper, on and on until the lips rot from their faces, their vocal cords slide away. They will never truly think again, never know the meaning of the words they try to utter, only flutter endlessly on the edge of remembering. Still they will try to speak, bone scraping on bone as their ruined jaws move, and they will not know why.

One by one they will fall. In the streets they will fall, legs no longer working, arms too broken to drag them forward. Inside buildings they will fall, tumbling down stairs and collapsing in hallways, slipping behind beds and in closets, curling into the gap between toilet and wall, not knowing, not seeing, not understanding these trappings of the places they once called home. They will sink to the bottoms of rivers and oceans, and lie down in fields, and tumble from mountainsides, and fall apart on the gravel edges of highways.

One by one they will stop moving, flesh and bone and brain too broken to do anything more. And in that silence and stillness they will struggle – trapped and ruined, they will still yearn, still hunger, always reaching for that which was taken from them. That which they granted to so many of us, in such great numbers.

To stop. To sleep. To rest, just rest, and let the darkness come.

# STEPHEN JONES
# & KIM NEWMAN

## Necrology: 2010

AS THE FIRST DECADE of the 21st century comes to an end, we once again remember the passing of writers, artists, performers and technicians who, during their lifetimes, made significant contributions to the horror, science fiction and fantasy genres (or left their mark on popular culture and music in other, often fascinating, ways) . . .

### AUTHORS/ARTISTS/COMPOSERS

**Tsutomu Yamaguchi,** the only man to be officially recognised by the Japanese government as surviving both the atomic bombings of Hiroshima and Nagasaki during World War II, died of stomach cancer on January 4, aged 93. On August 6, 1945, he was in Hiroshima on business when the bomb was dropped. He returned home the following day to Nagasaki, and despite his injuries resumed work on August 9, the date the second atomic bomb was detonated. He later wrote a book about his experiences.

American editor and literary agent **Knox** [Breckenridge] **Burger,** who published Kurt Vonnegut's first story in *Collier's* magazine in 1950, died after a long illness the same day, aged 87. Vonnegut dedicated his collection *Welcome to the Monkey House* to him.

Italian scriptwriter **Piero De Bernardi** died on January 8, aged

83. One of seven credited writers on Sergio Leone's *Once Upon a Time in America*, he also scripted *Il mistero del tempio indiano* (aka *Vengeance of Kali*) and *Dottor Jekyll e genyile signora*, and contributed dialogue to *Ghosts – Italian Style*.

Welsh-born scriptwriter and lyricist **Julian** [Bensley] **More** died in France of cancer on January 15, aged 81. He wrote the original play *Expresso Bongo* was based on, contributed to the screenplay of *The Valley of Gwangi* and scripted *Incense for the Damned* (aka *Blood Suckers*), based on the novel by Simon Raven.

"The Father of Japanese SF", author and translator **Takumi Shibano** (aka "Rei Kozumi"), died of pneumonia on January 16, aged 83. He founded the country's first fanzine, *Uchujin* (*Cosmic Dust*), in 1957, with the most recent issue appearing in 2009. Tukumi sold his first SF story in 1950 under a pseudonym, and he went on to write three YA novels and contribute non-fiction to a wide variety of publications, including *Locus* and the *Encyclopedia of Science Fiction*.

**Roger Gaillard**, the curator of Switzerland's Maison d'Ailleurs science fiction museum from 1989 to 1996, died on January 22, aged 73. He also edited or co-edited a number of anthologies of essays about SF.

American TV writer **Barry E. Blitzer**, one of the creators of the cartoon show *Goober and the Ghost Chasers* (1973–75), died of complications from abdominal surgery on January 27, aged 80. He also worked on *The Jetsons*, *The Flintstones*, *Get Smart*, *Land of the Lost*, *Partridge Family 2200 AD*, *The Lost Saucer* and *The Flintstone Kids*.

Prolific American SF writer **Kage Baker** died after a long battle with cancer on January 31, aged 57. She had undergone surgery in December 2009 for a brain tumour. Best known for her sprawling time travel "Company" series, which began with a story in *Asimov's* in 1997, it went on to encompass nine novels, three novellas and two collections, with more to come. Her other books include the fantasies *The Anvil of the World* and its sequel, *The House of the Stag*, the YA novel *The Hotel Under the Sand*, and the pirate novella *Or Else My Lady Keeps the Key*. Some of her other short fiction is collected in *Mother Aegypt and Other Stories* and *Dark Mondays*. Baker taught Elizabethan English to stage actors for twenty years.

American music composer, producer and drummer **Richard Delvy** (Richard Delvecchio) died of aspiration pneumonia after a long illness on February 6, aged 67. The drummer for the first California surf band, the Bel-Airs, he became the lead singer with another band, the Challengers, in 1961. Delvy arranged and sang the memorable theme song for the American version of the movie *The Green Slime* (1968), and he produced music for the cartoon TV series *My Favorite Martian* and *The Groovy Ghoulies*. He also owned the copyright to the classic surf hit "Wipeout".

Veteran British-born SF and fantasy humorist **William Tenn** (Philip Klass, aka "Kenneth Putnam") died of congestive heart failure at his home in Pennsylvania on February 7, aged 89. His first SF story appeared in *Astounding Science Fiction* in 1946, and he went on to publish fiction in many other pulp magazines of the time, including *Planet Stories*, *Thrilling Wonder Stories*, *Famous Fantastic Mysteries*, *Fantastic Adventures*, *Galaxy Science Fiction*, *Marvel Science Stories* and *Weird Tales*. His short story collections include *Of All Possible Worlds*, *The Human Angle*, *Time in Advance*, *The Square Root of Man* and two volumes of *The Complete Science Fiction of William Tenn* from NESFA Press: *Immodest Proposals* and *Here Comes Civilization*. Tenn's single novel was *Of Men and Monsters*, published in 1968; his novella *A Lamp for Medusa* appeared in book form the same year, he edited the SF anthology *Children of Wonder* and his non-fiction was collected in the Hugo Award-nominated *Dancing Naked: The Unexpurgated William Tenn*. He was named Author Emeritus by the SFWA in 1999.

British children's author **David Severn** (David Storr Unwin) died on February 11, aged 91. The son of publisher Sir Stanley Unwin, his more than thirty books include *Dream Gold*, *Drumbeats!*, *The Future Took Us* and *The Wishing Bone*.

Japanese SF translator **Hisashi Asakura** (Zenji Otani), whose works include Philip K. Dick's *Do Androids Dream of Electric Sheep?*, died on February 14, aged 79.

American writer and editor **Jim** (James Judson) **Harmon** died of a heart attack on February 16, aged 76. With Forrest J Ackerman as his agent, during the 1950s and '60s he contributed a number of stories to magazines such as *Amazing Stories*,

*Future Science Fiction*, *Galaxy*, *If*, *The Magazine of Fantasy & Science Fiction* and *Venture*, and the best of these were collected in 2004 in *Harmon's Galaxy*. In the early 1960s he collaborated with Ron Haydock on adult paperbacks with titles like *The Man Who Made Maniacs*, *Wanton Witch*, *Silent Siren* and *Ape Rape*, while his only SF novel, *The Contested Earth*, was written in 1959 but not published until 2007. Harmon and Haydock also scripted and appeared in Ray Dennis Steckler's movie *The Lemon Grove Kids Meet the Monsters*. After contributing articles to *Fantastic Monsters of the Movies* in the early 1960s, from 1973 to 1974 Harmon was West Coast editor of Curtis Magazines' *Monsters of the Movies*, Marvel Comics' nine-issue rival to *Famous Monsters of Filmland*. As "Mr Nostalgia", Harmon became the ancknowledged expert on classic radio shows and published a number of non-fiction works on the subject, including *The Great Radio Heroes* (1967) and *Radio Mystery and Adventure and Its Appearance in Film, Television and Other Media*. He also wrote *The Great Movie Serials* (with Don Glut) and *The Godzilla Book*, and edited and contributed to two volumes of the *It's That Time Again* anthology series featuring old-time radio characters.

American space artist **Robert T.** (Theodore) **McCall** died of heart failure on February 26, aged 90. He created the poster art for *2001: A Space Odyssey* and *Star Trek: The Motion Picture*, along with paintings for various SF magazines, postage stamps and NASA mission patches. Some of his artwork was collected in *The Art of Robert McCall: A Celebration of Our Future in Space* (1992).

British bookseller and 1930s fan-turned-author **Eric C.** (Cyril) **Williams** died at the age of 91. A contributor to such early fanzines as *The Satellite*, between 1968 and 1981 he published ten SF novels, including *Monkman Comes Down*, *The Time Injection*, *The Call of Utopia*, *Project: Renaissance*, *Largesse from Triangulum* and *Homo Telekins*, and his short fiction was reprinted in such anthologies as *New Writings in SF 5* and *Weird Shadows from Beyond*.

**John Clifford**, whose single feature film credit was co-writer of *Carnival of Souls* (1962) with director Herk Harvey, died of a heart attack on March 2, aged 91. Clifford also worked as a radio joke writer, an educational and industrial film writer, Western novelist and songwriter (with Angelo Badalamenti for Nina Simone).

British politician, author and former leader of the Labour Party **Michael** [Mackintosh] **Foot**, who wrote the 1995 biography of H.G. Wells, *The History of Mr Wells*, died on March 3, aged 96.

American film composer [William] **Paul Dunlap** died on March 11, aged 90. Although he claimed that he would much preferred to have been remembered for his piano concerto or choral piece, he is best known for his music for such "inferior" movies as *Lost Continent* (1951), *Target Earth* (1954), *I Was a Teenage Werewolf*, *Teenage Frankenstein*, *Blood of Dracula* (aka *Blood is My Heritage*), *How to Make a Monster*, *Frankenstein 1970*, *Invisible Invaders*, *The Four Skulls of Jonathan Drake*, *The Angry Red Planet*, *The Three Stooges Meet Hercules*, *The Three Stooges in Orbit*, *Black Zoo*, *Shock Corridor*, *Cyborg 2087*, *Destination Inner Space*, *Dimension 5* (aka *Dimension Four*), *Castle of Evil* and *The Destructors*, along with numerous Westerns. He reportedly consigned all his movie recordings and sheet music to landfill many years earlier.

Australian children's and YA writer **Patricia Wrightson** OBE (Alice Patricia Furlonger) died on March 15, aged 88. Starting in 1955 with the award-winning *The Crooked Snake*, her twenty-seven novels (many of which drew upon Aboriginal mythology) include *The Nargun and the Stars*, *The Ice Is Coming*, *The Dark Bright Water*, *Journey Beyond the Wind*, *A Little Fear*, *Moon-Dark* and *Balyet*. She was awarded the Hans Christian Andersen Medal in 1986 for her lifetime achievement in writing for young people.

Newberry Medal-winning American children's author **Sid Fleischman** (Albert Sidney Fleischman), died on March 17, the day after he turned 90. His more than fifty books include *The Ghost in the Noonday Sun*, *The Midnight Horse* and *The 13th Floor*. He also wrote scripts for movies (as "A.S. Fleischman") and TV.

42-year-old British graphic artist **John** ("Johnny") **Hicklenton** (aka "John Deadstock") ended his life at Switzerland's Dignitas clinic on March 19. He had been suffering from multiple sclerosis for more than a decade. Best known for his work on "Judge

Dredd" in *2000 AD*, he also illustrated *Third World War*, *Nemesis the Warlock* and *Zombie World: Tree of Death*. For the last six years of his life he was followed by a television crew that chronicled his battle with MS for the award-winning documentary *Here's Johnny*.

British children's author **William** [James Carter] **Mayne** (aka "Martin Cobalt"/"Dynely James") died on March 23, aged 82. Beginning in 1953, he wrote more than 100 books, including the "Earthfasts" time-slip trilogy (*Earthfasts*, *Cradlefasts* and *Candlefasts*), *The Member for the Marsh*, the Carnegie Medal-winning *A Grass Rope*, *A Game of Dark*, *Hob and the Goblins*, *Skiffy*, *Kelpie* and *Low Tide*, winner of the Guardian children's fiction prize. As "Charles Molin" he also edited the 1967 anthology *Ghosts, Spooks and Spectres*. In 2004, Mayne was convicted of eleven counts of sexual abuse of young girls between 1960 and 1973. He was jailed for two-and-half years, banned from working with children, and put on the sex offenders' register for life.

77-year-old American comic book artist and editor **Dick Giordano** died of complications from pneumonia on March 27, while being treated for leukaemia. He joined Charlton Comics in 1952, eventually rising to Editor-in-Chief of the line by the mid-1960s, where he looked after such characters as "Captain Atom", "Blue Beetle" and "Thunderbolt". Giordano moved to DC Comics in 1967, editing such titles as *Beware the Creeper*, *Bomba the Jungle Boy*, *Deadman*, *The Spectre*, *Blackhawk*, *The Witching Hour* and *Hawk and Dove*. As an artist, he pencilled Neal Adams' *Green Lantern/Green Arrow* series and inked *Batman*, *Wonder Woman* and many other titles. For Marvel he worked on the "Sons of the Tiger" series for *The Deadly Hands of Kung Fu*, as well as inking the first DC/Marvel crossover, *Superman vs. the Amazing Spider-Man*, in 1976, and the special *Superman vs. Muhammad Ali* two years later. As Vice President and Executive Editor at DC from 1983 to 1993 he oversaw the development of such post-modern re-imaginings as George Perez's *Crisis on Infinite Worlds*, John Byrne's *The Man of Steel*, Frank Miller's *The Dark Knight Returns* and Alan Moore's *Watchmen*. Giordano adapted Peter O'Donnell's *Modesty Blaise* for DC in 1994, and he continued to contribute to various graphic projects up to the time of his death.

American horror writer and psychologist **Joel S. Ross** died following a brief illness on April 2, aged 62. His one novel was *Eye For an Eye* (2004).

Female Japanese manga artist and writer [Chiyoko] **"Shio" Satō** (aka "Sugar Salt") died of brain cancer on April 4, aged 57. She was best known for *The Dreaming Planet* (*Yumemiru Wakusei*) and *One Zero*, and her short story "The Changeling".

Veteran American animator **Tom Ray** (Thomas Archer Ray) died on April 6, aged 90. He worked at Warner Bros., MGM and UPA, before returning to Warner Bros. in the late 1950s to work with Robert McKimson and Chuck Jones on numerous *Bugs Bunny*, *Road Runner*, *Speedy Gonzalez*, *Foghorn Leghorn* and *Pepe Le Pew* cartoon shorts. Ray's many other credits include such TV specials and series as *How the Grinch Stole Christmas!* (narrated by Boris Karloff), *The Night Before Christmas* (1968), *Horton Hears a Who!* (1970), *The Phantom Tollbooth*, *Heavy Traffic*, *Coonskin*, *The All-New Super Friends Hour*, *Scooby's All Star Laff-A-Lympics*, *Bugs Bunny's Howl-Oween Special*, *Challenge of the Super Friends*, *The Godzilla Show*, *Spider-Woman*, *Flash Gordon* (1979–80), *The Grinch Grinches the Cat in the Hat*, *Flash Gordon: The Greatest Adventure of All*, *Winnie the Pooh and a Day for Eeyore*, *Daffy Duck's Movie: Fantastic Island*, *The Incredible Hulk* (1982–83), *Dungeons & Dragons* (1983–85), *Defenders of Earth*, *The Transformers*, *Dino-Riders*, *Daffy Duck's Quackbusters*, *RoboCop* (1988), *Darkwing Duck*, *Tiny Toon Adventures*, *Animaniacs* and *The Real Adventures of Jonny Quest*.

American SF and wildlife artist **John** [Carl] **Schoenherr**, best known for his distinctive cover paintings on *Astounding/Analog* magazine during the 1950s and '60s, died on April 8, aged 74. He started his career by contributing interior illustrations to *Amazing* in 1956, while still a student, quickly graduating to a full-time artist with work in *Fantastic*, *Infinity* and *The Magazine of Fantasy and Science Fiction*, along with numerous book covers. He won the Hugo Award in 1965 and the Caldecott Medal in 1988.

Irish SF fan **Peggy White**, who was married to author James White from 1955 until his death in 1999, died the same day, aged 82.

**George H.** (Harry) **Scithers**, the founding editor of *Asimov's Science Fiction* magazine in 1977, died on April 19, aged 80. He had suffered a massive heart attack two days earlier. He began his career in the field in 1959 when he started editing the Hugo Award-winning sword and sorcery fanzine *Amra*, and he went on to also edit *Amazing Stories* from 1982 to 1986 and the revival of *Weird Tales* (with Darrell Schweitzer and John Betancourt) from 1987 to 2007. He compiled the anthologies *The Conan Swordbook* and *The Conan Grimoire* (both with L. Sprague de Camp) and *The Conan Reader* from material that appeared in *Amra*, along with eleven volumes of stories from *Asimov's*, *Tales from the Spaceport Bar* and *Another Round at the Spaceport Bar* (both with Schweitzer), and two volumes of *Cat Tales: Fantastic Feline Fiction*. Scithers' non-fiction books include *The Con-Committee Chairman's Guide*, *On Writing Science Fiction: The Editors Strike Back* (with Schweitzer and John M. Ford) and *Constructing Scientifiction and Fantasy* (with John Ashmead and Schweitzer). He was also a short fiction writer and the founder of Owlswick Press. Scithers won two Hugo Awards for Best Professional Editor and the World Fantasy Life Achievement Award in 2002.

77-year-old American scriptwriter and producer **Myles Wilder**, the son of B-movie director W. Lee Wilder and the nephew of Billy Wilder, died of complications from diverticulitis (a digestive disease) on April 20. He contributed the scripts and/or original story to his father's productions *Phantom from Space*, *Killers from Space*, *The Snow Creature*, *Manfish* (aka *Calypso*), *Fright* and *Bluebeard's Ten Honeymoons*, along with episodes of TV's *Mr Terrific*, *Get Smart*, *The Flying Nun*, *The Ghost & Mrs Muir* and the cartoon series *The Addams Family*, *Inch High Private Eye*, *Korg: 70,000 B.C.*, *Partridge Family 2200 AD* and *Valley of the Dinosaurs*. He retired from televison in 1994 and grew avocados in California.

American paperback book cover and pin-up artist **Ernest Chiriaka** (Anastassios Kyriakakos) died on April 27, aged 96. His work appeared on everything from Gold Medal books to the Esquire Pin-up Calendars of the 1950s.

Prolific Italian screenwriter **Furio Scarpelli** died of heart failure in April 28, aged 90. Nominated for three Oscars, his credits include *Hercules* (1958), *The Witches* (1967) and *The Good, the Bad and the Ugly*.

American SF author **Sharon Webb**, who based much of her fiction on her work as a nurse, died of a heart attack on April 30, aged 74. She began her career writing for *The Magazine of Fantasy and Science Fiction* (as "Rob Webb"), *Asimov's* and other magazines, and her novels include the trilogy *Earthchild*, *Earthsong* and *Ramsong*, *The Adventures of Terra Tarkington, R.N.*, *Pestis 18* and *The Half Life*.

British author **Peter O'Donnell** (aka "Madeleine Brent"), who created the comic-strip heroine Modesty Blaise for London's *Evening Standard* newspaper in 1963, died of complications from Parkinson's disease on May 3, aged 90. He continued the female adventurer's exploits in eleven novels and two short story collections, although two film adaptations (1966 and 2004) and a 1982 TV pilot didn't do the character justice. The strip ran for 10,104 daily episodes, finally ending in 2001. O'Donnell also worked on the cartoon strips *Belinda*, *For Better or Worse*, *Tug Transom*, *Romeo Brown*, *Eve* and *Garth*, and he scripted the 1968 Hammer film *The Vengeance of She*.

American script supervisor **Robert Gary** (aka "Bob Gary"), whose credits include *The Magic Sword*, *What Ever Happened to Baby Jane?*, *The Outer Limits*, *The Strangler*, *Hush . . . Hush, Sweet Charlotte*, *Highway to Heaven* and all four *Star Trek* TV series, died the same day, aged 90.

Novelist and aviation author **Robert J. Serling** (Jerome Robert Serling), the older brother of Rod Serling, died of cancer on May 6, aged 92. He served as an aviation expert on his brother's *Twilight Zone* episode "The Odyssey of Flight 33", and his novels include *Something's Alive on the Titanic* and the bestseller *The President's Plane is Missing*, the latter made into a TV movie in 1973.

Freelance journalist **David Everitt** died of complications from amyotrophic lateral sclerosis (aka Lou Gehrig's disease) on May 7, aged 57. Between 1981 and 1985 he co-edited *Fangoria* magazine with Bob Martin. He also contributed articles and interviews to *Starlog*, *Comics Scene* and *Entertainment Weekly*, and wrote a number of reference books (several with his cousin, Harold Schecter).

Legendary American artist **Frank Frazetta** (Frank Frazzetta) died of complications from a stroke on May 10, aged 82. Credited with popularising Robert E. Howard's character "Conan" with his series of distinctive paperback covers for Lancer Books in the late 1960s and early '70s, Frazetta began his career in the 1950s working on such comic strips as *Flash Gordon*, *Buck Rogers*, *Thun'da King of the Congo*, *The Shining Knight*, *Ghost Rider*, *Johnny Comet* and EC's SF titles. For nearly a decade he also "ghosted" Al Capp's *Li'l Abner* newspaper strip. In the 1960s Frazetta branched out into book covers (notably the works of Edgar Rice Burroughs), periodicals such as *Creepy*, *Eerie*, *Playboy* and *Mad Magazine*, calendars, record album sleeves, movie posters and merchandise. He also co-created the 1983 animated film *Fire & Ice* with Ralph Bashki. His work has been collected in numerous books and he won three Chesley Awards, the Hugo Award, the World Fantasy Award, the Spectrum Grandmaster Award and the World Fantasy Lifetime Achievement Award. Frazetta's 1971 painting for *Conan the Destroyer* sold for $1.5 million at the San Diego Comic Convention. Following his death, Frazetta's four children were embroiled in a very public family feud involving the artist's body of work, estimated to be worth tens of millions of dollars.

On May 16, Florida police discovered a blue van and an arm belonging to 55-year-old comic book writer **Stephen J. Perry**, the original scriptwriter on the 1980s cartoon TV show *Thundercats*. The writer had been missing from his home for more than two weeks under suspicious circumstances, and police confirmed that he was dead and a victim of homicide. One of his roommates was subsequently charged with first-degree murder. Perry contributed stories to such comics as *T.H.U.N.D.E.R. Agents*, *Creepy* (1985), *Bizarre Adventures*, *Epic Illustrated* and *Star Comics*, and he also worked on such animated TV series as *Silverhawks*, *Spider-Man Unlimited*, *Godzilla: The Series*, *Gargoyles*, *Extreme Ghostbusters*, *Batman: The Animated Series*, *Conan and the Young Warriors* and *Starcom: The U.S. Space Force*.

64-year-old American author and technical writer **George M.** (McDonald) **Ewing** died of a massive heart attack in the parking lot of his workplace on May 18. His first story, "Black Fly", appeared in *Analog* in 1974, and he contributed fiction to a number of other magazines, including *Asimov's*.

American comic book artist/writer and TV animation director **Howard "Howie" Post** died of complications from Alzheimer's disease on May 21, aged 83. He began his career in comics in the mid-1940s with strips in such titles as *Wonderland Comics*, *More Fun Comics* and *Comic Cavalcade*. He then moved on to Atlas Comics, where he worked on such horror titles as *Journey Into Mystery*, *Uncanny Tales* and *Mystery Tales*. By the early 1960s Post had joined Harvey Comics, where he was drawing such characters as "Hot Stuff the Little Devil", "Spooky the Tuff Little Ghost", "Wendy the Good Little Witch" and the "Ghostly Trio". During the mid-1960s he wrote and directed a number of cartoon shorts for Famous Studios, including *Poor Little Witch Girl* (1965), *From Nags to Witches* (1966) and *Trick or Cheat* (1966), all featuring the voice of Shari Lewis as "Honey Halfwitch". Post then created the prehistoric teen comic *Anthro* for DC, which ran for six issues from 1968 to 1969, and drew the syndicated newspaper strip *The Dropouts* from 1968-81.

Mathematician, puzzle-maker and author **Martin Gardner** died on May 22, aged 95. From 1977 to 1986 he wrote a column for *Asimov's* magazine that featured puzzles in the form of short SF stories. Some of these were collected in *Science Fiction Puzzle Tales* and *Puzzles from Other Worlds*. An expert on the works of Lewis Carroll, Gardner also published *The Annotated Alice* (1960), while his short fiction was collected in *The No-Sided Professor and Other Tales of Fantasy, Humor, Mystery and Philosophy*. His 1999 novel *Visitors from Oz: The Wild Adventures of Dorothy, the Scarecrow and the Tin Woodman* was a sequel to L. Frank Baum's classic series.

American novelist **Arthur Herzog III**, whose first book was the 1974 killer bee novel *The Swarm* (filmed four years later), died of complications from a stroke on May 26, aged 83. Herzog's other books include the novels *Earthbound, Heat, IQ 83, Make Us Happy* and *Glad to Be Here*, along with the short story collection *Beyond Sci-Fi*. He was married six times.

Australian-born author **Randolph Snow**, whose novels include the post-apocalypse *Tourmaline* and the fantasy *The Girl Green as Elderflower* died on May 30, aged 74.

62-year-old American dancer and choreographer **Jeanne Robinson** (Jeanne Marie Rubbicco), who collaborated with her husband, author Spider Robinson, on the Hugo and Nebula Award-winning *Analog* story "Stardance" (1977), died in Vancouver, Canada, the same day, of biliary tract cancer. The couple expanded their story into the 1979 novel *Stardance* and two sequels, *Starseed* and *Starmind*.

American artist and author **Ray Capella** (Raul Garcia Capella) died of complications from Alzheimer's disease on June 6, aged 77. His artwork was featured on numerous book and magazine covers, while his short fiction was included in the anthologies *Warlocks and Warriors*, *The Year's Best Fantasy Stories 3* and *Swords Against Darkness 1*, and collected in *The Leopard of Poitain* (1985).

Pioneering American SF writer **Frank K.** (King) **Kelly** died on June 11, the day before his 96th birthday. His first story appeared in the pulp magazine *Wonder Stories* in 1931, and he published nine more stories until he stopped writing fiction four years later. Some of his work was collected in the 1979 collection *Starship Invincible*. Kelly also worked as a journalist and speechwriter for US President Harry S. Truman, and he co-founded the Center for the Study of Democratic Institutions and the Nuclear Age Peace Foundation. In 1996 he was inducted into the First Fandom Hall of Fame.

American comics artist **Al Williamson**, who was taught art by *Tarzan* illustrator Burne Hogarth in the 1940s and became friends with Wally Wood and Roy Krenkel, died on June 13, aged 79. Best known for his contributions to the EC comics titles *Weird Science* and *Weird Fantasy* during the 1950s, he also worked on such strips as *Flash Gordon*, *Secret Agent X-9/Secret Agent Corrigan* and *Star Wars*. He was a contributor to *Creepy* and *Eerie*, and illustrated a number of Edgar Rice Burroughs books during the 1960s. In later years he worked primarily as an inker, first at DC Comics and then at Marvel.

American editor, bibliographer, translator and critic **Everett F.** (Franklin) **Bleiler**, whose pioneering *The Checklist of Fantastic Literature: A Bibliography of Fantasy, Weird and Science Fiction Books Published in the English Language* was published in 1948, died the same day, aged 90. With T.E. Ditky he also co-edited the first annual "Year's Best" anthology series, *The Best Science Fiction Stories*, which ran from 1949 to 1954. Bleiler began working at Dover Publications in 1955, where he edited numerous collections and anthologies of genre fiction, eventually becoming executive president in 1977. In 1986 he joined Charles Scribner's Sons. His other reference works include *Science Fiction Writers: Critical Studies of the Major Authors from the Early Nineteenth Century to the Present Day*, *Supernatural Fiction Writers: Fantasy and Horror*, *The Guide to Supernatural Fiction* and, in collaboration with his son Richard Bleiler, the Hugo Award-nominated *Science-Fiction: The Early Years* and *Science-Fiction: The Gernsback Years*. Although written ten decades earlier, his novels *Firefang: A Mythic Fantasy* and *The Invisible Murder* were both finally published in 2006. Bleiler won the World Fantasy Special Award – Professional in 1978, the World Fantasy Life Achievent Award a decade later, and the 1984 SFRA Pilgrim Award. He was also presented with a First Fandom Award in 1994, and named a Living Legend by the International Horror Guild in 2004.

Irish writer and businessman **Stephen Gilbert,** best known for his 1968 novel *Ratman's Notebooks*, which was the basis for the films *Willard* (twice) and *Ben*, died on June 23. He was 97, and his other SF and fantasy novels include *Landslide*, *Monkeyface* and *The Burnaby Experiments: An Account of the Life and Work of John Burnaby and Marcus Brownlow*.

Eccentric and reclusive author and artist **F. (Fergus) Gwynplaine "Froggy" MacIntyre** (aka "Timothy C. Allen", "Paul G. Jeffrey" and "Oleg V. Bredikhine") apparently committed suicide on the morning of June 25 by setting fire to four different areas of the one-bedroom Brooklyn apartment where he had lived for the past twenty-five years. The intense fire vapourised the writer's belongings and his body was burned beyond recognition. He was thought to be aged around 59 or 60. MacIntyre was remarkably secretive about his past and his identity, claiming he was born a twin with minor deformities in Perthshire, Scotland, and subsequently sent to live in Australia by his parents. In an obituary published in the June *Locus*, he revealed that George Scithers (who died in April) had been his editor, agent and mentor. MacIntyre's books include the 1994 steampunk novel *The Woman Between the Worlds*, the *Tom Swift* YA adventure *The DNA Disaster* (under the house name "Victor Appleton") and a collection of verse, *MacIntyre's Improbable Bestiary: Perverse Verse & Odious Odes*. His short fiction was published in such magazines as *Asimov's Science Fiction*, *Amazing Stories* and *Weird Tales*, and he was a regular contributor to the "Curiosities" column in the back of *The Magazine of Fantasy & Science Fiction*. MacIntyre admitted to inventing details of his own biography, but also claimed that, while living in the UK during the 1960s, he published SF and horror for Badger Books under various names and worked as a crew member on such TV series as *The Prisoner* and *The Champions*. He also reportedly wrote part of Jerzy Kosinski's 1984 novel *Pinball*. His story "The Clockwork Horror" appeared in *The Mammoth Book of Best New Horror Volume Eighteen*. In 2000 MacIntyre was found guilty of a third-degree misdemeanour assault on a female neighbour. Depressed about losing his job as a night printer, he seemed to leave an enigmatic farewell message in e-mails to friends, on his website (where he claimed to be moving back to Australia), and in an online review of the restored version of *Metropolis*, in which he said "All good things come to a happy ending". His body was eventually positively identified using DNA testing.

British scriptwriter and playright **Alan** [Frederick] **Plater** CBE died of cancer the same day, aged 75. His credits include *Shades of Darkness* ("Feet Foremost", based on the story by L.P. Hartley), *Bewitched* (based on the story by Edith Wharton), *The Adventures of Sherlock Holmes* ("The Solitary Cyclist"), *The Return of Sherlock Holmes* ("The Man With the Twisted Lip") and the near-future mini-series *A Very British Coup*.

British "hard" science fiction writer **James P.** (Patrick) **Hogan** died in Ireland on July 12, aged 69. A prolific novelist, he began his career in 1977 with *Inherit the Stars*, the first in his "Giants" series, and his many other books include *The Genesis Machine*, *The Two Faces of Tomorrow*, *Thrice Upon Time*, *Voyage from Yesteryear*, *The Proteus Operation*, *Endgame Enigma*, *The Mirror Maze*, *The Infinity Gambit*, *The Multiplex Man*, *Realtime Interrupt*, *Paths to Otherwhere*, *Bug Park*, *Star Child*, *Outward Bound*, *The Legend That Was Earth*, *Martian Knightlife*, *The*

*Anguished Dawn*, *Echoes of an Alien Sky*, *Moonflower* and *Migration*, along with the "Code of the Lifemaker" duology and the "Cradle of Saturn" series. Hogan's short fiction is collected in *Minds Machines & Evolution*, *Rockets Redheads and Revolution* and *Catastrophes Chaos and Convolutions*. He was also the author of the non-fiction collections *Mind Matters* and *Kicking the Sacred Cow*.

70-year-old American underground comic book writer **Harvey Pekar** was found dead from an an accidental overdose of anti-depressant drugs in his Ohio home on the same day. He had been suffering from prostate cancer, asthma, high blood pressure and depression. Pekar began publishing his autobiographical comics series *American Splendor* in 1976, and he was portrayed by Paul Giamatti in the 2003 Oscar-nominated film of the same name. In 1988 he annoyed talk-show host David Letterman so much that he was banned from the NBC-TV show. Pekar was buried in Cleveland's Lake View Cemetery, next to "The Untouchables" crime-buster Elliot Ness.

Canadian **Richard Langlois** (aka "Lee Richard"/"Richard Lee"), a pioneering historian and scholar of French-language comics, died of cancer in Quebec on July 19, aged 68.

American screenwriter **Tom** (Thomas) [Frank] **Mankiewicz**, the son of famed Hollywood writer-director Joseph L. Mankiewicz, died of cancer on July 31, aged 68. Best known for his scripts for the James Bond films *Diamonds Are Forever*, *Live and Let Die* and *The Man with the Golden Gun*, his other screenwriting credits include *Ladyhawke* and *Dragnet* (1987). Mankiewicz also worked as a "creative consultant" on the scripts for *Superman* (1978) and its sequel, *Superman II*, and he directed *Dragnet*, *Delirious* and an episode of TV's *Tales from the Crypt*.

Prolific Italian screenwriter **Suso Cecchi d'Amico** (Giovanna Cecchi), best known for her work with Luchino Visconti, died the same day, aged 96. In 1972 she co-scripted the TV mini-series *The Adventures of Pinocchio* featuring comedy team Franco and Ciccio.

Spanish comic book artist and portrait painter **Fernando Fernández** [Sanchez] died on August 9, aged 70. During the 1950s and '60s he worked (uncredited) on many war and romance titles from British imprint Fleetway Publications.

Fernández also contributed eleven strips to James Warren's horror title *Vampirella* in the early 1970s (including the acclaimed "Rendezvous"), and in 1982 his adaptation of "Bram Stoker's Dracula" in oil paints was serialised in the Spanish edition of *Creepy* magazine. He also adapted a number of stories by Isaac Asimov to comics.

**Elain Koster** (Elain Landis) who, as publisher at New American Library in the 1970s, paid $400,000 for the paperback rights to Stephen King's *Carrie* after the book had sold disappointingly in hardcover, died on August 10, aged 69. She also oversaw the SF list at NAL, and was president and publisher at Dutton before starting her own literary agency in 1998.

Scriptwriter **Raphael Hayes**, who wrote the 1959 Three Stooges movie *Have Rocket, Will Travel*, died on August 14, aged 95. His other writing credits include episodes of TV's *Lights Out*, *Suspense*, *Steve Canyon* and *Voyage to the Bottom of the Sea*.

**Susan M. Garret**, who began publishing fan fiction in her *Doctor Who* fanzine *Time Winds* in 1983, died of cancer the same day, aged 49. Her *Forever Knight* TV novelisation *Intimations of Mortality* was published by Berkeley in 1997.

American scriptwriter **Jackson** [Clark] **Gillis** died on August 19, two days before his 94th birthday. He wrote episodes of *Adventures of Superman*, Disney's *The Hardy Boys* serials, *The Man from U.N.C.L.E.*, *The Girl from U.N.C.L.E.*, *Tarzan*, *Lost in Space*, *The Wild Wild West*, *Land of the Giants*, *The Snoop Sisters* ("A Black Day for Bluebeard" featuring Vincent Price), *The New Adventures of Wonder Woman*, *Jason of Star Command*, *Knight Rider*, and the 1976 Rod Serling TV movie *Time Travelers*. In 1957 Gillis scripted a feature version of the 1950s *Superman* show, *Superman and the Secret Planet*, which was never produced, and he also co-wrote a pilot script for Irwin Allen's proposed 1967 TV series *Jules Verne's Journey to the Center of the Earth*, which was also never made. One of Gillis' original *Superman* scripts was later rewritten as a 1994 episode of *The New Adventures of Superman*.

American songwriter **George David Weiss** died on August 23, aged 89. His credits include such standards as "What a Wonderful World", "Can't Help Falling in Love", "The Lion Sleeps Tonight" and "Stay with Me Baby".

American author **Rebecca V. Neason** died after a long illness on August 31, aged 55. She had suffered from fibromyalgia for many years. Neason made her publishing debut in 1993 with the *Star Trek: The Next Generation* novel *Guises of the Mind*, and her other books include the fantasy novels *The Oak and the Cross*, *The Thirteenth Scroll* and *The Truest Power*, along with two *Highlander* TV tie-ins: *The Path* and *Shadow of Obsession*.

**Larry Ashmead**, who was an editor at such American publishing houses as Doubleday, Simon & Schuster, and Lippincott for almost fifty years, died of pneumonia on September 3, aged 78. He was Isaac Asimov's editor at Doubleday, where he also looked after J.G. Ballard and Philip K. Dick, amongst other authors.

Bibliographical researcher, critic and editor [Richard] **Neil Barron** died on September 5, aged 76. He edited the seminal 1976 critical reference work *Anatomy of Wonder* and then expanded it over four further editions. His other books include *Fantasy Literature: A Reader's Guide*, *Horror Literature: A Reader's Guide*, *What Do I Read Next?* and *Fantasy and Horror: A Critical and Historical Guide to Literature and Illustration, Film, TV, Radio, and the Internet*. Barron also founded *Science Fiction & Fantasy Book Review* and edited the magazine from 1979 to 1980 and from 1982 to 1983. He received a Pilgrim Award from the Science Fiction Research Association in 1982 for his contributions to SF criticism.

Veteran British SF and fantasy author **E. (Edwin) C. (Charles) Tubb** (aka "Charles Grey", "King Lang", "Gill Hunt", "Brian Shaw" etc.) died in his sleep on on September 10, aged 90. From 1951 onwards, he published more than 130 novels and over 230 stories (often pseudonymously) in such magazines as *Astounding/ Analog*, *Authentic Science Fiction* (which he edited from 1956 to 1957), *Galaxy*, *Nebula*, *New Worlds*, *Science Fantasy*, *Vision of Tomorrow* and others. His many books include *Saturn Patrol*, *Alien Dust*, *The Space-Born*, *The Possessed*, *Death God's Doom*, *The Sleeping City*, the *Space: 1999* tie-in *Earthbound*, the "Cap Kennedy" series (1973–83) and the "Dumarest of Terra" series that began in 1967 with *The Winds of Gath* and ran for thirty-three volumes (with the final book appearing in 2009). *Mirror of the Night* was a collection of the author's horror fiction, published by Sarob Press in 2003. He also wrote Westerns and a trilogy based on Roman history, and his 1955 story "Little Girl Lost" was adapted as an episode of Rod Serling's TV series *Night Gallery*. Tubb was Guest of Honour at the 1970 World SF Convention in Germany, and he left behind a number of unpublished manuscripts.

British TV scriptwriter and producer **Louis [Frank] Marks** died on September 17, aged 81. An expert on the Italian Renaissance, Marks scripted several episodes of *Doctor Who* (including "Day of the Daleks" and "The Masque of Mandragora") and *Doomwatch*, he was script editor on the *Dead of Night* episode "The Exorcism" and Nigel Kneale's *The Stone Tape*, and he produced such series as *Centre Play* (which included two Edgar Allan Poe adaptations) and a 1993 version of Franz Kafka's *The Trial*, scripted by Harold Pinter.

45-year-old American urban fantasy author **Jennifer Rardin** (Jennifer Pringle), who wrote the "Jaz Parks" CIA assassin/vampire hunter series, apparently committed suicide on September 20. The first novel in the sequence, *Once Bitten, Twice Shy*, was published in October 2007. It was followed by *Another One Bites the Dust*, *Biting the Bullet*, *Bitten to Death*, *One More Bite*, *Bite Marks*, *Bitten in Two* and the posthumously published *The Deadliest Bite*. She also wrote a YA novel, *Shadowstruck*.

Award-winning British music composer **Geoffrey Burgon** died after a short illness on September 21, aged 69. He composed music for the 1970s *Doctor Who* serials "Terror of the Zygons" and "The Seeds of Doom", and his other credits include *Treasure of Abbott Thomas* (based on the story by M.R. James), *Monty Python's Life of Brian*, *Bewitched* (based on the story by Edith Wharton), *Play for Today*: "Z for Zachariah", the BBC adaptations of C.S. Lewis' *The Lion the Witch & the Wardrobe* (1988), *Prince Caspian and the Voyage of the Dawn Treader* and *The Silver Chair*, plus *Ghost Stories for Christmas*, in which Christopher Lee portrayed M.R. James.

British Sherlock Holmes scholar and actor **Bernard [Hurst] Davies** died the same day, aged 86. He joined the Sherlock Holmes Society of London in 1958 and subsequently published a number of articles that redefined Holmesian research (these were collected in 2008 in the two-volume *Holmes and Watson*

*Country: Travels in Search of a Solution*). He served as chairman of the Sherlock Holmes Society of London from 1983 to 1986 and in 1973 co-founded the Dracula Society with fellow actor Bruce Wightman. As an actor, Davies appeared in a 1969 episode of *Doctor Who* ("The War Games") playing a German soldier.

One of the most powerful agents in the genre, **Ralph M. (Mario) Vicinanza**, died of a cerebral aneurysm in his sleep on September 25. He was 60. Vicinanza had worked in publishing for forty years, and his client list included such authors as Stephen King, Robert Heinlein, Robert Silverberg, Frank Herbert, Kim Stanley Robinson, Michael Marshall Smith, the Dalai Lama and many others. He began his career as a foreign rights agent at the Scott Meredith Agency, a role he continued for agents such as Kirby McCauley, Lurton Blassingame and Eleanor Wood. In 1978 he founded his own agency, Ralph M. Vicinanza Ltd, and he formed the media production and management company Created By in 1998. In recent years, Vincinanza was credited as an executive producer on a number of film and TV projects based on his clients' work, including *Snow Wonder* (Connie Willis), *Jumper* (Steven Gould), *The Wee Free Men* (Terry Pratchett), *FlashForward* (Robert J. Sawyer) and *Game of Thrones* (George R.R. Martin). At the time of his death, a film version of *The Forever War* (Joe Haldeman) was in development.

Legendary American TV writer and producer **Stephen J. Cannell**, creator of *The Rockford Files* and numerous other hit shows, died of complications from melanoma on September 30, aged 69. Despite suffering from dyslexia, his more than 300 television scripts include episodes of *The Greatest American Hero*, *Stingray* and *Silk Stalkings*, along with the TV movies *Dr Scorpion*, *The Night Rider*, the Disney pilot *The 100 Lives of Black Jack Savage*, and the direct-to-video movies *Dead Above Ground*, *It Waits* and *The Tooth Fairy*. As a producer, Cannell's credits include *Midnight Offerings*, *Them*, *Demon Hunter* and *The Garden*, and he was also the author of sixteen novels.

British SF author **Lan Wright** (Lionel Perry Wright) died on October 1, aged 87. His first story was published in *New Worlds* in 1952, and his short fiction continued to appear in that magazine, along with such titles as *Nebula Science Fiction* and *Science*

*Fiction Adventures*, for the next decade. Wright's books include *Who Speaks of Conquest?*, *A Man Called Destiny*, *Assignment Luther*, *Space Born* (aka *Exile from Xanadu*), *The Creeping Shroud* (aka *The Last Hope of Earth*) and *A Planet Called Pavanne* (aka *The Pictures of Pavanne*).

American screenwriter and political activist **Willam W.** (Wallace) **Norton** [Jr] died of a heart aneurysm the same day, aged 85. His credits include the psycho thriller *Poor Albert and Little Annie*, *Big Bad Mama*, *Day of the Animals* and the original story for *Body Count*. He also produced the 1964 nudie *How to Succeed with Girls*, written by his son, Bill L. Norton. In 1958, William Norton was called before the House Un-American Activities Committee for being a member of the Communist Party. He moved to Ireland in 1985 where, along with his second wife Eleanor, he was convicted of trying to smuggle guns to the IRA in Northern Ireland and served nearly two years in a French prison. Upon his release, the couple moved to Nicaragua, where he shot and killed a robber who broke into their home.

**Betty Bond** (Betty Gough Fulsom), the widow of pulp author Nelson S. Bond (who died in 2006), died of a heart attack on October 2, aged 94. The couple were married for seventy-two years, and she was closely involved in her husband's writing career – typing his manuscripts and handling finances. She also had her own career in radio and TV broadcasting, including hosting her own shows in the 1950s.

British illustrator **Brian Williams** died on October 4, aged 54. After contributing work to the gaming magazine *White Dwarf*, he worked on the interactive *Lone Wolf* series of books by Joe Dever and the spin-off novels by John Grant.

Pioneering Australian bibliographer **Donald H.** (Henry) **Tuck** died on October 11, aged 87. He published *A Handbook of Science Fiction and Fantasy* (1954; revised and expanded 1959) and the three-volume *The Encyclopedia of Science Fiction and Fantasy Through 1968: A Bibliographic Survey of the Fields of Science Fiction, Fantasy, and Weird Fiction Through 1968* (1974, 1978 and 1983), winning a World Fantasy Special Award – Non-Professional and a Hugo Award for the third volume. He was a Guest of Honour at the first Australian World SF Convention in 1975, but was unable to attend.

Prolific Belgium SF writer **Alain le Bussy** died of complications following a throat operation on October 14, aged around 63. A regular Eurocon attendee, he wrote more than thirty novels and was editor of the fanzine *Xuensè*.

*Penthouse* publisher and film producer **Bob Guccione** (Robert Charles Joseph Edward Sabatini Guccione) died after a long battle with lung cancer on October 20, aged 79. Guccione also published the glossy science fiction magazine *Omni*, which ran as a print title from 1978 to 1995, and then in an electronic version for another three years. At one time one of the richest men in America, a series of poor investments eventually resulted in him losing most of his $4 billion fortune.

American TV writer **Coleman Jacoby** (Coleman Jacobs), who scripted the 1958 "Bilko's Vampire" episode of *The Phil Silver's Show*, died of pancreatic cancer the same day, aged 95. His other credits include the 1979 special *The Halloween That Almost Wasn't*, featuring Judd Hirsch as "Count Dracula".

Award-winning British children's author **Eva Ibbotson** also died on October 20, aged 85. Ibbotson was born in Vienna, Austria, and her books for youngsters include *The Great Ghost Rescue*, *The Secret of Platform 13*, *The Star of Kazan*, *Journey to the River Sea*, *The Dragonfly Pool* and *The Ogre of Oglefort*. She won the Romantic Novelists' Association award for her 1982 adult novel *Magic Flutes*.

90-year-old American cartoonist **Alex Anderson Jr**, who co-created the TV characters Rocky and Bullwinkle with Jay Ward and Bill Scott, died after a long battle with Alzheimer's disease on October 22. He was the first artist to draw the adventures of the flying squirrel and his moose friend, but had no involvement in the subsequent TV series. Anderson also worked on "Mighty Mouse" for his uncle Paul Terry's Terrytoons cartoons and, with college friend Ward, he also co-created such characters as "Crusader Rabbit" and "Dudley Do-Right". However, two years after Ward's death, Anderson had to sue Jay Ward Productions to gain official acknowledgement as a co-creator of Rocky, Bullwinkle and Dudley Do-Right.

Swiss-born Swedish artist **Hans Arnold** died on October 25, aged 85. Probably best known for his cover illustration for the *ABBA Greatest Hits* album, Arnold was Sweden's premier horror artist, illustrating numerous stories in the weekly magazines from the 1950s to the 1970s, some of which were later collected in a book on the subject. He also created a popular TV cartoon show, *Matulda och Megasen*, and founded a fan club, the Swedish Horror Academy.

British scriptwriter **Mervyn** [Oliver] **Haisman** who, with writing partner Henry Lincoln, was a credited writer on the 1968 Boris Karloff/Christopher Lee/Barbara Steele film *Curse of the Crimson Altar* (aka *The Crimson Cult*), loosely based on an H.P. Lovecraft story, died of heart failure in Spain on October 29, aged 82. Haisman and Lincoln also scripted "The Abominable Snowman", "The Web of Fear" and "The Dominators" stories for the BBC's *Doctor Who* in the 1960s, creating the "Yeti" monsters and the character of "Colonel Lethbridge-Stewart" portrayed by Nicholas Courtney. Haisman's other credits include the episodic BBC series *Jane*, based on the popular World War II newspaper strip, and the subsequent movie *Jane and the Lost City*, along with the New Zealand TV series *Twist in the Tale* hosted by William Shatner.

Japanese *anime* scriptwriter and novelist **Takeshi Shudo** died of a subarachnoid haemorrhage the same day, aged 61. A winner of the first Anime Grand Prix screenwriting award in 1983, he is credited with turning the *Pokémon* video game into a worldwide phenomenon through TV and movies.

**Glen** [Howard] **GoodKnight** [II], an American Tolkein enthusiast who founded the Mythopoeic Society in 1967 and the annual Mythcon convention in 1970, died on November 3, aged 69. He also edited the society's scholarly journal *Mythlore* (1970–98) and created a monthly news bulletin entitled *Mythprint*. A retired elementary school teacher, GoodKnight (his real name) had been in poor health for several years.

American fan and art collector **Bob** (Robert) **Doyle**, who chaired the 1989 World Fantasy Convention in Seattle, Washington, died of pancreatic problems in November.

British fan and bookseller **Paul** "Gamma" **Gamble** died of kidney failure after a long illness on November 15, aged 61. He worked at London's Forbidden Planet for many years.

American author **John** [William] **Steakley** [Jr] died after a long illness on November 27, aged 59. Best known for his 1990 book *Vampire$*, which was made into a movie by John Carpenter, he sold his first short fiction to *Amazing Stories* in the early 1980s and his first novel, *Armor*, was published in 1984. Steakley was Toastmaster at the 1998 World Horror Convention in Phoenix, Arizona.

Italian-born American comics artist **John P. D'Agostino, Sr** (aka "Jon D'Agostino") died of bone cancer on November 28, aged 81. Best known for his work for Archie Comics, Charlton and Gold Key, he began his career as a colourist at Timely Comics in the 1940s and subsequently worked as an artist on such titles as *Romantic Hearts*, *Dark Mysteries* and *Space Adventures* ("Rocky Jones, Space Ranger"). Under the pseudonym "Johnny Dee" he lettered the first three issues of *The Amazing Spider-Man*, and his later credits at Marvel include issues of *G.I. Joe*, *Marvel Two-in-One* and *A Real American Hero*.

American SF and mystery fan and author **Len J. Moffatt** who, with his wife June, helped found Bouchercon, died on November 30, aged 87. Following World War II, he wrote some stories for the pulp magazines, including "Father's Vampire" (with Alvin Taylor), which appeared in the May 1952 issue of *Weird Tales*. A member of First Fandom, Moffatt also published such fanzines as *JDM Bibliophile* (devoted to the work of John D. MacDonald) and the FAPAzine *Moonshine*.

American TV scriptwriter **Herman Groves** died on December 5, 83. His credits include Disney's *The Whiz Kid and the Mystery at Riverton*, *The Whiz Kid and the Carnival Caper* and *The Strongest Man in the World*, along with episodes of *Lost in Space*, *Bewitched*, *The Bionic Woman*, *Battlestar Galactica* (1978) and *Fantasy Island*.

DC Comics freelance colourist **Adrienne Roy** died after a year-long battle against ovarian cancer on December 14, aged 57. She is best remembered for her sixteen-year run on *Detective Comics* (202 issues, including the 50th anniversary issue featuring Sherlock Holmes), fifteen years on *Batman* (189 issues) and fourteen years with *New Teen Titans*. Her many other credits include *Flash Gordon*, *The Phantom*, *Doc Savage*, *The Shadow Strikes*, *Brave and the Bold*, *Gotham Knights*, *Shadow of the Bat* and *Crisis on Infinite Earths*. During her more than two-decade career at DC she coloured more than 50,000 pages of art and her name appeared on more *Batman* comics than anybody other than creator Bob Kane. She was also the centrefold in the first issue of *Tattoo* magazine.

New Zealand-born Australian author **Ruth Park**, whose children's books include the time-travel fantasy *Playing Beatie Bow* (1980) died on December 16, aged 93.

American scriptwriter **Norm Liebmann**, who co-wrote and developed the CBS-TV series *The Munsters* (1964–66), died on December 20. In 1968 he scripted the half-hour pilot *Mad Mad Scientist* (aka *Guess What I Did Today?*) for NBC, which also starred Fred Gwynne.

French-born British children's author **Elisabeth Beresford** MBE, who is best known for creating "The Wombles", died in the Channel Islands on December 24, aged 84. The eco-friendly furry characters appeared in numerous books, two TV series and even a movie, *Wombling Free* (1977). Beresford also wrote the "Magic" series, beginning with *Awkward Magic* in 1964, and she created the 1990 ITV series *Bertie the Bat*.

## PERFORMERS/PERSONALITIES

Japanese actor **Tetsuo Narikawa**, who starred as the alter-ego of the cybernetic super-hero in the 1970s TV series *Spectreman*, died on January 1, aged 65.

Pioneering French-born female comedienne **Jean Carroll** (Celine Zeigman), who played one of the mermaids in John Lamb's *Mermaids of Tiburon* (1962), died in a New York hospital the same day, aged 98. She also appeared in *The Legend of Lylah Clare* and an early episode of Boris Karloff's *Thriller*.

English-born Irish actor **Donal Donnelly** died of cancer in Chicago, Illinois, on January 4, aged 78. Best known for co-starring in the 1965 comedy *The Knack . . . and How to Get It*, he also appeared in episodes of TV's *The New Adventures of Charlie Chan*, *The Avengers*, *Out of the Unknown* and *Orson Welles' Great Mysteries*.

86-year-old Mexican actress **Beatriz** [Eugenia] **Baz,** who co-starred with Boris Karloff in *House of Evil* (1968), died in El Paso, Texas, on January 5.

**Beverly** [Elaine] **Aadland,** who earned notoriety as Errol

Flynn's last girlfriend, died of complications of diabetes and congestive heart failure the same day, aged 67. Starting when she was fifteen years old, the 34-28-34 dancer had a torrid two-year affair with the actor that ended with his death at the age of 50.

American adult film star **Juliet Anderson** (Juliet Carr), who appeared on screen as "Aunt Peg", died on January 11, aged 71. She had suffered from Crohn's disease for most of her life. Her numerous credits include *The Beast That Killed Women*, *Fantasex Island* and *Tattoo Vampire*. Anderson later became one of the first female producers of X-rated movies.

New Zealand actress **Elizabeth Moody**, best remembered as the flesh-eating mother in Peter Jackson's 1992 zombie comedy *Braindead* (aka *Dead Alive*), died on January 12, aged 70. She also appeared in *The Scarecrow* (featuring John Carradine), *Turn of the Blade* and Jackson's *Heavenly Creatures*, along with the extended version of *The Lord of the Rings: The Fellowship of the Ring*.

Hollywood stuntman and actor **Fred "Crunch" Krone** (Fredrick A. Krone) died of cancer the same day, aged 79. Although he worked predominantly in the Western genre, his credits also include *Hand of Death*, Disney's *The Love Bug*, and *Megaforce*, along with episodes of such TV shows as *Captain Midnight*, *The Green Hornet*, *I Dream of Jeannie*, *Lost in Space* (playing various monsters) and *Search Control*.

R&B singer **Teddy Pendergrass** (Theodore DeReese Pendergrass) died of complications from colon cancer on January 13, aged 59. A car accident in 1982 left him paralysed from the chest down, but he continued to perform from a wheelchair. In the early 1970s he was the lead singer with Harold Melvin & the Blue Notes, who had hits with "If You Don't Know Me by Now", "The Love I Lost" and "Don't Leave Me This Way". After going solo in 1977, Pendergrass released a number of successful albums and, despite announcing his retirement in 2006, continued to perform up to November 2008.

British actor **Mark Jones**, who played an Imperial Officer in the *Star Wars* sequel *The Empire Strikes Back*, died on January 14, aged 70. His other credits include Peter Brooks' *Marat/Sade*, *The Sexplorer* (aka *Girl from Starship Venus*), *The Medusa*

*Touch, Don't Open Till Christmas* and episodes of TV's *A.D.A.M.*, *Doctor Who* ("The Seeds of Doom"), *The New Avengers*, *Tales of the Unexpected* and *Red Dwarf*.

63-year-old Canadian folk singer-songwriter **Kate McGarrigle**, best known for her work with sister Anna, died of clear-cell sarcoma, a rare form of cancer, on January 18. At one time she was married to American musician Loudon Wainwright III.

British film star **Jean [Merilyn] Simmons** OBE died of lung cancer on January 22, just over a week before her 81st birthday. Her many movies include *Meet Sexton Blake*, *Great Expectations* (both 1946 and 1991 versions), *Black Narcissus*, *Uncle Silas* (based on the novel by Sheridan Le Fanu), *Hamlet* (1948, as the doomed "Ophelia"), *So Long at the Fair*, *Footsteps in the Fog*, *Mr Sycamore*, *Dominique* (aka *Dominique is Dead*) and the mini-series *The Dain Curse*. In recent years she contributed voice work to *Final Fantasy: The Spirits Within*, *Howl's Moving Castle* (based on the novel by Diana Wynne Jones) and *Thru the Moebius Strip*. On TV Simmons appeared in an episode of the 1980s *Alfred Hitchcock Presents*, the 1990s revival of *Dark Shadows* (as "Elizabeth Collins Stoddard") and *Star Trek: The Next Generation*. She became a US citizen in 1956, and was married to actor Stewart Granger (1950–60) and writer/director Richard Brooks (1960–77).

American character actor and director **Johnny Seven** (John Anthony Fetto II, aka "John Seven") died of lung cancer the same day, a month before his 84th birthday. He appeared in such TV shows as *Inner Sanctum*, *One Step Beyond*, *Batman*, *Get Smart* and *The Wild Wild West*. Seven also appeared in the 1968 sci-spy film *The Destructors*.

American actor and dancer **James Mitchell**, best known for his role as scheming tycoon "Palmer Cortlandt, Sr." in more than 400 episodes of the ABC-TV daytime soap opera *All My Children*, died of chronic obstructive pulmonary disease on January 22. He was 89. Mitchell also appeared in *White Savage* (aka *White Captive*) and the 1943 *Phantom of the Opera* (uncredited).

American TV actor and singer **Pernell Roberts** (Pernell Elvin Roberts, Jr), who starred in both *Bonanza* and the *M\*A\*S\*H* spin-off *Trapper John, M.D.*, died of pancreatic cancer on January 24, aged 81. He also appeared in episodes of *Shirley*

*Temple Theatre, One Step Beyond, The Girl from U.N.C.L.E., The Wild Wild West, Night Gallery, The Sixth Sense, The Six Million Dollar Man, Man from Atlantis* and the 1989 mini-series *Around the World in 80 Days.*

Diminutive character actress **Zelda Rubinstein**, who played eccentric psychic "Tangina" in *Poltergeist* (1982) and its two sequels, *Poltergeist II: The Other Side* and *Poltergeist III*, died of complications from a heart attack on January 27, aged 76. Rubinstein was also in *Anguish, Teen Witch, Timemaster, Little Witches, Sinbad: The Battle of the Dark Knights, Wishcraft, Angels with Angles* and *Southland Tales*, along with episodes of TV's *Whiz Kids, Faerie Tale Theatre, Tales from the Crypt, Poltergeist: The Legacy* and *The Pretender*. She voiced "Atrocia Frankenstone" in an episode of *The Flintstone Comedy Show*, narrated the Fox Family Channel series *The Scariest Places on Earth*, and appeared as herself in the video footage preceding Universal Studios' disappointing Revenge of the Mummy: The Ride.

Irish-born stuntman **Martin Grace** died of an aneurysm in a hospital in Spain the same day. He was 67, and had been injured in a cycling accident a couple of months earlier. After playing one of the Thals in *Dr. Who and the Daleks* (starring Peter Cushing), Grace became a stuntman on the James Bond series, starting with *You Only Live Twice* and continuing through *Live and Let Die* and *The Man with the Golden Gun*. With *The Spy Who Loved Me*, he became Roger Moore's stunt double, a role he repeated in *Moonraker, For Your Eyes Only, Octopussy* and *A View to a Kill*. His many other films include Hammer's *Moon Zero Two, Horror Hospital, Superman* (1978), *Raiders of the Lost Ark, Indiana Jones and the Temple of Doom, Brazil, Enemy Mine, Willow, High Spirits, Indiana Jones and the Last Crusade, Erik the Viking, The NeverEnding Story II* and *Afraid of the Dark*. He also worked on the TV series *Space: 1999.*

American actress **Helen Talbot** (Helen Darling) died on January 29, aged 85. She had a small role in *The Lady and the Monster* (aka *The Lady and the Doctor*) and starred in the Republic serials *Operator 99* and *King of the Forest Rangers*. Talbot retired from the screen in 1945.

British actress and singer **Paddie O'Neil** OBE (Adalena Lillian Nail), who was married to actor Alfred Marks from 1952 until his death in 1996, died on January 31, aged 83. She appeared in episodes of TV's *Rentaghost*, *Woof!* and *Virtual Murder*.

**Justin Mentell**, who appeared in *G-Force* (2009), was killed on February 1 when his jeep veered off a highway in rural Wisconsin and hit two trees. The 27-year-old actor was not wearing a seatbelt at the time.

American character actor **Bernard Kates** died of sepsis and pneumonia on February 2, aged 87. His film credits include *Seedpeople*, *The Phantom* (1996) and *Robo Warriors*. On TV he was in episodes of *Suspense*, *Captain Video and His Video Rangers*, *One Step Beyond*, *Shirley Temple's Storybook*, *Alfred Hitchcock Presents*, *The Outer Limits*, *Star Trek: The Next Generation* (as "Dr Sigmund Freud") and *3rd Rock from the Sun*.

Australian actor, screenwriter, producer and director **John** [Neil] **McCallum** CBE, who was married to actress Googie Withers since 1948, died on February 3, aged 91. He starred with his wife in the British mermaid comedy *Miranda*.

American actress **Frances Reid**, who starred as matriarch "Alice Horton" in NBC's daytime soap opera *Days of Our Lives* for forty-four years, died the same day, aged 95. She also appeared in *Seconds*, *The Andromeda Strain* (1971), and episodes of TV's *Lights Out*, *Hallmark Hall of Fame* ("Berkeley Square"), *Alfred Hitchcock Presents*, *The Alfred Hitchcock Hour*, *Matt Helm* and *Project U.F.O.*

British character actor **Ian** [Gillett] **Carmichael** OBE, best remembered for playing upper-class Englishmen (including "Bertie Wooster" and "Lord Peter Wimsey" on TV), died after a short illness on February 4, aged 89. He appeared in the films *Ghost Ship* (1952), *Meet Mr Lucifer*, *The Magnificent Seven Deadly Sins*, *From Beyond the Grave* (based on stories by R. Chetwynd-Hayes) and Hammer Films' 1979 remake of *The Lady Vanishes*. Carmichael was also the narrator of the 1980s Cosgrove Hall series *The Wind in the Willows* and *Oh! Mr Toad*.

Italian actor **Peter Martell** (Pietro Martellanza) died the same day, aged 72. His many credits include *War Between the Planets*, *Night of the Blood Monster* (with Christopher Lee) and *Momo*. After a career slump that was highlighted by the 1999 documentary *Starring Peter Martell*, the actor returned to the screen as "Dracula" in Jess Franco's *Killer Barbys vs. Dracula* in 2002, and he also appeared in the German horror movies *Tears of Kali* and *The Angels' Melancholia*.

British jazz saxophonist Sir **John**(ny) [Phillip William] **Dankworth** died after a long illness on February 6, aged 82. He composed the music for *Morgan: A Suitable Case for Treatment* (aka *Morgan!*), *Modesty Blaise* (1966), *The Magus* and *10 Rillington Place*, as well as the now-forgotten ATV series *The Voodoo Factor* and the original theme for *The Avengers*. Dankworth was married to jazz singer Cleo Laine since 1958.

American stuntman and actor **Robert F.** (Frances) **Hoy** (aka "Bob Hoy") died of pneumonia on February 8, aged 82. Best known for his recurring role as "Joe Butler" in TV's *The High Chaparral*, he also appeared (often uncredited) in *Revenge of the Creature*, *The Mole People*, *Man of a Thousand Faces*, Disney's *The Love Bug*, *Earth II*, *Scream Blacula Scream*, *The Astral Factor* (aka *Invisible Strangler*), *Helter Skelter* (1976), *The Legend of the Lone Ranger* and *The Return of the Six Million Dollar Man and the Bionic Woman*, along with episodes of *The Man from U.N.C.L.E.*, *The Green Hornet*, *Star Trek*, *Night Gallery*, *Search*, *Matt Helm*, *Future Cop*, *The Six Million Dollar Man*, *Fantasy Island*, *The New Adventures of Wonder Woman*, *Salvage 1*, *B.J. and the Bear* ("A Coffin with a View" featuring John Carradine) and *Beauty and the Beast*. Hoy co-founded the Stuntmen's Association of Motion Pictures in 1961 and was a lifetime member of the organisation.

American actress **Caroline** [Margaret] **McWilliams**, who starred in the short-lived supernatural sit-com *Nearly Departed* (1989) with Eric Idle, died of complications of multiple myeloma on February 11, aged 64. Her credits include episodes of *The Incredible Hulk*, *Project U.F.O.*, *Lois & Clark: The New Adventures of Superman* and the TV movie *The Aliens Are Coming*.

British Guiana-born actor and calypso singer **Cy Grant** died on February 13, aged 90. Best remembered as the voice of "Lieutenant Green" in TV's *Captain Scarlet and the Mysterons*, Grant appeared in the films *Doppelgänger* (aka *Journey to the Far Side of the Sun*), *Shaft in Africa* and *At the Earth's Core* (with Peter Cushing), along with episodes of *Blakes 7* and *Metal Mickey*.

British stuntman and character actor **Max Faulkner** died the same day, aged 78. He appeared (often uncredited) in *Behemoth the Sea Monster* (aka *The Giant Behemoth*), *Dr Crippen*, *The Ipcress File*, *Bedazzled* (1967), *Blind Terror* (aka *See No Evil*), *Trial by Combat* (aka *A Dirty Knight's Work*), *Krull*, Clive Barker's *Nightbreed* and the James Bond film *GoldenEye*, along with episodes of TV's *The Prisoner*, *Randall and Hopkirk (Deceased)*, *Doctor Who*, *The Rivals of Sherlock Holmes*, *Space: 1999*, *Survivors* (1977), *Blakes 7*, *The Day of the Triffids* (1981), *The Adventures of Sherlock Holmes* and *Robin of Sherwood*.

**Doug Fieger** (Douglas Lars Fieger), lead singer, songwriter and rhythm guitarist with Los Angeles power pop band The Knack, died of metastatic lung cancer on February 14, aged 57. The group's 1979 hit "My Sharona" topped the US charts for six weeks.

British TV character actor **George** [Edward] **Waring**, who appeared in five different roles in *Coronation Street*, died of cancer on February 15. He was 84. Waring also appeared in episodes of the now-forgotten BBC SF series *The Big Pull* (1962), *Doctor Who* ("The Ice Warriors"), *Doomwatch*, *Survivors* and the 1970s children's horror anthology series *Shadows*.

Delightful British character actor and director **Lionel** [Charles] **Jeffries** died on February 19, aged 83. After making an uncredited appearance in Alfred Hitchcock's *Stage Fright*, he appeared in *The Black Rider*, Hammer's *The Quatermass Xperiment* (aka *The Creeping Unknown*), *The Revenge of Frankenstein*, *The Scarlet Blade*, *Tarzan the Magnificent* (with John Carradine), *First Men in the Moon* (opposite Ray Harryhausen's Lunar inhabitants), *Oh Dad Poor Dad Mama's Hung You in the Closet and I'm Feeling So Sad*, *Rocket to the Moon* (aka *Those Fantastic Flying Fools*), *Chitty Chitty Bang Bang*, *Whoever Slew Auntie Roo?* and the 1990 TV movie *Jekyll & Hyde*. He was also a regular on the children's fantasy series *Woof!* and turned up in a vampire episode of *Lexx*. As a writer-director, Jeffries' credits include *The Railway Children*, *The Amazing Mr Blunden*, *Wombling Free* and *The Water Babies*.

Adult film star and director **Jamie Gillis** (James Ira Gurman), who portrayed a hardcore "Count Dracula" in *Dracula Sucks* and *Dracula Exotica*, died of cancer the same day, aged 66. As an aspiring theatre actor and mime artist he entered the porn film industry in the early 1970s and appeared (often under various pseudonyms) in more than 500 films and "loops" before he retired from the screen at the end of 2007. His numerous credits (not all porn) include *Devil's Due*, *Hypnorotica*, *Invasion of the Love Drones*, *Night of the Zombies*, *Pandora's Mirror*, *Pleasure Zone*, *Blue Voodoo*, *Erotic Zone*, *Ten Little Maidens*, *Deranged*, *The Dark Angel*, *The Phantom of the Cabaret* and *The Phantom of the Cabaret II* (both as "The Phantom"), *Alien Space Avenger*, *Robo Fox II: The Collector*, *Mummy Dearest*, *Curse of the Catwoman*, *Forever Night*, *Dark Garden* and *Die You Zombie Bastards!*

American character actor and voice artist **Sandy Kenyon** (Sanford Klein) died on February 20, aged 87. He appeared in *When Time Ran Out . . .*, *The Loch Ness Horror*, *Lifepod* and episodes of TV's *Steve Canyon*, *One Step Beyond*, *Thriller*, *The Twilight Zone*, *The Outer Limits*, *The Wild Wild West*, *The Invaders* and *The Bionic Woman*.

Welsh actor **Robin Davies** (Robert Richard Davies) died of lung cancer on February 22, aged 56. A former child actor, he appeared in *If . . .*, *The Blood of Satan's Claw* (aka *Satan's Skin*), *Britannia Hospital*, the first season of TV's *Catweazle* and an episode of *Doomwatch*.

The body of [Joshua] **Andrew Koenig**, the son of *Star Trek* actor Walter Koenig, was discovered in a densely wooded area of the 1,000-acre Stanley Park in Vancouver, Canada, on February 25. The 41-year-old actor and film-maker had been reported missing by his family on the 16th, and it was subsequently determined that he had committed suicide by hanging a couple of days before his body was found. Koenig suffered from depression and had reportedly stopped taking his medication. He had small roles in the SF movie *InAlienable* (scripted by his father) and an episode of TV's *Star Trek: Deep Space Nine*. He also played "The Joker" in the 2003 short film *Batman: Dead End*.

American character actor **Richard Devon**, who played "Satan"

516   STEPHEN JONES & KIM NEWMAN

in Roger Corman's *The Undead* (1957), died of vascular disease on February 26, aged 83. Devon was also in Corman's *The Saga of the Viking Women and Their Voyage to the Waters of the Great Sea Serpent* and *War of the Satellites*, and his other credits include *Blood of Dracula* (aka *Blood is My Heritage*), *The Three Stooges Go Around the World in a Daze*, *The Silencers*, *The Seventh Sign* and episodes of TV's *Space Patrol*, *One Step Beyond*, *The Twilight Zone*, *The Monkees*, *Get Smart*, *Planet of the Apes* and *Quark*.

Busy British character actor and Shakespearean artist **Martin [Benjamin] Benson** died on February 28, aged 91. Best remembered for his role as American gangster "Mr Solo" in the James Bond movie *Goldfinger*, he also appeared in *The Strange World of Planet X* (aka *Cosmic Monsters*), *The 3 Worlds of Gulliver*, *Gorgo*, Hammer's *Captain Clegg* (aka *Night Creatures*, with Peter Cushing), *Battle Beneath the Earth* and *The Omen*, along with episodes of TV's *Colonel March of Scotland Yard* (with Boris Karloff), *The New Adventures of Charlie Chan*, *Invisible Man* (1959), *One Step Beyond*, *The Champions*, *Thriller* (1976), *Tales of the Unexpected* and *The Hitch Hiker's Guide to the Galaxy* (as the "Vogon Captain").

Tony Award-nominated American stage and screen actress **Nan [Clow] Martin** died of complications from emphysema on March 4, aged 82. A former fashion model, her film credits include *A Nightmare on Elm Street III: Dream Warriors* (as Freddy Krueger's mother) and *Last Gasp*, and she appeared in episodes of *The Twilight Zone* (both the original and revived series), *The Invaders*, *Bewitched*, *The Sixth Sense*, *Star Trek: The Next Generation*, *Harry and the Hendersons*, *The Adventures of Brisco County Jr.* and *The Invisible Man* (2000). Her son, Zen Gesner, starred in the South African TV series *The Adventures of Sinbad* (1996–98).

British-born leading man **Richard Stapley** (aka "Richard Wyler") died of kidney failure in Palm Springs, California, on March 5, aged 86. As hero "Denis de Beaulieu" he starred opposite Charles Laughton and Boris Karloff in *The Strange Door* (1951), and he also appeared in the "Jungle Jim" movie *Jungle Man-Eaters*, Jess Franco's *The Girl from Rio* (aka *Future Women/Rio 70*), *Dick Smart 2007* and Alfred Hitchcock's *Frenzy* (uncredited).

British actress **Carol Marsh** (Norma Lilian Simpson), best known for her role as "Lucy" opposite Christopher Lee's Count in Hammer's *Dracula* (aka *Horror of Dracula*), died on March 6, aged 84. She also appeared in *Brighton Rock*, *Alice in Wonderland* (1949), *Helter Skelter*, *The Tempest* (1951) and *Scrooge* (1951). Marsh continued to appear on TV until the mid-1970s.

Troubled Canadian-born actor **Corey** [Ian] **Haim** died in a Burbank, California, hospital of pulmonary oedema (thickening of the heart muscles) on March 10. He was 38 and had battled drug and alcohol problems for years. As a child actor he co-starred as "Sam" in the cult vampire movie *The Lost Boys* (1987), and his other credits include *Silver Bullet* (based on the novella by Stephen King), *Watchers* (based on the novel by Dean R. Koontz), *Dream a Little Dream*, *Prayer of the Rollerboys*, *The Double 0 Kid*, *Double Switch*, *Dream a Little Dream 2*, *Fever Lake*, *Merlin* (1998), *The Back Lot Murders*, *Lost Boys: The Tribe*, *Crank: High Voltage* and an episode of *PSI Factor: Chronicles of the Paranormal*.

Singer and actress **Evelyn** [Mildred] **Dall** (Evelyn Mildred Fuss), the American-born "Blonde Bombshell" who appeared in a few 1930s and '40s musical-comedy films on both sides of the Atlantic, died the same day, aged 92. Her credits include *King Arthur Was a Gentleman* (with Arthur Askey) and the time-travel comedy *Time Flies* (with Tommy Handley).

American NFL football star-turned-actor **Merlin Olsen** died of malignant pleural mesothelioma on March 11, aged 69. A former player with the Los Angeles Rams, he went on to portray "Jonathan Garvey" in TV's *Little House on the Prairie* and appeared in the 1978 TV movie *A Fire in the Sky*.

Hollywood leading man **Peter Graves** (Peter Duesler Aurness), best remembered for his role as "Jim Phelps" on both the 1960s and 1980s series of TV's *Mission Impossible*, died of a heart attack on March 14, four days before his 84th birthday. The younger brother of actor James Arness, Graves also appeared in *Red Planet Mars*, *Killers from Space*, *The Night of the Hunter* (1955), Roger Corman's *It Conquered the World*, *Beginning of the End*, *Scream of the Wolf* (based on the story by David Case), *Where Have All the People Gone*, *The Clonus Horror*, *Death*

*Car on the Freeway*, *Addams Family Values* and *Looney Tunes: Back in Action*, along with episodes of *The Invaders*, *Fantasy Island*, *Buck Rodgers in the 25th Century* and *Hammer House of Mystery and Suspense* ("Tennis Court").

American character actor and vocal teacher **Lisle Wilson** died the same day, aged 66. He appeared in *Sisters* (aka *Blood Sisters*), *The Incredible Melting Man* and episodes of TV's *ALF* and *Tales from the Crypt*.

Diminutive three-foot, one-inch character actor **David Joseph Steinberg** died on March 15, aged 45. He played the loyal "Meegosh" in *Willow*, and his other movie credits include *Epic Movie* and *Transylmania*, along with episodes of TV's *Are You Afraid of the Dark?* and *Charmed*.

**Alex Chilton**, singer and guitarist with the influential early 1970s rock goup Big Star, died of a heart attack on March 17, aged 59. Chilton was also a former member of the Box Tops.

American leading man **Fess Parker** (Fess Elisha Parker, Jr), who starred as both frontiersmen "Davy Crockett" and "Daniel Boone" on TV, died on March 18, aged 85. The theme song "The Ballad of Davy Crockett" from the 1950s Disney TV series *Davy Crockett, King of the Wild Frontier* was #1 for sixteen weeks. Parker began his career as the voice of the chauffeur in *Harvey* (1950) and he went on to appear in *Them!* and an episode of *The Alfred Hitchcock Hour*. He retired from the screen in 1974 and went into the lucrative real-estate business.

American Doo-Wop singer **Johnny Maestro** (John Peter Mastrangelo) died of cancer on March 24, aged 70. As lead singer for the Crests he is best remembered for the hit teen anthem "16 Candles" (which reached #2 in the US charts in 1958). Maestro later sang with such groups as the Del-Satins and the Brooklyn Bridge.

45-year-old American actor and producer **John** [Patrick] **McGarr** was killed on the morning of March 25 while attending a horror film convention in Indianapolis when he was hit by a car being driven by a drunk driver. His credits include *House of the Wolf Man* and *Mondo Holocausto!*

**Robert** [Martin] **Culp**, who starred as debonair secret agent "Kelly Robinson" opposite Bill Cosby on NBC-TV's *I Spy*

(1965–68), died on March 26, aged 79. He apparently suffered a heart attack while out walking and died from head injuries he sustained in the fall. A former cartoonist, he appeared in *Silent Night Deadly Night III: Better Watch Out!*, *Xtro 3: Watch the Skies*, *Santa's Slay* and the TV movies *Now is Tomorrow*, *A Name for Evil*, *A Cold Night's Death*, Gene Roddenberry's pilot *Spectre*, *Calendar Girl Murders* and the 1994 reunion *I Spy Returns*. Culp also co-starred as CIA agent "Bill Maxwell" on ABC's *The Greatest American Hero* (1981–86), and he appeared in episodes of *Alfred Hitchcock Presents*, *Shirley Temple Theatre* ("The House of the Seven Gables"), *The Alfred Hitchcock Hour*, *The Outer Limits* (including Harlan Ellison's "Demon with a Glass Hand"), *The Man from U.N.C.L.E.*, *Get Smart*, *Highway to Heaven*, *The Ray Bradbury Theatre*, *The New Adventures of Superman*, *Viper*, *Conan* ("Red Sonja") and *The Dead Zone*. He was married five times, including to actress France Nuyen for three years in the late 1960s.

Canadian-born Hollywood actress, singer and playwright **June Havoc** (Ellen Evangeline Hovick), died in Stamford, Connecticut, on March 28, aged 97. A former vaudeville child star (as "Baby June") with her older sister, Rose Louise (aka stripper "Gypsy Rose Lee"), she appeared in *A Return to Salem's Lot* and an episode of *The Outer Limits*. It has been speculated that Havoc's estranged relationship with her sister was the inspiration for Henry Farrell's 1960 novel *What Ever Happened to Baby Jane?*

American actor **John Forsythe** (John Lincoln Freund), the voice of the unseen "Charles Townsend" on the ABC-TV series *Charlie's Angels* and the subsequent two movies, died of complications from pneumonia on April 1, aged 92. He appeared in Alfred Hitchcock's *The Trouble with Harry*, *In Cold Blood*, *Cruise Into Terror*, *Mysterious Two* and *Scrooged* (as a zombie). Forsythe also portrayed patriarch "Blake Carrington" on *Dynasty* for eight years, and his other credits include episodes of *Kraft Theatre* ("Wuthering Heights"), *Suspense*, *Alfred Hitchcock Presents* and *The Alfred Hitchcock Hour*.

**Buddy Gorman**, who temporarily replaced Bennie Bartlett as "Butch" in several Bowery Boys/Dead End Kids movies in the early 1950s, died the same day, aged 88. He appeared in

*Whistling in Brooklyn*, the 1945 serial *The Master Key*, *The Perils of Pauline* (1947) and the Bowery Boys comedy *Ghost Chasers*. After retiring from the screen, Gorman and his wife opened a magic and novelty store in Los Angeles.

American navy Vice Admiral **Chuck Griffiths** (Charles Henry Griffiths), who played Kenneth Tobey's executive officer on board the submarine in *It Came from Beneath the Sea* (1955), also died on April 1, aged 88.

Former WWE and WWF wrestler **Chris "Champagne" Kanyon** (Chris Klucsaritis, aka "Mortis"), one of the first openly gay American professional wrestlers, committed suicide by overdosing on medication in his New York apartment on April 2. He was 40 years old and suffered from a recently diagnosed bipolar disorder.

British actor and playwright **Corin** [William] **Redgrave**, the middle brother of Vanessa and Lynn, died after a short illness on April 6, aged 70. He appeared on the screen in *A Study in Terror* (uncredited), *The Magus*, *Excalibur*, *The Woman in White* (1997), *Doctor Sleep* (aka *Close Your Eyes*) and episodes of *The Avengers*, *Mystery and Imagination* (as "Jonathan Harker" in "Dracula") and *Ultraviolet*. His final role was in the 2009 BBC TV movie of Henry James' *The Turn of the Screw*, playing the same role his father, Michael, did in the 1961 adaptation, *The Innocents*. Redgrave's second wife was actress Kika Markham.

28-year-old American stuntwoman **April** [Erin] **Stirton** was killed in a motorcycle accident in Los Angeles the same day. Her credits include *The Dead Undead* (starring Luke Goss and Forrest J Ackerman!), Clint Eastwood's *Hereafter* and an episode of TV's *True Blood*.

Canadian actor **Eddie Carroll**, who had been the voice of Disney's "Jiminy Cricket" from 1973 onwards, died of a brain tumour on April 6. He was 76.

British actor **Christopher Cazenove** (Christopher de Lerisson Cazenove), best known to American audiences as "Ben Carrington" in *Dynasty*, died of septicaemia on April 7, aged 64. He reportedly began drinking heavily after the death of his eldest son in a road accident in 1999. The son of a brigadier in the Coldstream Guards, Cazenove appeared in the TV movie *Dead*

*Man's Island* and episodes of *The Rivals of Sherlock Holmes*, *Thriller* (1974), *Hammer House of Horror* ("Children of the Full Moon"), *Hammer House of Mystery and Suspense*, *Tales from the Crypt* and *Charmed*. Cazenove was married to actress Angharad Rees from 1973 to 1994.

Austrian-born British actor **James Aubrey** [Tregidgo], who made his memorable screen debut as the feral schoolboy "Ralph" in *Lord of the Flies* (1963), died of pancreatitis on April 8, aged 62. Ten years after his first film, he returned to the screen in *The Sex Thief* (which was released in the US in an X-rated version), and followed it with appearances in Norman J. Warren's *Terror*, *The Hunger*, *The American Way* (aka *Riders of the Storm*), *The Rift*, *A Demon in My View* and episodes of *Tales of the Unexpected* and *Worlds Beyond*.

We must aver, he's really most sincerely dead: four-foot, seven-inch **Meinhardt** [Frank] **Raabe**, who played the uncredited "Munchkin Coroner" who examined The Wicked Witch of the West in *The Wizard of Oz* (1939) died of a heart attack on April 9, aged 94. For thirty years, as "Little Oscar, the World's Smallest Chef", he worked as a spokesperson for the Oscar Mayer hot dog company.

Likeable American TV actor **Peter** [Abraham] **Haskell** died of a heart attack on April 12, aged 75. His credits include the TV movies *The Eyes of Charles Sand*, *The Phantom of Hollywood*, *The Suicide Club* and *Mandrake*, along with episodes of TV's *The Outer Limits*, *The Man from U.N.C.L.E.*, *The Green Hornet*, *Land of the Giants*, *The Bionic Woman*, *Fantasy Island* and the 1980s remake of *Alfred Hitchcock Presents*. Haskell also appeared in the movies *Child's Play 2*, *Child's Play 3* and *Robot Wars*.

American character actor **Robert Brubaker** died on April 15, aged 93. He appeared (often uncredited) in the movies *Man of a Thousand Faces* (as *Unholy Three* director "Jack Conway"), *Seven Days in May*, *Seconds* and *The Brotherhood of the Bell*, along with episodes of TV's *Steve Canyon*, *Men Into Space*, *The Twilight Zone*, *Moon Pilot*, *The Outer Limits*, *The Man from U.N.C.L.E.*, *Voyage to the Bottom of the Sea*, *Tarzan*, *The Invaders*, *The Sixth Sense* and *Search Control*.

Memorable American character actor **Michael Pataki**, who

portrayed both the Count and his ancestor in *Dracula's Dog* (aka *Zoltan, Hound of Dracula*), died of cancer on April 16, aged 72. Pataki also played another bloodsucker in *Grave of the Vampire* (aka *Seed of Evil*), and his other credits include *Dream No Evil*, *The Return of Count Yorga*, *The Baby*, *The Bat People*, *Love at First Bite*, *Graduation Day*, *Dead & Buried*, *Remo: The Adventure Begins* (aka *Remo: Unarmed and Dangerous*), *Death House* and *Halloween 4: The Return of Michael Myers*. On TV he appeared in episodes of *The Twilight Zone*, *My Favorite Martian*, *Voyage to the Bottom of the Sea*, *Batman*, *Mr Terrific*, *Star Trek* (he was apparently the first character on the show to speak Klingon), *The Flying Nun* (in a recurring role), *The Sixth Sense*, *The Invisible Man*, *The Amazing Spider-Man* (as regular "Capt. Barbera"), *Beyond Westworld*, *Automan*, *Star Trek: The Next Generation* and *The Highwayman*. Pataki also directed two films for Charles Band: the cult horror movie *Mansion of the Doomed* (aka *The Terror of Dr Chaney*) and the softcore musical comedy *Cinderella* (aka *The Other Cinderella*), plus an episode of TV's *The Hardy Boys/Nancy Drew Mysteries*.

Scottish actor and poet **Tom Fleming** OBE (Thomas Kelman Fleming), who appeared in a 1954 BBC adaptation of John Buchan's *Witch Wood*, died on April 18, aged 82. More famously, as the "Voice of the BBC", he was the commentator for the TV coverage of the Queen's coronation, the Silver Jubilee, the enthronement of two Popes and Princess Diana's funeral.

American stuntman and actor **Mike Adams** (Michael Gene Adams) a former President of the Stuntman's Association of Motion Pictures, died of a stroke the same day, aged 60. His numerous credits include *The Manitou*, *Prophecy*, *The Sword and the Sorcerer*, *Spacehunter: Adventures in the Forbidden Zone*, *WarGames*, *My Science Project*, *Ratboy*, *RoboCop 2* and *RoboCop 3*, *Mr Destiny*, *Coneheads*, *Mighty Joe Young* (1998), *Herbie Fully Loaded* and *Dark Moon Rising* (aka *Wolf Moon*).

American voice and character actor **Allen Swift** (Ira Stadlen) died of complications from a fall on April 18, aged 86. He contributed a number of voices (including Dracula's) to the cartoon movies *Mad Monster Party?* and *The Mad, Mad, Mad Monsters*, amongst numerous other credits.

Sparkling blonde actress, dancer and commediene [Michele] **Dorothy Provine** died of emphysema on April 25, aged 75. Best remembered for her role in *The 30 Foot Bride of Candy Rock* (opposite a solo Lou Costello in his last film), she also appeared in *It's a Mad Mad Mad Mad World*, *One Spy Too Many*, *Kiss the Girls and Make Them Die*, and episodes of *Alfred Hitchcock Presents* and *The Man from U.N.C.L.E.* She mostly retired from the screen in 1968, after marrying British-born director Robert Day.

American actress **Helen Wagner**, who had played "Nancy Hughes" on the CBS daytime soap opera *As the World Turns* for a record-breaking fifty-four years, died on May 1, aged 91. In 1954 she appeared in two episodes of *Inner Sactum*.

53-year-old American stuntman, actor and film-maker **Danny Aiello III**, the son of actor Danny Aiello, died of pancreatic cancer the same day. His many credits include *Splash*, *A Return to Salem's Lot*, *Ghostbusters II*, *Jacob's Ladder*, *Kate & Leopold*, *Stuart Little 2*, *13 Going on 30*, *The Forgotten*, *The Invasion*, *Halloween II* (2009), *The Box* and episodes of the US TV version of *Life on Mars*.

Less than a month after the death of her older brother Corin, **Lynn [Rachel] Redgrave** OBE died of breast cancer on May 2, aged 67. Her credits include *Every Thing You Always Wanted to Know About Sex\* \*But Were Afraid to Ask*, *The Turn of the Screw* (1974), *The Happy Hooker*, *Disco Beaver from Outer Space* (as "Dr Van Helsing"), *The Bad Seed* (1985), *Midnight*, *What Ever Happened to Baby Jane?* (1991), *Toothless*, *Gods and Monsters*, *The Lion of Oz* (as the voice of "The Wicked Witch of the East"), David Cronenberg's *Spider*, *Hansel & Gretel* (2002), *Peter Pan* (2003), and two episodes of TV's *Fantasy Island*.

Japanese actor **Kei Satô** (Keinosuke Sato) died the same day, aged 81. His many credits include *Onibaba*, *Kaidan*, *Kuroneko*, *Curse of the Ghost* and the 1984 *Godzilla*.

Prolific British character actor **Jimmy Gardner** (Edward Charles James Gardner) died on May 3, aged 85. Playwright John Osborne's personal driver before he became an actor, Gardner appeared in Hammer's *The Curse of the Mummy's Tomb*, *10 Rillington Place*, Hitchcock's *Frenzy*, *The Company* *of Wolves, Harry Potter and the Prisoner of Azkaban* (as "Ernie, the Bus Driver"), *Finding Neverland* and episodes of *The Lion the Witch and the Wardrobe* (1967, as "Mr Beaver"), *Doctor Who, The Avengers, Thriller* (1974), *The Young Indiana Jones Chronicles* and *My Hero*.

Spanish-American singer, dancer and actress **Adele Mara** (Adelaide Delgado) died on May 7, aged 87. Originally a performer with Xavier Cugat and his Orchestra, she was signed by a Columbia Pictures talent scout in 1942 before moving on to Republic Studios. Her credits include starring roles in *The Vampire's Ghost, The Catman of Paris* and *Curse of the Faceless Man*, plus episodes of *Thriller* ("What Beckoning Ghost?") and *The Alfred Hitchcock Hour*. She retired from the screen in the late 1970s, and was married to TV writer-producer Roy Huggins until his death in 2002.

"The Queen of Curves", busty, blonde British pin-up model [Phyllis] **Pamela Green** (aka "Rita Landré"/"Princess Sommar"), who played one of the murder victims in Michael Powell's controversial *Peeping Tom*, died of leukaemia the same day, aged 81. The "glamour" model's other films include *Naked as Nature Intended, The Day the Earth Caught Fire* (uncredited), *The Naked World of Harrison Marks* and *Legend of the Werewolf* (with Peter Cushing). She also worked as an uncredited assistant still photographer on that film, plus *The Ghoul* (1975) and the 1966 James Bond spoof *Casino Royale*. From 1953 to 1961 Green lived with photographer/film-maker George Harrison Marks.

Groundbreaking singer, dancer and actress **Lena** [Mary Calhoun] **Horne** died of heart failure on May 9, aged 92. Her first job, at the age of 16, was performing at the legendary Cotton Club in Harlem. Her film appearances include *Cabin in the Sky* and *The Wiz* (as "Glinda the Good").

American actress and dancer **Doris Eaton** [Travis], the last surviving member of the famous Ziegfeld Follies, died of an aneurysm on May 11, aged 106. She made her screen debut in 1921, and her final movie credit was in 1999.

**Phyllis Douglas** (Phyllis Callow), one of the last surviving cast members of *Gone With the Wind* (she played a two-year-old) died on May 12, aged 73. The daughter of assistant director

Ridgeway Callow, during the 1960s she also had small roles in George Pal's *Atlantis the Lost Continent* and episodes of TV's *Batman* and *Star Trek*.

Composer and organist **Rosa Rio** (Elizabeth Raub), whose professional career spanned more than ninety years, died on May 13, aged 107. She had been suffering from intestinal flu. A child prodigy, she began playing music accompaniments to silent films at the age of 10. During the 1930s and '40s Rio was a staff organist for NBC Radio, where she worked on such shows as *The Shadow* starring Orson Welles. Her last performace was in 2009.

**Peter Steele** (Petrus T. Ratajczyk), the fanged six-foot, eight-inch tall lead singer and primary songwriter with New York goth-metal band Type O Negative, died of heart failure on May 14, aged 48. The band's songs were used in such movies as *I Know What You Did Last Summer*, *Bride of Chucky* and *Freddy vs. Jason*, and appeared on the soundtracks of various computer games. In 2005, Steele spent time in prison for drug possession and assault.

Italian-American singer **Ronnie James Dio** (Ronald James Padavona), former frontman with heavy metal bands Rainbow, Black Sabbath and the eponymous Dio, died of stomach cancer on May 16, aged 67. He appeared in the 2006 movie *Tenacious D in the Pick of Destiny*. Dio is credited with creating the "horns" gesture with his fingers, which is still widely used at rock concerts.

39-year-old British-born screenwriter, producer and director **Simon Monjack**, the widower of actress Brittany Murphy, died at the couple's home in Los Angeles on May 23. He reportedly died from pneumonia, which was also the cause of his wife's death five months earlier. Questions were subsequently raised about the already controversial Monjack's handling of Murphy's finances following her untimely death.

**Paul** [Dedrick] **Gray**, bass player with the American heavy metal band Slipknot, was found dead in an Iowa hotel room on May 24, aged 38. Gray wrote a song for the soundtrack of *Resident Evil* and the band appeared in the 2002 remake of *Rollerball*.

British stage and television ventriloquist **Ray** (Raymond) **Alan** died the same day, aged 79. Best known for his slightly tipsy toff dummy "Lord Charles" and the puppets "Tich" and "Quackers", his first success was with the puppet "Mikki the Martian" on the children's TV show *Toytown* (1958). Alan appeared with Laurel and Hardy on their final tour in 1954, and he also worked as a scriptwriter for 1960s sitcoms and variety shows under the pseudonym "Ray Whyberd". He later had three crime novels published.

**Pat** (Patricia) **Stevens**, who voiced "Velma Dinkley" in TV's *Scooby-Doo* cartoons from 1974 to 1979, died on May 26, aged 64.

Canadian-born TV presenter, actor and author **Art Linkletter** (Gordon Arthur Kelly), best known as the host of *People Are Funny* and author of *Kids Say the Darndest Things*, died in Bel-Air, California, the same day, aged 97. He hosted the grand opening of Disneyland in 1955, and turned up as himself in the 1967 *Batman* episode "Catwoman Goes to College". Linkletter's daughter committed suicide in 1969 and his son was killed in a car accident in 1980.

Silent movie actress **Yvonne Howell** (Julia Rose Shevlin), the former wife of Oscar-winning film director George Stevens, died on May 27, aged 104. She was the last of the "Mack Sennett Bathing Beauty" pin-ups of the 1920s and retired from the screen in 1928, without ever having made a talking picture.

42-year-old former child star **Gary** [Wayne] **Coleman**, the diminutive star of NBC's hit sitcom *Diff'rent Strokes* (1978–86), died on May 28. Following a fall at his home two days earlier, the four-foot, eight-inch actor suffered an intercranial haemorrhage and chronic renal failure that left him in a coma. His ex-wife made the decision to turn off his life-support. Coleman, who had a congenital kidney condition that stunted his growth, appeared in *The Kid with the Broken Halo*, *The Fantastic World of D.C. Collins*, *Like Father Like Santa* (aka *The Christmas Takeover*), *A Christmas Carol* (2003), *An American Carol* and episodes of *Buck Rogers in the 25th Century* (as child genius "Hieronymous Fox"), *Amazing Stories*, *Unhappily Ever After* (as "The Devil") and *Homeboys in Outer Space*. Coleman's troubled adult career was marred by bankruptcy, various court appearances and feigned suicide attempts.

Often unpredictable actor, director and photographer **Dennis [Lee] Hopper** died of prostate cancer on May 29, aged 74. Infamous for his hellraising ways in the 1960s and '70s, he beat his drug and alcohol addiction and settled down in later life to become a highly respected character actor. Hopper's early appearances include *Rebel Without a Cause, Giant, The Story of Mankind* (with Vincent Price), *Night Tide, Queen of Blood* (with Basil Rathbone), Roger Corman's *The Trip*, The Monkees' *Head* (uncredited) and an episode of *The Twilight Zone*. Then in 1969, Hopper co-wrote, directed and starred in the counter-culture classic *Easy Rider*, made for just $400,000. It was a huge box-office success, but Hopper's career went into decline during the 1970s until Francis Ford Coppola gave him a supporting role as a drugged-out photojournalist in *Apocalypse Now*. His later credits include *My Science Project, The American Way* (aka *Riders of the Storm*), *The Texas Chainsaw Massacre 2*, David Lynch's *Blue Velvet, Super Mario Bros., Witch Hunt* (as "H. Phillip Lovecraft"), *Waterworld, Space Truckers, Jason and the Argonauts* (2000), *Firestarter 2: Rekindled, Unspeakable, House of 9, The Crow: Wicked Prayer*, George A. Romero's *Land of the Dead, Hoboken Hollow* and *Memory*. Hopper also starred in the rarely-seen SF TV series *Flatland* (2002), filmed in Hong Kong.

30-year-old American adult film actor **Tom Dong** (Herbert Wong), whose credits include *Perverted Planet 4*, was killed with a Samurai sword-style movie prop on June 1 when he went to the aid of a man allegedly being attacked by fellow porn actor **Steven Driver** (Stephen Clancy Hill) outside the offices of Ultima DVD Inc. in Van Nuys, California. Following a long stand-off with police four days later, 30-year-old Hill fell to his death off a cliff on the outskirts of Los Angeles after being hit by a "less than lethal munition".

American actress **Rue McClanahan** (Eddi-Rue McClanahan), who played "Blanche Devereaux" on NBC-TV's *The Golden Girls* (1985–92), died of a massive cerebral haemorrhage on June 2, aged 76. A former Broadway star, she appeared in *Five Minutes to Live* (aka *Door-to-Door Maniac*), *How to Succeed with Girls* (aka *The Peeping Phantom*), *They Might Be Giants, Topper* (1979), *The Wickedest Witch, The Dreamer of Oz,*

*Starship Troopers*, *A Saintly Switch* and episodes of *Darkroom*, *Fantasy Island*, *Nightmare Classics* ("The Strange Case of Dr Jekyll and Mr Hyde"), *Touched by an Angel* and *Wonderfalls*. McClanahan also took over the role of "Madame Morrible" on Broadway in *Wicked* in 2005.

Hollywood child star **Dorothy** [Adelle] **DeBorba** died the same day of emphysema, aged 85. She appeared in a number of "Our Gang" comedy shorts during the early 1930s. As a curly-haired child she retired from the screen in 1933 and went on to appear in advertisements for lemonade and ice cream.

**Marvin Isley**, the youngest of The Isley Brothers, died of complications from diabetes on June 6. The bass player was 56 and had had to have both legs amputated. He joined the American R&B, soul and funk group in 1973, and among their biggest hits were "This Old Heart of Mine (Is Weak for You)", "That Lady" and "Fight the Power". The Isley Brothers were elected to the Rock and Roll Hall of Fame in 1992.

**Stuart Cable**, the former drummer with Welsh group Stereophonics, was found dead at his home in the early hours of June 7. He had choked to death on his own vomit after effectively drinking himself to death after a three-day alcohol binge. The 40-year-old was thrown out of the band in 2003 after falling out with singer Kelly Jones, who was unhappy about Cable's alcohol and drug abuse.

Sudan-born Greek actor and stage director **Andréas Voutsinas**, who starred as "Count Dracula" in *Les Charlots contre Dracula* (1980), died of a respiratory infection in Athens on June 8, aged 79. A drama coach to both Warren Beatty and Jane Fonda (on *Barbarella*), Voutsinas also appeared in *Spirits of the Dead* (Roger Vadim's "Metzengerstein") and Mel Brooks' *History of the World: Part 1*.

German silent screen star **Daisy D'Ora** (Daisy Freiin von Freyberg zu Eisenberg), who appeared in G.W. Pabst's 1929 *Pandora's Box* with Louise Brooks, died on June 12, aged 97. She remembered Adolf Hitler, whom she met many times, as "the most terrible pianist".

Country musician and actor **Jimmy** [Ray] **Dean** died on June 13, aged 81. In 1961 he had a #1 hit in the US with his song "Big Bad John". A distant cousin of film legend James Dean, he founded Jimmy Dean Pure Pork Sausage in 1969 and was a spokesperson for the company for more than twenty years. Dean appeared in the James Bond movie *Diamonds Are Forever* and a couple of episodes of TV's *Fantasy Island*.

Polish actress **Elzbieta** [Justyna] **Czyzewska** died of oesophageal cancer in New York on June 17, aged 72. She appeared in *The Saragossa Manuscript* and the 1991 remake of *A Kiss Before Dying*.

38-year-old German actor **Frank Giering** was found dead in his Berlin apartment on June 23. The cause of death was internal bleeding from alcohol poisoning. His films include *Funny Games* and *Anatomy 2*.

**Pete Quaife** (Peter Alexander Greenlaw "Pete" Quaife), the original bassist with the Kinks from 1963 to 1969, died in Denmark of kidney failure the same day, aged 66. He had been undergoing kidney dialysis for nearly a decade. Quaife played on all the British band's early hits, including "You Really Got Me", "All Day and All of the Night", "Dedicated Follower of Fashion" and "Waterloo Sunset". He later became a cartoonist and artist.

Actor-turned-Emmy Award-winning director and acting coach **Corey Allen** (Alan Cohen) died of complications from Parkinson's disease on June 27, two days before his 76th birthday. During the 1950s and '60s he appeared in *The Mad Magician* (uncredited), *The Night of the Hunter* (1955, uncredited), *Rebel Without a Cause* and episodes of *Alfred Hitchcock Presents* and *Men Into Space*. In the early 1970s he started directing TV shows such as *The New People*, *Tucker's Witch*, *The Powers of Matthew Star*, *Otherworld* and *Star Trek: The Next Generation*, the TV movies *The Man in the Santa Claus Suit* and *I-Man*, along with an adult version of *Pinocchio* (1971). Allen was a former roommate of Dennis Hopper's, and his father Carl was a Las Vegas casino manager, who famously punched out two of Frank Sinatra's teeth during a confrontation at the Sands Hotel in 1967.

Legendary voice-over artist **Ron Gans** (Ronald Kenneth Gans, aka "Ron Kennedy") died of complications from pneumonia on June 29, aged 78. Gans's sonorous tones could be heard on numerous exploitation trailers during the 1970s for such movies as *Caged Heat*, *Terminal Island* and *The Little*

*Girl Who Lives Down the Lane*, and he had small roles in *Killers from Space*, *The Wild Racers*, *Tarzan and the Jungle Boy*, *The Student Nurses*, *Coffy* and *Hell Night*. He also did voice work for *Deathsport*, *Heartbeeps* and *Not of This Earth* (1988), plus TV's *Lost in Space*, *Buck Rogers in the 25th Century*, *Welcome to Pooh Corner* (as "Eeyore"), *Transformers* (1985–86, as "Drag Strip"), *Star Trek: The Next Generation*, *Pryde of the X-Men* (as "Magneto") and *Captain Planet and the Planeteers*.

American singer **Ilene Woods** (Jacquelyn Ruth Woods), who was the voice of the titular cartoon character in Walt Disney's *Cinderella* (1950), died of complications from Alzheimer's disease on July 1, aged 81.

Shakespearan actor **Geoffrey Hutchings**, who appeared (as different characters) in the TV movies of Terry Pratchett's *Hogfather* and *The Colour of Magic*, died of meningitis the same day, aged 71. His final stage appearance was in *The Shawshank Redemption* (2009), as the prison librarian.

American blaxploitation actress [Lawrence] **Vonetta McGee**, who played the love interest in *Blacula* (1972), died of cardiac arrest on July 9, aged 65. Her other credits include *The Norliss Tapes*, *Repo Man*, *Brother Future* and an episode of *Whiz Kids*.

Bohemian American poet, cartoonist and singer **Tuli Kupferberg** (Naphtali Kupferberg), co-founder of the mid-1960s folk-rock group The Fugs, died on July 12, aged 86.

Voice actor and pulp adventure writer **Peter Fernandez**, best known for dubbing all the main voices in *Speed Racer* for the English-language version of the 1960s *anime* TV show, died of lung cancer on July 15, aged 83. Fernandez also did voice work for *Mothra*, *Ebirah Horror of the Deep*, *The Tempter*, *The Super Inframan*, *Dogs of Hell*, *Blood Link*, *2019: After the Fall of New York*, *Silent Madness*, *Day of the Dead*, and such TV series as *Astroboy*, *The Space Giants*, *Marine Boy*, *Ultraman*, *Star Blazers*, *Thunderbirds 2086*, *The Adventures of the Galaxy Rangers* and many others. He had a cameo as a local announcer in the 2008 live-action movie of *Speed Racer*.

Grizzled American character actor **James** [Richard] **Gammon** died of cancer of the adrenal glands and liver on July 16, aged 70. A former TV cameraman, he made his acting debut in 1966 and his credits include Stephen King's *Silver Bullet, Made in Heaven, The Milagro Beanfield War, Cabin Boy, Natural Born Killers, The Iron Giant, The Cell* and *Altered*, along with episodes of TV's *The Wild Wild West, Captain Nice, The Invaders, Batman, Monster Squad* and *The Young Indiana Jones Chronicles*.

French actress **Cécil Aubrey** (Anne-José Madeleine Henriette Bénard) died of lung cancer on July 19, aged 81. She co-starred with Tyrone Power and Orson Welles in the 1950 British costume drama *The Black Rose*, and appeared in the French and German versions of *Bluebeard* the following year. In the 1960s Aubrey retired from acting and became a scriptwriter and director of children's TV series, including the popular *Belle et Sébastian*, based on her own novel.

1940s American actress and former Coca-Cola pin-up model, **Rebel Randall** (Alaine Brandes) died on July 22, aged 89. She had small roles (often uncredited) in *Turnabout, The Lone Rider in Ghost Town* (aka *Ghost Mine*), *Arabian Nights, Seven Doors to Death, A Thousand and One Nights* and *The Shadow Returns*. In the 1950s Randall became the only female radio DJ in Hollywood.

American actor **Maury Chaykin** died of kidney problems brought on by a heart-valve infection in a Toronto hospital on July 27, his 61st birthday. Best known for portraying Rex Stout's eccentric investigator in the A&E series of *Nero Wolfe* TV movies (2000–02), the rotund actor also appeared in *Overdrawn at the Memory Bank* (based on the SF story by John Varley), *Curtains, WarGames, Of Unknown Origin, Def-Con 4, The Vindicator, Millennium* (another Varley adaptation), *Mr Destiny, Jacob Two Two Meets the Hooded Fang* and *Static* (aka *Glitch*). He had a recurring role in four episodes of the TV series of *Seeing Things* (1981–87), and also turned up in the revived *The Twilight Zone* (George Clayton Johnson's "A Game of Pool") and episodes of *PSI Factor: Chronicles of the Paranormal, Lexx, Andromeda, Stargate SG-1*, the pilot for *Eureka* (aka *A Town Called Eureka*) and the mini-series *Superstorm*. Chaykin had dual American and Canadian nationality.

American singer, musician and record producer **Mitch Miller** (Mitchell William Miller) died on July 31, aged 99. An avowed hater of rock 'n' roll music, he was best known during the 1950s and '60s for such hits as "The Yellow Rose of Texas" (which topped the US charts and sold over a million copies) and the theme songs for such movies as *The Longest Day* and *Major Dundee*. He can also be heard on the soundtrack of *Piranha* (2010). Miller's NBC-TV show *Sing Along with Mitch* ran from 1961 to 1966.

British actor **John Louis Mansi** (John Patrick Adams), best remembered for his role as incompetent Gestapo agent "Von Smallhausen" in the BBC sitcom *'Allo, 'Allo!*, died of lung cancer on August 6, aged 83. He also appeared uncredited in the movies *Help!* and *Tales from the Crypt* (1972), and was in the BBC's 1966 series of *The Woman in White* and epsiodes of *The Adventures of Don Quick* and *Hammer House of Horror* ("The Thirteenth Reunion").

Oscar-winning Hollywood actress **Patricia Neal** (Patsy Louise Neal) died of lung cancer on August 8, aged 84. She appeared in *The Day the Earth Stood Still* (1951) and its British "remake" *Stranger from Venus*, *The Night Digger*, *Happy Mother's Day Love George*, *Ghost Story* (based on the novel by Peter Straub) and an episode of TV's *Ghost Story/Circle of Fear* scripted by Jimmy Sangster. In 1965, Neal suffered a series of debilitating strokes that put her in a coma for twenty-one days before she managed her own rehabilitation. She famously had a secret three-year affair with the older and married Gary Cooper, her co-star in *The Fountainhead* (1949), before marrying British author Roald Dahl from 1953 until their divorce in 1983. Glenda Jackson portrayed the actress in the 1981 TV movie *The Patricia Neal Story*.

British drummer and bandleader **Jack** [Russell] **Parnell** died of cancer the same day, aged 87. He had also been suffering from the lung disorder chronic obstructive pulmonary disease. As musical director for ATV (then run by his uncle, Val) he orchestrated such TV programmes as *The Muppet Show* and a 1976 version of *Peter Pan* starring Mia Farrow, Danny Kaye and Sir John Gielgud. He also apparently worked on the soundtracks for the films *Eye of the Devil* (aka *13*) and *It's Alive III: Island of the Alive*.

70-year-old American character actor and voice artist **George**

[Ralph] **DiCenzo** died of sepsis after a long illness on August 9. He began his career as an associate producer on the TV series *Dark Shadows* and an assistant to the producer on the spin-off movie, *House of Dark Shadows* (in which he also had an uncredited role). Switching to acting, he appeared in *The Invasion of Carol Enders*, *The Night Strangler*, *The Norliss Tapes*, *Helter Skelter* (1976), *Close Encounters of the Third Kind*, *The Ninth Configuration*, *Starflight: The Plane That Couldn't Land* (aka *Starflight One*), *The Tom Swift and Linda Craig Mystery Hour*, *Back to the Future*, *18 Again!* (1988) and *The Exorcist III*, along with episodes of TV's *Kung Fu*, *Space Academy*, *Alfred Hitchcock Presents* (1985) and *M.A.N.T.I.S.* As a voice actor, DiCenzo contributed to *Space Sentinels*, *Spider-Man and His Amazing Friends* (as "Captain America"), *Blackstar* (as "John Blackstar"), *Challenge of the GoBots*, *Galtar and the Golden Lance*, *Batman* (1994), *She-Ra Princess of Power* (as the villain, "Hordak") and the spin-off movies *The Secret of the Sword* and *He-Man: A Christmas Special*. On Broadway, he appeared opposite Nathan Lane in George C. Scott's 1991 revival of *On Borrowed Time*.

German actor, painter and musician **Bruno S** (Bruno Schleinstein) died of heart failure on August 11, aged 78. After spending more than twenty years in various institutions, he was cast by Werner Herzog in the title role of *The Enigma of Kaspar Hauser* (1974).

Hungarian-born actress **Ahna Capri** (Anna Marie Nanasi) died in Los Angeles on August 19 from injuries sustained in a car crash eleven days earlier. The 66-year-old had been in a coma ever since her car collided with a five-ton truck. Best remembered for her role as "Tania" in *Enter the Dragon*, the buxom blonde also appeared in *One of Our Spies is Missing*, *The Brotherhood of Satan* and *Piranha* (1972), along with episodes of *The Wild Wild West*, *The Man from U.N.C.L.E.*, *The Invaders*, *Matt Helm* and *Man from Atlantis*. She retired from acting at the end of the 1970s.

American child actor **Christopher** [Dylan] **Shea**, the voice of "Linus van Pelt" in the *Peanuts* animated specials *A Boy Named Charlie Brown*, *A Charlie Brown Christmas*, *Charlie Brown's All-Stars*, *It's the Great Pumpkin Charlie Brown*, *You're in Love*

*Charlie Brown* and *He's Your Dog Charlie Brown*, died the same day, aged 52. He also appeared in two episodes of *The Invaders*.

American comedian **Robert Schimmel** died on September 3 of complications from a car accident eight days earlier, when his daughter swerved to avoid another vehicle and crashed into the side of the freeway. The 60-year-old appeared in the movies *Blankman* and *Scary Movie 2*.

62-year-old **Mike Edwards** (aka "Dev Pramada"), a founding member of 1970s British rock group ELO (Electric Light Orchestra), was killed instantly in a freak accident the same day, when the van he was driving on a Devon road was crushed by a giant bale of hay that rolled out of a field. The cellist was identified by police using photographs and YouTube footage. Edwards was with the Birmingham band from 1972 to 1975.

Portly American character actor [William] **Glenn Shadix**, who appeared as the interior decorator in Tim Burton's *Beetle Juice*, died following a fall at home on September 7. He was 58 and had been using a wheelchair due to mobility problems. Shadix also had roles in Burton's *The Nightmare Before Christmas* (as the "Mayor") and *Planet of the Apes* remake, and his other credits include *Heathers*, *Nightlife*, *Meet the Applegates*, *Sleepwalkers*, *Demolition Man*, *Multiplicity*, *Bartok the Magnificent*, and episodes of *Hercules: The Legendary Journeys*, *Sabrina the Teenage Witch* and *Carnivàle*. He also voiced "Lonnie the Shark" in four episodes of the cartoon series *The Mask*, and contributed voice work to numerous other TV cartoon shows and video games.

Canadian voice actress **Billie Mae Richards** (Billie Mae Dinsmore, aka "Billy/Billie Richards") died after suffering several strokes on September 10, aged 88. Her many credits include *Rudolph the Red-Nosed Reindeer*, *Willy McBean and His Magic Machine*, *The Daydreamer*, *Rudolph's Shiny New Year*, *Rudolph and Frosty's Christmas in July*, *The Trolls and the Christmas Express*, *The Care Bears Movie*, *Care Bears Movie II: A New Generation* and episodes of TV's *King Kong* (1966), *Spider-Man*, *The Undersea Adventures of Captain Nemo* and *The Care Bears*. Richards also appeared in such shows as *War of* *the* Worlds, *My Secret Identity* and *The Hidden Room*, along with the movie *Shadow Builder*.

Veteran American leading man **Kevin McCarthy** died on September 11, aged 96. Best remembered for warning the world that "They're here already!" in the 1956 version of Jack Finny's *Invasion of the Body Snatchers*, he also appeared in the 1978 remake, plus *Between Time and Timbuktu, Exo-Man, Piranha* (1978), *Hero at Large, The Howling, Twilight Zone: The Movie, Invitation to Hell, The Midnight Hour, Dark Tower, Innerspace, The Sleeping Car, Eve of Destruction* (uncredited), *Ghoulies III: Ghoulies Go to College, Duplicates, Matinee* (uncredited), *Mommy, Addams Family Reunion, Looney Tunes: Back in Action, Fallen Angels, Slipstream* (2007), *Trail of the Screaming Forehead* and *Her Morbid Desires*. McCarthy also turned up in numerous TV shows, including episodes of *Lights Out, Inner Sanctum, The Twilight Zone, Way Out, Great Ghost Stories, The Alfred Hitchcock Hour, The Man from U.N.C.L.E.*, the pilot *Ghostbreakers, The Invaders, The Wild Wild West, Fantasy Island, Tales from the Crypt* and *Early Edition*.

Busy American character actor **Harold Gould** (Harold V. Goldstein) died of prostate cancer the same day, aged 86. His credits include *The Couch* (based on a story by Robert Bloch), *The Satan Bug*, William Castle's *Project X, The Man in the Santa Claus Suit, Get Smart Again!, Stuart Little* and Disney's *The Strongest Man in the World*, the 1997 remake of *The Love Bug*, and the 2003 remake of *Freaky Friday*, along with episodes of TV's *The Alfred Hitchcock Hour, The Twilight Zone, The Man from U.N.C.L.E., Mister Ed, Get Smart, The Green Hornet, The Invaders, The Flying Nun, The Wild Wild West, I Dream of Jeannie, Dinosaurs, The Ray Bradbury Theatre, The New Adventures of Superman, The Outer Limits* (1996) and *Touched by an Angel*.

British character actor **Nicholas Selby** [James Ivor Selby], who was orginally offered the role of "Alastair Lethbridge-Stewart" in the 1968 *Doctor Who* serial "The Web of Fear", died on September 14, aged 85. He appeared in a 1960 TV adaptation of *Night of the Big Heat*, based on the SF novel by John Lymington, along with episodes of *The Avengers, Alfred Hitchcock Presents, Strange Report, Doomwatch, The Rivals of Sherlock Holmes,*

*The Storyteller* and *The Young Indiana Jones Chronicles*. A member of the Royal Shakespeare Company, Selby also portrayed "Egeus" in Peter Hall's 1968 film of *A Midsummer Night's Dream* and "Duncan" in Roman Polanski's 1971 version of *Macbeth*, and his stage appearances include the *Bell, Book and Candle* in 1957 and the 1974 play *Sherlock Holmes*.

British character actor **Frank Jarvis**, who was usually cast as crooks or policemen in films and on TV, died on September 15, aged 69. His credits include the first episode of *Adam Adamant Lives!* and three series of *Doctor Who*.

Rugged American character actor **John Crawford** (Alfred Crawford Richardson) died of complications from a stroke on September 21, aged 90. His many appearances include *The Phantom of 42nd Street*, *The Time of Their Lives* (with Abbott and Costello as ghosts), the serials *G-Men Never Forget, Dangers of the Canadian Mounted, Ghost of Zorro, Radar Patrol vs. Sky King, The Invisible Monster, Zombies of the Stratosphere, Blackhawk* and *Commado Cody: Sky Marshall of the Universe, Invasion USA, Captain Sinbad, Jason and the Argonauts, I Saw What You Did* (1965), *The Poseidon Adventure* (1972), *The Severed Arm, The Towering Inferno* and *The Boogens*. On TV Crawford appeared in episodes of *Adventures of Superman* (1952–53), *Matinee Theatre* ("Wuthering Heights", 1953), *13 Demon Street* (hosted by Lon Chaney, Jr), *The Twilight Zone, Batman, Star Trek, The Time Tunnel, Voyage to the Bottom of the Sea, Tarzan, Lost in Space, The Wild Wild West, Land of the Giants, The Invisible Man* (1975), *The Bionic Woman, The Incredible Hulk, The Amazing Spider-Man, Salvage 1, The Powers of Matthew Star, Matt Houston, Knight Rider* and the unaired 1967 pilot *The Man from the 25th Century*.

Hollywood "B" movie actress **Grace Bradley** died the same day, her birthday, aged 97. After appearing in a number of films during the 1930s and early '40s, including *The Invisible Killer*, she became the fifth and final wife of cowboy actor William Boyd, best known for his long portrayal of "Hopalong Cassidy" in movies and on TV. He was 42 and she was 23 at the time, and they remained married for thirty-five years, until his death in 1972.

English-born Canadian character actress **Jackie Burroughs** died of cancer on September 22, aged 71. She moved with her family to Toronto when she was 13, and her credits include *Heavy Metal, Overdrawn at the Memory Bank* (based on John Varley's story), Stephen King's *The Dead Zone* (1983), *The Care Bears Movie, Carnival of Shadows, Food of the Gods II, Whispers* (based on the novel by Dean R. Koontz), *Bleeders* (aka *Hemoglobin*, based on "The Lurking Fear" by H.P. Lovecraft), *Willard* (2003), *RE-Generation* (aka *The Limb Salesman*), *Into the Labyrinth* and episodes of *The All New Ewoks*, the 1980s *Twilight Zone, Smallville* and *Dead Like Me*. During the 1960s, Burroughs was married to lead guitarist and singer Zal Yanovsky, a founding member of the rock band The Lovin' Spoonful.

Five-times married singer and actor **Eddie Fisher** (Edwin John Fisher), who famously married and divorced Debbie Reynolds, Elizabeth Taylor and Connie Stevens, died of complications from hip surgery the same day, aged 82. One of the biggest pop idols of the 1950s ("Thinking of You") and the father of *Star Wars* actress Carrie Fisher, he also made an uncredited appearance in Taylor's 1959 movie *Suddenly, Last Summer*, based on the play by Tennessee Williams.

Former Argentinian professional basketball player and WWF wrestler **Jorge "Giant" Gonzáles** died of complications from diabetes and giantism on September 22, aged 44. He was seven foot, six inches tall and appeared in the 1994 TV movie *Hercules in the Underworld*.

**Art Gilmore** (Arthur Wells Gilmore), whose crisp tones introduced numerous TV series and narrated around 3,000 movie trailers from the 1940s to the 1960s, died on September 25, aged 98. Gilmore's voice introduced such shows as *Climax!* and *Highway Patrol*, while his distinctive pitch helped sell the trailers for Disney's *Dumbo, It's a Wonderful Life, The War of the Worlds*, Alfred Hitchcock's *Vertigo* and *Fahrenheit 451*, amongst many others. Gilmore also turned up in small roles in *When Worlds Collide, Francis in the Navy* and an episode of *Captain Midnight*, and his voice can be heard in *The Reluctant Dragon, The Unsuspected, King of the Rocket Men, Rear Window, Tobor the Great, Around the World in Eighty Days, Rodan! The Flying Monster* and *The Nutty Professor*.

Veteran Hollywood actress **Gloria Stuart** (Gloria Frances

Stewart), best known by modern audiences for her Oscar-nominated role as the centenarian survivor in James Cameron's 1997 blockbuster *Titanic*, died of respiratory failure on September 26, aged 100. She had been diagnosed with lung cancer five years earlier. A founding member of the Screen Actors Guild, the actress made her movie debut in 1932, and she starred in James Whale's *The Old Dark House* (opposite Boris Karloff) and *The Invisible Man* (with Claude Rains), along with *Secret of the Blue Room*, *Roman Scandals*, *Gift of Gab* (with cameos by Karloff and Bela Lugosi) and William Castle's *The Whistler*. Disillusioned with the types of parts she was getting, Stuart retired from the screen in 1946, but returned to TV in 1975 with supporting roles in *The Legend of Lizzie Borden*, *The Two Worlds of Jennie Logan* and episodes of *Manimal*, *The Invisible Man* (2001) and *Touched by an Angel*.

Oscar-nominated American character actor **Joe Mantell** (Joseph Mantel), who played the travelling salesman in the diner sequence in Alfred Hitchcock's *The Birds* (1963), died on September 29, aged 94. He also appeared in episodes of TV's *Suspense*, *Lights Out*, *Inner Sanctum*, *Alfred Hitchcock Presents*, *One Step Beyond*, *The Twilight Zone* (including Richard Matheson's "Steel"), *The Man from U.N.C.L.E.* and *Fantasy Island*. Mantell is probably best remembered for uttering the final line in Roman Polanski's *Chinatown* (1974): "Forget it, Jake, it's Chinatown."

Hollywood star **Tony Curtis** (Bernard Schwartz) died of cardiac arrest at his home in Las Vegas on September 30, aged 85. One of the actor's earliest film roles was in Universal's 1950 talking mule comedy *Francis* (billed as "Anthony Curtis"), and he went on to appear in *Son of Ali Baba*, *Houdini* (1953), *The Vikings*, *The List of Adrian Messenger*, *Chamber of Horrors* (uncredited), *The Boston Strangler*, *The Manitou* (based on the novel by Graham Masterton), *BrainWaves*, *Lobster Man from Mars*, *Tarzan in Manhattan*, *Midnight*, *The Mummy Lives*, *Stargames* and *Reflections of Evil*. His other credits include episodes of TV's *The Flintstones* (as "Stony Curtis") and *The New Adventures of Superman*, and his voice was also heard (uncredited) in Roman Polanski's *Rosemary's Baby* (1968). Curtis was also an avid painter. He was married five times, most notably to *Psycho* star Janet Leigh, with whom he had two daughters, actresses Jamie Lee Curtis and Kelly Curtis.

British character actress **Brenda** [Rose] **Cowling** died of a stroke on October 2, aged 85. She made her (uncredited) film debut in Alfred Hitchcock's *Stage Fright* and went on to appear in the 1972 short *The Man and the Snake* (based on the story by Ambrose Bierce), *Jabberwocky*, *Pink Floyd The Wall*, Leon Garfield's *The Ghost Downstairs*, the James Bond film *Octopussy* and *Dream Lover*, along with episodes of *The Avengers*, *The Rivals of Sherlock Holmes*, *Shadows* ("Time Out of Mind"), *Hammer House of Horror* ("The Two Faces of Evil"), *Goodnight Sweetheart* and *Jonathan Creek* on TV.

British slapstick comedian Sir **Norman Wisdom** died in an Isle of Man nursing home on October 4, aged 95. He had suffered a series of strokes over the preceding six months that had led to a deterioration in his mental and physical health. Best known for his series of "little man" comedy films during the 1950s and '60s (you either love 'em or hate 'em), in later years Wisdom appeared in *Five Children & It* (as a character named "Nesbitt", after the story's author, E. Nesbit) and the 2008 direct-to-video release *Evil Calls*. In 1998 he shot scenes for a yet-to-be-completed SF comedy, *Cosmic! Lost and Found*, which also apparently involved John Landis and Ray Harryhausen. Wisdom was the national comedy hero of Albania. Christopher Fowler's story, "Norman Wisdom and the Angel of Death", appeared in *Best New Horror 4* and *The Mammoth Book of the Best of Best New Horror*.

The "King of Rock and Soul", Grammy Award-winning American singer/composer **Solomon Burke** (James Solomon Burke) died on October 10 at Amsterdam's Schiphol Airport after arriving on a flight from Los Angeles. He was 70. Burke co-wrote the song "Everybody Needs Somebody to Love" and had a hit with "Cry to Me" in the early 1960s and again twenty years later when it was featured on the soundtrack of *Dirty Dancing*. An undertaker with his own mortuary business in LA, Burke fathered twenty-one children. He was inducted into the Rock and Roll Hall of Fame in 2001.

British leading man **Simon MacCorkindale** died of bowel and lung cancer on October 14, aged 58. He had been battling the disease for four years. MacCorkindale starred as the shape-changing "Professor Jonathan Chase" in the short-lived NBC-TV series *Manimal* (1983), and reprised the role in a 1998 episode of *Night Man*. The actor's other credits include *Quatermass/The Quatermass Conclusion* (1979), *The Sword and the Sorcerer*, *Jaws 3-D* (co-scripted by Richard Matheson), *Wing Commander* and *13hrs*, plus episodes of *Beasts* (created by Nigel Kneale), *Hammer House of Horror*, *Fantasy Island*, *Earth: Final Conflict*, *Dark Realm*, *Relic Hunter* and *Poltergeist: The Legacy* (in the recurring role of "Reed Horton"). MacCorkindale co-scripted and directed the TV movie *The House That Mary Built* starring his second wife, Susan George, and he also co-produced the TV series *Adventure Inc*. His first marriage to actress Fiona Fullerton ended in divorce in 1982.

**Johnny Sheffield** (John Matthew Sheffied Cassan, aka "John Sheffield"), the child actor who portrayed Tarzan's adopted son in eight films, died of a heart attack after falling off a ladder on October 15, aged 79. Following a stint at the age of seven in the original Broadway stage production of *On Borrowed Time*, he was cast by MGM as "Boy" opposite Johnny Weissmuller's Ape Man and Maureen O'Sullivan's Jane in *Tarzan Finds a Son!* (1939). He went on to reprise the role in *Tarzan's Secret Treasure*, *Tarzan's New York Adventure*, and the cheaper RKO series *Tarzan Triumphs*, *Tarazan's Desert Mystery* (with dinosaurs!), *Tarzan and the Amazons*, *Tarzan and the Leopard Woman* and *Tarzan and the Huntress*, before outgrowing the role. Monogram Pictures then starred him in a series of twelve low-budget *Bomba, the Jungle Boy* adventures from 1949–55. Following the final film in the series, *Lord of the Jungle*, Sheffield left showbusiness and worked in real estate, lobster importing and building restoration.

American actress **Barbara Billingsley** (Barbara Lillian Combes), best remembered as sensible mother "June Cleaver" in the 1950s TV series *Leave It to Beaver*, died from a rheumatoid disease on October 16, aged 94. The former model also appeared in the 1953 *Invaders from Mars* (uncredited), the TV movie *Bay Coven*, plus episodes of *Mork & Mindy*, *Amazing Stories*, *Monsters* ("Reaper", based on a story by Robert Bloch) and *Mysterious Ways*.

Another famous TV parent, American character actor **Tom Bosley** (Thomas Edward Bosley), died of a staph infection and cancer on October 19, aged 83. He had been battling lung cancer. Well known for starring in such popular TV series as *Happy Days*, *Murder She Wrote* and *Father Dowling Investigates*, Bosley also appeared in *Miracle on 34th Street* (1973), *Death Cruise*, *The Night That Panicked America*, *Wicked Stepmother*, *Little Bigfoot 2: The Journey Home*, *Mary Christmas and The Fallen Ones*, along with episodes of *Hallmark Hall of Fame* ("Arsenic and Old Lace"), *The Girl from U.N.C.L.E.* ("The Faustus Affair"), *Get Smart*, *Night Gallery*, *Bewitched*, *The Sixth Sense*, *Kolchak: The Night Stalker*, *Tales of the Unexpected*, *Out of This World*, *Early Edition* and *Touched by an Angel*.

Fussy Scotish character actor [Clement] **Graham Crowden** died the same day, aged 87. His films include *Morgan: A Suitable Case for Treatment*, *If . . .*, *The Night Digger*, *The Ruling Class*, *The Amazing Mr Blunden*, *The Final Programme* (based on the novel by Michael Moorcock), *O Lucky Man!*, *The Little Prince*, *Jabberwocky*, *For Your Eyes Only*, *Britannia Hospital*, *The Company of Wolves* and a 1996 version of *Gulliver's Travels*. On TV Crowden was in a 1959 version of *Trilby*, plus episodes of *The Indian Tales of Rudyard Kipling*, *Mystery and Imagination* ("The Curse of the Mummy"), *The Adventures of Don Quick*, *Catweazle*, *Star Maidens*, *The 10th Kingdom* and *Dr Terrible's House of Horrible*. In 1974 he was offered the title role of *Doctor Who* following the departure of Jon Pertwee, but turned it down. However, he did turn up as the villainous "Soldeed" in the show's 1979 sequence "The Horns of Nimon".

German-born singer **Ari Up** (Ariane Daniele Forster), who was Sex Pistol John Lydon's step-daughter and a founding member of the British all-girl punk-reggae band The Slits, died of cancer in Los Angeles on October 20. She was 48.

American character actor and film historian **Don Leifert** (Donald L. Leifert, Jr) died on October 23, aged 59. He appeared in the no-budget SF and horror movies *The Alien Factor*, *Fiend*, *Nightbeast*, *The Galaxy Invader*, *Blood Massacre* and *Crawler* for Maryland independent film-maker Don Dohler.

Jamaican-born reggae singer **Gregory Isaacs** died of lung cancer in his London home on October 25, aged 59. The smooth-voiced singer released an estimated 500 albums and was best known for his 1982 hit "Night Nurse". He was arrested more than fifty times on drug and illegal firearms charges.

The body of 53-year-old **Lisa Blount** was found at her Arkansas home on October 27, although the actress most likely died two days earlier. Best known for her role in *An Officer and a Gentleman*, Blount also appeared in the movies *Dead and Buried*, *What Waits Below*, *Radioactive Dreams*, *Annihilator*, *Nightflyers* (based on the novel by George R.R. Martin), John Carpenter's *Prince of Darkness*, *Needful Things* (uncredited) and *Stalked*, along with episodes of TV's *The Hitchhiker* and *Starman*.

Actor **James** [Gordon] **MacArthur**, best known for playing "Danny 'Danno' Williams" opposite Jack Lord's "Steve McGarrett" on CBS-TV's *Hawaii Five-O* (1968–79), died on October 28, aged 72. He was the last surviving main cast member of the original series. The adopted son of playwright Charles MacArthur and America's "First Lady of the American Stage", Helen Hayes, MacArthur also appeared in Disney's *Swiss Family Robinson*, *The Bedford Incident* and episodes of *The Alfred Hitchcock Hour*, *Tarzan*, *Fantasy Island*, *Time Express* (starring Vincent Price) and *Superboy*.

American character actor **Robert Ellenstein** died the same day, aged 87. He began his career playing "Quasimodo" in a two-part 1950 *Robert Montgomery Presents* adaptation of *The Hunchback of Notre Dame* on live TV. His other credits include *Mandrake the Magician* (1954), *Love at First Bite* and *Star Trek: The Voyage Home*, plus episodes of *Climax!*, *One Step Beyond*, *Thriller* (1961), *The Man from U.N.C.L.E.*, *Get Smart*, *The Wild Wild West*, *The Bionic Woman*, *A Man Called Sloane*, *V* (1984) and *Star Trek: The Next Gerneration*.

**Maurice Murphy** MBE, the principal trumpet player with the London Symphony Orchestra (LSO), also died on October 28, aged 75. His distinctive playing can be heard on the soundtracks for *Star Wars*, *The Empire Strikes Back*, *Return of the Jedi*, *Star Wars: Episode I: The Phantom Menace*, *Summer of Sam*, *Star Wars: Episode III: Revenge of the Sith*, *The Golden Compass*, *The Dark Knight* and *Fantastic Mr Fox*.

Acclaimed Hollywood actress **Jill Clayburgh** died of chronic lymphocytic leukaemia on November 5, aged 66. Her credits include *The Terminal Man* (based on the novel by Michael Crichton) and the TV sequel *Phenomenon II*.

**Marie Osborne** [Yeats] (Helen Alice Myres) who, as "Baby Marie Osborne" was one of the first American child stars of the silent screen, died on November 11, six days after her 99th birthday. Between 1914 and 1919 she appeared in twenty-eight silent movies, before becoming a stand-in and uncredited extra in various 1930s and '40s productions, including *The Last Days of Pompeii*. From the mid-1950s until the mid-1970s, she worked as a wardrobe costumer on such films as *Around the World in Eighty Days*, *Cleopatra* and *The Legend of Lylah Clare*. At the height of her fame she was earning $300 a week (when the average American was making less than $1,000 per year) and Baby Marie Osborne dolls were sold around the world.

Polish-born actress and author **Ingrid Pitt** (Ingoushka Petrov) died of heart failure while on her way to a dinner in her honour in London on November 23, two days after her 73rd birthday. She had been in poor health for some time. In the early 1970s she became a horror icon when Hammer Films starred her in *The Vampire Lovers* (based on J. Sheridan Le Fanu's "Carmilla") and *Countess Dracula*. Her other film credits include the Spanish *Sound of Horror*, *The Omegans*, *The House That Dripped Blood* (in a segment based on Robert Bloch's "The Cloak"), *The Wicker Man* (1973), *Artemis 81*, *The House*, *Underworld* (aka *Transmutations*, based on a story by Clive Barker), *The Asylum*, the short *Green Fingers*, *Minotaur*, Hammer's *Beyond the Rave* and *Sea of Dust*, and she also appeared on TV in episodes of *Doctor Who* ("The Time Monster" and "Warriors of the Deep") and *Thriller* (1975). The actress wrote the non-fiction studies *The Ingrid Pitt Bedside Companion for Vampire Lovers*, *The Ingrid Pitt Bedside Companion for Ghosthunters* and *The Ingrid Pitt Book of Murder, Torture & Depravity*, as well as contributing a regular column to *Shivers* magazine and an Introduction and story to *The Mammoth Book of Vampire Stories by Women*. Her 1999 autobiography was titled *Life's a Scream*. In 2010 Ingrid Pitt was Special Media Guest at the World Horror Convention in Brighton, England.

British leading lady **Joyce Howard**, who co-starred with

James Mason in the psychological chiller *The Night Has Eyes* (aka *Terror House*, 1942), died the same day in Santa Monica, California. She was 88. Howard also appeared in the old dark lighthouse comedy-mystery *Back-Room Boy* with Arthur Askey. After marrying actor Basil Sydney, she retired from acting in the early 1960s, becoming a novelist, playwright and, eventually, an excutive story editor and executive at Paramount TV in Los Angeles.

Danish stage and screen actor **Palle Huld,** who was reputed to be the inpiration for cartoon character "Tintin", died on November 26, aged 98. In 1928, the fifteen-year-old Huld won a newspaper competition for an aspiring journalist to celebrate the centennial of Jules Verne by travelling around the world in fourty-four days by any means except flying. The first Tintin strip, *Tintin in the Land of the Soviets*, appeared in a Belgian newspaper the following year.

Versatile Canadian-born Hollywood actor **Leslie [William] Nielsen,** who starred as the starship commander in the 1956 classic *Forbidden Planet* (based on William Shakespeare's *The Tempest*), died in Florida from pneumonia on November 28 while battling a staph infection. He was 84. His movie credits include the underrated *Dark Intruder, The Reluctant Astronaut, Change of Mind, Night Slaves, The Aquarians, Hauser's Memory* (based on the novel Curt Siodmak), *The Resurrection of Zachary Wheeler, The Poseidon Adventure* (1972), *The Return of Charlie Chan, Project: Kill, Day of the Animals, Prom Night* (1980), *Creepshow* (based on stories by Stephen King), *Harvey* (1996) and *Santa Who?*. Although he was often cast as the "heavy", with *Airplane!* in 1980, Nielsen began a second career appearing in comedy spoofs such as *The Creature Wasn't Nice, Repossessed, Dracula: Dead and Loving It* (as "Count Dracula"), *2001: A Space Travesty, Scary Movie 3* and *Scary Movie 4, Superhero Movie, Stan Helsing* and *Spanish Movie*. On TV the busy actor appeared in episodes of *Lights Out* (including adaptations of stories by John D. MacDonald, August Derleth and M.R. James), *Suspense* (including "The Black Prophet" with Boris Karloff as Rasputin), *Tales of Tomorrow* (including a two-part adaptation "Twenty Thousand Leagues Under the Sea"), *Robert Montgomery Presents* (including a version of "The House of Seven Gables"), *Thriller*, *Alfred Hitchcock Presents*, *The Alfred Hitchcock Hour* ("The Magic Shop", based on the story by John Collier), *Voyage to the Bottom of the Sea*, *The Wild Wild West*, *Cimarron Strip* ("The Beast That Walks Like a Man"), *The Man from U.N.C.L.E.*, *Night Gallery*, *The Evil Touch*, *Lucan*, *Fantasy Island*, *The Ray Bradbury Theatre* and *Highway to Heaven*.

. Mexican *luchador enmascarado* **El Hijo de Cien Caras** (Eusacio "Tacho" Jimínez Ibarra) was shot dead by two assassins while sitting in his car in Coyoacan, Mexico, on November 29. The masked wrestler was aged 32 and had bought the rights to his stage name as a way of linking himself to the famed wrestler Cien Caras ("Hundred Faces"), to whom he was not related. He also wrestled under the names "Frankenstein" and "Suplex".

American character actor **Ted Sorel** (Theodore Eliopoulos) died of Lyme's disease on November 30, aged 74. His credits include *Doctor Franken*, *The Clairvoyant* (aka *The Killing Hour*), *The Tempest* (1983), H.P. Lovecraft's *From Beyond* (as "Dr Edward Pretorius"), *Basket Case 2* and an episode of TV's *Star Trek: Deep Space Nine*.

Adult film star, director and producer **John Leslie** [Nuzzo] died on December 5, aged 65. As an actor, his more than 300 porno films since the mid-1970s include *Dracula Sucks*, *Pleasure Zone*, *Fantasex Island*, *Erotic Zone*, *The Lust Potion of Doctor F*, *Friday the 13th: A Nude Beginning*, *Fatal Erection*, *The Cat Woman* and *Beauty and the Beast* (1988) and its sequel. He also turned up (uncredited) in the 1984 horror movie, *The Prey*. Among Leslie's more than 140 credits as a director are *The Cat Woman*, *The Chameleon*, *Mad Love* (1989), *Laying the Ghost* and *Curse of the Catwoman*.

Japanese voice actor **Takeshi Watabe** (Masato Maeno), who worked on numerous *anime* TV series such as *Dragonball*, *Dragon Quest*, *Doraemon*, *Detective Conan*, *Paranoia Agent* and *Strike Witches*, along with the 1986 film *Fist of the North Star* (1986), died on December 13, aged 74.

American character actress **Neva** [Louise] **Patterson**, who played "Eleanor Dupres" in the 1980s TV movie *V* and the miniseries *V: The Final Battle*, died of complications from a broken hip on December 14, aged 90. She also appeared in the Steve

Martin comedy *All of Me*, along with episodes of *Lights Out*, *Suspense*, *Moment of Fear*, *Ghost Story*, *Tales of the Unexpected* (aka *Twist in the Tale*) and *Logan's Run*.

Innovative American musician and visual artist **Captain Beefheart** (Donald Van Vliet) died after a long battle with multiple sclerosis on December 17, aged 69. He recorded twelve studio albums with The Magic Band between 1965 and 1982.

American character actor **Steve Landesberg** died after a long battle with cancer on December 20, aged 65. He made guest appearances on such TV shows as *When Things Were Rotten*, *Harry and the Hendersons* and *Dinosaurs*.

American radio and television announcer **Fred Foy** (Frederick William Foy), who provided the opening "Hi-Yo, Silver!" narration for ABC Radio's *The Lone Ranger* (1948–54), died on December 22, aged 89. Foy also announced *The Green Hornet* and *Challenge of the Yukon* series for radio and *The Lone Ranger* TV series (1949–57). He was inducted into the Radio Hall of Fame in 2000.

Adult film actress **Viper** (Stephanie Green, aka "Stephanie Bishop"), best known for her trademark full body snake tattoo, died of lung cancer on December 24, aged 51. A former ballet dancer and US marine, her porn movies include *Jane Bond Meets Thunderballs*, *Future Sodom*, *Dreams in the Forbidden Zone*, *Voodoo Lust: The Possession*, *Debbie Does the Devil in Dallas* and *Captain Hooker & Peter Porn*. She abruptly left the X-rated movie industry in 1991 and later worked as a hair-stylist and phlebotomist.

American R&B singer and songwriter **Teena Marie** (Mary Christine Brockert) died in her sleep on December 26, aged 54. She had suffered a grand mal seizure a month earlier. A protégé of funk music legend Rick James, the Grammy Award-nominated singer released thirteen studio albums from the mid-1970s onwards, and had hits with such songs as "I'm Just a Sucker For Your Love" and "Lovergirl". In 1964 she appeared in an episode of TV's *The Beverly Hillbillies*.

Prolific French actor **Bernard-Pierre Donnadieu** died of cancer on December 27, aged 61. His many credits include Roman Polanski's *The Tenant* and George Sluizer's *The Vanishing*.

Prolific American character actor **Bill Erwin** (William Lindsey

Erwin) died on December 29, aged 96. Best known for his numerous Western roles, he was also in *The Brass Bottle*, *How Awful About Allan*, *Tarantulas: The Deadly Cargo*, *Somewhere in Time*, Wes Craven's *Invitation to Hell*, *The Willies*, *Menno's Mind* and *A Crack in the Floor*, along with episodes of TV's *Alfred Hitchcock Presents*, *Science Fiction Theatre*, *The Twilight Zone*, *Mister Ed*, *The Invaders*, *The Wild Wild West*, *Get Smart*, *Struck by Lightning*, *Voyagers!*, *ABC Weekend Specials* ("Henry Hamilton Graduate Ghost"), *Highway to Heaven*, *Star Trek: The Next Generation*, *Quantum Leap* and *Lois & Clark: The New Adventures of Superman*. Erwin was also the voice of "Grandfather" in the animated *The Land Before Time*.

Swedish-born actor **Per** [Oscar Heinrich] **Oscarsson**, who portrayed "The Monster" in Calvin Floyd's *Victor Frankenstein* (aka *Terror of Frankenstein*, 1977), was apparently killed with his wife, Kia Ostling, early on December 31 when a fire burned their rural home in the small Swedish town of Skara to the ground. He was 83 and she was 67. Oscarsson's other credits include *The Night Visitor*, *Endless Night*, *The Sleep of Death* (based on the story by J. Sheridan Le Fanu) and the second and third movies in Stieg Larsson's "Millennium" trilogy.

## FILM/TV TECHNICIANS & PRODUCERS

**Gary "Tex" Brockette** died of cancer on January 1, aged 62. A former actor – he appeared in *Mark of the Witch*, the Rod Serling-narrated *Encounter with the Unknown* and *Ice Pirates* (as "Percy the Robot") – he worked as an assistant director on *R.L. Stine's The Haunting Hour: Don't Think About It* and *Sirens of the Caribbean*. Brockette also co-scripted and associate-produced the dinosaur comedy *Tammy and the T-Rex* and was script supervisor for *Mannequin: On the Move*.

American music producer, arranger and songwriter **Willie Mitchell** died of cardiac arrest on January 5, aged 81. A former session musician, he is best known for his work during the 1970s with Al Green on such hit songs as "Let's Stay Together", "I'm Still in Love with You" and "Tired of Being Alone".

American "claymation" animator **Art Clokey** (Arthur Charles Farrington), died of a gall bladder infection on January 8, aged

88. Best known for creating the green "Gumby" character in the 1960s for a short-lived TV series (successfully revived 1988–2002), he also directed the series *Davey and Goliath* and *Gumby: The Movie* (1995).

The "King of the Paparazzi", **Felice Quinto**, died of pneumonia at his home in Rockville, Maryland, on January 16, aged 80. The pioneering Italian-born celebrity photographer is widely believed to be the inspiration for the aggressive character "Paparazzo" in Frederico Fellini's 1960 movie *La Dolce Vita*. For a time Quinto was also Elizabeth Taylor's personal photographer.

69-year-old British special effects designer **Ian Scoones** died of liver cancer in Spain on January 20. He began his career working as an uncredited special effects assistant with Les Bowie on such Hammer films as *Taste of Fear* (aka *Scream of Fear*), *The Shadow of the Cat*, *Captain Clegg* (aka *Night Creatures*), *The Damned* (aka *These Are the Damned*), *The Kiss of the Vampire*, *She* (1965), *Frankenstein Created Woman*, *The Mummy's Shroud* and *Quatermass and the Pit* (aka *Five Million Miles to Earth*). Scoones also worked on *Dr Jekyll and Mr Hyde* (1980), *The Dark Crystal*, *Nineteen Eighty-Four*, *Haunted Honeymoon*, the *Max Headroom* pilot, and *The Mystery of Edwin Drood* (1993), along with episodes of *Blake's 7*, *Doctor Who*, *Hammer House of Horror* and *Hammer House of Mystery and Suspense*.

American stage actor **Ed Ragozzino**, who directed the 1977 docu-drama *Sasquatch, the Legend of Bigfoot*, died of cancer on January 30, aged 79.

American film producer, journalist and author **David Brown** who, with Richard D. Zanuck produced Steven Spielberg's *Jaws*, died of kidney failure on February 1, aged 93. His other credits include *SSSSnake*, *Jaws 2*, *The Island*, *Cocoon*, *Cocoon: The Return*, *Kiss the Girls*, *Deep Impact* and *Along Came a Spider*.

**Fred** [Walter Frederick] **Morrison**, inventor of the "Frisbee", died of cancer on February 9, aged 90. Early versions were called "Whirlo-Way", "Flyin-Saucers" and "Pluto Platter", before Morrison sold the rights to toy company Wham-O in 1957. It has since sold more than 200 million Frisbees.

British-born studio executive **Gareth Wigan** who, while at 20th Century Fox in the 1970s championed a little film called *Star Wars*, died of cancer in Los Angeles on February 13, aged

78. Wigan's other credits include *All That Jazz*, *Alien* and *Bram Stoker's Dracula*. His first wife was singer/actress Georgia Brown.

American animation director **Rudy** (Rudolph) **Larriva**, who created the opening titles for the original series of *The Twilight Zone*, died on February 19, aged 94. As an animator, he worked on numerous "Merrie Melodies" and "Looney Tunes" shorts in the 1930s, '40s and '50s, as well as the "Mr Magoo" cartoons. His many other credits include *Popeye the Sailor*, *The Lone Ranger*, *Sabrina and the Groovie Goolies*, *My Favorite Martians*, *Tarzan Lord of the Jungle*, *The New Adventures of Batman*, *Space Sentinels*, *Fangface*, *The Plastic Man Comedy/Adventure Show*, *Thundarr the Barbarian*, *The Scooby and Scrappy-Doo Puppy Hour* and a TV version of *Beauty and the Beast* (1983).

Regional American film-maker and actor **Russ** (Russell) **Marker** died on February 22, aged 83. He wrote, produced and directed the obscure 1963 SF movie *The Yesterday Machine* and co-scripted and directed *Demon from Devil's Lake*, which was eventually completed by James A. Sullivan as *Night Fright* (aka *E.T.N.: The Extraterrestrial Nastie*). As well as appearing in a small role in the latter film, Marker was also in Edgar Ulmer's *Beyond the Time Barrier*.

British-born cinematographer and TV commercial director **Derek** [James] **Vanlint** died in Toronto, Canada, on February 23, aged 77. He shot *Alien* and *Dragonslayer*, and was responsible for the miniature photography on *X-Men*.

British dancer, choreographer and director **Wendy Toye** CBE (Beryl May Jessie Toye), who created the dance for the mechanical doll in *The Thief of Bagdad* (1940), died on February 27, aged 92. In the 1950s she choreographed the Broadway production of *Peter Pan*, starring Boris Karloff as "Captain Hook". Toye also directed the best segment of *Three Cases of Murder* ("In the Picture"), an episode of *Tales of the Unexpected* (based on her 1952 short film) and a 1961 TV version of the opera *Orpheus in the Underworld*.

French-Canadian still photographer **Pierre Vinet** died in New Zealand of mesothelioma on March 3. Best known for his work on such Peter Jackson films as *Braindead* (aka *Dead Alive*), *Heavenly Creatures*, *The Frighteners*, *The Lord of the Rings* trilogy and *King Kong* (2005), his other credits include *Hercules and the Amazon Women*, *Hercules and the Lost Kingdom*, *Kull the Conqueror*, *Battlefield Earth: A Saga of the Year 3000*, *Willard* (2003), *The Chronicles of Narnia: The Lion the Witch and the Wardrobe* and *The Water Horse*.

Russian film director **Vladamir Chebotaryov** died on March 4, aged 88. He co-directed the 1961 SF film *The Amphibian Man* with Gennadi Kazansky.

American screenwriter and independent rural filmmaker **Charles B.** (Chuck) **Pierce** died on March 5, aged 71. Amongst his credits are the documentary-style *The Legend of Boggy Creek*, *The Town That Dreaded Sundown*, *The Evictors* and *The Barbaric Beast of Boggy Creek Part II*. He also worked as a set decorator on *The Phantom Tollbooth*, *Pretty Maids All in a Row*, *Earth II*, *The Invasion of Carol Enders*, *The Night Strangler*, *Wicked Wicked*, *Scream Blacula Scream*, *Killer Bees*, *The Return of the Man from U.N.C.L.E.: The Fifteen Years Later Affair* and episodes of TV's *The Twilight Zone* (1985) and *MacGyver*. Pierce made cameo appearances in some of his own films, and also turned up as a preacher in *The Aurora Encounter*.

Innovative British cinematographer **Tony** (Anthony) **Imi** died on March 8, aged 72. His many credits include *Percy's Progress* (aka *It's Not the Size That Counts*, with Vincent Price), *The Slipper and the Rose: The Story of Cinderella*, *A Christmas Carol* (1984), *Enemy Mine*, *The Haunting of Helen Walker* (based on *Turn of the Screw* by Henry James) and *Lighthouse* (aka *Dead of Night*). For TV he worked on *The Indian Tales of Rudyard Kipling*, *Adam Adamant Lives!*, *Doctor Who* ("The Faceless Ones") and *The Return of Sherlock Holmes*.

American cinematographer, film historian and movie preservationist **Karl Malkames** died the same day, aged 83. As an editor, he cut the negative for the 1971 alternate version of John Barrymore's *Dr Jekyll and Mr Hyde* (1920).

Production designer **John D. Jefferies, Sr** who, with his brother Matt, created the design of the original phaser pistol for TV's *Star Trek*, died of lung cancer on March 25, aged 73. His other credits include the series *The Greatest American Hero* and *Misfits of Science*, plus the movies *Just Visiting*, *I Still Know*

*What You Did Last Summer*, *Austin Powers: The Spy Who Shagged Me* and *Black Knight*.

**Gregg** (Gregory) **Peters**, who was unit production manager on the original *Star Trek* TV series (1967–69), died of complications from Parkinson's disease on March 27, aged 84. He also served as an assistant director and associate producer on the show. Peters' other credits include such TV series as *The Outer Limits* and *The Immortal*.

British special effects technician and matte painter **Bob** (Robert) **Cuff** died in April, aged 87. He produced matte paintings (working with John Mackey, often uncredited) for *The Day of the Triffids* (1962), *Dr Strangelove or: How I Learned to Stop Worrying and Love the Bomb*, *The Masque of the Red Death* (1964), *First Men in the Moon*, Hammer's *One Million B.C.* and *Dracula Has Risen from the Grave*, *Life of Brian*, *The Princess Bride*, *The Adventures of Baron Munchausen* and *Erik the Viking*. Cuff also worked on the special effects for *2001: A Space Odyssey* and *The Vengeance of She*. Along with Les Bowie, Cuff and Mackey formed Abacus Productions, which produced TV commercials, including Orson Welles' spots for Domecq sherry.

Controversial British music manager, songwriter and singer **Malcolm** [Robert Andrew] **McLaren** died in Switzerland after a long battle with cancer on April 9, aged 64. During the 1970s he famously managed such acts as The Sex Pistols, the New York Dolls, Adam Ant, Bow Wow Wow and Boy George, and is widely credited with creating the "Punk Rock" movement. He lived with clothes designer Vivienne Westwood for a number of years and was portrayed by David Hayman in the 1986 film *Sid and Nancy*. In 1999 McLaren announced that he was standing for Mayor of London.

American film editor **Dede Allen** (Dorothea Corothers Allen) died of a stroke on April 17, aged 86. Starting her career as a messenger at Columbia Pictures, she went on to edit *Terror from the Year 5000*, *Slaughterhouse-Five*, *The Wiz* and *The Addams Family*, amongst many other titles. With *Bonnie and Clyde* (1967) she was the first editor – either male or female – to receive sole onscreen credit at the beginning of a movie.

"The Godfather of *anime*", American producer and scriptwriter **Carl Macek**, died of a heart attack the same day, aged 58.

In 1985 he edited together three different Japanese *anime* series to create the popular *Robotech* series. He followed it with various sequels and spin-offs, and his other credits include the English-language versions of *Lupin the Third: The Castle of Cagliostro*, *Vampire Hunter D*, *Wicked City*, *Cyber Ninja*, the *Crying Freeman* series, *Casshan: Robot Hunter* and *2009: Lost Memories*, along with *Heavy Metal 2000*. Macek also co-edited the studies *McGill's Survey of the Cinema* and *Film Noir: An Encyclopedic Reference to the American Style*, and he wrote *The Art of Heavy Metal: Animation for the Eighties* and the novel *War Eagles*, the latter based on a 1930s film treatment by Merian C. Cooper.

British televison and theatre production designer [Arthur] **David Myerscough-Jones** died of cancer in France on April 21, aged 75. Through the late 1960s and early '70s he worked on *Doctor Who* ("The Web of Fear", "The Ambassadors of Death" and "Day of the Daleks"), and his other credits include Jonathan Miller's TV version of *A Midsummer Night's Dream* starring Nigel Davenport and a 1989 adaptation of *The Yellow Wallpaper*, based on the short story by Charlotte Perkins Gilman.

American-born Mexican director and actor **Alberto Mariscal** (Adalberto Ramírez Álvarez Mariscal) died in Los Angeles on April 24, aged 84. With Alfredo B. Crevenna he co-directed the 1960s horror comedies *House of the Frights*, *Bring Me the Vampire* and *La huella macabre*, and his other films include *Kalimán el hombre increíble* and its sequel *Kalimán en el siniestro mundo de Humanón*, *La tumba de Matías* and *Danik el viajero del tiempo*. As an actor, Mariscal appeared in *El monstruo resucitado*, *Santo contra el rey del crimen* and *Neutrón contra el criminal sádico*.

Pioneering American sexploitation writer, director and editor **Joseph W. Sarno** died after a short illness on April 26, aged 89. Under a wide variety of names he worked on both hard- and softcore films, including *Pandora and the Magic Box*, *The Devil's Plaything*, *A Touch of Genie* and *Oversexed*, among numerous other titles.

British film producer **Roy [William] Baird** died the same day, aged 76. After working as a first assistant director or production manager on such films as *Devils of Darkness*, *The Collector*

(1965), *Morgan: A Suitable Case for Treatment* (aka *Morgan!*), *Island of Terror* (starring Peter Cushing) and the James Bond spoof *Casino Royale* (1966), he went on to produce such titles as *Our Mother's House*, Lindsay Anderson's *If . . .*, Ken Russell's *The Devils* and *The Final Programme*, based on the novel by Michael Moorcock.

Costume designer **Cecelia** [Doidge] **Ripper**, the widow of veteran British character actor Michael Ripper (who died in 2000), died of cancer on April 29, aged 66. Her credits include several episodes of TV's *Tales of the Unexpected* and *The Witches and the Grinnygog* (based on the children's novel by Dorothy Edwards).

American music and entertainment lawyer **Peter Lopez**, whose clients included Michael Jackson, The Eagles and Michael Bublé, shot himself to death outside his home on April 30. Lopez was 60, and was married to actress Catherine Bach.

Innovative French cinematographer **William Lubtchansky** died of heart disease in Paris on May 4, aged 72. Part of the French "New Wave" movement of the 1960s and '70s, he worked with director Jean-Luc Godard six times and also photographed Alain Jessua's *Frankenstein 90* (1984).

**David** [Edward] **Durston** (aka "Richard Kent"/"Spencer Logan"), who wrote and directed the 1970 film *I Drink Your Blood*, died of pneumonia on May 6, aged 88. He also scripted a couple of episodes of the 1950s TV series *Tales of Tomorrow*.

**Michael Levesque**, who directed the 1971 cult classic *Werewolves on Wheels*, died of cancer on May 14, aged 66. As an art/production designer he worked on *The Trip*, *Phantom of the Paradise*, *Ilsa Harem Keeper of the Oil Sheiks* (uncredited), *The Incredible Melting Man* and several Russ Meyer movies.

American TV animation producer **Peter** [Eugene] **Keefe** died on May 27, aged 57. His credits include such juvenile series as *Voltron: Defender of the Universe*, *Saber Rider and the Star Sheriffs*, *Denver the Last Dinosaur*, *Widget the World Watcher*, *Twinkle the Dream Being* and the direct-to-video *Nine Dog Christmas*.

Veteran Hollywood cinematographer **William A.** (Ashman) **Fraker** died of cancer on May 31, aged 86. The six-times Oscar nominee's credits include *Incubus* (1966), *Games*, *The President's*

*Analyst*, *Rosemary's Baby*, *The Day of the Dolphin*, *Fritz Lang Interviewed by William Friedkin*, *Coonskin*, *Lipstick* (additional photography), *Exorcist II: The Heretic*, *Close Encounters of the Third Kind* (additional American scenes), *Heaven Can Wait* (1978), *1941*, *WarGames*, *SpaceCamp*, *Memoirs of an Invisible Man*, *Street Fighter* and *The Island of Dr Moreau* (1996). He also shot *The Ghost of Sierra de Cobre*, the pilot for *The Haunted*, Leslie Stevens' unproduced companion TV series to *The Outer Limits*, and *The Unknown*, another pilot that eventually aired on that series as "The Form of Things Unknown". Fraker also directed *A Reflection of Fear*, *The Legend of the Lone Ranger* and an episode of TV's *The Flash*.

"Mr Radio Drama", **Himan** (Hyman) **Brown**, who in 1941 created, produced and directed ABC Radio's *Inner Sanctum Mysteries*, died on June 4, six weeks short of his 100th birthday. The show was later adapted into a series of films by Universal starring Lon Chaney, Jr, and also a 1954 TV series. His other radio shows included *Dick Tracy*, *The Adventures of the Thin Man*, *Flash Gordon*, *Terry and the Pirates* and *CBS Radio Mystery Theatre*. "I am firmly convinced that nothing visual can touch audio," said Brown in a 2003 interview. "The magic word is imagination."

American movie producer **Steven** [Daniel] **Reuther**, who founded Douglas/Reuther Productions with actor Michael Douglas, died after a long battle with cancer on June 5, aged 58. His credits include *Big Man on Campus*, *Hider in the House*, *The Ghost and the Darkness* and *Face/Off*. Reuther was married to actress Helen Shaver from 1979 to 1982.

Veteran British cinematographer, scriptwriter, producer and director **Ronald Neame** CBE died in Los Angeles of complications from a fall on June 16, aged 99. While working at Elstree Studios in the 1920s, one of Neame's first jobs in the industry was as an assistant cameraman on Alfred Hitchcock's *Blackmail* (1929), the first talking pictured filmed in the UK. He went on to photograph *The Crimes of Stephen Hawke* (starring Tod Slaughter), the Edgar Wallace adaptation *The Gaunt Stranger* (aka *The Phantom Strikes*) and Noël Coward's *Blithe Spirit*. Neame produced and co-scripted David Lean's classic adaptation of Charles Dickens' *Great Expectations*

(1946) before he turned to directing in 1950. His later credits in that department include *Scrooge* (1970), *The Poseidon Adventure* (1972) and *Meteor*.

Independent American movie producer **Elliott Kastner** died of cancer in London on June 30, aged 80. A former music talent agent who worked extensively in Europe, he produced *Tam Lin* (aka *The Devil's Widow*), *The Nightcomers, Absolution, The First Deadly Sin, Nomads, Angel Heart, White of the Eye, Zombie High, Jack's Back* and the 1988 remake of *The Blob*. Kastner was the stepfather of actor Cary Elwes.

Prolific British cinematographer [George] **Alan Hume** died on July 13, aged 85. He began his career in the camera department working in various capacities on *Thunder Rock, Great Expectations* (1946), *Svengali, The Green Man, Tarzan the Magnificent* and a number of early *Carry On* films. From 1960 onwards he photographed many more *Carry On* titles (including *Carry On Spying* and *Carry On Screaming!*); the James Bond films *The Spy Who Loved Me* (Hume shot the stunning pre-credit skiing sequence), *For Your Eyes Only, Octopussy* and *A View to a Kill*, plus Hammer's *The Kiss of the Vampire, Dr Terror's House of Horrors, Captain Nemo and the Underwater City, From Beyond the Grave* (based on stories by R. Chetwynd-Hayes), *The Legend of Hell House* (based on the novel by Richard Matheson), *Cleopatra Jones and the Casino of Gold*, the Edgar Rice Burroughs adaptations *The Land That Time Forgot* (1975), *At the Earth's Core* and *The People That Time Forgot, Trial By Combat* (aka *A Dirty Knight's Work*), *Wombling Free, Gulliver's Travels* (1977), *Warlords of Atlantis, The Legacy, Arabian Adventure*, Disney's *The Watcher in the Woods, Caveman, The Hunchback of Notre Dame* (1982), *Star Wars Episode VI: The Empire Strikes Back* (he fell out with the producers over their treatment of director Richard Marquand and was replaced by his assistant), *Supergirl, Lifeforce, Jack the Ripper* (1988), *Without a Clue, Eve of Destruction* and *20,000 Leagues Under the Sea* (1997), along with episodes of TV's *The Avengers, Star Maidens, Space Precinct* and *Tales from the Crypt*.

American art director and production designer **Robert F.** (Francis) **Boyle** died on August 2, aged 100. His long career includes such films as *The Wolf Man* (1941), *Invisible Agent*, *Who Done It?*, *White Savage* (aka *White Captive*), *Flesh and Fantasy*, *Abbott and Costello Go to Mars*, *It Came from Outer Space*, *Cape Fear* (1962), Hitchcock's *The Birds*, *In Cold Blood*, *Explorers* and *Dragnet* (1987). In 2008 Boyle was presented with an honorary Oscar at the 80th Academy Awards, making him the oldest Oscar winner to date.

American film and TV producer **David L. Wolper** died of congestive heart failure and complications from Parkinson's disease on August 10, aged 82. Best known for such "event" mini-series as *Roots*, *The Thorn Birds* and *North and South*, his other credits include *The Incredible World of James Bond*, *The Hellstrom Chronicle*, *Willy Wonka & the Chocolate Factory*, *Monsters! Mysteries or Myths?*, *The Man Who Saw Tomorrow*, *The Mystic Warrior*, *Without Warning* (1994) and *The Mists of Avalon* (based on the novel by Marion Zimmer Bradley).

**Edward O. Denault**, who was an assistant director on *The Twilight Zone* (mostly directing the linking material featuring Rod Serling) and many other TV series during the 1960s, died of heart failure on August 21, aged 86. As a production manager he later worked on *Sole Survivor*, *The Brotherhood of the Bell*, *Something Evil*, *The Horror at 37,000 Feet* and an episode of *The Wild Wild West*. Denault also produced the 1984 movie *The Last Starfighter* and was involved with the *Max Headroom* TV series.

Japanese *anime* writer-director **Satoshi Kon** died of pancreatic cancer on August 23, aged 46. His films include *Perfect Blue*, *Millennium Actress*, *Tokyo Godfathers* and *Paprika*.

Workmanlike British film director and editor **Clive** [Stanley] **Donner** died of Alzheimer's disease on September 6, aged 84. His credits include *Vampira* (aka *Old Dracula*, starring David Niven as the Count), the 1976 TV movie *Rogue Mail*, the Gene Roddenberry pilot *Spectre*, *The Thief of Baghdad* (1978), *The Nude Bomb* (aka *The Return of Maxwell Smart*), *Charlie Chan and the Curse of the Dragon Queen*, *A Christmas Carol* (1984), *Arthur the King* (aka *Merlin and the Sword*) and *Babes in Toyland* (1986). As an editor, Donner worked on *Pandora and the Flying Dutchman* (uncredited) and *Scrooge* (1951), and he co-scripted the 1966 episode of the BBC TV series *Out of the*

*Unknown*, "The Machine Stops", based on the SF novel by E.M. Forster. He was also set to direct the 1980 sequel *Romance of the Pink Panther*, but star Peter Sellers (who had worked with Donner on *What's New Pussycat?*) died before production began.

French film director, writer and producer **Claude Chabrol**, a founding father of the celebrated "New Wave" movement, died on September 12, aged 80. His credits include *Bluebeard* (1963), *The Champagne Murders*, *Le boucher*, *Death Rite*, *Alice or the Last Escapade*, *Dr M* and *Hell* (based on the 1964 film script by Henri-Georges Clouzot). He contributed two episodes to the 1980 series *Fantômas*, and filmed a 1981 TV version of Edgar Allan Poe's *Le système du docteur Goudron et du professeur Plume*. Chabrol was married to actress Stéphane Audran from 1964 to 1980.

British TV scriptwriter and producer **Louis [Frank] Marks** died on September 17, aged 82. He wrote four *Doctor Who* stories – "Planet of the Giants" (1964), "Day of the Daleks" (1972), "Planet of Evil" (1975) and "The Masque of Mandragora" (1976). Marks also scripted three episodes of *Doomwatch* and he was script editor for the 1972 *Dead of Night* episode "The Exorcism".

American puppeteer and actor **Van [Charles] Snowden** died of cancer on September 22, aged 71. He was the puppeteer for the "Crypt Keeper" in the TV series *Tales from the Crypt* and the movies *Tales from the Crypt: Demon Knight*, *Casper* and *Bordello of Blood*. Snowden's other credits include *Beetle Juice*, *Child's Play 2*, *Child's Play 3*, *Dracula* (1992), *The X Files* and such shows as *Pufnstuf*, *The Bugaloos*, *Sigmund and the Sea Monsters*, *Land of the Lost* and *Pee-wee's Playhouse*.

British-born cinematographer **Neil Lisk** died in Los Angeles the same day. His credits include *Sasquatch Mountain* (aka *Devil on the Mountain*), *War Wolves*, *I Spit on Your Grave* (2010), *Mongolian Death Worm* and *Night of the Alien*.

American film and TV director **Arthur Penn**, best known for his 1967 version of *Bonnie and Clyde*, died of congestive heart failure on September 28, the day after his 88th birthday. After getting his start with live television in the mid-1950s, his other movie credits include *Mickey One* and *Dead of Winter*.

56-year-old Oscar-nominated film editor **Sally** [JoAnne] **Menke**, best known for her collaborations with director Quentin Tarantino, was found dead the same day on a hiking trail in the hills near Los Angeles' Griffith Park. She had become separated while out hiking with friends on the hottest day since records began 133 years earlier. Menke worked on such movies as *Teenage Mutant Ninja Turtles* (1990), *Nightwatch* and Tarantino's *Death Proof*.

Russian-born **Andy** (Andreus) **Alback**, who was president of United Artists during the *Heaven's Gate* debacle (Michael Cimino's Western only made back $1.5 million of its $44 million cost at the US box office), died in New York City on September 29, aged 89. Alback had more success with other films at UA, including the two James Bond movies *Moonraker* and *For Your Eyes Only*.

**Roy Ward Baker** (Roy Horace Baker), the veteran British director of the Marilyn Monroe film *Don't Bother to Knock* and the "Titanic" drama *A Night to Remember*, died on October 5, aged 93. In later years he became a prolific if journeyman director for Hammer Films, Amicus Productions and Tyburn Film Productions with such movies as *Quatermass and the Pit* (aka *Five Million Years to Earth*), *The Anniversary*, *Moon Zero Two*, *The Vampire Lovers*, *Scars of Dracula*, *Dr Jekyll and Sister Hyde*, *Asylum* (based on stories by Robert Bloch), *The Vault of Horror*, *—And Now the Screaming Starts!* (based on the novella by David Case), *The Legend of the 7 Golden Vampires* (aka *The 7 Brothers Meet Dracula*), *The Monster Club* (based on the book by R. Chetwynd-Hayes) and *The Masks of Death* (featuring Peter Cushing as "Sherlock Holmes"). Baker's other credits include the time-travel fantasy *The House in the Square* (aka *I'll Never Forget You*), plus episodes of *The Avengers*, *The Champions*, Hammer's *Journey to the Unknown* (Robert Bloch's "The Indian Spirit Guide"), *Randall and Hopkirk (Deceased)* and *Sherlock Holmes and Doctor Watson*.

French-born cinematographer **Michael Hugo**, who shot the "Kolchak" pilot TV movie *The Night Stalker*, died of cancer in Las Vegas on October 12, aged 80. His other credits include The Monkees' *Head*, *The Phynx*, *Earth II*, *Bug*, *The Manitou* (based on the novel by Graham Masterton), *Terror Out of the Sky*,

*Pandemonium* and *High Desert Kill,* along with episodes of *Tales of the Unexpected* (aka *Twist in the Tale*) and *Matt Houston.*

British cinematographer **Robert** [William] **Paynter,** who photographed John Landis' groundbreaking video for *Michael Jackson's Thriller,* died on October 20, aged 82. His other credits include *The Nightcomers* (a prequel to Henry James' *Turn of the Screw*), *Superman II, The Final Conflict,* Landis' *An American Werewolf in London, Curtains, Superman III, The Muppets Take Manhattan, Scream For Help, Little Shop of Horrors* (1986), *The Secret Garden* (1987) and the live-action segments in *Rock-a-Doodle,* along with additional photography on *Saturn 3.* Paynter also had a cameo as a doctor in John Landis' 2010 comedy *Burke and Hare.*

Director and actor **Lamont Johnson** died of congestive heart failure on October 24, aged 88. His films include *The Groundstar Conspiracy, You'll Like My Mother, Lipstick,* and *Spacehunter Adventures in the Forbidden Zone* in 3-D, along with episodes of TV's *Matinee Theatre* ("Jane Eyre", and "Dracula" starring John Carradine), *Steve Canyon, The Twilight Zone* ("Five Characters in Search of an Exit", "Kick the Can" and six others), *The Name of the Game* ("The White Birch", featuring Boris Karloff) and *Faerie Tale Theatre.* In the early 1950s Johnson portrayed "Tarzan" on the radio, and he also appeared in episodes of *Climax!* ("The Thirteenth Chair"), *Alfred Hitchcock Presents* and *Steve Canyon.*

British-born TV and documentary director **Eric** [Albert] **Fullilove,** whose credits include the weekly 1973 anthology series *The Evil Touch,* died of heart failure in Australia the same day, aged 85.

Japanese producer, writer and director **Yoshinobu Nishizaki** (Hirofumi Nishizaki), co-creator of the 1970s *anime* TV series *Space Crusier Yamato* (aka *Star Blazers*) and the various movie spin-offs, died on November 7, aged 74.

Italian-born movie producer **Dino De Laurentiis** (Agostino De Laurentiis) died in Beverly Hills, California, on November 10, aged 91. An often controversial figure, he began his career in Italy working with Carlo Ponti and Federico Fellini and producing the fantasy epic *Ulysses,* before churning out genre product like *Goliath and the Vampires, Matchless,* Mario

Bava's *Danger: Diabolik*, *Barbarella*, *Lipstick*, the 1976 version of *King Kong*, *The White Buffalo*, *Orca*, the 1980 version of *Flash Gordon*, *Amityville II: The Possession*, *Conan the Barbarian* and *Conan the Destroyer*, *Dune*, *Manhunter*, *King Kong Lives*, *Army of Darkness*, *Hannibal*, *Red Dragon*, *Hannibal Rising*, and the Stephen King adaptations *The Dead Zone*, *Cat's Eye*, *Silver Bullet*, *Maximum Overdrive* (directed by King) and *Sometimes They Come Back*. After the failure of his Dinocitta' Studios complex in Rome, De Laurentiis moved to America in the mid-1970s and in 1984 he unveiled the DEG Film Studios in Wilmington, North Carolina, which he was forced to sell just four years later. His first wife was Italian actress Silvana Mangano.

American TV production executive **William** [Edwin] **Self** died of a heart attack on November 15, aged 89. A former actor (*The Thing from Another World*), his many production credits include *Voyage to the Bottom of the Sea* (1964–68), *Lost in Space* (1965–68), the 1967 pilot *Dick Tracy* (featuring Victor Buono), *Batman* (1966–68), *The Green Hornet* (1966–67), *The Time Tunnel* (1966–67), *The Ghost & Mrs Muir* (1968–69) and *Land of the Giants* (1968–69).

64-year-old Hollywood publicist **Ronni Chasen** died on November 16 when she was shot to death while driving home from the *Burlesque* premier and after-party. Chasen was hit at least five times in the chest, which caused her to crash her Mercedes into a lamp post in a Beverly Hills street. No motive was established. A publicist for thirty-seven years, her work included the *Cocoon* franchise. 43-year-old Harold Martin Smith, a "person of interest" to the police investigation, subsequently shot himself to death with a handgun that ballistics matched to a bullet recovered from Chasen's body.

Japanese animator and *anime* writer and director **Umanosuke Iida** died on November 26, aged 49. His credits include the 2001–2 vampire TV series *Herushingu* (aka *Hellsing*).

**Irvin** (Isadore) **Kershner**, who was one of George Lucas' instructors at the University of Southern California Film School and directed the first *Star Wars* sequel, *The Empire Strikes Back* (1980), died of cancer on November 27, aged 87. Given his first break by producer Roger Corman in 1958, Kershner went on to direct such films as *Eyes of Laura Mars*, the "other" James Bond movie *Never Say Never Again* and *RoboCop 2*, along with an episode of TV's *Amazing Stories* and the pilot for *SeaQuest DSV*, after which he retired.

British make-up artist **Jane Royle** (Irene Jane Buchan Shortt) died on December 13, aged 78. She worked on *The Rocky Horror Picture Show* (uncredited), *Murder by Decree*, *Dracula* (1979), *Flash Gordon* (1980), *Dragonslayer*, *The Company of Wolves*, *Legend*, *Young Sherlock Holmes*, *Who Framed Roger Rabbit*, *Indiana Jones and the Last Crusade*, *Alien³*, *Lost in Space*, the James Bond films *GoldenEye* and *The World is Not Enough*, *Batman Begins* and the first three *Harry Potter* movies. Royle also worked on the TV series *The Avengers* (1965–69) and *The Champions*.

Iconoclastic French director **Jean Rollin** (Jean Michel Rollin Le Gentil) died on December 15 after a long illness. He was 72. Beginning with *Le viol du vampire* (*The Rape of the Vampire*) in 1968, he churned out a string of often erotic horror movies that usually relied more on imagination than budget. These included *La vampire nue* (*The Nude Vampire*), *Le frisson des vampires* (*The Shiver of the Vampires*), *Vierges et vampires* (*Requiem for a Vampire* aka *Caged Virgins*), *Curse of the Living Dead* (aka *The Démoniacs*), *Lèvres de sang* (*Lips of Blood*), *The Grapes of Death*, *Fascination*, *Zombie Lake* (as "J.A. Laser"), *La morte vivante* (*The Living Dead Girl*), *Les deux orphelines vampires* (*The Two Vampire Orphans*), *La fiancée de Dracula*, *La nuit des Horloges* (*The Night of the Clocks*) and *La masque de la Médusa*. Rollin also contributed a dream sequence to Jesus Franco's *Among the Living Dead*, as well as directing hardcore movies under the pseudonyms "Michel Gentil" and "Robert Xavier". He also scripted, produced and acted in his films, and was the author of a number of novels, including a novelisation of *Les deux orphelines vampires*.

Hollywood actor-turned-screenwriter, producer and director **Blake Edwards** (William Blake Crump), best known for his successful series of *Pink Panther* movies, died of complications from pneumonia the same day, aged 88. He began his career as an (often uncredited) actor in such films as *A Guy Named Joe* and *Strangler of the Swamp*, before going on to write the original stories for *The Atomic Kid* and *The Couch* (scripted by Robert Bloch). Edwards' own films as a director include the genre-inspired *The Pink Panther Strikes Again*, the ghostly TV movie *Justin Case*, and the body-swap comedy *Switch*. His second wife was singer and actress Julie Andrews.

American TV scriptwriter **Aron Abrams**, who co-produced and wrote six episodes of the NBC SF sit-com *3rd Rock from the Sun* (1999–2001), was found dead in his hotel room in Waikoloa, Hawaii, on Christmas Day. It is thought that the 50-year-old died of a heart attack. He also scripted an episode of *Big Wolf on Campus* and the 2007 TV movie *I'm in Hell*.

American special effects supervisor and model maker **Grant McCune** died of cancer on December 27, aged 67. He shared a 1978 Academy Award for Best Visual Effects with John Dykstra for his work on "R2-D2" and the miniatures in the original *Star Wars* (he also appeared in the film as a "Death Star Gunner"). McCune's numerous other credits include the pilot for *Battlestar Galactica* (1978), *Star Trek: The Motion Picture*, *Firefox*, *Starflight: The Plane That Couldn't Land*, *Lifeforce*, *Spaceballs*, *My Stepmother is an Alien*, *Ghostbusters II*, *Batman Forever*, *Sphere* and *Thirteen Days*.

# USEFUL ADDRESSES

THE FOLLOWING LISTING OF organisations, publications, dealers and individuals is designed to present readers and authors with further avenues to explore. Although I can personally recommend many of those listed on the following pages, neither the publisher nor myself can take any responsibility for the services they offer. Please also note that the information below is only a guide and is subject to change without notice.

—The Editor

## ORGANISATIONS

**The Australian Horror Writers Association** (*www.australian-horror.com*) is a non-profit organisation that formed as a way of providing a unified voice and a sense of community for Australian (and New Zealand) writers of horror/dark fiction, while furthering the development and evolution of this genre within Australia. AHWA aims to become the focal point and first point of reference for Australian writers and fans of the dark side of literature, and to improve the acceptance and understanding of what horror is to a wider audience. For more information mail to: Australian Horror Writers Association, Post Office, Elphinstone, Victoria 3448, Australia. E-mail: *ahwa@australianhorror.com*

**The British Fantasy Society** (*www.britishfantasysociety.org*) was founded in 1971 and publishes the newsletter *Prism* and the magazines *Dark Horizons* and *New Horizons* featuring articles, interviews and fiction, along with occasional special booklets. The BFS also enjoys a lively online community – there is an e-mail news-feed, a discussion board with numerous links, and a CyberStore selling various publications. FantasyCon is one of the UK's friendliest conventions and there are social gatherings and meet-the-author events organised around Britain. For yearly membership details, e-mail: *secretary@ britishfantasysociety.org.uk*. You can also join online through the CyberStore.

**The Friends of Arthur Machen** (*www.machensoc.demon. co.uk*) is a literary society whose objectives include encouraging a wider recognition of Machen's work and providing a focus for critical debate. Members get a hardcover journal, *Faunus*, twice a year, and also the informative newsletter *Machenalia*. For membership details, contact Jeremy Cantwell, FOAM Treasurer, Apt.5, 26 Hervey Road, Blackheath, London SE3 8BS, UK.

**The Friends of the Merril Collection** (*www.friendsofmerril. org*) is a volunteer organisation that provides support and assistance to the largest public collection of science fiction, fantasy and horror books in North America. Details about annual membership and donations are available from the website or by contacting The Friends of the Merril Collection, c/o Lillian H. Smith Branch, Toronto Public Library, 239 College Street, 3rd Floor, Toronto, Ontario M5T 1R5, Canada. E-mail: *ltoolis@tpl.toronto.on.ca*

**A Ghostly Company** (*www.aghostlycompany.org.uk*) is an informal group of like-minded people, whose members are known within the society as "Companions". It publishes a regular newsletter that appears four times a year, containing members' letters, book reviews, a section for book sales and wanted, and other news. *The Silent Companion* is an annual fiction magazine containing previously unpublished fiction by members. The society also holds an Annual General Meeting, which coincides with a gathering or "Black Pilgrimage" to places associated with actual ghost stories or the lives of their authors. Membership falls due in January of each year and is open to anyone from the UK or overseas. Details are on the website, or contact the Membership Secretary: Katherine Haynes, 150 Elstree Park,

Barnet Lane, Borehamwood, Hertfordshire WD6 2RP, UK. E-mail: *tony.college@fsmail.net*

**The Horror Writers Association** (*www.horror.org*) is a world-wide organisation of writers and publishing professionals dedicated to promoting the interests of writers of horror and dark fantasy. It was formed in the early 1980s. Interested individuals may apply for active, affiliate or associate membership. Active membership is limited to professional writers. HWA publishes a monthly online newsletter, and sponsors the annual Bram Stoker Awards. Apply online or write to HWA Membership, PO Box 50577, Palo Alto, CA 94303, USA.

**World Fantasy Convention** (*www.worldfantasy.org*) is an annual convention held in a different (usually American) city each year, oriented particularly towards serious readers and genre professionals.

**World Horror Convention** (*www.worldhorrorsociety.org*) is a smaller, more relaxed, event. It is aimed specifically at horror fans and professionals, and held in a different city (usually American) each year.

## SELECTED SMALL PRESS PUBLISHERS

**Anomalous Books.** E-mail: *anomalousbooks@anomalous books. com*

**Apex Publications LLC** (*www.apexbookcompany.com*), PO Box 24323, Lexington, KY 40524, USA. E-mail: *jason@ apexdigest.com*

**Ash-Tree Press** (*www.ash-tree.bc.ca*), PO Box 1360, Ashcroft, British Columbia, Canada V0K 1A0. E-mail: *ashtree@ash-tree.bc.ca*

**Atomic Fez Publishing** (*www.atomicfez.com*).

**Bad Moon Books/Eclipse** (*www.badmoonbooks.com*), 1854 W. Chateau Avenue, Anaheim, CA 92804-4527, USA.

**Bards and Sages Publishing** (*www.bardsandsages.com*), 201 Leed Avenue, Bellmawr, NJ 08031, USA.

**BearManor Media** (*www.bearmanormedia.com*), PO Box 71426, Albany, GA 31708, USA.

**Big Mouth House** (*www.bigmouthhouse.net*), 150 Pleasant Street #306, Easthampton, MA 01027, USA. E-mail: *info@ bigmouthhouse.net*

**Blue Room Publishing** (*www.blueroompublishing.com*), PO Box 134, Newtown Square, PA 19073, USA. E-mail: *editor@blueroompublishing.com*

**Cemetery Dance Publications** (*www.cemeterydance.com*), 132-B Industry Lane, Unit #7, Forest Hill, MD 21050, USA. E-mail: *info@cemeterydance.com*

**ChiZine Publications** (*www.chizinepub.com*). E-mail: *info@chizinepub.com*

**Chômu Press** (*info@chomupress.com*), 70 Hill Street, Richmond, Surrey TW9 1TW, UK. E-mail: *info@chomupress.com*

**Cutting Block Press** (*www.cuttingblock.net*), 6911 Riverton Drive, Austin, TX 78729, USA. E-mail: *info@cuttingblock.net*

**Damnation Books, LLC** (*www.damnationbooks.com*), PO Box 3931, Santa Rosa, CA 95402, USA.

**Dark Regions Press/Ghost House** (*www.darkregions.com*), PO Box 1264, Colusa, CA 95932, USA.

**Earthling Publications** (*www.earthlingpub.com*), PO Box 413, Northborough, MA 01532, USA. E-mail: *earthlingpub@yahoo.com*

**Edge Science Fiction and Fantasy Publishing** (*www.edgewebsite.com*), PO Box 1714, Calgary, Alberta T2P 2L7, Canada.

**Gauntlet Publications** (*www.gauntletpress.com*), 5307 Arroyo Street, Colorado Springs, CO 80922, USA. E-mail: *info@gauntletpress.com*

**Gothic Press** (*www.gothicpress.com*), 2272 Quail Oak, Baton Rouge, LA 70808-9023, USA.

**Gray Friar Press** (*www.grayfriarpress.com*), 9 Abbey Terrace, Whitby, North Yorkshire Y021 3HQ, UK. E-mail: *gary.fry@virgin.net*

**Hippocampus Press** (*www.hippocampuspress.com*), PO Box 641, New York, NY 10156, USA. E-mail: *info@hippocampuspress.com*

**IDW Publishing** (*www.idwpublishing.com*), 5080 Santa Fe Street, San Diego, CA 92109, USA.

**Lachesis Publishing** (*www.lachesispublishing.com*), Kingston, Nova Scotia, Canada B0P 1R0.

**McFarland & Company, Inc., Publishers** (*www.mcfarlandpub.com*), Box 611, Jefferson, NC 28640, USA.

**MonkeyBrain Books** (*www.monkeybrainbooks.com*), 11204 Crossland Drive, Austin, TX 78726, USA. E-mail: *info@monkey brainbooks.com*

**Mortbury Press** (*mortburypress.webs.com/*), Shiloh, Nantglas, Llandrindod Wells, Powys LD1 6PF, UK. E-mail: *mortburypress@ yahoo.com*

**Mutation Press** (*www.mutationpress.com*), 1 Craiglea Place, Edinburgh EH10 5QA, Scotland.

**Mythos Books, LLC** (*www.mythosbooks.com*), 351 Lake Ridge Road, Poplar Bluff, MO 63901, USA.

**NewCon Press** (*www.newconpress.co.uk*).

**Nightjar Press** (*nightjarpress.wordpress.com*), 38 Belfield Road, Manchester M20 6BH, UK.

**Night Shade Books** (*www.nightshadebooks.com*), 1661 Tennessee Street, #3H, San Francisco, CA 94107, USA. E-mail: *night@.nightshadebooks.com*

**Obverse Books** (*www.obversebooks.co.uk*). E-mail: *info@ obversebooks.co.uk*

**Pendragon Press** (*www.pendragonpress.net*), PO Box 12, Maesteg, Mid Glamorgan CF34 0XG, UK. E-mail: *chris@ pendragonpress.co.uk*

**P'rea Press** (*www.preapress.com*), 34 Osborne Road, Lane Cove, NSW 2066, Australia. E-mail: *dannyL58@hotmail.com*

**PS Publishing Ltd** (*www.pspublishing.co.uk*), Grosvenor House, 1 New Road, Hornsea HU18 1PG, UK. E-mail: *editor@ pspublishing.co.uk*

**Raw Dog Screaming Press** (*www.rawdogscreaming.com*), 2802 Farris Lane, Bowie, MD 20715, USA. E-mail: *books@ rawdogscreaming.com*

**Read Raw Press**, 11 Market Road, Carluke ML8 4BL, UK.

**Sam's Dot Publishing** (*www.samsdotpublishing.com*), PO Box 782, Cedar Rapids, IA 52406-0782, USA. E-mail: *sdpshowcase@yahoo.com*

**Screaming Dreams** (*www.screamingdreams.com*), 25 Heol Evan Wynne, Pontlottyn, Bargoed, Mid Glamorgan CF81 9PQ, UK. E-mail: *steve@screamingdreams.com*

**Skullvines Press** (*www.skullvines.com*). E-mail: *mail@skullvines. com*

**Small Beer Press** (*www.smallbeerpress.com*), 150 Pleasant

Street #306, Easthampton, MA 01027, USA. E-mail: *info@ smallbeerpress.com*

**Strange Publications** (*www.strangepublications.com*), Attn: Aaron Polson, 3038 West 7th Street, Lawrence, KS 66049, USA. E-mail: *strange.pubs@gmail.com*

**Stygian Publications** (*www.necrotictissue.com*), PO Box 787, Forest Lake, MN 55025, USA. E-mail: *anthology@ nectrotictissue.com*

**Subterranean Press** (*www.subterraneanpress.com*), PO Box 190106, Burton, MI 48519, USA. E-mail: *subpress@earthlink. net*

**The Swan River Press** (*www.brianjshowers.com*). E-mail: *gothicdublin@gmail.com*

**Tartarus Press** (*tartaruspress.com*), Coverley House, Carlton-in-Coverdale, Leyburn, North Yorkshire DL8 4AY, UK. E-mail: *tartarus@pavilion.co.uk*

**Telos Publishing Ltd** (*www.telos.co.uk*), 17 Pendre Avenue, Prestatyn, Denbighshire LL19 9SH, UK. E-mail: *feedback@telos. co.uk*

**Ticonderoga Publications** (*www.ticonderogapublications. com*), PO Box 29, Greenwood, WA 6924, Australia.

**Undertow Publications** (*www.undertowbooks.com*), 1905 Faylee Crescent, Pickering, ON L1V 2T3, Canada. E-mail: *undertowbooks@gmail.com*

**University of Nevada Press** (*www.unpress.nevada.edu*), MS 0166, Reno, NV 89557-0166, USA.

**ZED Presents . . . Publishing** (*www.zombiesexist.com*), 424 W. Bakerview Road, Suite 105-272, Bellingham, WA 98226, USA.

## SELECTED MAGAZINES

**Albedo One** (*www.albedo1.com*) is Ireland's magazine of science fiction, fantasy and horror. The editorial address is Albedo One, 2 Post Road, Lusk, Co. Dublin, Ireland. E-mail: *bobn@yellowbrickroad.ie*

**Ansible** is a highly entertaining monthly SF and fantasy newsletter/gossip column edited by David Langford. It is available free electronically by sending an e-mail to: *ansible-request@dcs.gla.*

*ac.uk* with a subject line reading "subscribe", or you can receive the print version by sending a stamped and addressed envelope to Ansible, 94 London Road, Reading, Berks RG1 5AU, UK. Back issues, links and book lists are also available online.

**Black Gate: Adventures in Fantasy Literature** (*www.blackgate. com*) is an attractive pulp-style publication that includes heroic fantasy and horror fiction. Subscriptions are available from: New Epoch Press, 815 Oak Street, St. Charles, IL 60174, USA. E-mail: *john@blackgate.com*

**Black Static** (*www.ttapress.com*) is the UK's premier horror fiction magazine. Published bi-monthly, six- and twelve-issue subscriptions are available from TTA Press, 5 Martins Lane, Witcham, Ely, Cambridgeshire CB6 2LB, UK, or from the secure TTA website. E-mail: *blackstatic@ttapress.com*

**Cemetery Dance Magazine** (*www.cemeterydance.com*) is edited by Richard Chizmar and includes fiction up to 5,000 words, interviews, articles and columns by many of the biggest names in horror. For subscription information contact: Cemetery Dance Publications, PO Box 623, Forest Hill, MD 21050, USA. E-mail: *info@cemeterydance.com*

**GUD: Greatest Uncommon Denominator Magazine** (www. *gudmagazine.com*) is a paperback magazine of fiction and poetry published twice yearly by Greatest Uncommon Denominator Publishing, PO Box 1537, Laconia, NH 03247, USA. E-mail: *editor@gudmagazine.com*

**Locus** (*www.locusmag.com*) is the monthly newspaper of the SF/fantasy/horror field. Contact: Locus Publications, PO Box 13305, Oakland, CA 94661, USA. Subscription information with other rates and order forms are also available on the website. E-mail: *locus@locusmag.com*

**Locus Online** (*www.locusmag.com/news*) is an excellent online source for the latest news and reviews.

**The Magazine of Fantasy & Science Fiction** (*www.fandsf. com*) has been publishing some of the best imaginative fiction for more than sixty years. Edited by Gordon Van Gelder, and now published bi-monthly, single copies or an annual subscription are available by US cheques or credit card from: Fantasy & Science Fiction, PO Box 3447, Hoboken, NJ 07030, USA, or you can subscribe via the new website.

**Morpheus Tales** (*www.morpheustales.com*), 116 Muriel Street, London N1 9QU, UK. *www.myspace.com/morpheustales*

**The Paperback Fanatic** (*www.thepaperbackfanatic.com*) has become a mostly subscription-only title after changing to a more attractive digest format. This is a shame, because it is quite simply the best magazine available dedicated to old paperbacks and the people who produced and published them. Each issue includes interviews, articles and numerous full-colour cover reproductions. E-mail: *thepaperbackfanatic@sky.com*

**Rabbit Hole** is a semi-regular newsletter about Harlan Ellison®. A subscription is available from The Harlan Ellison® Recording Collection, PO Box 55548, Sherman Oaks, CA 91413-0548, USA.

**Rue Morgue** (*www.rue-morgue.com*) is a glossy monthly magazine edited by Dave Alexander and subtitled "Horror in Culture & Entertainment". Each issue is packed with full-colour features and reviews of new films, books, comics, music and game releases. Subscriptions are available from: Marrs Media Inc., 2926 Dundas Street West, Toronto, ON M6P 1Y8, Canada, or by credit card on the website. E-mail: *info@rue-morgue.com*. *Rue Morgue* also runs the Festival of Fear: Canadian National Horror Expo in Toronto. Every Friday you can log on to a new show at Rue Morgue Radio at *www.ruemorgueradio.com* and your horror shopping online source, the Rue Morgue Marketplace, is at *www.ruemorguemarketplace.com*

**Space and Time: The Magazine of Fantasy, Horror, and Science Fiction** (*www.spaceandtimemagazine.com*) is published quarterly. Single issues and subscriptions are available from the website or from the new address: Space and Time Magazine, 458 Elizabeth Avenue #5348, Somerset, NJ 08873, USA. In the UK and Europe, copies can be ordered from BBR Distributing, PO Box 625, Sheffield S1 3GY, UK.

**Subterranean Press Magazine** (*www.supterraneanpress.com/magazine*).

**Supernatural Tales** (*suptales.blogspot.com*) is a twice-yearly fiction magazine edited by David Longhorn. Three-issue subscriptions are available via post (UK cheques or PayPal only) to: Supernatural Tales, 291 Eastbourne Avenue, Gateshead NE8 4NN, UK. E-mail: *davidlonghorn@hotmail.com*

**Video WatcHDog** (*www.videowatchdog.com*) describes itself as "The Perfectionist's Guide to Fantastic Video" and is published bi-monthly. One-year (six issues) subscriptions are available from: *orders@videowatchdog.com*

**Weird Tales** (*www.weirdtalesmagazine.com*) continues to seek out that which is most weird and unsettling for the reader's own edification and alarm. Single copies or a six-issue subscription are available from: Wildside Press, 9710 Traville Gateway Drive #234, Rockville, MD 20850-7408, USA. E-mail: *info@weirdtales.net*. For subscriptions in the UK contact: Cold Tonnage Books, 22 Kings Lane, Windlesham, Surrey, GU20 6JQ, UK (*andy@coldtonnage.co.uk*).

**Writing Magazine** (*www.writingmagazine.co.uk*) is the UK's best-selling magazine aimed at writers and poets and those who want to be. It is published by Warners Group Publications plc, 5th Floor, 31–32 Park Row, Leeds LS1 SJD, UK. E-mail: *writingmagazine@warnersgroup.co.uk*

## DEALERS

**Ted Ball**, who co-owned the late and lamented Fantasy Centre bookstore, has set up a new mail-order business, with catalogues issued by e-mail (with a few print copies for those who do not have Internet access). Orders by post (E.W. Ball, 3 Barmouth Avenue, Andover Road, London N7 7HT, UK). Tel: +44 (0)20 7272-3046. E-mail: *tedball@btinternet.com*. Payment by PayPal or a cheque in UK pounds drawn on a UK bank.

**Bookfellows/Mystery and Imagination Books** (*www.mystery andimagination.com*) is owned and operated by Malcolm and Christine Bell, who have been selling fine and rare books since 1975. This clean and neatly organised store includes SF/fantasy/horror/mystery, along with all other areas of popular literature. Many editions are signed, and catalogues are issued regularly. Credit cards accepted. Open seven days a week at 238 N. Brand Blvd., Glendale, CA 91203, USA. Tel: (818) 545-0206. Fax: (818) 545-0094. E-mail: *bookfellows@gowebway.com*

**Borderlands Books** (*www.borderlands-books.com*) is a nicely designed store with friendly staff and an impressive stock of new and used books from both sides of the Atlantic.

866 Valencia Street (at 19th), San Francisco, CA 94110, USA. Tel: (415) 824-8203 or (888) 893-4008 (toll free in the US). Credit cards accepted. World-wide shipping. E-mail: *office@ borderlands-books.com*

**Cold Tonnage Books** (*www.coldtonnage.com*) offers excellent mail order new and used SF/fantasy/horror, art, reference, limited editions etc. Write to: Andy & Angela Richards, Cold Tonnage Books, 22 Kings Lane, Windlesham, Surrey GU20 6JQ, UK. Credit cards accepted. Tel: +44 (0)1276-475388. E-mail: *andy@coldtonnage.com*

**Ken Cowley** issues a bumper catalogue filled with a huge number of titles both old and new, many from his own extensive collection. Write to: Ken Cowley, Trinity Cottage, 153 Old Church Road, Clevedon, North Somerset BS21 7TU, UK. Tel: +44 (0)1275-872247. E-mail: *kencowley@blueyonder.co.uk*

**Richard Dalby** issues an annual Christmas catalogue of used ghost stories and other supernatural volumes at very reasonable prices. Write to: Richard Dalby, 4 Westbourne Park, Scarborough, North Yorkshire Y012 4AT. Tel: +44 (0)1723-377049.

**Dark Delicacies** (*www.darkdel.com*) is a Burbank, California, store specialising in horror books, toys, vampire merchandise and signings. They also do mail order and run money-saving book club and membership discount deals. 3512 W. Magnolia Blvd, Burbank, CA 91505, USA. Tel: (818) 556-6660. Credit cards accepted. E-mail: *darkdel@darkdel.com*

**DreamHaven Books & Comics** (*www.dreamhavenbooks. com*) store and mail order offers new and used SF/fantasy/horror/ art and illustrated etc. with regular catalogues (both print and e-mail). Write to: 2301 E. 38th Street, Minneapolis, MN 55406, USA. Credit cards accepted. Tel: (612) 823-6070. E-mail: *dream@dreamhavenbooks.com*

**Fantastic Literature** (*www.fantasticliterature.com*) mail order offers the UK's biggest online out-of-print SF/fantasy/horror genre bookshop. Fanzines, pulps and vintage paperbacks as well. Write to: Simon and Laraine Gosden, Fantastic Literature, 35 The Ramparts, Rayleigh, Essex SS6 8PY, UK. Credit cards and PayPal accepted. Tel/Fax: +44 (0)1268-747564. E-mail: *sgosden@ netcomuk.co.uk*

**Horrorbles** (*www.horrorbles.com*), 6731 West Roosevelt

Road, Berwyn, IL 60402, USA. Small, friendly Chicago store selling horror and sci-fi toys, memorabilia and magazines that has monthly specials and in-store signings. Specialises in exclusive "Basil Gogos" and "Svengoolie" items. Tel: (708) 484-7370. E-mail: *store@horrorbles.com*

**Iliad Bookshop** (*www.iliadbooks.com*), 5400 Cahuenga Blvd., North Hollywood, CA 91601, USA. General used bookstore that has a very impressive genre section, reasonable prices and knowledgeable staff. They have recently expanded their fiction section into an adjacent building. Tel: (818) 509-2665.

**Kayo Books** (*www.kayobooks.com*) is a bright, clean treasure-trove of used SF/fantasy/horror/mystery/pulps spread over two floors. Titles are stacked alphabetically by subject, and there are many bargains to be had. Credit cards accepted. Visit the store (Wednesday–Saturday, 11:00am to 6:00pm) at 814 Post Street, San Francisco, CA 94109, USA or order off their website. Tel: (415) 749-0554. E-mail: *kayo@kayobooks.com*

**Porcupine Books** offers regular catalogues and extensive mail-order lists of used fantasy/horror/SF titles via e-mail *brian@ porcupine.demon.co.uk* or write to: 37 Coventry Road, Ilford, Essex IG1 4QR, UK. Tel: +44 (0)20 8554-3799.

**Kirk Ruebotham** (*www.ukbookworld.com/members/kirk*) is a mail-order only dealer, who specialises in out-of-print and second-hand horror/SF/fantasy/crime and related non-fiction at very good prices, with regular catalogues. Write to: 16 Beaconsfield Road, Runcorn, Cheshire WA7 4BX, UK. Tel: +44 (0)1928-560540. E-mail: *kirk.ruebotham@ntlworld.com*

**The Talking Dead** is run by Bob and Julie Wardzinski and offers reasonably priced paperbacks, rare pulps and hardcovers, with catalogues issued *very* occasionally. They accept wants lists and are also the exclusive supplier of back issues of *Interzone*. Credit cards accepted. Contact them at: 12 Rosamund Avenue, Merley, Wimborne, Dorset BH21 1TE, UK. Tel: +44 (0)1202-849212 (9:00am–9:00pm). E-mail: *books@thetalkingdead.fsnet.co.uk*

**Ygor's Books** specialises in out-of-print science fiction, fantasy and horror titles, including British, signed, speciality press and limited editions. They also buy books, letters and original art in these fields. E-mail: *ygorsbooks@earthlink.net*

## ONLINE

**All Things Horror** (*www.allthingshorror.co.uk*) is a genre interview site run by Johnny Mains that mainly focuses on authors, editors, artists and movie stars of the 1960s, 1970s and 1980s. It also caters to reviews of both films and books, and features a short fiction section that is open to submissions.

**Cast Macabre** (*www.castmacabre.org*) is the premium horror fiction podcast that is "bringing Fear to your ears", offering a free horror short story every week.

**Fantastic Fiction** (*www.fantasticfiction.co.uk*) features more than 2,000 best-selling author biographies with all their latest books, covers and descriptions.

**FEARnet** (*www.fearnet.com*) is a digital cable channel dedicated to all things horror, including news, free movie downloads (sadly not available to those outside North America) and Mick Garris' online talk show *Post Mortem*.

**Hellnotes** (*www.hellnotes.com*) offers news and reviews of novels, collections, magazines, anthologies, non-fiction works, and chapbooks. Materials for review should be sent to editor and publisher David B. Silva, Hellnotes, 5135 Chapel View Court, North Las Vegas, NV 89031, USA. E-mail: *news@hellnotes.com* or *dbsilva13@gmail.com*

**The Irish Journal of Gothic and Horror Studies** (*irishgothic horrorjournal.homestead.com*) features a diverse range of articles and reviews, along with a regular "Lost Souls" feature focusing on overlooked individuals in the genre.

**SF Site** (*www.sfsite.com*) has been posted twice each month since 1997. Presently, it publishes around thirty to fifty reviews of SF, fantasy and horror from mass-market publishers and some small press. They also maintain link pages for Author and Fan Tribute Sites and other facets including pages for Interviews, Fiction, Science Fact, Bookstores, Small Press, Publishers, E-zines and Magazines, Artists, Audio, Art Galleries, Newsgroups and Writers' Resources. Periodically, they add features such as author and publisher reading lists.

**Vault of Evil** (*www.vaultofevil.wordpress.com*) is a site dedicated to celebrating the best in British horror with special emphasis on UK anthologies (although they apparently don't care much for this series!). There is also a lively forum devoted to many different themes at *www.vaultofevil. proboards.com*